British Mystery Multipack Volume 1

The Good Soldier
Haunted Hotel
The Red House Mystery

Ford Madox Ford

Wilkie Collins

A. A. Milne

The Good Soldier by Ford Madox Ford. First published in 1915.

Haunted Hotel by Wilkie Collins. First published as *The Haunted Hotel: A Mystery of Modern Venice* in 1876.

The Red House Mystery by A. A. Milne. First published in 1922.

ISBN-10: 151879095X
ISBN-13: 978-1518790959

CONTENTS

THE GOOD SOLDIER

BY

FORD MADOX FORD

PART 1

I

THIS is the saddest story I have ever heard. We had known the Ashburnhams for nine seasons of the town of Nauheim with an extreme intimacy—or, rather with an acquaintanceship as loose and easy and yet as close as a good glove's with your hand. My wife and I knew Captain and Mrs Ashburnham as well as it was possible to know anybody, and yet, in another sense, we knew nothing at all about them. This is, I believe, a state of things only possible with English people of whom, till today, when I sit down to puzzle out what I know of this sad affair, I knew nothing whatever. Six months ago I had never been to England, and, certainly, I had never sounded the depths of an English heart. I had known the shallows.

I don't mean to say that we were not acquainted with many English people. Living, as we perforce lived, in Europe, and being, as we perforce were, leisured Americans, which is as much as to say that we were un-American, we were thrown very much into the society of the nicer English. Paris, you see, was our home. Somewhere between Nice and Bordighera provided yearly winter quarters for us, and Nauheim always received us from July to September. You will gather from this statement that one of us had, as the saying is, a "heart", and, from the statement that my wife is dead, that she was the sufferer.

Captain Ashburnham also had a heart. But, whereas a yearly month or so at Nauheim tuned him up to exactly the right pitch for the rest of the twelvemonth, the two months or so were only just enough to keep poor Florence alive from year to year. The reason for his heart was, approximately, polo, or too much hard sportsmanship in his youth. The reason for poor Florence's broken years was a storm at sea upon our first crossing to Europe, and the immediate reasons for our imprisonment in that continent were doctor's orders. They said that even the short Channel crossing might well kill the poor thing.

When we all first met, Captain Ashburnham, home on sick leave from an India to which he was never to return, was thirty-three; Mrs Ashburnham Leonora—was thirty-one. I was thirty-six and poor Florence thirty. Thus today Florence would have been thirty-nine and Captain Ashburnham forty-two; whereas I am forty-five and Leonora forty. You will perceive, therefore, that our friendship has been a young-middle-aged affair, since we were all of us of quite quiet dispositions, the Ashburnhams being more particularly what in England it is the custom to call "quite good people".

They were descended, as you will probably expect, from the Ashburnham who accompanied Charles I to the scaffold, and, as you must also expect with this class of English people, you would never have noticed it. Mrs Ashburnham was a Powys; Florence was a Hurlbird of Stamford, Connecticut, where, as you know, they are more old-fashioned than even the inhabitants of Cranford, England, could have been. I myself am a Dowell of Philadelphia, Pa., where, it is historically true, there are more old English families than you would find in any six English counties taken together. I carry about with me, indeed—as if it were the only thing that invisibly anchored me to any spot upon the globe—the title deeds of my farm, which once covered several blocks between Chestnut and Walnut Streets. These title deeds are of wampum, the grant of an Indian chief to the first Dowell, who left Farnham in Surrey in company with William Penn. Florence's people, as is so often the case with the inhabitants of

Connecticut, came from the neighbourhood of Fordingbridge, where the Ashburnhams' place is. From there, at this moment, I am actually writing.

You may well ask why I write. And yet my reasons are quite many. For it is not unusual in human beings who have witnessed the sack of a city or the falling to pieces of a people to desire to set down what they have witnessed for the benefit of unknown heirs or of generations infinitely remote; or, if you please, just to get the sight out of their heads.

Some one has said that the death of a mouse from cancer is the whole sack of Rome by the Goths, and I swear to you that the breaking up of our little four-square coterie was such another unthinkable event. Supposing that you should come upon us sitting together at one of the little tables in front of the club house, let us say, at Homburg, taking tea of an afternoon and watching the miniature golf, you would have said that, as human affairs go, we were an extraordinarily safe castle. We were, if you will, one of those tall ships with the white sails upon a blue sea, one of those things that seem the proudest and the safest of all the beautiful and safe things that God has permitted the mind of men to frame. Where better could one take refuge? Where better?

Permanence? Stability? I can't believe it's gone. I can't believe that that long, tranquil life, which was just stepping a minuet, vanished in four crashing days at the end of nine years and six weeks. Upon my word, yes, our intimacy was like a minuet, simply because on every possible occasion and in every possible circumstance we knew where to go, where to sit, which table we unanimously should choose; and we could rise and go, all four together, without a signal from any one of us, always to the music of the Kur orchestra, always in the temperate sunshine, or, if it rained, in discreet shelters. No, indeed, it can't be gone. You can't kill a minuet de la cour. You may shut up the music-book, close the harpsichord; in the cupboard and presses the rats may destroy the white satin favours. The mob may sack Versailles; the Trianon may fall, but surely the minuet—the minuet itself is dancing itself away into the furthest stars, even as our minuet of the Hessian bathing places must be stepping itself still. Isn't there any heaven where old beautiful dances, old beautiful intimacies prolong themselves? Isn't there any Nirvana pervaded by the faint thrilling of instruments that have fallen into the dust of wormwood but that yet had frail, tremulous, and everlasting souls?

No, by God, it is false! It wasn't a minuet that we stepped; it was a prison—a prison full of screaming hysterics, tied down so that they might not outsound the rolling of our carriage wheels as we went along the shaded avenues of the Taunus Wald.

And yet I swear by the sacred name of my creator that it was true. It was true sunshine; the true music; the true splash of the fountains from the mouth of stone dolphins. For, if for me we were four people with the same tastes, with the same desires, acting—or, no, not acting—sitting here and there unanimously, isn't that the truth? If for nine years I have possessed a goodly apple that is rotten at the core and discover its rottenness only in nine years and six months less four days, isn't it true to say that for nine years I possessed a goodly apple? So it may well be with Edward Ashburnham, with Leonora his wife and with poor dear Florence. And, if you come to think of it, isn't it a little odd that the physical rottenness of at least two pillars of our four-square house never presented itself to my mind as a menace to its security? It doesn't so present itself now though the two of them are actually dead. I don't know....

I know nothing—nothing in the world—of the hearts of men. I only know that I am alone—horribly alone. No hearthstone will ever again witness, for me, friendly intercourse. No smoking-room will ever be other than peopled with incalculable simulacra amidst smoke wreaths. Yet, in the name of God, what should I know if I don't know the life of the hearth and of the smoking-room, since my whole life has been passed in those places? The warm hearthside!—Well, there was Florence: I believe that for the twelve years her life lasted, after the storm that seemed irretrievably to have weakened her heart—I don't believe that for one minute she was out of my sight, except when she was safely tucked up in bed and I should be downstairs, talking to some good fellow or other in some lounge or smoking-room or taking my final turn with a cigar before going to bed. I don't, you understand, blame Florence. But how can she have known what she knew? How could she have got to know it? To know it so fully. Heavens! There doesn't seem to have been the actual time. It must have been when I was taking my baths, and my Swedish exercises, being manicured. Leading the life I did, of the sedulous, strained nurse, I had to do something to keep myself fit. It must have been then! Yet even that can't have been enough time to get the tremendously long conversations full of worldly wisdom that Leonora has reported to me since their deaths. And is it possible to imagine that during our prescribed walks in Nauheim and the neighbourhood she found time to carry on the protracted negotiations which she did carry on between Edward Ashburnham and his wife? And isn't it incredible that during all that time Edward and Leonora never spoke a word to each other in private? What is one to think of humanity?

For I swear to you that they were the model couple. He was as devoted as it was possible to be without appearing fatuous. So well set up, with such honest blue eyes, such a touch of stupidity, such a warm goodheartedness! And she—so tall, so splendid in the saddle, so fair! Yes, Leonora was extraordinarily fair and so extraordinarily the real thing that she seemed too good to be true. You don't, I mean, as a rule, get it all so superlatively together. To be the county family, to look the county family, to be so appropriately and perfectly wealthy; to be so perfect in manner—even just to the saving touch of insolence that seems to be necessary. To have all that and to be all that! No, it was too good to be true. And yet, only this afternoon, talking over the whole matter she said to me: "Once I tried to have a lover but I was so sick at the heart, so utterly worn out that I had to send him away." That struck me as the most amazing thing I had ever heard. She said "I was actually in a man's arms. Such a nice chap! Such a dear fellow! And I was saying to myself, fiercely, hissing it between my teeth, as they say in novels—and really clenching them together: I was saying to myself: 'Now, I'm in for it and I'll really have a good time for once in my life—for once in my life!' It was in the dark, in a carriage, coming back from a hunt ball. Eleven miles we had to drive! And then suddenly the bitterness of the endless poverty, of the endless acting—it fell on me like a blight, it spoilt everything. Yes, I had to realize that I had been spoilt even for the good time when it came. And I burst out crying and I cried and I cried for the whole eleven miles. Just imagine me crying! And just imagine me making a fool of the poor dear chap like that. It certainly wasn't playing the game, was it now?"

I don't know; I don't know; was that last remark of hers the remark of a harlot, or is it what every decent woman, county family or not county family, thinks at the bottom of her heart? Or thinks all the time for the matter of that? Who knows?

Yet, if one doesn't know that at this hour and day, at this pitch of civilization to which we have attained, after all the preachings of all the moralists, and all the teachings of all the mothers to all the daughters in saecula saeculorum... but perhaps that is what all mothers teach all daughters, not with lips but with the eyes, or with heart whispering to heart. And, if one doesn't know as much as that about the first thing in the world, what does one know and why is one here?

I asked Mrs Ashburnham whether she had told Florence that and what Florence had said and she answered:—"Florence didn't offer any comment at all. What could she say? There wasn't anything to be said. With the grinding poverty we had to put up with to keep up appearances, and the way the poverty came about—you know what I mean—any woman would have been justified in taking a lover and presents too. Florence once said about a very similar position—she was a little too well-bred, too American, to talk about mine—that it was a case of perfectly open riding and the woman could just act on the spur of the moment. She said it in American of course, but that was the sense of it. I think her actual words were: 'That it was up to her to take it or leave it....'"

I don't want you to think that I am writing Teddy Ashburnham down a brute. I don't believe he was. God knows, perhaps all men are like that. For as I've said what do I know even of the smoking-room? Fellows come in and tell the most extraordinarily gross stories—so gross that they will positively give you a pain. And yet they'd be offended if you suggested that they weren't the sort of person you could trust your wife alone with. And very likely they'd be quite properly offended—that is if you can trust anybody alone with anybody. But that sort of fellow obviously takes more delight in listening to or in telling gross stories—more delight than in anything else in the world. They'll hunt languidly and dress languidly and dine languidly and work without enthusiasm and find it a bore to carry on three minutes' conversation about anything whatever and yet, when the other sort of conversation begins, they'll laugh and wake up and throw themselves about in their chairs. Then, if they so delight in the narration, how is it possible that they can be offended—and properly offended—at the suggestion that they might make attempts upon your wife's honour? Or again: Edward Ashburnham was the cleanest looking sort of chap;—an excellent magistrate, a first rate soldier, one of the best landlords, so they said, in Hampshire, England. To the poor and to hopeless drunkards, as I myself have witnessed, he was like a painstaking guardian. And he never told a story that couldn't have gone into the columns of the Field more than once or twice in all the nine years of my knowing him. He didn't even like hearing them; he would fidget and get up and go out to buy a cigar or something of that sort. You would have said that he was just exactly the sort of chap that you could have trusted your wife with. And I trusted mine and it was madness. And yet again you have me. If poor Edward was dangerous because of the chastity of his expressions—and they say that is always the hall-mark of a libertine—what about myself? For I solemnly avow that not only have I never so much as hinted at an impropriety in my conversation in the whole of my days; and more than that, I will vouch for the cleanness of my thoughts and the absolute chastity of my life. At what, then, does it all work out? Is the whole thing a folly and a mockery? Am I no better than a eunuch or is the proper man—the man with the right to existence—a raging stallion forever neighing after his neighbour's womankind?

I don't know. And there is nothing to guide us. And if everything is so nebulous about a matter so elementary as the morals of sex, what is there to guide us in the more subtle morality of all other personal contacts, associations, and activities? Or are we meant to act on impulse alone? It is all a darkness.

II

I DON'T know how it is best to put this thing down—whether it would be better to try and tell the story from the beginning, as if it were a story; or whether to tell it from this distance of time, as it reached me from the lips of Leonora or from those of Edward himself.

So I shall just imagine myself for a fortnight or so at one side of the fireplace of a country cottage, with a sympathetic soul opposite me. And I shall go on talking, in a low voice while the sea sounds in the distance and overhead the great black flood of wind polishes the bright stars. From time to time we shall get up and go to the door and look out at the great moon and say: "Why, it is nearly as bright as in Provence!" And then we shall come back to the fireside, with just the touch of a sigh because we are not in that Provence where even the saddest stories are gay. Consider the lamentable history of Peire Vidal. Two years ago Florence and I motored from Biarritz to Las Tours, which is in the Black Mountains. In the middle of a tortuous valley there rises up an immense pinnacle and on the pinnacle are four castles—Las Tours, the Towers. And the immense mistral blew down that valley which was the way from France into Provence so that the silver grey olive leaves appeared like hair flying in the wind, and the tufts of rosemary crept into the iron rocks that they might not be torn up by the roots.

It was, of course, poor dear Florence who wanted to go to Las Tours. You are to imagine that, however much her bright personality came from Stamford, Connecticut, she was yet a graduate of Poughkeepsie. I never could imagine how she did it—the queer, chattery person that she was. With the far-away look in her eyes—which wasn't, however, in the least romantic—I mean that she didn't look as if she were seeing poetic dreams, or looking through you, for she hardly ever did look at you!—holding up one hand as if she wished to silence any objection—or any comment for the matter of that—she would talk. She would talk about William the Silent, about Gustave the Loquacious, about Paris frocks, about how the poor dressed in 1337, about Fantin-Latour, about the Paris-Lyons-Mediterranée train-deluxe, about whether it would be worth while to get off at Tarascon and go across the windswept suspension-bridge, over the Rhone to take another look at Beaucaire.

We never did take another look at Beaucaire, of course—beautiful Beaucaire, with the high, triangular white tower, that looked as thin as a needle and as tall as the Flatiron, between Fifth and Broadway—Beaucaire with the grey walls on the top of the pinnacle surrounding an acre and a half of blue irises, beneath the tallness of the stone pines, What a beautiful thing the stone pine is!...

No, we never did go back anywhere. Not to Heidelberg, not to Hamelin, not to Verona, not to Mont Majour—not so much as to Carcassonne itself. We talked of it, of course, but I guess Florence got all she wanted out of one look at a place. She had the seeing eye.

I haven't, unfortunately, so that the world is full of places to which I want to return—towns with the blinding white sun upon them; stone pines against the blue of the sky; corners of gables, all carved and painted with stags and scarlet flowers and crowstepped gables with the little saint at the top; and grey and pink palazzi and walled towns a mile or so back from the sea, on the Mediterranean, between Leghorn and Naples. Not one of them did we see more than once, so that the whole world for me is like spots of colour in an immense canvas. Perhaps if it weren't so I should have something to catch hold of now.

Is all this digression or isn't it digression? Again I don't know. You, the listener, sit opposite me. But you are so silent. You don't tell me anything. I am, at any rate, trying to get you to see what sort of life it was I led with Florence and what Florence was like. Well, she was bright; and she danced. She seemed to dance over the floors of castles and over seas and over and over and over the salons of modistes and over the plages of the Riviera like a gay tremulous beam, reflected from water upon a ceiling. And my function in life was to keep that bright thing in existence. And it was almost as difficult as trying to catch with your hand that dancing reflection. And the task lasted for years.

Florence's aunts used to say that I must be the laziest man in Philadelphia. They had never been to Philadelphia and they had the New England conscience. You see, the first thing they said to me when I called in on Florence in the little ancient, colonial, wooden house beneath the high, thin-leaved elms—the first question they asked me was not how I did but what did I do. And I did nothing. I suppose I ought to have done something, but I didn't see any call to do it. Why does one do things? I just drifted in and wanted Florence. First I had drifted in on Florence at a Browning tea, or something of the sort in Fourteenth Street, which was then still residential. I don't know why I had gone to New York; I don't know why I had gone to the tea. I don't see why Florence should have gone to that sort of spelling bee. It wasn't the place at which, even then, you expected to find a Poughkeepsie graduate. I guess Florence wanted to raise the culture of the Stuyvesant crowd and did it as she might have gone in slumming. Intellectual slumming, that was what it was. She always wanted to leave the world a little more elevated than she found it. Poor dear thing, I have heard her lecture Teddy Ashburnham by the hour on the difference between a Franz Hals and a Wouvermans and why the Pre-Mycenaean statues were cubical with knobs on the top. I wonder what he made of it? Perhaps he was thankful.

I know I was. For do you understand my whole attentions, my whole endeavours were to keep poor dear Florence on to topics like the finds at Cnossos and the mental spirituality of Walter Pater. I had to keep her at it, you understand, or she might die. For I was solemnly informed that if she became excited over anything or if her emotions were really stirred her little heart might cease to beat. For twelve years I had to watch every word that any person uttered in any conversation and I had to head it off what the English call "things"—off love, poverty, crime, religion and the rest of it. Yes, the first doctor that we had when she was carried off the ship at Havre assured me that this must be done. Good God, are all these fellows monstrous idiots, or is there a freemasonry between all of them from end to end of the earth?... That is what makes me think of that fellow Peire Vidal.

Because, of course, his story is culture and I had to head her towards culture and at the same time it's so funny and she hadn't got to laugh, and it's so full of love and she wasn't to think of love. Do you know the story? Las Tours of the Four Castles had for chatelaine Blanche Somebody-or-other who was called as a term of commendation, La Louve—the She-Wolf. And Peire Vidal the Troubadour paid his court to La Louve. And she wouldn't have anything to do with him. So, out of compliment to her—the things people do when they're in love!—he dressed himself up in wolfskins and went up into the Black Mountains. And the shepherds of the Montagne Noire and their dogs mistook him for a wolf and he was torn with the fangs and beaten with clubs. So they carried him back to Las Tours and La

Louve wasn't at all impressed. They polished him up and her husband remonstrated seriously with her. Vidal was, you see, a great poet and it was not proper to treat a great poet with indifference.

So Peire Vidal declared himself Emperor of Jerusalem or somewhere and the husband had to kneel down and kiss his feet though La Louve wouldn't. And Peire set sail in a rowing boat with four companions to redeem the Holy Sepulchre. And they struck on a rock somewhere, and, at great expense, the husband had to fit out an expedition to fetch him back. And Peire Vidal fell all over the Lady's bed while the husband, who was a most ferocious warrior, remonstrated some more about the courtesy that is due to great poets. But I suppose La Louve was the more ferocious of the two. Anyhow, that is all that came of it. Isn't that a story?

You haven't an idea of the queer old-fashionedness of Florence's aunts—the Misses Hurlbird, nor yet of her uncle. An extraordinarily lovable man, that Uncle John. Thin, gentle, and with a "heart" that made his life very much what Florence's afterwards became. He didn't reside at Stamford; his home was in Waterbury where the watches come from. He had a factory there which, in our queer American way, would change its functions almost from year to year. For nine months or so it would manufacture buttons out of bone. Then it would suddenly produce brass buttons for coachmen's liveries. Then it would take a turn at embossed tin lids for candy boxes. The fact is that the poor old gentleman, with his weak and fluttering heart, didn't want his factory to manufacture anything at all. He wanted to retire. And he did retire when he was seventy. But he was so worried at having all the street boys in the town point after him and exclaim: "There goes the laziest man in Waterbury!" that he tried taking a tour round the world. And Florence and a young man called Jimmy went with him. It appears from what Florence told me that Jimmy's function with Mr Hurlbird was to avoid exciting topics for him. He had to keep him, for instance, out of political discussions. For the poor old man was a violent Democrat in days when you might travel the world over without finding anything but a Republican. Anyhow, they went round the world.

I think an anecdote is about the best way to give you an

idea of what the old gentleman was like. For it is perhaps important that you should know what the old gentleman was; he had a great deal of influence in forming the character of my poor dear wife.

Just before they set out from San Francisco for the South Seas old Mr Hurlbird said he must take something with him to make little presents to people he met on the voyage. And it struck him that the things to take for that purpose were oranges—because California is the orange country—and comfortable folding chairs. So he bought I don't know how many cases of oranges—the great cool California oranges, and half-a-dozen folding chairs in a special case that he always kept in his cabin. There must have been half a cargo of fruit.

For, to every person on board the several steamers that they employed—to every person with whom he had so much as a nodding acquaintance, he gave an orange every morning. And they lasted him right round the girdle of this mighty globe of ours. When they were at North Cape, even, he saw on the horizon, poor dear thin man that he was, a lighthouse. "Hello," says he to himself, "these fellows must be very lonely. Let's take them some oranges." So he had a boatload of his fruit out and had himself rowed to the lighthouse on the horizon. The folding chairs he lent to any lady that he came across and liked or who seemed tired and invalidish on the ship. And so, guarded against his heart and, having his niece with him, he went round the world....

He wasn't obtrusive about his heart. You wouldn't have known he had one. He only left it to the physical laboratory at Waterbury for the benefit of science, since he considered it to be quite an extraordinary kind of heart. And the joke of the matter was that, when, at the age of eighty-four, just five days before poor Florence, he died of bronchitis there was found to be absolutely nothing the matter with that organ. It had certainly jumped or squeaked or something just sufficiently to take in the doctors, but it appears that that was because of an odd formation of the lungs. I don't much understand about these matters.

I inherited his money because Florence died five days after him. I wish I hadn't. It was a great worry. I had to go out to Waterbury just after Florence's death because the poor dear old fellow had left a good many charitable bequests and I had to appoint trustees. I didn't like the idea of their not being properly handled.

Yes, it was a great worry. And just as I had got things roughly settled I received the extraordinary cable from Ashburnham begging me to come back and have a talk with him. And immediately afterwards came one from Leonora saying, "Yes, please do come. You could be so helpful." It was as if he had sent the cable without consulting her and had afterwards told her. Indeed, that was pretty much what had happened, except that he had told the girl and the girl told the wife. I arrived, however, too late to be of any good if I could have been of any good. And then I had my first taste of English life. It was amazing. It was overwhelming. I never shall forget the polished cob that Edward, beside me, drove; the animal's action, its high-stepping, its skin that was like satin. And the peace! And the red cheeks! And the beautiful, beautiful old house.

Just near Branshaw Teleragh it was and we descended on it from the high, clear, windswept waste of the New Forest. I tell you it was amazing to arrive there from Waterbury. And it came into my head—for Teddy Ashburnham, you remember, had cabled to me to "come and have a talk" with him—that it was unbelievable that anything essentially calamitous could happen to that place and those people. I tell you it was the very spirit of peace. And Leonora, beautiful and smiling, with her coils of yellow hair, stood on the top doorstep, with a butler and footman and a maid or so behind her. And she just said: "So glad you've come," as if I'd run down to lunch from a town ten miles away, instead of having come half the world over at the call of two urgent telegrams.

The girl was out with the hounds, I think. And that poor devil beside me was in an agony. Absolute, hopeless, dumb agony such as passes the mind of man to imagine.

III

IT was a very hot summer, in August, 1904; and Florence had already been taking the baths for a month. I don't know how it feels to be a patient at one of those places. I never was a patient anywhere. I daresay the patients get a home feeling and some sort of anchorage in the spot. They seem to like the bath attendants, with their cheerful faces, their air of authority, their white linen. But, for myself, to be at Nauheim gave me a sense—what shall I say?—a sense almost of nakedness—the nakedness that one feels on the sea-shore or in any great open space. I had no attachments, no accumulations. In one's own home it is as if little, innate sympathies draw one to particular chairs that seem to enfold one in an embrace, or take one along particular streets that seem friendly when others may be hostile. And, believe me, that feeling is a very important part of life. I know it well, that have been for so long a wanderer upon the face of public resorts. And one is too polished up. Heaven knows I was never an untidy man. But the feeling that I had when, whilst poor Florence was taking her morning bath, I stood upon the carefully swept steps of the Englischer Hof, looking at the carefully arranged trees in tubs upon the carefully arranged gravel whilst carefully arranged people walked past in carefully calculated gaiety, at the carefully calculated hour, the tall trees of the public gardens, going up to the right; the reddish stone of the baths—or were they white half-timber châlets? Upon my word I have forgotten, I who was there so often. That will give you the measure of how much I was in the landscape. I could find my way blindfolded to the hot rooms, to the douche rooms, to the fountain in the centre of the quadrangle where the rusty water gushes out. Yes, I could find my way blindfolded. I know the exact distances. From the Hotel Regina you took one hundred and eighty-seven paces, then, turning sharp, left-handed, four hundred and twenty took you straight down to the fountain. From the Englischer Hof, starting on the sidewalk, it was ninety-seven paces and the same four hundred and twenty, but turning lefthanded this time.

And now you understand that, having nothing in the world to do—but nothing whatever! I fell into the habit of counting my footsteps. I would walk with Florence to the baths. And, of course, she entertained me with her conversation. It was, as I have said, wonderful what she could make conversation out of. She walked very lightly, and her hair was very nicely done, and she dressed beautifully and very expensively. Of course she had money of her own, but I shouldn't have minded. And yet you know I can't remember a single one of her dresses. Or I can remember just one, a very simple one of blue figured silk—a Chinese pattern—very full in the skirts and broadening out over the shoulders. And her hair was copper-coloured, and the heels of her shoes were exceedingly high, so that she tripped upon the points of her toes. And when she came to the door of the bathing place, and when it opened to receive her, she would look back at me with a little coquettish smile, so that her cheek appeared to be caressing her shoulder.

I seem to remember that, with that dress, she wore an immensely broad Leghorn hat—like the Chapeau de Paille of Rubens, only very white. The hat would be tied with a lightly knotted scarf of the same stuff as her dress. She knew how to give value to her blue eyes. And round her neck would be some simple pink, coral beads. And her complexion had a perfect clearness, a perfect smoothness...

Yes, that is how I most exactly remember her, in that dress, in that hat, looking over her shoulder at me so that the eyes flashed very blue—dark pebble blue...

And, what the devil! For whose benefit did she do it? For that of the bath attendant? of the passers-by? I don't know. Anyhow, it can't have been for me, for never, in all the years of her life, never on any possible occasion, or in any other place did she so smile to me, mockingly, invitingly. Ah, she was a riddle; but then, all other women are riddles. And it occurs to me that some way back I began a sentence that I have never finished... It was about the feeling that I had when I stood on the steps of my hotel every morning before starting out to fetch Florence back from the bath. Natty, precise, well-brushed, conscious of being rather small amongst the long English, the lank Americans, the rotund Germans, and the obese Russian Jewesses, I should stand there, tapping a cigarette on the outside of my case, surveying for a moment the world in the sunlight. But a day was to come when I was never to do it again alone. You can imagine, therefore, what the coming of the Ashburnhams meant to me. I have forgotten the aspect of many things, but I shall never forget the aspect of the dining-room of the Hotel Excelsior on that evening—and on so many other evenings. Whole castles have vanished from my memory, whole cities that I have never visited again, but that white room, festooned with papier-maché fruits and flowers; the tall windows; the many tables; the black screen round the door with three golden cranes flying upward on each panel; the palm-tree in the centre of the room; the swish of the waiter's feet; the cold expensive elegance; the mien of the diners as they came in every evening—their air of earnestness as if they must go through a meal prescribed by the Kur authorities and their air of sobriety as if they must seek not by any means to enjoy their meals—those things I shall not easily forget. And then, one evening, in the twilight, I saw Edward Ashburnham lounge round the screen into the room. The head waiter, a man with a face all grey—in what subterranean nooks or corners do people cultivate those absolutely grey complexions?—went with the timorous patronage of these creatures towards him and held out a grey ear to be whispered into. It was generally a disagreeable ordeal for newcomers but Edward Ashburnham bore it like an Englishman and a gentleman. I could see his lips form a word of three syllables—remember I had nothing in the world to do but to notice these niceties—and immediately I knew that he must be Edward Ashburnham, Captain, Fourteenth Hussars, of Branshaw House, Branshaw Teleragh. I knew it because every evening just before dinner, whilst I waited in the hall, I used, by the courtesy of Monsieur Schontz, the proprietor, to inspect the little police reports that each guest was expected to sign upon taking a room.

The head waiter piloted him immediately to a vacant table, three away from my own—the table that the Grenfalls of Falls River, N.J., had just vacated. It struck me that that was not a very nice table for the newcomers, since the sunlight, low though it was, shone straight down upon it, and the same idea seemed to come at the same moment into Captain Ashburnham's head. His face hitherto had, in the wonderful English fashion, expressed nothing whatever. Nothing. There was in it neither joy nor despair; neither hope nor fear; neither boredom nor satisfaction. He seemed to perceive no soul in that crowded room; he might have been walking in a jungle. I never came across such a perfect expression before and I never shall again. It was insolence and not insolence; it was modesty and not modesty. His hair was fair, extraordinarily ordered in a wave, running from the left temple to the right; his face was a light brick-red, perfectly uniform in tint up to the roots of the hair itself; his yellow moustache was as stiff as a toothbrush and I verily believe that he had his black smoking jacket thickened a little over the shoulder-blades so as to give himself the air of the slightest possible stoop. It would be like him to do that; that was the sort of thing he thought about. Martingales, Chiffney bits, boots; where you got the best soap, the best brandy, the name of the chap who rode a plater down the Khyber cliffs; the spreading power of number three shot before a charge of number four powder... by heavens, I hardly ever heard him talk of anything else. Not in all the years that I knew him did I hear him talk of anything but these subjects. Oh, yes, once he told me that I could buy my special shade of blue ties cheaper from a firm in Burlington Arcade than from my own people in New York. And I have bought my ties from that firm ever since. Otherwise I should not remember the name of the Burlington Arcade. I wonder what it looks like. I have never seen it. I imagine it to be two immense rows of pillars, like those of the Forum at Rome, with Edward Ashburnham striding down between them. But it probably isn't—the least like that. Once also he advised me to buy Caledonian Deferred, since they were due to rise. And I did buy them and they did rise. But of how he got the knowledge I haven't the faintest idea. It seemed to drop out of the blue sky.

And that was absolutely all that I knew of him until a month ago—that and the profusion of his cases, all of pigskin and stamped with his initials, E. F. A. There were gun cases, and collar cases, and shirt cases, and letter cases and cases each containing four bottles of medicine; and hat cases and helmet cases. It must have needed a whole herd of the Gadarene swine to make up his outfit. And, if I ever penetrated into his private room it would be to see him standing, with his coat and waistcoat off and the immensely long line of his perfectly elegant trousers from waist to boot heel. And he would have a slightly reflective air and he would be just opening one kind of case and just closing another.

Good God, what did they all see in him? for I swear there was all there was of him, inside and out; though they said he was a good soldier. Yet, Leonora adored him with a passion that was like an agony, and hated him with an agony that was as bitter as the sea. How could he arouse anything like a sentiment, in anybody?

What did he even talk to them about—when they were

under four eyes?—Ah, well, suddenly, as if by a flash of inspiration, I know. For all good soldiers are sentimentalists—all good soldiers of that type. Their profession, for one thing, is full of the big words, courage, loyalty, honour, constancy. And I have given a wrong impression of Edward Ashburnham if I have made you think that literally never in the course of our nine years of intimacy did he discuss what he would have called "the graver things." Even before his final outburst to me, at times, very late at night, say, he has blurted out something that gave an insight into the sentimental view of the cosmos that was his. He would say how much the society of a good woman could do towards redeeming you, and he would say that constancy was the finest of the virtues. He said it very stiffly, of course, but still as if the statement admitted of no doubt.

Constancy! Isn't that the queer thought? And yet, I must add that poor dear Edward was a great reader—he would pass hours lost in novels of a sentimental type—novels in which typewriter girls married Marquises and governesses Earls. And in his books, as a rule, the course of true love ran as smooth as buttered honey. And he was fond of poetry, of a certain type—and he could even read a perfectly sad love story. I have seen his eyes filled with tears at reading of a hopeless parting. And he loved, with a sentimental yearning, all children, puppies, and the feeble generally... .

So, you see, he would have plenty to gurgle about to a woman—with that and his sound common sense about martingales and his—still sentimental—experiences as a county magistrate; and with his intense, optimistic belief that the woman he was making love to at the moment was the one he was destined, at last, to be eternally constant to.... Well, I fancy he could put up a pretty good deal of talk when there was no man around to make him feel shy. And I was quite astonished, during his final burst out to me—at the very end of things, when the poor girl was on her way to that fatal Brindisi and he was trying to persuade himself and me that he had never really cared for her—I was quite astonished to observe how literary and how just his expressions were. He talked like quite a good book—a book not in the least cheaply sentimental. You see, I suppose he regarded me not so much as a man. I had to be regarded as a woman or a solicitor. Anyhow, it burst out of him on that horrible night. And then, next morning, he took me over to the Assizes and I saw how, in a perfectly calm and business-like way, he set to work to secure a verdict of not guilty for a poor girl, the daughter of one of his tenants, who had been accused of murdering her baby. He spent two hundred pounds on her defence... Well, that was Edward Ashburnham.

I had forgotten about his eyes. They were as blue as the sides of a certain type of box of matches. When you looked at them carefully you saw that they were perfectly honest, perfectly straightforward, perfectly, perfectly stupid. But the brick pink of his complexion, running perfectly level to the brick pink of his inner eyelids, gave them a curious, sinister expression—like a mosaic of blue porcelain set in pink china. And that chap, coming into a room, snapped up the gaze of every woman in it, as dexterously as a conjurer pockets billiard balls. It was most amazing. You know the man on the stage who throws up sixteen balls at once and they all drop into pockets all over his person, on his shoulders, on his heels, on the inner side of his sleeves; and he stands perfectly still and does nothing. Well, it was like that. He had rather a rough, hoarse voice.

And, there he was, standing by the table. I was looking at him, with my back to the screen. And suddenly, I saw two distinct expressions flicker across his immobile eyes. How the deuce did they do it, those unflinching blue eyes with the direct gaze? For the eyes themselves never moved, gazing over my shoulder towards the screen. And the gaze was perfectly level and perfectly direct and perfectly unchanging. I suppose that the lids really must have rounded themselves a little and perhaps the lips moved a little too, as if he should be saying: "There you are, my dear." At any rate, the expression was that of pride, of satisfaction, of the possessor. I saw him once afterwards, for a moment, gaze upon the sunny fields of Branshaw and say: "All this is my land!"

And then again, the gaze was perhaps more direct, harder if possible—hardy too. It was a measuring look; a challenging look. Once when we were at Wiesbaden watching him play in a polo match against the Bonner Hussaren I saw the same look come into his eyes, balancing the possibilities, looking over the ground. The German Captain, Count Baron Idigon von Lelöffel, was right up by their goal posts, coming with the ball in an easy canter in that tricky German fashion. The rest of the field were just anywhere. It was only a scratch sort of affair. Ashburnham was quite close to the rails not five yards from us and I heard him saying to himself: "Might just be done!" And he did it. Goodness! he swung that pony round with all its four legs spread out, like a cat dropping off a roof....

Well, it was just that look that I noticed in his eyes: "It might," I seem even now to hear him muttering to himself, "just be done."

I looked round over my shoulder and saw, tall, smiling brilliantly and buoyant—Leonora. And, little and fair, and as radiant as the track of sunlight along the sea—my wife.

That poor wretch! to think that he was at that moment in a perfect devil of a fix, and there he was, saying at the back of his mind: "It might just be done." It was like a chap in the middle of the eruption of a volcano, saying that he might just manage to bolt into the tumult and set fire to a haystack. Madness? Predestination? Who the devil knows?

Mrs Ashburnham exhibited at that moment more gaiety than I have ever since known her to show. There are certain classes of English people—the nicer ones when they have been to many spas, who seem to make a point of becoming much more than usually animated when they are introduced to my compatriots. I have noticed this often. Of course, they must first have accepted the Americans. But that once done, they seem to say to themselves: "Hallo, these women are so bright. We aren't going to be outdone in brightness." And for the time being they certainly aren't. But it wears off. So it was with Leonora—at least until she noticed me. She began, Leonora did—and perhaps it was that that gave me the idea of a touch of insolence in her character, for she never afterwards did any one single thing like it—she began by saying in quite a loud voice and from quite a distance:

"Don't stop over by that stuffy old table, Teddy. Come and sit by these nice people!"

And that was an extraordinary thing to say. Quite extraordinary. I couldn't for the life of me refer to total strangers as nice people. But, of course, she was taking a line of her own in which I at any rate—and no one else in the room, for she too had taken the trouble to read through the list of guests—counted any more than so many clean, bull terriers. And she sat down rather brilliantly at a vacant table, beside ours—one that was reserved for the Guggenheimers. And she just sat absolutely deaf to the remonstrances of the head waiter with his face like a grey ram's. That poor chap was doing his steadfast duty too. He knew that the Guggenheimers of Chicago, after they had stayed there a month and had worried the poor life out of him, would give him two dollars fifty and grumble at the tipping system. And he knew that Teddy Ashburnham and his wife would give him no trouble whatever except what the smiles of Leonora might cause in his apparently unimpressionable bosom—though you never can tell what may go on behind even a not quite spotless plastron!—And every week Edward Ashburnham would give him a solid, sound, golden English sovereign. Yet this stout fellow was intent on saving that table for the Guggenheimers of Chicago. It ended in Florence saying:

"Why shouldn't we all eat out of the same trough?—that's a nasty New York saying. But I'm sure we're all nice quiet people and there can be four seats at our table. It's round."

Then came, as it were, an appreciative gurgle from the Captain and I was perfectly aware of a slight hesitation—a quick sharp motion in Mrs Ashburnham, as if her horse had checked. But she put it at the fence all right, rising from the seat she had taken and sitting down opposite me, as it were, all in one motion. I never thought that Leonora looked her best in evening dress. She seemed to get it too clearly cut, there was no ruffling. She always affected black and her shoulders were too classical. She seemed to stand out of her corsage as a white marble bust might out of a black Wedgwood vase. I don't know.

I loved Leonora always and, today, I would very cheerfully lay down my life, what is left of it, in her service. But I am sure I never had the beginnings of a trace of what is called the sex instinct towards her. And I suppose—no I am certain that she never had it towards me. As far as I am concerned I think it was those white shoulders that did it. I seemed to feel when I looked at them that, if ever I should press my lips upon them that they would be slightly cold—not icily, not without a touch of human heat, but, as they say of baths, with the chill off. I seemed to feel chilled at the end of my lips when I looked at her...

No, Leonora always appeared to me at her best in a blue

tailor-made. Then her glorious hair wasn't deadened by her white shoulders. Certain women's lines guide your eyes to their necks, their eyelashes, their lips, their breasts. But Leonora's seemed to conduct your gaze always to her wrist. And the wrist was at its best in a black or a dog-skin glove and there was always a gold circlet with a little chain supporting a very small golden key to a dispatch box. Perhaps it was that in which she locked up her heart and her feelings.

Anyhow, she sat down opposite me and then, for the first time, she paid any attention to my existence. She gave me, suddenly, yet deliberately, one long stare. Her eyes too were blue and dark and the eyelids were so arched that they gave you the whole round of the irises. And it was a most remarkable, a most moving glance, as if for a moment a lighthouse had looked at me. I seemed to perceive the swift questions chasing each other through the brain that was behind them. I seemed to hear the brain ask and the eyes answer with all the simpleness of a woman who was a good hand at taking in qualities of a horse—as indeed she was. "Stands well; has plenty of room for his oats behind the girth. Not so much in the way of shoulders," and so on. And so her eyes asked: "Is this man trustworthy in money matters; is he likely to try to play the lover; is he likely to let his women be troublesome? Is he, above all, likely to babble about my affairs?"

And, suddenly, into those cold, slightly defiant, almost defensive china blue orbs, there came a warmth, a tenderness, a friendly recognition... oh, it was very charming and very touching—and quite mortifying. It was the look of a mother to her son, of a sister to her brother. It implied trust; it implied the want of any necessity for barriers. By God, she looked at me as if I were an invalid—as any kind woman may look at a poor chap in a bath chair. And, yes, from that day forward she always treated me and not Florence as if I were the invalid. Why, she would run after me with a rug upon chilly days. I suppose, therefore, that her eyes had made a favourable answer. Or, perhaps, it wasn't a favourable answer. And then Florence said: "And so the whole round table is begun." Again Edward Ashburnham gurgled slightly in his throat; but Leonora shivered a little, as if a goose had walked over her grave. And I was passing her the nickel-silver basket of rolls. Avanti!...

IV

So began those nine years of uninterrupted tranquillity. They were characterized by an extraordinary want of any communicativeness on the part of the Ashburnhams to which we, on our part, replied by leaving out quite as extraordinarily, and nearly as completely, the personal note. Indeed, you may take it that what characterized our relationship was an atmosphere of taking everything for granted. The given proposition was, that we were all "good people." We took for granted that we all liked beef underdone but not too underdone; that both men preferred a good liqueur brandy after lunch; that both women drank a very light Rhine wine qualified with Fachingen water—that sort of thing. It was also taken for granted that we were both sufficiently well off to afford anything that we could reasonably want in the way of amusements fitting to our station—that we could take motor cars and carriages by the day; that we could give each other dinners and dine our friends and we could indulge if we liked in economy. Thus, Florence was in the habit of having the Daily Telegraph sent to her every day from London. She was always an Anglo-maniac, was Florence; the Paris edition of the New York Herald was always good enough for me. But when we discovered that the Ashburnhams' copy of the London paper followed them from England, Leonora and Florence decided between them to suppress one subscription one year and the other the next. Similarly it was the habit of the Grand Duke of Nassau Schwerin, who came yearly to the baths, to dine once with about eighteen families of regular Kur guests. In return he would give a dinner of all the eighteen at once. And, since these dinners were rather expensive (you had to take the Grand Duke and a good many of his suite and any members of the diplomatic bodies that might be there)—Florence and Leonora, putting their heads together, didn't see why we shouldn't give the Grand Duke his dinner together. And so we did. I don't suppose the Serenity minded that economy, or even noticed it. At any rate, our joint dinner to the Royal Personage gradually assumed the aspect of a yearly function. Indeed, it grew larger and larger, until it became a sort of closing function for the season, at any rate as far as we were concerned. I don't in the least mean to say that we were the sort of persons who aspired to mix "with royalty." We didn't; we hadn't any claims; we were just "good people." But the Grand Duke was a pleasant, affable sort of royalty, like the late King Edward VII, and it was pleasant to hear him talk about the races and, very occasionally, as a bonne bouche, about his nephew, the Emperor; or to have him pause for a moment in his walk to ask after the progress of our cures or to be benignantly interested in the amount of money we had put on Lelöffel's hunter for the Frankfurt Welter Stakes.

But upon my word, I don't know how we put in our time. How does one put in one's time? How is it possible to have achieved nine years and to have nothing whatever to show for it? Nothing whatever, you understand. Not so much as a bone penholder, carved to resemble a chessman and with a hole in the top through which you could see four views of Nauheim. And, as for experience, as for knowledge of one's fellow beings—nothing either. Upon my word, I couldn't tell you offhand whether the lady who sold the so expensive violets at the bottom of the road that leads to the station, was cheating me or no; I can't say whether the porter who carried our traps across the station at Leghorn was a thief or no when he said that the regular tariff was a lira a parcel. The instances of honesty that one comes across in this world are just as amazing as the instances of dishonesty. After forty-five years of mixing with one's kind, one ought to have acquired the habit of being able to know something about one's fellow beings. But one doesn't.

I think the modern civilized habit—the modern English habit of taking every one for granted—is a good deal to blame for this. I have observed this matter long enough to know the queer, subtle thing that it is; to know how the faculty, for what it is worth, never lets you down.

Mind, I am not saying that this is not the most desirable type of life in the world; that it is not an almost unreasonably high standard. For it is really nauseating, when you detest it, to have to eat every day several slices of thin, tepid, pink india rubber, and it is disagreeable to have to drink brandy when you would prefer to be cheered up by warm, sweet Kümmel. And it is nasty to have to take a cold bath in the morning when what you want is really a hot one at night. And it stirs a little of the faith of your fathers that is deep down within you to have to have it taken for granted that you are an Episcopalian when really you are an old-fashioned Philadelphia Quaker.

But these things have to be done; it is the cock that the whole of this society owes to Aesculapius.

And the odd, queer thing is that the whole collection of rules applies to anybody—to the anybodies that you meet in hotels, in railway trains, to a less degree, perhaps, in steamers, but even, in the end, upon steamers. You meet a man or a woman and, from tiny and intimate sounds, from the slightest of movements, you know at once whether you are concerned with good people or with those who won't do. You know, this is to say, whether they will go rigidly through with the whole programme from the underdone beef to the Anglicanism. It won't matter whether they be short or tall; whether the voice squeak like a marionette or rumble like a town bull's; it won't matter whether they are Germans, Austrians, French, Spanish, or even Brazilians—they will be the Germans or Brazilians who take a cold bath every morning and who move, roughly speaking, in diplomatic circles.

But the inconvenient—well, hang it all, I will say it—the damnable nuisance of the whole thing is, that with all the taking for granted, you never really get an inch deeper than the things I have catalogued.

I can give you a rather extraordinary instance of this. I can't remember whether it was in our first year—the first year of us four at Nauheim, because, of course, it would have been the fourth year of Florence and myself—but it must have been in the first or second year. And that gives the measure at once of the extraordinariness of our discussion and of the swiftness with which intimacy had grown up between us. On the one hand we seemed to start out on the expedition so naturally and with so little preparation, that it was as if we must have made many such excursions before; and our intimacy seemed so deep....

Yet the place to which we went was obviously one to which Florence at least would have wanted to take us quite early, so that you would almost think we should have gone there together at the beginning of our intimacy. Florence was singularly expert as a guide to archaeological expeditions and there was nothing she liked so much as taking people round ruins and showing you the window from which some one looked down upon the murder of some one else. She only did it once; but she did it quite magnificently. She could find her way, with the sole help of Baedeker, as easily about any old monument as she could about any American city where the blocks are all square and the streets all numbered, so that you can go perfectly easily from Twenty-fourth to Thirtieth.

Now it happens that fifty minutes away from Nauheim, by a good train, is the ancient city of M——, upon a great pinnacle of basalt, girt with a triple road running sideways up its shoulder like a scarf. And at the top there is a castle—not a square castle like Windsor, but a castle all slate gables and high peaks with gilt weathercocks flashing bravely—the castle of St Elizabeth of Hungary. It has the disadvantage of being in Prussia; and it is always disagreeable to go into that country; but it is very old and there are many double-spired churches and it stands up like a pyramid out of the green valley of the Lahn. I don't suppose the Ashburnhams wanted especially to go there and I didn't especially want to go there myself. But, you understand, there was no objection. It was part of the cure to make an excursion three or four times a week. So that we were all quite unanimous in being grateful to Florence for providing the motive power. Florence, of course, had a motive of her own. She was at that time engaged in educating Captain Ashburnham—oh, of course, quite pour le bon motif! She used to say to Leonora: "I simply can't understand how you can let him live by your side and be so ignorant!" Leonora herself always struck me as being remarkably well educated. At any rate, she knew beforehand all that Florence had to tell her. Perhaps she got it up out of Baedeker before Florence was up in the morning. I don't mean to say that you would ever have known that Leonora knew anything, but if Florence started to tell us how Ludwig the Courageous wanted to have three wives at once—in which he differed from Henry VIII, who wanted them one after the other, and this caused a good deal of trouble—if Florence started to tell us this, Leonora would just nod her head in a way that quite pleasantly rattled my poor wife.

She used to exclaim: "Well, if you knew it, why haven't you told it all already to Captain Ashburnham? I'm sure he finds it interesting!" And Leonora would look reflectively at her husband and say: "I have an idea that it might injure his hand—the hand, you know, used in connection with horses' mouths...." And poor Ashburnham would blush and mutter and would say: "That's all right. Don't you bother about me."

I fancy his wife's irony did quite alarm poor Teddy; because one evening he asked me seriously in the smoking-room if I thought that having too much in one's head would really interfere with one's quickness in polo. It struck him, he said, that brainy Johnnies generally were rather muffs when they got on to four legs. I reassured him as best I could. I told him that he wasn't likely to take in enough to upset his balance. At that time the Captain was quite evidently enjoying being educated by Florence. She used to do it about three or four times a week under the approving eyes of Leonora and myself. It wasn't, you understand, systematic. It came in bursts. It was Florence clearing up one of the dark places of the earth, leaving the world a little lighter than she had found it. She would tell him the story of Hamlet; explain the form of a symphony, humming the first and second subjects to him, and so on; she would explain to him the difference between Arminians and Erastians; or she would give him a short lecture on the early history of the United States. And it was done in a way well calculated to arrest a young attention. Did you ever read Mrs Markham? Well, it was like that... .

But our excursion to M—— was a much larger, a much more full dress affair. You see, in the archives of the Schloss in that city there was a document which Florence thought would finally give her the chance to educate the whole lot of us together. It really worried poor Florence that she couldn't, in matters of culture, ever get the better of Leonora. I don't know what Leonora knew or what she didn't know, but certainly she was always there whenever Florence brought out any information. And she gave, somehow, the impression of really knowing what poor Florence gave the impression of having only picked up. I can't exactly define it. It was almost something physical. Have you ever seen a retriever dashing in play after a greyhound? You see the two running over a green field, almost side by side, and suddenly the retriever makes a friendly snap at the other. And the greyhound simply isn't there. You haven't observed it quicken its speed or strain a limb; but there it is, just two yards in front of the retriever's outstretched muzzle. So it was with Florence and Leonora in matters of culture.

But on this occasion I knew that something was up. I found Florence some days before, reading books like Ranke's History of the Popes, Symonds' Renaissance, Motley's Rise of the Dutch Republic and Luther's Table Talk.

I must say that, until the astonishment came, I got nothing but pleasure out of the little expedition. I like catching the two-forty; I like the slow, smooth roll of the great big trains—and they are the best trains in the world! I like being drawn through the green country and looking at it through the clear glass of the great windows. Though, of course, the country isn't really green. The sun shines, the earth is blood red and purple and red and green and red. And the oxen in the ploughlands are bright varnished brown and black and blackish purple; and the peasants are dressed in the black and white of magpies; and there are great Rocks of magpies too. Or the peasants' dresses in another field where there are little mounds of hay that will be grey-green on the sunny side and purple in the shadows—the peasants' dresses are vermilion with emerald green ribbons and purple skirts and white shirts and black velvet stomachers. Still, the impression is that you are drawn through brilliant green meadows that run away on each side to the dark purple fir-woods; the basalt pinnacles; the immense forests. And there is meadowsweet at the edge of the streams, and cattle. Why, I remember on that afternoon I saw a brown cow hitch its horns under the stomach of a black and white animal and the black and white one was thrown right into the middle of a narrow stream. I burst out laughing. But Florence was imparting information so hard and Leonora was listening so intently that no one noticed me. As for me, I was pleased to be off duty; I was pleased to think that Florence for the moment was indubitably out of mischief—because she was talking about Ludwig the Courageous (I think it was Ludwig the Courageous but I am not an historian) about Ludwig the Courageous of Hessen who wanted to have three wives at once and patronized Luther—something like that!—I was so relieved to be off duty, because she couldn't possibly be doing anything to excite herself or set her poor heart a-fluttering—that the incident of the cow was a real joy to me. I chuckled over it from time to time for the whole rest of the day. Because it does look very funny, you know, to see a black and white cow land on its back in the middle of a stream. It is so just exactly what one doesn't expect of a cow.

I suppose I ought to have pitied the poor animal; but I just didn't. I was out for enjoyment. And I just enjoyed myself. It is so pleasant to be drawn along in front of the spectacular towns with the peaked castles and the many double spires. In the sunlight gleams come from the city—gleams from the glass of windows; from the gilt signs of apothecaries; from the ensigns of the student corps high up in the mountains; from the helmets of the funny little soldiers moving their stiff little legs in white linen trousers. And it was pleasant to get out in the great big spectacular Prussian station with the hammered bronze ornaments and the paintings of peasants and flowers and cows; and to hear Florence bargain energetically with the driver of an ancient droschka drawn by two lean horses. Of course, I spoke German much more correctly than Florence, though I never could rid myself quite of the accent of the Pennsylvania Duitsch of my childhood. Anyhow, we were drawn in a sort of triumph, for five marks without any trinkgeld, right up to the castle. And we were taken through the museum and saw the fire-backs, the old glass, the old swords and the antique contraptions. And we went up winding corkscrew staircases and through the Rittersaal, the great painted hall where the Reformer and his friends met for the first time under the protection of the gentleman that had three wives at once and formed an alliance with the gentleman that had six wives, one after the other (I'm not really interested in these facts but they have a bearing on my story). And we went through chapels, and music rooms, right up immensely high in the air to a large old chamber, full of presses, with heavily-shuttered windows all round. And Florence became positively electric. She told the tired, bored custodian what shutters to open; so that the bright sunlight streamed in palpable shafts into the dim old chamber. She explained that this was Luther's bedroom and that just where the sunlight fell had stood his bed. As a matter of fact, I believe that she was wrong and that Luther only stopped, as it were, for lunch, in order to evade pursuit. But, no doubt, it would have been his bedroom if he could have been persuaded to stop the night. And then, in spite of the protest of the custodian, she threw open another shutter and came tripping back to a large glass case.

"And there," she exclaimed with an accent of gaiety, of triumph, and of audacity. She was pointing at a piece of paper, like the half-sheet of a letter with some faint pencil scrawls that might have been a jotting of the amounts we were spending during the day. And I was extremely happy at her gaiety, in her triumph, in her audacity. Captain Ashburnham had his hands upon the glass case. "There it is—the Protest." And then, as we all properly stage-managed our bewilderment, she continued: "Don't you know that is why we were all called Protestants? That is the pencil draft of the Protest they drew up. You can see the signatures of Martin Luther, and Martin Bucer, and Zwingli, and Ludwig the Courageous...."

I may have got some of the names wrong, but I know that Luther and Bucer were there. And her animation continued and I was glad. She was better and she was out of mischief. She continued, looking up into Captain Ashburnham's eyes: "It's because of that piece of paper that you're honest, sober, industrious, provident, and clean-lived. If it weren't for that piece of paper you'd be like the Irish or the Italians or the Poles, but particularly the Irish...."

And she laid one finger upon Captain Ashburnham's wrist.

I was aware of something treacherous, something frightful, something evil in the day. I can't define it and can't find a simile for it. It wasn't as if a snake had looked out of a hole. No, it was as if my heart had missed a beat. It was as if we were going to run and cry out; all four of us in separate directions, averting our heads. In Ashburnham's face I know that there was absolute panic. I was horribly frightened and then I discovered that the pain in my left wrist was caused by Leonora's clutching it:

"I can't stand this," she said with a most extraordinary passion; "I must get out of this." I was horribly frightened. It came to me for a moment, though I hadn't time to think it, that she must be a madly jealous woman—jealous of Florence and Captain Ashburnham, of all people in the world! And it was a panic in which we fled! We went right down the winding stairs, across the immense Rittersaal to a little terrace that overlooks the Lahn, the broad valley and the immense plain into which it opens out.

"Don't you see?" she said, "don't you see what's going on?" The panic again stopped my heart. I muttered, I stuttered—I don't know how I got the words out:

"No! What's the matter? Whatever's the matter?"

She looked me straight in the eyes; and for a moment I had the feeling that those two blue discs were immense, were overwhelming, were like a wall of blue that shut me off from the rest of the world. I know it sounds absurd; but that is what it did feel like.

"Don't you see," she said, with a really horrible bitterness, with a really horrible lamentation in her voice, "Don't you see that that's the cause of the whole miserable affair; of the whole sorrow of the world? And of the eternal damnation of you and me and them... ."

I don't remember how she went on; I was too frightened; I was too amazed. I think I was thinking of running to fetch assistance—a doctor, perhaps, or Captain Ashburnham. Or possibly she needed Florence's tender care, though, of course, it would have been very bad for Florence's heart. But I know that when I came out of it she was saying: "Oh, where are all the bright, happy, innocent beings in the world? Where's happiness? One reads of it in books!"

She ran her hand with a singular clawing motion upwards over her forehead. Her eyes were enormously distended; her face was exactly that of a person looking into the pit of hell and seeing horrors there. And then suddenly she stopped. She was, most amazingly, just Mrs Ashburnham again. Her face was perfectly clear, sharp and defined; her hair was glorious in its golden coils. Her nostrils twitched with a sort of contempt. She appeared to look with interest at a gypsy caravan that was coming over a little bridge far below us.

"Don't you know," she said, in her clear hard voice, "don't you know that I'm an Irish Catholic?"

IV

THOSE words gave me the greatest relief that I have ever had in my life. They told me, I think, almost more than I have ever gathered at any one moment—about myself. I don't think that before that day I had ever wanted anything very much except Florence. I have, of course, had appetites, impatiences...

Why, sometimes at a table d'hôte, when there would be, say, caviare handed round, I have been absolutely full of impatience for fear that when the dish came to me there should not be a satisfying portion left over by the other guests. I have been exceedingly impatient at missing trains. The Belgian State Railway has a trick of letting the French trains miss their connections at Brussels. That has always infuriated me. I have written about it letters to The Times that The Times never printed; those that I wrote to the Paris edition of the New York Herald were always printed, but they never seemed to satisfy me when I saw them. Well, that was a sort of frenzy with me.

It was a frenzy that now I can hardly realize. I can understand it intellectually. You see, in those days I was interested in people with "hearts." There was Florence, there was Edward Ashburnham—or, perhaps, it was Leonora that I was more interested in. I don't mean in the way of love. But, you see, we were both of the same profession—at any rate as I saw it. And the profession was that of keeping heart patients alive.

You have no idea how engrossing such a profession may become. Just as the blacksmith says: "By hammer and hand all Art doth stand," just as the baker thinks that all the solar system revolves around his morning delivery of rolls, as the postmaster-general believes that he alone is the preserver of society—and surely, surely, these delusions are necessary to keep us going—so did I and, as I believed, Leonora, imagine that the whole world ought to be arranged so as to ensure the keeping alive of heart patients. You have no idea how engrossing such a profession may become—how imbecile, in view of that engrossment, appear the ways of princes, of republics, of municipalities. A rough bit of road beneath the motor tyres, a couple of succeeding "thank'ee-marms" with their quick jolts would be enough to set me grumbling to Leonora against the Prince or the Grand Duke or the Free City through whose territory we might be passing. I would grumble like a stockbroker whose conversations over the telephone are incommoded by the ringing of bells from a city church. I would talk about medieval survivals, about the taxes being surely high enough. The point, by the way, about the missing of the connections of the Calais boat trains at Brussels was that the shortest possible sea journey is frequently of great importance to sufferers from the heart.

Now, on the Continent, there are two special heart cure places, Nauheim and Spa, and to reach both of these baths from England if in order to ensure a short sea passage, you come by Calais—you have to make the connection at Brussels. And the Belgian train never waits by so much the shade of a second for the one coming from Calais or from Paris. And even if the French train, are just on time, you have to run—imagine a heart patient running!—along the unfamiliar ways of the Brussels station and to scramble up the high steps of the moving train. Or, if you miss connection, you have to wait five or six hours.... I used to keep awake whole nights cursing that abuse. My wife used to run—she never, in whatever else she may have misled me, tried to give me the impression that she was not a gallant soul. But, once in the German Express, she would lean back, with one hand to her side and her eyes closed. Well, she was a good actress. And I would be in hell. In hell, I tell you. For in Florence I had at once a wife and an unattained mistress—that is what it comes to—and in the retaining of her in this world I had my occupation, my career, my ambition. It is not often that these things are united in one body. Leonora was a good actress too. By Jove she was good! I tell you, she would listen to me by the hour, evolving my plans for a shock-proof world. It is true that, at times, I used to notice about her an air of inattention as if she were listening, a mother, to the child at her knee, or as if, precisely, I were myself the patient.

You understand that there was nothing the matter with Edward Ashburnham's heart—that he had thrown up his commission and had left India and come half the world over in order to follow a woman who had really had a "heart" to Nauheim. That was the sort of sentimental ass he was. For, you understand, too, that they really needed to live in India, to economize, to let the house at Branshaw Teleragh.

Of course, at that date, I had never heard of the Kilsyte case. Ashburnham had, you know, kissed a servant girl in a railway train, and it was only the grace of God, the prompt functioning of the communication cord and the ready sympathy of what I believe you call the Hampshire Bench, that kept the poor devil out of Winchester Gaol for years and years. I never heard of that case until the final stages of Leonora's revelations....

But just think of that poor wretch.... I, who have surely the right, beg you to think of that poor wretch. Is it possible that such a luckless devil should be so tormented by blind and inscrutable destiny? For there is no other way to think of it. None. I have the right to say it, since for years he was my wife's lover, since he killed her, since he broke up all the pleasantnesses that there were in my life. There is no priest that has the right to tell me that I must not ask pity for him, from you, silent listener beyond the hearth-stone, from the world, or from the God who created in him those desires, those madnesses....

Of course, I should not hear of the Kilsyte case. I knew none of their friends; they were for me just good people—fortunate people with broad and sunny acres in a southern county. Just good people! By heavens, I sometimes think that it would have been better for him, poor dear, if the case had been such a one that I must needs have heard of it—such a one as maids and couriers and other Kur guests whisper about for years after, until gradually it dies away in the pity that there is knocking about here and there in the world. Supposing he had spent his seven years in Winchester Gaol or whatever it is that inscrutable and blind justice allots to you for following your natural but ill-timed inclinations—there would have arrived a stage when nodding gossips on the Kursaal terrace would have said, "Poor fellow," thinking of his ruined career. He would have been the fine soldier with his back now bent.... Better for him, poor devil, if his back had been prematurely bent.

Why, it would have been a thousand times better.... For, of course, the Kilsyte case, which came at the very beginning of his finding Leonora cold and unsympathetic, gave him a nasty jar. He left servants alone after that.

It turned him, naturally, all the more loose amongst women of his own class. Why, Leonora told me that Mrs Maidan—the woman he followed from Burma to Nauheim—assured her he awakened her attention by swearing that when he kissed the servant in the train he was driven to it. I daresay he was driven to it, by the mad passion to find an ultimately satisfying woman. I daresay he was sincere enough. Heaven help me, I daresay he was sincere enough in his love for Mrs Maidan. She was a nice little thing, a dear little dark woman with long lashes, of whom Florence grew quite fond. She had a lisp and a happy smile. We saw plenty of her for the first month of our acquaintance, then she died, quite quietly—of heart trouble.

But you know, poor little Mrs Maidan—she was so gentle, so young. She cannot have been more than twenty-three and she had a boy husband out in Chitral not more than twenty-four, I believe. Such young things ought to have been left alone. Of course Ashburnham could not leave her alone. I do not believe that he could. Why, even I, at this distance of time am aware that I am a little in love with her memory. I can't help smiling when I think suddenly of her—as you might at the thought of something wrapped carefully away in lavender, in some drawer, in some old house that you have long left. She was so—so submissive. Why, even to me she had the air of being submissive—to me that not the youngest child will ever pay heed to. Yes, this is the saddest story...

No, I cannot help wishing that Florence had left her alone—with her playing with adultery. I suppose it was; though she was such a child that one has the impression that she would hardly have known how to spell such a word. No, it was just submissiveness—to the importunities, to the tempestuous forces that pushed that miserable fellow on to ruin. And I do not suppose that Florence really made much difference. If it had not been for her that Ashburnham left his allegiance for Mrs Maidan, then it would have been some other woman. But still, I do not know. Perhaps the poor young thing would have died—she was bound to die, anyhow, quite soon—but she would have died without having to soak her noonday pillow with tears whilst Florence, below the window, talked to Captain Ashburnham about the Constitution of the United States.... Yes, it would have left a better taste in the mouth if Florence had let her die in peace....

Leonora behaved better in a sense. She just boxed Mrs Maidan's ears—yes, she hit her, in an uncontrollable access of rage, a hard blow on the side of the cheek, in the corridor of the hotel, outside Edward's rooms. It was that, you know, that accounted for the sudden, odd intimacy that sprang up between Florence and Mrs Ashburnham. Because it was, of course, an odd intimacy. If you look at it from the outside nothing could have been more unlikely than that Leonora, who is the proudest creature on God's earth, would have struck up an acquaintanceship with two casual Yankees whom she could not really have regarded as being much more than a carpet beneath her feet. You may ask what she had to be proud of. Well, she was a Powys married to an Ashburnham—I suppose that gave her the right to despise casual Americans as long as she did it unostentatiously. I don't know what anyone has to be proud of. She might have taken pride in her patience, in her keeping her husband out of the bankruptcy court. Perhaps she did.

At any rate that was how Florence got to know her. She came round a screen at the corner of the hotel corridor and found Leonora with the gold key that hung from her wrist caught in Mrs Maidan's hair just before dinner. There was not a single word spoken. Little Mrs Maidan was very pale, with a red mark down her left cheek, and the key would not come out of her black hair. It was Florence who had to disentangle it, for Leonora was in such a state that she could not have brought herself to touch Mrs Maidan without growing sick.

And there was not a word spoken. You see, under those four eyes—her own and Mrs Maidan's—Leonora could just let herself go as far as to box Mrs Maidan's ears. But the moment a stranger came along she pulled herself wonderfully up. She was at first silent and then, the moment the key was disengaged by Florence she was in a state to say: "So awkward of me... I was just trying to put the comb straight in Mrs Maidan's hair...."

Mrs Maidan, however, was not a Powys married to an Ashburnham; she was a poor little O'Flaherty whose husband was a boy of country parsonage origin. So there was no mistaking the sob she let go as she went desolately away along the corridor. But Leonora was still going to play up. She opened the door of Ashburnham's room quite ostentatiously, so that Florence should hear her address Edward in terms of intimacy and liking. "Edward," she called. But there was no Edward there.

You understand that there was no Edward there. It was then, for the only time of her career, that Leonora really compromised herself—She exclaimed.... "How frightful!... Poor little Maisie!..."

She caught herself up at that, but of course it was too late. It was a queer sort of affair....

I want to do Leonora every justice. I love her very dearly for one thing and in this matter, which was certainly the ruin of my small household cockle-shell, she certainly tripped up. I do not believe—and Leonora herself does not believe—that poor little Maisie Maidan was ever Edward's mistress. Her heart was really so bad that she would have succumbed to anything like an impassioned embrace. That is the plain English of it, and I suppose plain English is best. She was really what the other two, for reasons of their own, just pretended to be. Queer, isn't it? Like one of those sinister jokes that Providence plays upon one. Add to this that I do not suppose that Leonora would much have minded, at any other moment, if Mrs Maidan had been her husband's mistress. It might have been a relief from Edward's sentimental gurglings over the lady and from the lady's submissive acceptance of those sounds. No, she would not have minded.

But, in boxing Mrs Maidan's ears, Leonora was just striking the face of an intolerable universe. For, that afternoon she had had a frightfully painful scene with Edward.

As far as his letters went, she claimed the right to open them when she chose. She arrogated to herself the right because Edward's affairs were in such a frightful state and he lied so about them that she claimed the privilege of having his secrets at her disposal. There was not, indeed, any other way, for the poor fool was too ashamed of his lapses ever to make a clean breast of anything. She had to drag these things out of him.

It must have been a pretty elevating job for her. But that afternoon, Edward being on his bed for the hour and a half prescribed by the Kur authorities, she had opened a letter that she took to come from a Colonel Hervey. They were going to stay with him in Linlithgowshire for the month of September and she did not know whether the date fixed would be the eleventh or the eighteenth. The address on this letter was, in handwriting, as like Colonel Hervey's as one blade of corn is like another. So she had at the moment no idea of spying on him.

But she certainly was. For she discovered that Edward Ashburnham was paying a blackmailer of whom she had never heard something like three hundred pounds a year... It was a devil of a blow; it was like death; for she imagined that by that time she had really got to the bottom of her husband's liabilities. You see, they were pretty heavy. What had really smashed them up had been a perfectly common-place affair at Monte Carlo—an affair with a cosmopolitan harpy who passed for the mistress of a Russian Grand Duke. She exacted a twenty thousand pound pearl tiara from him as the price of her favours for a week or so. It would have pipped him a good deal to have found so much, and he was not in the ordinary way a gambler. He might, indeed, just have found the twenty thousand and the not slight charges of a week at an hotel with the fair creature. He must have been worth at that date five hundred thousand dollars and a little over. Well, he must needs go to the tables and lose forty thousand pounds.... Forty thousand solid pounds, borrowed from sharks! And even after that he must—it was an imperative passion—enjoy the favours of the lady. He got them, of course, when it was a matter of solid bargaining, for far less than twenty thousand, as he might, no doubt, have done from the first. I daresay ten thousand dollars covered the bill. Anyhow, there was a pretty solid hole in a fortune of a hundred thousand pounds or so. And Leonora had to fix things up; he would have run from money-lender to money-lender. And that was quite in the early days of her discovery of his infidelities—if you like to call them infidelities. And she discovered that one from public sources. God knows what would have happened if she had not discovered it from public sources. I suppose he would have concealed it from her until they were penniless. But she was able, by the grace of God, to get hold of the actual lenders of the money, to learn the exact sums that were needed. And she went off to England.

Yes, she went right off to England to her attorney and his while he was still in the arms of his Circe—at Antibes, to which place they had retired. He got sick of the lady quite quickly, but not before Leonora had had such lessons in the art of business from her attorney that she had her plan as clearly drawn up as was ever that of General Trochu for keeping the Prussians out of Paris in 1870. It was about as effectual at first, or it seemed so.

That would have been, you know, in 1895, about nine years before the date of which I am talking—the date of Florence's getting her hold over Leonora; for that was what it amounted to.... Well, Mrs Ashburnham had simply forced Edward to settle all his property upon her. She could force him to do anything; in his clumsy, good-natured, inarticulate way he was as frightened of her as of the devil. And he admired her enormously, and he was as fond of her as any man could be of any woman. She took advantage of it to treat him as if he had been a person whose estates are being managed by the Court of Bankruptcy. I suppose it was the best thing for him.

Anyhow, she had no end of a job for the first three years or so. Unexpected liabilities kept on cropping up—and that afflicted fool did not make it any easier. You see, along with the passion of the chase went a frame of mind that made him be extraordinarily ashamed of himself. You may not believe it, but he really had such a sort of respect for the chastity of Leonora's imagination that he hated—he was positively revolted at the thought that she should know that the sort of thing that he did existed in the world. So he would stick out in an agitated way against the accusation of ever having done anything. He wanted to preserve the virginity of his wife's thoughts. He told me that himself during the long walks we had at the last—while the girl was on the way to Brindisi.

So, of course, for those three years or so, Leonora had many agitations. And it was then that they really quarrelled.

Yes, they quarrelled bitterly. That seems rather extravagant. You might have thought that Leonora would be just calmly loathing and he lachrymosely contrite. But that was not it a bit... Along with Edward's passions and his shame for them went the violent conviction of the duties of his station—a conviction that was quite unreasonably expensive. I trust I have not, in talking of his liabilities, given the impression that poor Edward was a promiscuous libertine. He was not; he was a sentimentalist. The servant girl in the Kilsyte case had been pretty, but mournful of appearance. I think that, when he had kissed her, he had desired rather to comfort her. And, if she had succumbed to his blandishments I daresay he would have set her up in a little house in Portsmouth or Winchester and would have been faithful to her for four or five years. He was quite capable of that.

No, the only two of his affairs of the heart that cost him money were that of the Grand Duke's mistress and that which was the subject of the blackmailing letter that Leonora opened. That had been a quite passionate affair with quite a nice woman. It had succeeded the one with the Grand Ducal lady. The lady was the wife of a brother officer and Leonora had known all about the passion, which had been quite a real passion and had lasted for several years. You see, poor Edward's passions were quite logical in their progression upwards. They began with a servant, went on to a courtesan and then to a quite nice woman, very unsuitably mated. For she had a quite nasty husband who, by means of letters and things, went on blackmailing poor Edward to the tune of three or four hundred a year—with threats of the Divorce Court. And after this lady came Maisie Maidan, and after poor Maisie only one more affair and then—the real passion of his life. His marriage with Leonora had been arranged by his parents and, though he always admired her immensely, he had hardly ever pretended to be much more than tender to her, though he desperately needed her moral support, too....

But his really trying liabilities were mostly in the nature of generosities proper to his station. He was, according to Leonora, always remitting his tenants' rents and giving the tenants to understand that the reduction would be permanent; he was always redeeming drunkards who came before his magisterial bench; he was always trying to put prostitutes into respectable places—and he was a perfect maniac about children. I don't know how many ill-used people he did not pick up and provide with careers—Leonora has told me, but I daresay she exaggerated and the figure seems so preposterous that I will not put it down. All these things, and the continuance of them seemed to him to be his duty—along with impossible subscriptions to hospitals and Boy Scouts and to provide prizes at cattle shows and antivivisection societies....

Well, Leonora saw to it that most of these things were not continued. They could not possibly keep up Branshaw Manor at that rate after the money had gone to the Grand Duke's mistress. She put the rents back at their old figures; discharged the drunkards from their homes, and sent all the societies notice that they were to expect no more subscriptions. To the children, she was more tender; nearly all of them she supported till the age of apprenticeship or domestic service. You see, she was childless herself.

She was childless herself, and she considered herself to be to blame. She had come of a penniless branch of the Powys family, and they had forced upon her poor dear Edward without making the stipulation that the children should be brought up as

Catholics. And that, of course, was spiritual death to Leonora. I have given you a wrong impression if I have not made you see that Leonora was a woman of a strong, cold conscience, like all English Catholics. (I cannot, myself, help disliking this religion; there is always, at the bottom of my mind, in spite of Leonora, the feeling of shuddering at the Scarlet Woman, that filtered in upon me in the tranquility of the little old Friends' Meeting House in Arch Street, Philadelphia.) So I do set down a good deal of Leonora's mismanagement of poor dear Edward's case to the peculiarly English form of her religion. Because, of course, the only thing to have done for Edward would have been to let him sink down until he became a tramp of gentlemanly address, having, maybe, chance love affairs upon the highways. He would have done so much less harm; he would have been much less agonized too. At any rate, he would have had fewer chances of ruining and of remorse. For Edward was great at remorse. But Leonora's English Catholic conscience, her rigid principles, her coldness, even her very patience, were, I cannot help thinking, all wrong in this special case. She quite seriously and naïvely imagined that the Church of Rome disapproves of divorce; she quite seriously and naïvely believed that her church could be such a monstrous and imbecile institution as to expect her to take on the impossible job of making Edward Ashburnham a faithful husband. She had, as the English would say, the Nonconformist temperament. In the United States of North America we call it the New England conscience. For, of course, that frame of mind has been driven in on the English Catholics. The centuries that they have gone through—centuries of blind and malignant oppression, of ostracism from public employment, of being, as it were, a small beleagured garrison in a hostile country, and therefore having to act with great formality—all these things have combined to perform that conjuring trick. And I suppose that Papists in England are even technically Nonconformists.

Continental Papists are a dirty, jovial and unscrupulous crew. But that, at least, lets them be opportunists. They would have fixed poor dear Edward up all right. (Forgive my writing of these monstrous things in this frivolous manner. If I did not I should break down and cry.) In Milan, say, or in Paris, Leonora would have had her marriage dissolved in six months for two hundred dollars paid in the right quarter. And Edward would have drifted about until he became a tramp of the kind I have suggested. Or he would have married a barmaid who would have made him such frightful scenes in public places and would so have torn out his moustache and left visible signs upon his face that he would have been faithful to her for the rest of his days. That was what he wanted to redeem him....

For, along with his passions and his shames there went the dread of scenes in public places, of outcry, of excited physical violence; of publicity, in short. Yes, the barmaid would have cured him. And it would have been all the better if she drank; he would have been kept busy looking after her.

I know that I am right in this. I know it because of the Kilsyte case. You see, the servant girl that he then kissed was nurse in the family of the Nonconformist head of the county—whatever that post may be called. And that gentleman was so determined to ruin Edward, who was the chairman of the Tory caucus, or whatever it is—that the poor dear sufferer had the very devil of a time. They asked questions about it in the House of Commons; they tried to get the Hampshire magistrates degraded; they suggested to the War Ministry that Edward was not the proper person to hold the King's commission. Yes, he got it hot and strong.

The result you have heard. He was completely cured of philandering amongst the lower classes. And that seemed a real blessing to Leonora. It did not revolt her so much to be connected—it is a sort of connection—with people like Mrs Maidan, instead of with a little kitchenmaid.

In a dim sort of way, Leonora was almost contented when she arrived at Nauheim, that evening....

She had got things nearly straight by the long years of scraping in little stations in Chitral and Burma—stations where living is cheap in comparison with the life of a county magnate, and where, moreover, liaisons of one sort or another are normal and inexpensive too. So that, when Mrs Maidan came along—and the Maidan affair might have caused trouble out there because of the youth of the husband—Leonora had just resigned herself to coming home. With pushing and scraping and with letting Branshaw Teleragh, and with selling a picture and a relic of Charles I or so, had got—and, poor dear, she had never had a really decent dress to her back in all those years and years—she had got, as she imagined, her poor dear husband back into much the same financial position as had been his before the mistress of the Grand Duke had happened along. And, of course, Edward himself had helped her a little on the financial side. He was a fellow that many men liked. He was so presentable and quite ready to lend you his cigar puncher—that sort of thing. So, every now and then some financier whom he met about would give him a good, sound, profitable tip. And Leonora was never afraid of a bit of a gamble—English Papists seldom are, I do not know why.

So nearly all her investment turned up trumps, and Edward was really in fit case to reopen Branshaw Manor and once more to assume his position in the county. Thus Leonora had accepted Maisie Maidan almost with resignation—almost with a sigh of relief. She really liked the poor child—she had to like somebody. And, at any rate, she felt she could trust Maisie—she could trust her not to rook Edward for several thousands a week, for Maisie had refused to accept so much as a trinket ring from him. It is true that Edward gurgled and raved about the girl in a way that she had never yet experienced. But that, too, was almost a relief. I think she would really have welcomed it if he could have come across the love of his life. It would have given her a rest.

And there could not have been anyone better than poor little Mrs Maidan; she was so ill she could not want to be taken on expensive jaunts.... It was Leonora herself who paid Maisie's expenses to Nauheim. She handed over the money to the boy husband, for Maisie would never have allowed it; but the husband was in agonies of fear. Poor devil!

I fancy that, on the voyage from India, Leonora was as happy as ever she had been in her life. Edward was wrapped up, completely, in his girl—he was almost like a father with a child, trotting about with rugs and physic and things, from deck to deck. He behaved, however, with great circumspection, so that nothing leaked through to the other passengers. And Leonora had almost attained to the attitude of a mother towards Mrs Maidan. So it had looked very well—the benevolent, wealthy couple of good people, acting as saviours to the poor, dark-eyed, dying young thing. And that attitude of Leonora's towards Mrs Maidan no doubt partly accounted for the smack in the face. She was hitting a naughty child who had been stealing chocolates at an inopportune moment. It was certainly an inopportune moment. For, with the opening of that blackmailing letter from that injured brother officer, all the old terrors had redescended upon Leonora. Her road had again seemed to stretch out endless; she imagined that there might be hundreds and hundreds of such things that Edward was concealing from her—that they might necessitate more mortgagings, more pawnings of bracelets, more and always more horrors. She had spent an excruciating afternoon. The matter was one of a divorce case, of course, and she wanted to avoid publicity as much as Edward did, so that she saw the necessity of continuing the payments. And she did not so much mind that. They could find three hundred a year. But it was the horror of there being more such obligations.

She had had no conversation with Edward for many years—none that went beyond the mere arrangements for taking trains or engaging servants. But that afternoon she had to let him have it. And he had been just the same as ever. It was like opening a book after a decade to find the words the same. He had the same motives. He had not wished to tell her about the case because he had not wished her to sully her mind with the idea that there was such a thing as a brother officer who could be a blackmailer—and he had wanted to protect the credit of his old light of love. That lady was certainly not concerned with her husband. And he swore, and swore, and swore, that there was nothing else in the world against him. She did not believe him.

He had done it once too often—and she was wrong for the first time, so that he acted a rather creditable part in the matter. For he went right straight out to the post-office and spent several hours in coding a telegram to his solicitor, bidding that hard-headed man to threaten to take out at once a warrant against the fellow who was on his track. He said afterwards that it was a bit too thick on poor old Leonora to be ballyragged any more. That was really the last of his outstanding accounts, and he was ready to take his personal chance of the Divorce Court if the blackmailer turned nasty. He would face it out—the publicity, the papers, the whole bally show. Those were his simple words....

He had made, however, the mistake of not telling Leonora where he was going, so that, having seen him go to his room to fetch the code for the telegram, and seeing, two hours later, Maisie Maidan come out of his room, Leonora imagined that the two hours she had spent in silent agony Edward had spent with Maisie Maidan in his arms. That seemed to her to be too much. As a matter of fact, Maisie's being in Edward's room had been the result, partly of poverty, partly of pride, partly of sheer innocence. She could not, in the first place, afford a maid; she refrained as much as possible from sending the hotel servants on errands, since every penny was of importance to her, and she feared to have to pay high tips at the end of her stay. Edward had lent her one of his fascinating cases containing fifteen different sizes of scissors, and, having seen from her window, his departure for the post-office, she had taken the opportunity of returning the case. She could not see why she should not, though she felt a certain remorse at the thought that she had kissed the pillows of his bed. That was the way it took her.

But Leonora could see that, without the shadow of a doubt, the incident gave Florence a hold over her. It let Florence into things and Florence was the only created being who had any idea that the Ashburnhams were not just good people with nothing to their tails. She determined at once, not so much to give Florence the privilege of her intimacy—which would have been the payment of a kind of blackmail—as to keep Florence under observation until she could have demonstrated to Florence that she was not in the least jealous of poor Maisie. So that was why she had entered the dining room arm in arm with my wife, and why she had so markedly planted herself at our table. She never left us, indeed, for a minute that night, except just to run up to Mrs Maidan's room to beg her pardon and to beg her also to let Edward take her very markedly out into the gardens that night. She said herself, when Mrs Maidan came rather wistfully down into the lounge where we were all sitting: "Now, Edward, get up and take Maisie to the Casino. I want Mrs Dowell to tell me all about the families in Connecticut who came from Fordingbridge." For it had been discovered that Florence came of a line that had actually owned Branshaw Teleragh for two centuries before the Ashburnhams came there. And there she sat with me in that hall, long after Florence had gone to bed, so that I might witness her gay reception of that pair. She could play up.

And that enables me to fix exactly the day of our going to

the town of M——. For it was the very day poor Mrs Maidan died. We found her dead when we got back—pretty awful, that, when you come to figure out what it all means....

At any rate the measure of my relief when Leonora said that she was an Irish Catholic gives you the measure of my affection for that couple. It was an affection so intense that even to this day I cannot think of Edward without sighing. I do not believe that I could have gone on any more with them. I was getting too tired. And I verily believe, too, if my suspicion that Leonora was jealous of Florence had been the reason she gave for her outburst I should have turned upon Florence with the maddest kind of rage. Jealousy would have been incurable. But Florence's mere silly jibes at the Irish and at the Catholics could be apologized out of existence. And that I appeared to fix up in two minutes or so.

She looked at me for a long time rather fixedly and queerly while I was doing it. And at last I worked myself up to saying:

"Do accept the situation. I confess that I do not like your religion. But I like you so intensely. I don't mind saying that I have never had anyone to be really fond of, and I do not believe that anyone has ever been fond of me, as I believe you really to be."

"Oh, I'm fond enough of you," she said. "Fond enough to say that I wish every man was like you. But there are others to be considered." She was thinking, as a matter of fact, of poor Maisie. She picked a little piece of pellitory out of the breast-high wall in front of us. She chafed it for a long minute between her finger and thumb, then she threw it over the coping.

"Oh, I accept the situation," she said at last, "if you can."

VI

I REMEMBER laughing at the phrase, "accept the situation", which she seemed to repeat with a gravity too intense. I said to her something like:

"It's hardly as much as that. I mean, that I must claim the liberty of a free American citizen to think what I please about your co-religionists. And I suppose that Florence must have liberty to think what she pleases and to say what politeness allows her to say."

"She had better," Leonora answered, "not say one single word against my people or my faith." It struck me at the time, that there was an unusual, an almost threatening, hardness in her voice. It was almost as if she were trying to convey to Florence, through me, that she would seriously harm my wife if Florence went to something that was an extreme. Yes, I remember thinking at the time that it was almost as if Leonora were saying, through me to Florence:

"You may outrage me as you will; you may take all that I personally possess, but do not you care to say one single thing in view of the situation that that will set up—against the faith that makes me become the doormat for your feet."

But obviously, as I saw it, that could not be her meaning. Good people, be they ever so diverse in creed, do not threaten each other. So that I read Leonora's words to mean just no more than: "It would be better if Florence said nothing at all against my co-religionists, because it is a point that I am touchy about."

That was the hint that, accordingly, I conveyed to Florence when, shortly afterwards, she and Edward came down from the tower. And I want you to understand that, from that moment until after Edward and the girl and Florence were all dead together, I had never the remotest glimpse, not the shadow of a suspicion, that there was anything wrong, as the saying is. For five minutes, then, I entertained the possibility that Leonora might be jealous; but there was never another flicker in that flame-like personality. How in the world should I get it?

For, all that time, I was just a male sick nurse. And what chance had I against those three hardened gamblers, who were all in league to conceal their hands from me? What earthly chance? They were three to one—and they made me happy. Oh God, they made me so happy that I doubt if even paradise, that shall smooth out all temporal wrongs, shall ever give me the like. And what could they have done better, or what could they have done that could have been worse? I don't know....

I suppose that, during all that time I was a deceived husband and that Leonora was pimping for Edward. That was the cross that she had to take up during her long Calvary of a life....

You ask how it feels to be a deceived husband. Just Heavens, I do not know. It feels just nothing at all. It is not Hell, certainly it is not necessarily Heaven. So I suppose it is the intermediate stage. What do they call it? Limbo. No, I feel nothing at all about that. They are dead; they have gone before their Judge who, I hope, will open to them the springs of His compassion. It is not my business to think about it. It is simply my business to say, as Leonora's people say: "Requiem aeternam dona eis, Do mine, et lux perpetua luceat eis. In memoria aeterna erit...." But what were they? The just? The unjust? God knows! I think that the pair of them were only poor wretches, creeping over this earth in the shadow of an eternal wrath. It is very terrible....

It is almost too terrible, the picture of that judgement, as it appears to me sometimes, at nights. It is probably the suggestion of some picture that I have seen somewhere. But upon an immense plain, suspended in mid-air, I seem to see three figures, two of them clasped close in an intense embrace, and one intolerably solitary. It is in black and white, my picture of that judgement, an etching, perhaps; only I cannot tell an etching from a photographic reproduction. And the immense plain is the hand of God, stretching out for miles and miles, with great spaces above it and below it. And they are in the sight of God, and it is Florence that is alone.... And, do you know, at the thought of that intense solitude I feel an overwhelming desire to rush forward and comfort her. You cannot, you see, have acted as nurse to a person for twelve years without wishing to go on nursing them, even though you hate them with the hatred of the adder, and even in the palm of God. But, in the nights, with that vision of judgement before me, I know that I hold myself back. For I hate Florence. I hate Florence with such a hatred that I would not spare her an eternity of loneliness. She need not have done what she did. She was an American, a New Englander. She had not the hot passions of these Europeans. She cut out that poor imbecile of an Edward—and I pray God that he is really at peace, clasped close in the arms of that poor, poor girl! And, no doubt, Maisie Maidan will find her young husband again, and Leonora will burn, clear and serene, a northern light and one of the archangels of God. And me.... Well, perhaps, they will find me an elevator to run.... But Florence... .

She should not have done it. She should not have done it. It was playing it too low down. She cut out poor dear Edward from sheer vanity; she meddled between him and Leonora from a sheer, imbecile spirit of district visiting. Do you understand that, whilst she was Edward's mistress, she was perpetually trying to reunite him to his wife? She would gabble on to Leonora about forgiveness—treating the subject from the bright, American point of view. And Leonora would treat her like the whore she was. Once she said to Florence in the early morning:

"You come to me straight out of his bed to tell me that that is my proper place. I know it, thank you."

But even that could not stop Florence. She went on saying that it was her ambition to leave this world a little brighter by the passage of her brief life, and how thankfully she would leave Edward, whom she thought she had brought to a right frame of mind, if Leonora would only give him a chance. He needed, she said, tenderness beyond anything.

And Leonora would answer—for she put up with this outrage for years—Leonora, as I understand, would answer something like:

"Yes, you would give him up. And you would go on writing to each other in secret, and committing adultery in hired rooms. I know the pair of you, you know. No. I prefer the situation as it is." Half the time Florence would ignore Leonora's remarks. She would think they were not quite ladylike. The other half of the time she would try to persuade Leonora that her love for Edward was quite spiritual—on account of her heart. Once she said:

"If you can believe that of Maisie Maidan, as you say you do, why cannot you believe it of me?" Leonora was, I understand, doing her hair at that time in front of the mirror in her bedroom. And she looked round at Florence, to whom she did not usually vouchsafe a glance,—she looked round coolly and calmly, and said:

"Never do you dare to mention Mrs Maidan's name again. You murdered her. You and I murdered her between us. I am as much a scoundrel as you. I don't like to be reminded of it."

Florence went off at once into a babble of how could she have hurt a person whom she hardly knew, a person whom with the best intentions, in pursuance of her efforts to leave the world a little brighter, she had tried to save from Edward. That was how she figured it out to herself. She really thought that.... So Leonora said patiently:

"Very well, just put it that I killed her and that it's a painful subject. One does not like to think that one had killed someone. Naturally not. I ought never to have brought her from India." And that, indeed, is exactly how Leonora looked at it. It is stated a little baldly, but Leonora was always a great one for bald statements.

What had happened on the day of our jaunt to the ancient city of M—— had been this:

Leonora, who had been even then filled with pity and contrition for the poor child, on returning to our hotel had gone straight to Mrs Maidan's room. She had wanted just to pet her. And she had perceived at first only, on the clear, round table covered with red velvet, a letter addressed to her. It ran something like:

"Oh, Mrs Ashburnham, how could you have done it? I trusted you so. You never talked to me about me and Edward, but I trusted you. How could you buy me from my husband? I have just heard how you have—in the hall they were talking about it, Edward and the American lady. You paid the money for me to come here. Oh, how could you? How could you? I am going straight back to Bunny...." Bunny was Mrs Maidan's husband.

And Leonora said that, as she went on reading the letter, she had, without looking round her, a sense that that hotel room was cleared, that there were no papers on the table, that there were no clothes on the hooks, and that there was a strained silence—a silence, she said, as if there were something in the room that drank up such sounds as there were. She had to fight against that feeling, whilst she read the postscript of the letter.

"I did not know you wanted me for an adulteress," the postscript began. The poor child was hardly literate. "It was surely not right of you and I never wanted to be one. And I heard Edward call me a poor little rat to the American lady. He always called me a little rat in private, and I did not mind. But, if he called me it to her, I think he does not love me any more. Oh, Mrs Ashburnham, you knew the world and I knew nothing. I thought it would be all right if you thought it could, and I thought you would not have brought me if you did not, too. You should not have done it, and we out of the same convent...."

Leonora said that she screamed when she read that.

And then she saw that Maisie's boxes were all packed, and she began a search for Mrs Maidan herself—all over the hotel. The manager said that Mrs Maidan had paid her bill, and had gone up to the station to ask the Reiseverkehrsbureau to make her out a plan for her immediate return to Chitral. He imagined that he had seen her come back, but he was not quite certain. No one in the large hotel had bothered his head about the child. And she, wandering solitarily in the hall, had no doubt sat down beside a screen that had Edward and Florence on the other side. I never heard then or after what had passed between that precious couple. I fancy Florence was just about beginning her cutting out of poor dear Edward by addressing to him some words of friendly warning as to the ravages he might be making in the girl's heart. That would be the sort of way she would begin. And Edward would have sentimentally assured her that there was nothing in it; that Maisie was just a poor little rat whose passage to Nauheim his wife had paid out of her own pocket. That would have been enough to do the trick.

For the trick was pretty efficiently done. Leonora, with panic growing and with contrition very large in her heart, visited every one of the public rooms of the hotel—the dining-room, the lounge, the schreibzimmer, the winter garden. God knows what they wanted with a winter garden in an hotel that is only open from May till October. But there it was. And then Leonora ran—yes, she ran up the stairs—to see if Maisie had not returned to her rooms. She had determined to take that child right away from that hideous place. It seemed to her to be all unspeakable. I do not mean to say that she was not quite cool about it. Leonora was always Leonora. But the cold justice of the thing demanded that she should play the part of mother to this child who had come from the same convent. She figured it out to amount to that. She would leave Edward to Florence and to me—and she would devote all her time to providing that child with an atmosphere of love until she could be returned to her poor young husband. It was naturally too late.

She had not cared to look round Maisie's rooms at first. Now, as soon as she came in, she perceived, sticking out beyond the bed, a small pair of feet in high-heeled shoes. Maisie had died in the effort to strap up a great portmanteau. She had died so grotesquely that her little body had fallen forward into the trunk, and it had closed upon her, like the jaws of a gigantic alligator. The key was in her hand. Her dark hair, like the hair of a Japanese, had come down and covered her body and her face.

Leonora lifted her up—she was the merest featherweight—and laid her on the bed with her hair about her. She was smiling, as if she had just scored a goal in a hockey match. You understand she had not committed suicide. Her heart had just stopped. I saw her, with the long lashes on the cheeks, with the smile about the lips, with the flowers all about her. The stem of a white lily rested in her hand so that the spike of flowers was upon her shoulder. She looked like a bride in the sunlight of the mortuary candles that were all about her, and the white coifs of the two nuns that knelt at her feet with their faces hidden might have been two swans that were to bear her away to kissing-kindness land, or wherever it is. Leonora showed her to me. She would not let either of the others see her. She wanted, you know, to spare poor dear Edward's feelings. He never could bear the sight of a corpse. And, since she never gave him an idea that Maisie had written to her, he imagined that the death had been the most natural thing in the world. He soon got over it. Indeed, it was the one affair of his about which he never felt much remorse.

PART II

I

THE death of Mrs Maidan occurred on the 4th of August, 1904. And then nothing happened until the 4th of August, 1913. There is the curious coincidence of dates, but I do not know whether that is one of those sinister, as if half jocular and altogether merciless proceedings on the part of a cruel Providence that we call a coincidence. Because it may just as well have been the superstitious mind of Florence that forced her to certain acts, as if she had been hypnotized. It is, however, certain that the 4th of August always proved a significant date for her. To begin with, she was born on the 4th of August. Then, on that date, in the year 1899, she set out with her uncle for the tour round the world in company with a young man called Jimmy. But that was not merely a coincidence. Her kindly old uncle, with the supposedly damaged heart, was in his delicate way, offering her, in this trip, a birthday present to celebrate her coming of age. Then, on the 4th of August, 1900, she yielded to an action that certainly coloured her whole life—as well as mine. She had no luck. She was probably offering herself a birthday present that morning.... On the 4th of August, 1901, she married me, and set sail for Europe in a great gale of wind—the gale that affected her heart. And no doubt there, again, she was offering herself a birthday gift—the birthday gift of my miserable life. It occurs to me that I have never told you anything about my marriage. That was like this: I have told you, as I think, that I first met Florence at the Stuyvesants', in Fourteenth Street. And, from that moment, I determined with all the obstinacy of a possibly weak nature, if not to make her mine, at least to marry her. I had no occupation—I had no business affairs. I simply camped down there in Stamford, in a vile hotel, and just passed my days in the house, or on the verandah of the Misses Hurlbird. The Misses Hurlbird, in an odd, obstinate way, did not like my presence. But they were hampered by the national manners of these occasions. Florence had her own sitting-room. She could ask to it whom she liked, and I simply walked into that apartment. I was as timid as you will, but in that matter I was like a chicken that is determined to get across the road in front of an automobile. I would walk into Florence's pretty, little, old-fashioned room, take off my hat, and sit down.

Florence had, of course, several other fellows, too—strapping young New Englanders, who worked during the day in New York and spent only the evenings in the village of their birth. And, in the evenings, they would march in on Florence with almost as much determination as I myself showed. And I am bound to say that they were received with as much disfavour as was my portion—from the Misses Hurlbird....

They were curious old creatures, those two. It was almost as if they were members of an ancient family under some curse—they were so gentlewomanly, so proper, and they sighed so. Sometimes I would see tears in their eyes. I do not know that my courtship of Florence made much progress at first. Perhaps that was because it took place almost entirely during the daytime, on hot afternoons, when the clouds of dust hung like fog, right up as high as the tops of the thin-leaved elms. The night, I believe, is the proper season for the gentle feats of love, not a Connecticut July afternoon, when any sort of proximity is an almost appalling thought. But, if I never so much as kissed Florence, she let me discover very easily, in the course of a fortnight, her simple wants. And I could supply those wants....

She wanted to marry a gentleman of leisure; she wanted a European establishment. She wanted her husband to have an English accent, an income of fifty thousand dollars a year from real estate and no ambitions to increase that income. And—she faintly hinted—she did not want much physical passion in the affair. Americans, you know, can envisage such unions without blinking.

She gave cut this information in floods of bright talk—she would pop a little bit of it into comments over a view of the Rialto, Venice, and, whilst she was brightly describing Balmoral Castle, she would say that her ideal husband would he one who could get her received at the British Court. She had spent, it seemed, two months in Great Britain—seven weeks in touring from Stratford to Strathpeffer, and one as paying guest in an old English family near Ledbury, an impoverished, but still stately family, called Bagshawe. They were to have spent two months more in that tranquil bosom, but inopportune events, apparently in her uncle's business, had caused their rather hurried return to Stamford. The young man called Jimmy had remained in Europe to perfect his knowledge of that continent. He certainly did: he was most useful to us afterwards.

But the point that came out—that there was no mistaking—was that Florence was coldly and calmly determined to take no look at any man who could not give her a European settlement. Her glimpse of English home life had effected this. She meant, on her marriage, to have a year in Paris, and then to have her husband buy some real estate in the neighbourhood of Fordingbridge, from which place the Hurlbirds had come in the year 1688. On the strength of that she was going to take her place in the ranks of English county society. That was fixed.

I used to feel mightily elevated when I considered these details, for I could not figure out that amongst her acquaintances in Stamford there was any fellow that would fill the bill. The most of them were not as wealthy as I, and those that were were not the type to give up the fascinations of Wall Street even for the protracted companionship of Florence. But nothing really happened during the month of July. On the 1st of August Florence apparently told her aunts that she intended to marry me.

She had not told me so, but there was no doubt about the aunts, for, on that afternoon, Miss Florence Hurlbird, Senior, stopped me on my way to Florence's sitting-room and took me, agitatedly, into the parlour. It was a singular interview, in that old-fashioned colonial room, with the spindle-legged furniture, the silhouettes, the miniatures, the portrait of General Braddock, and the smell of lavender. You see, the two poor maiden ladies were in agonies—and they could not say one single thing direct. They would almost wring their hands and ask if I had considered such a thing as different temperaments. I assure you they were almost affectionate, concerned for me even, as if Florence were too bright for my solid and serious virtues.

For they had discovered in me solid and serious virtues. That might have been because I had once dropped the remark that I preferred General Braddock to General Washington. For the Hurlbirds had backed the losing side in the War of Independence, and had been seriously impoverished and quite efficiently oppressed for that reason. The Misses Hurlbird could never forget it.

Nevertheless they shuddered at the thought of a European career for myself and Florence. Each of them really wailed when they heard that that was what I hoped to give their niece. That may have been partly because they regarded Europe as a sink of iniquity, where strange laxities prevailed. They thought the Mother Country as Erastian as any other. And they carried their protests to extraordinary lengths, for them....

They even, almost, said that marriage was a sacrament; but neither Miss Florence nor Miss Emily could quite bring herself to utter the word. And they almost brought themselves to say that Florence's early life had been characterized by flirtations—something of that sort.

I know I ended the interview by saying:

"I don't care. If Florence has robbed a bank I am going to marry her and take her to Europe." And at that Miss Emily wailed and fainted. But Miss Florence, in spite of the state of her sister, threw herself on my neck and cried out: "Don't do it, John. Don't do it. You're a good young man," and she added, whilst I was getting out of the room to send Florence to her aunt's rescue:

"We ought to tell you more. But she's our dear sister's child."

Florence, I remember, received me with a chalk-pale face and the exclamation:

"Have those old cats been saying anything against me?" But I assured her that they had not and hurried her into the room of her strangely afflicted relatives. I had really forgotten all about that exclamation of Florence's until this moment. She treated me so very well—with such tact—that, if I ever thought of it afterwards I put it down to her deep affection for me.

And that evening, when I went to fetch her for a buggy-ride, she had disappeared. I did not lose any time. I went into New York and engaged berths on the "Pocahontas", that was to sail on the evening of the fourth of the month, and then, returning to Stamford, I tracked out, in the course of the day, that Florence had been driven to Rye Station. And there I found that she had taken the cars to Waterbury. She had, of course, gone to her uncle's. The old man received me with a stony, husky face. I was not to see Florence; she was ill; she was keeping her room. And, from something that he let drop—an odd Biblical phrase that I have forgotten—I gathered that all that family simply did not intend her to marry ever in her life.

I procured at once the name of the nearest minister and a rope ladder—you have no idea how primitively these matters were arranged in those days in the United States. I daresay that may be so still. And at one o'clock in the morning of the 4th of August I was standing in Florence's bedroom. I was so one-minded in my purpose that it never struck me there was anything improper in being, at one o'clock in the morning, in Florence's bedroom. I just wanted to wake her up. She was not, however, asleep. She expected me, and her relatives had only just left her. She received me with an embrace of a warmth.... Well, it was the first time I had ever been embraced by a woman—and it was the last when a woman's embrace has had in it any warmth for me.... I suppose it was my own fault, what followed. At any rate, I was in such a hurry to get the wedding over, and was so afraid of her relatives finding me there, that I must have received her advances with a certain amount of absence of mind. I was out of that room and down the ladder in under half a minute. She kept me waiting at the foot an unconscionable time—it was certainly three in the morning before we knocked up that minister. And I think that that wait was the only sign Florence ever showed of having a conscience as far as I was concerned, unless her lying for some moments in my arms was also a sign of conscience. I fancy that, if I had shown warmth then, she would have acted the proper wife to me, or would have put me back again. But, because I acted like a Philadelphia gentleman, she made me, I suppose, go through with the part of a male nurse. Perhaps she thought that I should not mind.

After that, as I gather, she had not any more remorse. She was only anxious to carry out her plans. For, just before she came down the ladder, she called me to the top of that grotesque implement that I went up and down like a tranquil jumping-jack. I was perfectly collected. She said to me with a certain fierceness:

"It is determined that we sail at four this afternoon? You are not lying about having taken berths?"

I understood that she would naturally be anxious to get away from the neighbourhood of her apparently insane relatives, so that I readily excused her for thinking that I should be capable of lying about such a thing. I made it, therefore, plain to her that it was my fixed determination to sail by the "Pocahontas". She said then—it was a moonlit morning, and she was whispering in my ear whilst I stood on the ladder. The hills that surround Waterbury showed, extraordinarily tranquil, around the villa. She said, almost coldly:

"I wanted to know, so as to pack my trunks." And she added: "I may be ill, you know. I guess my heart is a little like Uncle Hurlbird's. It runs in families."

I whispered that the "Pocahontas" was an extraordinarily steady boat....

Now I wonder what had passed through Florence's mind during the two hours that she had kept me waiting at the foot of the ladder. I would give not a little to know. Till then, I fancy she had had no settled plan in her mind. She certainly never mentioned her heart till that time. Perhaps the renewed sight of her Uncle Hurlbird had given her the idea. Certainly her Aunt Emily, who had come over with her to Waterbury, would have rubbed into her, for hours and hours, the idea that any accentuated discussions would kill the old gentleman. That would recall to her mind all the safeguards against excitement with which the poor silly old gentleman had been hedged in during their trip round the world. That, perhaps, put it into her head. Still, I believe there was some remorse on my account, too. Leonora told me that Florence said there was—for Leonora knew all about it, and once went so far as to ask her how she could do a thing so infamous. She excused herself on the score of an overmastering passion. Well, I always say that an overmastering passion is a good excuse for feelings. You cannot help them. And it is a good excuse for straight actions—she might have bolted with the fellow, before or after she married me. And, if they had not enough money to get along with, they might have cut their throats, or sponged on her family, though, of course, Florence wanted such a lot that it would have suited her very badly to have for a husband a clerk in a dry-goods store, which was what old Hurlbird would have made of that fellow. He hated him. No, I do not think that there is much excuse for Florence.

God knows. She was a frightened fool, and she was

fantastic, and I suppose that, at that time, she really cared for that imbecile. He certainly didn't care for her. Poor thing.... At any rate, after I had assured her that the "Pocahontas" was a steady ship, she just said: "You'll have to look after me in certain ways—like Uncle Hurlbird is looked after. I will tell you how to do it." And then she stepped over the sill, as if she were stepping on board a boat. I suppose she had burnt hers!

I had, no doubt, eye-openers enough. When we re-entered the Hurlbird mansion at eight o'clock the Hurlbirds were just exhausted. Florence had a hard, triumphant air. We had got married about four in the morning and had sat about in the woods above the town till then, listening to a mocking-bird imitate an old tom-cat. So I guess Florence had not found getting married to me a very stimulating process. I had not found anything much more inspiring to say than how glad I was, with variations. I think I was too dazed. Well, the Hurlbirds were too dazed to say much. We had breakfast together, and then Florence went to pack her grips and things. Old Hurlbird took the opportunity to read me a full-blooded lecture, in the style of an American oration, as to the perils for young American girlhood lurking in the European jungle. He said that Paris was full of snakes in the grass, of which he had had bitter experience. He concluded, as they always do, poor, dear old things, with the aspiration that all American women should one day be sexless—though that is not the way they put it.. ..

Well, we made the ship all right by one-thirty—an there was a tempest blowing. That helped Florence a good deal. For we were not ten minutes out from Sandy Hook before Florence went down into her cabin and her heart took her. An agitated stewardess came running up to me, and I went running down. I got my directions how to behave to my wife. Most of them came from her, though it was the ship doctor who discreetly suggested to me that I had better refrain from manifestations of affection. I was ready enough. I was, of course, full of remorse. It occurred to me that her heart was the reason for the Hurlbirds' mysterious desire to keep their youngest and dearest unmarried. Of course, they would be too refined to put the motive into words. They were old stock New Englanders. They would not want to have to suggest that a husband must not kiss the back of his wife's neck. They would not like to suggest that he might, for the matter of that. I wonder, though, how Florence got the doctor to enter the conspiracy—the several doctors.

Of course her heart squeaked a bit—she had the same configuration of the lungs as her Uncle Hurlbird. And, in his company, she must have heard a great deal of heart talk from specialists. Anyhow, she and they tied me pretty well down—and Jimmy, of course, that dreary boy—what in the world did she see in him? He was lugubrious, silent, morose. He had no talent as a painter. He was very sallow and dark, and he never shaved sufficiently. He met us at Havre, and he proceeded to make himself useful for the next two years, during which he lived in our flat in Paris, whether we were there or not. He studied painting at Julien's, or some such place....

That fellow had his hands always in the pockets of his odious, square-shouldered, broad-hipped, American coats, and his dark eyes were always full of ominous appearances. He was, besides, too fat. Why, I was much the better man....

And I daresay Florence would have given me the better. She showed signs of it. I think, perhaps, the enigmatic smile with which she used to look back at me over her shoulder when she went into the bathing place was a sort of invitation. I have mentioned that. It was as if she were saying: "I am going in here. I am going to stand so stripped and white and straight—and you are a man...." Perhaps it was that....

No, she cannot have liked that fellow long. He looked like sallow putty. I understand that he had been slim and dark and very graceful at the time of her first disgrace. But, loafing about in Paris, on her pocket-money and on the allowance that old Hurlbird made him to keep out of the United States, had given him a stomach like a man of forty, and dyspeptic irritation on top of it. God, how they worked me! It was those two between them who really elaborated the rules. I have told you something about them—how I had to head conversations, for all those eleven years, off such topics as love, poverty, crime, and so on. But, looking over what I have written, I see that I have unintentionally misled you when I said that Florence was never out of my sight. Yet that was the impression that I really had until just now. When I come to think of it she was out of my sight most of the time.

You see, that fellow impressed upon me that what Florence

needed most of all were sleep and privacy. I must never enter her room without knocking, or her poor little heart might flutter away to its doom. He said these things with his lugubrious croak, and his black eyes like a crow's, so that I seemed to see poor Florence die ten times a day—a little, pale, frail corpse. Why, I would as soon have thought of entering her room without her permission as of burgling a church. I would sooner have committed that crime. I would certainly have done it if I had thought the state of her heart demanded the sacrilege. So at ten o'clock at night the door closed upon Florence, who had gently, and, as if reluctantly, backed up that fellow's recommendations; and she would wish me good night as if she were a cinquecento Italian lady saying good-bye to her lover. And at ten o'clock of the next morning there she would come out the door of her room as fresh as Venus rising from any of the couches that are mentioned in Greek legends.

Her room door was locked because she was nervous about thieves; but an electric contrivance on a cord was understood to be attached to her little wrist. She had only to press a bulb to raise the house. And I was provided with an axe—an axe!—great gods, with which to break down her door in case she ever failed to answer my knock, after I knocked really loud several times. It was pretty well thought out, you see.

What wasn't so well thought out were the ultimate consequences—our being tied to Europe. For that young man rubbed it so well into me that Florence would die if she crossed the Channel—he impressed it so fully on my mind that, when later Florence wanted to go to Fordingbridge, I cut the proposal short—absolutely short, with a curt no. It fixed her and it frightened her. I was even backed up by all the doctors. I seemed to have had endless interviews with doctor after doctor, cool, quiet men, who would ask, in reasonable tones, whether there was any reason for our going to England—any special reason. And since I could not see any special reason, they would give the verdict: "Better not, then." I daresay they were honest enough, as things go. They probably imagined that the mere associations of the steamer might have effects on Florence's nerves. That would be enough, that and a conscientious desire to keep our money on the Continent.

It must have rattled poor Florence pretty considerably, for

you see, the main idea—the only main idea of her heart, that was otherwise cold—was to get to Fordingbridge and be a county lady in the home of her ancestors. But Jimmy got her, there: he shut on her the door of the Channel; even on the fairest day of blue sky, with the cliffs of England shining like mother of pearl in full view of Calais, I would not have let her cross the steamer gangway to save her life. I tell you it fixed her.

It fixed her beautifully, because she could not announce herself as cured, since that would have put an end to the locked bedroom arrangements. And, by the time she was sick of Jimmy—which happened in the year 1903—she had taken on Edward Ashburnham. Yes, it was a bad fix for her, because Edward could have taken her to Fordingbridge, and, though he could not give her Branshaw Manor, that home of her ancestors being settled on his wife, she could at least have pretty considerably queened it there or thereabouts, what with our money and the support of the Ashburnhams. Her uncle, as soon as he considered that she had really settled down with me—and I sent him only the most glowing accounts of her virtue and constancy—made over to her a very considerable part of his fortune for which he had no use. I suppose that we had, between us, fifteen thousand a year in English money, though I never quite knew how much of hers went to Jimmy. At any rate, we could have shone in Fordingbridge. I never quite knew, either, how she and Edward got rid of Jimmy. I fancy that fat and disreputable raven must have had his six golden front teeth knocked down his throat by Edward one morning whilst I had gone out to buy some flowers in the Rue de la Paix, leaving Florence and the flat in charge of those two. And serve him very right, is all that I can say. He was a bad sort of blackmailer; I hope Florence does not have his company in the next world.

As God is my Judge, I do not believe that I would have separated those two if I had known that they really and passionately loved each other. I do not know where the public morality of the case comes in, and, of course, no man really knows what he would have done in any given case. But I truly believe that I would have united them, observing ways and means as decent as I could. I believe that I should have given them money to live upon and that I should have consoled myself somehow. At that date I might have found some young thing, like Maisie Maidan, or the poor girl, and I might have had some peace. For peace I never had with Florence, and hardly believe that I cared for her in the way of love after a year or two of it. She became for me a rare and fragile object, something burdensome, but very frail. Why it was as if I had been given a thin-shelled pullet's egg to carry on my palm from Equatorial Africa to Hoboken. Yes, she became for me, as it were, the subject of a bet—the trophy of an athlete's achievement, a parsley crown that is the symbol of his chastity, his soberness, his abstentions, and of his inflexible will. Of intrinsic value as a wife, I think she had none at all for me. I fancy I was not even proud of the way she dressed.

But her passion for Jimmy was not even a passion, and, mad as the suggestion may appear, she was frightened for her life. Yes, she was afraid of me. I will tell you how that happened. I had, in the old days, a darky servant, called Julius, who valeted me, and waited on me, and loved me, like the crown of his head. Now, when we left Waterbury to go to the "Pocahontas", Florence entrusted to me one very special and very precious leather grip. She told me that her life might depend on that grip, which contained her drugs against heart attacks. And, since I was never much of a hand at carrying things, I entrusted this, in turn, to Julius, who was a grey-haired chap of sixty or so, and very picturesque at that. He made so much impression on Florence that she regarded him as a sort of father, and absolutely refused to let me take him to Paris. He would have inconvenienced her.

Well, Julius was so overcome with grief at being left behind that he must needs go and drop the precious grip. I saw red, I saw purple. I flew at Julius. On the ferry, it was, I filled up one of his eyes; I threatened to strangle him. And, since an unresisting negro can make a deplorable noise and a deplorable spectacle, and, since that was Florence's first adventure in the married state, she got a pretty idea of my character. It affirmed in her the desperate resolve to conceal from me the fact that she was not what she would have called "a pure woman". For that was really the mainspring of her fantastic actions. She was afraid that I should murder her....

So she got up the heart attack, at the earliest possible opportunity, on board the liner. Perhaps she was not so very much to be blamed. You must remember that she was a New

Englander, and that New England had not yet come to loathe darkies as it does now. Whereas, if she had come from even so little south as Philadelphia, and had been an oldish family, she would have seen that for me to kick Julius was not so outrageous an act as for her cousin, Reggie Hurlbird, to say—as I have heard him say to his English butler—that for two cents he would bat him on the pants. Besides, the medicine-grip did not bulk as largely in her eyes as it did in mine, where it was the symbol of the existence of an adored wife of a day. To her it was just a useful lie....

Well, there you have the position, as clear as I can make it—the husband an ignorant fool, the wife a cold sensualist with imbecile fears—for I was such a fool that I should never have known what she was or was not—and the blackmailing lover. And then the other lover came along....

Well, Edward Ashburnham was worth having. Have I conveyed to you the splendid fellow that he was—the fine soldier, the excellent landlord, the extraordinarily kind, careful and industrious magistrate, the upright, honest, fair-dealing, fair-thinking, public character? I suppose I have not conveyed it to you. The truth is, that I never knew it until the poor girl came along—the poor girl who was just as straight, as splendid and as upright as he. I swear she was. I suppose I ought to have known. I suppose that was, really, why I liked him so much—so infinitely much. Come to think of it, I can remember a thousand little acts of kindliness, of thoughtfulness for his inferiors, even on the Continent. Look here, I know of two families of dirty, unpicturesque, Hessian paupers that that fellow, with an infinite patience, rooted up, got their police reports, set on their feet, or exported to my patient land. And he would do it quite inarticulately, set in motion by seeing a child crying in the street. He would wrestle with dictionaries, in that unfamiliar tongue.... Well, he could not bear to see a child cry. Perhaps he could not bear to see a woman and not give her the comfort of his physical attractions. But, although I liked him so intensely, I was rather apt to take these things for granted. They made me feel comfortable with him, good towards him; they made me trust him. But I guess I thought it was part of the character of any English gentleman. Why, one day he got it into his head that the head waiter at the Excelsior had been crying—the fellow with the grey face and grey whiskers. And then he spent the best part of a week, in correspondence and up at the British consul's, in getting the fellow's wife to come back from London and bring back his girl baby. She had bolted with a Swiss scullion. If she had not come inside the week he would have gone to London himself to fetch her. He was like that. Edward Ashburnham was like that, and I thought it was only the duty of his rank and station. Perhaps that was all that it was—but I pray God to make me discharge mine as well. And, but for the poor girl, I daresay that I should never have seen it, however much the feeling might have been over me. She had for him such enthusiasm that, although even now I do not understand the technicalities of English life, I can gather enough. She was with them during the whole of our last stay at Nauheim.

Nancy Rufford was her name; she was Leonora's only friend's only child, and Leonora was her guardian, if that is the correct term. She had lived with the Ashburnhams ever since she had been of the age of thirteen, when her mother was said to have committed suicide owing to the brutalities of her father. Yes, it is a cheerful story.... Edward always called her "the girl", and it was very pretty, the evident affection he had for her and she for him. And Leonora's feet she would have kissed—those two were for her the best man and the best woman on earth—and in heaven. I think that she had not a thought of evil in her head—the poor girl....

Well, anyhow, she chanted Edward's praises to me for the hour together, but, as I have said, I could not make much of it. It appeared that he had the D.S.O., and that his troop loved him beyond the love of men. You never saw such a troop as his. And he had the Royal Humane Society's medal with a clasp. That meant, apparently, that he had twice jumped off the deck of a troopship to rescue what the girl called "Tommies", who had fallen overboard in the Red Sea and such places. He had been twice recommended for the V.C., whatever that might mean, and, although owing to some technicalities he had never received that apparently coveted order, he had some special place about his sovereign at the coronation. Or perhaps it was some post in the Beefeaters'. She made him out like a cross between Lohengrin and the Chevalier Bayard. Perhaps he was.... But he was too silent a fellow to make that side of him really decorative.

I remember going to him at about that time and asking him what the D.S.O. was, and he grunted out:

"It's a sort of a thing they give grocers who've honourably supplied the troops with adulterated coffee in war-time"—something of that sort. He did not quite carry conviction to me, so, in the end, I put it directly to Leonora. I asked her fully and squarely—prefacing the question with some remarks, such as those that I have already given you, as to the difficulty one has in really getting to know people when one's intimacy is conducted as an English acquaintanceship—I asked her whether her husband was not really a splendid fellow—along at least the lines of his public functions. She looked at me with a slightly awakened air—with an air that would have been almost startled if Leonora could ever have been startled.

"Didn't you know?" she asked. "If I come to think of it there is not a more splendid fellow in any three counties, pick them where you will—along those lines." And she added, after she had looked at me reflectively for what seemed a long time:

"To do my husband justice there could not be a better man on the earth. There would not be room for it—along those lines."

"Well," I said, "then he must really be Lohengrin and the Cid in one body. For there are not any other lines that count."

Again she looked at me for a long time.

"It's your opinion that there are no other lines that count?" she asked slowly.

"Well," I answered gaily, "you're not going to accuse him of not being a good husband, or of not being a good guardian to your ward?"

She spoke then, slowly, like a person who is listening to the sounds in a sea-shell held to her ear—and, would you believe it?—she told me afterwards that, at that speech of mine, for the first time she had a vague inkling of the tragedy that was to follow so soon—although the girl had lived with them for eight years or so:

"Oh, I'm not thinking of saying that he is not the best of husbands, or that he is not very fond of the girl."

And then I said something like:

"Well, Leonora, a man sees more of these things than even a wife. And, let me tell you, that in all the years I've known

Edward he has never, in your absence, paid a moment's attention to any other woman—not by the quivering of an eyelash. I should have noticed. And he talks of you as if you were one of the angels of God."

"Oh," she came up to the scratch, as you could be sure Leonora would always come up to the scratch, "I am perfectly sure that he always speaks nicely of me."

I daresay she had practice in that sort of scene—people must have been always complimenting her on her husband's fidelity and adoration. For half the world—the whole of the world that knew Edward and Leonora believed that his conviction in the Kilsyte affair had been a miscarriage of justice—a conspiracy of false evidence, got together by Nonconformist adversaries. But think of the fool that I was....

II

LET me think where we were. Oh, yes... that conversation took place on the 4th of August, 1913. I remember saying to her that, on that day, exactly nine years before, I had made their acquaintance, so that it had seemed quite appropriate and like a birthday speech to utter my little testimonial to my friend Edward. I could quite confidently say that, though we four had been about together in all sorts of places, for all that length of time, I had not, for my part, one single complaint to make of either of them. And I added, that that was an unusual record for people who had been so much together. You are not to imagine that it was only at Nauheim that we met. That would not have suited Florence.

I find, on looking at my diaries, that on the 4th of September, 1904, Edward accompanied Florence and myself to Paris, where we put him up till the twenty-first of that month. He made another short visit to us in December of that year—the first year of our acquaintance. It must have been during this visit that he knocked Mr Jimmy's teeth down his throat. I daresay Florence had asked him to come over for that purpose. In 1905 he was in Paris three times—once with Leonora, who wanted some frocks. In 1906 we spent the best part of six weeks together at Mentone, and Edward stayed with us in Paris on his way back to London. That was how it went.

The fact was that in Florence the poor wretch had got hold of a Tartar, compared with whom Leonora was a sucking kid. He must have had a hell of a time. Leonora wanted to keep him for—what shall I say—for the good of her church, as it were, to show that Catholic women do not lose their men. Let it go at that, for the moment. I will write more about her motives later, perhaps. But Florence was sticking on to the proprietor of the home of her ancestors. No doubt he was also a very passionate lover. But I am convinced that he was sick of Florence within three years of even interrupted companionship and the life that she led him....

If ever Leonora so much as mentioned in a letter that they had had a woman staying with them—or, if she so much as mentioned a woman's name in a letter to me—off would go a desperate cable in cipher to that poor wretch at Branshaw, commanding him on pain of an instant and horrible disclosure to come over and assure her of his fidelity. I daresay he would have faced it out; I daresay he would have thrown over Florence and taken the risk of exposure. But there he had Leonora to deal with. And Leonora assured him that, if the minutest fragment of the real situation ever got through to my senses, she would wreak upon him the most terrible vengeance that she could think of. And he did not have a very easy job. Florence called for more and more attentions from him as the time went on. She would make him kiss her at any moment of the day; and it was only by his making it plain that a divorced lady could never assume a position in the county of Hampshire that he could prevent her from making a bolt of it with him in her train. Oh, yes, it was a difficult job for him.

For Florence, if you please, gaining in time a more composed view of nature, and overcome by her habits of garrulity, arrived at a frame of mind in which she found it almost necessary to tell me all about it—nothing less than that. She said that her situation was too unbearable with regard to me.

She proposed to tell me all, secure a divorce from me, and go with Edward and settle in California.... I do not suppose that she was really serious in this. It would have meant the extinction of all hopes of Branshaw Manor for her. Besides she had got it into her head that Leonora, who was as sound as a roach, was consumptive. She was always begging Leonora, before me, to go and see a doctor. But, none the less, poor Edward seems to have believed in her determination to carry him off. He would not have gone; he cared for his wife too much. But, if Florence had put him at it, that would have meant my getting to know of it, and his incurring Leonora's vengeance. And she could have made it pretty hot for him in ten or a dozen different ways. And she assured me that she would have used every one of them. She was determined to spare my feelings. And she was quite aware that, at that date, the hottest she could have made it for him would have been to refuse, herself, ever to see him again....

Well, I think I have made it pretty clear. Let me come to the 4th of August, 1913, the last day of my absolute ignorance—and, I assure you, of my perfect happiness. For the coming of that dear girl only added to it all.

On that 4th of August I was sitting in the lounge with a rather odious Englishman called Bagshawe, who had arrived that night, too late for dinner. Leonora had just gone to bed and I was waiting for Florence and Edward and the girl to come back from a concert at the Casino. They had not gone there all together. Florence, I remember, had said at first that she would remain with Leonora, and me, and Edward and the girl had gone off alone. And then Leonora had said to Florence with perfect calmness:

"I wish you would go with those two. I think the girl ought to have the appearance of being chaperoned with Edward in these places. I think the time has come." So Florence, with her light step, had slipped out after them. She was all in black for some cousin or other. Americans are particular in those matters.

We had gone on sitting in the lounge till towards ten, when Leonora had gone up to bed. It had been a very hot day, but there it was cool. The man called Bagshawe had been reading The Times on the other side of the room, but then he moved over to me with some trifling question as a prelude to suggesting an acquaintance. I fancy he asked me something About the poll-tax on Kur-guests, and whether it could not be sneaked out of. He was that sort of person.

Well, he was an unmistakable man, with a military figure, rather exaggerated, with bulbous eyes that avoided your own, and a pallid complexion that suggested vices practised in secret along with an uneasy desire for making acquaintance at whatever cost.... The filthy toad...

He began by telling me that he came from Ludlow Manor, near Ledbury. The name had a slightly familiar sound, though I could not fix it in my mind. Then he began to talk about a duty on hops, about Californian hops, about Los Angeles, where he had been. He fencing for a topic with which he might gain my affection.

And then, quite suddenly, in the bright light of the street, I saw Florence running. It was like that—I saw Florence running with a face whiter than paper and her hand on the black stuff over her heart. I tell you, my own heart stood still; I tell you I could not move. She rushed in at the swing doors. She looked round that place of rush chairs, cane tables and newspapers. She saw me and opened her lips. She saw the man who was talking to me. She stuck her hands over her face as if she wished to push her eyes out. And she was not there any more.

I could not move; I could not stir a finger. And then that man said:

"By Jove: Florry Hurlbird." He turned upon me with an oily and uneasy sound meant for a laugh. He was really going to ingratiate himself with me. "Do you know who that is?" he asked. "The last time I saw that girl she was coming out of the bedroom of a young man called Jimmy at five o'clock in the morning. In my house at Ledbury. You saw her recognize me." He was standing on his feet, looking down at me. I don't know what I looked like. At any rate, he gave a sort of gurgle and then stuttered:

"Oh, I say...." Those were the last words I ever heard of Mr Bagshawe's. A long time afterwards I pulled myself out of the lounge and went up to Florence's room. She had not locked the door—for the first time of our married life. She was lying, quite respectably arranged, unlike Mrs Maidan, on her bed. She had a little phial that rightly should have contained nitrate of amyl, in her right hand. That was on the 4th of August, 1913.

PART III

I

THE odd thing is that what sticks out in my recollection of the rest of that evening was Leonora's saying:

"Of course you might marry her," and, when I asked whom, she answered:

"The girl."

Now that is to me a very amazing thing—amazing for the light of possibilities that it casts into the human heart. For I had never had the slightest conscious idea of marrying the girl; I never had the slightest idea even of caring for her. I must have talked in an odd way, as people do who are recovering from an anaesthetic. It is as if one had a dual personality, the one I being entirely unconscious of the other. I had thought nothing; I had said such an extraordinary thing. I don't know that analysis of my own psychology matters at all to this story. I should say that it didn't or, at any rate, that I had given enough of it. But that odd remark of mine had a strong influence upon what came after. I mean, that Leonora would probably never have spoken to me at all about Florence's relations with Edward if I hadn't said, two hours after my wife's death:

"Now I can marry the girl."

She had, then, taken it for granted that I had been suffering all that she had been suffering, or, at least, that I had permitted all that she had permitted. So that, a month ago, about a week after the funeral of poor Edward, she could say to me in the most natural way in the world—I had been talking about the duration of my stay at Branshaw—she said with her clear, reflective intonation:

"Oh, stop here for ever and ever if you can." And then she added, "You couldn't be more of a brother to me, or more of a counsellor, or more of a support. You are all the consolation I have in the world. And isn't it odd to think that if your wife hadn't been my husband's mistress, you would probably never have been here at all?"

That was how I got the news—full in the face, like that. I didn't say anything and I don't suppose I felt anything, unless maybe it was with that mysterious and unconscious self that underlies most people. Perhaps one day when I am unconscious or walking in my sleep I may go and spit upon poor Edward's grave. It seems about the most unlikely thing I could do; but there it is. No, I remember no emotion of any sort, but just the clear feeling that one has from time to time when one hears that some Mrs So-and-So is au mieux with a certain gentleman. It made things plainer, suddenly, to my curiosity. It was as if I thought, at that moment, of a windy November evening, that, when I came to think it over afterwards, a dozen unexplained things would fit themselves into place. But I wasn't thinking things over then. I remember that distinctly. I was just sitting back, rather stiffly, in a deep arm-chair. That is what I remember. It was twilight.

Branshaw Manor lies in a little hollow with lawns across it and pine-woods on the fringe of the dip. The immense wind, coming from across the forest, roared overhead. But the view from the window was perfectly quiet and grey. Not a thing stirred, except a couple of rabbits on the extreme edge of the lawn. It was Leonora's own little study that we were in and we were waiting for the tea to be brought. I, as I said, was sitting in the deep chair, Leonora was standing in the window twirling the wooden acorn at the end of the window-blind cord desultorily round and round. She looked across the lawn and said, as far as I can remember:

"Edward has been dead only ten days and yet there are rabbits on the lawn."

I understand that rabbits do a great deal of harm to the short grass in England. And then she turned round to me and said without any adornment at all, for I remember her exact words:

"I think it was stupid of Florence to commit suicide."

I cannot tell you the extraordinary sense of leisure that we two seemed to have at that moment. It wasn't as if we were waiting for a train, it wasn't as if we were waiting for a meal—it was just that there was nothing to wait for. Nothing. There was an extreme stillness with the remote and intermittent sound of the wind. There was the grey light in that brown, small room.

And there appeared to be nothing else in the world. I knew then that Leonora was about to let me into her full confidence. It was as if—or no, it was the actual fact that—Leonora with an odd English sense of decency had determined to wait until Edward had been in his grave for a full week before she spoke. And with some vague motive of giving her an idea of the extent to which she must permit herself to make confidences, I said slowly—and these words too I remember with exactitude—"Did Florence commit suicide? I didn't know."

I was just, you understand, trying to let her know that, if she were going to speak she would have to talk about a much wider range of things than she had before thought necessary.

So that that was the first knowledge I had that Florence had committed suicide. It had never entered my head. You may think that I had been singularly lacking in suspiciousness; you may consider me even to have been an imbecile. But consider the position.

In such circumstances of clamour, of outcry, of the crash of many people running together, of the professional reticence of such people as hotel-keepers, the traditional reticence of such "good people" as the Ashburnhams—in such circumstances it is some little material object, always, that catches the eye and that appeals to the imagination. I had no possible guide to the idea of suicide and the sight of the little flask of nitrate of amyl in Florence's hand suggested instantly to my mind the idea of the failure of her heart. Nitrate of amyl, you understand, is the drug that is given to relieve sufferers from angina pectoris.

Seeing Florence, as I had seen her, running with a white face and with one hand held over her heart, and seeing her, as I immediately afterwards saw her, lying upon her bed with the so familiar little brown flask clenched in her fingers, it was natural enough for my mind to frame the idea. As happened now and again, I thought, she had gone out without her remedy and, having felt an attack coming on whilst she was in the gardens, she had run in to get the nitrate in order, as quickly as possible, to obtain relief. And it was equally inevitable my mind should frame the thought that her heart, unable to stand the strain of the running, should have broken in her side. How could I have known that, during all the years of our married life, that little brown flask had contained, not nitrate of amyl, but prussic acid?

It was inconceivable.

Why, not even Edward Ashburnham, who was, after all more intimate with her than I was, had an inkling of the truth. He just thought that she had dropped dead of heart disease. Indeed, I fancy that the only people who ever knew that Florence had committed suicide were Leonora, the Grand Duke, the head of the police and the hotel-keeper. I mention these last three because my recollection of that night is only the sort of pinkish effulgence from the electric-lamps in the hotel lounge. There seemed to bob into my consciousness, like floating globes, the faces of those three. Now it would be the bearded, monarchical, benevolent head of the Grand Duke; then the sharp-featured, brown, cavalry-moustached feature of the chief of police; then the globular, polished and high-collared vacuousness that represented Monsieur Schontz, the proprietor of the hotel. At times one head would be there alone, at another the spiked helmet of the official would be close to the healthy baldness of the prince; then M. Schontz's oiled locks would push in between the two. The sovereign's soft, exquisitely trained voice would say, "Ja, ja, ja!" each word dropping out like so many soft pellets of suet; the subdued rasp of the official would come: "Zum Befehl Durchlaucht," like five revolver-shots; the voice of M. Schontz would go on and on under its breath like that of an unclean priest reciting from his breviary in the corner of a railway-carriage. That was how it presented itself to me.

They seemed to take no notice of me; I don't suppose that I was even addressed by one of them. But, as long as one or the other, or all three of them were there, they stood between me as if, I being the titular possessor of the corpse, had a right to be present at their conferences. Then they all went away and I was left alone for a long time.

And I thought nothing; absolutely nothing. I had no ideas; I had no strength. I felt no sorrow, no desire for action, no inclination to go upstairs and fall upon the body of my wife. I just saw the pink effulgence, the cane tables, the palms, the globular match-holders, the indented ash-trays. And then Leonora came to me and it appears that I addressed to her that singular remark:

"Now I can marry the girl."

But I have given you absolutely the whole of my

recollection of that evening, as it is the whole of my recollection of the succeeding three or four days. I was in a state just simply cataleptic. They put me to bed and I stayed there; they brought me my clothes and I dressed; they led me to an open grave and I stood beside it. If they had taken me to the edge of a river, or if they had flung me beneath a railway train, I should have been drowned or mangled in the same spirit. I was the walking dead.

Well, those are my impressions.

What had actually happened had been this. I pieced it together afterwards. You will remember I said that Edward Ashburnham and the girl had gone off, that night, to a concert at the Casino and that Leonora had asked Florence, almost immediately after their departure, to follow them and to perform the office of chaperone. Florence, you may also remember, was all in black, being the mourning that she wore for a deceased cousin, Jean Hurlbird. It was a very black night and the girl was dressed in cream-coloured muslin, that must have glimmered under the tall trees of the dark park like a phosphorescent fish in a cupboard. You couldn't have had a better beacon.

And it appears that Edward Ashburnham led the girl not up the straight allée that leads to the Casino, but in under the dark trees of the park. Edward Ashburnham told me all this in his final outburst. I have told you that, upon that occasion, he became deucedly vocal. I didn't pump him. I hadn't any motive. At that time I didn't in the least connect him with my wife. But the fellow talked like a cheap novelist.—Or like a very good novelist for the matter of that, if it's the business of a novelist to make you see things clearly. And I tell you I see that thing as clearly as if it were a dream that never left me. It appears that, not very far from the Casino, he and the girl sat down in the darkness upon a public bench. The lights from that place of entertainment must have reached them through the tree-trunks, since, Edward said, he could quite plainly see the girl's face—that beloved face with the high forehead, the queer mouth, the tortured eyebrows, and the direct eyes. And to Florence, creeping up behind them, they must have presented the appearance of silhouettes. For I take it that Florence came creeping up behind them over the short grass to a tree that, I quite well remember, was immediately behind that public seat. It was not a very difficult feat for a woman instinct with jealousy.

The Casino orchestra was, as Edward remembered to tell me, playing the Rakocsy march, and although it was not loud enough, at that distance, to drown the voice of Edward Ashburnham it was certainly sufficiently audible to efface, amongst the noises of the night, the slight brushings and rustlings that might have been made by the feet of Florence or by her gown in coming over the short grass. And that miserable woman must have got it in the face, good and strong. It must have been horrible for her. Horrible! Well, I suppose she deserved all that she got.

Anyhow, there you have the picture, the immensely tall trees, elms most of them, towering and feathering away up into the black mistiness that trees seem to gather about them at night; the silhouettes of those two upon the seat; the beams of light coming from the Casino, the woman all in black peeping with fear behind the tree-trunk. It is melodrama; but I can't help it.

And then, it appears, something happened to Edward Ashburnham. He assured me—and I see no reason for disbelieving him—that until that moment he had had no idea whatever of caring for the girl. He said that he had regarded her exactly as he would have regarded a daughter. He certainly loved her, but with a very deep, very tender and very tranquil love. He had missed her when she went away to her convent-school; he had been glad when she had returned. But of more than that he had been totally unconscious. Had he been conscious of it, he assured me, he would have fled from it as from a thing accursed. He realized that it was the last outrage upon Leonora. But the real point was his entire unconsciousness. He had gone with her into that dark park with no quickening of the pulse, with no desire for the intimacy of solitude. He had gone, intending to talk about polo-ponies, and tennis-racquets; about the temperament of the reverend Mother at the convent she had left and about whether her frock for a party when they got home should be white or blue. It hadn't come into his head that they would talk about a single thing that they hadn't always talked about; it had not even come into his head that the tabu which extended around her was not inviolable. And then, suddenly, that—He was very careful to assure me that at that time there was no physical motive about his declaration. It did not appear to him to be a matter of a dark night and a propinquity and so on. No, it was simply of her effect on the moral side of his life that he appears to have talked. He said that he never had the slightest notion to enfold her in his arms or so much as to touch her hand. He swore that he did not touch her hand. He said that they sat, she at one end of the bench, he at the other; he leaning slightly towards her and she looking straight towards the light of the Casino, her face illuminated by the lamps. The expression upon her face he could only describe as "queer". At another time, indeed, he made it appear that he thought she was glad. It is easy to imagine that she was glad, since at that time she could have had no idea of what was really happening. Frankly, she adored Edward Ashburnham. He was for her, in everything that she said at that time, the model of humanity, the hero, the athlete, the father of his country, the law-giver. So that for her, to be suddenly, intimately and overwhelmingly praised must have been a matter for mere gladness, however overwhelming it were. It must have been as if a god had approved her handiwork or a king her loyalty. She just sat still and listened, smiling. And it seemed to her that all the bitterness of her childhood, the terrors of her tempestuous father, the bewailings of her cruel-tongued mother were suddenly atoned for. She had her recompense at last. Because, of course, if you come to figure it out, a sudden pouring forth of passion by a man whom you regard as a cross between a pastor and a father might, to a woman, have the aspect of mere praise for good conduct. It wouldn't, I mean, appear at all in the light of an attempt to gain possession. The girl, at least, regarded him as firmly anchored to his Leonora. She had not the slightest inkling of any infidelities. He had always spoken to her of his wife in terms of reverence and deep affection. He had given her the idea that he regarded Leonora as absolutely impeccable and as absolutely satisfying. Their union had appeared to her to be one of those blessed things that are spoken of and contemplated with reverence by her church.

So that, when he spoke of her as being the person he cared most for in the world, she naturally thought that he meant to except Leonora and she was just glad. It was like a father saying that he approved of a marriageable daughter... And Edward, when he realized what he was doing, curbed his tongue at once. She was just glad and she went on being just glad.

I suppose that that was the most monstrously wicked thing that Edward Ashburnham ever did in his life. And yet I am so near to all these people that I cannot think any of them wicked. It is impossible of me to think of Edward Ashburnham as anything but straight, upright and honourable. That, I mean, is, in spite of everything, my permanent view of him. I try at times by dwelling on some of the things that he did to push that image of him away, as you might try to push aside a large pendulum. But it always comes back—the memory of his innumerable acts of kindness, of his efficiency, of his unspiteful tongue. He was such a fine fellow.

So I feel myself forced to attempt to excuse him in this as in so many other things. It is, I have no doubt, a most monstrous thing to attempt to corrupt a young girl just out of a convent. But I think Edward had no idea at all of corrupting her. I believe that he simply loved her. He said that that was the way of it and I, at least, believe him and I believe too that she was the only woman he ever really loved. He said that that was so; and he did enough to prove it. And Leonora said that it was so and Leonora knew him to the bottom of his heart.

I have come to be very much of a cynic in these matters; I mean that it is impossible to believe in the permanence of man's or woman's love. Or, at any rate, it is impossible to believe in the permanence of any early passion. As I see it, at least, with regard to man, a love affair, a love for any definite woman—is something in the nature of a widening of the experience. With each new woman that a man is attracted to there appears to come a broadening of the outlook, or, if you like, an acquiring of new territory. A turn of the eyebrow, a tone of the voice, a queer characteristic gesture—all these things, and it is these things that cause to arise the passion of love—all these things are like so many objects on the horizon of the landscape that tempt a man to walk beyond the horizon, to explore. He wants to get, as it were, behind those eyebrows with the peculiar turn, as if he desired to see the world with the eyes that they overshadow. He wants to hear that voice applying itself to every possible proposition, to every possible topic; he wants to see those characteristic gestures against every possible background. Of the question of the sex-instinct I know very little and I do not think that it counts for very much in a really great passion. It can be aroused by such nothings—by an untied shoelace, by a glance of the eye in passing—that I think it might be left out of the calculation. I don't mean to say that any great passion can exist without a desire for consummation. That seems to me to be a commonplace and to be therefore a matter needing no comment at all. It is a thing, with all its accidents, that must be taken for granted, as, in a novel, or a biography, you take it for granted that the characters have their meals with some regularity. But the real fierceness of desire, the real heat of a passion long continued and withering up the soul of a man is the craving for identity with the woman that he loves. He desires to see with the same eyes, to touch with the same sense of touch, to hear with the same ears, to lose his identity, to be enveloped, to be supported. For, whatever may be said of the relation of the sexes, there is no man who loves a woman that does not desire to come to her for the renewal of his courage, for the cutting asunder of his difficulties. And that will be the mainspring of his desire for her. We are all so afraid, we are all so alone, we all so need from the outside the assurance of our own worthiness to exist. So, for a time, if such a passion come to fruition, the man will get what he wants. He will get the moral support, the encouragement, the relief from the sense of loneliness, the assurance of his own worth. But these things pass away; inevitably they pass away as the shadows pass across sundials. It is sad, but it is so. The pages of the book will become familiar; the beautiful corner of the road will have been turned too many times. Well, this is the saddest story. And yet I do believe that for every man there comes at last a woman—or no, that is the wrong way of formulating it. For every man there comes at last a time of life when the woman who then sets her seal upon his imagination has set her seal for good. He will travel over no more horizons; he will never again set the knapsack over his shoulders; he will retire from those scenes. He will have gone out of the business. That at any rate was the case with Edward and the poor girl. It was quite literally the case. It was quite literally the case that his passions—for the mistress of the Grand Duke, for Mrs Basil, for little Mrs Maidan, for Florence, for whom you will—these passions were merely preliminary canters compared to his final race with death for her. I am certain of that. I am not going to be so American as to say that all true love demands some sacrifice. It doesn't. But I think that love will be truer and more permanent in which self-sacrifice has been exacted. And, in the case of the other women, Edward just cut in and cut them out as he did with the polo-ball from under the nose of Count Baron von Lelöffel. I don't mean to say that he didn't wear himself as thin as a lath in the endeavour to capture the other women; but over her he wore himself to rags and tatters and death—in the effort to leave her alone.

And, in speaking to her on that night, he wasn't, I am convinced, committing a baseness. It was as if his passion for her hadn't existed; as if the very words that he spoke, without knowing that he spoke them, created the passion as they went along. Before he spoke, there was nothing; afterwards, it was the integral fact of his life. Well, I must get back to my story.

And my story was concerning itself with Florence—with Florence, who heard those words from behind the tree. That of course is only conjecture, but I think the conjecture is pretty well justified. You have the fact that those two went out, that she followed them almost immediately afterwards through the darkness and, a little later, she came running back to the hotel with that pallid face and the hand clutching her dress over her heart. It can't have been only Bagshawe. Her face was contorted with agony before ever her eyes fell upon me or upon him beside me. But I dare say Bagshawe may have been the determining influence in her suicide. Leonora says that she had that flask, apparently of nitrate of amyl, but actually of prussic acid, for many years and that she was determined to use it if ever I discovered the nature of her relationship with that fellow Jimmy. You see, the mainspring of her nature must have been vanity. There is no reason why it shouldn't have been; I guess it is vanity that makes most of us keep straight, if we do keep straight, in this world.

If it had been merely a matter of Edward's relations with the girl I dare say Florence would have faced it out. She would no doubt have made him scenes, have threatened him, have appealed to his sense of humour, to his promises. But Mr Bagshawe and the fact that the date was the 4th of August must have been too much for her superstitious mind. You see, she had two things that she wanted. She wanted to be a great lady, installed in Branshaw Teleragh. She wanted also to retain my respect.

She wanted, that is to say, to retain my respect for as long as she lived with me. I suppose, if she had persuaded Edward Ashburnham to bolt with her she would have let the whole thing go with a run. Or perhaps she would have tried to exact from me a new respect for the greatness of her passion on the lines of all for love and the world well lost. That would be just like Florence.

In all matrimonial associations there is, I believe, one constant factor—a desire to deceive the person with whom one lives as to some weak spot in one's character or in one's career. For it is intolerable to live constantly with one human being who perceives one's small meannesses. It is really death to do so—that is why so many marriages turn out unhappily.

I, for instance, am a rather greedy man; I have a taste for good cookery and a watering tooth at the mere sound of the names of certain comestibles. If Florence had discovered this secret of mine I should have found her knowledge of it so unbearable that I never could have supported all the other privations of the régime that she extracted from me. I am bound to say that Florence never discovered this secret.

Certainly she never alluded to it; I dare say she never took sufficient interest in me.

And the secret weakness of Florence—the weakness that she could not bear to have me discover, was just that early escapade with the fellow called Jimmy. Let me, as this is in all probability the last time I shall mention Florence's name, dwell a little upon the change that had taken place in her psychology. She would not, I mean, have minded if I had discovered that she was the mistress of Edward Ashburnham. She would rather have liked it. Indeed, the chief trouble of poor Leonora in those days was to keep Florence from making, before me, theatrical displays, on one line or another, of that very fact. She wanted, in one mood, to come rushing to me, to cast herself on her knees at my feet and to declaim a carefully arranged, frightfully emotional, outpouring as to her passion. That was to show that she was like one of the great erotic women of whom history tells us. In another mood she would desire to come to me disdainfully and to tell me that I was considerably less than a man and that what had happened was what must happen when a real male came along. She wanted to say that in cool, balanced and sarcastic sentences. That was when she wished to appear like the heroine of a French comedy. Because of course she was always play acting.

But what she didn't want me to know was the fact of her first escapade with the fellow called Jimmy. She had arrived at figuring out the sort of low-down Bowery tough that that fellow was. Do you know what it is to shudder, in later life, for some small, stupid action—usually for some small, quite genuine piece of emotionalism—of your early life? Well, it was that sort of shuddering that came over Florence at the thought that she had surrendered to such a low fellow. I don't know that she need have shuddered. It was her footling old uncle's work; he ought never to have taken those two round the world together and shut himself up in his cabin for the greater part of the time. Anyhow, I am convinced that the sight of Mr Bagshawe and the thought that Mr Bagshawe—for she knew that unpleasant and toadlike personality—the thought that Mr Bagshawe would almost certainly reveal to me that he had caught her coming out of Jimmy's bedroom at five o'clock in the morning on the 4th of August, 1900—that was the determining influence in her suicide. And no doubt the effect of the date was too much for her superstitious personality. She had been born on the 4th of August; she had started to go round the world on the 4th of August; she had become a low fellow's mistress on the 4th of August. On the same day of the year she had married me; on that 4th she had lost Edward's love, and Bagshawe had appeared like a sinister omen—like a grin on the face of Fate. It was the last straw. She ran upstairs, arranged herself decoratively upon her bed—she was a sweetly pretty woman with smooth pink and white cheeks, long hair, the eyelashes falling like a tiny curtain on her cheeks. She drank the little phial of prussic acid and there she lay.—Oh, extremely charming and clear-cut—looking with a puzzled expression at the electric-light bulb that hung from the ceiling, or perhaps through it, to the stars above. Who knows? Anyhow, there was an end of Florence.

You have no idea how quite extraordinarily for me that was the end of Florence. From that day to this I have never given her another thought; I have not bestowed upon her so much as a sigh. Of course, when it has been necessary to talk about her to Leonora, or when for the purpose of these writings I have tried to figure her out, I have thought about her as I might do about a problem in algebra. But it has always been as a matter for study, not for remembrance. She just went completely out of existence, like yesterday's paper.

I was so deadly tired. And I dare say that my week or ten days of affaissement—of what was practically catalepsy—was just the repose that my exhausted nature claimed after twelve years of the repression of my instincts, after twelve years of playing the trained poodle. For that was all that I had been. I suppose that it was the shock that did it—the several shocks. But I am unwilling to attribute my feelings at that time to anything so concrete as a shock. It was a feeling so tranquil. It was as if an immensely heavy—an unbearably heavy knapsack, supported upon my shoulders by straps, had fallen off and left my shoulders themselves that the straps had cut into, numb and without sensation of life. I tell you, I had no regret. What had I to regret? I suppose that my inner soul—my dual personality—had realized long before that Florence was a personality of paper—that she represented a real human being with a heart, with feelings, with sympathies and with emotions only as a bank-note represents a certain quantity of gold. I know that sort of feeling came to the surface in me the moment the man Bagshawe told me that he had seen her coming out of that fellow's bedroom. I thought suddenly that she wasn't real; she was just a mass of talk out of guidebooks, of drawings out of fashion-plates. It is even possible that, if that feeling had not possessed me, I should have run up sooner to her room and might have prevented her drinking the prussic acid. But I just couldn't do it; it would have been like chasing a scrap of paper—an occupation ignoble for a grown man.

And, as it began, so that matter has remained. I didn't care whether she had come out of that bedroom or whether she hadn't. It simply didn't interest me. Florence didn't matter.

I suppose you will retort that I was in love with Nancy Rufford and that my indifference was therefore discreditable. Well, I am not seeking to avoid discredit. I was in love with Nancy Rufford as I am in love with the poor child's memory, quietly and quite tenderly in my American sort of way. I had never thought about it until I heard Leonora state that I might now marry her. But, from that moment until her worse than death, I do not suppose that I much thought about anything else.

I don't mean to say that I sighed about her or groaned; I just wanted to marry her as some people want to go to Carcassonne.

Do you understand the feeling—the sort of feeling that you must get certain matters out of the way, smooth out certain fairly negligible complications before you can go to a place that has, during all your life, been a sort of dream city? I didn't attach much importance to my superior years. I was forty-five, and she, poor thing, was only just rising twenty-two. But she was older than her years and quieter. She seemed to have an odd quality of sainthood, as if she must inevitably end in a convent with a white coif framing her face. But she had frequently told me that she had no vocation; it just simply wasn't there—the desire to become a nun. Well, I guess that I was a sort of convent myself; it seemed fairly proper that she should make her vows to me. No, I didn't see any impediment on the score of age. I dare say no man does and I was pretty confident that with a little preparation, I could make a young girl happy. I could spoil her as few young girls have ever been spoiled; and I couldn't regard myself as personally repulsive. No man can, or if he ever comes to do so, that is the end of him. But, as soon as I came out of my catalepsy, I seemed to perceive that my problem—that what I had to do to prepare myself for getting into contact with her, was just to get back into contact with life. I had been kept for twelve years in a rarefied atmosphere; what I then had to do was a little fighting with real life, some wrestling with men of business, some travelling amongst larger cities, something harsh, something masculine. I didn't want to present myself to Nancy Rufford as a sort of an old maid. That was why, just a fortnight after Florence's suicide, I set off for the United States.

II

IMMEDIATELY after Florence's death Leonora began to put the leash upon Nancy Rufford and Edward. She had guessed what had happened under the trees near the Casino. They stayed at Nauheim some weeks after I went, and Leonora has told me that that was the most deadly time of her existence. It seemed like a long, silent duel with invisible weapons, so she said. And it was rendered all the more difficult by the girl's entire innocence. For Nancy was always trying to go off alone with Edward—as she had been doing all her life, whenever she was home for holidays. She just wanted him to say nice things to her again.

You see, the position was extremely complicated. It was as complicated as it well could be, along delicate lines. There was the complication caused by the fact that Edward and Leonora never spoke to each other except when other people were present. Then, as I have said, their demeanours were quite perfect. There was the complication caused by the girl's entire innocence; there was the further complication that both Edward and Leonora really regarded the girl as their daughter. Or it might be more precise to say that they regarded her as being Leonora's daughter. And Nancy was a queer girl; it is very difficult to describe her to you.

She was tall and strikingly thin; she had a tortured mouth, agonized eyes, and a quite extraordinary sense of fun. You, might put it that at times she was exceedingly grotesque and at times extraordinarily beautiful. Why, she had the heaviest head of black hair that I have ever come across; I used to wonder how she could bear the weight of it. She was just over twenty-one and at times she seemed as old as the hills, at times not much more than sixteen. At one moment she would be talking of the lives of the saints and at the next she would be tumbling all over the lawn with the St Bernard puppy. She could ride to hounds like a Maenad and she could sit for hours perfectly still, steeping handkerchief after handkerchief in vinegar when Leonora had one of her headaches. She was, in short, a miracle of patience who could be almost miraculously impatient. It was, no doubt, the convent training that effected that. I remember that one of her letters to me, when she was about sixteen, ran something like:

"On Corpus Christi"—or it may have been some other saint's day, I cannot keep these things in my head—"our school played Roehampton at Hockey. And, seeing that our side was losing, being three goals to one against us at halftime, we retired into the chapel and prayed for victory. We won by five goals to three." And I remember that she seemed to describe afterwards a sort of saturnalia. Apparently, when the victorious fifteen or eleven came into the refectory for supper, the whole school jumped upon the tables and cheered and broke the chairs on the floor and smashed the crockery—for a given time, until the Reverend Mother rang a hand-bell. That is of course the Catholic tradition—saturnalia that can end in a moment, like the crack of a whip. I don't, of course, like the tradition, but I am bound to say that it gave Nancy—or at any rate Nancy had—a sense of rectitude that I have never seen surpassed. It was a thing like a knife that looked out of her eyes and that spoke with her voice, just now and then. It positively frightened me. I suppose that I was almost afraid to be in a world where there could be so fine a standard. I remember when she was about fifteen or sixteen on going back to the convent I once gave her a couple of English sovereigns as a tip. She thanked me in a peculiarly heartfelt way, saying that it would come in extremely handy. I asked her why and she explained. There was a rule at the school that the pupils were not to speak when they walked through the garden from the chapel to the refectory. And, since this rule appeared to be idiotic and arbitrary, she broke it on purpose day after day. In the evening the children were all asked if they had committed any faults during the day, and every evening Nancy confessed that she had broken this particular rule. It cost her sixpence a time, that being the fine attached to the offence. Just for the information I asked her why she always confessed, and she answered in these exact words:

"Oh, well, the girls of the Holy Child have always been noted for their truthfulness. It's a beastly bore, but I've got to do it."

I dare say that the miserable nature of her childhood, coming before the mixture of saturnalia and discipline that was her convent life, added something to her queernesses. Her father was a violent madman of a fellow, a major of one of what I believe are called the Highland regiments. He didn't drink, but he had an ungovernable temper, and the first thing that Nancy could remember was seeing her father strike her mother with his clenched fist so that her mother fell over sideways from the breakfast-table and lay motionless. The mother was no doubt an irritating woman and the privates of that regiment appeared to have been irritating, too, so that the house was a place of outcries and perpetual disturbances. Mrs Rufford was Leonora's dearest friend and Leonora could be cutting enough at times. But

I fancy she was as nothing to Mrs Rufford. The Major would come in to lunch harassed and already spitting out oaths after an unsatisfactory morning's drilling of his stubborn men beneath a hot sun. And then Mrs Rufford would make some cutting remark and pandemonium would break loose. Once, when she had been about twelve, Nancy had tried to intervene between the pair of them. Her father had struck her full upon the forehead a blow so terrible that she had lain unconscious for three days. Nevertheless, Nancy seemed to prefer her father to her mother. She remembered rough kindnesses from him. Once or twice when she had been quite small he had dressed her in a clumsy, impatient, but very tender way. It was nearly always impossible to get a servant to stay in the family and, for days at a time, apparently, Mrs Rufford would be incapable. I fancy she drank. At any rate, she had so cutting a tongue that even Nancy was afraid of her—she so made fun of any tenderness, she so sneered at all emotional displays. Nancy must have been a very emotional child.

Then one day, quite suddenly, on her return from a ride at Fort William, Nancy had been sent, with her governess, who had a white face, right down South to that convent school. She had been expecting to go there in two months' time. Her mother disappeared from her life at that time. A fortnight later Leonora came to the convent and told her that her mother was dead. Perhaps she was. At any rate, I never heard until the very end what became of Mrs Rufford. Leonora never spoke of her.

And then Major Rufford went to India, from which he returned very seldom and only for very short visits; and Nancy lived herself gradually into the life at Branshaw Teleragh. I think that, from that time onwards, she led a very happy life, till the end. There were dogs and horses and old servants and the Forest. And there were Edward and Leonora, who loved her.

I had known her all the time—I mean, that she always came to the Ashburnhams' at Nauheim for the last fortnight of their stay—and I watched her gradually growing. She was very cheerful with me. She always even kissed me, night and morning, until she was about eighteen. And she would skip about and fetch me things and laugh at my tales of life in Philadelphia. But, beneath her gaiety, I fancy that there lurked some terrors. I remember one day, when she was just eighteen, during one of her father's rare visits to Europe, we were sitting in the gardens, near the iron-stained fountain. Leonora had one of her headaches and we were waiting for Florence and Edward to come from their baths. You have no idea how beautiful Nancy looked that morning.

We were talking about the desirability of taking tickets in lotteries—of the moral side of it, I mean. She was all in white, and so tall and fragile; and she had only just put her hair up, so that the carriage of her neck had that charming touch of youth and of unfamiliarity. Over her throat there played the reflection from a little pool of water, left by a thunderstorm of the night before, and all the rest of her features were in the diffused and luminous shade of her white parasol. Her dark hair just showed beneath her broad, white hat of pierced, chip straw; her throat was very long and leaned forward, and her eyebrows, arching a little as she laughed at some old-fashionedness in my phraseology, had abandoned their tense line. And there was a little colour in her cheeks and light in her deep blue eyes. And to think that that vivid white thing, that saintly and swanlike being—to think that... Why, she was like the sail of a ship, so white and so definite in her movements. And to think that she will never... Why, she will never do anything again. I can't believe it...

Anyhow, we were chattering away about the morality of lotteries. And then, suddenly, there came from the arcades behind us the overtones of her father's unmistakable voice; it was as if a modified foghorn had boomed with a reed inside it. I looked round to catch sight of him. A tall, fair, stiffly upright man of fifty, he was walking away with an Italian baron who had had much to do with the Belgian Congo. They must have been talking about the proper treatment of natives, for I heard him say:

"Oh, hang humanity!"

When I looked again at Nancy her eyes were closed and her face was more pallid than her dress, which had at least some pinkish reflections from the gravel. It was dreadful to see her with her eyes closed like that.

"Oh!" she exclaimed, and her hand that had appeared to be groping, settled for a moment on my arm. "Never speak of it. Promise never to tell my father of it. It brings back those dreadful dreams..." And, when she opened her eyes she looked straight into mine. "The blessed saints," she said, "you would think they would spare you such things. I don't believe all the sinning in the world could make one deserve them."

They say the poor thing was always allowed a light at night, even in her bedroom.... And yet, no young girl could more archly and lovingly have played with an adored father. She was always holding him by both coat lapels; cross-questioning him as to how he spent his time; kissing the top of his head. Ah, she was well-bred, if ever anyone was.

The poor, wretched man cringed before her—but she could not have done more to put him at his ease. Perhaps she had had lessons in it at her convent. It was only that peculiar note of his voice, used when he was overbearing or dogmatic, that could unman her—and that was only visible when it came unexpectedly. That was because the bad dreams that the blessed saints allowed her to have for her sins always seemed to her to herald themselves by the booming sound of her father's voice. It was that sound that had always preceded his entrance for the terrible lunches of her childhood... .

I have reported, earlier in this chapter, that Leonora said, during that remainder of their stay at Nauheim, after I had left, it had seemed to her that she was fighting a long duel with unseen weapons against silent adversaries. Nancy, as I have also said, was always trying to go off with Edward alone. That had been her habit for years. And Leonora found it to be her duty to stop that. It was very difficult. Nancy was used to having her own way, and for years she had been used to going off with Edward, ratting, rabbiting, catching salmon down at Fordingbridge, district-visiting of the sort that Edward indulged in, or calling on the tenants. And at Nauheim she and Edward had always gone up to the Casino alone in the evenings—at any rate, whenever Florence did not call for his attendance. It shows the obviously innocent nature of the regard of those two that even Florence had never had any idea of jealousy. Leonora had cultivated the habit of going to bed at ten o'clock.

I don't know how she managed it, but, for all the time they were at Nauheim, she contrived never to let those two be alone together, except in broad daylight, in very crowded places. If a Protestant had done that it would no doubt have awakened a self-consciousness in the girl. But Catholics, who have always reservations and queer spots of secrecy, can manage these things better. And I dare say that two things made this easier—the death of Florence and the fact that Edward was obviously sickening. He appeared, indeed, to be very ill; his shoulders began to be bowed; there were pockets under his eyes; he had extraordinary moments of inattention.

And Leonora describes herself as watching him as a fierce cat watches an unconscious pigeon in a roadway. In that silent watching, again, I think she was a Catholic—of a people that can think thoughts alien to ours and keep them to themselves. And the thoughts passed through her mind; some of them even got through to Edward with never a word spoken. At first she thought that it might be remorse, or grief, for the death of Florence that was oppressing him. But she watched and watched, and uttered apparently random sentences about Florence before the girl, and she perceived that he had no grief and no remorse. He had not any idea that Florence could have committed suicide without writing at least a tirade to him. The absence of that made him certain that it had been heart disease. For Florence had never undeceived him on that point. She thought it made her seem more romantic.

No, Edward had no remorse. He was able to say to himself that he had treated Florence with gallant attentiveness of the kind that she desired until two hours before her death. Leonora gathered that from the look in his eyes, and from the way he straightened his shoulders over her as she lay in her coffin—from that and a thousand other little things. She would speak suddenly about Florence to the girl and he would not start in the least; he would not even pay attention, but would sit with bloodshot eyes gazing at the tablecloth. He drank a good deal, at that time—a steady soaking of drink every evening till long after they had gone to bed.

For Leonora made the girl go to bed at ten, unreasonable though that seemed to Nancy. She would understand that, whilst they were in a sort of half mourning for Florence, she ought not to be seen at public places, like the Casino; but she could not see why she should not accompany her uncle upon his evening strolls though the park. I don't know what Leonora put up as an excuse—something, I fancy, in the nature of a nightly orison that she made the girl and herself perform for the soul of Florence. And then, one evening, about a fortnight later, when the girl, growing restive at even devotional exercises, clamoured once more to be allowed to go for a walk with Edward, and when Leonora was really at her wits' end, Edward gave himself into her hands. He was just standing up from dinner and had his face averted.

But he turned his heavy head and his bloodshot eyes upon his wife and looked full at her.

"Doctor von Hauptmann," he said, "has ordered me to go to bed immediately after dinner. My heart's much worse."

He continued to look at Leonora for a long minute—with a sort of heavy contempt. And Leonora understood that, with his speech, he was giving her the excuse that she needed for separating him from the girl, and with his eyes he was reproaching her for thinking that he would try to corrupt Nancy.

He went silently up to his room and sat there for a long time—until the girl was well in bed—reading in the Anglican prayer-book. And about half-past ten she heard his footsteps pass her door, going outwards. Two and a half hours later they came back, stumbling heavily.

She remained, reflecting upon this position until the last night of their stay at Nauheim. Then she suddenly acted. For, just in the same way, suddenly after dinner, she looked at him and said:

"Teddy, don't you think you could take a night off from your doctor's orders and go with Nancy to the Casino. The poor child has had her visit so spoiled."

He looked at her in turn for a long, balancing minute.

"Why, yes," he said at last.

Nancy jumped out of her chair and kissed him. Those two words, Leonora said, gave her the greatest relief of any two syllables she had ever heard in her life. For she realized that Edward was breaking up, not under the desire for possession, but from the dogged determination to hold his hand. She could relax some of her vigilance.

Nevertheless, she sat in the darkness behind her half-closed jalousies, looking over the street and the night and the trees until, very late, she could hear Nancy's clear voice coming closer and saying:

"You did look an old guy with that false nose." There had been some sort of celebration of a local holiday up in the Kursaal. And Edward replied with his sort of sulky good nature:

"As for you, you looked like old Mother Sideacher."

The girl came swinging along, a silhouette beneath a gas-lamp; Edward, another, slouched at her side. They were talking just as they had talked any time since the girl had been seventeen; with the same tones, the same joke about an old beggar woman who always amused them at Branshaw. The girl, a little later, opened Leonora's door whilst she was still kissing Edward on the forehead as she had done every night.

"We've had a most glorious time," she said. "He's ever so much better. He raced me for twenty yards home. Why are you all in the dark?"

Leonora could hear Edward going about in his room, but, owing to the girl's chatter, she could not tell whether he went out again or not. And then, very much later, because she thought that if he were drinking again something must be done to stop it, she opened for the first time, and very softly, the never-opened door between their rooms. She wanted to see if he had gone out again. Edward was kneeling beside his bed with his head hidden in the counterpane. His arms, outstretched, held out before him a little image of the Blessed Virgin—a tawdry, scarlet and Prussian blue affair that the girl had given him on her first return from the convent. His shoulders heaved convulsively three times, and heavy sobs came from him before she could close the door. He was not a Catholic; but that was the way it took him.

Leonora slept for the first time that night with a sleep from which she never once started.

III

AND then Leonora completely broke down—on the day that they returned to Branshaw Teleragh. It is the infliction of our miserable minds—it is the scourge of atrocious but probably just destiny that no grief comes by itself. No, any great grief, though the grief itself may have gone, leaves in its place a train of horrors, of misery, and despair. For Leonora was, in herself, relieved. She felt that she could trust Edward with the girl and she knew that Nancy could be absolutely trusted. And then, with the slackening of her vigilance, came the slackening of her entire mind. This is perhaps the most miserable part of the entire story. For it is miserable to see a clean intelligence waver; and Leonora wavered.

You are to understand that Leonora loved Edward with a passion that was yet like an agony of hatred. And she had lived with him for years and years without addressing to him one word of tenderness. I don't know how she could do it. At the beginning of that relationship she had been just married off to him. She had been one of seven daughters in a bare, untidy Irish manor-house to which she had returned from the convent I have so often spoken of. She had left it just a year and she was just nineteen. It is impossible to imagine such inexperience as was hers. You might almost say that she had never spoken to a man except a priest. Coming straight from the convent, she had gone in behind the high walls of the manor-house that was almost more cloistral than any convent could have been. There were the seven girls, there was the strained mother, there was the worried father at whom, three times in the course of that year, the tenants took pot-shots from behind a hedge. The women-folk, upon the whole, the tenants respected. Once a week each of the girls, since there were seven of them, took a drive with the mother in the old basketwork chaise drawn by a very fat, very lumbering pony. They paid occasionally a call, but even these were so rare that, Leonora has assured me, only three times in the year that succeeded her coming home from the convent did she enter another person's house. For the rest of the time the seven sisters ran about in the neglected gardens between the unpruned espaliers. Or they played lawn-tennis or fives in an angle of a great wall that surrounded the garden—an angle from which the fruit trees had long died away. They painted in water-colour; they embroidered; they copied verses into albums. Once a week they went to Mass; once a week to the confessional, accompanied by an old nurse. They were happy since they had known no other life.

It appeared to them a singular extravagance when, one day, a photographer was brought over from the county town and photographed them standing, all seven, in the shadow of an old apple tree with the grey lichen on the raddled trunk. But it wasn't an extravagance.

Three weeks before Colonel Powys had written to Colonel Ashburnham:

"I say, Harry, couldn't your Edward marry one of my girls? It would be a god-send to me, for I'm at the end of my tether and, once one girl begins to go off, the rest of them will follow." He went on to say that all his daughters were tall, upstanding, clean-limbed and absolutely pure, and he reminded Colonel Ashburnham that, they having been married on the same day, though in different churches, since the one was a Catholic and the other an Anglican—they had said to each other, the night before, that, when the time came, one of their sons should marry one of their daughters. Mrs Ashburnham had been a Powys and remained Mrs Powys' dearest friend. They had drifted about the world as English soldiers do, seldom meeting, but their women always in correspondence one with another. They wrote about minute things such as the teething of Edward and of the earlier daughters or the best way to repair a Jacob's ladder in a stocking. And, if they met seldom, yet it was often enough to keep each other's personalities fresh in their minds, gradually growing a little stiff in the joints, but always with enough to talk about and with a store of reminiscences. Then, as his girls began to come of age when they must leave the convent in which they were regularly interned during his years of active service, Colonel Powys retired from the army with the necessity of making a home for them. It happened that the Ashburnhams had never seen any of the Powys girls, though, whenever the four parents met in London, Edward Ashburnham was always of the party. He was at that time twenty-two and, I believe, almost as pure in mind as Leonora herself. It is odd how a boy can have his virgin intelligence untouched in this world.

That was partly due to the careful handling of his mother, partly to the fact that the house to which he went at Winchester had a particularly pure tone and partly to Edward's own peculiar aversion from anything like coarse language or gross stories. At Sandhurst he had just kept out of the way of that sort of thing. He was keen on soldiering, keen on mathematics, on land-surveying, on politics and, by a queer warp of his mind, on literature. Even when he was twenty-two he would pass hours reading one of Scott's novels or the Chronicles of Froissart. Mrs

Ashburnham considered that she was to be congratulated, and almost every week she wrote to Mrs Powys, dilating upon her satisfaction.

Then, one day, taking a walk down Bond Street with her son, after having been at Lord's, she noticed Edward suddenly turn his head round to take a second look at a well-dressed girl who had passed them. She wrote about that, too, to Mrs Powys, and expressed some alarm. It had been, on Edward's part, the merest reflex action. He was so very abstracted at that time owing to the pressure his crammer was putting upon him that he certainly hadn't known what he was doing.

It was this letter of Mrs Ashburnham's to Mrs Powys that had caused the letter from Colonel Powys to Colonel Ashburnham—a letter that was half-humorous, half longing. Mrs Ashburnham caused her husband to reply, with a letter a little more jocular—something to the effect that Colonel Powys ought to give them some idea of the goods that he was marketing. That was the cause of the photograph. I have seen it, the seven girls, all in white dresses, all very much alike in feature—all, except Leonora, a little heavy about the chins and a little stupid about the eyes. I dare say it would have made Leonora, too, look a little heavy and a little stupid, for it was not a good photograph. But the black shadow from one of the branches of the apple tree cut right across her face, which is all but invisible. There followed an extremely harassing time for Colonel and Mrs Powys. Mrs Ashburnham had written to say that, quite sincerely, nothing would give greater ease to her maternal anxieties than to have her son marry one of Mrs Powys' daughters if only he showed some inclination to do so. For, she added, nothing but a love-match was to be thought of in her Edward's case. But the poor Powys couple had to run things so very fine that even the bringing together of the young people was a desperate hazard.

The mere expenditure upon sending one of the girls over from Ireland to Branshaw was terrifying to them; and whichever girl they selected might not be the one to ring Edward's bell. On the other hand, the expenditure upon mere food and extra sheets for a visit from the Ashburnhams to them was terrifying, too. It would mean, mathematically, going short in so many meals themselves, afterwards. Nevertheless, they chanced it, and all the three Ashburnhams came on a visit to the lonely manor-house.

They could give Edward some rough shooting, some rough fishing and a whirl of femininity; but I should say the girls made really more impression upon Mrs Ashburnham than upon Edward himself. They appeared to her to be so clean run and so safe. They were indeed so clean run that, in a faint sort of way, Edward seems to have regarded them rather as boys than as girls. And then, one evening, Mrs Ashburnham had with her boy one of those conversations that English mothers have with English sons. It seems to have been a criminal sort of proceeding, though I don't know what took place at it. Anyhow, next morning Colonel Ashburnham asked on behalf of his son for the hand of Leonora. This caused some consternation to the Powys couple, since Leonora was the third daughter and Edward ought to have married the eldest. Mrs Powys, with her rigid sense of the proprieties, almost wished to reject the proposal. But the Colonel, her husband, pointed out that the visit would have cost them sixty pounds, what with the hire of an extra servant, of a horse and car, and with the purchase of beds and bedding and extra tablecloths. There was nothing else for it but the marriage. In that way Edward and Leonora became man and wife.

I don't know that a very minute study of their progress towards complete disunion is necessary. Perhaps it is. But there are many things that I cannot well make out, about which I cannot well question Leonora, or about which Edward did not tell me. I do not know that there was ever any question of love from Edward to her. He regarded her, certainly, as desirable amongst her sisters. He was obstinate to the extent of saying that if he could not have her he would not have any of them. And, no doubt, before the marriage, he made her pretty speeches out of books that he had read. But, as far as he could describe his feelings at all, later, it seems that, calmly and without any quickening of the pulse, he just carried the girl off, there being no opposition. It had, however, been all so long ago that it seemed to him, at the end of his poor life, a dim and misty affair. He had the greatest admiration for Leonora.

He had the very greatest admiration. He admired her for her truthfulness, for her cleanness of mind, and the clean-runness of her limbs, for her efficiency, for the fairness of her skin, for the gold of her hair, for her religion, for her sense of duty. It was a satisfaction to take her about with him.

But she had not for him a touch of magnetism. I suppose, really, he did not love her because she was never mournful; what really made him feel good in life was to comfort somebody who would be darkly and mysteriously mournful. That he had never had to do for Leonora. Perhaps, also, she was at first too obedient. I do not mean to say that she was submissive—that she deferred, in her judgements, to his. She did not. But she had been handed over to him, like some patient medieval virgin; she had been taught all her life that the first duty of a woman is to obey. And there she was.

In her, at least, admiration for his qualities very soon became love of the deepest description. If his pulses never quickened she, so I have been told, became what is called an altered being when he approached her from the other side of a dancing-floor. Her eyes followed him about full of trustfulness, of admiration, of gratitude, and of love. He was also, in a great sense, her pastor and guide—and he guided her into what, for a girl straight out of a convent, was almost heaven. I have not the least idea of what an English officer's wife's existence may be like. At any rate, there were feasts, and chatterings, and nice men who gave her the right sort of admiration, and nice women who treated her as if she had been a baby. And her confessor approved of her life, and Edward let her give little treats to the girls of the convent she had left, and the Reverend Mother approved of him. There could not have been a happier girl for five or six years. For it was only at the end of that time that clouds began, as the saying is, to arise. She was then about twenty-three, and her purposeful efficiency made her perhaps have a desire for mastery. She began to perceive that Edward was extravagant in his largesses. His parents died just about that time, and Edward, though they both decided that he should continue his soldiering, gave a great deal of attention to the management of Branshaw through a steward. Aldershot was not very far away, and they spent all his leaves there.

And, suddenly, she seemed to begin to perceive that his generosities were almost fantastic. He subscribed much too much to things connected with his mess, he pensioned off his father's servants, old or new, much too generously. They had a large income, but every now and then they would find themselves hard up. He began to talk of mortgaging a farm or two, though it never actually came to that.

She made tentative efforts at remonstrating with him. Her father, whom she saw now and then, said that Edward was much too generous to his tenants; the wives of his brother officers remonstrated with her in private; his large subscriptions made it difficult for their husbands to keep up with them. Ironically enough, the first real trouble between them came from his desire to build a Roman Catholic chapel at Branshaw. He wanted to do it to honour Leonora, and he proposed to do it very expensively. Leonora did not want it; she could perfectly well drive from Branshaw to the nearest Catholic Church as often as she liked. There were no Roman Catholic tenants and no Roman Catholic servants except her old nurse who could always drive with her. She had as many priests to stay with her as could be needed—and even the priests did not want a gorgeous chapel in that place where it would have merely seemed an invidious instance of ostentation. They were perfectly ready to celebrate Mass for Leonora and her nurse, when they stayed at Branshaw, in a cleaned-up outhouse. But Edward was as obstinate as a hog about it. He was truly grieved at his wife's want of sentiment—at her refusal to receive that amount of public homage from him. She appeared to him to be wanting in imagination—to be cold and hard. I don't exactly know what part her priests played in the tragedy that it all became; I dare say they behaved quite creditably but mistakenly. But then, who would not have been mistaken with Edward? I believe he was even hurt that Leonora's confessor did not make strenuous efforts to convert him. There was a period when he was quite ready to become an emotional Catholic.

I don't know why they did not take him on the hop; but they have queer sorts of wisdoms, those people, and queer sorts of tact. Perhaps they thought that Edward's too early conversion would frighten off other Protestant desirables from marrying Catholic girls. Perhaps they saw deeper into Edward than he saw himself and thought that he would make a not very creditable convert. At any rate they—and Leonora—left him very much alone. It mortified him very considerably. He has told me that if Leonora had then taken his aspirations seriously everything would have been different. But I dare say that was nonsense. At any rate, it was over the question of the chapel that they had their first and really disastrous quarrel. Edward at that time was not well; he supposed himself to be overworked with his regimental affairs—he was managing the mess at the time. And Leonora was not well—she was beginning to fear that their union might be sterile. And then her father came over from Glasmoyle to stay with them.

Those were troublesome times in Ireland, I understand. At any rate, Colonel Powys had tenants on the brain—his own tenants having shot at him with shot-guns. And, in conversation with Edward's land-steward, he got it into his head that Edward managed his estates with a mad generosity towards his tenants. I understand, also, that those years—the 'nineties—were very bad for farming. Wheat was fetching only a few shillings the hundred; the price of meat was so low that cattle hardly paid for raising; whole English counties were ruined. And Edward allowed his tenants very high rebates.

To do both justice Leonora has since acknowledged that she was in the wrong at that time and that Edward was following out a more far-seeing policy in nursing his really very good tenants over a bad period. It was not as if the whole of his money came from the land; a good deal of it was in rails. But old Colonel Powys had that bee in his bonnet and, if he never directly approached Edward himself on the subject, he preached unceasingly, whenever he had the opportunity, to Leonora. His pet idea was that Edward ought to sack all his own tenants and import a set of farmers from Scotland. That was what they were doing in Essex. He was of opinion that Edward was riding hotfoot to ruin.

That worried Leonora very much—it worried her dreadfully; she lay awake nights; she had an anxious line round her mouth. And that, again, worried Edward. I do not mean to say that Leonora actually spoke to Edward about his tenants—but he got to know that some one, probably her father, had been talking to her about the matter. He got to know it because it was the habit of his steward to look in on them every morning about breakfast-time to report any little happenings. And there was a farmer called Mumford who had only paid half his rent for the last three years. One morning the land-steward reported that Mumford would be unable to pay his rent at all that year.

Edward reflected for a moment and then he said something like:

"Oh well, he's an old fellow and his family have been our tenants for over two hundred years. Let him off altogether."

And then Leonora—you must remember that she had reason for being very nervous and unhappy at that time—let out a sound that was very like a groan. It startled Edward, who more than suspected what was passing in her mind—it startled him into a state of anger. He said sharply:

"You wouldn't have me turn out people who've been earning money for us for centuries—people to whom we have responsibilities—and let in a pack of Scotch farmers?"

He looked at her, Leonora said, with what was practically a glance of hatred and then, precipitately, he left the breakfast-table. Leonora knew that it probably made it all the worse that he had been betrayed into a manifestation of anger before a third party. It was the first and last time that he ever was betrayed into such a manifestation of anger. The land-steward, a moderate and well-balanced man whose family also had been with the Ashburnhams for over a century, took it upon himself to explain that he considered Edward was pursuing a perfectly proper course with his tenants. He erred perhaps a little on the side of generosity, but hard times were hard times, and every one had to feel the pinch, landlord as well as tenants. The great thing was not to let the land get into a poor state of cultivation. Scotch farmers just skinned your fields and let them go down and down. But Edward had a very good set of tenants who did their best for him and for themselves. These arguments at that time carried very little conviction to Leonora. She was, nevertheless, much concerned by Edward's outburst of anger. The fact is that Leonora had been practising economies in her department. Two of the under-housemaids had gone and she had not replaced them; she had spent much less that year upon dress. The fare she had provided at the dinners they gave had been much less bountiful and not nearly so costly as had been the case in preceding years, and Edward began to perceive a hardness and determination in his wife's character. He seemed to see a net closing round him—a net in which they would be forced to live like one of the comparatively poor county families of the neighbourhood. And, in the mysterious way in which two people, living together, get to know each other's thoughts without a word spoken, he had known, even before his outbreak, that Leonora was worrying about his managing of the estates. This appeared to him to be intolerable. He had, too, a great feeling of self-contempt because he had been betrayed into speaking harshly to Leonora before that land-steward. She imagined that his nerve must be deserting him, and there can have been few men more miserable than Edward was at that period. You see, he was really a very simple soul—very simple. He imagined that no man can satisfactorily accomplish his life's work without loyal and whole-hearted cooperation of the woman he lives with. And he was beginning to perceive dimly that, whereas his own traditions were entirely collective, his wife was a sheer individualist. His own theory—the feudal theory of an over-lord doing his best by his dependents, the dependents meanwhile doing their best for the over-lord—this theory was entirely foreign to Leonora's nature. She came of a family of small Irish landlords—that hostile garrison in a plundered country. And she was thinking unceasingly of the children she wished to have. I don't know why they never had any children—not that I really believe that children would have made any difference. The dissimilarity of Edward and Leonora was too profound. It will give you some idea of the extraordinary naïveté of Edward Ashburnham that, at the time of his marriage and for perhaps a couple of years after, he did not really know how children are produced. Neither did Leonora. I don't mean to say that this state of things continued, but there it was. I dare say it had a good deal of influence on their mentalities. At any rate, they never had a child. It was the Will of God.

It certainly presented itself to Leonora as being the Will of God—as being a mysterious and awful chastisement of the Almighty. For she had discovered shortly before this period that her parents had not exacted from Edward's family the promise that any children she should bear should be brought up as Catholics. She herself had never talked of the matter with either her father, her mother, or her husband. When at last her father had let drop some words leading her to believe that that was the fact, she tried desperately to extort the promise from Edward. She encountered an unexpected obstinacy. Edward was perfectly willing that the girls should be Catholic; the boys must be Anglican. I don't understand the bearing of these things in

English society. Indeed, Englishmen seem to me to be a little mad in matters of politics or of religion. In Edward it was particularly queer because he himself was perfectly ready to become a Romanist. He seemed, however, to contemplate going over to Rome himself and yet letting his boys be educated in the religion of their immediate ancestors. This may appear illogical, but I dare say it is not so illogical as it looks. Edward, that is to say, regarded himself as having his own body and soul at his own disposal. But his loyalty to the traditions of his family would not permit him to bind any future inheritors of his name or beneficiaries by the death of his ancestors. About the girls it did not so much matter. They would know other homes and other circumstances. Besides, it was the usual thing. But the boys must be given the opportunity of choosing—and they must have first of all the Anglican teaching. He was perfectly unshakable about this.

Leonora was in an agony during all this time. You will have to remember she seriously believed that children who might be born to her went in danger, if not absolutely of damnation, at any rate of receiving false doctrine. It was an agony more terrible than she could describe. She didn't indeed attempt to describe it, but I could tell from her voice when she said, almost negligently, "I used to lie awake whole nights. It was no good my spiritual advisers trying to console me." I knew from her voice how terrible and how long those nights must have seemed and of how little avail were the consolations of her spiritual advisers. Her spiritual advisers seemed to have taken the matter a little more calmly. They certainly told her that she must not consider herself in any way to have sinned. Nay, they seem even to have extorted, to have threatened her, with a view to getting her out of what they considered to be a morbid frame of mind. She would just have to make the best of things, to influence the children when they came, not by propaganda, but by personality. And they warned her that she would be committing a sin if she continued to think that she had sinned. Nevertheless, she continued to think that she had sinned.

Leonora could not be aware that the man whom she loved passionately and whom, nevertheless, she was beginning to try to rule with a rod of iron—that this man was becoming more and more estranged from her. He seemed to regard her as being not only physically and mentally cold, but even as being actually wicked and mean. There were times when he would almost shudder if she spoke to him. And she could not understand how he could consider her wicked or mean. It only seemed to her a sort of madness in him that he should try to take upon his own shoulders the burden of his troop, of his regiment, of his estate and of half of his country. She could not see that in trying to curb what she regarded as megalomania she was doing anything wicked. She was just trying to keep things together for the sake of the children who did not come. And, little by little, the whole of their intercourse became simply one of agonized discussion as to whether Edward should subscribe to this or that institution or should try to reclaim this or that drunkard. She simply could not see it.

Into this really terrible position of strain, from which there appeared to be no issue, the Kilsyte case came almost as a relief. It is part of the peculiar irony of things that Edward would certainly never have kissed that nurse-maid if he had not been trying to please Leonora. Nurse-maids do not travel first-class, and, that day, Edward travelled in a third-class carriage in order to prove to Leonora that he was capable of economies. I have said that the Kilsyte case came almost as a relief to the strained situation that then existed between them. It gave Leonora an opportunity of backing him up in a whole-hearted and absolutely loyal manner. It gave her the opportunity of behaving to him as he considered a wife should behave to her husband.

You see, Edward found himself in a railway carriage with a quite pretty girl of about nineteen. And the quite pretty girl of about nineteen, with dark hair and red cheeks and blue eyes, was quietly weeping. Edward had been sitting in his corner thinking about nothing at all. He had chanced to look at the nurse-maid; two large, pretty tears came out of her eyes and dropped into her lap. He immediately felt that he had got to do something to comfort her. That was his job in life. He was desperately unhappy himself and it seemed to him the most natural thing in the world that they should pool their sorrows. He was quite democratic; the idea of the difference in their station never seems to have occurred to him. He began to talk to her. He discovered that her young man had been seen walking out with Annie of Number 54. He moved over to her side of the carriage.

He told her that the report probably wasn't true; that, after all, a young man might take a walk with Annie from Number 54 without its denoting anything very serious. And he assured me that he felt at least quite half-fatherly when he put his arm around her waist and kissed her. The girl, however, had not forgotten the difference of her station.

All her life, by her mother, by other girls, by schoolteachers, by the whole tradition of her class she had been warned against gentlemen. She was being kissed by a gentleman. She screamed, tore herself away; sprang up and pulled a communication cord.

Edward came fairly well out of the affair in the public estimation; but it did him, mentally, a good deal of harm.

IV

IT is very difficult to give an all-round impression of an man. I wonder how far I have succeeded with Edward Ashburnham. I dare say I haven't succeeded at all. It is ever very difficult to see how such things matter. Was it the important point about poor Edward that he was very well built, carried himself well, was moderate at the table and led a regular life—that he had, in fact, all the virtues that are usually accounted English? Or have I in the least succeeded in conveying that he was all those things and had all those virtues? He certainly was them and had them up to the last months of his life. They were the things that one would set upon his tombstone. They will, indeed, be set upon his tombstone by his widow.

And have I, I wonder, given the due impression of how his life was portioned and his time laid out? Because, until the very last, the amount of time taken up by his various passions was relatively small. I have been forced to write very much about his passions, but you have to consider—I should like to be able to make you consider—that he rose every morning at seven, took a cold bath, breakfasted at eight, was occupied with his regiment from nine until one; played polo or cricket with the men when it was the season for cricket, till tea-time. Afterwards he would occupy himself with the letters from his land-steward or with the affairs of his mess, till dinner-time. He would dine and pass the evening playing cards, or playing billiards with Leonora or at social functions of one kind or another. And the greater part of his life was taken up by that—by far the greater part of his life. His love-affairs, until the very end, were sandwiched in at odd moments or took place during the social evenings, the dances and dinners. But I guess I have made it hard for you, O silent listener, to get that impression. Anyhow, I hope I have not given you the idea that Edward Ashburnham was a pathological case. He wasn't. He was just a normal man and very much of a sentimentalist. I dare say the quality of his youth, the nature of his mother's influence, his ignorances, the crammings that he received at the hands of army coaches—I dare say that all these excellent influences upon his adolescence were very bad for him. But we all have to put up with that sort of thing and no doubt it is very bad for all of us. Nevertheless, the outline of Edward's life was an outline perfectly normal of the life of a hard-working, sentimental and efficient professional man.

That question of first impressions has always bothered me a good deal—but quite academically. I mean that, from time to time I have wondered whether it were or were not best to trust to one's first impressions in dealing with people. But I never had anybody to deal with except waiters and chambermaids and the Ashburnhams, with whom I didn't know that I was having any dealings. And, as far as waiters and chambermaids were concerned, I have generally found that my first impressions were correct enough. If my first idea of a man was that he was civil, obliging, and attentive, he generally seemed to go on being all those things. Once, however, at our Paris flat we had a maid who appeared to be charming and transparently honest. She stole, nevertheless, one of Florence's diamond rings. She did it, however, to save her young man from going to prison. So here, as somebody says somewhere, was a special case.

And, even in my short incursion into American business life—an incursion that lasted during part of August and nearly the whole of September—I found that to rely upon first impressions was the best thing I could do. I found myself automatically docketing and labelling each man as he was introduced to me, by the run of his features and by the first words that he spoke. I can't, however, be regarded as really doing business during the time that I spent in the United States. I was just winding things up. If it hadn't been for my idea of marrying the girl I might possibly hav looked for something to do in my own country. For my experiences there were vivid and amusing. It was exactly as if I had come out of a museum into a riotous fancy-dress ball. During my life with Florence I had almost come to forget that there were such things as fashions or occupations or the greed of gain. I had, in fact, forgotten that there was such a thing as a dollar and that a dollar can be extremely desirable if you don't happen to possess one. And I had forgotten, too, that there was such a thing as gossip that mattered. In that particular, Philadelphia was the most amazing place I have ever been in in my life. I was not in that city for more than a week or ten days and I didn't there transact anything much in the way of business; nevertheless, the number of times that I was warned by everybody against everybody else was simply amazing. A man I didn't know would come up behind my lounge chair in the hotel, and, whispering cautiously beside my ear, would warn me against some other man that I equally didn't know but who would be standing by the bar. I don't know what they thought I was there to do—perhaps to buy out the city's debt or get a controlling hold of some railway interest. Or, perhaps, they imagined that I wanted to buy a newspaper, for they were either politicians or reporters, which, of course, comes to the same thing. As a matter of fact, my property in Philadelphia was mostly real estate in the old-fashioned part of the city and all I wanted to do there was just to satisfy myself that the houses were in good repair and the doors kept properly painted. I wanted also to see my relations, of whom I had a few. These were mostly professional people and they were mostly rather hard up because of the big bank failure in 1907 or thereabouts. Still, they were very nice. They would have been nicer still if they hadn't, all of them, had what appeared to me to be the mania that what they called influences were working against them. At any rate, the impression of that city was one of old-fashioned rooms, rather English than American in type, in which handsome but careworn ladies, cousins of my own, talked principally about mysterious movements that were going on against them. I never got to know what it was all about; perhaps they thought I knew or perhaps there weren't any movements at all. It was all very secret and subtle and subterranean. But there was a nice young fellow called Carter who was a sort of second-nephew of mine, twice removed. He was handsome and dark and gentie and tall and modest. I understand also that he was a good cricketer. He was employed by the real-estate agents who collected my rents. It was he, therefore, who took me over my own property and I saw a good deal of him and of a nice girl called Mary, to whom he was engaged. At that time I did, what I certainly shouldn't do now—I made some careful inquiries as to his character. I discovered from his employers that he was just all that he appeared, honest, industrious, high-spirited, friendly and ready to do anyone a good turn. His relatives, however, as they were mine, too—seemed to have something darkly mysterious against him. I imagined that he must have been mixed up in some case of graft or that he had at least betrayed several innocent and trusting maidens. I pushed, however, that particular mystery home and discovered it was only that he was a Democrat. My own people were mostly Republicans. It seemed to make it worse and more darkly mysterious to them that young Carter was what they called a sort of a Vermont Democrat which was the whole ticket and no mistake. But I don't know what it means. Anyhow, I suppose that my money will go to him when I die—I like the recollection of his friendly image and of the nice girl he was engaged to. May Fate deal very kindly with them.

I have said just now that, in my present frame of mind, nothing would ever make me make inquiries as to the character of any man that I liked at first sight. (The little digression as to my Philadelphia experiences was really meant to lead around to this.) For who in this world can give anyone a character? Who in this world knows anything of any other heart—or of his own? I don't mean to say that one cannot form an average estimate of the way a person will behave. But one cannot be certain of the way any man will behave in every case—and until one can do that a "character" is of no use to anyone. That, for instance, was the way with Florence's maid in Paris. We used to trust that girl with blank cheques for the payment of the tradesmen. For quite a time she was so trusted by us. Then, suddenly, she stole a ring. We should not have believed her capable of it; she would not have believed herself capable of it. It was nothing in her character. So, perhaps, it was with Edward Ashburnham.

Or, perhaps, it wasn't. No, I rather think it wasn't. It is

difficult to figure out. I have said that the Kilsyte case eased the immediate tension for him and Leonora. It let him see that she was capable of loyalty to him; it gave her her chance to show that she believed in him. She accepted without question his statement that, in kissing the girl, he wasn't trying to do more than administer fatherly comfort to a weeping child. And, indeed, his own world—including the magistrates—took that view of the case. Whatever people say, one's world can be perfectly charitable at times... But, again, as I have said, it did Edward a great deal of harm.

That, at least, was his view of it. He assured me that, before that case came on and was wrangled about by counsel with all sorts of dirty-mindedness that counsel in that sort of case can impute, he had not had the least idea that he was capable of being unfaithful to Leonora. But, in the midst of that tumult—he says that it came suddenly into his head whilst he was in the witness-box—in the midst of those august ceremonies of the law there came suddenly into his mind the recollection of the softness of the girl's body as he had pressed her to him. And, from that moment, that girl appeared desirable to him—and Leonora completely unattractive.

He began to indulge in day-dreams in which he approached the nurse-maid more tactfully and carried the matter much further. Occasionally he thought of other women in terms of wary courtship—or, perhaps, it would be more exact to say that he thought of them in terms of tactful comforting, ending in absorption. That was his own view of the case. He saw himself as the victim of the law. I don't mean to say that he saw himself as a kind of Dreyfus. The law, practically, was quite kind to him. It stated that in its view Captain Ashburnham had been misled by an ill-placed desire to comfort a member of the opposite sex, and it fined him five shilling for his want of tact, or of knowledge of the world. But Edward maintained that it had put ideas into his head.

I don't believe it, though he certainly did. He was twenty-seven then, and his wife was out of sympathy with him—some crash was inevitable. There was between them a momentary rapprochement; but it could not last. It made it, probably, all the worse that, in that particular matter, Leonara had come so very well up to the scratch. For, whilst Edward respected her more and was grateful to her, it made her seem by so much the more cold in other matters that were near his heart—his responsibilities, his career, his tradition. It brought his despair of her up to a point of exasperation—and it riveted on him the idea that he might find some other woman who would give him the moral support that he needed. He wanted to be looked upon as a sort of Lohengrin.

At that time, he says, he went about deliberately looking for some woman who could help him. He found several—for there were quite a number of ladies in his set who were capable of agreeing with this handsome and fine fellow that the duties of a feudal gentleman were feudal. He would have liked to pass his days talking to one or other of these ladies. But there was always an obstacle—if the lady were married there would be a husband who claimed the greater part of her time and attention. If, on the other hand, it were an unmarried girl, he could not see very much of her for fear of compromising her. At that date, you understand, he had not the least idea of seducing any one of these ladies. He wanted only moral support at the hands of some female, because he found men difficult to talk to about ideals. Indeed, I do not believe that he had, at any time, any idea of making any one his mistress. That sounds queer; but I believe it is quite true as a statement of character.

It was, I believe, one of Leonora's priests—a man of the world—who suggested that she should take him to Monte Carlo. He had the idea that what Edward needed, in order to fit him for the society of Leonora, was a touch of irresponsibility. For Edward, at that date, had much the aspect of a prig. I mean that, if he played polo and was an excellent dancer he did the one for the sake of keeping himself fit and the other because it was a social duty to show himself at dances, and, when there, to dance well. He did nothing for fun except what he considered to be his work in life. As the priest saw it, this must for ever estrange him from Leonora—not because Leonora set much store by the joy of life, but because she was out of sympathy with Edward's work. On the other hand, Leonora did like to have a good time, now and then, and, as the priest saw it, if Edward could be got to like having a good time now and then, too, there would be a bond of sympathy between them. It was a good idea, but it worked out wrongly.

It worked out, in fact, in the mistress of the Grand Duke. In anyone less sentimental than Edward that would not have mattered. With Edward it was fatal. For, such was his honourable nature, that for him to enjoy a woman's favours made him feel that she had a bond on him for life. That was the way it worked out in practice. Psychologically it meant that he could not have a mistress without falling violently in love with her. He was a serious person—and in this particular case it was very expensive. The mistress of the Grand Duke—a Spanish dancer of passionate appearance—singled out Edward for her glances at a ball that was held in their common hotel. Edward was tall, handsome, blond and very wealthy as she understood—and Leonora went up to bed early. She did not care for public dances, but she was relieved to see that Edward appeared to be having a good time with several amiable girls. And that was the end of Edward—for the Spanish dancer of passionate appearance wanted one night of him for his beaux yeux. He took her into the dark gardens and, remembering suddenly the girl of the Kilsyte case, he kissed her. He kissed her passionately, violently, with a sudden explosion of the passion that had been bridled all his life—for Leonora was cold, or at any rate, well behaved. La Dolciquita liked this reversion, and he passed the night in her bed.

When the palpitating creature was at last asleep in his arms he discovered that he was madly, was passionately, was overwhelmingly in love with her. It was a passion that had arisen like fire in dry corn. He could think of nothing else; he could live for nothing else. But La Dolciquita was a reasonable creature without an ounce of passion in her. She wanted a certain satisfaction of her appetites and Edward had appealed to her the night before. Now that was done with, and, quite coldly, she said that she wanted money if he was to have any more of her. It was a perfectly reasonable commercial transaction. She did not care two buttons for Edward or for any man and he was asking her to risk a very good situation with the Grand Duke. If Edward could put up sufficient money to serve as a kind of insurance against accident she was ready to like Edward for a time that would be covered, as it were, by the policy. She was getting fifty thousand dollars a year from her Grand Duke; Edward would have to pay a premium of two years' hire for a month of her society. There would not be much risk of the Grand Duke's finding it out and it was not certain that he would give her the keys of the street if he did find out. But there was the risk—a twenty per cent risk, as she figured it out. She talked to Edward as if she had been a solicitor with an estate to sell—perfectly quietly and perfectly coldly without any inflections in her voice. She did not want to be unkind to him; but she could see no reason for being kind to him. She was a virtuous business woman with a mother and two sisters and her own old age to be provided comfortably for. She did not expect more than a five years' further run. She was twenty-four and, as she said: "We Spanish women are horrors at thirty." Edward swore that he would provide for her for life if she would come to him and leave off talking so horribly; but she only shrugged one shoulder slowly and contemptuously. He tried to convince this woman, who, as he saw it, had surrendered to him her virtue, that he regarded it as in any case his duty to provide for her, and to cherish her and even to love her—for life. In return for her sacrifice he would do that. In return, again, for his honourable love she would listen for ever to the accounts of his estate. That was how he figured it out.

She shrugged the same shoulder with the same gesture and held out her left hand with the elbow at her side:

"Enfin, mon ami," she said, "put in this hand the price of that tiara at Forli's or..." And she turned her back on him.

Edward went mad; his world stood on its head; the palms in front of the blue sea danced grotesque dances. You see, he believed in the virtue, tenderness and moral support of women. He wanted more than anything to argue with La Dolciquita; to retire with her to an island and point out to her the damnation of her point of view and how salvation can only be found in true love and the feudal system. She had once been his mistress, he reflected, and by all the moral laws she ought to have gone on being his mistress or at the very least his sympathetic confidante. But her rooms were closed to him; she did not appear in the hotel. Nothing: blank silence. To break that down he had to have twenty thousand pounds. You have heard what happened. He spent a week of madness; he hungered; his eyes sank in; he shuddered at Leonora's touch. I dare say that nine-tenths of what he took to be his passion for La Dolciquita was really discomfort at the thought that he had been unfaithful to Leonora. He felt uncommonly bad, that is to say—oh, unbearably bad, and he took it all to be love. Poor devil, he was incredibly naïve. He drank like a fish after Leonora was in bed and he spread himself over the tables, and this went on for about a fortnight. Heaven knows what would have happened; he would have thrown away every penny that he possessed.

On the night after he had lost about forty thousand pounds and whilst the whole hotel was whispering about it, La Dolciquita walked composedly into his bedroom. He was too drunk to recognize her, and she sat in his arm-chair, knitting and holding smelling salts to her nose—for he was pretty far gone with alcoholic poisoning—and, as soon as he was able to understand her, she said:

"Look here, mon ami, do not go to the tables again. Take a good sleep now and come and see me this afternoon."

He slept till the lunch-hour. By that time Leonora had heard the news. A Mrs Colonel Whelan had told her. Mrs Colonel Whelan seems to have been the only sensible person who was ever connected with the Ashburnhams. She had argued it out that there must be a woman of the harpy variety connected with Edward's incredible behaviour and mien; and she advised Leonora to go straight off to Town—which might have the effect of bringing Edward to his senses—and to consult her solicitor and her spiritual adviser. She had better go that very morning; it was no good arguing with a man in Edward's condition.

Edward, indeed, did not know that she had gone. As soon as he awoke he went straight to La Dolciquita's room and she stood him his lunch in her own apartments. He fell on her neck and wept, and she put up with it for a time. She was quite a good-natured woman. And, when she had calmed him down with Eau de Mélisse, she said: "Look here, my friend, how much money have you left? Five thousand dollars? Ten?" For the rumour went that Edward had lost two kings' ransoms a night for fourteen nights and she imagined that he must be near the end of his resources.

The Eau de Mélisse had calmed Edward to such an extent that, for the moment, he really had a head on his shoulders. He did nothing more than grunt:

"And then?"

"Why," she answered, "I may just as well have the ten thousand dollars as the tables. I will go with you to Antibes for a week for that sum."

Edward grunted: "Five." She tried to get seven thousand five hundred; but he stuck to his five thousand and the hotel expenses at Antibes. The sedative carried him just as far as that and then he collapsed again. He had to leave for Antibes at three; he could not do without it. He left a note for Leonora saying that he had gone off for a week with the Clinton Morleys, yachting.

He did not enjoy himself very much at Antibes. La Dolciquita could talk of nothing with any enthusiasm except money, and she tired him unceasingly, during every waking hour, for presents of the most expensive description. And, at the end of a week, she just quietly kicked him out. He hung about in Antibes for three days. He was cured of the idea that he had any duties towards La Dolciquita—feudal or otherwise. But his sentimentalism required of him an attitude of Byronic gloom—as if his court had gone into half-mourning. Then his appetite suddenly returned, and he remembered Leonora. He found at his hotel at Monte Carlo a telegram from Leonora, dispatched from London, saying; "Please return as soon as convenient." He could not understand why Leonora should have abandoned him so precipitately when she only thought that he had gone yachting with the Clinton Morleys. Then he discovered that she had left the hotel before he had written the note. He had a pretty rocky journey back to town; he was frightened out of his life—and Leonora had never seemed so desirable to him.

V

I CALL this the Saddest Story, rather than "The Ashburnham Tragedy", just because it is so sad, just because there was no current to draw things along to a swift and inevitable end. There is about it none of the elevation that accompanies tragedy; there is about it no nemesis, no destiny. Here were two noble people—for I am convinced that both Edward and Leonora had noble natures—here, then, were two noble natures, drifting down life, like fireships afloat on a lagoon and causing miseries, heart-aches, agony of the mind and death. And they themselves steadily deteriorated. And why? For what purpose? To point what lesson? It is all a darkness.

There is not even any villain in the story—for even Major Basil, the husband of the lady who next, and really, comforted the unfortunate Edward—even Major Basil was not a villain in this piece. He was a slack, loose, shiftless sort of fellow—but he did not do anything to Edward. Whilst they were in the same station in Burma he borrowed a good deal of money—though, really, since Major Basil had no particular vices, it was difficult to know why he wanted it. He collected—different types of horses' bits from the earliest times to the present day—but, since he did not prosecute even this occupation with any vigour, he cannot have needed much money for the acquirement, say, of the bit of Genghis Khan's charger—if Genghis Khan had a charger. And when I say that he borrowed a good deal of money from Edward I do not mean to say that he had more than a thousand pounds from him during the five years that the connection lasted. Edward, of course, did not have a great deal of money; Leonora was seeing to that. Still, he may have had five hundred pounds a year English, for his menus plaisirs—for his regimental subscriptions and for keeping his men smart. Leonora hated that; she would have preferred to buy dresses for herself or to have devoted the money to paying off a mortgage. Still, with her sense of justice, she saw that, since she was managing a property bringing in three thousand a year with a view to re-establishing it as a property of five thousand a year and since the property really, if not legally, belonged to Edward, it was reasonable and just that Edward should get a slice of his own. Of course she had the devil of a job.

I don't know that I have got the financial details exactly right. I am a pretty good head at figures, but my mind, still, sometimes mixes up pounds with dollars and I get a figure wrong. Anyhow, the proposition was something like this: Properly worked and without rebates to the tenants and keeping up schools and things, the Branshaw estate should have brought in about five thousand a year when Edward had it. It brought in actually about four. (I am talking in pounds, not dollars.) Edward's excesses with the Spanish Lady had reduced its value to about three—as the maximum figure, without reductions.

Leonora wanted to get it back to five.

She was, of course, very young to be faced with such a proposition—twenty-four is not a very advanced age. So she did things with a youthful vigour that she would, very likely, have made more merciful, if she had known more about life. She got Edward remarkably on the hop. He had to face her in a London hotel, when he crept back from Monte Carlo with his poor tail between his poor legs. As far as I can make out she cut short his first mumblings and his first attempts at affectionate speech with words something like: "We're on the verge of ruin. Do you intend to let me pull things together? If not I shall retire to Hendon on my jointure." (Hendon represented a convent to which she occasionally went for what is called a "retreat" in Catholic circles.) And poor dear Edward knew nothing—absolutely nothing. He did not know how much money he had, as he put it, "blued" at the tables. It might have been a quarter of a million for all he remembered. He did not know whether she knew about La Dolciquita or whether she imagined that he had gone off yachting or had stayed at Monte Carlo. He was just dumb and he just wanted to get into a hole and not have to talk. Leonora did not make him talk and she said nothing herself.

I do not know much about English legal procedure—I cannot, I mean, give technical details of how they tied him up. But I know that, two days later, without her having said more than I have reported to you, Leonora and her attorney had become the trustees, as I believe it is called, of all Edward's property, and there was an end of Edward as the good landlord and father of his people. He went out. Leonora then had three thousand a year at her disposal. She occupied Edward with getting himself transferred to a part of his regiment that was in Burma—if that is the right way to put it. She herself had an interview, lasting a week or so—with Edward's land-steward. She made him understand that the estate would have to yield up to its last penny. Before they left for India she had let Branshaw for seven years at a thousand a year. She sold two Vandykes and a little silver for eleven thousand pounds and she raised, on mortgage, twenty-nine thousand. That went to Edward's money-lending friends in Monte Carlo. So she had to get the twenty-nine thousand back, for she did not regard the Vandykes and the silver as things she would have to replace. They were just frills to the Ashburnham vanity. Edward cried for two days over the disappearance of his ancestors and then she wished she had not done it; but it did not teach her anything and it lessened such esteem as she had for him. She did not also understand that to let Branshaw affected him with a feeling of physical soiling—that it was almost as bad for him as if a woman belonging to him had become a prostitute. That was how it did affect him; but I dare say she felt just as bad about the Spanish dancer.

So she went at it. They were eight years in India, and during the whole of that time she insisted that they must be self-supporting—they had to live on his Captain's pay, plus the extra allowance for being at the front. She gave him the five hundred a year for Ashburnham frills, as she called it to herself—and she considered she was doing him very well.

Indeed, in a way, she did him very well—but it was not his way. She was always buying him expensive things which, as it were, she took off her own back. I have, for instance, spoken of Edward's leather cases. Well, they were not Edward's at all; they were Leonora's manifestations. He liked to be clean, but he preferred, as it were, to be threadbare. She never understood that, and all that pigskin was her idea of a reward to him for putting her up to a little speculation by which she made eleven hundred pounds. She did, herself, the threadbare business. When they went up to a place called Simla, where, as I understand, it is cool in the summer and very social—when they went up to Simla for their healths it was she who had him prancing around, as we should say in the United States, on a thousand-dollar horse with the gladdest of glad rags all over him. She herself used to go into "retreat". I believe that was very good for her health and it was also very inexpensive.

It was probably also very good for Edward's health, because he pranced about mostly with Mrs Basil, who was a nice woman and very, very kind to him. I suppose she was his mistress, but I never heard it from Edward, of course. I seem to gather that they carried it on in a high romantic fashion, very proper to both of them—or, at any rate, for Edward; she seems to have been a tender and gentle soul who did what he wanted. I do not mean to say that she was without character; that was her job, to do what Edward wanted. So I figured it out, that for those five years, Edward wanted long passages of deep affection kept up in long, long talks and that every now and then they "fell," which would give Edward an opportunity for remorse and an excuse to lend the Major another fifty. I don't think that Mrs Basil considered it to be "falling"; she just pitied him and loved him.

You see, Leonora and Edward had to talk about something during all these years. You cannot be absolutely dumb when you live with a person unless you are an inhabitant of the North of England or the State of Maine. So Leonora imagined the cheerful device of letting him see the accounts of his estate and discussing them with him. He did not discuss them much; he was trying to behave prettily. But it was old Mr Mumford—the farmer who did not pay his rent—that threw Edward into Mrs Basil's arms. Mrs Basil came upon Edward in the dusk, in the Burmese garden, with all sorts of flowers and things. And he was cutting up that crop—with his sword, not a walking-stick. He was also carrying on and cursing in a way you would not believe.

She ascertained that an old gentleman called Mumford had been ejected from his farm and had been given a little cottage rent-free, where he lived on ten shillings a week from a farmers' benevolent society, supplemented by seven that was being allowed him by the Ashburnham trustees. Edward had just discovered that fact from the estate accounts. Leonora had left them in his dressing-room and he had begun to read them before taking off his marching-kit. That was how he came to have a sword. Leonora considered that she had been unusually generous to old Mr Mumford in allowing him to inhabit a cottage, rent-free, and in giving him seven shillings a week. Anyhow, Mrs Basil had never seen a man in such a state as Edward was. She had been passionately in love with him for quite a time, and he had been longing for her sympathy and admiration with a passion as deep. That was how they came to speak about it, in the Burmese garden, under the pale sky, with sheaves of severed vegetation, misty and odorous, in the night around their feet. I think they behaved themselves with decorum for quite a time after that, though Mrs Basil spent so many hours over the accounts of the Ashburnham estate that she got the name of every field by heart. Edward had a huge map of his lands in his harness-room and Major Basil did not seem to mind. I believe that people do not mind much in lonely stations. It might have lasted for ever if the Major had not been made what is called a brevet-colonel during the shuffling of troops that went on just before the South African War. He was sent off somewhere else and, of course, Mrs Basil could not stay with Edward. Edward ought, I suppose, to have gone to the Transvaal. It would have done him a great deal of good to get killed. But Leonora would not let him; she had heard awful stories of the extravagance of the hussar regiment in war-time—how they left hundred-bottle cases of champagne, at five guineas a bottle, on the veldt and so on. Besides, she preferred to see how Edward was spending his five hundred a year. I don't mean to say that Edward had any grievance in that. He was never a man of the deeds of heroism sort and it was just as good for him to be sniped at up in the hills of the North Western frontier, as to be shot at by an old gentleman in a tophat at the bottom of some spruit. Those are more or less his words about it. I believe he quite distinguished himself over there. At any rate, he had had his D.S.O. and was made a brevet-major. Leonora, however, was not in the least keen on his soldiering. She hated also his deeds of heroism. One of their bitterest quarrels came after he had, for the second time, in the Red Sea, jumped overboard from the troopship and rescued a private soldier. She stood it the first time and even complimented him. But the Red Sea was awful, that trip, and the private soldiers seemed to develop a suicidal craze. It got on Leonora's nerves; she figured Edward, for the rest of that trip, jumping overboard every ten minutes. And the mere cry of "Man overboard" is a disagreeable, alarming and disturbing thing. The ship gets stopped and there are all sorts of shouts. And Edward would not promise not to do it again, though, fortunately, they struck a streak of cooler weather when they were in the Persian Gulf. Leonora had got it into her head that Edward was trying to commit suicide, so I guess it was pretty awful for her when he would not give the promise. Leonora ought never to have been on that troopship; but she got there somehow, as an economy.

Major Basil discovered his wife's relation with Edward just before he was sent to his other station. I don't know whether that was a blackmailer's adroitness or just a trick of destiny. He may have known of it all the time or he may not. At any rate, he got hold of, just about then, some letters and things. It cost Edward three hundred pounds immediately. I do not know how it was arranged; I cannot imagine how even a blackmailer can make his demands. I suppose there is some sort of way of saving your face. I figure the Major as disclosing the letters to Edward with furious oaths, then accepting his explanations that the letters were perfectly innocent if the wrong construction were not put upon them. Then the Major would say: "I say, old chap, I'm deuced hard up. Couldn't you lend me three hundred or so?" I fancy that was how it was. And, year by year, after that there would come a letter from the Major, saying that he was deuced hard up and couldn't Edward lend him three hundred or so? Edward was pretty hard hit when Mrs Basil had to go away. He really had been very fond of her, and he remained faithful to her memory for quite a long time. And Mrs Basi had loved him very much and continued to cherish a hope of reunion with him. Three days ago there came a quite proper but very lamentable letter from her to Leonora, asking to be given particulars as to Edward's death. She had read the advertisement of it in an Indian paper. I think she must have been a very nice woman....

And then the Ashburnhams were moved somewhere up towards a place or a district called Chitral. I am no good at geography of the Indian Empire. By that time they had settled down into a model couple and they never spoke in private to each other. Leonora had given up even showing the accounts of the Ashburnham estate to Edward. He thought that that was because she had piled up such a lot of money that she did not want him to know how she was getting on any more. But, as a matter of fact, after five or six years it had penetrated to her mind that it was painful to Edward to have to look on at the accounts of his estate and have no hand in the management of it. She was trying to do him a kindness. And, up in Chitral, poor dear little Maisie Maidan came along....

That was the most unsettling to Edward of all his affairs. It made him suspect that he was inconstant. The affair with the Dolciquita he had sized up as a short attack of madness like hydrophobia. His relations with Mrs Basil had not seemed to him to imply moral turpitude of a gross kind. The husband had been complaisant; they had really loved each other; his wife was very cruel to him and had long ceased to be a wife to him. He thought that Mrs Basil had been his soul-mate, separated from him by an unkind fate—something sentimental of that sort.

But he discovered that, whilst he was still writing long weekly letters to Mrs Basil, he was beginning to be furiously impatient if he missed seeing Maisie Maidan during the course of the day. He discovered himself watching the doorways with impatience; he discovered that he disliked her boy husband very much for hours at a time. He discovered that he was getting up at unearthly hours in order to have time, later in the morning, to go for a walk with Maisie Maidan. He discovered himself using little slang words that she used and attaching a sentimental value to those words. These, you understand, were discoveries that came so late that he could do nothing but drift. He was losing weight; his eyes were beginning to fall in; he had touches of bad fever. He was, as he described it, pipped.

And, one ghastly hot day, he suddenly heard himself say to Leonora:

"I say, couldn't we take Mrs Maidan with us to Europe and drop her at Nauheim?"

He hadn't had the least idea of saying that to Leonora. He had merely been standing, looking at an illustrated paper, waiting for dinner. Dinner was twenty minutes late or the Ashburnhams would not have been alone together. No, he hadn't had the least idea of framing that speech. He had just been standing in a silent agony of fear, of longing, of heat, of fever. He was thinking that they were going back to Branshaw in a month and that Maisie Maidan was going to remain behind and die. And then, that had come out.

The punkah swished in the darkened room; Leonora lay exhausted and motionless in her cane lounge; neither of them stirred. They were both at that time very ill in indefinite ways.

And then Leonora said:

"Yes. I promised it to Charlie Maidan this afternoon. I have offered to pay her ex's myself."

Edward just saved himself from saying: "Good God!" You see, he had not the least idea of what Leonora knew—about Maisie, about Mrs Basil, even about La Dolciquita. It was a pretty enigmatic situation for him. It struck him that Leonora must be intending to manage his loves as she managed his money affairs and it made her more hateful to him—and more worthy of respect.

Leonora, at any rate, had managed his money to some

purpose. She had spoken to him, a week before, for the first time in several years—about money. She had made twenty-two thousand pounds out of the Branshaw land and seven by the letting of Branshaw furnished. By fortunate investments—in which Edward had helped her—she had made another six or seven thousand that might well become more. The mortgages were all paid off, so that, except for the departure of the two Vandykes and the silver, they were as well off as they had been before the Dolciquita had acted the locust. It was Leonora's great achievement. She laid the figures before Edward, who maintained an unbroken silence.

"I propose," she said, "that you should resign from the Army and that we should go back to Branshaw. We are both too ill to stay here any longer."

Edward said nothing at all.

"This," Leonora continued passionlessly, "is the great day of my life."

Edward said:

"You have managed the job amazingly. You are a wonderful woman." He was thinking that if they went back to Branshaw they would leave Maisie Maidan behind. That thought occupied him exclusively. They must, undoubtedly, return to Branshaw; there could be no doubt that Leonora was too ill to stay in that place. She said:

"You understand that the management of the whole of the expenditure of the income will be in your hands. There will be five thousand a year." She thought that he cared very much about the expenditure of an income of five thousand a year and that the fact that she had done so much for him would rouse in him some affection for her. But he was thinking exclusively of Maisie Maidan—of Maisie, thousands of miles away from him. He was seeing the mountains between them—blue mountains and the sea and sunlit plains. He said:

"That is very generous of you." And she did not know whether that were praise or a sneer. That had been a week before. And all that week he had passed in an increasing agony at the thought that those mountains, that sea, and those sunlit plains would be between him and Maisie Maidan. That thought shook him in the burning nights: the sweat poured from him and he trembled with cold, in the burning noons—at that thought.

He had no minute's rest; his bowels turned round and round within him: his tongue was perpetually dry and it seemed to him that the breath between his teeth was like air from a pest-house.

He gave no thought to Leonora at all; he had sent in his papers. They were to leave in a month. It seemed to him to be his duty to leave that place and to go away, to support Leonora. He did his duty.

It was horrible, in their relationship at that time, that whatever she did caused him to hate her. He hated her when he found that she proposed to set him up as the Lord of Branshaw again—as a sort of dummy lord, in swaddling clothes. He imagined that she had done this in order to separate him from Maisie Maidan. Hatred hung in all the heavy nights and filled the shadowy corners of the room. So when he heard that she had offered to the Maidan boy to take his wife to Europe with him, automatically he hated her since he hated all that she did. It seemed to him, at that time, that she could never be other than cruel even if, by accident, an act of hers were kind.... Yes, it was a horrible situation.

But the cool breezes of the ocean seemed to clear up that hatred as if it had been a curtain. They seemed to give him back admiration for her, and respect. The agreeableness of having money lavishly at command, the fact that it had bought for him the companionship of Maisie Maidan—these things began to make him see that his wife might have been right in the starving and scraping upon which she had insisted. He was at ease; he was even radiantly happy when he carried cups of bouillon for Maisie Maidan along the deck. One night, when he was leaning beside Leonora, over the ship's side, he said suddenly:

"By jove, you're the finest woman in the world. I wish we could be better friends."

She just turned away without a word and went to her cabin. Still, she was very much better in health.

And now, I suppose, I must give you Leonora's side of the case....

That is very difficult. For Leonora, if she preserved an unchanged front, changed very frequently her point of view. She had been drilled—in her tradition, in her upbringing—to keep her mouth shut. But there were times, she said, when she was so near yielding to the temptation of speaking that afterwards she shuddered to think of those times. You must postulate that what she desired above all things was to keep a shut mouth to the world; to Edward and to the women that he loved. If she spoke she would despise herself.

From the moment of his unfaithfulness with La Dolciquita she never acted the part of wife to Edward. It was not that she intended to keep herself from him as a principle, for ever. Her spiritual advisers, I believe, forbade that. But she stipulated that he must, in some way, perhaps symbolical, come back to her. She was not very clear as to what she meant; probably she did not know herself. Or perhaps she did.

There were moments when he seemed to be coming back to her; there were moments when she was within a hair of yielding to her physical passion for him. In just the same way, at moments, she almost yielded to the temptation to denounce Mrs Basil to her husband or Maisie Maidan to hers. She desired then to cause the horrors and pains of public scandals. For, watching Edward more intently and with more straining of ears than that which a cat bestows upon a bird overhead, she was aware of the progress of his passion for each of these ladies. She was aware of it from the way in which his eyes returned to doors and gateways; she knew from his tranquillities when he had received satisfactions.

At times she imagined herself to see more than was warranted. She imagined that Edward was carrying on intrigues with other women with two at once, with three. For whole periods she imagined him to be a monster of libertinage and she could not see that he could have anything against her. She left him his liberty; she was starving herself to build up his fortunes; she allowed herself none of the joys of femininity—no dresses, no jewels—hardly even friendships, for fear they should cost money.

And yet, oddly, she could not but be aware that both Mrs Basil and Maisie Maidan were nice women. The curious, discounting eye which one woman can turn on another did not prevent her seeing that Mrs Basil was very good to Edward and Mrs Maidan very good for him. That seemed her to be a monstrous and incomprehensible working of Fate's. Incomprehensible! Why, she asked herself again and again, did none of the good deeds that she did for her husband ever come through to him, or appear to hime as good deeds? By what trick of mania could not he let her be as good to him as Mrs Basil was? Mrs Basil was not so extraordinarily dissimilar to herself. She was, it was true, tall, dark, with soft mournful voice and a great kindness of manner for every created thing, from punkah men to flowers on the trees. But she was not so well read as Lenora, at any rate in learned books. Leonora could not stand novels. But, even with all her differences, Mrs Basil did not appear to Leonora to differ so very much from herself. She was truthful, honest and, for the rest, just a woman. And Leonora had a vague sort of idea that, to a man, all women are the same after three weeks of close intercourse. She thought that the kindness should no longer appeal, the soft and mournful voice no longer thrill, the tall darkness no longer give a man the illusion that he was going into the depths of an unexplored wood. She could not understand how Edward could go on and on maundering over Mrs Basil. She could not see why he should continue to write her long letters after their separation. After that, indeed, she had a very bad time.

She had at that period what I will call the "monstrous" theory of Edward. She was always imagining him ogling at every woman that he came across. She did not, that year, go into "retreat" at Simla because she was afraid that he would corrupt her maid in her absence. She imagined him carrying on intrigues with native women or Eurasians. At dances she was in a fever of watchfulness.

She persuaded herself that this was because she had a dread of scandals. Edward might get himself mixed up with a marriageable daughter of some man who would make a row or some husband who would matter. But, really, she acknowledged afterwards to herself, she was hoping that, Mrs Basil being out of the way, the time might have come when Edward should return to her. All that period she passed in an agony of jealousy and fear—the fear that Edward might really become promiscuous in his habits.

So that, in an odd way, she was glad when Maisie Maidan came along—and she realized that she had not, before, been afraid of husbands and of scandals, since, then, she did her best to keep Maisie's husband unsuspicious. She wished to appear so trustful of Edward that Maidan could not possibly have any suspicions. It was an evil position for her. But Edward was very ill and she wanted to see him smile again. She thought that if he could smile again through her agency he might return, through gratitude and satisfied love—to her. At that time she thought that Edward was a person of light and fleeting passions. And she could understand Edward's passion for Maisie, since Maisie was one of those women to whom other women will allow magnetism. She was very pretty; she was very young; in spite of her heart she was very gay and light on her feet. And Leonora was really very fond of Maisie, who was fond enough of Leonora. Leonora, indeed, imagined that she could manage this affair all right. She had no thought of Maisie's being led into adultery; she imagined that if she could take Maisie and Edward to Nauheim, Edward would see enough of her to get tired of her pretty little chatterings, and of the pretty little motions of her hands and feet. And she thought she could trust Edward. For there was not any doubt of Maisie's passion for Edward. She raved about him to Leonora as Leonora had heard girls rave about drawing masters in schools. She was perpetually asking her boy husband why he could not dress, ride, shoot, play polo, or even recite sentimental poems, like their major. And young Maidan had the greatest admiration for Edward, and he adored, was bewildered by and entirely trusted his wife. It appeared to him that Edward was devoted to Leonora. And Leonora imagined that when poor Maisie was cured of her hear and Edward had seen enough of her, he would return to her. She had the vague, passionate idea that, when Edward had exhausted a number of other types of women he must turn to her. Why should not her type have its turn in his heart? She imagined that, by now, she understood him better, that she understood better his vanities and that, by making him happier, she could arouse his love.

Florence knocked all that on the head....

PART IV

I

I HAVE, I am aware, told this story in a very rambling way so that it may be difficult for anyone to find their path through what may be a sort of maze. I cannot help it. I have stuck to my idea of being in a country cottage with a silent listener, hearing between the gusts of the wind and amidst the noises of the distant sea, the story as it comes. And, when one discusses an affair—a long, sad affair—one goes back, one goes forward. One remembers points that one has forgotten and one explains them all the more minutely since one recognizes that one has forgotten to mention them in their proper places and that one may have given, by omitting them, a false impression. I console myself with thinking that this is a real story and that, after all, real stories are probably told best in the way a person telling a story would tell them. They will then seem most real.

At any rate, I think I have brought my story up to the date of Maisie Maidan's death. I mean that I have explained everything that went before it from the several points of view that were necessary—from Leonora's, from Edward's and, to some extent, from my own. You have the facts for the trouble of finding them; you have the points of view as far as I could ascertain or put them. Let me imagine myself back, then, at the day of Maisie's death—or rather at the moment of Florence's dissertation on the Protest, up in the old Castle of the town of M——. Let us consider Leonora's point of view with regard to Florence; Edward's, of course, I cannot give you, for Edward naturally never spoke of his affair with my wife. (I may, in what follows, be a little hard on Florence; but you must remember that I have been writing away at this story now for six months and reflecting longer and longer upon these affairs.) And the longer I think about them the more certain I become that Florence was a contaminating influence—she depressed and deteriorated poor Edward; she deteriorated, hopelessly, the miserable Leonora. There is no doubt that she caused Leonora's character to deteriorate. If there was a fine point about Leonora it was that she was proud and that she was silent. But that pride and that silence broke when she made that extraordinary outburst, in the shadowy room that contained the Protest, and in the little terrace looking over the river. I don't mean to say that she was doing a wrong thing. She was certainly doing right in trying to warn me that Florence was making eyes at her husband. But, if she did the right thing, she was doing it in the wrong way. Perhaps she should have reflected longer; she should have spoken, if she wanted to speak, only after reflection. Or it would have been better if she had acted—if, for instance, she had so chaperoned Florence that private communication between her and Edward became impossible. She should have gone eavesdropping; she should have watched outside bedroom doors. It is odious; but that is the way the job is done. She should have taken Edward away the moment Maisie was dead. No, she acted wrongly.... And yet, poor thing, is it for me to condemn her—and what did it matter in the end? If it had not been Florence, it would have been some other... Still, it might have been a better woman than my wife. For Florence was vulgar; Florence was a common flirt who would not, at the last, lacher prise; and Florence was an unstoppable talker. You could not stop her; nothing would stop her. Edward and Leonora were at least proud and reserved people. Pride and reserve are not the only things in life; perhaps they are not even the best things. But if they happen to be your particular virtues you will go all to pieces if you let them go. And Leonora let them go. She let them go before poor Edward did even. Consider her position when she burst out over the Luther-Protest.... Consider her agonies....

You are to remember that the main passion of her life was to get Edward back; she had never, till that moment, despaired of getting him back. That may seem ignoble; but you have also to remember that her getting him back represented to her not only a victory for herself. It would, as it appeared to her, have been a victory for all wives and a victory for her Church. That was how it presented itself to her. These things are a little inscrutable. I don't know why the getting back of Edward should have represented to her a victory for all wives, for Society and for her Church. Or, maybe, I have a glimmering of it. She saw life as a perpetual sex-battle between husbands who desire to be unfaithful to their wives, and wives who desire to recapture their husbands in the end. That was her sad and modest view of matrimony. Man, for her, was a sort of brute who must have his divagations, his moments of excess, his nights out, his, let us say, rutting seasons. She had read few novels, so that the idea of a pure and constant love succeeding the sound of wedding bells had never been very much presented to her. She went, numbed and terrified, to the Mother Superior of her childhood's convent with the tale of Edward's infidelities with the Spanish dancer, and all that the old nun, who appeared to her to be infinitely wise, mystic and reverend, had done had been to shake her head sadly and to say:

"Men are like that. By the blessing of God it will all come right in the end."

That was what was put before her by her spiritual advisers as her programme in life. Or, at any rate, that was how their teachings came through to her—that was the lesson she told me she had learned of them. I don't know exactly what they taught her. The lot of women was patience and patience and again patience—ad majorem Dei gloriam—until upon the appointed day, if God saw fit, she should have her reward. If then, in the end, she should have succeeded in getting Edward back she would have kept her man within the limits that are all that wifehood has to expect. She was even taught that such excesses in men are natural, excusable—as if they had been children.

And the great thing was that there should be no scandal before the congregation. So she had clung to the idea of getting Edward back with a fierce passion that was like an agony. She had looked the other way; she had occupied herself solely with one idea. That was the idea of having Edward appear, when she did get him back, wealthy, glorious as it were, on account of his lands, and upright. She would show, in fact, that in an unfaithful world one Catholic woman had succeeded in retaining the fidelity of her husband. And she thought she had come near her desires.

Her plan with regard to Maisie had appeared to be working admirably. Edward had seemed to be cooling off towards the girl. He did not hunger to pass every minute of the time at Nauheirn beside the child's recumbent form; he went out to polo matches; he played auction bridge in the evenings; he was cheerful and bright. She was certain that he was not trying to seduce that poor child; she was beginning to think that he had never tried to do so. He seemed in fact to be dropping back into what he had been for Maisie in the beginning—a kind, attentive, superior officer in the regiment, paying gallant attentions to a bride. They were as open in their little flirtations as the dayspring from on high. And Maisie had not appeared to fret when he went off on excursions with us; she had to lie down for so many hours on her bed every afternoon, and she had not appeared to crave for the attentions of Edward at those times. And Edward was beginning to make little advances to Leonora. Once or twice, in private—for he often did it before people—he had said: "How nice you look!" or "What a pretty dress!" She had gone with Florence to Frankfurt, where they dress as well as in Paris, and had got herself a gown or two. She could afford it, and Florence was an excellent adviser as to dress. She seemed to have got hold of the clue to the riddle.

Yes, Leonora seemed to have got hold of the clue to the riddle. She imagined herself to have been in the wrong to some extent in the past. She should not have kept Edward on such a tight rein with regard to money. She thought she was on the right tack in letting him—as she had done only with fear and irresolution—have again the control of his income. He came even a step towards her and acknowledged, spontaneously, that she had been right in husbanding, for all those years, their resources. He said to her one day:

"You've done right, old girl. There's nothing I like so much as to have a little to chuck away. And I can do it, thanks to you."

That was really, she said, the happiest moment of her life. And he, seeming to realize it, had ventured to pat her on the shoulder. He had, ostensibly, come in to borrow a safety-pin of her. And the occasion of her boxing Maisie's ears, had, after it was over, riveted in her mind the idea that there was no intrigue between Edward and Mrs Maidan. She imagined that, from henceforward, all that she had to do was to keep him well supplied with money and his mind amused with pretty girls. She was convinced that he was coming back to her. For that month she no longer repelled his timid advances that never went very far. For he certainly made timid advances. He patted her on the shoulder; he whispered into her ear little jokes about the odd figures that they saw up at the Casino. It was not much to make a little joke—but the whispering of it was a precious intimacy....

And then—smash—it all went. It went to pieces at the moment when Florence laid her hand upon Edward's wrist, as it lay on the glass sheltering the manuscript of the Protest, up in the high tower with the shutters where the sunlight here and there streamed in. Or, rather, it went when she noticed the look in Edward's eyes as he gazed back into Florence's. She knew that look.

She had known—since the first moment of their meeting, since the moment of our all sitting down to dinner together—that Florence was making eyes at Edward. But she had seen so many women make eyes at Edward—hundreds and hundreds of women, in railway trains, in hotels, aboard liners, at street corners. And she had arrived at thinking that Edward took little stock in women that made eyes at him. She had formed what was, at that time, a fairly correct estimate of the methods of, the reasons for, Edward's loves. She was certain that hitherto they had consisted of the short passion for the Dolciquita, the real sort of love for Mrs Basil, and what she deemed the pretty courtship of Maisie Maidan. Besides she despised Florence so haughtily that she could not imagine Edward's being attracted by her. And she and Maisie were a sort of bulwark round him. She wanted, besides, to keep her eyes on Florence—for Florence knew that she had boxed Maisie's ears. And Leonora desperately desired that her union with Edward should appear to be flawless. But all that went....

With the answering gaze of Edward into Florence's blue and uplifted eyes, she knew that it had all gone. She knew that that gaze meant that those two had had long conversations of an intimate kind—about their likes and dislikes, about their natures, about their views of marriage. She knew what it meant that she, when we all four walked out together, had always been with me ten yards ahead of Florence and Edward. She did not imagine that it had gone further than talks about their likes and dislikes, about their natures or about marriage as an institution. But, having watched Edward all her life, she knew that that laying on of hands, that answering of gaze with gaze, meant that the thing was unavoidable. Edward was such a serious person.

She knew that any attempt on her part to separate those two would be to rivet on Edward an irrevocable passion; that, as I have before told you, it was a trick of Edward's nature to believe that the seducing of a woman gave her an irrevocable hold over him for life. And that touching of hands, she knew, would give that woman an irrevocable claim—to be seduced. And she so despised Florence that she would have preferred it to be a parlour-maid. There are very decent parlour-maids.

And, suddenly, there came into her mind the conviction that Maisie Maidan had a real passion for Edward; that this would break her heart—and that she, Leonora, would be responsible for that. She went, for the moment, mad. She clutched me by the wrist; she dragged me down those stairs and across that whispering Rittersaal with the high painted pillars, the high painted chimney-piece. I guess she did not go mad enough.

She ought to have said:

"Your wife is a harlot who is going to be my husband's mistress.. ." That might have done the trick. But, even in her madness, she was afraid to go as far as that. She was afraid that, if she did, Edward and Florence would make a bolt of it, and that, if they did that, she would lose forever all chance of getting him back in the end. She acted very badly to me.

Well, she was a tortured soul who put her Church before the interests of a Philadelphia Quaker. That is all right—I daresay the Church of Rome is the more important of the two.

A week after Maisie Maidan's death she was aware that Florence had become Edward's mistress. She waited outside Florence's door and met Edward as he came away. She said nothing and he only grunted. But I guess he had a bad time.

Yes, the mental deterioration that Florence worked in Leonora was extraordinary; it smashed up her whole life and all her chances. It made her, in the first place, hopeless—for she could not see how, after that, Edward could return to her—after a vulgar intrigue with a vulgar woman. His affair with Mrs Basil, which was now all that she had to bring, in her heart, against him, she could not find it in her to call an intrigue. It was a love affair—a pure enough thing in its way. But this seemed to her to be a horror—a wantonness, all the more detestable to her, because she so detested Florence. And Florence talked....

That was what was terrible, because Florence forced

Leonora herself to abandon her high reserve—Florence and the situation. It appears that Florence was in two minds whether to confess to me or to Leonora. Confess she had to. And she pitched at last on Leonora, because if it had been me she would have had to confess a great deal more. Or, at least, I might have guessed a great deal more, about her "heart", and about Jimmy. So she went to Leonora one day and began hinting and hinting. And she enraged Leonora to such an extent that at last Leonora said:

"You want to tell me that you are Edward's mistress. You can be. I have no use for him." That was really a calamity for Leonora, because, once started, there was no stopping the talking. She tried to stop—but it was not to be done. She found it necessary to send Edward messages through Florence; for she would not speak to him. She had to give him, for instance, to understand that if I ever came to know of his intrigue she would ruin him beyond repair. And it complicated matters a good deal that Edward, at about this time, was really a little in love with her. He thought that he had treated her so badly; that she was so fine. She was so mournful that he longed to comfort her, and he thought himself such a blackguard that there was nothing he would not have done to make amends. And Florence communicated these items of information to Leonora.

I don't in the least blame Leonora for her coarseness to Florence; it must have done Florence a world of good. But I do blame her for giving way to what was in the end a desire for communicativeness. You see that business cut her off from her Church. She did not want to confess what she was doing because she was afraid that her spiritual advisers would blame her for deceiving me. I rather imagine that she would have preferred damnation to breaking my heart. That is what it works out at. She need not have troubled.

But, having no priests to talk to, she had to talk to someone, and as Florence insisted on talking to her, she talked back, in short, explosive sentences, like one of the damned. Precisely like one of the damned. Well, if a pretty period in hell on this earth can spare her any period of pain in Eternity—where there are not any periods—I guess Leonora will escape hell fire.

Her conversations with Florence would be like this.

Florence would happen in on her, whilst she was doing her wonderful hair, with a proposition from Edward, who seems about that time to have conceived the naïve idea that he might become a polygamist. I daresay it was Florence who put it into his head. Anyhow, I am not responsible for the oddities of the human psychology. But it certainly appears that at about that date Edward cared more for Leonora than he had ever done before—or, at any rate, for a long time. And, if Leonora had been a person to play cards and if she had played her cards well, and if she had had no sense of shame and so on, she might then have shared Edward with Florence until the time came for jerking that poor cuckoo out of the nest. Well, Florence would come to Leonora with some such proposition. I do not mean to say that she put it baldly, like that. She stood out that she was not Edward's mistress until Leonora said that she had seen Edward coming out of her room at an advanced hour of the night. That checked Florence a bit; but she fell back upon her "heart" and stuck out that she had merely been conversing with Edward in order to bring him to a better frame of mind. Florence had, of course, to stick to that story; for even Florence would not have had the face to implore Leonora to grant her favours to Edward if she had admitted that she was Edward's mistress. That could not be done. At the same time Florence had such a pressing desire to talk about something. There would have been nothing else to talk about but a rapprochement between that estranged pair. So Florence would go on babbling and Leonora would go on brushing her hair. And then Leonora would say suddenly something like:

"I should think myself defiled if Edward touched me now that he has touched you."

That would discourage Florence a bit; but after a week or so, on another morning she would have another try.

And even in other things Leonora deteriorated. She had promised Edward to leave the spending of his own income in his own hands. And she had fully meant to do that. I daresay she would have done it too; though, no doubt, she would have spied upon his banking account in secret. She was not a Roman Catholic for nothing. But she took so serious a view of Edward's unfaithfulness to the memory of poor little Maisie that she could not trust him any more at all.

So when she got back to Branshaw she started, after less than a month, to worry him about the minutest items of his expenditure. She allowed him to draw his own cheques, but there was hardly a cheque that she did not scrutinize—except for a private account of about five hundred a year which, tacitly, she allowed him to keep for expenditure on his mistress or mistresses. He had to have his jaunts to Paris; he had to send expensive cables in cipher to Florence about twice a week. But she worried him about his expenditure on wines, on fruit trees, on harness, on gates, on the account at his blacksmith's for work done to a new patent Army stirrup that he was trying to invent. She could not see why he should bother to invent a new Army stirrup, and she was really enraged when, after the invention was mature, he made a present to the War Office of the designs and the patent rights. It was a remarkably good stirrup.

I have told you, I think, that Edward spent a great deal of time, and about two hundred pounds for law fees on getting a poor girl, the daughter of one of his gardeners, acquitted of a charge of murdering her baby. That was positively the last act of Edward's life. It came at a time when Nancy Rufford was on her way to India; when the most horrible gloom was over the household; when Edward himself was in an agony and behaving as prettily as he knew how. Yet even then Leonora made him a terrible scene about this expenditure of time and trouble. She sort of had the vague idea that what had passed with the girl and the rest of it ought to have taught Edward a lesson—the lesson of economy. She threatened to take his banking account away from him again. I guess that made him cut his throat. He might have stuck it out otherwise—but the thought that he had lost Nancy and that, in addition, there was nothing left for him but a dreary, dreary succession of days in which he could be of no public service... Well, it finished him.

It was during those years that Leonora tried to get up a love affair of her own with a fellow called Bayham—a decent sort of fellow. A really nice man. But the affair was no sort of success. I have told you about it already... .

II

WELL, that about brings me up to the date of my receiving, in Waterbury, the laconic cable from Edward to the effect that he wanted me to go to Branshaw and have a chat. I was pretty busy at the time and I was half minded to send him a reply cable to the effect that I would start in a fortnight. But I was having a long interview with old Mr Hurlbird's attorneys and immediately afterwards I had to have a long interview with the Misses Hurlbird, so I delayed cabling.

I had expected to find the Misses Hurlbird excessively old—in the nineties or thereabouts. The time had passed so slowly that I had the impression that it must have been thirty years since I had been in the United States. It was only twelve years. Actually Miss Hurlbird was just sixty-one and Miss Florence Hurlbird fifty-nine, and they were both, mentally and physically, as vigorous as could be desired. They were, indeed, more vigorous, mentally, than suited my purpose, which was to get away from the United States as quickly as I could. The Hurlbirds were an exceedingly united family—exceedingly united except on one set of points. Each of the three of them had a separate doctor, whom they trusted implicitly—and each had a separate attorney. And each of them distrusted the other's doctor and the other's attorney. And, naturally, the doctors and the attorneys warned one all the time—against each other. You cannot imagine how complicated it all became for me. Of course I had an attorney of my own—recommended to me by young Carter, my Philadelphia nephew.

I do not mean to say that there was any unpleasantness of a grasping kind. The problem was quite another one—a moral dilemma. You see, old Mr Hurlbird had left all his property to Florence with the mere request that she would have erected to him in the city of Waterbury, Ill., a memorial that should take the form of some sort of institution for the relief of sufferers from the heart. Florence's money had all come to me—and with it old Mr Hurlbird's. He had died just five days before Florence.

Well, I was quite ready to spend a round million dollars on the relief of sufferers from the heart. The old gentleman had left about a million and a half; Florence had been worth about eight hundred thousand—and as I figured it out, I should cut up at about a million myself. Anyhow, there was ample money. But I naturally wanted to consult the wishes of his surviving relatives and then the trouble really began. You see, it had been discovered that Mr Hurlbird had had nothing whatever the matter with his heart. His lungs had been a little affected all through his life and he had died of bronchitis. It struck Miss Florence Hurlbird that, since her brother had died of lungs and not of heart, his money ought to go to lung patients. That, she considered, was what her brother would have wished. On the other hand, by a kink, that I could not at the time understand, Miss Hurlbird insisted that I ought to keep the money all to myself. She said that she did not wish for any monuments to the Hurlbird family. At the time I thought that that was because of a New England dislike for necrological ostentation. But I can figure out now, when I remember certain insistent and continued questions that she put to me, about Edward Ashburnham, that there was another idea in her mind. And Leonora has told me that, on Florence's dressing-table, beside her dead body, there had lain a letter to Miss Hurlbird—a letter which Leonora posted without telling me. I don't know how Florence had time to write to her aunt; but I can quite understand that she would not like to go out of the world without making some comments. So I guess Florence had told Miss Hurlbird a good bit about Edward Ashburnham in a few scrawled words—and that that was why the old lady did not wish the name of Hurlbird perpetuated. Perhaps also she thought that I had earned the Hurlbird money. It meant a pretty tidy lot of discussing, what with the doctors warning each other about the bad effects of discussions on the health of the old ladies, and warning me covertly against each other, and saying that old Mr Hurlbird might have died of heart, after all, in spite of the diagnosis of his doctor. And the solicitors all had separate methods of arranging about how the money should be invested and entrusted and bound. Personally, I wanted to invest the money so that the interest could be used for the relief of sufferers from the heart. If old Mr Hurlbird had not died of any defects in that organ he had considered that it was defective. Moreover, Florence had certainly died of her heart, as I saw it. And when Miss Florence Hurlbird stood out that the money ought to go to chest sufferers I was brought to thinking that there ought to be a chest institution too, and I advanced the sum that I was ready to provide to a million and a half of dollars. That would have given seven hundred and fifty thousand to each class of invalid. I did not want money at all badly. All I wanted it for was to be able to give Nancy Rufford a good time. I did not know much about housekeeping expenses in England where, I presumed, she would wish to live. I knew that her needs at that time were limited to good chocolates, and a good horse or two, and simple, pretty frocks. Probably she would want more than that later on. But even if I gave a million and a half dollars to these institutions I should still have the equivalent of about twenty thousand a year English, and I considered that Nancy could have a pretty good time on that or less. Anyhow, we had a stiff set of arguments up at the Hurlbird mansion which stands on a bluff over the town. It may strike you, silent listener, as being funny if you happen to be European. But moral problems of that description and the giving of millions to institutions are immensely serious matters in my country. Indeed, they are the staple topics for consideration amongst the wealthy classes. We haven't got peerage and social climbing to occupy us much, and decent people do not take interest in politics or elderly people in sport. So that there were real tears shed by both Miss Hurlbird and Miss Florence before I left that city. I left it quite abruptly. Four hours after Edward's telegram came another from Leonora, saying: "Yes, do come. You could be so helpful." I simply told my attorney that there was the million and a half; that he could invest it as he liked, and that the purposes must be decided by the Misses Hurlbird. I was, anyhow, pretty well worn out by all the discussions. And, as I have never heard yet from the Misses Hurlbird, I rather think that Miss Hurlbird, either by revelations or by moral force, has persuaded Miss Florence that no memorial to their names shall be erected in the city of Waterbury, Conn. Miss Hurlbird wept dreadfully when she heard that I was going to stay with the Ashburnhams, but she did not make any comments. I was aware, at that date, that her niece had been seduced by that fellow Jimmy before I had married her—but I contrived to produce on her the impression that I thought Florence had been a model wife. Why, at that date I still believed that Florence had been perfectly virtuous after her marriage to me. I had not figured it out that she could have played it so low down as to continue her intrigue with that fellow under my roof.

Well, I was a fool. But I did not think much about Florence at that date. My mind was occupied with what was happening at Branshaw. I had got it into my head that the telegrams had something to do with Nancy. It struck me that she might have shown signs of forming an attachment for some undesirable fellow and that Leonora wanted me to come back and marry her out of harm's way. That was what was pretty firmly in my mind. And it remained in my mind for nearly ten days after my arrival at that beautiful old place. Neither Edward nor Leonora made any motion to talk to me about anything other than the weather and the crops. Yet, although there were several young fellows about, I could not see that any one in particular was distinguished by the girl's preference. She certainly appeared illish and nervous, except when she woke up to talk gay nonsense to me. Oh, the pretty thing that she was....

I imagined that what must have happened was that the undesirable young man had been forbidden the place and that Nancy was fretting a little. What had happened was just Hell. Leonora had spoken to Nancy; Nancy had spoken to Edward; Edward had spoken to Leonora—and they had talked and talked. And talked. You have to imagine horrible pictures of gloom and half lights, and emotions running through silent nights—through whole nights. You have to imagine my beautiful Nancy appearing suddenly to Edward, rising up at the foot of his bed, with her long hair falling, like a split cone of shadow, in the glimmer of a night-light that burned beside him. You have to imagine her, a silent, a no doubt agonized figure, like a spectre, suddenly offering herself to him—to save his reason! And you have to imagine his frantic refusal—and talk. And talk! My God!

And yet, to me, living in the house, enveloped with the charm of the quiet and ordered living, with the silent, skilled servants whose mere laying out of my dress clothes was like a caress—to me who was hourly with them they appeared like tender, ordered and devoted people, smiling, absenting themselves at the proper intervals; driving me to meets—just good people! How the devil—how the devil do they do it?

At dinner one evening Leonora said—she had just opened a telegram:

"Nancy will be going to India, tomorrow, to be with her father."

No one spoke. Nancy looked at her plate; Edward went on eating his pheasant. I felt very bad; I imagined that it would be up to me to propose to Nancy that evening. It appeared to me to be queer that they had not given me any warning of Nancy's departure—But I thought that that was only English manners—some sort of delicacy that I had not got the hang of. You must remember that at that moment I trusted in Edward and Leonora and in Nancy Rufford, and in the tranquility of ancient haunts of peace, as I had trusted in my mother's love. And that evening Edward spoke to me.

What in the interval had happened had been this:

Upon her return from Nauheim Leonora had completely broken down—because she knew she could trust Edward. That seems odd but, if you know anything about breakdowns, you will know that by the ingenious torments that fate prepares for us, these things come as soon as, a strain having relaxed, there is nothing more to be done. It is after a husband's long illness and death that a widow goes to pieces; it is at the end of a long rowing contest that a crew collapses and lies forward upon its oars. And that was what happened to Leonora.

From certain tones in Edward's voice; from the long, steady stare that he had given her from his bloodshot eyes on rising from the dinner table in the Nauheim hotel, she knew that, in the affair of the poor girl, this was a case in which Edward's moral scruples, or his social code, or his idea that it would be playing it too low down, rendered Nancy perfectly safe. The girl, she felt sure, was in no danger at all from Edward. And in that she was perfectly right. The smash was to come from herself.

She relaxed; she broke; she drifted, at first quickly, then with an increasing momentum, down the stream of destiny. You may put it that, having been cut off from the restraints of her religion, for the first time in her life, she acted along the lines of her instinctive desires. I do not know whether to think that, in that she was no longer herself; or that, having let loose the bonds of her standards, her conventions and her traditions, she was being, for the first time, her own natural self. She was torn between her intense, maternal love for the girl and an intense jealousy of the woman who realizes that the man she loves has met what appears to be the final passion of his life. She was divided between an intense disgust for Edward's weakness in conceiving this passion, an intense pity for the miseries that he was enduring, and a feeling equally intense, but one that she hid from herself—a feeling of respect for Edward's determination to keep himself, in this particular affair, unspotted.

And the human heart is a very mysterious thing. It is impossible to say that Leonora, in acting as she then did, was not filled with a sort of hatred of Edward's final virtue. She wanted, I think, to despise him. He was, she realized gone from her for good. Then let him suffer, let him agonize; let him, if possible, break and go to that Hell that is the abode of broken resolves. She might have taken a different line. It would have been so easy to send the girl away to stay with some friends; to have taken her away herself upon some pretext or other. That would not have cured things but it would have been the decent line,... But, at that date, poor Leonora was incapable of taking any line whatever.

She pitied Edward frightfully at one time—and then she acted along the lines of pity; she loathed him at another and then she acted as her loathing dictated. She gasped, as a person dying of tuberculosis gasps for air. She craved madly for communication with some other human soul. And the human soul that she selected was that of the girl.

Perhaps Nancy was the only person that she could have talked to. With her necessity for reticences, with her coldness of manner, Leonora had singularly few intimates. She had none at all, with the exception of the Mrs Colonel Whelen, who had advised her about the affair with La Dolciquita, and the one or two religious, who had guided her through life. The Colonel's wife was at that time in Madeira; the religious she now avoided. Her visitors' book had seven hundred names in it; there was not a soul that she could speak to. She was Mrs Ashburnham of Branshaw Teleragh.

She was the great Mrs Ashburnham of Branshaw and she lay all day upon her bed in her marvellous, light, airy bedroom with the chintzes and the Chippendale and the portraits of deceased Ashburnhams by Zoffany and Zucchero. When there was a meet she would struggle up—supposing it were within driving distance—and let Edward drive her and the girl to the cross-roads or the country house. She would drive herself back alone; Edward would ride off with the girl. Ride Leonora could not, that season—her head was too bad. Each pace of her mare was an anguish.

But she drove with efficiency and precision; she smiled at the Gimmers and Ffoulkes and the Hedley Seatons. She threw with exactitude pennies to the boys who opened gates for her; she sat upright on the seat of the high dog-cart; she waved her hands to Edward and Nancy as they rode off with the hounds, and every one could hear her clear, high voice, in the chilly weather, saying: "Have a good time!"

Poor forlorn woman!...

There was, however, one spark of consolation. It came from the fact that Rodney Bayham, of Bayham, followed her always with his eyes. It had been three years since she had tried her abortive love-affair with him. Yet still, on the winter mornings he would ride up to her shafts and just say: "Good day," and look at her with eyes that were not imploring, but seemed to say: "You see, I am still, as the Germans say, A. D.—at disposition."

It was a great consolation, not because she proposed ever to take him up again, but because it showed her that there was in the world one faithful soul in riding-breeches. And it showed her that she was not losing her looks.

And, indeed, she was not losing her looks. She was forty, but she was as clean run as on the day she had left the convent—as clear in outline, as clear coloured in the hair, as dark blue in the eyes. She thought that her looking-glass told her this; but there are always the doubts.... Rodney Bayham's eyes took them away.

It is very singular that Leonora should not have aged at all. I suppose that there are some types of beauty and even of youth made for the embellishments that come with enduring sorrow. That is too elaborately put. I mean that Leonora, if everything had prospered, might have become too hard and, maybe, overbearing. As it was she was tuned down to appearing efficient—and yet sympathetic. That is the rarest of all blends. And yet I swear that Leonora, in her restrained way, gave the impression of being intensely sympathetic. When she listened to you she appeared also to be listening to some sound that was going on in the distance. But still, she listened to you and took in what you said, which, since the record of humanity is a record of sorrows, was, as a rule, something sad.

I think that she must have taken Nancy through many terrors of the night and many bad places of the day. And that would account for the girl's passionate love for the elder woman. For Nancy's love for Leonora was an admiration that is awakened in Catholics by their feeling for the Virgin Mary and for various of the saints. It is too little to say that the girl would have laid her life at Leonora's feet. Well, she laid there the offer of her virtue—and her reason. Those were sufficient instalments of her life. It would today be much better for Nancy Rufford if she were dead.

Perhaps all these reflections are a nuisance; but they crowd on me. I will try to tell the story.

You see—when she came back from Nauheim Leonora began to have her headaches—headaches lasting through whole days, during which she could speak no word and could bear to hear no sound. And, day after day, Nancy would sit with her, silent and motionless for hours, steeping handkerchiefs in vinegar and water, and thinking her own thoughts. It must have been very bad for her—and her meals alone with Edward must have been bad for her too—and beastly bad for Edward. Edward, of course, wavered in his demeanour, What else could he do? At times he would sit silent and dejected over his untouched food. He would utter nothing but monosyllables when Nancy spoke to him. Then he was simply afraid of the girl falling in love with him. At other times he would take a little wine; pull himself together; attempt to chaff Nancy about a stake and binder hedge that her mare had checked at, or talk about the habits of the Chitralis. That was when he was thinking that it was rough on the poor girl that he should have become a dull companion. He realized that his talking to her in the park at Nauheim had done her no harm.

But all that was doing a great deal of harm to Nancy. It gradually opened her eyes to the fact that Edward was a man with his ups and downs and not an invariably gay uncle like a nice dog, a trustworthy horse or a girl friend. She would find him in attitudes of frightful dejection, sunk into his armchair in the study that was half a gun-room. She would notice through the open door that his face was the face of an old, dead man, when he had no one to talk to. Gradually it forced itself upon her attention that there were profound differences between the pair that she regarded a her uncle and her aunt. It was a conviction that came very slowly.

It began with Edward's giving an oldish horse to a young fellow called Selmes. Selmes' father had been ruined by fraudulent solicitor and the Selmes family had had to sell their hunters. It was a case that had excited a good deal of sympathy in that part of the county. And Edward, meeting the young man one day, unmounted, and seeing him to be very unhappy, had offered to give him an old Irish cob upon which he was riding. It was a silly sort of thing to do really. The horse was worth from thirty to forty pounds and Edward might have known that the gift would upset his wife. But Edward just had to comfort that unhappy young man whose father he had known all his life. And what made it all the worse was that young Selmes could not afford to keep the horse even. Edward recollected this, immediately after he had made the offer, and said quickly:

"Of course I mean that you should stable the horse at Branshaw until you have time to turn round or want to sell him and get a better."

Nancy went straight home and told all this to Leonora who was lying down. She regarded it as a splendid instance of Edward's quick consideration for the feelings and the circumstances of the distressed. She thought it would cheer Leonora up—because it ought to cheer any woman up to know that she had such a splendid husband. That was the last girlish thought she ever had. For Leonora, whose headache had left her collected but miserably weak, turned upon her bed and uttered words that were amazing to the girl:

"I wish to God," she said, "that he was your husband, and not mine. We shall be ruined. We shall be ruined. Am I never to have a chance?" And suddenly Leonora burst into a passion of tears. She pushed herself up from the pillows with one elbow and sat there—crying, crying, crying, with her face hidden in her hands and the tears falling through her fingers.

The girl flushed, stammered and whimpered as if she had been personally insulted.

"But if Uncle Edward..." she began.

"That man," said Leonora, with an extraordinary bitterness, "would give the shirt off his back and off mine—and off yours to any..." She could not finish the sentence.

At that moment she had been feeling an extraordinary hatred and contempt for her husband. All the morning and all the afternoon she had been lying there thinking that Edward and the girl were together—in the field and hacking it home at dusk. She had been digging her sharp nails into her palms.

The house had been very silent in the drooping winter weather. And then, after an eternity of torture, there had invaded it the sound of opening doors, of the girl's gay voice saying:

"Well, it was only under the mistletoe."... And there was Edward's gruff undertone. Then Nancy had come in, with feet that had hastened up the stairs and that tiptoed as they approached the open door of Leonora's room. Branshaw had a great big hall with oak floors and tiger skins. Round this hall there ran a gallery upon which Leonora's doorway gave. And even when she had the worst of her headaches she liked to have her door open—I suppose so that she might hear the approaching footsteps of ruin and disaster. At any rate she hated to be in a room with a shut door.

At that moment Leonora hated Edward with a hatred that was like hell, and she would have liked to bring her riding-whip down across the girl's face. What right had Nancy to be young and slender and dark, and gay at times, at times mournful? What right had she to be exactly the woman to make Leonora's husband happy? For Leonora knew that Nancy would have made Edward happy.

Yes, Leonora wished to bring her riding-whip down on Nancy's young face. She imagined the pleasure she would feel when the lash fell across those queer features; the plea sure she would feel at drawing the handle at the same moment toward her, so as to cut deep into the flesh and to leave a lasting wheal.

Well, she left a lasting wheal, and her words cut deeply into the girl's mind....

They neither of them spoke about that again. A fortnight went by—a fortnight of deep rains, of heavy fields, of bad scent. Leonora's headaches seemed to have gone for good. She hunted once or twice, letting herself be piloted by Bayham, whilst Edward looked after the girl. Then, one evening, when those three were dining alone, Edward said, in the queer, deliberate, heavy tones that came out of him in those days (he was looking at the table):

"I have been thinking that Nancy ought to do more for her father. He is getting an old man. I have written to Colonel Rufford, suggesting that she should go to him."

Leonora called out:

"How dare you? How dare you?"

The girl put her hand over her heart and cried out: "Oh, my sweet Saviour, help me!" That was the queer way she thought within her mind, and the words forced themselves to her lips. Edward said nothing.

And that night, by a merciless trick of the devil that pays attention to this sweltering hell of ours, Nancy Rufford had a letter from her mother. It came whilst Leonora was talking to Edward, or Leonora would have intercepted it as she had intercepted others. It was an amazing and a horrible letter.. ..

I don't know what it contained. I just average out from its effects on Nancy that her mother, having eloped with some worthless sort of fellow, had done what is called "sinking lower and lower". Whether she was actually on the streets I do not know, but I rather think that she eked out a small allowance that she had from her husband by that means of livelihood. And I think that she stated as much in her letter to Nancy and upbraided the girl with living in luxury whilst her mother starved. And it must have been horrible in tone, for Mrs Rufford was a cruel sort of woman at the best of times. It must have seemed to that poor girl, opening her letter, for distraction from another grief, up in her bedroom, like the laughter of a devil.

I just cannot bear to think of my poor dear girl at that moment....

And, at the same time, Leonora was lashing, like a cold fiend, into the unfortunate Edward. Or, perhaps, he was not so unfortunate; because he had done what he knew to be the right thing, he may be deemed happy. I leave it to you. At any rate, he was sitting in his deep chair, and Leonora came into his room—for the first time in nine years. She said:

"This is the most atrocious thing you have done in your atrocious life." He never moved and he never looked at her. God knows what was in Leonora's mind exactly.

I like to think that, uppermost in it was concern and horror at the thought of the poor girl's going back to a father whose voice made her shriek in the night. And, indeed, that motive was very strong with Leonora. But I think there was also present the thought that she wanted to go on torturing Edward with the girl's presence. She was, at that time, capable of that.

Edward was sunk in his chair; there were in the room two candles, hidden by green glass shades. The green shades were reflected in the glasses of the book-cases that contained not books but guns with gleaming brown barrels and fishing-rods in green baize over-covers. There was dimly to be seen, above a mantelpiece encumbered with spurs, hooves and bronze models of horses, a dark-brown picture of a white horse.

"If you think," Leonora said, "that I do not know that you are in love with the girl..." She began spiritedly, but she could not find any ending for the sentence. Edward did not stir; he never spoke. And then Leonora said:

"If you want me to divorce you, I will. You can marry her then. She's in love with you."

He groaned at that, a little, Leonora said. Then she went away.

Heaven knows what happened in Leonora after that. She certainly does not herself know. She probably said a good deal more to Edward than I have been able to report; but that is all that she has told me and I am not going to make up speeches. To follow her psychological development of that moment I think we must allow that she upbraided him for a great deal of their past life, whilst Edward sat absolutely silent. And, indeed, in speaking of it afterwards, she has said several times: "I said a great deal more to him than I wanted to, just because he was so silent." She talked, in fact, in the endeavour to sting him into speech.

She must have said so much that, with the expression of her grievance, her mood changed. She went back to her own room in the gallery, and sat there for a long time thinking. And she thought herself into a mood of absolute unselfishness, of absolute self-contempt, too. She said to herself that she was no good; that she had failed in all her efforts—in her efforts to get Edward back as in her efforts to make him curb his expenditure. She imagined herself to be exhausted; she imagined herself to be done. Then a great fear came over her.

She thought that Edward, after what she had said to him, must have committed suicide. She went out on to the gallery and listened; there was no sound in all the house except the regular beat of the great clock in the hall. But, even in her debased condition, she was not the person to hang about. She acted. She went straight to Edward's room, opened the door, and looked in.

He was oiling the breech action of a gun. It was an unusual thing for him to do, at that time of night, in his evening clothes. It never occurred to her, nevertheless, that he was going to shoot himself with that implement. She knew that he was doing it just for occupation—to keep himself from thinking. He looked up when she opened the door, his face illuminated by the light cast upwards from the round orifices in the green candle shades.

She said:

"I didn't imagine that I should find Nancy here." She thought that she owed that to him. He answered then:

"I don't imagine that you did imagine it." Those were the only words he spoke that night. She went, like a lame duck, back through the long corridors; she stumbled over the familiar tiger skins in the dark hall. She could hardly drag one limb after the other. In the gallery she perceived that Nancy's door was half open and that there was a light in the girl's room. A sudden madness possessed her, a desire for action, a thirst for self-explanation.

Their rooms all gave on to the gallery; Leonora's to the east, the girl's next, then Edward's. The sight of those three open doors, side by side, gaping to receive whom the chances of the black night might bring, made Leonora shudder all over her body. She went into Nancy's room.

The girl was sitting perfectly still in an armchair, very upright, as she had been taught to sit at the convent. She appeared to be as calm as a church; her hair fell, black and like a pall, down over both her shoulders. The fire beside her was burning brightly; she must have just put coals on. She was in a white silk kimono that covered her to the feet. The clothes that she had taken off were exactly folded upon the proper seats. Her long hands were one upon each arm of the chair that had a pink and white chintz back.

Leonora told me these things. She seemed to think it extraordinary that the girl could have done such orderly things as fold up the clothes she had taken off upon such a night—when Edward had announced that he was going to send her to her father, and when, from her mother, she had received that letter. The letter, in its envelope, was in her right hand.

Leonora did not at first perceive it. She said:

"What are you doing so late?"

The girl answered: "Just thinking."

They seemed to think in whispers and to speak below their breaths. Then Leonora's eyes fell on the envelope, and she recognized Mrs Rufford's handwriting.

It was one of those moments when thinking was impossible, Leonora said. It was as if stones were being thrown at her from every direction and she could only run. She heard herself exclaim: "Edward's dying—because of you. He's dying. He's worth more than either of us...."

The girl looked past her at the panels of the half-closed door.

"My poor father," she said, "my poor father." "You must stay here," Leonora answered fiercely. "You must stay here. I tell you you must stay here."

"I am going to Glasgow," Nancy answered. "I shall go to Glasgow tomorrow morning. My mother is in Glasgow."

It appears that it was in Glasgow that Mrs Rufford pursued her disorderly life. She had selected that city, not because it was more profitable but because it was the natal home of her husband to whom she desired to cause as much pain as possible.

"You must stay here," Leonora began, "to save Edward. He's dying for love of you."

The girl turned her calm eyes upon Leonora. "I know it," she said. "And I am dying for love of him."

Leonora uttered an "Ah," that, in spite of herself, was an "Ah" of horror and of grief.

"That is why," the girl continued, "I am going to Glasgow—to take my mother away from there." She added, "To the ends of the earth," for, if the last months had made her nature that of a woman, her phrases were still romantically those of a schoolgirl. It was as if she had grown up so quickly that there had not been time to put her hair up. But she added: "We're no good—my mother and I."

Leonora said, with her fierce calmness:

"No. No. You're not no good. It's I that am no good. You can't let that man go on to ruin for want of you. You must belong to him."

The girl, she said, smiled at her with a queer, far-away smile—as if she were a thousand years old, as if Leonora were a tiny child.

"I knew you would come to that," she said, very slowly. "But we are not worth it—Edward and I."

III

NANCY had, in fact, been thinking ever since Leonora had made that comment over the giving of the horse to young Selmes. She had been thinking and thinking, because she had had to sit for many days silent beside her aunt's bed. (She had always thought of Leonora as her aunt.) And she had had to sit thinking during many silent meals with Edward. And then, at times, with his bloodshot eyes and creased, heavy mouth, he would smile at her. And gradually the knowledge had come to her that Edward did not love Leonora and that Leonora hated Edward. Several things contributed to form and to harden this conviction. She was allowed to read the papers in those days—or, rather, since Leonora was always on her bed and Edward breakfasted alone and went out early, over the estate, she was left alone with the papers. One day, in the papers, she saw the portrait of a woman she knew very well. Beneath it she read the words: "The Hon. Mrs Brand, plaintiff in the remarkable divorce case reported on p. 8." Nancy hardly knew what a divorce case was. She had been so remarkably well brought up, and Roman Catholics do not practise divorce. I don't know how Leonora had done it exactly. I suppose she had always impressed it on Nancy's mind that nice women did not read these things, and that would have been enough to make Nancy skip those pages.

She read, at any rate, the account of the Brand divorce case—principally because she wanted to tell Leonora about it. She imagined that Leonora, when her headache left her, would like to know what was happening to Mrs Brand, who lived at Christchurch, and whom they both liked very well. The case occupied three days, and the report that Nancy first came upon was that of the third day. Edward, however, kept the papers of the week, after his methodical fashion, in a rack in his gun-room, and when she had finished her breakfast Nancy went to that quiet apartment and had what she would have called a good read. It seemed to her to be a queer affair. She could not understand why one counsel should be so anxious to know all about the movements of Mr Brand upon a certain day; she could not understand why a chart of the bedroom accommodation at Christchurch Old Hall should be produced in court. She did not even see why they should want to know that, upon a certain occasion, the drawing-room door was locked. It made her laugh; it appeared to be all so senseless that grown people should occupy themselves with such matters. It struck her, nevertheless, as odd that one of the counsel should cross-question Mr Brand so insistently and so impertinently as to his feelings for Miss Lupton. Nancy knew Miss Lupton of Ringwood very well—a jolly girl, who rode a horse with two white fetlocks. Mr Brand persisted that he did not love Miss Lupton.... Well, of course he did not love Miss Lupton; he was a married man. You might as well think of Uncle Edward loving... loving anybody but Leonora. When people were married there was an end of loving. There were, no doubt, people who misbehaved—but they were poor people—or people not like those she knew. So these matters presented themselves to Nancy's mind. But later on in the case she found that Mr Brand had to confess to a "guilty intimacy" with some one or other. Nancy imagined that he must have been telling some one his wife's secrets; she could not understand why that was a serious offence. Of course it was not very gentlemanly—it lessened her opinion of Mrs Brand. But since she found that Mrs Brand had condoned that offence, she imagined that they could not have been very serious secrets that Mr Brand had told. And then, suddenly, it was forced on her conviction that Mr Brand—the mild Mr Brand that she had seen a month or two before their departure to Nauheim, playing "Blind Man's Buff" with his children and kissing his wife when he caught her—Mr Brand and Mrs Brand had been on the worst possible terms. That was incredible.

Yet there it was—in black and white. Mr Brand drank; Mr Brand had struck Mrs Brand to the ground when he was drunk. Mr Brand was adjudged, in two or three abrupt words, at the end of columns and columns of paper, to have been guilty of cruelty to his wife and to have committed adultery with Miss Lupton. The last words conveyed nothing to Nancy—nothing real, that is to say. She knew that one was commanded not to commit adultery—but why, she thought, should one? It was probably something like catching salmon out of season—a thing one did not do. She gathered it had something to do with kissing, or holding some one in your arms.. ..

And yet the whole effect of that reading upon Nancy was mysterious, terrifying and evil. She felt a sickness—a sickness that grew as she read. Her heart beat painfully; she began to cry. She asked God how He could permit such things to be. And she was more certain that Edward did not love Leonora and that Leonora hated Edward. Perhaps, then, Edward loved some one else. It was unthinkable.

If he could love some one else than Leonora, her fierce unknown heart suddenly spoke in her side, why could it not be herself? And he did not love her.... This had occurred about a month before she got the letter from her mother. She let the matter rest until the sick feeling went off; it did that in a day or two. Then, finding that Leonora's headaches had gone, she suddenly told Leonora that Mrs Brand had divorced her husband. She asked what, exactly, it all meant.

Leonora was lying on the sofa in the hall; she was feeling so weak that she could hardly find the words. She answered just:

"It means that Mr Brand will be able to marry again."

Nancy said:

"But... but..." and then: "He will be able to marry Miss Lupton." Leonora just moved a hand in assent. Her eyes were shut.

"Then..." Nancy began. Her blue eyes were full of horror: her brows were tight above them; the lines of pain about her mouth were very distinct. In her eyes the whole of that familiar, great hall had a changed aspect. The andirons with the brass flowers at the ends appeared unreal; the burning logs were just logs that were burning and not the comfortable symbols of an indestructible mode of life. The flame fluttered before the high fireback; the St Bernard sighed in his sleep. Outside the winter rain fell and fell. And suddenly she thought that Edward might marry some one else; and she nearly screamed.

Leonora opened her eyes, lying sideways, with her face

upon the black and gold pillow of the sofa that was drawn half across the great fireplace.

"I thought," Nancy said, "I never imagined.... Aren't marriages sacraments? Aren't they indissoluble? I thought you were married. .. and..." She was sobbing. "I thought you were married or not married as you are alive or dead." "That," Leonora said, "is the law of the church. It is not the law of the land...."

"Oh yes," Nancy said, "the Brands are Protestants." She felt a sudden safeness descend upon her, and for an hour or so her mind was at rest. It seemed to her idiotic not to have remembered Henry VIII and the basis upon which Protestantism rests. She almost laughed at herself.

The long afternoon wore on; the flames still fluttered when the maid made up the fire; the St Bernard awoke and lolloped away towards the kitchen. And then Leonora opened her eyes and said almost coldly:

"And you? Don't you think you will get married?"

It was so unlike Leonora that, for the moment, the girl was frightened in the dusk. But then, again, it seemed a perfectly reasonable question. "I don't know," she answered. "I don't know that anyone wants to marry me."

"Several people want to marry you," Leonora said.

"But I don't want to marry," Nancy answered. "I should like to go on living with you and Edward. I don't think I am in the way or that I am really an expense. If I went you would have to have a companion. Or, perhaps, I ought to earn my living...."

"I wasn't thinking of that," Leonora answered in the same dull tone. "You will have money enough from your father. But most people want to be married."

I believe that she then asked the girl if she would not like to marry me, and that Nancy answered that she would marry me if she were told to; but that she wanted to go on living there. She added:

"If I married anyone I should want him to be like Edward."

She was frightened out of her life. Leonora writhed on her couch and called out: "Oh, God!..."

Nancy ran for the maid; for tablets of aspirin; for wet handkerchiefs. It never occurred to her that Leonora's expression of agony was for anything else than physical pain.

You are to remember that all this happened a month before Leonora went into the girl's room at night. I have been casting back again; but I cannot help it. It is so difficult to keep all these people going. I tell you about Leonora and bring her up to date; then about Edward, who has fallen behind. And then the girl gets hopelessly left behind. I wish I could put it down in diary form. Thus: On the 1st of September they returned from Nauheim. Leonora at once took to her bed. By the 1st of October they were all going to meets together. Nancy had already observed very fully that Edward was strange in his manner. About the 6th of that month Edward gave the horse to young Selmes, and Nancy had cause to believe that her aunt did not love her uncle. On the 20th she read the account of the divorce case, which is reported in the papers of the 18th and the two following days. On the 23rd she had the conversation with her aunt in the hall—about marriage in general and about her own possible marriage, her aunt's coming to her bedroom did not occur until the 12th of November....

Thus she had three weeks for introspection—for introspection beneath gloomy skies, in that old house, rendered darker by the fact that it lay in a hollow crowned by fir trees with their black shadows. It was not a good situation for a girl. She began thinking about love, she who had never before considered it as anything other than a rather humorous, rather nonsensical matter. She remembered chance passages in chance books—things that had not really affected her at all at the time. She remembered someone's love for the Princess Badrulbadour; she remembered to have heard that love was a flame, a thirst, a withering up of the vitals—though she did not know what the vitals were. She had a vague recollection that love was said to render a hopeless lover's eyes hopeless; she remembered a character in a book who was said to have taken to drink through love; she remembered that lovers' existences were said to be punctuated with heavy sighs. Once she went to the little cottage piano that was in the corner of the hall and began to play. It was a tinkly, reedy instrument, for none of that household had any turn for music. Nancy herself could play a few simple songs, and she found herself playing. She had been sitting on the window seat, looking out on the fading day. Leonora had gone to pay some calls; Edward was looking after some planting up in the new spinney. Thus she found herself playing on the old piano. She did not know how she came to be doing it. A silly lilting wavering tune came from before her in the dusk—a tune in which major notes with their cheerful insistence wavered and melted into minor sounds, as, beneath a bridge, the high lights on dark waters melt and waver and disappear into black depths. Well, it was a silly old tune....

It goes with the words—they are about a willow tree, I think: Thou art to all lost loves the best The only true plant found.

—That sort of thing. It is Herrick, I believe, and the music with the reedy, irregular, lilting sound that goes with Herrick, And it was dusk; the heavy, hewn, dark pillars that supported the gallery were like mourning presences; the fire had sunk to nothing—a mere glow amongst white ashes.... It was a sentimental sort of place and light and hour....

And suddenly Nancy found that she was crying. She was crying quietly; she went on to cry with long convulsive sobs. It seemed to her that everything gay, everything charming, all light, all sweetness, had gone out of life. Unhappiness; unhappiness; unhappiness was all around her. She seemed to know no happy being and she herself was agonizing....

She remembered that Edward's eyes were hopeless; she was certain that he was drinking too much; at times he sighed deeply. He appeared as a man who was burning with inward flame; drying up in the soul with thirst; withering up in the vitals. Then, the torturing conviction came to her—the conviction that had visited her again and again—that Edward must love some one other than Leonora. With her little, pedagogic sectarianism she remembered that Catholics do not do this thing. But Edward was a Protestant. Then Edward loved somebody....

And, after that thought, her eyes grew hopeless; she sighed as the old St Bernard beside her did. At meals she would feel an intolerable desire to drink a glass of wine, and then another and then a third. Then she would find herself grow gay.... But in half an hour the gaiety went; she felt like a person who is burning up with an inward flame; desiccating at the soul with thirst; withering up in the vitals. One evening she went into Edward's gun-room—he had gone to a meeting of the National Reserve Committee. On the table beside his chair was a decanter of whisky. She poured out a wineglassful and drank it off. Flame then really seemed to fill her body; her legs swelled; her face grew feverish. She dragged her tall height up to her room and lay in the dark. The bed reeled beneath her; she gave way to the thought that she was in Edward's arms; that he was kissing her on her face that burned; on her shoulders that burned, and on her neck that was on fire.

She never touched alcohol again. Not once after that did she have such thoughts. They died out of her mind; they left only a feeling of shame so insupportable that her brain could not take it in and they vanished. She imagined that her anguish at the thought of Edward's love for another person was solely sympathy for Leonora; she determined that the rest of her life must be spent in acting as Leonora's handmaiden—sweeping, tending, embroidering, like some Deborah, some medieval saint—I am not, unfortunately, up in the Catholic hagiology. But I know that she pictured herself as some personage with a depressed, earnest face and tightly closed lips, in a clear white room, watering flowers or tending an embroidery frame. Or, she desired to go with Edward to Africa and to throw herself in the path of a charging lion so that Edward might be saved for Leonora at the cost of her life. Well, along with her sad thoughts she had her childish ones. She knew nothing—nothing of life, except that one must live sadly. That she now knew. What happened to her on the night when she received at once the blow that Edward wished her to go to her father in India and the blow of the letter from her mother was this. She called first upon her sweet Saviour—and she thought of Our Lord as her sweet Saviour!—that He might make it impossible that she should go to India. Then she realized from Edward's demeanour that he was determined that she should go to India. It must then be right that she should go. Edward was always right in his determinations. He was the Cid; he was Lohengrin; he was the Chevalier Bayard.

Nevertheless her mind mutinied and revolted. She could not leave that house. She imagined that he wished her gone that she might not witness his amours with another girl. Well, she was prepared to tell him that she was ready to witness his amours with another young girl. She would stay there—to comfort Leonora.

Then came the desperate shock of the letter from her mother. Her mother said, I believe, something like: "You have no right to go on living your life of prosperity and respect. You ought to be on the streets with me. How do you know that you are even Colonel Rufford's daughter?" She did not know what these words meant. She thought of her mother as sleeping beneath the arches whilst the snow fell. That was the impression conveyed to her mind by the words "on the streets". A Platonic sense of duty gave her the idea that she ought to go to comfort her mother—the mother that bore her, though she hardly knew what the words meant. At the same time she knew that her mother had left her father with another man—therefore she pitied her father, and thought it terrible in herself that she trembled at the sound of her father's voice. If her mother was that sort of woman it was natural that her father should have had accesses of madness in which he had struck herself to the ground. And the voice of her conscience said to her that her first duty was to her parents. It was in accord with this awakened sense of duty that she undressed with great care and meticulously folded the clothes that she took off. Sometimes, but not very often, she threw them helter-skelter about the room.

And that sense of duty was her prevailing mood when Leonora, tall, clean-run, golden-haired, all in black, appeared in her doorway, and told her that Edward was dying of love for her. She knew then with her conscious mind what she had known within herself for months—that Edward was dying—actually and physically dying—of love for her. It seemed to her that for one short moment her spirit could say: "Domine, nunc dimittis,... Lord, now, lettest thou thy servant depart in peace." She imagined that she could cheerfully go away to Glasgow and rescue her fallen mother.

IV

AND it seemed to her to be in tune with the mood, with the hour, and with the woman in front of her to say that she knew Edward was dying of love for her and that she was dying of love for Edward. For that fact had suddenly slipped into place and become real for her as the niched marker on a whist tablet slips round with the pressure of your thumb. That rubber at least was made.

And suddenly Leonora seemed to have become different and she seemed to have become different in her attitude towards Leonora. It was as if she, in her frail, white, silken kimono, sat beside her fire, but upon a throne. It was as if Leonora, in her close dress of black lace, with the gleaming white shoulders and the coiled yellow hair that the girl had always considered the most beautiful thing in the world—it was as if Leonora had become pinched, shrivelled, blue with cold, shivering, suppliant. Yet Leonora was commanding her. It was no good commanding her. She was going on the morrow to her mother who was in Glasgow.

Leonora went on saying that she must stay there to save Edward, who was dying of love for her. And, proud and happy in the thought that Edward loved her, and that she loved him, she did not even listen to what Leonora said. It appeared to her that it was Leonora's business to save her husband's body; she, Nancy, possessed his soul—a precious thing that she would shield and bear away up in her arms—as if Leonora were a hungry dog, trying to spring up at a lamb that she was carrying. Yes, she felt as if Edward's love were a precious lamb that she were bearing away from a cruel and predatory beast. For, at that time, Leonora appeared to her as a cruel and predatory beast. Leonora, Leonora with her hunger, with her cruelty had driven Edward to madness. He must be sheltered by his love for her and by her love—her love from a great distance and unspoken, enveloping him, surrounding him, upholding him; by her voice speaking from Glasgow, saying that she loved, that she adored, that she passed no moment without longing, loving, quivering at the thought of him.

Leonora said loudly, insistently, with a bitterly imperative tone:

"You must stay here; you must belong to Edward. I will divorce him."

The girl answered:

"The Church does not allow of divorce. I cannot belong to your husband. I am going to Glasgow to rescue my mother."

The half-opened door opened noiselessly to the full. Edward was there. His devouring, doomed eyes were fixed on the girl's face; his shoulders slouched forward; he was undoubtedly half drunk and he had the whisky decanter in one hand, a slanting candlestick in the other. He said, with a heavy ferocity, to Nancy:

"I forbid you to talk about these things. You are to stay here until I hear from your father. Then you will go to your father."

The two women, looking at each other, like beasts about to spring, hardly gave a glance to him. He leaned against the door-post. He said again:

"Nancy, I forbid you to talk about these things. I am the master of this house." And, at the sound of his voice, heavy, male, coming from a deep chest, in the night with the blackness behind him, Nancy felt as if her spirit bowed before him, with folded hands. She felt that she would go to India, and that she desired never again to talk of these things.

Leonora said:

"You see that it is your duty to belong to him. He must not be allowed to go on drinking."

Nancy did not answer. Edward was gone; they heard him slipping and shambling on the polished oak of the stairs. Nancy screamed when there came the sound of a heavy fall. Leonora said again: "You see!"

The sounds went on from the hall below; the light of the candle Edward held flickered up between the hand rails of the gallery. Then they heard his voice:

"Give me Glasgow... Glasgow, in Scotland.. I want the number of a man called White, of Simrock Park, Glasgow... Edward White, Simrock Park, Glasgow... ten minutes... at this time of night..." His voice was quite level, normal, and patient. Alcohol took him in the legs, not the speech. "I can wait," his voice came again. "Yes, I know they have a number. I have been in communication with them before."

"He is going to telephone to your mother," Leonora said. "He will make it all right for her." She got up and closed the door. She came back to the fire, and added bitterly: "He can always make it all right for everybody, except me—excepting me!"

The girl said nothing. She sat there in a blissful dream. She seemed to see her lover sitting as he always sat, in a round-backed chair, in the dark hall—sitting low, with the receiver at his ear, talking in a gentle, slow voice, that he reserved for the telephone—and saving the world and her, in the black darkness. She moved her hand over the bareness of the base of her throat, to have the warmth of flesh upon it and upon her bosom.

She said nothing; Leonora went on talking....

God knows what Leonora said. She repeated that the girl must belong to her husband. She said that she used that phrase because, though she might have a divorce, or even a dissolution of the marriage by the Church, it would still be adultery that the girl and Edward would be committing. But she said that that was necessary; it was the price that the girl must pay for the sin of having made Edward love her, for the sin of loving her husband. She talked on and on, beside the fire. The girl must become an adulteress; she had wronged Edward by being so beautiful, so gracious, so good. It was sinful to be so good. She must pay the price so as to save the man she had wronged.

In between her pauses the girl could hear the voice of Edward, droning on, indistinguishably, with jerky pauses for replies. It made her glow with pride; the man she loved was working for her. He at least was resolved; was malely determined; knew the right thing. Leonora talked on with her eyes boring into Nancy's. The girl hardly looked at her and hardly heard her. After a long time Nancy said—after hours and hours:

"I shall go to India as soon as Edward hears from my father. I cannot talk about these things, because Edward does not wish it."

At that Leonora screamed out and wavered swiftly towards the closed door. And Nancy found that she was springing out of her chair with her white arms stretched wide. She was clasping the other woman to her breast; she was saying:

"Oh, my poor dear; oh, my poor dear." And they sat, crouching together in each other's arms, and crying and crying; and they lay down in the same bed, talking and talking, all through the night. And all through the night Edward could hear their voices through the wall. That was how it went.... Next morning they were all three as if nothing had happened. Towards eleven Edward came to Nancy, who was arranging some Christmas roses in a silver bowl. He put a telegram beside her on the table. "You can uncode it for yourself," he said. Then, as he went out of the door, he said: "You can tell your aunt I have cabled to Mr Dowell to come over. He will make things easier till you leave." The telegram when it was uncoded, read, as far as I can remember: "Will take Mrs Rufford to Italy. Undertake to do this for certain. Am devotedly attached to Mrs Rufford. Have no need of financial assistance. Did not know there was a daughter, and am much obliged to you for pointing out my duty.—White." It was something like that. Then the household resumed its wonted course of days until my arrival.

V

IT is this part of the story that makes me saddest of all. For I ask myself unceasingly, my mind going round and round in a weary, baffled space of pain—what should these people have done? What, in the name of God, should they have done?

The end was perfectly plain to each of them—it was perfectly manifest at this stage that, if the girl did not, in Leonora's phrase, "belong to Edward," Edward must die, the girl must lose her reason because Edward died—and, that after a time, Leonora, who was the coldest and the strongest of the three, would console herself by marrying Rodney Bayham and have a quiet, comfortable, good time. That end, on that night, whilst Leonora sat in the girl's bedroom and Edward telephoned down below—that end was plainly manifest. The girl, plainly, was half-mad already; Edward was half dead; only Leonora, active, persistent, instinct with her cold passion of energy, was "doing things". What then, should they have done? worked out in the extinction of two very splendid personalities—for Edward and the girl were splendid personalities, in order that a third personality, more normal, should have, after a long period of trouble, a quiet, comfortable, good time.

I am writing this, now, I should say, a full eighteen months after the words that end my last chapter. Since writing the words "until my arrival", which I see end that paragraph, I have seen again for a glimpse, from a swift train, Beaucaire with the beautiful white tower, Tarascon with the square castle, the great Rhone, the immense stretches of the Crau. I have rushed through all Provence—and all Provence no longer matters. It is no longer in the olive hills that I shall find my Heaven; because there is only Hell... .

Edward is dead; the girl is gone—oh, utterly gone; Leonora is having a good time with Rodney Bayham, and I sit alone in Branshaw Teleragh. I have been through Provence; I have seen Africa; I have visited Asia to see, in Ceylon, in a darkened room, my poor girl, sitting motionless, with her wonderful hair about her, looking at me with eyes that did not see me, and saying distinctly: "Credo in unum Deum omnipotentem.... Credo in unum Deum omnipotentem." Those are the only reasonable words she uttered; those are the only words, it appears, that she ever will utter. I suppose that they are reasonable words; it must be extraordinarily reasonable for her, if she can say that she believes in an Omnipotent Deity. Well, there it is. I am very tired of it all....

For, I daresay, all this may sound romantic, but it is tiring, tiring, tiring to have been in the midst of it; to have taken the tickets; to have caught the trains; to have chosen the cabins; to have consulted the purser and the stewards as to diet for the quiescent patient who did nothing but announce her belief in an Omnipotent Deity. That may sound romantic—but it is just a record of fatigue.

I don't know why I should always be selected to be serviceable. I don't resent it—but I have never been the least good. Florence selected me for her own purposes, and I was no good to her; Edward called me to come and have a chat with him, and I couldn't stop him cutting his throat.

And then, one day eighteen months ago, I was quietly writing in my room at Branshaw when Leonora came to me with a letter. It was a very pathetic letter from Colonel Rufford about Nancy. Colonel Rufford had left the army and had taken up an appointment at a tea-planting estate in Ceylon. His letter was pathetic because it was so brief, so inarticulate, and so business-like. He had gone down to the boat to meet his daughter, and had found his daughter quite mad. It appears that at Aden Nancy had seen in a local paper the news of Edward's suicide. In the Red Sea she had gone mad. She had remarked to Mrs Colonel Luton, who was chaperoning her, that she believed in an Omnipotent Deity. She hadn't made any fuss; her eyes were quite dry and glassy. Even when she was mad Nancy could behave herself.

Colonel Rufford said the doctor did not anticipate that there was any chance of his child's recovery. It was, nevertheless, possible that if she could see someone from Branshaw it might soothe her and it might have a good effect. And he just simply wrote to Leonora: "Please come and see if you can do it."

I seem to have lost all sense of the pathetic; but still, that simple, enormous request of the old colonel strikes me as pathetic. He was cursed by his atrocious temper; he had been cursed by a half-mad wife, who drank and went on the streets. His daughter was totally mad—and yet he believed in the goodness of human nature. He believed that Leonora would take the trouble to go all the way to Ceylon in order to soothe his daughter. Leonora wouldn't. Leonora didn't ever want to see Nancy again. I daresay that that, in the circumstances, was natural enough. At the same time she agreed, as it were, on public grounds, that someone soothing ought to go from Branshaw to Ceylon. She sent me and her old nurse, who had looked after Nancy from the time when the girl, a child of thirteen, had first come to Branshaw. So off I go, rushing through Provence, to catch the steamer at Marseilles. And I wasn't the least good when I got to Ceylon; and the nurse wasn't the least good. Nothing has been the least good. The doctors said, at Kandy, that if Nancy could be brought to England, the sea air, the change of climate, the voyage, and all the usual sort of things, might restore her reason. Of course, they haven't restored her reason. She is, I am aware, sitting in the hall, forty paces from where I am now writing. I don't want to be in the least romantic about it. She is very well dressed; she is quite quiet; she is very beautiful. The old nurse looks after her very efficiently.

Of course you have the makings of a situation here, but it is all very humdrum, as far as I am concerned. I should marry Nancy if her reason were ever sufficiently restored to let her appreciate the meaning of the Anglican marriage service. But it is probable that her reason will never be sufficiently restored to let her appreciate the meaning of the Anglican marriage service. Therefore I cannot marry her, according to the law of the land.

So here I am very much where I started thirteen years ago. I am the attendant, not the husband, of a beautiful girl, who pays no attention to me. I am estranged from Leonora, who married Rodney Bayham in my absence and went to live at Bayham. Leonora rather dislikes me, because she has got it into her head that I disapprove of her marriage with Rodney Bayham. Well, I disapprove of her marriage. Possibly I am jealous. Yes, no doubt I am jealous. In my fainter sort of way I seem to perceive myself following the lines of Edward Ashburnham. I suppose that I should really like to be a polygamist; with Nancy, and with Leonora, and with Maisie Maidan and possibly even with Florence. I am no doubt like every other man; only, probably because of my American origin I am fainter. At the same time I am able to assure you that I am a strictly respectable person. I have never done anything that the most anxious mother of a daughter or the most careful dean of a cathedral would object to. I have only followed, faintly, and in my unconscious desires, Edward Ashburnham. Well, it is all over. Not one of us has got what he really wanted. Leonora wanted Edward, and she has got Rodney Bayham, a pleasant enough sort of sheep. Florence wanted Branshaw, and it is I who have bought it from Leonora. I didn't really want it; what I wanted mostly was to cease being a nurse-attendant. Well, I am a nurse-attendant. Edward wanted Nancy Rufford, and I have got her. Only she is mad. It is a queer and fantastic world. Why can't people have what they want? The things were all there to content everybody; yet everybody has the wrong thing. Perhaps you can make head or tail of it; it is beyond me.

Is there any terrestial paradise where, amidst the whispering of the olive-leaves, people can be with whom they like and have what they like and take their ease in shadows and in coolness? Or are all men's lives like the lives of us good people—like the lives of the Ashburnhams, of the Dowells, of the Ruffords—broken, tumultuous, agonized, and unromantic, lives, periods punctuated by screams, by imbecilities, by deaths, by agonies? Who the devil knows?

For there was a great deal of imbecility about the closing scenes of the Ashburnham tragedy. Neither of those two women knew what they wanted. It was only Edward who took a perfectly clear line, and he was drunk most of the time. But, drunk or sober, he stuck to what was demanded by convention and by the traditions of his house. Nancy Rufford had to be exported to India, and Nancy Rufford hadn't to hear a word of love from him. She was exported to India and she never heard a word from Edward Ashburnham.

It was the conventional line; it was in tune with the tradition of Edward's house. I daresay it worked out for the greatest good of the body politic. Conventions and traditions, I suppose, work blindly but surely for the preservation of the normal type; for the extinction of proud, resolute and unusual individuals.

Edward was the normal man, but there was too much of the sentimentalist about him; and society does not need too many sentimentalists. Nancy was a splendid creature, but she had about her a touch of madness. Society does not need individuals with touches of madness about them. So Edward and Nancy found themselves steamrolled out and Leonora survives, the perfectly normal type, married to a man who is rather like a rabbit. For Rodney Bayham is rather like a rabbit, and I hear that Leonora is expected to have a baby in three months' time.

So those splendid and tumultuous creatures with their magnetism and their passions—those two that I really loved—have gone from this earth. It is no doubt best for them. What would Nancy have made of Edward if she had succeeded in living with him; what would Edward have made of her? For there was about Nancy a touch of cruelty—a touch of definite actual cruelty that made her desire to see people suffer. Yes, she desired to see Edward suffer. And, by God, she gave him hell.

She gave him an unimaginable hell. Those two women pursued that poor devil and flayed the skin off him as if they had done it with whips. I tell you his mind bled almost visibly. I seem to see him stand, naked to the waist, his forearms shielding his eyes, and flesh hanging from him in rags. I tell you that is no exaggeration of what I feel. It was as if Leonora and Nancy banded themselves together to do execution, for the sake of humanity, upon the body of a man who was at their disposal. They were like a couple of Sioux who had got hold of an Apache and had him well tied to a stake. I tell you there was no end to the tortures they inflicted upon him.

Night after night he would hear them talking; talking; maddened, sweating, seeking oblivion in drink, he would lie there and hear the voices going on and on. And day after day Leonora would come to him and would announce the results of their deliberations.

They were like judges debating over the sentence upon a criminal; they were like ghouls with an immobile corpse in a tomb beside them. I don't think that Leonora was any more to blame than the girl—though Leonora was the more active of the two. Leonora, as I have said, was the perfectly normal woman. I mean to say that in normal circumstances her desires were those of the woman who is needed by society. She desired children, decorum, an establishment; she desired to avoid waste, she desired to keep up appearances. She was utterly and entirely normal even in her utterly undeniable beauty. But I don't mean to say that she acted perfectly normally in this perfectly abnormal situation. All the world was mad around her and she herself, agonized, took on the complexion of a mad woman; of a woman very wicked; of the villain of the piece. What would you have? Steel is a normal, hard, polished substance. But, if you put it in a hot fire it will become red, soft, and not to be handled. If you put it in a fire still more hot it will drip away. It was like that with Leonora. She was made for normal circumstances—for Mr Rodney Bayham, who will keep a separate establishment, secretly, in Portsmouth, and make occasional trips to Paris and to Budapest.

In the case of Edward and the girl, Leonora broke and simply went all over the place. She adopted unfamiliar and therefore extraordinary and ungraceful attitudes of mind. At one moment she was all for revenge. After haranguing the girl for hours through the night she harangued for hours of the day the silent Edward. And Edward just once tripped up, and that was his undoing. Perhaps he had had too much whisky that afternoon. She asked him perpetually what he wanted. What did he want? What did he want? And all he ever answered was: "I have told you". He meant that he wanted the girl to go to her father in India as soon as her father should cable that he was ready to receive her. But just once he tripped up. To Leonora's eternal question he answered that all he desired in life was that—that he could pick himself together again and go on with his daily occupations if—the girl, being five thousand miles away, would continue to love him. He wanted nothing more, He prayed his God for nothing more. Well, he was a sentimentalist.

And the moment that she heard that, Leonora determined that the girl should not go five thousand miles away and that she should not continue to love Edward. The way she worked it was this:

She continued to tell the girl that she must belong to Edward; she was going to get a divorce; she was going to get a dissolution of marriage from Rome. But she considered it to be her duty to warn the girl of the sort of monster that Edward was. She told the girl of La Dolciquita, of Mrs Basil, of Maisie Maidan, of Florence. She spoke of the agonies that she had endured during her life with the man, who was violent, overbearing, vain, drunken, arrogant, and monstrously a prey to his sexual necessities. And, at hearing of the miseries her aunt had suffered—for Leonora once more had the aspect of an aunt to the girl—with the swift cruelty of youth and, with the swift solidarity that attaches woman to woman, the girl made her resolves. Her aunt said incessantly: "You must save Edward's life; you must save his life. All that he needs is a little period of satisfaction from you. Then he will tire of you as he has of the others. But you must save his life."

And, all the while, that wretched fellow knew—by a curious instinct that runs between human beings living together—exactly what was going on. And he remained dumb; he stretched out no finger to help himself. All that he required to keep himself a decent member of society was, that the girl, five thousand miles away, should continue to love him. They were putting a stopper upon that.

I have told you that the girl came one night to his room. And that was the real hell for him. That was the picture that never left his imagination—the girl, in the dim light, rising up at the foot of his bed. He said that it seemed to have a greenish sort of effect as if there were a greenish tinge in the shadows of the tall bedposts that framed her body. And she looked at him with her straight eyes of an unflinching cruelty and she said: "I am ready to belong to you—to save your life."

He answered: "I don't want it; I don't want it; I don't want it."

And he says that he didn't want it; that he would have hated himself; that it was unthinkable. And all the while he had the immense temptation to do the unthinkable thing, not from the physical desire but because of a mental certitude. He was certain that if she had once submitted to him she would remain his for ever. He knew that.

She was thinking that her aunt had said he had desired her to love him from a distance of five thousand miles. She said: "I can never love you now I know the kind of man you are. I will belong to you to save your life. But I can never love you."

It was a fantastic display of cruelty. She didn't in the least know what it meant—to belong to a man. But, at that Edward pulled himself together. He spoke in his normal tones; gruff, husky, overbearing, as he would have done to a servant or to a horse.

"Go back to your room," he said. "Go back to your room and go to sleep. This is all nonsense."

They were baffled, those two women.

And then I came on the scene.

VI

MY coming on the scene certainly calmed things down—for the whole fortnight that intervened between my arrival and the girl's departure. I don't mean to say that the endless talking did not go on at night or that Leonora did not send me out with the girl and, in the interval, give Edward a hell of a time. Having discovered what he wanted—that the girl should go five thousand miles away and love him steadfastly as people do in sentimental novels, she was determined to smash that aspiration. And she repeated to Edward in every possible tone that the girl did not love him; that the girl detested him for his brutality, his overbearingness, his drinking habits. She pointed out that Edward in the girl's eyes, was already pledged three or four deep. He was pledged to Leonora herself, to Mrs Basil, and to the memories of Maisie Maidan and to Florence. Edward never said anything.

Did the girl love Edward, or didn't she? I don't know. At that time I daresay she didn't though she certainly had done so before Leonora had got to work upon his reputation. She certainly had loved him for what I call the public side of his record—for his good soldiering, for his saving lives at sea, for the excellent landlord that he was and the good sportsman. But it is quite possible that all those things came to appear as nothing in her eyes when she discovered that he wasn't a good husband. For, though women, as I see them, have little or no feeling of responsibility towards a county or a country or a career—although they may be entirely lacking in any kind of communal solidarity—they have an immense and automatically working instinct that attaches them to the interest of womanhood. It is, of course, possible for any woman to cut out and to carry off any other woman's husband or lover. But I rather think that a woman will only do this if she has reason to believe that the other woman has given her husband a bad time. I am certain that if she thinks the man has been a brute to his wife she will, with her instinctive feeling for suffering femininity, "put him back", as the saying is. I don't attach any particular importance to these generalizations of mine. They may be right, they may be wrong; I am only an ageing American with very little knowledge of life. You may take my generalizations or leave them. But I am pretty certain that I am right in the case of Nancy Rufford—that she had loved Edward Ashburnham very deeply and tenderly.

It is nothing to the point that she let him have it good and strong as soon as she discovered that he had been unfaithful to Leonora and that his public services had cost more than Leonora thought they ought to have cost. Nancy would be bound to let him have it good and strong then. She would owe that to feminine public opinion; she would be driven to it by the instinct for self-preservation, since she might well imagine that if Edward had been unfaithful to Leonora, to Mrs Basil and to the memories of the other two, he might be unfaithful to herself. And, no doubt, she had her share of the sex instinct that makes women be intolerably cruel to the beloved person. Anyhow, I don't know whether, at this point, Nancy Rufford loved Edward Ashburnham. I don't know whether she even loved him when, on getting, at Aden, the news of his suicide she went mad. Because that may just as well have been for the sake of Leonora as for the sake of Edward. Or it may have been for the sake of both of them. I don't know. I know nothing. I am very tired. Leonora held passionately the doctrine that the girl didn't love Edward. She wanted desperately to believe that. It was a doctrine as necessary to her existence as a belief in the personal immortality of the soul. She said that it was impossible that Nancy could have loved Edward after she had given the girl her view of Edward's career and character. Edward, on the other hand, believed maunderingly that some essential attractiveness in himself must have made the girl continue to go on loving him—to go on loving him, as it were, in underneath her official aspect of hatred. He thought she only pretended to hate him in order to save her face and he thought that her quite atrocious telegram from Brindisi was only another attempt to do that—to prove that she had feelings creditable to a member of the feminine commonweal. I don't know. I leave it to you. There is another point that worries me a good deal in the aspects of this sad affair. Leonora says that, in desiring that the girl should go five thousand miles away and yet continue to love him, Edward was a monster of selfishness. He was desiring the ruin of a young life. Edward on the other hand put it to me that, supposing that the girl's love was a necessity to his existence, and, if he did nothing by word or by action to keep Nancy's love alive, he couldn't be called selfish. Leonora replied that showed he had an abominably selfish nature even though his actions might be perfectly correct. I can't make out which of them was right. I leave it to you.

It is, at any rate, certain that Edward's actions were perfectly—were monstrously, were cruelly—correct. He sat still and let Leonora take away his character, and let Leonora damn him to deepest hell, without stirring a finger. I daresay he was a fool; I don't see what object there was in letting the girl think worse of him than was necessary. Still there it is. And there it is also that all those three presented to the world the spectacle of being the best of good people. I assure you that during my stay for that fortnight in that fine old house, I never so much as noticed a single thing that could have affected that good opinion. And even when I look back, knowing the circumstances, I can't remember a single thing any of them said that could have betrayed them. I can't remember, right up to the dinner, when Leonora read out that telegram—not the tremor of an eyelash, not the shaking of a hand. It was just a pleasant country house-party.

And Leonora kept it up jolly well, for even longer than that—she kept it up as far as I was concerned until eight days after Edward's funeral. Immediately after that particular dinner—the dinner at which I received the announcement that Nancy was going to leave for India on the following day—I asked Leonora to let me have a word with her. She took me into her little sitting-room and I then said—I spare you the record of my emotions—that she was aware that I wished to marry Nancy; that she had seemed to favour my suit and that it appeared to be rather a waste of money upon tickets and rather a waste of time upon travel to let the girl go to India if Leonora thought that there was any chance of her marrying me.

And Leonora, I assure you, was the absolutely perfect British matron. She said that she quite favoured my suit; that she could not desire for the girl a better husband; but that she considered that the girl ought to see a little more of life before taking such an important step. Yes, Leonora used the words "taking such an important step". She was perfect. Actually, I think she would have liked the girl to marry me enough but my programme included the buying of the Kershaw's house about a mile away upon the Fordingbridge road, and settling down there with the girl. That didn't at all suit Leonora. She didn't want to have the girl within a mile and a half of Edward for the rest of their lives. Still, I think she might have managed to let me know, in some periphrasis or other, that I might have the girl if I would take her to Philadelphia or Timbuctoo. I loved Nancy very much—and Leonora knew it. However, I left it at that. I left it with the understanding that Nancy was going away to India on probation. It seemed to me a perfectly reasonable arrangement and I am a reasonable sort of man. I simply said that I should follow Nancy out to India after six months' time or so. Or, perhaps, after a year. Well, you see, I did follow Nancy out to India after a year.... I must confess to having felt a little angry with Leonora for not having warned me earlier that the girl would be going. I took it as one of the queer, not very straight methods that Roman Catholics seem to adopt in dealing with matters of this world. I took it that Leonora had been afraid I should propose to the girl or, at any rate, have made considerably greater advances to her than I did, if I had known earlier that she was going away so soon. Perhaps Leonora was right; perhaps Roman Catholics, with their queer, shifty ways, are always right. They are dealing with the queer, shifty thing that is human nature. For it is quite possible that, if I had known Nancy was going away so soon, I should have tried making love to her. And that would have produced another complication. It may have been just as well.

It is queer the fantastic things that quite good people will do in order to keep up their appearance of calm pococurantism. For Edward Ashburnham and his wife called me half the world over in order to sit on the back seat of a dog-cart whilst Edward drove the girl to the railway station from which she was to take her departure to India. They wanted, I suppose, to have a witness of the calmness of that function. The girl's luggage had been already packed and sent off before. Her berth on the steamer had been taken. They had timed it all so exactly that it went like clockwork. They had known the date upon which Colonel Rufford would get Edward's letter and they had known almost exactly the hour at which they would receive his telegram asking his daughter to come to him. It had all been quite beautifully and quite mercilessly arranged, by Edward himself. They gave Colonel Rufford, as a reason for telegraphing, the fact that Mrs Colonel Somebody or other would be travelling by that ship and that she would serve as an efficient chaperon for the girl. It was a most amazing business, and I think that it would have been better in the eyes of God if they had all attempted to gouge out each other's eyes with carving knives. But they were "good people". After my interview with Leonora I went desultorily into Edward's gun-room. I didn't know where the girl was and I thought I mind find her there. I suppose I had a vague idea of proposing to her in spite of Leonora. So, I presume, I don't come of quite such good people as the Ashburnhams. Edward was lounging in his chair smoking a cigar and he said nothing for quite five minutes. The candles glowed in the green shades; the reflections were green in the glasses of the book-cases that held guns and fishing-rods. Over the mantelpiece was the brownish picture of the white horse. Those were the quietest moments that I have ever known. Then, suddenly, Edward looked me straight in the eyes and said:

"Look here, old man, I wish you would drive with Nancy and me to the station tomorrow."

I said that of course I would drive with him and Nancy to the station on the morrow. He lay there for a long time, looking along the line of his knees at the fluttering fire, and then suddenly, in a perfectly calm voice, and without lifting his eyes, he said:

"I am so desperately in love with Nancy Rufford that I am dying of it."

Poor devil—he hadn't meant to speak of it. But I guess he just had to speak to somebody and I appeared to be like a woman or a solicitor. He talked all night.

Well, he carried out the programme to the last breath.

It was a very clear winter morning, with a good deal of frost in it. The sun was quite bright, the winding road between the heather and the bracken was very hard. I sat on the back-seat of the dog-cart; Nancy was beside Edward. They talked about the way the cob went; Edward pointed out with the whip a cluster of deer upon a coombe three-quarters of a mile away. We passed the hounds in the level bit of road beside the high trees going into Fordingbridge and Edward pulled up the dog-cart so that Nancy might say good-bye to the huntsman and cap him a last sovereign. She had ridden with those hounds ever since she had been thirteen.

The train was five minutes late and they imagined that that was because it was market-day at Swindon or wherever the train came from. That was the sort of thing they talked about. The train came in; Edward found her a first-class carriage with an elderly woman in it. The girl entered the carriage, Edward closed the door and then she put out her hand to shake mine. There was upon those people's faces no expression of any kind whatever. The signal for the train's departure was a very bright red; that is about as passionate a statement as I can get into that scene. She was not looking her best; she had on a cap of brown fur that did not very well match her hair. She said:

"So long," to Edward.

Edward answered: "So long."

He swung round on his heel and, large, slouching, and walking with a heavy deliberate pace, he went out of the station. I followed him and got up beside him in the high dog-cart. It was the most horrible performance I have ever seen.

And, after that, a holy peace, like the peace of God which passes all understanding, descended upon Branshaw Teleragh. Leonora went about her daily duties with a sort of triumphant smile—a very faint smile, but quite triumphant. I guess she had so long since given up any idea of getting her man back that it was enough for her to have got the girl out of the house and well cured of her infatuation. Once, in the hall, when Leonora was going out, Edward said, beneath his breath—but I just caught the words:

"Thou hast conquered, O pale Galilean." It was like his sentimentality to quote Swinburne. But he was perfectly quiet and he had given up drinking. The only thing that he ever said to me after that drive to the station was:

"It's very odd. I think I ought to tell you, Dowell, that I haven't any feelings at all about the girl now it's all over. Don't you worry about me. I'm all right." A long time afterwards he said: "I guess it was only a flash in the pan." He began to look after the estates again; he took all that trouble over getting off the gardener's daughter who had murdered her baby. He shook hands smilingly with every farmer in the market-place. He addressed two political meetings; he hunted twice. Leonora made him a frightful scene about spending the two hundred pounds on getting the gardener's daughter acquitted. Everything went on as if the girl had never existed. It was very still weather.

Well, that is the end of the story. And, when I come to look at it I see that it is a happy ending with wedding bells and all. The villains—for obviously Edward and the girl were villains—have been punished by suicide and madness. The heroine—the perfectly normal, virtuous and slightly deceitful heroine—has become the happy wife of a perfectly normal, virtuous and slightly deceitful husband. She will shortly become a mother of a perfectly normal, virtuous slightly deceitful son or daughter. A happy ending, that is what it works out at.

I cannot conceal from myself the fact that I now dislike Leonora. Without doubt I am jealous of Rodney Bayham. But I don't know whether it is merely a jealousy arising from the fact that I desired myself to possess Leonora or whether it is because to her were sacrificed the only two persons that I have ever really loved—Edward Ashburnham and Nancy Rufford. In order to set her up in a modern mansion, replete with every convenience and dominated by a quite respectable and eminently economical master of the house, it was necessary that Edward and Nancy Rufford should become, for me at least, no more than tragic shades.

I seem to see poor Edward, naked and reclining amidst darkness, upon cold rocks, like one of the ancient Greek damned, in Tartarus or wherever it was.

And as for Nancy... Well, yesterday at lunch she said suddenly:

"Shuttlecocks!"

And she repeated the word "shuttlecocks" three times. I know what was passing in her mind, if she can be said to have a mind, for Leonora has told me that, once, the poor girl said she felt like a shuttlecock being tossed backwards and forwards between the violent personalities of Edward and his wife. Leonora, she said, was always trying to deliver her over to Edward, and Edward tacitly and silently forced her back again. And the odd thing was that Edward himself considered that those two women used him like a shuttlecock. Or, rather, he said that they sent him backwards and forwards like a blooming parcel that someone didn't want to pay the postage on. And Leonora also imagined that Edward and Nancy picked her up and threw her down as suited their purely vagrant moods. So there you have the pretty picture. Mind, I am not preaching anything contrary to accepted morality. I am not advocating free love in this or any other case. Society must go on, I suppose, and society can only exist if the normal, if the virtuous, and the slightly deceitful flourish, and if the passionate, the headstrong, and the too-truthful are condemned to suicide and to madness. But I guess that I myself, in my fainter way, come into the category of the passionate, of the headstrong, and the too-truthful. For I can't conceal from myself the fact that I loved Edward Ashburnham—and that I love him because he was just myself. If I had had the courage and virility and possibly also the physique of Edward Ashburnham I should, I fancy, have done much what he did. He seems to me like a large elder brother who took me out on several excursions and did many dashing things whilst I just watched him robbing the orchards, from a distance. And, you see, I am just as much of a sentimentalist as he was.. ..

Yes, society must go on; it must breed, like rabbits. That is what we are here for. But then, I don't like society—much. I am that absurd figure, an American millionaire, who has bought one of the ancient haunts of English peace. I sit here, in Edward's gun-room, all day and all day in a house that is absolutely quiet. No one visits me, for I visit no one. No one is interested in me, for I have no interests. In twenty minutes or so I shall walk down to the village, beneath my own oaks, alongside my own clumps of gorse, to get the American mail. My tenants, the village boys and the tradesmen will touch their hats to me. So life peters out. I shall return to dine and Nancy will sit opposite me with the old nurse standing behind her. Enigmatic, silent, utterly well-behaved as far as her knife and fork go, Nancy will stare in front of her with the blue eyes that have over them strained, stretched brows. Once, or perhaps twice, during the meal her knife and fork will be suspended in mid-air as if she were trying to think of something that she had forgotten. Then she will say that she believes in an Omnipotent Deity or she will utter the one word "shuttle-cocks", perhaps. It is very extraordinary to see the perfect flush of health on her cheeks, to see the lustre of her coiled black hair, the poise of the head upon the neck, the grace of the white hands—and to think that it all means nothing—that it is a picture without a meaning. Yes, it is queer.

But, at any rate, there is always Leonora to cheer you up; I don't want to sadden you. Her husband is quite an economical person of so normal a figure that he can get quite a large proportion of his clothes ready-made. That is the great desideratum of life, and that is the end of my story. The child is to be brought up as a Romanist.

It suddenly occurs to me that I have forgotten to say how Edward met his death. You remember that peace had descended upon the house; that Leonora was quietly triumphant and that Edward said his love for the girl had been merely a passing phase. Well, one afternoon we were in the stables together, looking at a new kind of flooring that Edward was trying in a loose-box. Edward was talking with a good deal of animation about the necessity of getting the numbers of the Hampshire territorials up to the proper standard. He was quite sober, quite quiet, his skin was clear-coloured; his hair was golden and perfectly brushed; the level brick-dust red of his complexion went clean up to the rims of his eyelids; his eyes were porcelain blue and they regarded me frankly and directly. His face was perfectly expressionless; his voice was deep and rough. He stood well back upon his legs and said:

"We ought to get them up to two thousand three hundred and fifty." A stable-boy brought him a telegram and went away. He opened it negligently, regarded it without emotion, and, in complete silence, handed it to me. On the pinkish paper in a sprawled handwriting I read: "Safe Brindisi. Having rattling good time. Nancy."

Well, Edward was the English gentleman; but he was also, to the last, a sentimentalist, whose mind was compounded of indifferent poems and novels. He just looked up to the roof of the stable, as if he were looking to Heaven, and whispered something that I did not catch.

Then he put two fingers into the waistcoat pocket of his grey, frieze suit; they came out with a little neat pen-knife—quite a small pen-knife. He said to me:

"You might just take that wire to Leonora." And he looked at me with a direct, challenging, brow-beating glare. I guess he could see in my eyes that I didn't intend to hinder him. Why should I hinder him?

I didn't think he was wanted in the world, let his confounded tenants, his rifle-associations, his drunkards, reclaimed and unreclaimed, get on as they liked. Not all the hundreds and hundreds of them deserved that that poor devil should go on suffering for their sakes.

When he saw that I did not intend to interfere with him his eyes became soft and almost affectionate. He remarked:

"So long, old man, I must have a bit of a rest, you know."

I didn't know what to say. I wanted to say, "God bless you", for I also am a sentimentalist. But I thought that perhaps that would not be quite English good form, so I trotted off with the telegram to Leonora. She was quite pleased with it.

HAUNTED HOTEL

BY

WILKIE COLLINS

I

In the year 1860, the reputation of Doctor Wybrow as a London physician reached its highest point. It was reported on good authority that he was in receipt of one of the largest incomes derived from the practice of medicine in modern times.

One afternoon, towards the close of the London season, the Doctor had just taken his luncheon after a specially hard morning's work in his consulting-room, and with a formidable list of visits to patients at their own houses to fill up the rest of his day—when the servant announced that a lady wished to speak to him.

'Who is she?' the Doctor asked. 'A stranger?'

'Yes, sir.'

'I see no strangers out of consulting-hours. Tell her what the hours are, and send her away.'

'I have told her, sir.'

'Well?'

'And she won't go.'

'Won't go?' The Doctor smiled as he repeated the words. He was a humourist in his way; and there was an absurd side to the situation which rather amused him. 'Has this obstinate lady given you her name?' he inquired.

'No, sir. She refused to give any name—she said she wouldn't keep you five minutes, and the matter was too important to wait till to-morrow. There she is in the consulting-room; and how to get her out again is more than I know.'

Doctor Wybrow considered for a moment. His knowledge of women (professionally speaking) rested on the ripe experience of more than thirty years; he had met with them in all their varieties—especially the variety which knows nothing of the value of time, and never hesitates at sheltering itself behind the privileges of its sex. A glance at his watch informed him that he must soon begin his rounds among the patients who were waiting for him at their own houses. He decided forthwith on taking the only wise course that was open under the circumstances. In other words, he decided on taking to flight.

'Is the carriage at the door?' he asked.

'Yes, sir.'

'Very well. Open the house-door for me without making any noise, and leave the lady in undisturbed possession of the consulting-room. When she gets tired of waiting, you know what to tell her. If she asks when I am expected to return, say that I dine at my club, and spend the evening at the theatre. Now then, softly, Thomas! If your shoes creak, I am a lost man.'

He noiselessly led the way into the hall, followed by the servant on tip-toe.

Did the lady in the consulting-room suspect him? or did Thomas's shoes creak, and was her sense of hearing unusually keen? Whatever the explanation may be, the event that actually happened was beyond all doubt. Exactly as Doctor Wybrow passed his consulting-room, the door opened—the lady appeared on the threshold—and laid her hand on his arm.

'I entreat you, sir, not to go away without letting me speak to you first.'

The accent was foreign; the tone was low and firm. Her

fingers closed gently, and yet resolutely, on the Doctor's arm.

Neither her language nor her action had the slightest effect in inclining him to grant her request. The influence that instantly stopped him, on the way to his carriage, was the silent influence of her face. The startling contrast between the corpse-like pallor of her complexion and the overpowering life and light, the glittering metallic brightness in her large black eyes, held him literally spell-bound. She was dressed in dark colours, with perfect taste; she was of middle height, and (apparently) of middle age—say a year or two over thirty. Her lower features—the nose, mouth, and chin—possessed the fineness and delicacy of form which is oftener seen among women of foreign races than among women of English birth. She was unquestionably a handsome person—with the one serious drawback of her ghastly complexion, and with the less noticeable defect of a total want of tenderness in the expression of her eyes. Apart from his first emotion of surprise, the feeling she produced in the Doctor may be described as an overpowering feeling of professional curiosity. The case might prove to be something entirely new in his professional experience. 'It looks like it,' he thought; 'and it's worth waiting for.'

She perceived that she had produced a strong impression of some kind upon him, and dropped her hold on his arm.

'You have comforted many miserable women in your time,' she said. 'Comfort one more, to-day.'

Without waiting to be answered, she led the way back into the room.

The Doctor followed her, and closed the door. He placed her in the patients' chair, opposite the windows. Even in London the sun, on that summer afternoon, was dazzlingly bright. The radiant light flowed in on her. Her eyes met it unflinchingly, with the steely steadiness of the eyes of an eagle. The smooth pallor of her unwrinkled skin looked more fearfully white than ever. For the first time, for many a long year past, the Doctor felt his pulse quicken its beat in the presence of a patient.

Having possessed herself of his attention, she appeared, strangely enough, to have nothing to say to him. A curious apathy seemed to have taken possession of this resolute woman. Forced to speak first, the Doctor merely inquired, in the conventional phrase, what he could do for her.

The sound of his voice seemed to rouse her. Still looking straight at the light, she said abruptly: 'I have a painful question to ask.'

'What is it?'

Her eyes travelled slowly from the window to the Doctor's face. Without the slightest outward appearance of agitation, she put the 'painful question' in these extraordinary words:

'I want to know, if you please, whether I am in danger of going mad?'

Some men might have been amused, and some might have been alarmed. Doctor Wybrow was only conscious of a sense of disappointment. Was this the rare case that he had anticipated, judging rashly by appearances? Was the new patient only a hypochondriacal woman, whose malady was a disordered stomach and whose misfortune was a weak brain? 'Why do you come to me?' he asked sharply. 'Why don't you consult a doctor whose special employment is the treatment of the insane?'

She had her answer ready on the instant.

'I don't go to a doctor of that sort,' she said, 'for the very reason that he is a specialist: he has the fatal habit of judging everybody by lines and rules of his own laying down. I come to you, because my case is outside of all lines and rules, and because you are famous in your profession for the discovery of mysteries in disease. Are you satisfied?'

He was more than satisfied—his first idea had been the right idea, after all. Besides, she was correctly informed as to his professional position. The capacity which had raised him to fame and fortune was his capacity (unrivalled among his brethren) for the discovery of remote disease.

'I am at your disposal,' he answered. 'Let me try if I can find out what is the matter with you.'

He put his medical questions. They were promptly and plainly answered; and they led to no other conclusion than that the strange lady was, mentally and physically, in excellent health. Not satisfied with questions, he carefully examined the great organs of life. Neither his hand nor his stethoscope could discover anything that was amiss. With the admirable patience and devotion to his art which had distinguished him from the time when he was a student, he still subjected her to one test after another. The result was always the same. Not only was there no tendency to brain disease—there was not even a perceptible derangement of the nervous system. 'I can find nothing the matter with you,' he said. 'I can't even account for the extraordinary pallor of your complexion. You completely puzzle me.'

'The pallor of my complexion is nothing,' she answered a little impatiently. 'In my early life I had a narrow escape from death by poisoning. I have never had a complexion since—and my skin is so delicate, I cannot paint without producing a hideous rash. But that is of no importance. I wanted your opinion given positively. I believed in you, and you have disappointed me.' Her head dropped on her breast. 'And so it ends!' she said to herself bitterly.

The Doctor's sympathies were touched. Perhaps it might be more correct to say that his professional pride was a little hurt. 'It may end in the right way yet,' he remarked, 'if you choose to help me.'

She looked up again with flashing eyes, 'Speak plainly,' she said. 'How can I help you?'

'Plainly, madam, you come to me as an enigma, and you leave me to make the right guess by the unaided efforts of my art. My art will do much, but not all. For example, something must have occurred—something quite unconnected with the state of your bodily health—to frighten you about yourself, or you would never have come here to consult me. Is that true?'

She clasped her hands in her lap. 'That is true!' she said eagerly. 'I begin to believe in you again.'

'Very well. You can't expect me to find out the moral cause which has alarmed you. I can positively discover that there is no physical cause of alarm; and (unless you admit me to your confidence) I can do no more.'

She rose, and took a turn in the room. 'Suppose I tell you?' she said. 'But, mind, I shall mention no names!'

'There is no need to mention names. The facts are all I want.'

'The facts are nothing,' she rejoined. 'I have only my own impressions to confess—and you will very likely think me a fanciful fool when you hear what they are. No matter. I will do my best to content you—I will begin with the facts that you want. Take my word for it, they won't do much to help you.'

She sat down again. In the plainest possible words, she began the strangest and wildest confession that had ever reached the Doctor's ears.

II

'It is one fact, sir, that I am a widow,' she said. 'It is another fact, that I am going to be married again.'

There she paused, and smiled at some thought that occurred to her. Doctor Wybrow was not favourably impressed by her smile—there was something at once sad and cruel in it. It came slowly, and it went away suddenly. He began to doubt whether he had been wise in acting on his first impression. His mind reverted to the commonplace patients and the discoverable maladies that were waiting for him, with a certain tender regret.

The lady went on.

'My approaching marriage,' she said, 'has one embarrassing circumstance connected with it. The gentleman whose wife I am to be, was engaged to another lady when he happened to meet with me, abroad: that lady, mind, being of his own blood and family, related to him as his cousin. I have innocently robbed her of her lover, and destroyed her prospects in life. Innocently, I say—because he told me nothing of his engagement until after I had accepted him. When we next met in England—and when there was danger, no doubt, of the affair coming to my knowledge—he told me the truth. I was naturally indignant. He had his excuse ready; he showed me a letter from the lady herself, releasing him from his engagement. A more noble, a more high-minded letter, I never read in my life. I cried over it—I who have no tears in me for sorrows of my own! If the letter had left him any hope of being forgiven, I would have positively refused to marry him. But the firmness of it—without anger, without a word of reproach, with heartfelt wishes even for his happiness—the firmness of it, I say, left him no hope. He appealed to my compassion; he appealed to his love for me. You know what women are. I too was soft-hearted—I said, Very well: yes! In a week more (I tremble as I think of it) we are to be married.'

She did really tremble—she was obliged to pause and

compose herself, before she could go on. The Doctor, waiting for more facts, began to fear that he stood committed to a long story. 'Forgive me for reminding you that I have suffering persons waiting to see me,' he said. 'The sooner you can come to the point, the better for my patients and for me.'

The strange smile—at once so sad and so cruel—showed itself again on the lady's lips. 'Every word I have said is to the point,' she answered. 'You will see it yourself in a moment more.'

She resumed her narrative.

'Yesterday—you need fear no long story, sir; only yesterday—I was among the visitors at one of your English luncheon parties. A lady, a perfect stranger to me, came in late—after we had left the table, and had retired to the drawing-room. She happened to take a chair near me; and we were presented to each other. I knew her by name, as she knew me. It was the woman whom I had robbed of her lover, the woman who had written the noble letter. Now listen! You were impatient with me for not interesting you in what I said just now. I said it to satisfy your mind that I had no enmity of feeling towards the lady, on my side. I admired her, I felt for her—I had no cause to reproach myself. This is very important, as you will presently see. On her side, I have reason to be assured that the circumstances had been truly explained to her, and that she understood I was in no way to blame. Now, knowing all these necessary things as you do, explain to me, if you can, why, when I rose and met that woman's eyes looking at me, I turned cold from head to foot, and shuddered, and shivered, and knew what a deadly panic of fear was, for the first time in my life.'

The Doctor began to feel interested at last.

'Was there anything remarkable in the lady's personal appearance?' he asked.

'Nothing whatever!' was the vehement reply. 'Here is the true description of her:—The ordinary English lady; the clear cold blue eyes, the fine rosy complexion, the inanimately polite manner, the large good-humoured mouth, the too plump cheeks and chin: these, and nothing more.'

'Was there anything in her expression, when you first looked at her, that took you by surprise?'

'There was natural curiosity to see the woman who had been preferred to her; and perhaps some astonishment also, not to see a more engaging and more beautiful person; both those feelings restrained within the limits of good breeding, and both not lasting for more than a few moments—so far as I could see. I say, "so far," because the horrible agitation that she communicated to me disturbed my judgment. If I could have got to the door, I would have run out of the room, she frightened me so! I was not even able to stand up—I sank back in my chair; I stared horror-struck at the calm blue eyes that were only looking at me with a gentle surprise. To say they affected me like the eyes of a serpent is to say nothing. I felt her soul in them, looking into mine—looking, if such a thing can be, unconsciously to her own mortal self. I tell you my impression, in all its horror and in all its folly! That woman is destined (without knowing it herself) to be the evil genius of my life. Her innocent eyes saw hidden capabilities of wickedness in me that I was not aware of myself, until I felt them stirring under her look. If I commit faults in my life to come—if I am even guilty of crimes—she will bring the retribution, without (as I firmly believe) any conscious exercise of her own will. In one indescribable moment I felt all this—and I suppose my face showed it. The good artless creature was inspired by a sort of gentle alarm for me. "I am afraid the heat of the room is too much for you; will you try my smelling bottle?" I heard her say those kind words; and I remember nothing else—I fainted. When I recovered my senses, the company had all gone; only the lady of the house was with me. For the moment I could say nothing to her; the dreadful impression that I have tried to describe to you came back to me with the coming back of my life. As soon I could speak, I implored her to tell me the whole truth about the woman whom I had supplanted. You see, I had a faint hope that her good character might not really be deserved, that her noble letter was a skilful piece of hypocrisy—in short, that she secretly hated me, and was cunning enough to hide it. No! the lady had been her friend from her girlhood, was as familiar with her as if they had been sisters—knew her positively to be as good, as innocent, as incapable of hating anybody, as the greatest saint that ever lived. My one last hope, that I had only felt an ordinary forewarning of danger in the presence of an ordinary enemy, was a hope destroyed for ever. There was one more effort I could make, and I made it. I went next to the man whom I am to marry. I implored him to release me from my promise. He refused. I declared I would break my engagement. He showed me letters from his sisters, letters from his brothers, and his dear friends—all entreating him to think again before he made me his wife; all repeating reports of me in Paris, Vienna, and London, which are so many vile lies. "If you refuse to marry me," he said, "you admit that these reports are true—you admit that you are afraid to face society in the character of my wife." What could I answer? There was no contradicting him—he was plainly right: if I persisted in my refusal, the utter destruction of my reputation would be the result. I consented to let the wedding take place as we had arranged it—and left him. The night has passed. I am here, with my fixed conviction—that innocent woman is ordained to have a fatal influence over my life. I am here with my one question to put, to the one man who can answer it. For the last time, sir, what am I—a demon who has seen the avenging angel? or only a poor mad woman, misled by the delusion of a deranged mind?'

Doctor Wybrow rose from his chair, determined to close the interview.

He was strongly and painfully impressed by what he had heard. The longer he had listened to her, the more irresistibly the conviction of the woman's wickedness had forced itself on him. He tried vainly to think of her as a person to be pitied—a person with a morbidly sensitive imagination, conscious of the capacities for evil which lie dormant in us all, and striving earnestly to open her heart to the counter-influence of her own better nature; the effort was beyond him. A perverse instinct in him said, as if in words, Beware how you believe in her!

'I have already given you my opinion,' he said. 'There is no sign of your intellect being deranged, or being likely to be deranged, that medical science can discover—as I understand it. As for the impressions you have confided to me, I can only say that yours is a case (as I venture to think) for spiritual rather than for medical advice. Of one thing be assured: what you have said to me in this room shall not pass out of it. Your confession is safe in my keeping.'

She heard him, with a certain dogged resignation, to the end.

'Is that all?' she asked.

'That is all,' he answered.

She put a little paper packet of money on the table. 'Thank you, sir. There is your fee.'

With those words she rose. Her wild black eyes looked upward, with an expression of despair so defiant and so horrible in its silent agony that the Doctor turned away his head, unable to endure the sight of it. The bare idea of taking anything from her—not money only, but anything even that she had touched—suddenly revolted him. Still without looking at her, he said, 'Take it back; I don't want my fee.'

She neither heeded nor heard him. Still looking upward, she said slowly to herself, 'Let the end come. I have done with the struggle: I submit.'

She drew her veil over her face, bowed to the Doctor, and left the room.

He rang the bell, and followed her into the hall. As the servant closed the door on her, a sudden impulse of curiosity—utterly unworthy of him, and at the same time utterly irresistible—sprang up in the Doctor's mind. Blushing like a boy, he said to the servant, 'Follow her home, and find out her name.' For one moment the man looked at his master, doubting if his own ears had not deceived him. Doctor Wybrow looked back at him in silence. The submissive servant knew what that silence meant—he took his hat and hurried into the street.

The Doctor went back to the consulting-room. A sudden revulsion of feeling swept over his mind. Had the woman left an infection of wickedness in the house, and had he caught it? What devil had possessed him to degrade himself in the eyes of his own servant? He had behaved infamously—he had asked an honest man, a man who had served him faithfully for years, to turn spy! Stung by the bare thought of it, he ran out into the hall again, and opened the door. The servant had disappeared; it was too late to call him back. But one refuge from his contempt for himself was now open to him—the refuge of work. He got into his carriage and went his rounds among his patients.

If the famous physician could have shaken his own reputation, he would have done it that afternoon. Never before had he made himself so little welcome at the bedside. Never before had he put off until to-morrow the prescription which ought to have been written, the opinion which ought to have been given, to-day. He went home earlier than usual—

unutterably dissatisfied with himself.

The servant had returned. Dr. Wybrow was ashamed to question him. The man reported the result of his errand, without waiting to be asked.

'The lady's name is the Countess Narona. She lives at—'

Without waiting to hear where she lived, the Doctor acknowledged the all-important discovery of her name by a silent bend of the head, and entered his consulting-room. The fee that he had vainly refused still lay in its little white paper covering on the table. He sealed it up in an envelope; addressed it to the 'Poor-box' of the nearest police-court; and, calling the servant in, directed him to take it to the magistrate the next morning. Faithful to his duties, the servant waited to ask the customary question, 'Do you dine at home to-day, sir?'

After a moment's hesitation he said, 'No: I shall dine at the club.'

The most easily deteriorated of all the moral qualities is the quality called 'conscience.' In one state of a man's mind, his conscience is the severest judge that can pass sentence on him. In another state, he and his conscience are on the best possible terms with each other in the comfortable capacity of accomplices. When Doctor Wybrow left his house for the second time, he did not even attempt to conceal from himself that his sole object, in dining at the club, was to hear what the world said of the Countess Narona.

III

There was a time when a man in search of the pleasures of gossip sought the society of ladies. The man knows better now. He goes to the smoking-room of his club.

Doctor Wybrow lit his cigar, and looked round him at his brethren in social conclave assembled. The room was well filled; but the flow of talk was still languid. The Doctor innocently applied the stimulant that was wanted. When he inquired if anybody knew the Countess Narona, he was answered by something like a shout of astonishment. Never (the conclave agreed) had such an absurd question been asked before! Every human creature, with the slightest claim to a place in society, knew the Countess Narona. An adventuress with a European reputation of the blackest possible colour—such was the general description of the woman with the deathlike complexion and the glittering eyes.

Descending to particulars, each member of the club contributed his own little stock of scandal to the memoirs of the Countess. It was doubtful whether she was really, what she called herself, a Dalmatian lady. It was doubtful whether she had ever been married to the Count whose widow she assumed to be. It was doubtful whether the man who accompanied her in her travels (under the name of Baron Rivar, and in the character of her brother) was her brother at all. Report pointed to the Baron as a gambler at every 'table' on the Continent. Report whispered that his so-called sister had narrowly escaped being implicated in a famous trial for poisoning at Vienna—that she had been known at Milan as a spy in the interests of Austria—that her 'apartment' in Paris had been denounced to the police as nothing less than a private gambling-house—and that her present appearance in England was the natural result of the discovery. Only one member of the assembly in the smoking-room took the part of this much-abused woman, and declared that her character had been most cruelly and most unjustly assailed. But as the man was a lawyer, his interference went for nothing: it was naturally attributed to the spirit of contradiction inherent in his profession. He was asked derisively what he thought of the circumstances under which the Countess had become engaged to be married; and he made the characteristic answer, that he thought the circumstances highly creditable to both parties, and that he looked on the lady's future husband as a most enviable man.

Hearing this, the Doctor raised another shout of astonishment by inquiring the name of the gentleman whom the Countess was about to marry.

His friends in the smoking-room decided unanimously that the celebrated physician must be a second 'Rip-van-Winkle,' and that he had just awakened from a supernatural sleep of twenty years. It was all very well to say that he was devoted to his profession, and that he had neither time nor inclination to pick up fragments of gossip at dinner-parties and balls. A man who did not know that the Countess Narona had borrowed money at Homburg of no less a person than Lord Montbarry, and had then deluded him into making her a proposal of marriage, was a man who had probably never heard of Lord Montbarry himself. The younger members of the club, humouring the joke, sent a waiter for the 'Peerage'; and read aloud the memoir of the nobleman in question, for the Doctor's benefit—with illustrative morsels of information interpolated by themselves.

'Herbert John Westwick. First Baron Montbarry, of Montbarry, King's County, Ireland. Created a Peer for distinguished military services in India. Born, 1812. Forty-eight years old, Doctor, at the present time. Not married. Will be married next week, Doctor, to the delightful creature we have been talking about. Heir presumptive, his lordship's next brother, Stephen Robert, married to Ella, youngest daughter of the Reverend Silas Marden, Rector of Runnigate, and has issue, three daughters. Younger brothers of his lordship, Francis and Henry, unmarried. Sisters of his lordship, Lady Barville, married to Sir Theodore Barville, Bart.; and Anne, widow of the late Peter Norbury, Esq., of Norbury Cross. Bear his lordship's relations well in mind, Doctor. Three brothers Westwick, Stephen, Francis, and Henry; and two sisters, Lady Barville and Mrs. Norbury. Not one of the five will be present at the marriage; and not one of the five will leave a stone unturned to stop it, if the Countess will only give them a chance. Add to these hostile members of the family another offended relative not mentioned in the 'Peerage,' a young lady—'

A sudden outburst of protest in more than one part of the room stopped the coming disclosure, and released the Doctor from further persecution.

'Don't mention the poor girl's name; it's too bad to make a joke of that part of the business; she has behaved nobly under shameful provocation; there is but one excuse for Montbarry—he is either a madman or a fool.' In these terms the protest expressed itself on all sides. Speaking confidentially to his next neighbour, the Doctor discovered that the lady referred to was already known to him (through the Countess's confession) as the lady deserted by Lord Montbarry. Her name was Agnes Lockwood. She was described as being the superior of the Countess in personal attraction, and as being also by some years the younger woman of the two. Making all allowance for the follies that men committed every day in their relations with women, Montbarry's delusion was still the most monstrous delusion on record. In this expression of opinion every man present agreed—the lawyer even included. Not one of them could call to mind the innumerable instances in which the sexual influence has proved irresistible in the persons of women without even the pretension to beauty. The very members of the club whom the Countess (in spite of her personal disadvantages) could have most easily fascinated, if she had thought it worth her while, were the members who wondered most loudly at Montbarry's choice of a wife.

While the topic of the Countess's marriage was still the one topic of conversation, a member of the club entered the smoking-room whose appearance instantly produced a dead silence. Doctor Wybrow's next neighbour whispered to him, 'Montbarry's brother—Henry Westwick!'

The new-comer looked round him slowly, with a bitter smile.

'You are all talking of my brother,' he said. 'Don't mind me. Not one of you can despise him more heartily than I do. Go on, gentlemen—go on!'

But one man present took the speaker at his word. That man was the lawyer who had already undertaken the defence of the Countess.

'I stand alone in my opinion,' he said, 'and I am not ashamed of repeating it in anybody's hearing. I consider the Countess Narona to be a cruelly-treated woman. Why shouldn't she be Lord Montbarry's wife? Who can say she has a mercenary motive in marrying him?'

Montbarry's brother turned sharply on the speaker. 'I say it!' he answered.

The reply might have shaken some men. The lawyer stood on his ground as firmly as ever.

'I believe I am right,' he rejoined, 'in stating that his lordship's income is not more than sufficient to support his station in life; also that it is an income derived almost entirely from landed property in Ireland, every acre of which is entailed.'

Montbarry's brother made a sign, admitting that he had no objection to offer so far.

'If his lordship dies first,' the lawyer proceeded, 'I have been informed that the only provision he can make for his widow consists in a rent-charge on the property of no more than four hundred a year. His retiring pension and allowances, it is well known, die with him. Four hundred a year is therefore all that he can leave to the Countess, if he leaves her a widow.'

'Four hundred a year is not all,' was the reply to this. 'My brother has insured his life for ten thousand pounds; and he has settled the whole of it on the Countess, in the event of his death.'

This announcement produced a strong sensation. Men looked at each other, and repeated the three startling words, 'Ten thousand pounds!' Driven fairly to the wall, the lawyer made a last effort to defend his position.

'May I ask who made that settlement a condition of the marriage?' he said. 'Surely it was not the Countess herself?.'

Henry Westwick answered, 'It was the Countess's brother'; and added, 'which comes to the same thing.'

After that, there was no more to be said—so long, at least, as Montbarry's brother was present. The talk flowed into other channels; and the Doctor went home.

But his morbid curiosity about the Countess was not set at rest yet. In his leisure moments he found himself wondering whether Lord Montbarry's family would succeed in stopping the marriage after all. And more than this, he was conscious of a growing desire to see the infatuated man himself. Every day during the brief interval before the wedding, he looked in at the club, on the chance of hearing some news. Nothing had happened, so far as the club knew. The Countess's position was secure; Montbarry's resolution to be her husband was unshaken. They were both Roman Catholics, and they were to be married at the —el in Spanish Place. So much the Doctor discovered about them—and no more.

On the day of the wedding, after a feeble struggle with himself, he actually sacrificed his patients and their guineas, and slipped away secretly to see the marriage. To the end of his life, he was angry with anybody who reminded him of what he had done on that day!

The wedding was strictly private. A close carriage stood at the church door; a few people, mostly of the lower class, and mostly old women, were scattered about the interior of the building. Here and there Doctor Wybrow detected the faces of some of his brethren of the club, attracted by curiosity, like himself. Four persons only stood before the altar—the bride and bridegroom and their two witnesses. One of these last was an elderly woman, who might have been the Countess's companion or maid; the other was undoubtedly her brother, Baron Rivar. The bridal party (the bride herself included) wore their ordinary morning costume. Lord Montbarry, personally viewed, was a middle-aged military man of the ordinary type: nothing in the least remarkable distinguished him either in face or figure. Baron Rivar, again, in his way was another conventional representative of another well-known type. One sees his finely-pointed moustache, his bold eyes, his crisply-curling hair, and his dashing carriage of the head, repeated hundreds of times over on the Boulevards of Paris. The only noteworthy point about him was of the negative sort—he was not in the least like his sister. Even the officiating priest was only a harmless, humble-looking old man, who went through his duties resignedly, and felt visible rheumatic difficulties every time he bent his knees. The one remarkable person, the Countess herself, only raised her veil at the beginning of the ceremony, and presented nothing in her plain dress that was worth a second look. Never, on the face of it, was there a less interesting and less romantic marriage than this. From time to time the Doctor glanced round at the door or up at the galleries, vaguely anticipating the appearance of some protesting stranger, in possession of some terrible secret, commissioned to forbid the progress of the service. Nothing in the shape of an event occurred—nothing extraordinary, nothing dramatic. Bound fast together as man and wife, the two disappeared, followed by their witnesses, to sign the registers; and still Doctor Wybrow waited, and still he cherished the obstinate hope that something worth seeing must certainly happen yet.

The interval passed, and the married couple, returning to the church, walked together down the nave to the door. Doctor Wybrow drew back as they approached. To his confusion and surprise, the Countess discovered him. He heard her say to her husband, 'One moment; I see a friend.' Lord Montbarry bowed and waited. She stepped up to the Doctor, took his hand, and wrung it hard. He felt her overpowering black eyes looking at him through her veil. 'One step more, you see, on the way to the end!' She whispered those strange words, and returned to her husband. Before the Doctor could recover himself and follow her, Lord and Lady Montbarry had stepped into their carriage, and had driven away.

Outside the church door stood the three or four members of the club who, like Doctor Wybrow, had watched the ceremony out of curiosity. Near them was the bride's brother, waiting alone. He was evidently bent on seeing the man whom his sister had spoken to, in broad daylight. His bold eyes rested on the Doctor's face, with a momentary flash of suspicion in them. The cloud suddenly cleared away; the Baron smiled with charming courtesy, lifted his hat to his sister's friend, and walked off.

The members constituted themselves into a club conclave on the church steps. They began with the Baron. 'Damned ill-looking rascal!' They went on with Montbarry. 'Is he going to take that horrid woman with him to Ireland?' 'Not he! he can't face the tenantry; they know about Agnes Lockwood.' 'Well, but where is he going?' 'To Scotland.' 'Does she like that?' 'It's only for a fortnight; they come back to London, and go abroad.' 'And they will never return to England, eh?' 'Who can tell? Did you see how she looked at Montbarry, when she had to lift her veil at the beginning of the service? In his place, I should have bolted. Did you see her, Doctor?' By this time, Doctor Wybrow had remembered his patients, and had heard enough of the club gossip. He followed the example of Baron Rivar, and walked off.

'One step more, you see, on the way to the end,' he repeated to himself, on his way home. 'What end?'

IV

On the day of the marriage Agnes Lockwood sat alone in the little drawing-room of her London lodgings, burning the letters which had been written to her by Montbarry in the bygone time.

The Countess's maliciously smart description of her, addressed to Doctor Wybrow, had not even hinted at the charm that most distinguished Agnes—the artless expression of goodness and purity which instantly attracted everyone who approached her. She looked by many years younger than she really was. With her fair complexion and her shy manner, it seemed only natural to speak of her as 'a girl,' although she was now really advancing towards thirty years of age. She lived alone with an old nurse devoted to her, on a modest little income which was just enough to support the two. There were none of the ordinary signs of grief in her face, as she slowly tore the letters of her false lover in two, and threw the pieces into the small fire which had been lit to consume them. Unhappily for herself, she was one of those women who feel too deeply to find relief in tears. Pale and quiet, with cold trembling fingers, she destroyed the letters one by one without daring to read them again. She had torn the last of the series, and was still shrinking from throwing it after the rest into the swiftly destroying flame, when the old nurse came in, and asked if she would see 'Master Henry,'—meaning that youngest member of the Westwick family, who had publicly declared his contempt for his brother in the smoking-room of the club.

Agnes hesitated. A faint tinge of colour stole over her face.

There had been a long past time when Henry Westwick had owned that he loved her. She had made her confession to him, acknowledging that her heart was given to his eldest brother. He had submitted to his disappointment; and they had met thenceforth as cousins and friends. Never before had she associated the idea of him with embarrassing recollections. But now, on the very day when his brother's marriage to another woman had consummated his brother's treason towards her, there was something vaguely repellent in the prospect of seeing him. The old nurse (who remembered them both in their cradles) observed her hesitation; and sympathising of course with the man, put in a timely word for Henry. 'He says, he's going away, my dear; and he only wants to shake hands, and say good-bye.' This plain statement of the case had its effect. Agnes decided on receiving her cousin.

He entered the room so rapidly that he surprised her in the act of throwing the fragments of Montbarry's last letter into the fire. She hurriedly spoke first.

'You are leaving London very suddenly, Henry. Is it business? or pleasure?'

Instead of answering her, he pointed to the flaming letter, and to some black ashes of burnt paper lying lightly in the lower part of the fireplace.

'Are you burning letters?'

'Yes.'

'His letters?'

'Yes.'

He took her hand gently. 'I had no idea I was intruding on you, at a time when you must wish to be alone. Forgive me, Agnes—I shall see you when I return.'

She signed to him, with a faint smile, to take a chair.

'We have known one another since we were children,' she said. 'Why should I feel a foolish pride about myself in your presence? why should I have any secrets from you? I sent back all your brother's gifts to me some time ago. I have been advised to do more, to keep nothing that can remind me of him—in short, to burn his letters. I have taken the advice; but I own I shrank a little from destroying the last of the letters. No—not because it was the last, but because it had this in it.' She opened her hand, and showed him a lock of Montbarry's hair, tied with a morsel of golden cord. 'Well! well! let it go with the rest.'

She dropped it into the flame. For a while, she stood with her back to Henry, leaning on the mantel-piece, and looking into the fire. He took the chair to which she had pointed, with a strange contradiction of expression in his face: the tears were in his eyes, while the brows above were knit close in an angry frown. He muttered to himself, 'Damn him!'

She rallied her courage, and looked at him again when she spoke. 'Well, Henry, and why are you going away?'

'I am out of spirits, Agnes, and I want a change.'

She paused before she spoke again. His face told her plainly that he was thinking of her when he made that reply. She was grateful to him, but her mind was not with him: her mind was still with the man who had deserted her. She turned round again to the fire.

'Is it true,' she asked, after a long silence, 'that they have been married to-day?'

He answered ungraciously in the one necessary word:—'Yes.'

'Did you go to the church?'

He resented the question with an expression of indignant surprise. 'Go to the church?' he repeated. 'I would as soon go to—' He checked himself there. 'How can you ask?' he added in lower tones. 'I have never spoken to Montbarry, I have not even seen him, since he treated you like the scoundrel and the fool that he is.'

She looked at him suddenly, without saying a word. He understood her, and begged her pardon. But he was still angry. 'The reckoning comes to some men,' he said, 'even in this world. He will live to rue the day when he married that woman!'

Agnes took a chair by his side, and looked at him with a gentle surprise.

'Is it quite reasonable to be so angry with her, because your brother preferred her to me?' she asked.

Henry turned on her sharply. 'Do you defend the Countess, of all the people in the world?'

'Why not?' Agnes answered. 'I know nothing against her. On the only occasion when we met, she appeared to be a singularly timid, nervous person, looking dreadfully ill; and being indeed so ill that she fainted under the heat of my room. Why should we not do her justice? We know that she was innocent of any intention to wrong me; we know that she was not aware of my engagement—'

Henry lifted his hand impatiently, and stopped her. 'There is such a thing as being too just and too forgiving!' he interposed. 'I can't bear to hear you talk in that patient way, after the scandalously cruel manner in which you have been treated. Try to forget them both, Agnes. I wish to God I could help you to do it!'

Agnes laid her hand on his arm. 'You are very good to me, Henry; but you don't quite understand me. I was thinking of myself and my trouble in quite a different way, when you came in. I was wondering whether anything which has so entirely filled my heart, and so absorbed all that is best and truest in me, as my feeling for your brother, can really pass away as if it had never existed. I have destroyed the last visible things that remind me of him. In this world I shall see him no more. But is the tie that once bound us, completely broken? Am I as entirely parted from the good and evil fortune of his life as if we had never met and never loved? What do you think, Henry? I can hardly believe it.'

'If you could bring the retribution on him that he has deserved,' Henry Westwick answered sternly, 'I might be inclined to agree with you.'

As that reply passed his lips, the old nurse appeared again at the door, announcing another visitor.

'I'm sorry to disturb you, my dear. But here is little Mrs. Ferrari wanting to know when she may say a few words to you.'

Agnes turned to Henry, before she replied. 'You remember Emily Bidwell, my favourite pupil years ago at the village school, and afterwards my maid? She left me, to marry an Italian courier, named Ferrari—and I am afraid it has not turned out very well. Do you mind my having her in here for a minute or two?'

Henry rose to take his leave. 'I should be glad to see Emily again at any other time,' he said. 'But it is best that I should go now. My mind is disturbed, Agnes; I might say things to you, if I stayed here any longer, which—which are better not said now. I shall cross the Channel by the mail to-night, and see how a few weeks' change will help me.' He took her hand. 'Is there anything in the world that I can do for you?' he asked very earnestly. She thanked him, and tried to release her hand. He held it with a tremulous lingering grasp. 'God bless you, Agnes!' he said in faltering tones, with his eyes on the ground. Her face flushed again, and the next instant turned paler than ever; she knew his heart as well as he knew it himself—she was too distressed to speak. He lifted her hand to his lips, kissed it fervently, and, without looking at her again, left the room. The nurse hobbled after him to the head of the stairs: she had not forgotten the time when the younger brother had been the unsuccessful rival of the elder for the hand of Agnes. 'Don't be down-hearted, Master Henry,' whispered the old woman, with the unscrupulous common sense of persons in the lower rank of life. 'Try her again, when you come back!'

Left alone for a few moments, Agnes took a turn in the room, trying to compose herself. She paused before a little water-colour drawing on the wall, which had belonged to her mother: it was her own portrait when she was a child. 'How much happier we should be,' she thought to herself sadly, 'if we never grew up!'

The courier's wife was shown in—a little meek melancholy woman, with white eyelashes, and watery eyes, who curtseyed deferentially and was troubled with a small chronic cough. Agnes shook hands with her kindly. 'Well, Emily, what can I do for you?'

The courier's wife made rather a strange answer: 'I'm afraid to tell you, Miss.'

'Is it such a very difficult favour to grant? Sit down, and let me hear how you are going on. Perhaps the petition will slip out while we are talking. How does your husband behave to you?'

Emily's light grey eyes looked more watery than ever. She shook her head and sighed resignedly. 'I have no positive complaint to make against him, Miss. But I'm afraid he doesn't care about me; and he seems to take no interest in his home—I may almost say he's tired of his home. It might be better for both of us, Miss, if he went travelling for a while—not to mention the money, which is beginning to be wanted sadly.' She put her handkerchief to her eyes, and sighed again more resignedly than ever.

'I don't quite understand,' said Agnes. 'I thought your husband had an engagement to take some ladies to Switzerland and Italy?'

'That was his ill-luck, Miss. One of the ladies fell ill—and the others wouldn't go without her. They paid him a month's salary as compensation. But they had engaged him for the autumn and winter—and the loss is serious.'

'I am sorry to hear it, Emily. Let us hope he will soon have another chance.'

'It's not his turn, Miss, to be recommended when the next applications come to the couriers' office. You see, there are so many of them out of employment just now. If he could be privately recommended—' She stopped, and left the unfinished sentence to speak for itself.

Agnes understood her directly. 'You want my recommendation,' she rejoined. 'Why couldn't you say so at once?'

Emily blushed. 'It would be such a chance for my husband,' she answered confusedly. 'A letter, inquiring for a good courier (a six months' engagement, Miss!) came to the office this morning. It's another man's turn to be chosen—and the secretary will recommend him. If my husband could only send his testimonials by the same post—with just a word in your name, Miss—it might turn the scale, as they say. A private recommendation between gentlefolks goes so far.' She stopped again, and sighed again, and looked down at the carpet, as if she had some private reason for feeling a little ashamed of herself.

Agnes began to be rather weary of the persistent tone of mystery in which her visitor spoke. 'If you want my interest with any friend of mine,' she said, 'why can't you tell me the name?'

The courier's wife began to cry. 'I'm ashamed to tell you, Miss.'

For the first time, Agnes spoke sharply. 'Nonsense, Emily! Tell me the name directly—or drop the subject—whichever you like best.'

Emily made a last desperate effort. She wrung her handkerchief hard in her lap, and let off the name as if she had been letting off a loaded gun:—'Lord Montbarry!'

Agnes rose and looked at her.

'You have disappointed me,' she said very quietly, but with a look which the courier's wife had never seen in her face before. 'Knowing what you know, you ought to be aware that it is impossible for me to communicate with Lord Montbarry. I always supposed you had some delicacy of feeling. I am sorry to find that I have been mistaken.'

Weak as she was, Emily had spirit enough to feel the reproof. She walked in her meek noiseless way to the door. 'I beg your pardon, Miss. I am not quite so bad as you think me. But I beg your pardon, all the same.'

She opened the door. Agnes called her back. There was something in the woman's apology that appealed irresistibly to her just and generous nature. 'Come,' she said; 'we must not part in this way. Let me not misunderstand you. What is it that you expected me to do?'

Emily was wise enough to answer this time without any reserve. 'My husband will send his testimonials, Miss, to Lord Montbarry in Scotland. I only wanted you to let him say in his letter that his wife has been known to you since she was a child, and that you feel some little interest in his welfare on that account. I don't ask it now, Miss. You have made me understand that I was wrong.'

Had she really been wrong? Past remembrances, as well as present troubles, pleaded powerfully with Agnes for the courier's wife. 'It seems only a small favour to ask,' she said, speaking under the impulse of kindness which was the strongest impulse in her nature. 'But I am not sure that I ought to allow my name to be mentioned in your husband's letter. Let me hear again exactly what he wishes to say.' Emily repeated the words—and then offered one of those suggestions, which have a special value of their own to persons unaccustomed to the use of their pens. 'Suppose you try, Miss, how it looks in writing?' Childish as the idea was, Agnes tried the experiment. 'If I let you mention me,' she said, 'we must at least decide what you are to say.' She wrote the words in the briefest and plainest form:—'I venture to state that my wife has been known from her childhood to Miss Agnes Lockwood, who feels some little interest in my welfare on that account.' Reduced to this one sentence, there was surely nothing in the reference to her name which implied that Agnes had permitted it, or that she was even aware of it. After a last struggle with herself, she handed the written paper to Emily. 'Your husband must copy it exactly, without altering anything,' she stipulated. 'On that condition, I grant your request.' Emily was not only thankful—she was really touched. Agnes hurried the little woman out of the room. 'Don't give me time to repent and take it back again,' she said. Emily vanished.

'Is the tie that once bound us completely broken? Am I as entirely parted from the good and evil fortune of his life as if we had never met and never loved?' Agnes looked at the clock on the mantel-piece. Not ten minutes since, those serious questions had been on her lips. It almost shocked her to think of the common-place manner in which they had already met with their reply. The mail of that night would appeal once more to Montbarry's remembrance of her—in the choice of a servant.

Two days later, the post brought a few grateful lines from Emily. Her husband had got the place. Ferrari was engaged, for six months certain, as Lord Montbarry's courier.

THE SECOND PART

V

After only one week of travelling in Scotland, my lord and my lady returned unexpectedly to London. Introduced to the mountains and lakes of the Highlands, her ladyship positively declined to improve her acquaintance with them. When she was asked for her reason, she answered with a Roman brevity, 'I have seen Switzerland.'

For a week more, the newly-married couple remained in London, in the strictest retirement. On one day in that week the nurse returned in a state of most uncustomary excitement from an errand on which Agnes had sent her. Passing the door of a fashionable dentist, she had met Lord Montbarry himself just leaving the house. The good woman's report described him, with malicious pleasure, as looking wretchedly ill. 'His cheeks are getting hollow, my dear, and his beard is turning grey. I hope the dentist hurt him!'

Knowing how heartily her faithful old servant hated the man who had deserted her, Agnes made due allowance for a large infusion of exaggeration in the picture presented to her. The main impression produced on her mind was an impression of nervous uneasiness. If she trusted herself in the streets by daylight while Lord Montbarry remained in London, how could she be sure that his next chance-meeting might not be a meeting with herself? She waited at home, privately ashamed of her own undignified conduct, for the next two days. On the third day the fashionable intelligence of the newspapers announced the departure of Lord and Lady Montbarry for Paris, on their way to Italy.

Mrs. Ferrari, calling the same evening, informed Agnes that her husband had left her with all reasonable expression of conjugal kindness; his temper being improved by the prospect of going abroad. But one other servant accompanied the travellers—Lady Montbarry's maid, rather a silent, unsociable woman, so far as Emily had heard. Her ladyship's brother, Baron Rivar, was already on the Continent. It had been arranged that he was to meet his sister and her husband at Rome.

One by one the dull weeks succeeded each other in the life of Agnes. She faced her position with admirable courage, seeing her friends, keeping herself occupied in her leisure hours with reading and drawing, leaving no means untried of diverting her mind from the melancholy remembrance of the past. But she had loved too faithfully, she had been wounded too deeply, to feel in any adequate degree the influence of the moral remedies which she employed. Persons who met with her in the ordinary relations of life, deceived by her outward serenity of manner, agreed that 'Miss Lockwood seemed to be getting over her disappointment.' But an old friend and school companion who happened to see her during a brief visit to London, was inexpressibly distressed by the change that she detected in Agnes. This lady was Mrs. Westwick, the wife of that brother of Lord Montbarry who came next to him in age, and who was described in the 'Peerage' as presumptive heir to the title. He was then away, looking after his interests in some mining property which he possessed in America. Mrs. Westwick insisted on taking Agnes back with her to her home in Ireland. 'Come and keep me company while my husband is away. My three little girls will make you their playfellow, and the only stranger you will meet is the governess, whom I answer for your liking beforehand. Pack up your things, and I will call for you to-morrow on my way to the train.' In those hearty terms the invitation was given. Agnes thankfully accepted it. For three happy months she lived under the roof of her friend. The girls hung round her in tears at her departure; the youngest of them wanted to go back with Agnes to London. Half in jest, half in earnest, she said to her old friend at parting, 'If your governess leaves you, keep the place open for me.' Mrs. Westwick laughed. The wiser children took it seriously, and promised to let Agnes know.

On the very day when Miss Lockwood returned to London, she was recalled to those associations with the past which she was most anxious to forget. After the first kissings and greetings were over, the old nurse (who had been left in charge at the lodgings) had some startling information to communicate, derived from the courier's wife.

'Here has been little Mrs. Ferrari, my dear, in a dreadful state of mind, inquiring when you would be back. Her husband has left Lord Montbarry, without a word of warning—and nobody knows what has become of him.'

Agnes looked at her in astonishment. 'Are you sure of what you are saying?' she asked.

The nurse was quite sure. 'Why, Lord bless you! the news comes from the couriers' office in Golden Square—from the secretary, Miss Agnes, the secretary himself!' Hearing this, Agnes began to feel alarmed as well as surprised. It was still early in the evening. She at once sent a message to Mrs. Ferrari, to say that she had returned.

In an hour more the courier's wife appeared, in a state of agitation which it was not easy to control. Her narrative, when she was at last able to speak connectedly, entirely confirmed the nurse's report of it.

After hearing from her husband with tolerable regularity from Paris, Rome, and Venice, Emily had twice written to him afterwards—and had received no reply. Feeling uneasy, she had gone to the office in Golden Square, to inquire if he had been heard of there. The post of the morning had brought a letter to the secretary from a courier then at Venice. It contained startling news of Ferrari. His wife had been allowed to take a copy of it, which she now handed to Agnes to read.

The writer stated that he had recently arrived in Venice. He had previously heard that Ferrari was with Lord and Lady Montbarry, at one of the old Venetian palaces which they had hired for a term. Being a friend of Ferrari, he had gone to pay him a visit. Ringing at the door that opened on the canal, and failing to make anyone hear him, he had gone round to a side entrance opening on one of the narrow lanes of Venice. Here, standing at the door (as if she was waiting for him to try that way next), he found a pale woman with magnificent dark eyes, who proved to be no other than Lady Montbarry herself.

She asked, in Italian, what he wanted. He answered that he wanted to see the courier Ferrari, if it was quite convenient. She at once informed him that Ferrari had left the palace, without assigning any reason, and without even leaving an address at which his monthly salary (then due to him) could be paid. Amazed at this reply, the courier inquired if any person had offended Ferrari, or quarrelled with him. The lady answered, 'To my knowledge, certainly not. I am Lady Montbarry; and I can positively assure you that Ferrari was treated with the greatest kindness in this house. We are as much astonished as you are at his extraordinary disappearance. If you should hear of him, pray let us know, so that we may at least pay him the money which is due.'

After one or two more questions (quite readily answered) relating to the date and the time of day at which Ferrari had left the palace, the courier took his leave.

He at once entered on the necessary investigations—without the slightest result so far as Ferrari was concerned. Nobody had seen him. Nobody appeared to have been taken into his confidence. Nobody knew anything (that is to say, anything of the slightest importance) even about persons so distinguished as Lord and Lady Montbarry. It was reported that her ladyship's English maid had left her, before the disappearance of Ferrari, to return to her relatives in her own country, and that Lady Montbarry had taken no steps to supply her place. His lordship was described as being in delicate health. He lived in the strictest retirement—nobody was admitted to him, not even his own countrymen. A stupid old woman was discovered who did the housework at the palace, arriving in the morning and going away again at night. She had never seen the lost courier—she had never even seen Lord Montbarry, who was then confined to his room. Her ladyship, 'a most gracious and adorable mistress,' was in constant attendance on her noble husband. There was no other servant then in the house (so far as the old woman knew) but herself. The meals were sent in from a restaurant. My lord, it was said, disliked strangers. My lord's brother-in-law, the Baron, was generally shut up in a remote part of the palace, occupied (the gracious mistress said) with experiments in chemistry. The experiments sometimes made a nasty smell. A doctor had latterly been called in to his lordship—an Italian doctor, long resident in Venice. Inquiries being addressed to this gentleman (a physician of undoubted capacity and respectability), it turned out that he also had never seen Ferrari, having been summoned to the palace (as his memorandum book showed) at a date subsequent to the courier's disappearance. The doctor described Lord Montbarry's malady as bronchitis. So far, there was no reason to feel any anxiety, though the attack was a sharp one. If alarming symptoms should appear, he had arranged with her ladyship to call in another physician. For the rest, it was impossible to speak too highly of my lady; night and day, she was at her lord's bedside.

With these particulars began and ended the discoveries made by Ferrari's courier-friend. The police were on the look-out for the lost man—and that was the only hope which could be held forth for the present, to Ferrari's wife.

'What do you think of it, Miss?' the poor woman asked eagerly. 'What would you advise me to do?'

Agnes was at a loss how to answer her; it was an effort even to listen to what Emily was saying. The references in the courier's letter to Montbarry—the report of his illness, the melancholy picture of his secluded life—had reopened the old wound. She was not even thinking of the lost Ferrari; her mind was at Venice, by the sick man's bedside.

'I hardly know what to say,' she answered. 'I have had no experience in serious matters of this kind.'

'Do you think it would help you, Miss, if you read my husband's letters to me? There are only three of them—they won't take long to read.'

Agnes compassionately read the letters.

They were not written in a very tender tone. 'Dear Emily,' and 'Yours affectionately'—these conventional phrases, were the only phrases of endearment which they contained. In the first letter, Lord Montbarry was not very favourably spoken of:—'We leave Paris to-morrow. I don't much like my lord. He is proud and cold, and, between ourselves, stingy in money matters. I have had to dispute such trifles as a few centimes in the hotel bill; and twice already, some sharp remarks have passed between the newly-married couple, in consequence of her ladyship's freedom in purchasing pretty tempting things at the shops in Paris. "I can't afford it; you must keep to your allowance." She has had to hear those words already. For my part, I like her. She has the nice, easy foreign manners—she talks to me as if I was a human being like herself.'

The second letter was dated from Rome.

'My lord's caprices' (Ferrari wrote) 'have kept us perpetually on the move. He is becoming incurably restless. I suspect he is uneasy in his mind. Painful recollections, I should say—I find him constantly reading old letters, when her ladyship is not present. We were to have stopped at Genoa, but he hurried us on. The same thing at Florence. Here, at Rome, my lady insists on resting. Her brother has met us at this place. There has been a quarrel already (the lady's maid tells me) between my lord and the Baron. The latter wanted to borrow money of the former. His lordship refused in language which offended Baron Rivar. My lady pacified them, and made them shake hands.'

The third, and last letter, was from Venice.

'More of my lord's economy! Instead of staying at the hotel, we have hired a damp, mouldy, rambling old palace. My lady insists on having the best suites of rooms wherever we go—and the palace comes cheaper for a two months' term. My lord tried to get it for longer; he says the quiet of Venice is good for his nerves. But a foreign speculator has secured the palace, and is going to turn it into an hotel. The Baron is still with us, and there have been more disagreements about money matters. I don't like the Baron—and I don't find the attractions of my lady grow on me. She was much nicer before the Baron joined us. My lord is a punctual paymaster; it's a matter of honour with him; he hates parting with his money, but he does it because he has given his word. I receive my salary regularly at the end of each month—not a franc extra, though I have done many things which are not part of a courier's proper work. Fancy the Baron trying to borrow money of me! he is an inveterate gambler. I didn't believe it when my lady's maid first told me so—but I have seen enough since to satisfy me that she was right. I have seen other things besides, which—well! which don't increase my respect for my lady and the Baron. The maid says she means to give warning to leave. She is a respectable British female, and doesn't take things quite so easily as I do. It is a dull life here. No going into company—no company at home—not a creature sees my lord—not even the consul, or the banker. When he goes out, he goes alone, and generally towards nightfall. Indoors, he shuts himself up in his own room with his books, and sees as little of his wife and the Baron as possible. I fancy things are coming to a crisis here. If my lord's suspicions are once awakened, the consequences will be terrible. Under certain provocations, the noble Montbarry is a man who would stick at nothing. However, the pay is good—and I can't afford to talk of leaving the place, like my lady's maid.'

Agnes handed back the letters—so suggestive of the penalty paid already for his own infatuation by the man who had deserted her!—with feelings of shame and distress, which made her no fit counsellor for the helpless woman who depended on her advice.

'The one thing I can suggest,' she said, after first speaking some kind words of comfort and hope, 'is that we should consult a person of greater experience than ours. Suppose I write and ask my lawyer (who is also my friend and trustee) to come and advise us to-morrow after his business hours?'

Emily eagerly and gratefully accepted the suggestion. An hour was arranged for the meeting on the next day; the correspondence was left under the care of Agnes; and the courier's wife took her leave.

Weary and heartsick, Agnes lay down on the sofa, to rest and compose herself. The careful nurse brought in a reviving cup of tea. Her quaint gossip about herself and her occupations while Agnes had been away, acted as a relief to her mistress's overburdened mind. They were still talking quietly, when they were startled by a loud knock at the house door. Hurried footsteps ascended the stairs. The door of the sitting-room was thrown open violently; the courier's wife rushed in like a mad woman. 'He's dead! They've murdered him!' Those wild words were all she could say. She dropped on her knees at the foot of the sofa—held out her hand with something clasped in it—and fell back in a swoon.

The nurse, signing to Agnes to open the window, took the necessary measures to restore the fainting woman. 'What's this?' she exclaimed. 'Here's a letter in her hand. See what it is, Miss.'

The open envelope was addressed (evidently in a feigned hand-writing) to 'Mrs. Ferrari.' The post-mark was 'Venice.' The contents of the envelope were a sheet of foreign note-paper, and a folded enclosure.

On the note-paper, one line only was written. It was again in a feigned handwriting, and it contained these words:

'To console you for the loss of your husband'

Agnes opened the enclosure next.

It was a Bank of England note for a thousand pounds.

VI

The next day, the friend and legal adviser of Agnes Lockwood, Mr. Troy, called on her by appointment in the evening.

Mrs. Ferrari—still persisting in the conviction of her husband's death—had sufficiently recovered to be present at the consultation. Assisted by Agnes, she told the lawyer the little that was known relating to Ferrari's disappearance, and then produced the correspondence connected with that event. Mr. Troy read (first) the three letters addressed by Ferrari to his wife; (secondly) the letter written by Ferrari's courier-friend, describing his visit to the palace and his interview with Lady Montbarry; and (thirdly) the one line of anonymous writing which had accompanied the extraordinary gift of a thousand pounds to Ferrari's wife.

Well known, at a later period, as the lawyer who acted for Lady Lydiard, in the case of theft, generally described as the case of 'My Lady's Money,' Mr. Troy was not only a man of learning and experience in his profession—he was also a man who had seen something of society at home and abroad. He possessed a keen eye for character, a quaint humour, and a kindly nature which had not been deteriorated even by a lawyer's professional experience of mankind. With all these personal advantages, it is a question, nevertheless, whether he was the fittest adviser whom Agnes could have chosen under the circumstances. Little Mrs. Ferrari, with many domestic merits, was an essentially commonplace woman. Mr. Troy was the last person living who was likely to attract her sympathies—he was the exact opposite of a commonplace man.

'She looks very ill, poor thing!' In these words the lawyer opened the business of the evening, referring to Mrs. Ferrari as unceremoniously as if she had been out of the room.

'She has suffered a terrible shock,' Agnes answered.

Mr. Troy turned to Mrs. Ferrari, and looked at her again, with the interest due to the victim of a shock. He drummed absently with his fingers on the table. At last he spoke to her.

'My good lady, you don't really believe that your husband is dead?'

Mrs. Ferrari put her handkerchief to her eyes. The word 'dead' was ineffectual to express her feelings. 'Murdered!' she said sternly, behind her handkerchief.

'Why? And by whom?' Mr. Troy asked.

Mrs. Ferrari seemed to have some difficulty in answering. 'You have read my husband's letters, sir,' she began. 'I believe he discovered—' She got as far as that, and there she stopped.

'What did he discover?'

There are limits to human patience—even the patience of a bereaved wife. This cool question irritated Mrs. Ferrari into expressing herself plainly at last.

'He discovered Lady Montbarry and the Baron!' she answered, with a burst of hysterical vehemence. 'The Baron is no more that vile woman's brother than I am. The wickedness of those two wretches came to my poor dear husband's knowledge. The lady's maid left her place on account of it. If Ferrari had gone away too, he would have been alive at this moment. They have killed him. I say they have killed him, to prevent it from getting to Lord Montbarry's ears.' So, in short sharp sentences, and in louder and louder accents, Mrs. Ferrari stated her opinion of the case.

Still keeping his own view in reserve, Mr. Troy listened with an expression of satirical approval.

'Very strongly stated, Mrs. Ferrari,' he said. 'You build up your sentences well; you clinch your conclusions in a workmanlike manner. If you had been a man, you would have made a good lawyer—you would have taken juries by the scruff of their necks. Complete the case, my good lady—complete the case. Tell us next who sent you this letter, enclosing the bank-note. The "two wretches" who murdered Mr. Ferrari would hardly put their hands in their pockets and send you a thousand pounds. Who is it—eh? I see the post-mark on the letter is "Venice." Have you any friend in that interesting city, with a large heart, and a purse to correspond, who has been let into the secret and who wishes to console you anonymously?'

It was not easy to reply to this. Mrs. Ferrari began to feel the first inward approaches of something like hatred towards Mr. Troy. 'I don't understand you, sir,' she answered. 'I don't think this is a joking matter.'

Agnes interfered, for the first time. She drew her chair a little nearer to her legal counsellor and friend.

'What is the most probable explanation, in your opinion?' she asked.

'I shall offend Mrs. Ferrari if I tell you,' Mr. Troy answered.

'No, sir, you won't!' cried Mrs. Ferrari, hating Mr. Troy undisguisedly by this time.

The lawyer leaned back in his chair. 'Very well,' he said, in his most good-humoured manner. 'Let's have it out. Observe, madam, I don't dispute your view of the position of affairs at the palace in Venice. You have your husband's letters to justify you; and you have also the significant fact that Lady Montbarry's maid did really leave the house. We will say, then, that Lord Montbarry has presumably been made the victim of a foul wrong—that Mr. Ferrari was the first to find it out—and that the guilty persons had reason to fear, not only that he would acquaint Lord Montbarry with his discovery, but that he would be a principal witness against them if the scandal was made public in a court of law. Now mark! Admitting all this, I draw a totally different conclusion from the conclusion at which you have arrived. Here is your husband left in this miserable household of three, under very awkward circumstances for him. What does he do? But for the bank-note and the written message sent to you with it, I should say that he had wisely withdrawn himself from association with a disgraceful discovery and exposure, by taking secretly to flight. The money modifies this view—unfavourably so far as Mr. Ferrari is concerned. I still believe he is keeping out of the way. But I now say he is paid for keeping out of the way—and that bank-note there on the table is the price of his absence, sent by the guilty persons to his wife.'

Mrs. Ferrari's watery grey eyes brightened suddenly; Mrs. Ferrari's dull drab-coloured complexion became enlivened by a glow of brilliant red.

'It's false!' she cried. 'It's a burning shame to speak of my husband in that way!'

'I told you I should offend you!' said Mr. Troy.

Agnes interposed once more—in the interests of peace. She took the offended wife's hand; she appealed to the lawyer to reconsider that side of his theory which reflected harshly on Ferrari. While she was still speaking, the servant interrupted her by entering the room with a visiting-card. It was the card of Henry Westwick; and there was an ominous request written on it in pencil. 'I bring bad news. Let me see you for a minute downstairs.' Agnes immediately left the room.

Alone with Mrs. Ferrari, Mr. Troy permitted his natural kindness of heart to show itself on the surface at last. He tried to make his peace with the courier's wife.

'You have every claim, my good soul, to resent a reflection cast upon your husband,' he began. 'I may even say that I respect you for speaking so warmly in his defence. At the same time, remember, that I am bound, in such a serious matter as this, to tell you what is really in my mind. I can have no intention of offending you, seeing that I am a total stranger to you and to Mr. Ferrari. A thousand pounds is a large sum of money; and a poor man may excusably be tempted by it to do nothing worse than to keep out of the way for a while. My only interest, acting on your behalf, is to get at the truth. If you will give me time, I see no reason to despair of finding your husband yet.'

Ferrari's wife listened, without being convinced: her narrow little mind, filled to its extreme capacity by her unfavourable opinion of Mr. Troy, had no room left for the process of correcting its first impression. 'I am much obliged to you, sir,' was all she said. Her eyes were more communicative—her eyes added, in their language, 'You may say what you please; I will never forgive you to my dying day.'

Mr. Troy gave it up. He composedly wheeled his chair around, put his hands in his pockets, and looked out of window.

After an interval of silence, the drawing-room door was opened.

Mr. Troy wheeled round again briskly to the table, expecting to see Agnes. To his surprise there appeared, in her place, a perfect stranger to him—a gentleman, in the prime of life, with a marked expression of pain and embarrassment on his handsome face. He looked at Mr. Troy, and bowed gravely.

'I am so unfortunate as to have brought news to Miss Agnes Lockwood which has greatly distressed her,' he said. 'She has retired to her room. I am requested to make her excuses, and to speak to you in her place.'

Having introduced himself in those terms, he noticed Mrs. Ferrari, and held out his hand to her kindly. 'It is some years since we last met, Emily,' he said. 'I am afraid you have almost forgotten the "Master Henry" of old times.' Emily, in some little confusion, made her acknowledgments, and begged to know if she could be of any use to Miss Lockwood. 'The old nurse is with her,' Henry answered; 'they will be better left together.' He turned once more to Mr. Troy. 'I ought to tell you,' he said, 'that my name is Henry Westwick. I am the younger brother of the late Lord Montbarry.'

'The late Lord Montbarry!' Mr. Troy exclaimed.

'My brother died at Venice yesterday evening. There is the telegram.' With that startling answer, he handed the paper to Mr. Troy.

The message was in these words:

'Lady Montbarry, Venice. To Stephen Robert Westwick, Newbury's Hotel, London. It is useless to take the journey. Lord Montbarry died of bronchitis, at 8.40 this evening. All needful details by post.'

'Was this expected, sir?' the lawyer asked.

'I cannot say that it has taken us entirely by surprise,' Henry answered. 'My brother Stephen (who is now the head of the family) received a telegram three days since, informing him that alarming symptoms had declared themselves, and that a second physician had been called in. He telegraphed back to say that he had left Ireland for London, on his way to Venice, and to direct that any further message might be sent to his hotel. The reply came in a second telegram. It announced that Lord Montbarry was in a state of insensibility, and that, in his brief intervals of consciousness, he recognised nobody. My brother was advised to wait in London for later information. The third telegram is now in your hands. That is all I know, up to the present time.'

Happening to look at the courier's wife, Mr. Troy was struck by the expression of blank fear which showed itself in the woman's face.

'Mrs. Ferrari,' he said, 'have you heard what Mr. Westwick has just told me?'

'Every word of it, sir.'

'Have you any questions to ask?'

'No, sir.'

'You seem to be alarmed,' the lawyer persisted. 'Is it still about your husband?'

'I shall never see my husband again, sir. I have thought so all along, as you know. I feel sure of it now.'

'Sure of it, after what you have just heard?'

'Yes, sir.'

'Can you tell me why?'

'No, sir. It's a feeling I have. I can't tell why.'

'Oh, a feeling?' Mr. Troy repeated, in a tone of compassionate contempt. 'When it comes to feelings, my good soul—!' He left the sentence unfinished, and rose to take his leave of Mr. Westwick. The truth is, he began to feel puzzled himself, and he did not choose to let Mrs. Ferrari see it. 'Accept the expression of my sympathy, sir,' he said to Mr. Westwick politely. 'I wish you good evening.'

Henry turned to Mrs. Ferrari as the lawyer closed the door. 'I have heard of your trouble, Emily, from Miss Lockwood. Is there anything I can do to help you?'

'Nothing, sir, thank you. Perhaps, I had better go home after what has happened? I will call to-morrow, and see if I can be of any use to Miss Agnes. I am very sorry for her.' She stole away, with her formal curtsey, her noiseless step, and her obstinate resolution to take the gloomiest view of her husband's case.

Henry Westwick looked round him in the solitude of the little drawing-room. There was nothing to keep him in the house, and yet he lingered in it. It was something to be even near Agnes—to see the things belonging to her that were scattered about the room. There, in the corner, was her chair, with her embroidery on the work-table by its side. On the little easel near the window was her last drawing, not quite finished yet. The book she had been reading lay on the sofa, with her tiny pencil-case in it to mark the place at which she had left off. One after another, he looked at the objects that reminded him of the woman whom he loved—took them up tenderly—and laid them down again with a sigh. Ah, how far, how unattainably far from him, she was still! 'She will never forget Montbarry,' he thought to himself as he took up his hat to go. 'Not one of us feels his death as she feels it. Miserable, miserable wretch—how she loved him!'

In the street, as Henry closed the house-door, he was stopped by a passing acquaintance—a wearisome inquisitive man—doubly unwelcome to him, at that moment. 'Sad news, Westwick, this about your brother. Rather an unexpected death, wasn't it? We never heard at the club that Montbarry's lungs were weak. What will the insurance offices do?'

Henry started; he had never thought of his brother's life insurance. What could the offices do but pay? A death by bronchitis, certified by two physicians, was surely the least disputable of all deaths. 'I wish you hadn't put that question into my head!' he broke out irritably. 'Ah!' said his friend, 'you think the widow will get the money? So do I! so do I!'

VII

Some days later, the insurance offices (two in number) received the formal announcement of Lord Montbarry's death, from her ladyship's London solicitors. The sum insured in each office was five thousand pounds—on which one year's premium only had been paid. In the face of such a pecuniary emergency as this, the Directors thought it desirable to consider their position. The medical advisers of the two offices, who had recommended the insurance of Lord Montbarry's life, were called into council over their own reports. The result excited some interest among persons connected with the business of life insurance. Without absolutely declining to pay the money, the two offices (acting in concert) decided on sending a commission of inquiry to Venice, 'for the purpose of obtaining further information.'

Mr. Troy received the earliest intelligence of what was going on. He wrote at once to communicate his news to Agnes; adding, what he considered to be a valuable hint, in these words:

'You are intimately acquainted, I know, with Lady Barville, the late Lord Montbarry's eldest sister. The solicitors employed by her husband are also the solicitors to one of the two insurance offices. There may possibly be something in the report of the commission of inquiry touching on Ferrari's disappearance. Ordinary persons would not be permitted, of course, to see such a document. But a sister of the late lord is so near a relative as to be an exception to general rules. If Sir Theodore Barville puts it on that footing, the lawyers, even if they do not allow his wife to look at the report, will at least answer any discreet questions she may ask referring to it. Let me hear what you think of this suggestion, at your earliest convenience.'

The reply was received by return of post. Agnes declined to avail herself of Mr. Troy's proposal.

'My interference, innocent as it was,' she wrote, 'has already been productive of such deplorable results, that I cannot and dare not stir any further in the case of Ferrari. If I had not consented to let that unfortunate man refer to me by name, the late Lord Montbarry would never have engaged him, and his wife would have been spared the misery and suspense from which she is suffering now. I would not even look at the report to which you allude if it was placed in my hands—I have heard more than enough already of that hideous life in the palace at Venice. If Mrs. Ferrari chooses to address herself to Lady Barville (with your assistance), that is of course quite another thing. But, even in this case, I must make it a positive condition that my name shall not be mentioned. Forgive me, dear Mr. Troy! I am very unhappy, and very unreasonable—but I am only a woman, and you must not expect too much from me.'

Foiled in this direction, the lawyer next advised making the attempt to discover the present address of Lady Montbarry's English maid. This excellent suggestion had one drawback: it could only be carried out by spending money—and there was no money to spend. Mrs. Ferrari shrank from the bare idea of making any use of the thousand-pound note. It had been deposited in the safe keeping of a bank. If it was even mentioned in her hearing, she shuddered and referred to it, with melodramatic fervour, as 'my husband's blood-money!'

So, under stress of circumstances, the attempt to solve the mystery of Ferrari's disappearance was suspended for a while.

It was the last month of the year 1860. The commission of inquiry was already at work; having begun its investigations on December 6. On the 10th, the term for which the late Lord

Montbarry had hired the Venetian palace, expired. News by telegram reached the insurance offices that Lady Montbarry had been advised by her lawyers to leave for London with as little delay as possible. Baron Rivar, it was believed, would accompany her to England, but would not remain in that country, unless his services were absolutely required by her ladyship. The Baron, 'well known as an enthusiastic student of chemistry,' had heard of certain recent discoveries in connection with that science in the United States, and was anxious to investigate them personally.

These items of news, collected by Mr. Troy, were duly communicated to Mrs. Ferrari, whose anxiety about her husband made her a frequent, a too frequent, visitor at the lawyer's office. She attempted to relate what she had heard to her good friend and protectress. Agnes steadily refused to listen, and positively forbade any further conversation relating to Lord Montbarry's wife, now that Lord Montbarry was no more. 'You have Mr. Troy to advise you,' she said; 'and you are welcome to what little money I can spare, if money is wanted. All I ask in return is that you will not distress me. I am trying to separate myself from remembrances—' her voice faltered; she paused to control herself—'from remembrances,' she resumed, 'which are sadder than ever since I have heard of Lord Montbarry's death. Help me by your silence to recover my spirits, if I can. Let me hear nothing more, until I can rejoice with you that your husband is found.'

Time advanced to the 13th of the month; and more information of the interesting sort reached Mr. Troy. The labours of the insurance commission had come to an end—the report had been received from Venice on that day.

VIII

On the 14th the Directors and their legal advisers met for the reading of the report, with closed doors. These were the terms in which the Commissioners related the results of their inquiry: 'Private and confidential.

'We have the honour to inform our Directors that we arrived

in Venice on December 6, 1860. On the same day we proceeded to the palace inhabited by Lord Montbarry at the time of his last illness and death.

'We were received with all possible courtesy by Lady Montbarry's brother, Baron Rivar. "My sister was her husband's only attendant throughout his illness," the Baron informed us. "She is overwhelmed by grief and fatigue—or she would have been here to receive you personally. What are your wishes, gentlemen? and what can I do for you in her ladyship's place?"

'In accordance with our instructions, we answered that the death and burial of Lord Montbarry abroad made it desirable to obtain more complete information relating to his illness, and to the circumstances which had attended it, than could be conveyed in writing. We explained that the law provided for the lapse of a certain interval of time before the payment of the sum assured, and we expressed our wish to conduct the inquiry with the most respectful consideration for her ladyship's feelings, and for the convenience of any other members of the family inhabiting the house.

'To this the Baron replied, "I am the only member of the family living here, and I and the palace are entirely at your disposal." From first to last we found this gentleman perfectly straightforward, and most amiably willing to assist us.

'With the one exception of her ladyship's room, we went over the whole of the palace the same day. It is an immense place only partially furnished. The first floor and part of the second floor were the portions of it that had been inhabited by Lord Montbarry and the members of the household. We saw the bedchamber, at one extremity of the palace, in which his lordship died, and the small room communicating with it, which he used as a study. Next to this was a large apartment or hall, the doors of which he habitually kept locked, his object being (as we were informed) to pursue his studies uninterruptedly in perfect solitude. On the other side of the large hall were the bedchamber occupied by her ladyship, and the dressing-room in which the maid slept previous to her departure for England. Beyond these were the dining and reception rooms, opening into an antechamber, which gave access to the grand staircase of the palace.

'The only inhabited rooms on the second floor were the

sitting-room and bedroom occupied by Baron Rivar, and another room at some distance from it, which had been the bedroom of the courier Ferrari.

'The rooms on the third floor and on the basement were completely unfurnished, and in a condition of great neglect. We inquired if there was anything to be seen below the basement—and we were at once informed that there were vaults beneath, which we were at perfect liberty to visit.

'We went down, so as to leave no part of the palace unexplored. The vaults were, it was believed, used as dungeons in the old times—say, some centuries since. Air and light were only partially admitted to these dismal places by two long shafts of winding construction, which communicated with the back yard of the palace, and the openings of which, high above the ground, were protected by iron gratings. The stone stairs leading down into the vaults could be closed at will by a heavy trap-door in the back hall, which we found open. The Baron himself led the way down the stairs. We remarked that it might be awkward if that trap-door fell down and closed the opening behind us. The Baron smiled at the idea. "Don't be alarmed, gentlemen," he said; "the door is safe. I had an interest in seeing to it myself, when we first inhabited the palace. My favourite study is the study of experimental chemistry—and my workshop, since we have been in Venice, is down here."

'These last words explained a curious smell in the vaults, which we noticed the moment we entered them. We can only describe the smell by saying that it was of a twofold sort—faintly aromatic, as it were, in its first effect, but with some after-odour very sickening in our nostrils. The Baron's furnaces and retorts, and other things, were all there to speak for themselves, together with some packages of chemicals, having the name and address of the person who had supplied them plainly visible on their labels. "Not a pleasant place for study," Baron Rivar observed, "but my sister is timid. She has a horror of chemical smells and explosions—and she has banished me to these lower regions, so that my experiments may neither be smelt nor heard." He held out his hands, on which we had noticed that he wore gloves in the house. "Accidents will happen sometimes," he said, "no matter how careful a man may be. I burnt my hands severely in trying a new combination the other day, and they are only recovering now."

'We mention these otherwise unimportant incidents, in order to show that our exploration of the palace was not impeded by any attempt at concealment. We were even admitted to her ladyship's own room—on a subsequent occasion, when she went out to take the air. Our instructions recommended us to examine his lordship's residence, because the extreme privacy of his life at Venice, and the remarkable departure of the only two servants in the house, might have some suspicious connection with the nature of his death. We found nothing to justify suspicion.

'As to his lordship's retired way of life, we have conversed on the subject with the consul and the banker—the only two strangers who held any communication with him. He called once at the bank to obtain money on his letter of credit, and excused himself from accepting an invitation to visit the banker at his private residence, on the ground of delicate health. His lordship wrote to the same effect on sending his card to the consul, to excuse himself from personally returning that gentleman's visit to the palace. We have seen the letter, and we beg to offer the following copy of it. "Many years passed in India have injured my constitution. I have ceased to go into society; the one occupation of my life now is the study of Oriental literature. The air of Italy is better for me than the air of England, or I should never have left home. Pray accept the apologies of a student and an invalid. The active part of my life is at an end." The self-seclusion of his lordship seems to us to be explained in these brief lines. We have not, however, on that account spared our inquiries in other directions. Nothing to excite a suspicion of anything wrong has come to our knowledge.

'As to the departure of the lady's maid, we have seen the woman's receipt for her wages, in which it is expressly stated that she left Lady Montbarry's service because she disliked the Continent, and wished to get back to her own country. This is not an uncommon result of taking English servants to foreign parts. Lady Montbarry has informed us that she abstained from engaging another maid in consequence of the extreme dislike which his lordship expressed to having strangers in the house, in the state of his health at that time.

'The disappearance of the courier Ferrari is, in itself, unquestionably a suspicious circumstance. Neither her ladyship nor the Baron can explain it; and no investigation that we could make has thrown the smallest light on this event, or has justified us in associating it, directly or indirectly, with the object of our inquiry. We have even gone the length of examining the portmanteau which Ferrari left behind him. It contains nothing but clothes and linen—no money, and not even a scrap of paper in the pockets of the clothes. The portmanteau remains in charge of the police.

'We have also found opportunities of speaking privately to the old woman who attends to the rooms occupied by her ladyship and the Baron. She was recommended to fill this situation by the keeper of the restaurant who has supplied the meals to the family throughout the period of their residence at the palace. Her character is most favourably spoken of. Unfortunately, her limited intelligence makes her of no value as a witness. We were patient and careful in questioning her, and we found her perfectly willing to answer us; but we could elicit nothing which is worth including in the present report.

'On the second day of our inquiries, we had the honour of an interview with Lady Montbarry. Her ladyship looked miserably worn and ill, and seemed to be quite at a loss to understand what we wanted with her. Baron Rivar, who introduced us, explained the nature of our errand in Venice, and took pains to assure her that it was a purely formal duty on which we were engaged. Having satisfied her ladyship on this point, he discreetly left the room.

'The questions which we addressed to Lady Montbarry related mainly, of course, to his lordship's illness. The answers, given with great nervousness of manner, but without the slightest appearance of reserve, informed us of the facts that follow:

'Lord Montbarry had been out of order for some time past—nervous and irritable. He first complained of having taken cold on November 13 last; he passed a wakeful and feverish night, and remained in bed the next day. Her ladyship proposed sending for medical advice. He refused to allow her to do this, saying that he could quite easily be his own doctor in such a trifling matter as a cold. Some hot lemonade was made at his request, with a view to producing perspiration. Lady Montbarry's maid having left her at that time, the courier Ferrari (then the only servant in the house) went out to buy the lemons. Her ladyship made the drink with her own hands. It was successful in producing perspiration—and Lord Montbarry had some hours of sleep afterwards. Later in the day, having need of Ferrari's services, Lady Montbarry rang for him. The bell was not answered. Baron Rivar searched for the man, in the palace and out of it, in vain. From that time forth not a trace of Ferrari could be discovered. This happened on November 14.

'On the night of the 14th, the feverish symptoms accompanying his lordship's cold returned. They were in part perhaps attributable to the annoyance and alarm caused by Ferrari's mysterious disappearance. It had been impossible to conceal the circumstance, as his lordship rang repeatedly for the courier; insisting that the man should relieve Lady Montbarry and the Baron by taking their places during the night at his bedside.

'On the 15th (the day on which the old woman first came to do the housework), his lordship complained of sore throat, and of a feeling of oppression on the chest. On this day, and again on the 16th, her ladyship and the Baron entreated him to see a doctor. He still refused. "I don't want strange faces about me; my cold will run its course, in spite of the doctor,"—that was his answer. On the 17th he was so much worse that it was decided to send for medical help whether he liked it or not. Baron Rivar, after inquiry at the consul's, secured the services of Doctor Bruno, well known as an eminent physician in Venice, with the additional recommendation of having resided in England, and having made himself acquainted with English forms of medical practice.

'Thus far our account of his lordship's illness has been derived from statements made by Lady Montbarry. The narrative will now be most fitly continued in the language of the doctor's own report, herewith subjoined.

'"My medical diary informs me that I first saw the English Lord Montbarry, on November 17. He was suffering from a sharp attack of bronchitis. Some precious time had been lost, through his obstinate objection to the presence of a medical man at his bedside. Generally speaking, he appeared to be in a delicate state of health. His nervous system was out of order—he was at once timid and contradictory. When I spoke to him in English, he answered in Italian; and when I tried him in Italian, he went back to English. It mattered little—the malady had already made such progress that he could only speak a few words at a time, and those in a whisper.

"'I at once applied the necessary remedies. Copies of my prescriptions (with translation into English) accompany the present statement, and are left to speak for themselves.

"'For the next three days I was in constant attendance on my patient. He answered to the remedies employed—improving slowly, but decidedly. I could conscientiously assure Lady Montbarry that no danger was to be apprehended thus far. She was indeed a most devoted wife. I vainly endeavoured to induce her to accept the services of a competent nurse; she would allow nobody to attend on her husband but herself. Night and day this estimable woman was at his bedside. In her brief intervals of repose, her brother watched the sick man in her place. This brother was, I must say, very good company, in the intervals when we had time for a little talk. He dabbled in chemistry, down in the horrid under-water vaults of the palace; and he wanted to show me some of his experiments. I have enough of chemistry in writing prescriptions—and I declined. He took it quite good-humouredly.

"'I am straying away from my subject. Let me return to the sick lord.

"'Up to the 20th, then, things went well enough. I was quite unprepared for the disastrous change that showed itself, when I paid Lord Montbarry my morning visit on the 21st. He had relapsed, and seriously relapsed. Examining him to discover the cause, I found symptoms of pneumonia—that is to say, in unmedical language, inflammation of the substance of the lungs. He breathed with difficulty, and was only partially able to relieve himself by coughing. I made the strictest inquiries, and was assured that his medicine had been administered as carefully as usual, and that he had not been exposed to any changes of temperature. It was with great reluctance that I added to Lady Montbarry's distress; but I felt bound, when she suggested a consultation with another physician, to own that I too thought there was really need for it.

"'Her ladyship instructed me to spare no expense, and to get the best medical opinion in Italy. The best opinion was happily within our reach. The first and foremost of Italian physicians is Torello of Padua. I sent a special messenger for the great man. He arrived on the evening of the 21st, and confirmed my opinion that pneumonia had set in, and that our patient's life was in danger. I told him what my treatment of the case had been, and he approved of it in every particular. He made some valuable suggestions, and (at Lady Montbarry's express request) he consented to defer his return to Padua until the following morning.

'"We both saw the patient at intervals in the course of the night. The disease, steadily advancing, set our utmost resistance at defiance. In the morning Doctor Torello took his leave. 'I can be of no further use,' he said to me. 'The man is past all help—and he ought to know it.'

'"Later in the day I warned my lord, as gently as I could, that his time had come. I am informed that there are serious reasons for my stating what passed between us on this occasion, in detail, and without any reserve. I comply with the request.

'"Lord Montbarry received the intelligence of his approaching death with becoming composure, but with a certain doubt. He signed to me to put my ear to his mouth. He whispered faintly, 'Are you sure?' It was no time to deceive him; I said, 'Positively sure.' He waited a little, gasping for breath, and then he whispered again, 'Feel under my pillow.' I found under his pillow a letter, sealed and stamped, ready for the post. His next words were just audible and no more—'Post it yourself.' I answered, of course, that I would do so—and I did post the letter with my own hand. I looked at the address. It was directed to a lady in London. The street I cannot remember. The name I can perfectly recall: it was an Italian name—'Mrs. Ferrari.'

'"That night my lord nearly died of asphyxia. I got him through it for the time; and his eyes showed that he understood me when I told him, the next morning, that I had posted the letter. This was his last effort of consciousness. When I saw him again he was sunk in apathy. He lingered in a state of insensibility, supported by stimulants, until the 25th, and died (unconscious to the last) on the evening of that day.

'"As to the cause of his death, it seems (if I may be excused for saying so) simply absurd to ask the question. Bronchitis, terminating in pneumonia—there is no more doubt that this, and this only, was the malady of which he expired, than that two and two make four. Doctor Torello's own note of the case is added here to a duplicate of my certificate, in order (as I am informed) to satisfy some English offices in which his lordship's life was insured. The English offices must have been founded by that celebrated saint and doubter, mentioned in the New Testament, whose name was Thomas!"

'Doctor Bruno's evidence ends here.

'Reverting for a moment to our inquiries addressed to Lady Montbarry, we have to report that she can give us no information on the subject of the letter which the doctor posted at Lord Montbarry's request. When his lordship wrote it? what it contained? why he kept it a secret from Lady Montbarry (and from the Baron also); and why he should write at all to the wife of his courier? these are questions to which we find it simply impossible to obtain any replies. It seems even useless to say that the matter is open to suspicion. Suspicion implies conjecture of some kind—and the letter under my lord's pillow baffles all conjecture. Application to Mrs. Ferrari may perhaps clear up the mystery. Her residence in London will be easily discovered at the Italian Couriers' Office, Golden Square.

'Having arrived at the close of the present report, we have now to draw your attention to the conclusion which is justified by the results of our investigation.

'The plain question before our Directors and ourselves appears to be this: Has the inquiry revealed any extraordinary circumstances which render the death of Lord Montbarry open to suspicion? The inquiry has revealed extraordinary circumstances beyond all doubt—such as the disappearance of Ferrari, the remarkable absence of the customary establishment of servants in the house, and the mysterious letter which his lordship asked the doctor to post. But where is the proof that any one of these circumstances is associated—suspiciously and directly associated—with the only event which concerns us, the event of Lord Montbarry's death? In the absence of any such proof, and in the face of the evidence of two eminent physicians, it is impossible to dispute the statement on the certificate that his lordship died a natural death. We are bound, therefore, to report, that there are no valid grounds for refusing the payment of the sum for which the late Lord Montbarry's life was assured.

'We shall send these lines to you by the post of to-morrow, December 10; leaving time to receive your further instructions (if any), in reply to our telegram of this evening announcing the conclusion of the inquiry.'

IX

'Now, my good creature, whatever you have to say to me, out with it at once! I don't want to hurry you needlessly; but these are business hours, and I have other people's affairs to attend to besides yours.'

Addressing Ferrari's wife, with his usual blunt good-humour, in these terms, Mr. Troy registered the lapse of time by a glance at the watch on his desk, and then waited to hear what his client had to say to him.

'It's something more, sir, about the letter with the thousand-pound note,' Mrs. Ferrari began. 'I have found out who sent it to me.'

Mr. Troy started. 'This is news indeed!' he said. 'Who sent you the letter?'

'Lord Montbarry sent it, sir.'

It was not easy to take Mr. Troy by surprise. But Mrs. Ferrari threw him completely off his balance. For a while he could only look at her in silent surprise. 'Nonsense!' he said, as soon as he had recovered himself. 'There is some mistake—it can't be!'

'There is no mistake,' Mrs. Ferrari rejoined, in her most positive manner. 'Two gentlemen from the insurance offices called on me this morning, to see the letter. They were completely puzzled—especially when they heard of the bank-note inside. But they know who sent the letter. His lordship's doctor in Venice posted it at his lordship's request. Go to the gentlemen yourself, sir, if you don't believe me. They were polite enough to ask if I could account for Lord Montbarry's writing to me and sending me the money. I gave them my opinion directly—I said it was like his lordship's kindness.'

'Like his lordship's kindness?' Mr. Troy repeated, in blank amazement.

'Yes, sir! Lord Montbarry knew me, like all the other members of his family, when I was at school on the estate in Ireland. If he could have done it, he would have protected my poor dear husband. But he was helpless himself in the hands of my lady and the Baron—and the only kind thing he could do was to provide for me in my widowhood, like the true nobleman he was!'

'A very pretty explanation!' said Mr. Troy. 'What did your visitors from the insurance offices think of it?'

'They asked if I had any proof of my husband's death.'

'And what did you say?'

'I said, "I give you better than proof, gentlemen; I give you my positive opinion."'

'That satisfied them, of course?'

'They didn't say so in words, sir. They looked at each other—and wished me good-morning.'

'Well, Mrs. Ferrari, unless you have some more extraordinary news for me, I think I shall wish you good-morning too. I can take a note of your information (very startling information, I own); and, in the absence of proof, I can do no more.'

'I can provide you with proof, sir—if that is all you want,' said Mrs. Ferrari, with great dignity. 'I only wish to know, first, whether the law justifies me in doing it. You may have seen in the fashionable intelligence of the newspapers, that Lady Montbarry has arrived in London, at Newbury's Hotel. I propose to go and see her.'

'The deuce you do! May I ask for what purpose?'

Mrs. Ferrari answered in a mysterious whisper. 'For the purpose of catching her in a trap! I shan't send in my name—I shall announce myself as a person on business, and the first words I say to her will be these: "I come, my lady, to acknowledge the receipt of the money sent to Ferrari's widow." Ah! you may well start, Mr. Troy! It almost takes you off your guard, doesn't it? Make your mind easy, sir; I shall find the proof that everybody asks me for in her guilty face. Let her only change colour by the shadow of a shade—let her eyes only drop for half an instant—I shall discover her! The one thing I want to know is, does the law permit it?'

'The law permits it,' Mr. Troy answered gravely; 'but whether her ladyship will permit it, is quite another question. Have you really courage enough, Mrs. Ferrari, to carry out this notable scheme of yours? You have been described to me, by Miss Lockwood, as rather a nervous, timid sort of person—and, if I may trust my own observation, I should say you justify the description.'

'If you had lived in the country, sir, instead of living in London,' Mrs. Ferrari replied, 'you would sometimes have seen even a sheep turn on a dog. I am far from saying that I am a bold woman—quite the reverse. But when I stand in that wretch's presence, and think of my murdered husband, the one of us two who is likely to be frightened is not me. I am going there now, sir. You shall hear how it ends. I wish you good-morning.'

With those brave words the courier's wife gathered her mantle about her, and walked out of the room.

Mr. Troy smiled—not satirically, but compassionately. 'The little simpleton!' he thought to himself. 'If half of what they say of Lady Montbarry is true, Mrs. Ferrari and her trap have but a poor prospect before them. I wonder how it will end?'

All Mr. Troy's experience failed to forewarn him of how it did end.

X

In the mean time, Mrs. Ferrari held to her resolution. She went straight from Mr. Troy's office to Newbury's Hotel.

Lady Montbarry was at home, and alone. But the authorities of the hotel hesitated to disturb her when they found that the visitor declined to mention her name. Her ladyship's new maid happened to cross the hall while the matter was still in debate. She was a Frenchwoman, and, on being appealed to, she settled the question in the swift, easy, rational French way. 'Madame's appearance was perfectly respectable. Madame might have reasons for not mentioning her name which Miladi might approve. In any case, there being no orders forbidding the introduction of a strange lady, the matter clearly rested between Madame and Miladi. Would Madame, therefore, be good enough to follow Miladi's maid up the stairs?'

In spite of her resolution, Mrs. Ferrari's heart beat as if it would burst out of her bosom, when her conductress led her into an ante-room, and knocked at a door opening into a room beyond. But it is remarkable that persons of sensitively-nervous organisation are the very persons who are capable of forcing themselves (apparently by the exercise of a spasmodic effort of will) into the performance of acts of the most audacious courage. A low, grave voice from the inner room said, 'Come in.' The maid, opening the door, announced, 'A person to see you, Miladi, on business,' and immediately retired. In the one instant while these events passed, timid little Mrs. Ferrari mastered her own throbbing heart; stepped over the threshold, conscious of her clammy hands, dry lips, and burning head; and stood in the presence of Lord Montbarry's widow, to all outward appearance as supremely self-possessed as her ladyship herself.

It was still early in the afternoon, but the light in the room was dim. The blinds were drawn down. Lady Montbarry sat with her back to the windows, as if even the subdued daylight were disagreeable to her. She had altered sadly for the worse in her personal appearance, since the memorable day when Doctor Wybrow had seen her in his consulting-room. Her beauty was gone—her face had fallen away to mere skin and bone; the contrast between her ghastly complexion and her steely glittering black eyes was more startling than ever. Robed in dismal black, relieved only by the brilliant whiteness of her widow's cap—reclining in a panther-like suppleness of attitude on a little green sofa—she looked at the stranger who had intruded on her, with a moment's languid curiosity, then dropped her eyes again to the hand-screen which she held between her face and the fire. 'I don't know you,' she said. 'What do you want with me?'

Mrs. Ferrari tried to answer. Her first burst of courage had already worn itself out. The bold words that she had determined to speak were living words still in her mind, but they died on her lips.

There was a moment of silence. Lady Montbarry looked round again at the speechless stranger. 'Are you deaf?' she asked. There was another pause. Lady Montbarry quietly looked back again at the screen, and put another question. 'Do you want money?'

'Money!' That one word roused the sinking spirit of the courier's wife. She recovered her courage; she found her voice. 'Look at me, my lady, if you please,' she said, with a sudden outbreak of audacity.

Lady Montbarry looked round for the third time. The fatal words passed Mrs. Ferrari's lips.

'I come, my lady, to acknowledge the receipt of the money sent to Ferrari's widow.'

Lady Montbarry's glittering black eyes rested with steady attention on the woman who had addressed her in those terms. Not the faintest expression of confusion or alarm, not even a momentary flutter of interest stirred the deadly stillness of her face. She reposed as quietly, she held the screen as composedly, as ever. The test had been tried, and had utterly failed.

There was another silence. Lady Montbarry considered with herself. The smile that came slowly and went away suddenly—the smile at once so sad and so cruel—showed itself on her thin lips. She lifted her screen, and pointed with it to a seat at the farther end of the room. 'Be so good as to take that chair,' she said.

Helpless under her first bewildering sense of failure—not knowing what to say or what to do next—Mrs. Ferrari mechanically obeyed. Lady Montbarry, rising on the sofa for the first time, watched her with undisguised scrutiny as she crossed the room—then sank back into a reclining position once more. 'No,' she said to herself, 'the woman walks steadily; she is not intoxicated—the only other possibility is that she may be mad.'

She had spoken loud enough to be heard. Stung by the insult, Mrs. Ferrari instantly answered her. 'I am no more drunk or mad than you are!'

'No?' said Lady Montbarry. 'Then you are only insolent? The ignorant English mind (I have observed) is apt to be insolent in the exercise of unrestrained English liberty. This is very noticeable to us foreigners among you people in the streets. Of course I can't be insolent to you, in return. I hardly know what to say to you. My maid was imprudent in admitting you so easily to my room. I suppose your respectable appearance misled her. I wonder who you are? You mentioned the name of a courier who left us very strangely. Was he married by any chance? Are you his wife? And do you know where he is?'

Mrs. Ferrari's indignation burst its way through all restraints. She advanced to the sofa; she feared nothing, in the fervour and rage of her reply.

'I am his widow—and you know it, you wicked woman! Ah! it was an evil hour when Miss Lockwood recommended my husband to be his lordship's courier—!'

Before she could add another word, Lady Montbarry sprang from the sofa with the stealthy suddenness of a cat—seized her by both shoulders—and shook her with the strength and frenzy of a madwoman. 'You lie! you lie! you lie!' She dropped her hold at the third repetition of the accusation, and threw up her hands wildly with a gesture of despair. 'Oh, Jesu Maria! is it possible?' she cried. 'Can the courier have come to me through that woman?' She turned like lightning on Mrs. Ferrari, and stopped her as she was escaping from the room. 'Stay here, you fool—stay here, and answer me! If you cry out, as sure as the heavens are above you, I'll strangle you with my own hands. Sit down again—and fear nothing. Wretch! It is I who am frightened—frightened out of my senses. Confess that you lied, when you used Miss Lockwood's name just now! No! I don't believe you on your oath; I will believe nobody but Miss Lockwood herself. Where does she live? Tell me that, you noxious stinging little insect—and you may go.' Terrified as she was, Mrs. Ferrari hesitated. Lady Montbarry lifted her hands threateningly, with the long, lean, yellow-white fingers outspread and crooked at the tips. Mrs. Ferrari shrank at the sight of them, and gave the address. Lady Montbarry pointed contemptuously to the door—then changed her mind. 'No! not yet! you will tell Miss Lockwood what has happened, and she may refuse to see me. I will go there at once, and you shall go with me. As far as the house—not inside of it. Sit down again. I am going to ring for my maid. Turn your back to the door—your cowardly face is not fit to be seen!'

She rang the bell. The maid appeared.

'My cloak and bonnet—instantly!'

The maid produced the cloak and bonnet from the bedroom.

'A cab at the door—before I can count ten!'

The maid vanished. Lady Montbarry surveyed herself in the glass, and wheeled round again, with her cat-like suddenness, to Mrs. Ferrari.

'I look more than half dead already, don't I?' she said with a grim outburst of irony. 'Give me your arm.'

She took Mrs. Ferrari's arm, and left the room. 'You have

nothing to fear, so long as you obey,' she whispered, on the way downstairs. 'You leave me at Miss Lockwood's door, and never see me again.'

In the hall they were met by the landlady of the hotel. Lady Montbarry graciously presented her companion. 'My good friend Mrs. Ferrari; I am so glad to have seen her.' The landlady accompanied them to the door. The cab was waiting. 'Get in first, good Mrs. Ferrari,' said her ladyship; 'and tell the man where to go.'

They were driven away. Lady Montbarry's variable humour changed again. With a low groan of misery, she threw herself back in the cab. Lost in her own dark thoughts, as careless of the woman whom she had bent to her iron will as if no such person sat by her side, she preserved a sinister silence, until they reached the house where Miss Lockwood lodged. In an instant, she roused herself to action. She opened the door of the cab, and closed it again on Mrs. Ferrari, before the driver could get off his box.

'Take that lady a mile farther on her way home!' she said, as she paid the man his fare. The next moment she had knocked at the house-door. 'Is Miss Lockwood at home?' 'Yes, ma'am.' She stepped over the threshold—the door closed on her.

'Which way, ma'am?' asked the driver of the cab.

Mrs. Ferrari put her hand to her head, and tried to collect her thoughts. Could she leave her friend and benefactress helpless at Lady Montbarry's mercy? She was still vainly endeavouring to decide on the course that she ought to follow—when a gentleman, stopping at Miss Lockwood's door, happened to look towards the cab-window, and saw her.

'Are you going to call on Miss Agnes too?' he asked.

It was Henry Westwick. Mrs. Ferrari clasped her hands in gratitude as she recognised him.

'Go in, sir!' she cried. 'Go in, directly. That dreadful woman is with Miss Agnes. Go and protect her!'

'What woman?' Henry asked.

The answer literally struck him speechless. With amazement and indignation in his face, he looked at Mrs. Ferrari as she pronounced the hated name of 'Lady Montbarry.' 'I'll see to it,' was all he said. He knocked at the house-door; and he too, in his turn, was let in.

XI

'Lady Montbarry, Miss.'

Agnes was writing a letter, when the servant astonished her by announcing the visitor's name. Her first impulse was to refuse to see the woman who had intruded on her. But Lady Montbarry had taken care to follow close on the servant's heels. Before Agnes could speak, she had entered the room.

'I beg to apologise for my intrusion, Miss Lockwood. I have a question to ask you, in which I am very much interested. No one can answer me but yourself.' In low hesitating tones, with her glittering black eyes bent modestly on the ground, Lady Montbarry opened the interview in those words.

Without answering, Agnes pointed to a chair. She could do this, and, for the time, she could do no more. All that she had read of the hidden and sinister life in the palace at Venice; all that she had heard of Montbarry's melancholy death and burial in a foreign land; all that she knew of the mystery of Ferrari's disappearance, rushed into her mind, when the black-robed figure confronted her, standing just inside the door. The strange conduct of Lady Montbarry added a new perplexity to the doubts and misgivings that troubled her. There stood the adventuress whose character had left its mark on society all over Europe—the Fury who had terrified Mrs. Ferrari at the hotel—inconceivably transformed into a timid, shrinking woman! Lady Montbarry had not once ventured to look at Agnes, since she had made her way into the room. Advancing to take the chair that had been pointed out to her, she hesitated, put her hand on the rail to support herself, and still remained standing. 'Please give me a moment to compose myself,' she said faintly. Her head sank on her bosom: she stood before Agnes like a conscious culprit before a merciless judge.

The silence that followed was, literally, the silence of fear on both sides. In the midst of it, the door was opened once more—and Henry Westwick appeared.

He looked at Lady Montbarry with a moment's steady attention—bowed to her with formal politeness—and passed on in silence. At the sight of her husband's brother, the sinking spirit of the woman sprang to life again. Her drooping figure became erect. Her eyes met Westwick's look, brightly defiant. She returned his bow with an icy smile of contempt.

Henry crossed the room to Agnes.

'Is Lady Montbarry here by your invitation?' he asked quietly.

'No.'

'Do you wish to see her?'

'It is very painful to me to see her.'

He turned and looked at his sister-in-law. 'Do you hear that?' he asked coldly.

'I hear it,' she answered, more coldly still.

'Your visit is, to say the least of it, ill-timed.'

'Your interference is, to say the least of it, out of place.'

With that retort, Lady Montbarry approached Agnes. The presence of Henry Westwick seemed at once to relieve and embolden her. 'Permit me to ask my question, Miss Lockwood,' she said, with graceful courtesy. 'It is nothing to embarrass you. When the courier Ferrari applied to my late husband for employment, did you—' Her resolution failed her, before she could say more. She sank trembling into the nearest chair, and, after a moment's struggle, composed herself again. 'Did you permit Ferrari,' she resumed, 'to make sure of being chosen for our courier by using your name?'

Agnes did not reply with her customary directness. Trifling as it was, the reference to Montbarry, proceeding from that woman of all others, confused and agitated her.

'I have known Ferrari's wife for many years,' she began. 'And I take an interest—'

Lady Montbarry abruptly lifted her hands with a gesture of entreaty. 'Ah, Miss Lockwood, don't waste time by talking of his wife! Answer my plain question, plainly!'

'Let me answer her,' Henry whispered. 'I will undertake to speak plainly enough.'

Agnes refused by a gesture. Lady Montbarry's interruption had roused her sense of what was due to herself. She resumed her reply in plainer terms.

'When Ferrari wrote to the late Lord Montbarry,' she said, 'he did certainly mention my name.'

Even now, she had innocently failed to see the object which her visitor had in view. Lady Montbarry's impatience became ungovernable. She started to her feet, and advanced to Agnes.

'Was it with your knowledge and permission that Ferrari used your name?' she asked. 'The whole soul of my question is in that. For God's sake answer me—Yes, or No!'

'Yes.'

That one word struck Lady Montbarry as a blow might have struck her. The fierce life that had animated her face the instant before, faded out of it suddenly, and left her like a woman turned to stone. She stood, mechanically confronting Agnes, with a stillness so wrapt and perfect that not even the breath she drew was perceptible to the two persons who were looking at her.

Henry spoke to her roughly. 'Rouse yourself,' he said. 'You have received your answer.'

She looked round at him. 'I have received my Sentence,' she rejoined—and turned slowly to leave the room.

To Henry's astonishment, Agnes stopped her. 'Wait a moment, Lady Montbarry. I have something to ask on my side. You have spoken of Ferrari. I wish to speak of him too.'

Lady Montbarry bent her head in silence. Her hand trembled as she took out her handkerchief, and passed it over her forehead. Agnes detected the trembling, and shrank back a step. 'Is the subject painful to you?' she asked timidly.

Still silent, Lady Montbarry invited her by a wave of the hand to go on. Henry approached, attentively watching his sister-in-law. Agnes went on.

'No trace of Ferrari has been discovered in England,' she said. 'Have you any news of him? And will you tell me (if you have heard anything), in mercy to his wife?'

Lady Montbarry's thin lips suddenly relaxed into their sad and cruel smile.

'Why do you ask me about the lost courier?' she said. 'You will know what has become of him, Miss Lockwood, when the time is ripe for it.'

Agnes started. 'I don't understand you,' she said. 'How shall I know? Will some one tell me?'

'Some one will tell you.'

Henry could keep silence no longer. 'Perhaps, your ladyship may be the person?' he interrupted with ironical politeness.

She answered him with contemptuous ease. 'You may be right, Mr. Westwick. One day or another, I may be the person who tells Miss Lockwood what has become of Ferrari, if—' She stopped; with her eyes fixed on Agnes.

'If what?' Henry asked.

'If Miss Lockwood forces me to it.'

Agnes listened in astonishment. 'Force you to it?' she repeated. 'How can I do that? Do you mean to say my will is stronger than yours?'

'Do you mean to say that the candle doesn't burn the moth, when the moth flies into it?' Lady Montbarry rejoined. 'Have you ever heard of such a thing as the fascination of terror? I am drawn to you by a fascination of terror. I have no right to visit you, I have no wish to visit you: you are my enemy. For the first time in my life, against my own will, I submit to my enemy. See! I am waiting because you told me to wait—and the fear of you (I swear it!) creeps through me while I stand here. Oh, don't let me excite your curiosity or your pity! Follow the example of Mr. Westwick. Be hard and brutal and unforgiving, like him. Grant me my release. Tell me to go.'

The frank and simple nature of Agnes could discover but one intelligible meaning in this strange outbreak.

'You are mistaken in thinking me your enemy,' she said. 'The wrong you did me when you gave your hand to Lord Montbarry was not intentionally done. I forgave you my sufferings in his lifetime. I forgive you even more freely now that he has gone.'

Henry heard her with mingled emotions of admiration and distress. 'Say no more!' he exclaimed. 'You are too good to her; she is not worthy of it.'

The interruption passed unheeded by Lady Montbarry. The simple words in which Agnes had replied seemed to have absorbed the whole attention of this strangely-changeable woman. As she listened, her face settled slowly into an expression of hard and tearless sorrow. There was a marked change in her voice when she spoke next. It expressed that last worst resignation which has done with hope.

'You good innocent creature,' she said, 'what does your amiable forgiveness matter? What are your poor little wrongs, in the reckoning for greater wrongs which is demanded of me? I am not trying to frighten you, I am only miserable about myself. Do you know what it is to have a firm presentiment of calamity that is coming to you—and yet to hope that your own positive conviction will not prove true? When I first met you, before my marriage, and first felt your influence over me, I had that hope. It was a starveling sort of hope that lived a lingering life in me until to-day. You struck it dead, when you answered my question about Ferrari.'

'How have I destroyed your hopes?' Agnes asked. 'What connection is there between my permitting Ferrari to use my name to Lord Montbarry, and the strange and dreadful things you are saying to me now?'

'The time is near, Miss Lockwood, when you will discover that for yourself. In the mean while, you shall know what my fear of you is, in the plainest words I can find. On the day when I took your hero from you and blighted your life—I am firmly persuaded of it!—you were made the instrument of the retribution that my sins of many years had deserved. Oh, such things have happened before to-day! One person has, before now, been the means of innocently ripening the growth of evil in another. You have done that already—and you have more to do yet. You have still to bring me to the day of discovery, and to the punishment that is my doom. We shall meet again—here in England, or there in Venice where my husband died—and meet for the last time.'

In spite of her better sense, in spite of her natural superiority to superstitions of all kinds, Agnes was impressed by the terrible earnestness with which those words were spoken. She turned pale as she looked at Henry. 'Do you understand her?' she asked.

'Nothing is easier than to understand her,' he replied contemptuously. 'She knows what has become of Ferrari; and she is confusing you in a cloud of nonsense, because she daren't own the truth. Let her go!'

If a dog had been under one of the chairs, and had barked, Lady Montbarry could not have proceeded more impenetrably with the last words she had to say to Agnes.

'Advise your interesting Mrs. Ferrari to wait a little longer,' she said. 'You will know what has become of her husband, and you will tell her. There will be nothing to alarm you. Some trifling event will bring us together the next time—as trifling, I dare say, as the engagement of Ferrari. Sad nonsense, Mr. Westwick, is it not? But you make allowances for women; we all talk nonsense. Good morning, Miss Lockwood.'

She opened the door—suddenly, as if she was afraid of being

called back for the second time—and left them.

XII

'Do you think she is mad?' Agnes asked.

'I think she is simply wicked. False, superstitious, inveterately cruel—but not mad. I believe her main motive in coming here was to enjoy the luxury of frightening you.'

'She has frightened me. I am ashamed to own it—but so it is.'

Henry looked at her, hesitated for a moment, and seated himself on the sofa by her side.

'I am very anxious about you, Agnes,' he said. 'But for the fortunate chance which led me to call here to-day—who knows what that vile woman might not have said or done, if she had found you alone? My dear, you are leading a sadly unprotected solitary life. I don't like to think of it; I want to see it changed—especially after what has happened to-day. No! no! it is useless to tell me that you have your old nurse. She is too old; she is not in your rank of life—there is no sufficient protection in the companionship of such a person for a lady in your position. Don't mistake me, Agnes! what I say, I say in the sincerity of my devotion to you.' He paused, and took her hand. She made a feeble effort to withdraw it—and yielded. 'Will the day never come,' he pleaded, 'when the privilege of protecting you may be mine? when you will be the pride and joy of my life, as long as my life lasts?' He pressed her hand gently. She made no reply. The colour came and went on her face; her eyes were turned away from him. 'Have I been so unhappy as to offend you?' he asked.

She answered that—she said, almost in a whisper, 'No.'

'Have I distressed you?'

'You have made me think of the sad days that are gone.' She said no more; she only tried to withdraw her hand from his for the second time. He still held it; he lifted it to his lips.

'Can I never make you think of other days than those—of the happier days to come? Or, if you must think of the time that is passed, can you not look back to the time when I first loved you?'

She sighed as he put the question. 'Spare me, Henry,' she answered sadly. 'Say no more!'

The colour again rose in her cheeks; her hand trembled in his. She looked lovely, with her eyes cast down and her bosom heaving gently. At that moment he would have given everything he had in the world to take her in his arms and kiss her. Some mysterious sympathy, passing from his hand to hers, seemed to tell her what was in his mind. She snatched her hand away, and suddenly looked up at him. The tears were in her eyes. She said nothing; she let her eyes speak for her. They warned him—without anger, without unkindness—but still they warned him to press her no further that day.

'Only tell me that I am forgiven,' he said, as he rose from the sofa.

'Yes,' she answered quietly, 'you are forgiven.'

'I have not lowered myself in your estimation, Agnes?'

'Oh, no!'

'Do you wish me to leave you?'

She rose, in her turn, from the sofa, and walked to her writing-table before she replied. The unfinished letter which she had been writing when Lady Montbarry interrupted her, lay open on the blotting-book. As she looked at the letter, and then looked at Henry, the smile that charmed everybody showed itself in her face.

'You must not go just yet,' she said: 'I have something to tell you. I hardly know how to express it. The shortest way perhaps will be to let you find it out for yourself. You have been speaking of my lonely unprotected life here. It is not a very happy life, Henry—I own that.' She paused, observing the growing anxiety of his expression as he looked at her, with a shy satisfaction that perplexed him. 'Do you know that I have anticipated your idea?' she went on. 'I am going to make a great change in my life—if your brother Stephen and his wife will only consent to it.' She opened the desk of the writing-table while she spoke, took a letter out, and handed it to Henry.

He received it from her mechanically. Vague doubts, which he hardly understood himself, kept him silent. It was impossible that the 'change in her life' of which she had spoken could mean that she was about to be married—and yet he was conscious of a perfectly unreasonable reluctance to open the letter. Their eyes met; she smiled again. 'Look at the address,' she said. 'You ought to know the handwriting—but I dare say you don't.'

He looked at the address. It was in the large, irregular, uncertain writing of a child. He opened the letter instantly.

'Dear Aunt Agnes,—Our governess is going away. She has had money left to her, and a house of her own. We have had cake and wine to drink her health. You promised to be our governess if we wanted another. We want you. Mamma knows nothing about this. Please come before Mamma can get another governess. Your loving Lucy, who writes this. Clara and Blanche have tried to write too. But they are too young to do it. They blot the paper.'

'Your eldest niece,' Agnes explained, as Henry looked at her in amazement. 'The children used to call me aunt when I was staying with their mother in Ireland, in the autumn. The three girls were my inseparable companions—they are the most charming children I know. It is quite true that I offered to be their governess, if they ever wanted one, on the day when I left them to return to London. I was writing to propose it to their mother, just before you came.'

'Not seriously!' Henry exclaimed.

Agnes placed her unfinished letter in his hand. Enough of it had been written to show that she did seriously propose to enter the household of Mr. and Mrs. Stephen Westwick as governess to their children! Henry's bewilderment was not to be expressed in words.

'They won't believe you are in earnest,' he said.

'Why not?' Agnes asked quietly.

'You are my brother Stephen's cousin; you are his wife's old friend.'

'All the more reason, Henry, for trusting me with the charge of their children.'

'But you are their equal; you are not obliged to get your living by teaching. There is something absurd in your entering their service as a governess!'

'What is there absurd in it? The children love me; the mother loves me; the father has shown me innumerable instances of his true friendship and regard. I am the very woman for the place—and, as to my education, I must have completely forgotten it indeed, if I am not fit to teach three children the eldest of whom is only eleven years old. You say I am their equal. Are there no other women who serve as governesses, and who are the equals of the persons whom they serve? Besides, I don't know that I am their equal. Have I not heard that your brother Stephen was the next heir to the title? Will he not be the new lord? Never mind answering me! We won't dispute whether I am right or wrong in turning governess—we will wait the event. I am weary of my lonely useless existence here, and eager to make my life more happy and more useful, in the household of all others in which I should like most to have a place. If you will look again, you will see that I have these personal considerations still to urge before I finish my letter. You don't know your brother and his wife as well as I do, if you doubt their answer. I believe they have courage enough and heart enough to say Yes.'

Henry submitted without being convinced.

He was a man who disliked all eccentric departures from custom and routine; and he felt especially suspicious of the change proposed in the life of Agnes. With new interests to occupy her mind, she might be less favourably disposed to listen to him, on the next occasion when he urged his suit. The influence of the 'lonely useless existence' of which she complained, was distinctly an influence in his favour. While her heart was empty, her heart was accessible. But with his nieces in full possession of it, the clouds of doubt overshadowed his prospects. He knew the sex well enough to keep these purely selfish perplexities to himself. The waiting policy was especially the policy to pursue with a woman as sensitive as Agnes. If he once offended her delicacy he was lost. For the moment he wisely controlled himself and changed the subject.

'My little niece's letter has had an effect,' he said, 'which the child never contemplated in writing it. She has just reminded me of one of the objects that I had in calling on you to-day.'

Agnes looked at the child's letter. 'How does Lucy do that?' she asked.

'Lucy's governess is not the only lucky person who has had money left her,' Henry answered. 'Is your old nurse in the house?'

'You don't mean to say that nurse has got a legacy?'

'She has got a hundred pounds. Send for her, Agnes, while I show you the letter.'

He took a handful of letters from his pocket, and looked through them, while Agnes rang the bell. Returning to him, she noticed a printed letter among the rest, which lay open on the table. It was a 'prospectus,' and the title of it was 'Palace Hotel Company of Venice (Limited).' The two words, 'Palace' and 'Venice,' instantly recalled her mind to the unwelcome visit of Lady Montbarry. 'What is that?' she asked, pointing to the title.

Henry suspended his search, and glanced at the prospectus. 'A really promising speculation,' he said. 'Large hotels always pay well, if they are well managed. I know the man who is appointed to be manager of this hotel when it is opened to the public; and I have such entire confidence in him that I have become one of the shareholders of the Company.'

The reply did not appear to satisfy Agnes. 'Why is the hotel called the "Palace Hotel"?' she inquired.

Henry looked at her, and at once penetrated her motive for asking the question. 'Yes,' he said, 'it is the palace that Montbarry hired at Venice; and it has been purchased by the Company to be changed into an hotel.'

Agnes turned away in silence, and took a chair at the farther end of the room. Henry had disappointed her. His income as a younger son stood in need, as she well knew, of all the additions that he could make to it by successful speculation. But she was unreasonable enough, nevertheless, to disapprove of his attempting to make money already out of the house in which his brother had died. Incapable of understanding this purely sentimental view of a plain matter of business, Henry returned to his papers, in some perplexity at the sudden change in the manner of Agnes towards him. Just as he found the letter of which he was in search, the nurse made her appearance. He glanced at Agnes, expecting that she would speak first. She never even looked up when the nurse came in. It was left to Henry to tell the old woman why the bell had summoned her to the drawing-room.

'Well, nurse,' he said, 'you have had a windfall of luck. You have had a legacy left you of a hundred pounds.'

The nurse showed no outward signs of exultation. She waited a little to get the announcement of the legacy well settled in her mind—and then she said quietly, 'Master Henry, who gives me that money, if you please?'

'My late brother, Lord Montbarry, gives it to you.' (Agnes instantly looked up, interested in the matter for the first time. Henry went on.) 'His will leaves legacies to the surviving old servants of the family. There is a letter from his lawyers, authorising you to apply to them for the money.'

In every class of society, gratitude is the rarest of all human virtues. In the nurse's class it is extremely rare. Her opinion of the man who had deceived and deserted her mistress remained the same opinion still, perfectly undisturbed by the passing circumstance of the legacy.

'I wonder who reminded my lord of the old servants?' she said. 'He would never have heart enough to remember them himself!'

Agnes suddenly interposed. Nature, always abhorring monotony, institutes reserves of temper as elements in the composition of the gentlest women living. Even Agnes could, on rare occasions, be angry. The nurse's view of Montbarry's character seemed to have provoked her beyond endurance.

'If you have any sense of shame in you,' she broke out, 'you ought to be ashamed of what you have just said! Your ingratitude disgusts me. I leave you to speak with her, Henry—you won't mind it!' With this significant intimation that he too had dropped out of his customary place in her good opinion, she left the room.

The nurse received the smart reproof administered to her with every appearance of feeling rather amused by it than not. When the door had closed, this female philosopher winked at Henry.

'There's a power of obstinacy in young women,' she remarked. 'Miss Agnes wouldn't give my lord up as a bad one, even when he jilted her. And now she's sweet on him after he's dead. Say a word against him, and she fires up as you see. All obstinacy! It will wear out with time. Stick to her, Master Henry—stick to her!'

'She doesn't seem to have offended you,' said Henry.

'She?' the nurse repeated in amazement—'she offend me? I like her in her tantrums; it reminds me of her when she was a baby. Lord bless you! when I go to bid her good-night, she'll give me a big kiss, poor dear—and say, Nurse, I didn't mean it! About this money, Master Henry? If I was younger I should spend it in dress and jewellery. But I'm too old for that. What shall I do with my legacy when I have got it?'

'Put it out at interest,' Henry suggested. 'Get so much a year for it, you know.' 'How much shall I get?' the nurse asked.

'If you put your hundred pounds into the Funds, you will get between three and four pounds a year.'

The nurse shook her head. 'Three or four pounds a year? That won't do! I want more than that. Look here, Master Henry. I don't care about this bit of money—I never did like the man who has left it to me, though he was your brother. If I lost it all to-morrow, I shouldn't break my heart; I'm well enough off, as it is, for the rest of my days. They say you're a speculator. Put me in for a good thing, there's a dear! Neck-or-nothing—and that for the Funds!' She snapped her fingers to express her contempt for security of investment at three per cent.

Henry produced the prospectus of the Venetian Hotel Company. 'You're a funny old woman,' he said. 'There, you dashing speculator—there is neck-or-nothing for you! You must keep it a secret from Miss Agnes, mind. I'm not at all sure that she would approve of my helping you to this investment.'

The nurse took out her spectacles. 'Six per cent., guaranteed,' she read; 'and the Directors have every reason to believe that ten per cent., or more, will be ultimately realised to the shareholders by the hotel.' 'Put me into that, Master Henry! And, wherever you go, for Heaven's sake recommend the hotel to your friends!'

So the nurse, following Henry's mercenary example, had her pecuniary interest, too, in the house in which Lord Montbarry had died.

Three days passed before Henry was able to visit Agnes again. In that time, the little cloud between them had entirely passed away. Agnes received him with even more than her customary kindness. She was in better spirits than usual. Her letter to Mrs. Stephen Westwick had been answered by return of post; and her proposal had been joyfully accepted, with one modification. She was to visit the Westwicks for a month—and, if she really liked teaching the children, she was then to be governess, aunt, and cousin, all in one—and was only to go away in an event which her friends in Ireland persisted in contemplating, the event of her marriage.

'You see I was right,' she said to Henry.

He was still incredulous. 'Are you really going?' he asked.

'I am going next week.'

'When shall I see you again?'

'You know you are always welcome at your brother's house. You can see me when you like.' She held out her hand. 'Pardon me for leaving you—I am beginning to pack up already.'

Henry tried to kiss her at parting. She drew back directly.

'Why not? I am your cousin,' he said.

'I don't like it,' she answered.

Henry looked at her, and submitted. Her refusal to grant him his privilege as a cousin was a good sign—it was indirectly an act of encouragement to him in the character of her lover.

On the first day in the new week, Agnes left London on her way to Ireland. As the event proved, this was not destined to be the end of her journey. The way to Ireland was only the first stage on a roundabout road—the road that led to the palace at Venice.

THE THIRD PART

XIII

In the spring of the year 1861, Agnes was established at the country-seat of her two friends—now promoted (on the death of the first lord, without offspring) to be the new Lord and Lady Montbarry. The old nurse was not separated from her mistress. A place, suited to her time of life, had been found for her in the pleasant Irish household. She was perfectly happy in her new sphere; and she spent her first half-year's dividend from the Venice Hotel Company, with characteristic prodigality, in presents for the children.

Early in the year, also, the Directors of the life insurance offices submitted to circumstances, and paid the ten thousand pounds. Immediately afterwards, the widow of the first Lord Montbarry (otherwise, the dowager Lady Montbarry) left England, with Baron Rivar, for the United States. The Baron's object was announced, in the scientific columns of the newspapers, to be investigation into the present state of experimental chemistry in the great American republic. His sister informed inquiring friends that she accompanied him, in the hope of finding consolation in change of scene after the bereavement that had fallen on her. Hearing this news from Henry Westwick (then paying a visit at his brother's house), Agnes was conscious of a certain sense of relief. 'With the Atlantic between us,' she said, 'surely I have done with that terrible woman now!'

Barely a week passed after those words had been spoken, before an event happened which reminded Agnes of 'the terrible woman' once more.

On that day, Henry's engagements had obliged him to return to London. He had ventured, on the morning of his departure, to press his suit once more on Agnes; and the children, as he had anticipated, proved to be innocent obstacles in the way of his success. On the other hand, he had privately secured a firm ally in his sister-in-law. 'Have a little patience,' the new Lady Montbarry had said, 'and leave me to turn the influence of the children in the right direction. If they can persuade her to listen to you—they shall!'

The two ladies had accompanied Henry, and some other guests who went away at the same time, to the railway station, and had just driven back to the house, when the servant announced that 'a person of the name of Rolland was waiting to see her ladyship.'

'Is it a woman?'

'Yes, my lady.'

Young Lady Montbarry turned to Agnes.

'This is the very person,' she said, 'whom your lawyer thought likely to help him, when he was trying to trace the lost courier.'

'You don't mean the English maid who was with Lady Montbarry at Venice?'

'My dear! don't speak of Montbarry's horrid widow by the name which is my name now. Stephen and I have arranged to call her by her foreign title, before she was married. I am "Lady Montbarry," and she is "the Countess." In that way there will be no confusion.—Yes, Mrs. Rolland was in my service before she became the Countess's maid. She was a perfectly trustworthy person, with one defect that obliged me to send her away—a sullen temper which led to perpetual complaints of her in the servants' hall. Would you like to see her?'

Agnes accepted the proposal, in the faint hope of getting some information for the courier's wife. The complete defeat of every attempt to trace the lost man had been accepted as final by Mrs. Ferrari. She had deliberately arrayed herself in widow's mourning; and was earning her livelihood in an employment which the unwearied kindness of Agnes had procured for her in London. The last chance of penetrating the mystery of Ferrari's disappearance seemed to rest now on what Ferrari's former fellow-servant might be able to tell. With highly-wrought expectations, Agnes followed her friend into the room in which Mrs. Rolland was waiting.

A tall bony woman, in the autumn of life, with sunken eyes and iron-grey hair, rose stiffly from her chair, and saluted the ladies with stern submission as they opened the door. A person of unblemished character, evidently—but not without visible drawbacks. Big bushy eyebrows, an awfully deep and solemn voice, a harsh unbending manner, a complete absence in her figure of the undulating lines characteristic of the sex, presented Virtue in this excellent person under its least alluring aspect. Strangers, on a first introduction to her, were accustomed to wonder why she was not a man.

'Are you pretty well, Mrs. Rolland?'

'I am as well as I can expect to be, my lady, at my time of life.'

'Is there anything I can do for you?'

'Your ladyship can do me a great favour, if you will please speak to my character while I was in your service. I am offered a place, to wait on an invalid lady who has lately come to live in this neighbourhood.'

'Ah, yes—I have heard of her. A Mrs. Carbury, with a very pretty niece I am told. But, Mrs. Rolland, you left my service some time ago. Mrs. Carbury will surely expect you to refer to the last mistress by whom you were employed.'

A flash of virtuous indignation irradiated Mrs. Rolland's sunken eyes. She coughed before she answered, as if her 'last mistress' stuck in her throat.

'I have explained to Mrs. Carbury, my lady, that the person I last served—I really cannot give her her title in your ladyship's presence!—has left England for America. Mrs. Carbury knows that I quitted the person of my own free will, and knows why, and approves of my conduct so far. A word from your ladyship will be amply sufficient to get me the situation.'

'Very well, Mrs. Rolland, I have no objection to be your reference, under the circumstances. Mrs. Carbury will find me at home to-morrow until two o'clock.'

'Mrs. Carbury is not well enough to leave the house, my lady. Her niece, Miss Haldane, will call and make the inquiries, if your ladyship has no objection.'

'I have not the least objection. The pretty niece carries her own welcome with her. Wait a minute, Mrs. Rolland. This lady is Miss Lockwood—my husband's cousin, and my friend. She is anxious to speak to you about the courier who was in the late Lord Montbarry's service at Venice.'

Mrs. Rolland's bushy eyebrows frowned in stern disapproval of the new topic of conversation. 'I regret to hear it, my lady,' was all she said.

'Perhaps you have not been informed of what happened after you left Venice?' Agnes ventured to add. 'Ferrari left the palace secretly; and he has never been heard of since.'

Mrs. Rolland mysteriously closed her eyes—as if to exclude some vision of the lost courier which was of a nature to disturb a respectable woman. 'Nothing that Mr. Ferrari could do would surprise me,' she replied in her deepest bass tones.

'You speak rather harshly of him,' said Agnes.

Mrs. Rolland suddenly opened her eyes again. 'I speak harshly of nobody without reason,' she said. 'Mr. Ferrari behaved to me, Miss Lockwood, as no man living has ever behaved—before or since.'

'What did he do?'

Mrs. Rolland answered, with a stony stare of horror:— 'He took liberties with me.'

Young Lady Montbarry suddenly turned aside, and put her handkerchief over her mouth in convulsions of suppressed laughter.

Mrs. Rolland went on, with a grim enjoyment of the bewilderment which her reply had produced in Agnes: 'And when I insisted on an apology, Miss, he had the audacity to say that the life at the palace was dull, and he didn't know how else to amuse himself!'

'I am afraid I have hardly made myself understood,' said Agnes. 'I am not speaking to you out of any interest in Ferrari. Are you aware that he is married?'

'I pity his wife,' said Mrs. Rolland.

'She is naturally in great grief about him,' Agnes proceeded.

'She ought to thank God she is rid of him,' Mrs. Rolland interposed.

Agnes still persisted. 'I have known Mrs. Ferrari from her childhood, and I am sincerely anxious to help her in this matter. Did you notice anything, while you were at Venice, that would account for her husband's extraordinary disappearance? On what sort of terms, for instance, did he live with his master and mistress?'

'On terms of familiarity with his mistress,' said Mrs. Rolland, 'which were simply sickening to a respectable English servant. She used to encourage him to talk to her about all his affairs—

how he got on with his wife, and how pressed he was for money, and such like—just as if they were equals. Contemptible—that's what I call it.'

'And his master?' Agnes continued. 'How did Ferrari get on with Lord Montbarry?'

'My lord used to live shut up with his studies and his sorrows,' Mrs. Rolland answered, with a hard solemnity expressive of respect for his lordship's memory. 'Mr. Ferrari got his money when it was due; and he cared for nothing else. "If I could afford it, I would leave the place too; but I can't afford it." Those were the last words he said to me, on the morning when I left the palace. I made no reply. After what had happened (on that other occasion) I was naturally not on speaking terms with Mr. Ferrari.'

'Can you really tell me nothing which will throw any light on this matter?'

'Nothing,' said Mrs. Rolland, with an undisguised relish of the disappointment that she was inflicting.

'There was another member of the family at Venice,' Agnes resumed, determined to sift the question to the bottom while she had the chance. 'There was Baron Rivar.'

Mrs. Rolland lifted her large hands, covered with rusty black gloves, in mute protest against the introduction of Baron Rivar as a subject of inquiry. 'Are you aware, Miss,' she began, 'that I left my place in consequence of what I observed—?'

Agnes stopped her there. 'I only wanted to ask,' she explained, 'if anything was said or done by Baron Rivar which might account for Ferrari's strange conduct.'

'Nothing that I know of,' said Mrs. Rolland. 'The Baron and Mr. Ferrari (if I may use such an expression) were "birds of a feather," so far as I could see—I mean, one was as unprincipled as the other. I am a just woman; and I will give you an example. Only the day before I left, I heard the Baron say (through the open door of his room while I was passing along the corridor), "Ferrari, I want a thousand pounds. What would you do for a thousand pounds?" And I heard Mr. Ferrari answer, "Anything, sir, as long as I was not found out." And then they both burst out laughing. I heard no more than that. Judge for yourself, Miss.'

Agnes reflected for a moment. A thousand pounds was the

sum that had been sent to Mrs. Ferrari in the anonymous letter. Was that enclosure in any way connected, as a result, with the conversation between the Baron and Ferrari? It was useless to press any more inquiries on Mrs. Rolland. She could give no further information which was of the slightest importance to the object in view. There was no alternative but to grant her dismissal. One more effort had been made to find a trace of the lost man, and once again the effort had failed.

They were a family party at the dinner-table that day. The only guest left in the house was a nephew of the new Lord Montbarry—the eldest son of his sister, Lady Barville. Lady Montbarry could not resist telling the story of the first (and last) attack made on the virtue of Mrs. Rolland, with a comically-exact imitation of Mrs. Rolland's deep and dismal voice. Being asked by her husband what was the object which had brought that formidable person to the house, she naturally mentioned the expected visit of Miss Haldane. Arthur Barville, unusually silent and pre-occupied so far, suddenly struck into the conversation with a burst of enthusiasm. 'Miss Haldane is the most charming girl in all Ireland!' he said. 'I caught sight of her yesterday, over the wall of her garden, as I was riding by. What time is she coming to-morrow? Before two? I'll look into the drawing-room by accident—I am dying to be introduced to her!'

Agnes was amused by his enthusiasm. 'Are you in love with Miss Haldane already?' she asked.

Arthur answered gravely, 'It's no joking matter. I have been all day at the garden wall, waiting to see her again! It depends on Miss Haldane to make me the happiest or the wretchedest man living.'

'You foolish boy! How can you talk such nonsense?'

He was talking nonsense undoubtedly. But, if Agnes had only known it, he was doing something more than that. He was innocently leading her another stage nearer on the way to Venice.

XIV

As the summer months advanced, the transformation of the Venetian palace into the modern hotel proceeded rapidly towards completion.

The outside of the building, with its fine Palladian front looking on the canal, was wisely left unaltered. Inside, as a matter of necessity, the rooms were almost rebuilt—so far at least as the size and the arrangement of them were concerned. The vast saloons were partitioned off into 'apartments' containing three or four rooms each. The broad corridors in the upper regions afforded spare space enough for rows of little bedchambers, devoted to servants and to travellers with limited means. Nothing was spared but the solid floors and the finely-carved ceilings. These last, in excellent preservation as to workmanship, merely required cleaning, and regilding here and there, to add greatly to the beauty and importance of the best rooms in the hotel. The only exception to the complete re-organization of the interior was at one extremity of the edifice, on the first and second floors. Here there happened, in each case, to be rooms of such comparatively moderate size, and so attractively decorated, that the architect suggested leaving them as they were. It was afterwards discovered that these were no other than the apartments formerly occupied by Lord Montbarry (on the first floor), and by Baron Rivar (on the second). The room in which Montbarry had died was still fitted up as a bedroom, and was now distinguished as Number Fourteen. The room above it, in which the Baron had slept, took its place on the hotel-register as Number Thirty-Eight. With the ornaments on the walls and ceilings cleaned and brightened up, and with the heavy old-fashioned beds, chairs, and tables replaced by bright, pretty, and luxurious modern furniture, these two promised to be at once the most attractive and the most comfortable bedchambers in the hotel. As for the once-desolate and disused ground floor of the building, it was now transformed, by means of splendid dining-rooms, reception-rooms, billiard-rooms, and smoking-rooms, into a palace by itself. Even the dungeon-like vaults beneath, now lighted and ventilated on the most approved modern plan, had been turned as if by magic into kitchens, servants' offices, ice-rooms, and wine cellars, worthy of the splendour of the grandest hotel in Italy, in the now bygone period of seventeen years since.

Passing from the lapse of the summer months at Venice, to the lapse of the summer months in Ireland, it is next to be recorded that Mrs. Rolland obtained the situation of attendant on the invalid Mrs. Carbury; and that the fair Miss Haldane, like a female Caesar, came, saw, and conquered, on her first day's visit to the new Lord Montbarry's house.

The ladies were as loud in her praises as Arthur Barville himself. Lord Montbarry declared that she was the only perfectly pretty woman he had ever seen, who was really unconscious of her own attractions. The old nurse said she looked as if she had just stepped out of a picture, and wanted nothing but a gilt frame round her to make her complete. Miss Haldane, on her side, returned from her first visit to the Montbarrys charmed with her new acquaintances. Later on the same day, Arthur called with an offering of fruit and flowers for Mrs. Carbury, and with instructions to ask if she was well enough to receive Lord and Lady Montbarry and Miss Lockwood on the morrow. In a week's time, the two households were on the friendliest terms. Mrs. Carbury, confined to the sofa by a spinal malady, had been hitherto dependent on her niece for one of the few pleasures she could enjoy, the pleasure of having the best new novels read to her as they came out. Discovering this, Arthur volunteered to relieve Miss Haldane, at intervals, in the office of reader. He was clever at mechanical contrivances of all sorts, and he introduced improvements in Mrs. Carbury's couch, and in the means of conveying her from the bedchamber to the drawing-room, which alleviated the poor lady's sufferings and brightened her gloomy life. With these claims on the gratitude of the aunt, aided by the personal advantages which he unquestionably possessed, Arthur advanced rapidly in the favour of the charming niece. She was, it is needless to say, perfectly well aware that he was in love with her, while he was himself modestly reticent on the subject—so far as words went. But she was not equally quick in penetrating the nature of her own feelings towards Arthur. Watching the two young people with keen powers of observation, necessarily concentrated on them by the complete seclusion of her life, the invalid lady discovered signs of roused sensibility in Miss

Haldane, when Arthur was present, which had never yet shown themselves in her social relations with other admirers eager to pay their addresses to her. Having drawn her own conclusions in private, Mrs. Carbury took the first favourable opportunity (in Arthur's interests) of putting them to the test.

'I don't know what I shall do,' she said one day, 'when Arthur goes away.'

Miss Haldane looked up quickly from her work. 'Surely he is not going to leave us!' she exclaimed.

'My dear! he has already stayed at his uncle's house a month longer than he intended. His father and mother naturally expect to see him at home again.'

Miss Haldane met this difficulty with a suggestion, which could only have proceeded from a judgment already disturbed by the ravages of the tender passion. 'Why can't his father and mother go and see him at Lord Montbarry's?' she asked. 'Sir Theodore's place is only thirty miles away, and Lady Barville is Lord Montbarry's sister. They needn't stand on ceremony.'

'They may have other engagements,' Mrs. Carbury remarked.

'My dear aunt, we don't know that! Suppose you ask Arthur?'

'Suppose you ask him?'

Miss Haldane bent her head again over her work. Suddenly as it was done, her aunt had seen her face—and her face betrayed her.

When Arthur came the next day, Mrs. Carbury said a word to him in private, while her niece was in the garden. The last new novel lay neglected on the table. Arthur followed Miss Haldane into the garden. The next day he wrote home, enclosing in his letter a photograph of Miss Haldane. Before the end of the week, Sir Theodore and Lady Barville arrived at Lord Montbarry's, and formed their own judgment of the fidelity of the portrait. They had themselves married early in life—and, strange to say, they did not object on principle to the early marriages of other people. The question of age being thus disposed of, the course of true love had no other obstacles to encounter. Miss Haldane was an only child, and was possessed of an ample fortune. Arthur's career at the university had been creditable, but certainly not brilliant enough to present his withdrawal in the light of a disaster. As Sir Theodore's eldest son, his position was already made for him. He was two-and-twenty years of age; and the young lady was eighteen. There was really no producible reason for keeping the lovers waiting, and no excuse for deferring the wedding-day beyond the first week in September. In the interval, while the bride and bridegroom would be necessarily absent on the inevitable tour abroad, a sister of Mrs. Carbury volunteered to stay with her during the temporary separation from her niece. On the conclusion of the honeymoon, the young couple were to return to Ireland, and were to establish themselves in Mrs. Carbury's spacious and comfortable house.

These arrangements were decided upon early in the month of August. About the same date, the last alterations in the old palace at Venice were completed. The rooms were dried by steam; the cellars were stocked; the manager collected round him his army of skilled servants; and the new hotel was advertised all over Europe to open in October.

XV

(MISS AGNES LOCKWOOD TO MRS. FERRARI)

'I promised to give you some account, dear Emily, of the marriage of Mr. Arthur Barville and Miss Haldane. It took place ten days since. But I have had so many things to look after in the absence of the master and mistress of this house, that I am only able to write to you to-day.

'The invitations to the wedding were limited to members of the families on either side, in consideration of the ill health of Miss Haldane's aunt. On the side of the Montbarry family, there were present, besides Lord and Lady Montbarry, Sir Theodore and Lady Barville; Mrs. Norbury (whom you may remember as his lordship's second sister); and Mr. Francis Westwick, and Mr. Henry Westwick. The three children and I attended the ceremony as bridesmaids. We were joined by two young ladies, cousins of the bride and very agreeable girls. Our dresses were white, trimmed with green in honour of Ireland; and we each had a handsome gold bracelet given to us as a present from the bridegroom. If you add to the persons whom I have already mentioned, the elder members of Mrs. Carbury's family, and the old servants in both houses—privileged to drink the healths of the married pair at the lower end of the room—you will have the list of the company at the wedding-breakfast complete.

'The weather was perfect, and the ceremony (with music) was beautifully performed. As for the bride, no words can describe how lovely she looked, or how well she went through it all. We were very merry at the breakfast, and the speeches went off on the whole quite well enough. The last speech, before the party broke up, was made by Mr. Henry Westwick, and was the best of all. He offered a happy suggestion, at the end, which has produced a very unexpected change in my life here.

'As well as I remember, he concluded in these words:—"On one point, we are all agreed—we are sorry that the parting hour is near, and we should be glad to meet again. Why should we not meet again? This is the autumn time of the year; we are most of us leaving home for the holidays. What do you say (if you have no engagements that will prevent it) to joining our young married friends before the close of their tour, and renewing the social success of this delightful breakfast by another festival in honour of the honeymoon? The bride and bridegroom are going to Germany and the Tyrol, on their way to Italy. I propose that we allow them a month to themselves, and that we arrange to meet them afterwards in the North of Italy—say at Venice."

'This proposal was received with great applause, which was changed into shouts of laughter by no less a person than my dear old nurse. The moment Mr. Westwick pronounced the word "Venice," she started up among the servants at the lower end of the room, and called out at the top of her voice, "Go to our hotel, ladies and gentlemen! We get six per cent. on our money already; and if you will only crowd the place and call for the best of everything, it will be ten per cent. in our pockets in no time. Ask Master Henry!"

'Appealed to in this irresistible manner, Mr. Westwick had no choice but to explain that he was concerned as a shareholder in a new Hotel Company at Venice, and that he had invested a small sum of money for the nurse (not very considerately, as I think) in the speculation. Hearing this, the company, by way of humouring the joke, drank a new toast:—Success to the nurse's hotel, and a speedy rise in the dividend!

'When the conversation returned in due time to the more

serious question of the proposed meeting at Venice, difficulties began to present themselves, caused of course by invitations for the autumn which many of the guests had already accepted. Only two members of Mrs. Carbury's family were at liberty to keep the proposed appointment. On our side we were more at leisure to do as we pleased. Mr. Henry Westwick decided to go to Venice in advance of the rest, to test the accommodation of the new hotel on the opening day. Mrs. Norbury and Mr. Francis Westwick volunteered to follow him; and, after some persuasion, Lord and Lady Montbarry consented to a species of compromise. His lordship could not conveniently spare time enough for the journey to Venice, but he and Lady Montbarry arranged to accompany Mrs. Norbury and Mr. Francis Westwick as far on their way to Italy as Paris. Five days since, they took their departure to meet their travelling companions in London; leaving me here in charge of the three dear children. They begged hard, of course, to be taken with papa and mamma. But it was thought better not to interrupt the progress of their education, and not to expose them (especially the two younger girls) to the fatigues of travelling.

'I have had a charming letter from the bride, this morning, dated Cologne. You cannot think how artlessly and prettily she assures me of her happiness. Some people, as they say in Ireland, are born to good luck—and I think Arthur Barville is one of them.

'When you next write, I hope to hear that you are in better health and spirits, and that you continue to like your employment. Believe me, sincerely your friend,—A. L.'

Agnes had just closed and directed her letter, when the eldest of her three pupils entered the room with the startling announcement that Lord Montbarry's travelling-servant had arrived from Paris! Alarmed by the idea that some misfortune had happened, she ran out to meet the man in the hall. Her face told him how seriously he had frightened her, before she could speak. 'There's nothing wrong, Miss,' he hastened to say. 'My lord and my lady are enjoying themselves at Paris. They only want you and the young ladies to be with them.' Saying these amazing words, he handed to Agnes a letter from Lady Montbarry.

'Dearest Agnes,' (she read), 'I am so charmed with the

delightful change in my life—it is six years, remember, since I last travelled on the Continent—that I have exerted all my fascinations to persuade Lord Montbarry to go on to Venice. And, what is more to the purpose, I have actually succeeded! He has just gone to his room to write the necessary letters of excuse in time for the post to England. May you have as good a husband, my dear, when your time comes! In the mean while, the one thing wanting now to make my happiness complete, is to have you and the darling children with us. Montbarry is just as miserable without them as I am—though he doesn't confess it so freely. You will have no difficulties to trouble you. Louis will deliver these hurried lines, and will take care of you on the journey to Paris. Kiss the children for me a thousand times—and never mind their education for the present! Pack up instantly, my dear, and I will be fonder of you than ever. Your affectionate friend, Adela Montbarry.'

Agnes folded up the letter; and, feeling the need of composing herself, took refuge for a few minutes in her own room.

Her first natural sensations of surprise and excitement at the prospect of going to Venice were succeeded by impressions of a less agreeable kind. With the recovery of her customary composure came the unwelcome remembrance of the parting words spoken to her by Montbarry's widow:—'We shall meet again—here in England, or there in Venice where my husband died—and meet for the last time.'

It was an odd coincidence, to say the least of it, that the march of events should be unexpectedly taking Agnes to Venice, after those words had been spoken! Was the woman of the mysterious warnings and the wild black eyes still thousands of miles away in America? Or was the march of events taking her unexpectedly, too, on the journey to Venice? Agnes started out of her chair, ashamed of even the momentary concession to superstition which was implied by the mere presence of such questions as these in her mind.

She rang the bell, and sent for her little pupils, and announced their approaching departure to the household. The noisy delight of the children, the inspiriting effort of packing up in a hurry, roused all her energies. She dismissed her own absurd misgivings from consideration, with the contempt that they deserved. She worked as only women can work, when their hearts are in what they do. The travellers reached Dublin that day, in time for the boat to England. Two days later, they were with Lord and Lady Montbarry at Paris.

THE FOURTH PART

XVI

It was only the twentieth of September, when Agnes and the children reached Paris. Mrs. Norbury and her brother Francis had then already started on their journey to Italy—at least three weeks before the date at which the new hotel was to open for the reception of travellers.

The person answerable for this premature departure was Francis Westwick.

Like his younger brother Henry, he had increased his pecuniary resources by his own enterprise and ingenuity; with this difference, that his speculations were connected with the Arts. He had made money, in the first instance, by a weekly newspaper; and he had then invested his profits in a London theatre. This latter enterprise, admirably conducted, had been rewarded by the public with steady and liberal encouragement. Pondering over a new form of theatrical attraction for the coming winter season, Francis had determined to revive the languid public taste for the ballet by means of an entertainment of his own invention, combining dramatic interest with dancing. He was now, accordingly, in search of the best dancer (possessed of the indispensable personal attractions) who was to be found in the theatres of the Continent. Hearing from his foreign correspondents of two women who had made successful first appearances, one at Milan and one at Florence, he had arranged to visit those cities, and to judge of the merits of the dancers for himself, before he joined the bride and bridegroom. His widowed sister, having friends at Florence whom she was anxious to see, readily accompanied him. The Montbarrys remained at Paris, until it was time to present themselves at the family meeting in Venice. Henry found them still in the French capital, when he arrived from London on his way to the opening of the new hotel.

Against Lady Montbarry's advice, he took the opportunity of

renewing his addresses to Agnes. He could hardly have chosen a more unpropitious time for pleading his cause with her. The gaieties of Paris (quite incomprehensibly to herself as well as to everyone about her) had a depressing effect on her spirits. She had no illness to complain of; she shared willingly in the ever-varying succession of amusements offered to strangers by the ingenuity of the liveliest people in the world—but nothing roused her: she remained persistently dull and weary through it all. In this frame of mind and body, she was in no humour to receive Henry's ill-timed addresses with favour, or even with patience: she plainly and positively refused to listen to him. 'Why do you remind me of what I have suffered?' she asked petulantly. 'Don't you see that it has left its mark on me for life?'

'I thought I knew something of women by this time,' Henry said, appealing privately to Lady Montbarry for consolation. 'But Agnes completely puzzles me. It is a year since Montbarry's death; and she remains as devoted to his memory as if he had died faithful to her—she still feels the loss of him, as none of us feel it!'

'She is the truest woman that ever breathed the breath of life,' Lady Montbarry answered. 'Remember that, and you will understand her. Can such a woman as Agnes give her love or refuse it, according to circumstances? Because the man was unworthy of her, was he less the man of her choice? The truest and best friend to him (little as he deserved it) in his lifetime, she naturally remains the truest and best friend to his memory now. If you really love her, wait; and trust to your two best friends—to time and to me. There is my advice; let your own experience decide whether it is not the best advice that I can offer. Resume your journey to Venice to-morrow; and when you take leave of Agnes, speak to her as cordially as if nothing had happened.'

Henry wisely followed this advice. Thoroughly understanding him, Agnes made the leave-taking friendly and pleasant on her side. When he stopped at the door for a last look at her, she hurriedly turned her head so that her face was hidden from him. Was that a good sign? Lady Montbarry, accompanying Henry down the stairs, said, 'Yes, decidedly! Write when you get to Venice. We shall wait here to receive letters from Arthur and his wife, and we shall time our departure for Italy accordingly.'

A week passed, and no letter came from Henry. Some days

later, a telegram was received from him. It was despatched from Milan, instead of from Venice; and it brought this strange message:—'I have left the hotel. Will return on the arrival of Arthur and his wife. Address, meanwhile, Albergo Reale, Milan.'

Preferring Venice before all other cities of Europe, and having arranged to remain there until the family meeting took place, what unexpected event had led Henry to alter his plans? and why did he state the bare fact, without adding a word of explanation? Let the narrative follow him—and find the answer to those questions at Venice.

XVII

The Palace Hotel, appealing for encouragement mainly to English and American travellers, celebrated the opening of its doors, as a matter of course, by the giving of a grand banquet, and the delivery of a long succession of speeches.

Delayed on his journey, Henry Westwick only reached Venice in time to join the guests over their coffee and cigars. Observing the splendour of the reception rooms, and taking note especially of the artful mixture of comfort and luxury in the bedchambers, he began to share the old nurse's view of the future, and to contemplate seriously the coming dividend of ten per cent. The hotel was beginning well, at all events. So much interest in the enterprise had been aroused, at home and abroad, by profuse advertising, that the whole accommodation of the building had been secured by travellers of all nations for the opening night. Henry only obtained one of the small rooms on the upper floor, by a lucky accident—the absence of the gentleman who had written to engage it. He was quite satisfied, and was on his way to bed, when another accident altered his prospects for the night, and moved him into another and a better room.

Ascending on his way to the higher regions as far as the first floor of the hotel, Henry's attention was attracted by an angry voice protesting, in a strong New England accent, against one of the greatest hardships that can be inflicted on a citizen of the United States—the hardship of sending him to bed without gas in his room.

The Americans are not only the most hospitable people to be found on the face of the earth—they are (under certain conditions) the most patient and good-tempered people as well. But they are human; and the limit of American endurance is found in the obsolete institution of a bedroom candle. The American traveller, in the present case, declined to believe that his bedroom was in a complete finished state without a gas-burner. The manager pointed to the fine antique decorations (renewed and regilt) on the walls and the ceiling, and explained that the emanations of burning gas-light would certainly spoil them in the course of a few months. To this the traveller replied that it was possible, but that he did not understand decorations. A bedroom with gas in it was what he was used to, was what he wanted, and was what he was determined to have. The compliant manager volunteered to ask some other gentleman, housed on the inferior upper storey (which was lit throughout with gas), to change rooms. Hearing this, and being quite willing to exchange a small bedchamber for a large one, Henry volunteered to be the other gentleman. The excellent American shook hands with him on the spot. 'You are a cultured person, sir,' he said; 'and you will no doubt understand the decorations.'

Henry looked at the number of the room on the door as he opened it. The number was Fourteen.

Tired and sleepy, he naturally anticipated a good night's rest. In the thoroughly healthy state of his nervous system, he slept as well in a bed abroad as in a bed at home. Without the slightest assignable reason, however, his just expectations were disappointed. The luxurious bed, the well-ventilated room, the delicious tranquillity of Venice by night, all were in favour of his sleeping well. He never slept at all. An indescribable sense of depression and discomfort kept him waking through darkness and daylight alike. He went down to the coffee-room as soon as the hotel was astir, and ordered some breakfast. Another unaccountable change in himself appeared with the appearance of the meal. He was absolutely without appetite. An excellent omelette, and cutlets cooked to perfection, he sent away untasted—he, whose appetite never failed him, whose digestion was still equal to any demands on it!

The day was bright and fine. He sent for a gondola, and was rowed to the Lido.

Out on the airy Lagoon, he felt like a new man. He had not left the hotel ten minutes before he was fast asleep in the gondola. Waking, on reaching the landing-place, he crossed the Lido, and enjoyed a morning's swim in the Adriatic. There was only a poor restaurant on the island, in those days; but his appetite was now ready for anything; he ate whatever was offered to him, like a famished man. He could hardly believe, when he reflected on it, that he had sent away untasted his excellent breakfast at the hotel.

Returning to Venice, he spent the rest of the day in the picture-galleries and the churches. Towards six o'clock his gondola took him back, with another fine appetite, to meet some travelling acquaintances with whom he had engaged to dine at the table d'hote.

The dinner was deservedly rewarded with the highest approval by every guest in the hotel but one. To Henry's astonishment, the appetite with which he had entered the house mysteriously and completely left him when he sat down to table. He could drink some wine, but he could literally eat nothing. 'What in the world is the matter with you?' his travelling acquaintances asked. He could honestly answer, 'I know no more than you do.'

When night came, he gave his comfortable and beautiful bedroom another trial. The result of the second experiment was a repetition of the result of the first. Again he felt the all-pervading sense of depression and discomfort. Again he passed a sleepless night. And once more, when he tried to eat his breakfast, his appetite completely failed him!

This personal experience of the new hotel was too extraordinary to be passed over in silence. Henry mentioned it to his friends in the public room, in the hearing of the manager. The manager, naturally zealous in defence of the hotel, was a little hurt at the implied reflection cast on Number Fourteen. He invited the travellers present to judge for themselves whether Mr. Westwick's bedroom was to blame for Mr. Westwick's sleepless nights; and he especially appealed to a grey-headed gentleman, a guest at the breakfast-table of an English traveller, to take the lead in the investigation. 'This is Doctor Bruno, our first physician in Venice,' he explained. 'I appeal to him to say if there are any unhealthy influences in Mr. Westwick's room.'

Introduced to Number Fourteen, the doctor looked round him with a certain appearance of interest which was noticed by everyone present. 'The last time I was in this room,' he said, 'was on a melancholy occasion. It was before the palace was changed into an hotel. I was in professional attendance on an English nobleman who died here.' One of the persons present inquired the name of the nobleman. Doctor Bruno answered (without the slightest suspicion that he was speaking before a brother of the dead man), 'Lord Montbarry.'

Henry quietly left the room, without saying a word to anybody.

He was not, in any sense of the term, a superstitious man. But he felt, nevertheless, an insurmountable reluctance to remaining in the hotel. He decided on leaving Venice. To ask for another room would be, as he could plainly see, an offence in the eyes of the manager. To remove to another hotel, would be to openly abandon an establishment in the success of which he had a pecuniary interest. Leaving a note for Arthur Barville, on his arrival in Venice, in which he merely mentioned that he had gone to look at the Italian lakes, and that a line addressed to his hotel at Milan would bring him back again, he took the afternoon train to Padua—and dined with his usual appetite, and slept as well as ever that night.

The next day, a gentleman and his wife (perfect strangers to the Montbarry family), returning to England by way of Venice, arrived at the hotel and occupied Number Fourteen.

Still mindful of the slur that had been cast on one of his best bedchambers, the manager took occasion to ask the travellers the next morning how they liked their room. They left him to judge for himself how well they were satisfied, by remaining a day longer in Venice than they had originally planned to do, solely for the purpose of enjoying the excellent accommodation offered to them by the new hotel. 'We have met with nothing like it in Italy,' they said; 'you may rely on our recommending you to all our friends.'

On the day when Number Fourteen was again vacant, an English lady travelling alone with her maid arrived at the hotel, saw the room, and at once engaged it.

The lady was Mrs. Norbury. She had left Francis Westwick at Milan, occupied in negotiating for the appearance at his theatre of the new dancer at the Scala. Not having heard to the contrary, Mrs. Norbury supposed that Arthur Barville and his wife had already arrived at Venice. She was more interested in meeting the young married couple than in awaiting the result of the hard bargaining which delayed the engagement of the new dancer; and she volunteered to make her brother's apologies, if his theatrical business caused him to be late in keeping his appointment at the honeymoon festival.

Mrs. Norbury's experience of Number Fourteen differed entirely from her brother Henry's experience of the room.

Falling asleep as readily as usual, her repose was disturbed by a succession of frightful dreams; the central figure in every one of them being the figure of her dead brother, the first Lord Montbarry. She saw him starving in a loathsome prison; she saw him pursued by assassins, and dying under their knives; she saw him drowning in immeasurable depths of dark water; she saw him in a bed on fire, burning to death in the flames; she saw him tempted by a shadowy creature to drink, and dying of the poisonous draught. The reiterated horror of these dreams had such an effect on her that she rose with the dawn of day, afraid to trust herself again in bed. In the old times, she had been noted in the family as the one member of it who lived on affectionate terms with Montbarry. His other sister and his brothers were constantly quarrelling with him. Even his mother owned that her eldest son was of all her children the child whom she least liked. Sensible and resolute woman as she was, Mrs. Norbury shuddered with terror as she sat at the window of her room, watching the sunrise, and thinking of her dreams.

She made the first excuse that occurred to her, when her maid came in at the usual hour, and noticed how ill she looked. The woman was of so superstitious a temperament that it would have been in the last degree indiscreet to trust her with the truth. Mrs. Norbury merely remarked that she had not found the bed quite to her liking, on account of the large size of it. She was accustomed at home, as her maid knew, to sleep in a small bed. Informed of this objection later in the day, the manager regretted that he could only offer to the lady the choice of one other bedchamber, numbered Thirty-eight, and situated immediately over the bedchamber which she desired to leave. Mrs. Norbury accepted the proposed change of quarters. She was now about to pass her second night in the room occupied in the old days of the palace by Baron Rivar.

Once more, she fell asleep as usual. And, once more, the frightful dreams of the first night terrified her, following each other in the same succession. This time her nerves, already shaken, were not equal to the renewed torture of terror inflicted on them. She threw on her dressing-gown, and rushed out of her room in the middle of the night. The porter, alarmed by the banging of the door, met her hurrying headlong down the stairs, in search of the first human being she could find to keep her company. Considerably surprised at this last new manifestation of the famous 'English eccentricity,' the man looked at the hotel register, and led the lady upstairs again to the room occupied by her maid. The maid was not asleep, and, more wonderful still, was not even undressed. She received her mistress quietly. When they were alone, and when Mrs. Norbury had, as a matter of necessity, taken her attendant into her confidence, the woman made a very strange reply.

'I have been asking about the hotel, at the servants' supper to-night,' she said. 'The valet of one of the gentlemen staying here has heard that the late Lord Montbarry was the last person who lived in the palace, before it was made into an hotel. The room he died in, ma'am, was the room you slept in last night. Your room tonight is the room just above it. I said nothing for fear of frightening you. For my own part, I have passed the night as you see, keeping my light on, and reading my Bible. In my opinion, no member of your family can hope to be happy or comfortable in this house.'

'What do you mean?'

'Please to let me explain myself, ma'am. When Mr. Henry Westwick was here (I have this from the valet, too) he occupied the room his brother died in (without knowing it), like you. For two nights he never closed his eyes. Without any reason for it (the valet heard him tell the gentlemen in the coffee-room) he could not sleep; he felt so low and so wretched in himself. And what is more, when daytime came, he couldn't even eat while he was under this roof. You may laugh at me, ma'am—but even a servant may draw her own conclusions. It's my conclusion that something happened to my lord, which we none of us know about, when he died in this house. His ghost walks in torment until he can tell it—and the living persons related to him are the persons who feel he is near them. Those persons may yet see him in the time to come. Don't, pray don't stay any longer in this dreadful place! I wouldn't stay another night here myself—no, not for anything that could be offered me!'

Mrs. Norbury at once set her servant's mind at ease on this last point.

'I don't think about it as you do,' she said gravely. 'But I should like to speak to my brother of what has happened. We will go back to Milan.'

Some hours necessarily elapsed before they could leave the hotel, by the first train in the forenoon.

In that interval, Mrs. Norbury's maid found an opportunity of confidentially informing the valet of what had passed between her mistress and herself. The valet had other friends to whom he related the circumstances in his turn. In due course of time, the narrative, passing from mouth to mouth, reached the ears of the manager. He instantly saw that the credit of the hotel was in danger, unless something was done to retrieve the character of the room numbered Fourteen. English travellers, well acquainted with the peerage of their native country, informed him that Henry Westwick and Mrs. Norbury were by no means the only members of the Montbarry family. Curiosity might bring more of them to the hotel, after hearing what had happened. The manager's ingenuity easily hit on the obvious means of misleading them, in this case. The numbers of all the rooms were enamelled in blue, on white china plates, screwed to the doors. He ordered a new plate to be prepared, bearing the number, '13 A'; and he kept the room empty, after its tenant for the time being had gone away, until the plate was ready. He then re-numbered the room; placing the removed Number Fourteen on the door of his own room (on the second floor), which, not being to let, had not previously been numbered at all. By this device, Number Fourteen disappeared at once and for ever from the books of the hotel, as the number of a bedroom to let.

Having warned the servants to beware of gossiping with travellers, on the subject of the changed numbers, under penalty of being dismissed, the manager composed his mind with the reflection that he had done his duty to his employers. 'Now,' he thought to himself, with an excusable sense of triumph, 'let the whole family come here if they like! The hotel is a match for them.'

XVIII

Before the end of the week, the manager found himself in relations with 'the family' once more. A telegram from Milan announced that Mr. Francis Westwick would arrive in Venice on the next day; and would be obliged if Number Fourteen, on the first floor, could be reserved for him, in the event of its being vacant at the time.

The manager paused to consider, before he issued his directions.

The re-numbered room had been last let to a French gentleman. It would be occupied on the day of Mr. Francis Westwick's arrival, but it would be empty again on the day after. Would it be well to reserve the room for the special occupation of Mr. Francis? and when he had passed the night unsuspiciously and comfortably in 'No. 13 A,' to ask him in the presence of witnesses how he liked his bedchamber? In this case, if the reputation of the room happened to be called in question again, the answer would vindicate it, on the evidence of a member of the very family which had first given Number Fourteen a bad name. After a little reflection, the manager decided on trying the experiment, and directed that '13 A' should be reserved accordingly.

On the next day, Francis Westwick arrived in excellent spirits.

He had signed agreements with the most popular dancer in Italy; he had transferred the charge of Mrs. Norbury to his brother Henry, who had joined him in Milan; and he was now at full liberty to amuse himself by testing in every possible way the extraordinary influence exercised over his relatives by the new hotel. When his brother and sister first told him what their experience had been, he instantly declared that he would go to Venice in the interest of his theatre. The circumstances related to him contained invaluable hints for a ghost-drama. The title occurred to him in the railway: 'The Haunted Hotel.' Post that in red letters six feet high, on a black ground, all over London—

and trust the excitable public to crowd into the theatre!

Received with the politest attention by the manager, Francis met with a disappointment on entering the hotel. 'Some mistake, sir. No such room on the first floor as Number Fourteen. The room bearing that number is on the second floor, and has been occupied by me, from the day when the hotel opened. Perhaps you meant number 13 A, on the first floor? It will be at your service to-morrow—a charming room. In the mean time, we will do the best we can for you, to-night.'

A man who is the successful manager of a theatre is probably the last man in the civilized universe who is capable of being impressed with favourable opinions of his fellow-creatures. Francis privately set the manager down as a humbug, and the story about the numbering of the rooms as a lie.

On the day of his arrival, he dined by himself in the restaurant, before the hour of the table d'hote, for the express purpose of questioning the waiter, without being overheard by anybody. The answer led him to the conclusion that '13 A' occupied the situation in the hotel which had been described by his brother and sister as the situation of '14.' He asked next for the Visitors' List; and found that the French gentleman who then occupied '13 A,' was the proprietor of a theatre in Paris, personally well known to him. Was the gentleman then in the hotel? He had gone out, but would certainly return for the table d'hote. When the public dinner was over, Francis entered the room, and was welcomed by his Parisian colleague, literally, with open arms. 'Come and have a cigar in my room,' said the friendly Frenchman. 'I want to hear whether you have really engaged that woman at Milan or not.' In this easy way, Francis found his opportunity of comparing the interior of the room with the description which he had heard of it at Milan.

Arriving at the door, the Frenchman bethought himself of his travelling companion. 'My scene-painter is here with me,' he said, 'on the look-out for materials. An excellent fellow, who will take it as a kindness if we ask him to join us. I'll tell the porter to send him up when he comes in.' He handed the key of his room to Francis. 'I will be back in a minute. It's at the end of the corridor—13 A.'

Francis entered the room alone. There were the decorations on the walls and the ceiling, exactly as they had been described to him! He had just time to perceive this at a glance, before his attention was diverted to himself and his own sensations, by a grotesquely disagreeable occurrence which took him completely by surprise.

He became conscious of a mysteriously offensive odour in the room, entirely new in his experience of revolting smells. It was composed (if such a thing could be) of two mingling exhalations, which were separately-discoverable exhalations nevertheless. This strange blending of odours consisted of something faintly and unpleasantly aromatic, mixed with another underlying smell, so unutterably sickening that he threw open the window, and put his head out into the fresh air, unable to endure the horribly infected atmosphere for a moment longer.

The French proprietor joined his English friend, with his cigar already lit. He started back in dismay at a sight terrible to his countrymen in general—the sight of an open window. 'You English people are perfectly mad on the subject of fresh air!' he exclaimed. 'We shall catch our deaths of cold.'

Francis turned, and looked at him in astonishment. 'Are you really not aware of the smell there is in the room?' he asked.

'Smell!' repeated his brother-manager. 'I smell my own good cigar. Try one yourself. And for Heaven's sake shut the window!'

Francis declined the cigar by a sign. 'Forgive me,' he said. 'I will leave you to close the window. I feel faint and giddy—I had better go out.' He put his handkerchief over his nose and mouth, and crossed the room to the door.

The Frenchman followed the movements of Francis, in such a state of bewilderment that he actually forgot to seize the opportunity of shutting out the fresh air. 'Is it so nasty as that?' he asked, with a broad stare of amazement.

'Horrible!' Francis muttered behind his handkerchief. 'I never smelt anything like it in my life!'

There was a knock at the door. The scene-painter appeared. His employer instantly asked him if he smelt anything.

'I smell your cigar. Delicious! Give me one directly!'

'Wait a minute. Besides my cigar, do you smell anything else—vile, abominable, overpowering, indescribable, never-never-never-smelt before?'

The scene-painter appeared to be puzzled by the vehement energy of the language addressed to him. 'The room is as fresh and sweet as a room can be,' he answered. As he spoke, he looked back with astonishment at Francis Westwick, standing outside in the corridor, and eyeing the interior of the bedchamber with an expression of undisguised disgust.

The Parisian director approached his English colleague, and looked at him with grave and anxious scrutiny.

'You see, my friend, here are two of us, with as good noses as yours, who smell nothing. If you want evidence from more noses, look there!' He pointed to two little English girls, at play in the corridor. 'The door of my room is wide open—and you know how fast a smell can travel. Now listen, while I appeal to these innocent noses, in the language of their own dismal island. My little loves, do you sniff a nasty smell here—ha?' The children burst out laughing, and answered emphatically, 'No.' 'My good Westwick,' the Frenchman resumed, in his own language, 'the conclusion is surely plain? There is something wrong, very wrong, with your own nose. I recommend you to see a medical man.'

Having given that advice, he returned to his room, and shut out the horrid fresh air with a loud exclamation of relief. Francis left the hotel, by the lanes that led to the Square of St. Mark. The night-breeze soon revived him. He was able to light a cigar, and to think quietly over what had happened.

XIX

Avoiding the crowd under the colonnades, Francis walked slowly up and down the noble open space of the square, bathed in the light of the rising moon.

Without being aware of it himself, he was a thorough materialist. The strange effect produced on him by the room—following on the other strange effects produced on the other relatives of his dead brother—exercised no perplexing influence over the mind of this sensible man. 'Perhaps,' he reflected, 'my temperament is more imaginative than I supposed it to be—and this is a trick played on me by my own fancy? Or, perhaps, my friend is right; something is physically amiss with me? I don't feel ill, certainly. But that is no safe criterion sometimes. I am not going to sleep in that abominable room to-night—I can well wait till to-morrow to decide whether I shall speak to a doctor or not. In the mean time, the hotel doesn't seem likely to supply me with the subject of a piece. A terrible smell from an invisible ghost is a perfectly new idea. But it has one drawback. If I realise it on the stage, I shall drive the audience out of the theatre.'

As his strong common sense arrived at this facetious conclusion, he became aware of a lady, dressed entirely in black, who was observing him with marked attention. 'Am I right in supposing you to be Mr. Francis Westwick?' the lady asked, at the moment when he looked at her.

'That is my name, madam. May I inquire to whom I have the honour of speaking?'

'We have only met once,' she answered a little evasively, 'when your late brother introduced me to the members of his family. I wonder if you have quite forgotten my big black eyes and my hideous complexion?' She lifted her veil as she spoke, and turned so that the moonlight rested on her face.

Francis recognised at a glance the woman of all others whom he most cordially disliked—the widow of his dead brother, the first Lord Montbarry. He frowned as he looked at her. His experience on the stage, gathered at innumerable rehearsals with actresses who had sorely tried his temper, had accustomed him to speak roughly to women who were distasteful to him. 'I remember you,' he said. 'I thought you were in America!'

She took no notice of his ungracious tone and manner; she simply stopped him when he lifted his hat, and turned to leave her.

'Let me walk with you for a few minutes,' she quietly replied. 'I have something to say to you.'

He showed her his cigar. 'I am smoking,' he said.

'I don't mind smoking.'

After that, there was nothing to be done (short of downright brutality) but to yield. He did it with the worst possible grace. 'Well?' he resumed. 'What do you want of me?'

'You shall hear directly, Mr. Westwick. Let me first tell you what my position is. I am alone in the world. To the loss of my husband has now been added another bereavement, the loss of my companion in America, my brother—Baron Rivar.'

The reputation of the Baron, and the doubt which scandal

had thrown on his assumed relationship to the Countess, were well known to Francis. 'Shot in a gambling-saloon?' he asked brutally.

'The question is a perfectly natural one on your part,' she said, with the impenetrably ironical manner which she could assume on certain occasions. 'As a native of horse-racing England, you belong to a nation of gamblers. My brother died no extraordinary death, Mr. Westwick. He sank, with many other unfortunate people, under a fever prevalent in a Western city which we happened to visit. The calamity of his loss made the United States unendurable to me. I left by the first steamer that sailed from New York—a French vessel which brought me to Havre. I continued my lonely journey to the South of France. And then I went on to Venice.'

'What does all this matter to me?' Francis thought to himself. She paused, evidently expecting him to say something. 'So you have come to Venice?' he said carelessly. 'Why?'

'Because I couldn't help it,' she answered.

Francis looked at her with cynical curiosity. 'That sounds odd,' he remarked. 'Why couldn't you help it?'

'Women are accustomed to act on impulse,' she explained. 'Suppose we say that an impulse has directed my journey? And yet, this is the last place in the world that I wish to find myself in. Associations that I detest are connected with it in my mind. If I had a will of my own, I would never see it again. I hate Venice. As you see, however, I am here. When did you meet with such an unreasonable woman before? Never, I am sure!' She stopped, eyed him for a moment, and suddenly altered her tone. 'When is Miss Agnes Lockwood expected to be in Venice?' she asked.

It was not easy to throw Francis off his balance, but that extraordinary question did it. 'How the devil did you know that Miss Lockwood was coming to Venice?' he exclaimed.

She laughed—a bitter mocking laugh. 'Say, I guessed it!'

Something in her tone, or perhaps something in the audacious defiance of her eyes as they rested on him, roused the quick temper that was in Francis Westwick. 'Lady Montbarry—!' he began.

'Stop there!' she interposed. 'Your brother Stephen's wife calls herself Lady Montbarry now. I share my title with no woman. Call me by my name before I committed the fatal mistake of marrying your brother. Address me, if you please, as Countess Narona.'

'Countess Narona,' Francis resumed, 'if your object in claiming my acquaintance is to mystify me, you have come to the wrong man. Speak plainly, or permit me to wish you good evening.'

'If your object is to keep Miss Lockwood's arrival in Venice a secret,' she retorted, 'speak plainly, Mr. Westwick, on your side, and say so.'

Her intention was evidently to irritate him; and she succeeded. 'Nonsense!' he broke out petulantly. 'My brother's travelling arrangements are secrets to nobody. He brings Miss Lockwood here, with Lady Montbarry and the children. As you seem so well informed, perhaps you know why she is coming to Venice?'

The Countess had suddenly become grave and thoughtful. She made no reply. The two strangely associated companions, having reached one extremity of the square, were now standing before the church of St. Mark. The moonlight was bright enough to show the architecture of the grand cathedral in its wonderful variety of detail. Even the pigeons of St. Mark were visible, in dark closely packed rows, roosting in the archways of the great entrance doors.

'I never saw the old church look so beautiful by moonlight,' the Countess said quietly; speaking, not to Francis, but to herself. 'Good-bye, St. Mark's by moonlight! I shall not see you again.'

She turned away from the church, and saw Francis listening to her with wondering looks. 'No,' she resumed, placidly picking up the lost thread of the conversation, 'I don't know why Miss Lockwood is coming here, I only know that we are to meet in Venice.'

'By previous appointment?'

'By Destiny,' she answered, with her head on her breast, and her eyes on the ground. Francis burst out laughing. 'Or, if you like it better,' she instantly resumed, 'by what fools call Chance.' Francis answered easily, out of the depths of his strong common sense. 'Chance seems to be taking a queer way of bringing the meeting about,' he said. 'We have all arranged to meet at the Palace Hotel. How is it that your name is not on the Visitors' List? Destiny ought to have brought you to the Palace Hotel too.'

She abruptly pulled down her veil. 'Destiny may do that yet!' she said. 'The Palace Hotel?' she repeated, speaking once more to herself. 'The old hell, transformed into the new purgatory. The place itself! Jesu Maria! the place itself!' She paused and laid her hand on her companion's arm. 'Perhaps Miss Lockwood is not going there with the rest of you?' she burst out with sudden eagerness. 'Are you positively sure she will be at the hotel?'

'Positively! Haven't I told you that Miss Lockwood travels with Lord and Lady Montbarry? and don't you know that she is a member of the family? You will have to move, Countess, to our hotel.'

She was perfectly impenetrable to the bantering tone in which he spoke. 'Yes,' she said faintly, 'I shall have to move to your hotel.' Her hand was still on his arm—he could feel her shivering from head to foot while she spoke. Heartily as he disliked and distrusted her, the common instinct of humanity obliged him to ask if she felt cold.

'Yes,' she said. 'Cold and faint.'

'Cold and faint, Countess, on such a night as this?'

'The night has nothing to do with it, Mr. Westwick. How do you suppose the criminal feels on the scaffold, while the hangman is putting the rope around his neck? Cold and faint, too, I should think. Excuse my grim fancy. You see, Destiny has got the rope round my neck—and I feel it.'

She looked about her. They were at that moment close to the famous cafe known as 'Florian's.' 'Take me in there,' she said; 'I must have something to revive me. You had better not hesitate. You are interested in reviving me. I have not said what I wanted to say to you yet. It's business, and it's connected with your theatre.'

Wondering inwardly what she could possibly want with his theatre, Francis reluctantly yielded to the necessities of the situation, and took her into the cafe. He found a quiet corner in which they could take their places without attracting notice. 'What will you have?' he inquired resignedly. She gave her own orders to the waiter, without troubling him to speak for her.

'Maraschino. And a pot of tea.'

The waiter stared; Francis stared. The tea was a novelty (in connection with maraschino) to both of them. Careless whether she surprised them or not, she instructed the waiter, when her directions had been complied with, to pour a large wine-glass-full of the liqueur into a tumbler, and to fill it up from the teapot. 'I can't do it for myself,' she remarked, 'my hand trembles so.' She drank the strange mixture eagerly, hot as it was. 'Maraschino punch—will you taste some of it?' she said. 'I inherit the discovery of this drink. When your English Queen Caroline was on the Continent, my mother was attached to her Court. That much injured Royal Person invented, in her happier hours, maraschino punch. Fondly attached to her gracious mistress, my mother shared her tastes. And I, in my turn, learnt from my mother. Now, Mr. Westwick, suppose I tell you what my business is. You are manager of a theatre. Do you want a new play?'

'I always want a new play—provided it's a good one.'

'And you pay, if it's a good one?'

'I pay liberally—in my own interests.'

'If I write the play, will you read it?'

Francis hesitated. 'What has put writing a play into your head?' he asked.

'Mere accident,' she answered. 'I had once occasion to tell my late brother of a visit which I paid to Miss Lockwood, when I was last in England. He took no interest at what happened at the interview, but something struck him in my way of relating it. He said, "You describe what passed between you and the lady with the point and contrast of good stage dialogue. You have the dramatic instinct—try if you can write a play. You might make money." That put it into my head.'

Those last words seemed to startle Francis. 'Surely you don't want money!' he exclaimed.

'I always want money. My tastes are expensive. I have nothing but my poor little four hundred a year—and the wreck that is left of the other money: about two hundred pounds in circular notes—no more.'

Francis knew that she was referring to the ten thousand pounds paid by the insurance offices. 'All those thousands gone already!' he exclaimed.

She blew a little puff of air over her fingers. 'Gone like that!' she answered coolly.

'Baron Rivar?'

She looked at him with a flash of anger in her hard black eyes.

'My affairs are my own secret, Mr. Westwick. I have made you a proposal—and you have not answered me yet. Don't say No, without thinking first. Remember what a life mine has been. I have seen more of the world than most people, playwrights included. I have had strange adventures; I have heard remarkable stories; I have observed; I have remembered. Are there no materials, here in my head, for writing a play—if the opportunity is granted to me?' She waited a moment, and suddenly repeated her strange question about Agnes.

'When is Miss Lockwood expected to be in Venice?'

'What has that to do with your new play, Countess?'

The Countess appeared to feel some difficulty in giving that question its fit reply. She mixed another tumbler full of maraschino punch, and drank one good half of it before she spoke again.

'It has everything to do with my new play,' was all she said. 'Answer me.' Francis answered her.

'Miss Lockwood may be here in a week. Or, for all I know to the contrary, sooner than that.'

'Very well. If I am a living woman and a free woman in a week's time—or if I am in possession of my senses in a week's time (don't interrupt me; I know what I am talking about)—I shall have a sketch or outline of my play ready, as a specimen of what I can do. Once again, will you read it?'

'I will certainly read it. But, Countess, I don't understand—'

She held up her hand for silence, and finished the second tumbler of maraschino punch.

'I am a living enigma—and you want to know the right reading of me,' she said. 'Here is the reading, as your English phrase goes, in a nutshell. There is a foolish idea in the minds of many persons that the natives of the warm climates are imaginative people. There never was a greater mistake. You will find no such unimaginative people anywhere as you find in Italy, Spain, Greece, and the other Southern countries. To anything fanciful, to anything spiritual, their minds are deaf and blind by nature. Now and then, in the course of centuries, a great genius springs up among them; and he is the exception which proves the rule. Now see! I, though I am no genius—I am, in my little way (as I suppose), an exception too. To my sorrow, I have some of that imagination which is so common among the English and the Germans—so rare among the Italians, the Spaniards, and the rest of them! And what is the result? I think it has become a disease in me. I am filled with presentiments which make this wicked life of mine one long terror to me. It doesn't matter, just now, what they are. Enough that they absolutely govern me—they drive me over land and sea at their own horrible will; they are in me, and torturing me, at this moment! Why don't I resist them? Ha! but I do resist them. I am trying (with the help of the good punch) to resist them now. At intervals I cultivate the difficult virtue of common sense. Sometimes, sound sense makes a hopeful woman of me. At one time, I had the hope that what seemed reality to me was only mad delusion, after all—I even asked the question of an English doctor! At other times, other sensible doubts of myself beset me. Never mind dwelling on them now—it always ends in the old terrors and superstitions taking possession of me again. In a week's time, I shall know whether Destiny does indeed decide my future for me, or whether I decide it for myself. In the last case, my resolution is to absorb this self-tormenting fancy of mine in the occupation that I have told you of already. Do you understand me a little better now? And, our business being settled, dear Mr. Westwick, shall we get out of this hot room into the nice cool air again?'

They rose to leave the cafe. Francis privately concluded that the maraschino punch offered the only discoverable explanation of what the Countess had said to him.

XX

'Shall I see you again?' she asked, as she held out her hand to take leave. 'It is quite understood between us, I suppose, about the play?'

Francis recalled his extraordinary experience of that evening in the re-numbered room. 'My stay in Venice is uncertain,' he replied. 'If you have anything more to say about this dramatic venture of yours, it may be as well to say it now. Have you decided on a subject already? I know the public taste in England better than you do—I might save you some waste of time and trouble, if you have not chosen your subject wisely.'

'I don't care what subject I write about, so long as I write,' she answered carelessly. 'If you have got a subject in your head, give it to me. I answer for the characters and the dialogue.'

'You answer for the characters and the dialogue,' Francis repeated. 'That's a bold way of speaking for a beginner! I wonder if I should shake your sublime confidence in yourself, if I suggested the most ticklish subject to handle which is known to the stage? What do you say, Countess, to entering the lists with Shakespeare, and trying a drama with a ghost in it? A true story, mind! founded on events in this very city in which you and I are interested.'

She caught him by the arm, and drew him away from the crowded colonnade into the solitary middle space of the square. 'Now tell me!' she said eagerly. 'Here, where nobody is near us. How am I interested in it? How? how?'

Still holding his arm, she shook him in her impatience to hear the coming disclosure. For a moment he hesitated. Thus far, amused by her ignorant belief in herself, he had merely spoken in jest. Now, for the first time, impressed by her irresistible earnestness, he began to consider what he was about from a more serious point of view. With her knowledge of all that had passed in the old palace, before its transformation into an hotel, it was surely possible that she might suggest some explanation of what had happened to his brother, and sister, and himself. Or, failing to do this, she might accidentally reveal some event in her own experience which, acting as a hint to a competent dramatist, might prove to be the making of a play. The prosperity of his theatre was his one serious object in life. 'I may be on the trace of another "Corsican Brothers,"' he thought. 'A new piece of that sort would be ten thousand pounds in my pocket, at least.'

With these motives (worthy of the single-hearted devotion to dramatic business which made Francis a successful manager) he related, without further hesitation, what his own experience had been, and what the experience of his relatives had been, in the haunted hotel. He even described the outbreak of superstitious terror which had escaped Mrs. Norbury's ignorant maid. 'Sad stuff, if you look at it reasonably,' he remarked. 'But there is something dramatic in the notion of the ghostly influence making itself felt by the relations in succession, as they one after another enter the fatal room—until the one chosen relative comes who will see the Unearthly Creature, and know the terrible truth. Material for a play, Countess—first-rate material for a play!'

There he paused. She neither moved nor spoke. He stooped and looked closer at her.

What impression had he produced? It was an impression which his utmost ingenuity had failed to anticipate. She stood by his side—just as she had stood before Agnes when her question about Ferrari was plainly answered at last—like a woman turned to stone. Her eyes were vacant and rigid; all the life in her face had faded out of it. Francis took her by the hand. Her hand was as cold as the pavement that they were standing on. He asked her if she was ill.

Not a muscle in her moved. He might as well have spoken to the dead.

'Surely,' he said, 'you are not foolish enough to take what I have been telling you seriously?'

Her lips moved slowly. As it seemed, she was making an effort to speak to him.

'Louder,' he said. 'I can't hear you.'

She struggled to recover possession of herself. A faint light began to soften the dull cold stare of her eyes. In a moment more she spoke so that he could hear her.

'I never thought of the other world,' she murmured, in low dull tones, like a woman talking in her sleep.

Her mind had gone back to the day of her last memorable interview with Agnes; she was slowly recalling the confession that had escaped her, the warning words which she had spoken at that past time. Necessarily incapable of understanding this, Francis looked at her in perplexity. She went on in the same dull vacant tone, steadily following out her own train of thought, with her heedless eyes on his face, and her wandering mind far away from him.

'I said some trifling event would bring us together the next time. I was wrong. No trifling event will bring us together. I said I might be the person who told her what had become of Ferrari, if she forced me to it. Shall I feel some other influence than hers? Will he force me to it? When she sees him, shall I see him too?'

Her head sank a little; her heavy eyelids dropped slowly; she heaved a long low weary sigh. Francis put her arm in his, and made an attempt to rouse her.

'Come, Countess, you are weary and over-wrought. We have had enough talking to-night. Let me see you safe back to your hotel. Is it far from here?'

She started when he moved, and obliged her to move with him, as if he had suddenly awakened her out of a deep sleep.

'Not far,' she said faintly. 'The old hotel on the quay. My mind's in a strange state; I have forgotten the name.'

'Danieli's?'

'Yes!'

He led her on slowly. She accompanied him in silence as far as the end of the Piazzetta. There, when the full view of the moonlit Lagoon revealed itself, she stopped him as he turned towards the Riva degli Schiavoni. 'I have something to ask you. I want to wait and think.'

She recovered her lost idea, after a long pause.

'Are you going to sleep in the room to-night?' she asked.

He told her that another traveller was in possession of the room that night. 'But the manager has reserved it for me to-morrow,' he added, 'if I wish to have it.'

'No,' she said. 'You must give it up.'

'To whom?'

'To me!'

He started. 'After what I have told you, do you really wish to sleep in that room to-morrow night?'

'I must sleep in it.'

'Are you not afraid?'

'I am horribly afraid.'

'So I should have thought, after what I have observed in you to-night. Why should you take the room? You are not obliged to occupy it, unless you like.'

'I was not obliged to go to Venice, when I left America,' she answered. 'And yet I came here. I must take the room, and keep the room, until—' She broke off at those words. 'Never mind the rest,' she said. 'It doesn't interest you.'

It was useless to dispute with her. Francis changed the subject. 'We can do nothing to-night,' he said. 'I will call on you to-morrow morning, and hear what you think of it then.'

They moved on again to the hotel. As they approached the door, Francis asked if she was staying in Venice under her own name.

She shook her head. 'As your brother's widow, I am known here. As Countess Narona, I am known here. I want to be unknown, this time, to strangers in Venice; I am travelling under a common English name.' She hesitated, and stood still. 'What has come to me?' she muttered to herself. 'Some things I remember; and some I forget. I forgot Danieli's—and now I forget my English name.' She drew him hurriedly into the hall of the hotel, on the wall of which hung a list of visitors' names. Running her finger slowly down the list, she pointed to the English name that she had assumed:—'Mrs. James.'

'Remember that when you call to-morrow,' she said. 'My head is heavy. Good night.'

Francis went back to his own hotel, wondering what the events of the next day would bring forth. A new turn in his affairs had taken place in his absence. As he crossed the hall, he was requested by one of the servants to walk into the private office. The manager was waiting there with a gravely pre-occupied manner, as if he had something serious to say. He regretted to hear that Mr. Francis Westwick had, like other members of the family, discovered serious sources of discomfort in the new hotel. He had been informed in strict confidence of Mr. Westwick's extraordinary objection to the atmosphere of the bedroom upstairs. Without presuming to discuss the matter, he must beg to be excused from reserving the room for Mr. Westwick after what had happened.

Francis answered sharply, a little ruffled by the tone in which the manager had spoken to him. 'I might, very possibly, have declined to sleep in the room, if you had reserved it,' he said. 'Do you wish me to leave the hotel?'

The manager saw the error that he had committed, and hastened to repair it. 'Certainly not, sir! We will do our best to make you comfortable while you stay with us. I beg your pardon, if I have said anything to offend you. The reputation of an establishment like this is a matter of very serious importance. May I hope that you will do us the great favour to say nothing about what has happened upstairs? The two French gentlemen have kindly promised to keep it a secret.'

This apology left Francis no polite alternative but to grant the manager's request. 'There is an end to the Countess's wild scheme,' he thought to himself, as he retired for the night. 'So much the better for the Countess!'

He rose late the next morning. Inquiring for his Parisian friends, he was informed that both the French gentlemen had left for Milan. As he crossed the hall, on his way to the restaurant, he noticed the head porter chalking the numbers of the rooms on some articles of luggage which were waiting to go upstairs. One trunk attracted his attention by the extraordinary number of old travelling labels left on it. The porter was marking it at the moment—and the number was, '13 A.' Francis instantly looked at the card fastened on the lid. It bore the common English name, 'Mrs. James'! He at once inquired about the lady. She had arrived early that morning, and she was then in the Reading Room. Looking into the room, he discovered a lady in it alone. Advancing a little nearer, he found himself face to face with the Countess.

She was seated in a dark corner, with her head down and her arms crossed over her bosom. 'Yes,' she said, in a tone of weary impatience, before Francis could speak to her. 'I thought it best not to wait for you—I determined to get here before anybody else could take the room.'

'Have you taken it for long?' Francis asked.

'You told me Miss Lockwood would be here in a week's time. I have taken it for a week.'

'What has Miss Lockwood to do with it?'

'She has everything to do with it—she must sleep in the room. I shall give the room up to her when she comes here.'

Francis began to understand the superstitious purpose that she had in view. 'Are you (an educated woman) really of the same opinion as my sister's maid!' he exclaimed. 'Assuming your absurd superstition to be a serious thing, you are taking the wrong means to prove it true. If I and my brother and sister have seen nothing, how should Agnes Lockwood discover what was not revealed to us? She is only distantly related to the Montbarrys—she is only our cousin.'

'She was nearer to the heart of the Montbarry who is dead than any of you,' the Countess answered sternly. 'To the last day of his life, my miserable husband repented his desertion of her. She will see what none of you have seen—she shall have the room.'

Francis listened, utterly at a loss to account for the motives that animated her. 'I don't see what interest you have in trying this extraordinary experiment,' he said.

'It is my interest not to try it! It is my interest to fly from Venice, and never set eyes on Agnes Lockwood or any of your family again!'

'What prevents you from doing that?'

She started to her feet and looked at him wildly. 'I know no more what prevents me than you do!' she burst out. 'Some will that is stronger than mine drives me on to my destruction, in spite of my own self!' She suddenly sat down again, and waved her hand for him to go. 'Leave me,' she said. 'Leave me to my thoughts.'

Francis left her, firmly persuaded by this time that she was out of her senses. For the rest of the day, he saw nothing of her. The night, so far as he knew, passed quietly. The next morning he breakfasted early, determining to wait in the restaurant for the appearance of the Countess. She came in and ordered her breakfast quietly, looking dull and worn and self-absorbed, as she had looked when he last saw her. He hastened to her table, and asked if anything had happened in the night.

'Nothing,' she answered.

'You have rested as well as usual?'

'Quite as well as usual. Have you had any letters this morning? Have you heard when she is coming?'

'I have had no letters. Are you really going to stay here? Has your experience of last night not altered the opinion which you expressed to me yesterday?'

'Not in the least.'

The momentary gleam of animation which had crossed her face when she questioned him about Agnes, died out of it again when he answered her. She looked, she spoke, she ate her breakfast, with a vacant resignation, like a woman who had done with hopes, done with interests, done with everything but the mechanical movements and instincts of life.

Francis went out, on the customary travellers' pilgrimage to the shrines of Titian and Tintoret. After some hours of absence, he found a letter waiting for him when he got back to the hotel. It was written by his brother Henry, and it recommended him to return to Milan immediately. The proprietor of a French theatre, recently arrived from Venice, was trying to induce the famous dancer whom Francis had engaged to break faith with him and accept a higher salary.

Having made this startling announcement, Henry proceeded to inform his brother that Lord and Lady Montbarry, with Agnes and the children, would arrive in Venice in three days more. 'They know nothing of our adventures at the hotel,' Henry wrote; 'and they have telegraphed to the manager for the accommodation that they want. There would be something absurdly superstitious in our giving them a warning which would frighten the ladies and children out of the best hotel in Venice. We shall be a strong party this time—too strong a party for ghosts! I shall meet the travellers on their arrival, of course, and try my luck again at what you call the Haunted Hotel. Arthur Barville and his wife have already got as far on their way as Trent; and two of the lady's relations have arranged to accompany them on the journey to Venice.'

Naturally indignant at the conduct of his Parisian colleague, Francis made his preparations for returning to Milan by the train of that day.

On his way out, he asked the manager if his brother's telegram had been received. The telegram had arrived, and, to the surprise of Francis, the rooms were already reserved. 'I thought you would refuse to let any more of the family into the house,' he said satirically. The manager answered (with the due dash of respect) in the same tone. 'Number 13 A is safe, sir, in the occupation of a stranger. I am the servant of the Company; and I dare not turn money out of the hotel.'

Hearing this, Francis said good-bye—and said nothing more. He was ashamed to acknowledge it to himself, but he felt an irresistible curiosity to know what would happen when Agnes arrived at the hotel. Besides, 'Mrs. James' had reposed a confidence in him. He got into his gondola, respecting the confidence of 'Mrs. James.'

Towards evening on the third day, Lord Montbarry and his travelling companions arrived, punctual to their appointment.

'Mrs. James,' sitting at the window of her room watching for them, saw the new Lord land from the gondola first. He handed his wife to the steps. The three children were next committed to his care. Last of all, Agnes appeared in the little black doorway of the gondola cabin, and, taking Lord Montbarry's hand, passed in her turn to the steps. She wore no veil. As she ascended to the door of the hotel, the Countess (eyeing her through an opera-glass) noticed that she paused to look at the outside of the building, and that her face was very pale.

XXI

Lord and Lady Montbarry were received by the housekeeper; the manager being absent for a day or two on business connected with the affairs of the hotel.

The rooms reserved for the travellers on the first floor were three in number; consisting of two bedrooms opening into each other, and communicating on the left with a drawing-room. Complete so far, the arrangements proved to be less satisfactory in reference to the third bedroom required for Agnes and for the eldest daughter of Lord Montbarry, who usually slept with her on their travels. The bed-chamber on the right of the drawing-room was already occupied by an English widow lady. Other bedchambers at the other end of the corridor were also let in every case. There was accordingly no alternative but to place at the disposal of Agnes a comfortable room on the second floor. Lady Montbarry vainly complained of this separation of one of the members of her travelling party from the rest. The housekeeper politely hinted that it was impossible for her to ask other travellers to give up their rooms. She could only express her regret, and assure Miss Lockwood that her bed-chamber on the second floor was one of the best rooms in that part of the hotel.

On the retirement of the housekeeper, Lady Montbarry noticed that Agnes had seated herself apart, feeling apparently no interest in the question of the bedrooms. Was she ill? No; she felt a little unnerved by the railway journey, and that was all. Hearing this, Lord Montbarry proposed that she should go out with him, and try the experiment of half an hour's walk in the cool evening air. Agnes gladly accepted the suggestion. They directed their steps towards the square of St. Mark, so as to enjoy the breeze blowing over the lagoon. It was the first visit of Agnes to Venice. The fascination of the wonderful city of the waters exerted its full influence over her sensitive nature. The proposed half-hour of the walk had passed away, and was fast expanding to half an hour more, before Lord Montbarry could persuade his companion to remember that dinner was waiting for them. As they returned, passing under the colonnade, neither of them noticed a lady in deep mourning, loitering in the open space of the square. She started as she recognised Agnes walking with the new Lord Montbarry—hesitated for a moment—and then followed them, at a discreet distance, back to the hotel.

Lady Montbarry received Agnes in high spirits—with news of an event which had happened in her absence.

She had not left the hotel more than ten minutes, before a little note in pencil was brought to Lady Montbarry by the housekeeper. The writer proved to be no less a person than the widow lady who occupied the room on the other side of the drawing-room, which her ladyship had vainly hoped to secure for Agnes. Writing under the name of Mrs. James, the polite widow explained that she had heard from the housekeeper of the disappointment experienced by Lady Montbarry in the matter of the rooms. Mrs. James was quite alone; and as long as her bed-chamber was airy and comfortable, it mattered nothing to her whether she slept on the first or the second floor of the house. She had accordingly much pleasure in proposing to change rooms with Miss Lockwood. Her luggage had already been removed, and Miss Lockwood had only to take possession of the room (Number 13 A), which was now entirely at her disposal.

'I immediately proposed to see Mrs. James,' Lady Montbarry continued, 'and to thank her personally for her extreme kindness. But I was informed that she had gone out, without leaving word at what hour she might be expected to return. I have written a little note of thanks, saying that we hope to have the pleasure of personally expressing our sense of Mrs. James's courtesy to-morrow. In the mean time, Agnes, I have ordered your boxes to be removed downstairs. Go!—and judge for yourself, my dear, if that good lady has not given up to you the prettiest room in the house!'

With those words, Lady Montbarry left Miss Lockwood to make a hasty toilet for dinner.

The new room at once produced a favourable impression on Agnes. The large window, opening into a balcony, commanded an admirable view of the canal. The decorations on the walls and ceiling were skilfully copied from the exquisitely graceful designs of Raphael in the Vatican. The massive wardrobe possessed compartments of unusual size, in which double the number of dresses that Agnes possessed might have been conveniently hung at full length. In the inner corner of the room, near the head of the bedstead, there was a recess which had been turned into a little dressing-room, and which opened by a second door on the interior staircase of the hotel, commonly used by the servants. Noticing these aspects of the room at a glance, Agnes made the necessary change in her dress, as quickly as possible. On her way back to the drawing-room she was addressed by a chambermaid in the corridor who asked for her key. 'I will put your room tidy for the night, Miss,' the woman said, 'and I will then bring the key back to you in the drawing-room.'

While the chambermaid was at her work, a solitary lady, loitering about the corridor of the second storey, was watching her over the bannisters. After a while, the maid appeared, with her pail in her hand, leaving the room by way of the dressing-room and the back stairs. As she passed out of sight, the lady on the second floor (no other, it is needless to add, than the Countess herself) ran swiftly down the stairs, entered the bed-chamber by the principal door, and hid herself in the empty side compartment of the wardrobe. The chambermaid returned, completed her work, locked the door of the dressing-room on the inner side, locked the principal entrance-door on leaving the room, and returned the key to Agnes in the drawing-room.

The travellers were just sitting down to their late dinner, when one of the children noticed that Agnes was not wearing her watch. Had she left it in her bed-chamber in the hurry of changing her dress? She rose from the table at once in search of her watch; Lady Montbarry advising her, as she went out, to see to the security of her bed-chamber, in the event of there being thieves in the house. Agnes found her watch, forgotten on the toilet table, as she had anticipated. Before leaving the room again she acted on Lady Montbarry's advice, and tried the key in the lock of the dressing-room door. It was properly secured. She left the bed-chamber, locking the main door behind her.

Immediately on her departure, the Countess, oppressed by the confined air in the wardrobe, ventured on stepping out of her hiding place into the empty room.

Entering the dressing-room, she listened at the door, until the silence outside informed her that the corridor was empty. Upon this, she unlocked the door, and, passing out, closed it again softly; leaving it to all appearance (when viewed on the inner side) as carefully secured as Agnes had seen it when she tried the key in the lock with her own hand.

While the Montbarrys were still at dinner, Henry Westwick joined them, arriving from Milan.

When he entered the room, and again when he advanced to shake hands with her, Agnes was conscious of a latent feeling which secretly reciprocated Henry's unconcealed pleasure on meeting her again. For a moment only, she returned his look; and in that moment her own observation told her that she had silently encouraged him to hope. She saw it in the sudden glow of happiness which overspread his face; and she confusedly took refuge in the usual conventional inquiries relating to the relatives whom he had left at Milan.

Taking his place at the table, Henry gave a most amusing account of the position of his brother Francis between the mercenary opera-dancer on one side, and the unscrupulous manager of the French theatre on the other. Matters had proceeded to such extremities, that the law had been called on to interfere, and had decided the dispute in favour of Francis. On winning the victory the English manager had at once left Milan, recalled to London by the affairs of his theatre. He was accompanied on the journey back, as he had been accompanied on the journey out, by his sister. Resolved, after passing two nights of terror in the Venetian hotel, never to enter it again, Mrs. Norbury asked to be excused from appearing at the family festival, on the ground of ill-health. At her age, travelling fatigued her, and she was glad to take advantage of her brother's escort to return to England.

While the talk at the dinner-table flowed easily onward, the evening-time advanced to night—and it became necessary to think of sending the children to bed.

As Agnes rose to leave the room, accompanied by the eldest girl, she observed with surprise that Henry's manner suddenly changed. He looked serious and pre-occupied; and when his niece wished him good night, he abruptly said to her, 'Marian, I want to know what part of the hotel you sleep in?' Marian, puzzled by the question, answered that she was going to sleep, as usual, with 'Aunt Agnes.' Not satisfied with that reply, Henry next inquired whether the bedroom was near the rooms occupied by the other members of the travelling party. Answering for the child, and wondering what Henry's object could possibly be, Agnes mentioned the polite sacrifice made to her convenience by Mrs. James. 'Thanks to that lady's kindness,' she said, 'Marian and I are only on the other side of the drawing-room.' Henry made no remark; he looked incomprehensibly discontented as he opened the door for Agnes and her companion to pass out. After wishing them good night, he waited in the corridor until he saw them enter the fatal corner-room—and then he called abruptly to his brother, 'Come out, Stephen, and let us smoke!'

As soon as the two brothers were at liberty to speak together privately, Henry explained the motive which had led to his strange inquiries about the bedrooms. Francis had informed him of the meeting with the Countess at Venice, and of all that had followed it; and Henry now carefully repeated the narrative to his brother in all its details. 'I am not satisfied,' he added, 'about that woman's purpose in giving up her room. Without alarming the ladies by telling them what I have just told you, can you not warn Agnes to be careful in securing her door?'

Lord Montbarry replied, that the warning had been already given by his wife, and that Agnes might be trusted to take good care of herself and her little bed-fellow. For the rest, he looked upon the story of the Countess and her superstitions as a piece of theatrical exaggeration, amusing enough in itself, but unworthy of a moment's serious attention.

While the gentlemen were absent from the hotel, the room which had been already associated with so many startling circumstances, became the scene of another strange event in which Lady Montbarry's eldest child was concerned.

Little Marian had been got ready for bed as usual, and had (so far) taken hardly any notice of the new room. As she knelt down to say her prayers, she happened to look up at that part of the ceiling above her which was just over the head of the bed. The next instant she alarmed Agnes, by starting to her feet with a cry of terror, and pointing to a small brown spot on one of the white panelled spaces of the carved ceiling. 'It's a spot of blood!' the child exclaimed. 'Take me away! I won't sleep here!'

Seeing plainly that it would be useless to reason with her while she was in the room, Agnes hurriedly wrapped Marian in a dressing-gown, and carried her back to her mother in the drawing-room. Here, the ladies did their best to soothe and reassure the trembling girl. The effort proved to be useless; the impression that had been produced on the young and sensitive mind was not to be removed by persuasion. Marian could give no explanation of the panic of terror that had seized her. She was quite unable to say why the spot on the ceiling looked like the colour of a spot of blood. She only knew that she should die of terror if she saw it again. Under these circumstances, but one alternative was left. It was arranged that the child should pass the night in the room occupied by her two younger sisters and the nurse.

In half an hour more, Marian was peacefully asleep with her arm around her sister's neck. Lady Montbarry went back with Agnes to her room to see the spot on the ceiling which had so strangely frightened the child. It was so small as to be only just perceptible, and it had in all probability been caused by the carelessness of a workman, or by a dripping from water accidentally spilt on the floor of the room above.

'I really cannot understand why Marian should place such a shocking interpretation on such a trifling thing,' Lady Montbarry remarked.

'I suspect the nurse is in some way answerable for what has happened,' Agnes suggested. 'She may quite possibly have been telling Marian some tragic nursery story which has left its mischievous impression behind it. Persons in her position are sadly ignorant of the danger of exciting a child's imagination. You had better caution the nurse to-morrow.'

Lady Montbarry looked round the room with admiration. 'Is it not prettily decorated?' she said. 'I suppose, Agnes, you don't mind sleeping here by yourself.?'

Agnes laughed. 'I feel so tired,' she replied, 'that I was

thinking of bidding you good-night, instead of going back to the drawing-room.'

Lady Montbarry turned towards the door. 'I see your jewel-case on the table,' she resumed. 'Don't forget to lock the other door there, in the dressing-room.'

'I have already seen to it, and tried the key myself,' said Agnes. 'Can I be of any use to you before I go to bed?'

'No, my dear, thank you; I feel sleepy enough to follow your example. Good night, Agnes—and pleasant dreams on your first night in Venice.'

XXII

Having closed and secured the door on Lady Montbarry's departure, Agnes put on her dressing-gown, and, turning to her open boxes, began the business of unpacking. In the hurry of making her toilet for dinner, she had taken the first dress that lay uppermost in the trunk, and had thrown her travelling costume on the bed. She now opened the doors of the wardrobe for the first time, and began to hang her dresses on the hooks in the large compartment on one side.

After a few minutes only of this occupation, she grew weary of it, and decided on leaving the trunks as they were, until the next morning. The oppressive south wind, which had blown throughout the day, still prevailed at night. The atmosphere of the room felt close; Agnes threw a shawl over her head and shoulders, and, opening the window, stepped into the balcony to look at the view.

The night was heavy and overcast: nothing could be distinctly seen. The canal beneath the window looked like a black gulf; the opposite houses were barely visible as a row of shadows, dimly relieved against the starless and moonless sky. At long intervals, the warning cry of a belated gondolier was just audible, as he turned the corner of a distant canal, and called to invisible boats which might be approaching him in the darkness. Now and then, the nearer dip of an oar in the water told of the viewless passage of other gondolas bringing guests back to the hotel. Excepting these rare sounds, the mysterious night-silence of Venice was literally the silence of the grave.

Leaning on the parapet of the balcony, Agnes looked vacantly into the black void beneath. Her thoughts reverted to the miserable man who had broken his pledged faith to her, and who had died in that house. Some change seemed to have come over her since her arrival in Venice; some new influence appeared to be at work. For the first time in her experience of herself, compassion and regret were not the only emotions aroused in her by the remembrance of the dead Montbarry. A keen sense of the wrong that she had suffered, never yet felt by that gentle and forgiving nature, was felt by it now. She found herself thinking of the bygone days of her humiliation almost as harshly as Henry Westwick had thought of them—she who had rebuked him the last time he had spoken slightingly of his brother in her presence! A sudden fear and doubt of herself, startled her physically as well as morally. She turned from the shadowy abyss of the dark water as if the mystery and the gloom of it had been answerable for the emotions which had taken her by surprise. Abruptly closing the window, she threw aside her shawl, and lit the candles on the mantelpiece, impelled by a sudden craving for light in the solitude of her room.

The cheering brightness round her, contrasting with the black gloom outside, restored her spirits. She felt herself enjoying the light like a child!

Would it be well (she asked herself) to get ready for bed? No! The sense of drowsy fatigue that she had felt half an hour since was gone. She returned to the dull employment of unpacking her boxes. After a few minutes only, the occupation became irksome to her once more. She sat down by the table, and took up a guide-book. 'Suppose I inform myself,' she thought, 'on the subject of Venice?'

Her attention wandered from the book, before she had turned the first page of it.

The image of Henry Westwick was the presiding image in her memory now. Recalling the minutest incidents and details of the evening, she could think of nothing which presented him under other than a favourable and interesting aspect. She smiled to herself softly, her colour rose by fine gradations, as she felt the full luxury of dwelling on the perfect truth and modesty of his devotion to her. Was the depression of spirits from which she had suffered so persistently on her travels attributable, by any chance, to their long separation from each other—embittered perhaps by her own vain regret when she remembered her harsh reception of him in Paris? Suddenly conscious of this bold question, and of the self-abandonment which it implied, she returned mechanically to her book, distrusting the unrestrained liberty of her own thoughts. What lurking temptations to forbidden tenderness find their hiding-places in a woman's dressing-gown, when she is alone in her room at night! With her heart in the tomb of the dead Montbarry, could Agnes even think of another man, and think of love? How shameful! how unworthy of her! For the second time, she tried to interest herself in the guide-book—and once more she tried in vain. Throwing the book aside, she turned desperately to the one resource that was left, to her luggage—resolved to fatigue herself without mercy, until she was weary enough and sleepy enough to find a safe refuge in bed.

For some little time, she persisted in the monotonous occupation of transferring her clothes from her trunk to the wardrobe. The large clock in the hall, striking mid-night, reminded her that it was getting late. She sat down for a moment in an arm-chair by the bedside, to rest.

The silence in the house now caught her attention, and held it—held it disagreeably. Was everybody in bed and asleep but herself? Surely it was time for her to follow the general example? With a certain irritable nervous haste, she rose again and undressed herself. 'I have lost two hours of rest,' she thought, frowning at the reflection of herself in the glass, as she arranged her hair for the night. 'I shall be good for nothing to-morrow!'

She lit the night-light, and extinguished the candles—with one exception, which she removed to a little table, placed on the side of the bed opposite to the side occupied by the arm-chair. Having put her travelling-box of matches and the guide-book near the candle, in case she might be sleepless and might want to read, she blew out the light, and laid her head on the pillow.

The curtains of the bed were looped back to let the air pass freely over her. Lying on her left side, with her face turned away from the table, she could see the arm-chair by the dim night-light. It had a chintz covering—representing large bunches of roses scattered over a pale green ground. She tried to weary herself into drowsiness by counting over and over again the bunches of roses that were visible from her point of view. Twice her attention was distracted from the counting, by sounds outside—by the clock chiming the half-hour past twelve; and then again, by the fall of a pair of boots on the upper floor, thrown out to be cleaned, with that barbarous disregard of the comfort of others which is observable in humanity when it inhabits an hotel. In the silence that followed these passing disturbances, Agnes went on counting the roses on the arm-chair, more and more slowly. Before long, she confused herself in the figures—tried to begin counting again—thought she would wait a little first—felt her eyelids drooping, and her head reclining lower and lower on the pillow—sighed faintly—and sank into sleep.

How long that first sleep lasted, she never knew. She could only remember, in the after-time, that she woke instantly.

Every faculty and perception in her passed the boundary line between insensibility and consciousness, so to speak, at a leap. Without knowing why, she sat up suddenly in the bed, listening for she knew not what. Her head was in a whirl; her heart beat furiously, without any assignable cause. But one trivial event had happened during the interval while she had been asleep. The night-light had gone out; and the room, as a matter of course, was in total darkness.

She felt for the match-box, and paused after finding it. A vague sense of confusion was still in her mind. She was in no hurry to light the match. The pause in the darkness was, for the moment, agreeable to her.

In the quieter flow of her thoughts during this interval, she could ask herself the natural question:—What cause had awakened her so suddenly, and had so strangely shaken her nerves? Had it been the influence of a dream? She had not dreamed at all—or, to speak more correctly, she had no waking remembrance of having dreamed. The mystery was beyond her fathoming: the darkness began to oppress her. She struck the match on the box, and lit her candle.

As the welcome light diffused itself over the room, she turned from the table and looked towards the other side of the bed.

In the moment when she turned, the chill of a sudden terror gripped her round the heart, as with the clasp of an icy hand.

She was not alone in her room!

There—in the chair at the bedside—there, suddenly revealed under the flow of light from the candle, was the figure of a woman, reclining. Her head lay back over the chair. Her face, turned up to the ceiling, had the eyes closed, as if she was wrapped in a deep sleep.

The shock of the discovery held Agnes speechless and helpless. Her first conscious action, when she was in some degree mistress of herself again, was to lean over the bed, and to look closer at the woman who had so incomprehensibly stolen into her room in the dead of night. One glance was enough: she started back with a cry of amazement. The person in the chair was no other than the widow of the dead Montbarry—the woman who had warned her that they were to meet again, and that the place might be Venice!

Her courage returned to her, stung into action by the natural sense of indignation which the presence of the Countess provoked.

'Wake up!' she called out. 'How dare you come here? How did you get in? Leave the room—or I will call for help!'

She raised her voice at the last words. It produced no effect. Leaning farther over the bed, she boldly took the Countess by the shoulder and shook her. Not even this effort succeeded in rousing the sleeping woman. She still lay back in the chair, possessed by a torpor like the torpor of death—insensible to sound, insensible to touch. Was she really sleeping? Or had she fainted?

Agnes looked closer at her. She had not fainted. Her breathing was audible, rising and falling in deep heavy gasps. At intervals she ground her teeth savagely. Beads of perspiration stood thickly on her forehead. Her clenched hands rose and fell slowly from time to time on her lap. Was she in the agony of a dream? or was she spiritually conscious of something hidden in the room?

The doubt involved in that last question was unendurable. Agnes determined to rouse the servants who kept watch in the hotel at night.

The bell-handle was fixed to the wall, on the side of the bed by which the table stood.

She raised herself from the crouching position which she had assumed in looking close at the Countess; and, turning towards the other side of the bed, stretched out her hand to the bell. At the same instant, she stopped and looked upward. Her hand fell helplessly at her side. She shuddered, and sank back on the pillow.

What had she seen?

She had seen another intruder in her room.

Midway between her face and the ceiling, there hovered a human head—severed at the neck, like a head struck from the body by the guillotine.

Nothing visible, nothing audible, had given her any intelligible warning of its appearance. Silently and suddenly, the head had taken its place above her. No supernatural change had passed over the room, or was perceptible in it now. The dumbly-tortured figure in the chair; the broad window opposite the foot of the bed, with the black night beyond it; the candle burning on the table—these, and all other objects in the room, remained unaltered. One object more, unutterably horrid, had been added to the rest. That was the only change—no more, no less.

By the yellow candlelight she saw the head distinctly, hovering in mid-air above her. She looked at it steadfastly, spell-bound by the terror that held her.

The flesh of the face was gone. The shrivelled skin was darkened in hue, like the skin of an Egyptian mummy—except at the neck. There it was of a lighter colour; there it showed spots and splashes of the hue of that brown spot on the ceiling, which the child's fanciful terror had distorted into the likeness of a spot of blood. Thin remains of a discoloured moustache and whiskers, hanging over the upper lip, and over the hollows where the cheeks had once been, made the head just recognisable as the head of a man. Over all the features death and time had done their obliterating work. The eyelids were closed. The hair on the skull, discoloured like the hair on the face, had been burnt away in places. The bluish lips, parted in a fixed grin, showed the double row of teeth. By slow degrees, the hovering head (perfectly still when she first saw it) began to descend towards Agnes as she lay beneath. By slow degrees, that strange doubly-blended odour, which the Commissioners had discovered in the vaults of the old palace—which had sickened Francis Westwick in the bed-chamber of the new hotel—spread its fetid exhalations over the room. Downward and downward the hideous apparition made its slow progress, until it stopped close over Agnes—stopped, and turned slowly, so that the face of it confronted the upturned face of the woman in the chair.

There was a pause. Then, a supernatural movement disturbed the rigid repose of the dead face.

The closed eyelids opened slowly. The eyes revealed themselves, bright with the glassy film of death—and fixed their dreadful look on the woman in the chair.

Agnes saw that look; saw the eyelids of the living woman open slowly like the eyelids of the dead; saw her rise, as if in obedience to some silent command—and saw no more.

Her next conscious impression was of the sunlight pouring in at the window; of the friendly presence of Lady Montbarry at the bedside; and of the children's wondering faces peeping in at the door.

XXIII

'...You have some influence over Agnes. Try what you can do, Henry, to make her take a sensible view of the matter. There is really nothing to make a fuss about. My wife's maid knocked at her door early in the morning, with the customary cup of tea. Getting no answer, she went round to the dressing-room—found the door on that side unlocked—and discovered Agnes on the bed in a fainting fit. With my wife's help, they brought her to herself again; and she told the extraordinary story which I have just repeated to you. You must have seen for yourself that she has been over-fatigued, poor thing, by our long railway journeys: her nerves are out of order—and she is just the person to be easily terrified by a dream. She obstinately refuses, however, to accept this rational view. Don't suppose that I have been severe with her! All that a man can do to humour her I have done. I have written to the Countess (in her assumed name) offering to restore the room to her. She writes back, positively declining to return to it. I have accordingly arranged (so as not to have the thing known in the hotel) to occupy the room for one or two nights, and to leave Agnes to recover her spirits under my wife's care. Is there anything more that I can do? Whatever questions Agnes has asked of me I have answered to the best of my ability; she knows all that you told me about Francis and the Countess last night. But try as I may I can't quiet her mind. I have given up the attempt in despair, and left her in the drawing-room. Go, like a good fellow, and try what you can do to compose her.'

In those words, Lord Montbarry stated the case to his brother from the rational point of view. Henry made no remark, he went straight to the drawing-room.

He found Agnes walking rapidly backwards and forwards, flushed and excited. 'If you come here to say what your brother has been saying to me,' she broke out, before he could speak, 'spare yourself the trouble. I don't want common sense—I want a true friend who will believe in me.'

'I am that friend, Agnes,' Henry answered quietly, 'and you know it.'

'You really believe that I am not deluded by a dream?'

I know that you are not deluded—in one particular, at least.'

'In what particular?'

'In what you have said of the Countess. It is perfectly true—'

Agnes stopped him there. 'Why do I only hear this morning that the Countess and Mrs. James are one and the same person?' she asked distrustfully. 'Why was I not told of it last night?'

'You forget that you had accepted the exchange of rooms before I reached Venice,' Henry replied. 'I felt strongly tempted to tell you, even then—but your sleeping arrangements for the night were all made; I should only have inconvenienced and alarmed you. I waited till the morning, after hearing from my brother that you had yourself seen to your security from any intrusion. How that intrusion was accomplished it is impossible to say. I can only declare that the Countess's presence by your bedside last night was no dream of yours. On her own authority I can testify that it was a reality.'

'On her own authority?' Agnes repeated eagerly. 'Have you seen her this morning?'

'I have seen her not ten minutes since.'

'What was she doing?'

She was busily engaged in writing. I could not even get her to look at me until I thought of mentioning your name.'

'She remembered me, of course?'

'She remembered you with some difficulty. Finding that she wouldn't answer me on any other terms, I questioned her as if I had come direct from you. Then she spoke. She not only admitted that she had the same superstitious motive for placing you in that room which she had acknowledged to Francis—she even owned that she had been by your bedside, watching through the night, "to see what you saw," as she expressed it. Hearing this, I tried to persuade her to tell me how she got into the room. Unluckily, her manuscript on the table caught her eye; she returned to her writing. "The Baron wants money," she said; "I must get on with my play." What she saw or dreamed while she was in your room last night, it is at present impossible to discover. But judging by my brother's account of her, as well as by what I remember of her myself, some recent influence has been at work which has produced a marked change in this wretched woman for the worse. Her mind (since last night, perhaps) is partially deranged. One proof of it is that she spoke to me of the Baron as if he were still a living man. When Francis saw her, she declared that the Baron was dead, which is the truth. The United States Consul at Milan showed us the announcement of the death in an American newspaper. So far as I can see, such sense as she still possesses seems to be entirely absorbed in one absurd idea—the idea of writing a play for Francis to bring out at his theatre. He admits that he encouraged her to hope she might get money in this way. I think he did wrong. Don't you agree with me?'

Without heeding the question, Agnes rose abruptly from her chair.

'Do me one more kindness, Henry,' she said. 'Take me to the Countess at once.'

Henry hesitated. 'Are you composed enough to see her, after the shock that you have suffered?' he asked.

She trembled, the flush on her face died away, and left it deadly pale. But she held to her resolution. 'You have heard of what I saw last night?' she said faintly.

'Don't speak of it!' Henry interposed. 'Don't uselessly agitate yourself.'

'I must speak! My mind is full of horrid questions about it. I know I can't identify it—and yet I ask myself over and over again, in whose likeness did it appear? Was it in the likeness of Ferrari? or was it—?' she stopped, shuddering. 'The Countess knows, I must see the Countess!' she resumed vehemently. 'Whether my courage fails me or not, I must make the attempt. Take me to her before I have time to feel afraid of it!'

Henry looked at her anxiously. 'If you are really sure of your own resolution,' he said, 'I agree with you—the sooner you see her the better. You remember how strangely she talked of your influence over her, when she forced her way into your room in London?'

'I remember it perfectly. Why do you ask?'

'For this reason. In the present state of her mind, I doubt if she will be much longer capable of realizing her wild idea of you as the avenging angel who is to bring her to a reckoning for her evil deeds. It may be well to try what your influence can do while she is still capable of feeling it.'

He waited to hear what Agnes would say. She took his arm and led him in silence to the door.

They ascended to the second floor, and, after knocking, entered the Countess's room.

She was still busily engaged in writing. When she looked up from the paper, and saw Agnes, a vacant expression of doubt was the only expression in her wild black eyes. After a few moments, the lost remembrances and associations appeared to return slowly to her mind. The pen dropped from her hand. Haggard and trembling, she looked closer at Agnes, and recognised her at last. 'Has the time come already?' she said in low awe-struck tones. 'Give me a little longer respite, I haven't done my writing yet!'

She dropped on her knees, and held out her clasped hands entreatingly. Agnes was far from having recovered, after the shock that she had suffered in the night: her nerves were far from being equal to the strain that was now laid on them. She was so startled by the change in the Countess, that she was at a loss what to say or to do next. Henry was obliged to speak to her. 'Put your questions while you have the chance,' he said, lowering his voice. 'See! the vacant look is coming over her face again.'

Agnes tried to rally her courage. 'You were in my room last night—' she began. Before she could add a word more, the Countess lifted her hands, and wrung them above her head with a low moan of horror. Agnes shrank back, and turned as if to leave the room. Henry stopped her, and whispered to her to try again. She obeyed him after an effort. 'I slept last night in the room that you gave up to me,' she resumed. 'I saw—'

The Countess suddenly rose to her feet. 'No more of that,' she cried. 'Oh, Jesu Maria! do you think I want to be told what you saw? Do you think I don't know what it means for you and for me? Decide for yourself, Miss. Examine your own mind. Are you well assured that the day of reckoning has come at last? Are you ready to follow me back, through the crimes of the past, to the secrets of the dead?'

She returned again to the writing-table, without waiting to be answered. Her eyes flashed; she looked like her old self once more as she spoke. It was only for a moment. The old ardour and impetuosity were nearly worn out. Her head sank; she sighed heavily as she unlocked a desk which stood on the table. Opening a drawer in the desk, she took out a leaf of vellum, covered with faded writing. Some ragged ends of silken thread were still attached to the leaf, as if it had been torn out of a book.

'Can you read Italian?' she asked, handing the leaf to Agnes.

Agnes answered silently by an inclination of her head.

'The leaf,' the Countess proceeded, 'once belonged to a book in the old library of the palace, while this building was still a palace. By whom it was torn out you have no need to know. For what purpose it was torn out you may discover for yourself, if you will. Read it first—at the fifth line from the top of the page.'

Agnes felt the serious necessity of composing herself. 'Give me a chair,' she said to Henry; 'and I will do my best.' He placed himself behind her chair so that he could look over her shoulder and help her to understand the writing on the leaf. Rendered into English, it ran as follows:—

I have now completed my literary survey of the first floor of the palace. At the desire of my noble and gracious patron, the lord of this glorious edifice, I next ascend to the second floor, and continue my catalogue or description of the pictures, decorations, and other treasures of art therein contained. Let me begin with the corner room at the western extremity of the palace, called the Room of the Caryatides, from the statues which support the mantel-piece. This work is of comparatively recent execution: it dates from the eighteenth century only, and reveals the corrupt taste of the period in every part of it. Still, there is a certain interest which attaches to the mantel-piece: it conceals a cleverly constructed hiding-place, between the floor of the room and the ceiling of the room beneath, which was made during the last evil days of the Inquisition in Venice, and which is reported to have saved an ancestor of my gracious lord pursued by that terrible tribunal. The machinery of this curious place of concealment has been kept in good order by the present lord, as a species of curiosity. He condescended to show me the method of working it. Approaching the two Caryatides, rest your hand on the forehead (midway between the eyebrows) of the figure which is on your left as you stand opposite to the fireplace, then press the head inwards as if you were pushing it against the wall behind. By doing this, you set in motion the hidden machinery in the wall which turns the hearthstone on a pivot, and discloses the hollow place below. There is room enough in it for a man to lie easily at full length. The method of closing the cavity again is equally simple. Place both your hands on the temples of the figures; pull as if you were pulling it towards you—and the hearthstone will revolve into its proper position again.

'You need read no farther,' said the Countess. 'Be careful to remember what you have read.'

She put back the page of vellum in her writing-desk, locked it, and led the way to the door.

'Come!' she said; 'and see what the mocking Frenchman called "The beginning of the end."'

Agnes was barely able to rise from her chair; she trembled from head to foot. Henry gave her his arm to support her. 'Fear nothing,' he whispered; 'I shall be with you.'

The Countess proceeded along the westward corridor, and stopped at the door numbered Thirty-eight. This was the room which had been inhabited by Baron Rivar in the old days of the palace: it was situated immediately over the bedchamber in which Agnes had passed the night. For the last two days the room had been empty. The absence of luggage in it, when they opened the door, showed that it had not yet been let.

'You see?' said the Countess, pointing to the carved figure at the fire-place; 'and you know what to do. Have I deserved that you should temper justice with mercy?' she went on in lower tones. 'Give me a few hours more to myself. The Baron wants money—I must get on with my play.'

She smiled vacantly, and imitated the action of writing with her right hand as she pronounced the last words. The effort of concentrating her weakened mind on other and less familiar topics than the constant want of money in the Baron's lifetime, and the vague prospect of gain from the still unfinished play, had evidently exhausted her poor reserves of strength. When her request had been granted, she addressed no expressions of gratitude to Agnes; she only said, 'Feel no fear, miss, of my attempting to escape you. Where you are, there I must be till the end comes.'

Her eyes wandered round the room with a last weary and stupefied look. She returned to her writing with slow and feeble steps, like the steps of an old woman.

XXIV

Henry and Agnes were left alone in the Room of the Caryatides.

The person who had written the description of the palace—probably a poor author or artist—had correctly pointed out the defects of the mantel-piece. Bad taste, exhibiting itself on the most costly and splendid scale, was visible in every part of the work. It was nevertheless greatly admired by ignorant travellers of all classes; partly on account of its imposing size, and partly on account of the number of variously-coloured marbles which the sculptor had contrived to introduce into his design. Photographs of the mantel-piece were exhibited in the public rooms, and found a ready sale among English and American visitors to the hotel.

Henry led Agnes to the figure on the left, as they stood facing the empty fire-place. 'Shall I try the experiment,' he asked, 'or will you?' She abruptly drew her arm away from him, and turned back to the door. 'I can't even look at it,' she said. 'That merciless marble face frightens me!'

Henry put his hand on the forehead of the figure. 'What is there to alarm you, my dear, in this conventionally classical face?' he asked jestingly. Before he could press the head inwards, Agnes hurriedly opened the door. 'Wait till I am out of the room!' she cried. 'The bare idea of what you may find there horrifies me!' She looked back into the room as she crossed the threshold. 'I won't leave you altogether,' she said, 'I will wait outside.'

She closed the door. Left by himself, Henry lifted his hand once more to the marble forehead of the figure.

For the second time, he was checked on the point of setting the machinery of the hiding-place in motion. On this occasion, the interruption came from an outbreak of friendly voices in the corridor. A woman's voice exclaimed, 'Dearest Agnes, how glad I am to see you again!' A man's voice followed, offering to introduce some friend to 'Miss Lockwood.' A third voice (which Henry recognised as the voice of the manager of the hotel) became audible next, directing the housekeeper to show the ladies and gentlemen the vacant apartments at the other end of the corridor. 'If more accommodation is wanted,' the manager went on, 'I have a charming room to let here.' He opened the door as he spoke, and found himself face to face with Henry Westwick.

'This is indeed an agreeable surprise, sir!' said the manager cheerfully. 'You are admiring our famous chimney-piece, I see. May I ask, Mr. Westwick, how you find yourself in the hotel, this time? Have the supernatural influences affected your appetite again?'

'The supernatural influences have spared me, this time,' Henry answered. 'Perhaps you may yet find that they have affected some other member of the family.' He spoke gravely, resenting the familiar tone in which the manager had referred to his previous visit to the hotel. 'Have you just returned?' he asked, by way of changing the topic.

'Just this minute, sir. I had the honour of travelling in the same train with friends of yours who have arrived at the hotel—Mr. and Mrs. Arthur Barville, and their travelling companions. Miss Lockwood is with them, looking at the rooms. They will be here before long, if they find it convenient to have an extra room at their disposal.'

This announcement decided Henry on exploring the hiding-place, before the interruption occurred. It had crossed his mind, when Agnes left him, that he ought perhaps to have a witness, in the not very probable event of some alarming discovery taking place. The too-familiar manager, suspecting nothing, was there at his disposal. He turned again to the Caryan figure, maliciously resolving to make the manager his witness.

'I am delighted to hear that our friends have arrived at last,' he said. 'Before I shake hands with them, let me ask you a question about this queer work of art here. I see photographs of it downstairs. Are they for sale?'

'Certainly, Mr. Westwick!'

'Do you think the chimney-piece is as solid as it looks?' Henry proceeded. 'When you came in, I was just wondering whether this figure here had not accidentally got loosened from the wall behind it.' He laid his hand on the marble forehead, for the third time. 'To my eye, it looks a little out of the perpendicular. I almost fancied I could jog the head just now, when I touched it.' He pressed the head inwards as he said those words.

A sound of jarring iron was instantly audible behind the wall. The solid hearthstone in front of the fire-place turned slowly at the feet of the two men, and disclosed a dark cavity below. At the same moment, the strange and sickening combination of odours, hitherto associated with the vaults of the old palace and with the bed-chamber beneath, now floated up from the open recess, and filled the room.

The manager started back. 'Good God, Mr. Westwick!' he exclaimed, 'what does this mean?'

Remembering, not only what his brother Francis had felt in the room beneath, but what the experience of Agnes had been on the previous night, Henry was determined to be on his guard. 'I am as much surprised as you are,' was his only reply.

'Wait for me one moment, sir,' said the manager. 'I must stop the ladies and gentlemen outside from coming in.'

He hurried away—not forgetting to close the door after him. Henry opened the window, and waited there breathing the purer air. Vague apprehensions of the next discovery to come, filled his mind for the first time. He was doubly resolved, now, not to stir a step in the investigation without a witness.

The manager returned with a wax taper in his hand, which he lighted as soon as he entered the room.

'We need fear no interruption now,' he said. 'Be so kind, Mr. Westwick, as to hold the light. It is my business to find out what this extraordinary discovery means.'

Henry held the taper. Looking into the cavity, by the dim and flickering light, they both detected a dark object at the bottom of it. 'I think I can reach the thing,' the manager remarked, 'if I lie down, and put my hand into the hole.'

He knelt on the floor—and hesitated. 'Might I ask you, sir, to give me my gloves?' he said. 'They are in my hat, on the chair behind you.'

Henry gave him the gloves. 'I don't know what I may be going to take hold of,' the manager explained, smiling rather uneasily as he put on his right glove.

He stretched himself at full length on the floor, and passed his right arm into the cavity. 'I can't say exactly what I have got hold of,' he said. 'But I have got it.'

Half raising himself, he drew his hand out.

The next instant, he started to his feet with a shriek of terror. A human head dropped from his nerveless grasp on the floor, and rolled to Henry's feet. It was the hideous head that Agnes had seen hovering above her, in the vision of the night!

The two men looked at each other, both struck speechless by the same emotion of horror. The manager was the first to control himself. 'See to the door, for God's sake!' he said. 'Some of the people outside may have heard me.'

Henry moved mechanically to the door.

Even when he had his hand on the key, ready to turn it in the lock in case of necessity, he still looked back at the appalling object on the floor. There was no possibility of identifying those decayed and distorted features with any living creature whom he had seen—and, yet, he was conscious of feeling a vague and awful doubt which shook him to the soul. The questions which had tortured the mind of Agnes, were now his questions too. He asked himself, 'In whose likeness might I have recognised it before the decay set in? The likeness of Ferrari? or the likeness of—?' He paused trembling, as Agnes had paused trembling before him. Agnes! The name, of all women's names the dearest to him, was a terror to him now! What was he to say to her? What might be the consequence if he trusted her with the terrible truth?

No footsteps approached the door; no voices were audible outside. The travellers were still occupied in the rooms at the eastern end of the corridor.

In the brief interval that had passed, the manager had sufficiently recovered himself to be able to think once more of the first and foremost interests of his life—the interests of the hotel. He approached Henry anxiously.

'If this frightful discovery becomes known,' he said, 'the closing of the hotel and the ruin of the Company will be the inevitable results. I feel sure that I can trust your discretion, sir, so far?'

'You can certainly trust me,' Henry answered. 'But surely discretion has its limits,' he added, 'after such a discovery as we have made?'

The manager understood that the duty which they owed to the community, as honest and law-abiding men, was the duty to which Henry now referred. 'I will at once find the means,' he said, 'of conveying the remains privately out of the house, and I will myself place them in the care of the police authorities. Will you leave the room with me? or do you not object to keep watch here, and help me when I return?'

While he was speaking, the voices of the travellers made themselves heard again at the end of the corridor. Henry instantly consented to wait in the room. He shrank from facing the inevitable meeting with Agnes if he showed himself in the corridor at that moment.

The manager hastened his departure, in the hope of escaping notice. He was discovered by his guests before he could reach the head of the stairs. Henry heard the voices plainly as he turned the key. While the terrible drama of discovery was in progress on one side of the door, trivial questions about the amusements of Venice, and facetious discussions on the relative merits of French and Italian cookery, were proceeding on the other. Little by little, the sound of the talking grew fainter. The visitors, having arranged their plans of amusement for the day, were on their way out of the hotel. In a minute or two, there was silence once more.

Henry turned to the window, thinking to relieve his mind by looking at the bright view over the canal. He soon grew wearied of the familiar scene. The morbid fascination which seems to be exercised by all horrible sights, drew him back again to the ghastly object on the floor.

Dream or reality, how had Agnes survived the sight of it? As the question passed through his mind, he noticed for the first time something lying on the floor near the head. Looking closer, he perceived a thin little plate of gold, with three false teeth attached to it, which had apparently dropped out (loosened by the shock) when the manager let the head fall on the floor.

The importance of this discovery, and the necessity of not too readily communicating it to others, instantly struck Henry. Here surely was a chance—if any chance remained—of identifying the shocking relic of humanity which lay before him, the dumb witness of a crime! Acting on this idea, he took possession of the teeth, purposing to use them as a last means of inquiry when other attempts at investigation had been tried and had failed.

He went back again to the window: the solitude of the room began to weigh on his spirits. As he looked out again at the view, there was a soft knock at the door. He hastened to open it—and checked himself in the act. A doubt occurred to him. Was it the manager who had knocked? He called out, 'Who is there?'

The voice of Agnes answered him. 'Have you anything to tell me, Henry?'

He was hardly able to reply. 'Not just now,' he said, confusedly. 'Forgive me if I don't open the door. I will speak to you a little later.'

The sweet voice made itself heard again, pleading with him piteously. 'Don't leave me alone, Henry! I can't go back to the happy people downstairs.'

How could he resist that appeal? He heard her sigh—he heard the rustling of her dress as she moved away in despair. The very thing that he had shrunk from doing but a few minutes since was the thing that he did now! He joined Agnes in the corridor. She turned as she heard him, and pointed, trembling, in the direction of the closed room. 'Is it so terrible as that?' she asked faintly.

He put his arm round her to support her. A thought came to him as he looked at her, waiting in doubt and fear for his reply. 'You shall know what I have discovered,' he said, 'if you will first put on your hat and cloak, and come out with me.'

She was naturally surprised. 'Can you tell me your object in going out?' she asked.

He owned what his object was unreservedly. 'I want, before all things,' he said, 'to satisfy your mind and mine, on the subject of Montbarry's death. I am going to take you to the doctor who attended him in his illness, and to the consul who followed him to the grave.'

Her eyes rested on Henry gratefully. 'Oh, how well you understand me!' she said. The manager joined them at the same moment, on his way up the stairs. Henry gave him the key of the room, and then called to the servants in the hall to have a gondola ready at the steps. 'Are you leaving the hotel?' the manager asked. 'In search of evidence,' Henry whispered, pointing to the key. 'If the authorities want me, I shall be back in an hour.'

XXV

The day had advanced to evening. Lord Montbarry and the bridal party had gone to the Opera. Agnes alone, pleading the excuse of fatigue, remained at the hotel. Having kept up appearances by accompanying his friends to the theatre, Henry Westwick slipped away after the first act, and joined Agnes in the drawing-room.

'Have you thought of what I said to you earlier in the day?' he asked, taking a chair at her side. 'Do you agree with me that the one dreadful doubt which oppressed us both is at least set at rest?'

Agnes shook her head sadly. 'I wish I could agree with you, Henry—I wish I could honestly say that my mind is at ease.'

The answer would have discouraged most men. Henry's patience (where Agnes was concerned) was equal to any demands on it.

'If you will only look back at the events of the day,' he said, 'you must surely admit that we have not been completely baffled. Remember how Dr. Bruno disposed of our doubts:—"After thirty years of medical practice, do you think I am likely to mistake the symptoms of death by bronchitis?" If ever there was an unanswerable question, there it is! Was the consul's testimony doubtful in any part of it? He called at the palace to offer his services, after hearing of Lord Montbarry's death; he arrived at the time when the coffin was in the house; he himself saw the corpse placed in it, and the lid screwed down. The evidence of the priest is equally beyond dispute. He remained in the room with the coffin, reciting the prayers for the dead, until the funeral left the palace. Bear all these statements in mind, Agnes; and how can you deny that the question of Montbarry's death and burial is a question set at rest? We have really but one doubt left: we have still to ask ourselves whether the remains which I discovered are the remains of the lost courier, or not. There is the case, as I understand it. Have I stated it fairly?'

Agnes could not deny that he had stated it fairly.

"Then what prevents you from experiencing the same sense of relief that I feel?' Henry asked.

'What I saw last night prevents me,' Agnes answered. 'When we spoke of this subject, after our inquiries were over, you reproached me with taking what you called the superstitious view. I don't quite admit that—but I do acknowledge that I should find the superstitious view intelligible if I heard it expressed by some other person. Remembering what your brother and I once were to each other in the bygone time, I can understand the apparition making itself visible to me, to claim the mercy of Christian burial, and the vengeance due to a crime. I can even perceive some faint possibility of truth in the explanation which you described as the mesmeric theory—that what I saw might be the result of magnetic influence communicated to me, as I lay between the remains of the murdered husband above me and the guilty wife suffering the tortures of remorse at my bedside. But what I do not understand is, that I should have passed through that dreadful ordeal; having no previous knowledge of the murdered man in his lifetime, or only knowing him (if you suppose that I saw the apparition of Ferrari) through the interest which I took in his wife. I can't dispute your reasoning, Henry. But I feel in my heart of hearts that you are deceived. Nothing will shake my belief that we are still as far from having discovered the dreadful truth as ever.'

Henry made no further attempt to dispute with her. She had impressed him with a certain reluctant respect for her own opinion, in spite of himself.

'Have you thought of any better way of arriving at the truth?' he asked. 'Who is to help us? No doubt there is the Countess, who has the clue to the mystery in her own hands. But, in the present state of her mind, is her testimony to be trusted—even if she were willing to speak? Judging by my own experience, I should say decidedly not.'

'You don't mean that you have seen her again?' Agnes eagerly interposed.

'Yes. I disturbed her once more over her endless writing; and I insisted on her speaking out plainly.'

'Then you told her what you found when you opened the hiding-place?'

'Of course I did!' Henry replied. 'I said that I held her responsible for the discovery, though I had not mentioned her connection with it to the authorities as yet. She went on with her writing as if I had spoken in an unknown tongue! I was equally obstinate, on my side. I told her plainly that the head had been placed under the care of the police, and that the manager and I had signed our declarations and given our evidence. She paid not the slightest heed to me. By way of tempting her to speak, I added that the whole investigation was to be kept a secret, and that she might depend on my discretion. For the moment I thought I had succeeded. She looked up from her writing with a passing flash of curiosity, and said, "What are they going to do with it?"—meaning, I suppose, the head. I answered that it was to be privately buried, after photographs of it had first been taken. I even went the length of communicating the opinion of the surgeon consulted, that some chemical means of arresting decomposition had been used and had only partially succeeded—and I asked her point-blank if the surgeon was right? The trap was not a bad one—but it completely failed. She said in the coolest manner, "Now you are here, I should like to consult you about my play; I am at a loss for some new incidents." Mind! there was nothing satirical in this. She was really eager to read her wonderful work to me—evidently supposing that I took a special interest in such things, because my brother is the manager of a theatre! I left her, making the first excuse that occurred to me. So far as I am concerned, I can do nothing with her. But it is possible that your influence may succeed with her again, as it has succeeded already. Will you make the attempt, to satisfy your own mind? She is still upstairs; and I am quite ready to accompany you.'

Agnes shuddered at the bare suggestion of another interview with the Countess.

'I can't! I daren't!' she exclaimed. 'After what has happened in that horrible room, she is more repellent to me than ever. Don't ask me to do it, Henry! Feel my hand—you have turned me as cold as death only with talking of it!'

She was not exaggerating the terror that possessed her. Henry hastened to change the subject.

'Let us talk of something more interesting,' he said. 'I have a question to ask you about yourself. Am I right in believing that the sooner you get away from Venice the happier you will be?'

'Right?' she repeated excitedly. 'You are more than right! No words can say how I long to be away from this horrible place. But you know how I am situated—you heard what Lord Montbarry said at dinner-time?'

'Suppose he has altered his plans, since dinner-time?' Henry suggested.

Agnes looked surprised. 'I thought he had received letters from England which obliged him to leave Venice to-morrow,' she said.

'Quite true,' Henry admitted. 'He had arranged to start for England to-morrow, and to leave you and Lady Montbarry and the children to enjoy your holiday in Venice, under my care. Circumstances have occurred, however, which have forced him to alter his plans. He must take you all back with him to-morrow because I am not able to assume the charge of you. I am obliged to give up my holiday in Italy, and return to England too.'

Agnes looked at him in some little perplexity: she was not quite sure whether she understood him or not.

'Are you really obliged to go back?' she asked.

Henry smiled as he answered her. 'Keep the secret,' he said, 'or Montbarry will never forgive me!'

She read the rest in his face. 'Oh!' she exclaimed, blushing brightly, 'you have not given up your pleasant holiday in Italy on my account?'

'I shall go back with you to England, Agnes. That will be holiday enough for me.'

She took his hand in an irrepressible outburst of gratitude. 'How good you are to me!' she murmured tenderly. 'What should I have done in the troubles that have come to me, without your sympathy? I can't tell you, Henry, how I feel your kindness.'

She tried impulsively to lift his hand to her lips. He gently stopped her. 'Agnes,' he said, 'are you beginning to understand how truly I love you?'

That simple question found its own way to her heart. She owned the whole truth, without saying a word. She looked at him—and then looked away again.

He drew her nearer to him. 'My own darling!' he whispered—and kissed her. Softly and tremulously, the sweet lips lingered, and touched his lips in return. Then her head drooped. She put her arms round his neck, and hid her face on his bosom. They spoke no more.

The charmed silence had lasted but a little while, when it was mercilessly broken by a knock at the door.

Agnes started to her feet. She placed herself at the piano; the instrument being opposite to the door, it was impossible, when she seated herself on the music-stool, for any person entering the room to see her face. Henry called out irritably, 'Come in.'

The door was not opened. The person on the other side of it asked a strange question.

'Is Mr. Henry Westwick alone?'

Agnes instantly recognised the voice of the Countess. She hurried to a second door, which communicated with one of the bedrooms. 'Don't let her come near me!' she whispered nervously. 'Good night, Henry! good night!'

If Henry could, by an effort of will, have transported the Countess to the uttermost ends of the earth, he would have made the effort without remorse. As it was, he only repeated, more irritably than ever, 'Come in!'

She entered the room slowly with her everlasting manuscript in her hand. Her step was unsteady; a dark flush appeared on her face, in place of its customary pallor; her eyes were bloodshot and widely dilated. In approaching Henry, she showed a strange incapability of calculating her distances—she struck against the table near which he happened to be sitting. When she spoke, her articulation was confused, and her pronunciation of some of the longer words was hardly intelligible. Most men would have suspected her of being under the influence of some intoxicating liquor. Henry took a truer view—he said, as he placed a chair for her, 'Countess, I am afraid you have been working too hard: you look as if you wanted rest.'

She put her hand to her head. 'My invention has gone,' she said. 'I can't write my fourth act. It's all a blank—all a blank!'

Henry advised her to wait till the next day. 'Go to bed,' he suggested; 'and try to sleep.'

She waved her hand impatiently. 'I must finish the play,' she answered. 'I only want a hint from you. You must know something about plays. Your brother has got a theatre. You must often have heard him talk about fourth and fifth acts—you must have seen rehearsals, and all the rest of it.' She abruptly thrust the manuscript into Henry's hand. 'I can't read it to you,' she said; 'I feel giddy when I look at my own writing. Just run your eye over it, there's a good fellow—and give me a hint.'

Henry glanced at the manuscript. He happened to look at the list of the persons of the drama. As he read the list he started and turned abruptly to the Countess, intending to ask her for some explanation. The words were suspended on his lips. It was but too plainly useless to speak to her. Her head lay back on the rail of the chair. She seemed to be half asleep already. The flush on her face had deepened: she looked like a woman who was in danger of having a fit.

He rang the bell, and directed the man who answered it to send one of the chambermaids upstairs. His voice seemed to partially rouse the Countess; she opened her eyes in a slow drowsy way. 'Have you read it?' she asked.

It was necessary as a mere act of humanity to humour her. 'I will read it willingly,' said Henry, 'if you will go upstairs to bed. You shall hear what I think of it to-morrow morning. Our heads will be clearer, we shall be better able to make the fourth act in the morning.'

The chambermaid came in while he was speaking. 'I am afraid the lady is ill,' Henry whispered. 'Take her up to her room.' The woman looked at the Countess and whispered back, 'Shall we send for a doctor, sir?'

Henry advised taking her upstairs first, and then asking the manager's opinion. There was great difficulty in persuading her to rise, and accept the support of the chambermaid's arm. It was only by reiterated promises to read the play that night, and to make the fourth act in the morning, that Henry prevailed on the Countess to return to her room.

Left to himself, he began to feel a certain languid curiosity in relation to the manuscript. He looked over the pages, reading a line here and a line there. Suddenly he changed colour as he read—and looked up from the manuscript like a man bewildered. 'Good God! what does this mean?' he said to himself.

His eyes turned nervously to the door by which Agnes had left him. She might return to the drawing-room, she might want to see what the Countess had written. He looked back again at the passage which had startled him—considered with himself for a moment—and, snatching up the unfinished play, suddenly and softly left the room.

XXVI

Entering his own room on the upper floor, Henry placed the manuscript on his table, open at the first leaf. His nerves were unquestionably shaken; his hand trembled as he turned the pages, he started at chance noises on the staircase of the hotel.

The scenario, or outline, of the Countess's play began with no formal prefatory phrases. She presented herself and her work with the easy familiarity of an old friend.

'Allow me, dear Mr. Francis Westwick, to introduce to you the persons in my proposed Play. Behold them, arranged symmetrically in a line.

'My Lord. The Baron. The Courier. The Doctor. The

Countess.

'I don't trouble myself, you see, to invest fictitious family names. My characters are sufficiently distinguished by their social titles, and by the striking contrast which they present one with another.

The First Act opens— 'No! Before I open the First Act, I must announce, injustice to myself, that this Play is entirely the work of my own invention. I scorn to borrow from actual events; and, what is more extraordinary still, I have not stolen one of my ideas from the Modern French drama. As the manager of an English theatre, you will naturally refuse to believe this. It doesn't matter. Nothing matters—except the opening of my first act.

'We are at Homburg, in the famous Salon d'Or, at the height of the season. The Countess (exquisitely dressed) is seated at the green table. Strangers of all nations are standing behind the players, venturing their money or only looking on. My Lord is among the strangers. He is struck by the Countess's personal appearance, in which beauties and defects are fantastically mingled in the most attractive manner. He watches the Countess's game, and places his money where he sees her deposit her own little stake. She looks round at him, and says, "Don't trust to my colour; I have been unlucky the whole evening. Place your stake on the other colour, and you may have a chance of winning." My Lord (a true Englishman) blushes, bows, and obeys. The Countess proves to be a prophet. She loses again. My Lord wins twice the sum that he has risked.

'The Countess rises from the table. She has no more money, and she offers my Lord her chair.

'Instead of taking it, he politely places his winnings in her hand, and begs her to accept the loan as a favour to himself. The Countess stakes again, and loses again. My Lord smiles superbly, and presses a second loan on her. From that moment her luck turns. She wins, and wins largely. Her brother, the Baron, trying his fortune in another room, hears of what is going on, and joins my Lord and the Countess.

'Pay attention, if you please, to the Baron. He is delineated as a remarkable and interesting character.

'This noble person has begun life with a single-minded devotion to the science of experimental chemistry, very surprising in a young and handsome man with a brilliant future before him. A profound knowledge of the occult sciences has persuaded the Baron that it is possible to solve the famous problem called the "Philosopher's Stone." His own pecuniary resources have long since been exhausted by his costly experiments. His sister has next supplied him with the small fortune at her disposal: reserving only the family jewels, placed in the charge of her banker and friend at Frankfort. The Countess's fortune also being swallowed up, the Baron has in a fatal moment sought for new supplies at the gaming table. He proves, at starting on his perilous career, to be a favourite of fortune; wins largely, and, alas! profanes his noble enthusiasm for science by yielding his soul to the all-debasing passion of the gamester.

'At the period of the Play, the Baron's good fortune has deserted him. He sees his way to a crowning experiment in the fatal search after the secret of transmuting the baser elements into gold. But how is he to pay the preliminary expenses? Destiny, like a mocking echo, answers, How?

'Will his sister's winnings (with my Lord's money) prove large enough to help him? Eager for this result, he gives the Countess his advice how to play. From that disastrous moment the infection of his own adverse fortune spreads to his sister. She loses again, and again—loses to the last farthing.

'The amiable and wealthy Lord offers a third loan; but the scrupulous Countess positively refuses to take it. On leaving the table, she presents her brother to my Lord. The gentlemen fall into pleasant talk. My Lord asks leave to pay his respects to the Countess, the next morning, at her hotel. The Baron hospitably invites him to breakfast. My Lord accepts, with a last admiring glance at the Countess which does not escape her brother's observation, and takes his leave for the night.

'Alone with his sister, the Baron speaks out plainly. "Our affairs," he says, "are in a desperate condition, and must find a desperate remedy. Wait for me here, while I make inquiries about my Lord. You have evidently produced a strong impression on him. If we can turn that impression into money, no matter at what sacrifice, the thing must be done."

'The Countess now occupies the stage alone, and indulges in a soliloquy which develops her character.

'It is at once a dangerous and attractive character. Immense capacities for good are implanted in her nature, side by side with equally remarkable capacities for evil. It rests with circumstances to develop either the one or the other. Being a person who produces a sensation wherever she goes, this noble lady is naturally made the subject of all sorts of scandalous reports. To one of these reports (which falsely and abominably points to the Baron as her lover instead of her brother) she now refers with just indignation. She has just expressed her desire to leave Homburg, as the place in which the vile calumny first took its rise, when the Baron returns, overhears her last words, and says to her, "Yes, leave Homburg by all means; provided you leave it in the character of my Lord's betrothed wife!"

'The Countess is startled and shocked. She protests that she does not reciprocate my Lord's admiration for her. She even goes the length of refusing to see him again. The Baron answers, "I must positively have command of money. Take your choice, between marrying my Lord's income, in the interest of my grand discovery—or leave me to sell myself and my title to the first rich woman of low degree who is ready to buy me."

'The Countess listens in surprise and dismay. Is it possible that the Baron is in earnest? He is horribly in earnest. "The woman who will buy me," he says, "is in the next room to us at this moment. She is the wealthy widow of a Jewish usurer. She has the money I want to reach the solution of the great problem. I have only to be that woman's husband, and to make myself master of untold millions of gold. Take five minutes to consider what I have said to you, and tell me on my return which of us is to marry for the money I want, you or I."

'As he turns away, the Countess stops him.

'All the noblest sentiments in her nature are exalted to the highest pitch. "Where is the true woman," she exclaims, "who wants time to consummate the sacrifice of herself, when the man to whom she is devoted demands it? She does not want five minutes—she does not want five seconds—she holds out her hand to him, and she says, Sacrifice me on the altar of your glory! Take as stepping-stones on the way to your triumph, my love, my liberty, and my life!"

'On this grand situation the curtain falls. Judging by my first act, Mr. Westwick, tell me truly, and don't be afraid of turning my head:— Am I not capable of writing a good play?'

Henry paused between the First and Second Acts; reflecting, not on the merits of the play, but on the strange resemblance which the incidents so far presented to the incidents that had attended the disastrous marriage of the first Lord Montbarry.

Was it possible that the Countess, in the present condition of her mind, supposed herself to be exercising her invention when she was only exercising her memory?

The question involved considerations too serious to be made the subject of a hasty decision. Reserving his opinion, Henry turned the page, and devoted himself to the reading of the next act. The manuscript proceeded as follows:

'The Second Act opens at Venice. An interval of four months has elapsed since the date of the scene at the gambling table. The action now takes place in the reception-room of one of the Venetian palaces.

'The Baron is discovered, alone, on the stage. He reverts to the events which have happened since the close of the First Act. The Countess has sacrificed herself; the mercenary marriage has taken place—but not without obstacles, caused by difference of opinion on the question of marriage settlements.

'Private inquiries, instituted in England, have informed the Baron that my Lord's income is derived chiefly from what is called entailed property. In case of accidents, he is surely bound to do something for his bride? Let him, for example, insure his life, for a sum proposed by the Baron, and let him so settle the money that his widow shall have it, if he dies first.

'My Lord hesitates. The Baron wastes no time in useless discussion. "Let us by all means" (he says) "consider the marriage as broken off." My Lord shifts his ground, and pleads for a smaller sum than the sum proposed. The Baron briefly replies, "I never bargain." My lord is in love; the natural result follows—he gives way.

'So far, the Baron has no cause to complain. But my Lord's turn comes, when the marriage has been celebrated, and when the honeymoon is over. The Baron has joined the married pair at a palace which they have hired in Venice. He is still bent on solving the problem of the "Philosopher's Stone." His laboratory is set up in the vaults beneath the palace—so that smells from chemical experiments may not incommode the Countess, in the higher regions of the house. The one obstacle in the way of his grand discovery is, as usual, the want of money. His position at the present time has become truly critical. He owes debts of honour to gentlemen in his own rank of life, which must positively be paid; and he proposes, in his own friendly manner, to borrow the money of my Lord. My Lord positively refuses, in the rudest terms. The Baron applies to his sister to exercise her conjugal influence. She can only answer that her noble husband (being no longer distractedly in love with her) now appears in his true character, as one of the meanest men living. The sacrifice of the marriage has been made, and has already proved useless.

'Such is the state of affairs at the opening of the Second Act.

'The entrance of the Countess suddenly disturbs the Baron's reflections. She is in a state bordering on frenzy. Incoherent expressions of rage burst from her lips: it is some time before she can sufficiently control herself to speak plainly. She has been doubly insulted—first, by a menial person in her employment; secondly, by her husband. Her maid, an Englishwoman, has declared that she will serve the Countess no longer. She will give up her wages, and return at once to England. Being asked her reason for this strange proceeding, she insolently hints that the Countess's service is no service for an honest woman, since the Baron has entered the house. The Countess does, what any lady in her position would do; she indignantly dismisses the wretch on the spot.

'My Lord, hearing his wife's voice raised in anger, leaves the study in which he is accustomed to shut himself up over his books, and asks what this disturbance means. The Countess informs him of the outrageous language and conduct of her maid. My Lord not only declares his entire approval of the woman's conduct, but expresses his own abominable doubts of his wife's fidelity in language of such horrible brutality that no lady could pollute her lips by repeating it. "If I had been a man," the Countess says, "and if I had had a weapon in my hand, I would have struck him dead at my feet!"

'The Baron, listening silently so far, now speaks. "Permit me to finish the sentence for you," he says. "You would have struck your husband dead at your feet; and by that rash act, you would have deprived yourself of the insurance money settled on the widow—the very money which is wanted to relieve your brother from the unendurable pecuniary position which he now occupies!"

'The Countess gravely reminds the Baron that this is no joking matter. After what my Lord has said to her, she has little doubt that he will communicate his infamous suspicions to his lawyers in England. If nothing is done to prevent it, she may be divorced and disgraced, and thrown on the world, with no resource but the sale of her jewels to keep her from starving.

'At this moment, the Courier who has been engaged to travel with my Lord from England crosses the stage with a letter to take to the post. The Countess stops him, and asks to look at the address on the letter. She takes it from him for a moment, and shows it to her brother. The handwriting is my Lord's; and the letter is directed to his lawyers in London.

'The Courier proceeds to the post-office. The Baron and the Countess look at each other in silence. No words are needed. They thoroughly understand the position in which they are placed; they clearly see the terrible remedy for it. What is the plain alternative before them? Disgrace and ruin—or, my Lord's death and the insurance money!

'The Baron walks backwards and forwards in great agitation, talking to himself. The Countess hears fragments of what he is saying. He speaks of my Lord's constitution, probably weakened in India—of a cold which my Lord has caught two or three days since—of the remarkable manner in which such slight things as colds sometimes end in serious illness and death.

'He observes that the Countess is listening to him, and asks if she has anything to propose. She is a woman who, with many defects, has the great merit of speaking out. "Is there no such thing as a serious illness," she asks, "corked up in one of those bottles of yours in the vaults downstairs?"

'The Baron answers by gravely shaking his head. What is he afraid of?—a possible examination of the body after death? No: he can set any post-mortem examination at defiance. It is the process of administering the poison that he dreads. A man so distinguished as my Lord cannot be taken seriously ill without medical attendance. Where there is a Doctor, there is always danger of discovery. Then, again, there is the Courier, faithful to my Lord as long as my Lord pays him. Even if the Doctor sees nothing suspicious, the Courier may discover something. The poison, to do its work with the necessary secrecy, must be repeatedly administered in graduated doses. One trifling miscalculation or mistake may rouse suspicion. The insurance offices may hear of it, and may refuse to pay the money. As things are, the Baron will not risk it, and will not allow his sister to risk it in his place.

'My Lord himself is the next character who appears. He has repeatedly rung for the Courier, and the bell has not been answered. "What does this insolence mean?"

'The Countess (speaking with quiet dignity—for why should her infamous husband have the satisfaction of knowing how deeply he has wounded her?) reminds my Lord that the Courier has gone to the post. My Lord asks suspiciously if she has looked at the letter. The Countess informs him coldly that she has no curiosity about his letters. Referring to the cold from which he is suffering, she inquires if he thinks of consulting a medical man. My Lord answers roughly that he is quite old enough to be capable of doctoring himself.

'As he makes this reply, the Courier appears, returning from the post. My Lord gives him orders to go out again and buy some lemons. He proposes to try hot lemonade as a means of inducing perspiration in bed. In that way he has formerly cured colds, and in that way he will cure the cold from which he is suffering now.

'The Courier obeys in silence. Judging by appearances, he goes very reluctantly on this second errand.

'My Lord turns to the Baron (who has thus far taken no part in the conversation) and asks him, in a sneering tone, how much longer he proposes to prolong his stay in Venice. The Baron answers quietly, "Let us speak plainly to one another, my Lord. If you wish me to leave your house, you have only to say the word, and I go." My Lord turns to his wife, and asks if she can support the calamity of her brother's absence—laying a grossly insulting emphasis on the word "brother." The Countess preserves her impenetrable composure; nothing in her betrays the deadly hatred with which she regards the titled ruffian who has insulted her. "You are master in this house, my Lord," is all she says. "Do as you please."

'My Lord looks at his wife; looks at the Baron—and suddenly

alters his tone. Does he perceive in the composure of the Countess and her brother something lurking under the surface that threatens him? This is at least certain, he makes a clumsy apology for the language that he has used. (Abject wretch!)

'My Lord's excuses are interrupted by the return of the Courier with the lemons and hot water.

'The Countess observes for the first time that the man looks ill. His hands tremble as he places the tray on the table. My Lord orders his Courier to follow him, and make the lemonade in the bedroom. The Countess remarks that the Courier seems hardly capable of obeying his orders. Hearing this, the man admits that he is ill. He, too, is suffering from a cold; he has been kept waiting in a draught at the shop where he bought the lemons; he feels alternately hot and cold, and he begs permission to lie down for a little while on his bed.

'Feeling her humanity appealed to, the Countess volunteers to make the lemonade herself. My Lord takes the Courier by the arm, leads him aside, and whispers these words to him: "Watch her, and see that she puts nothing into the lemonade; then bring it to me with your own hands; and, then, go to bed, if you like."

'Without a word more to his wife, or to the Baron, my Lord leaves the room.

'The Countess makes the lemonade, and the Courier takes it to his master.

'Returning, on the way to his own room, he is so weak, and feels, he says, so giddy, that he is obliged to support himself by the backs of the chairs as he passes them. The Baron, always considerate to persons of low degree, offers his arm. "I am afraid, my poor fellow," he says, "that you are really ill." The Courier makes this extraordinary answer: "It's all over with me, Sir: I have caught my death."

'The Countess is naturally startled. "You are not an old man," she says, trying to rouse the Courier's spirits. "At your age, catching cold doesn't surely mean catching your death?" The Courier fixes his eyes despairingly on the Countess.

"My lungs are weak, my Lady," he says; "I have already had two attacks of bronchitis. The second time, a great physician joined my own doctor in attendance on me. He considered my recovery almost in the light of a miracle. Take care of yourself," he said. "If you have a third attack of bronchitis, as certainly as two and two make four, you will be a dead man. I feel the same inward shivering, my Lady, that I felt on those two former occasions—and I tell you again, I have caught my death in Venice."

'Speaking some comforting words, the Baron leads him to his room. The Countess is left alone on the stage.

'She seats herself, and looks towards the door by which the Courier has been led out. "Ah! my poor fellow," she says, "if you could only change constitutions with my Lord, what a happy result would follow for the Baron and for me! If you could only get cured of a trumpery cold with a little hot lemonade, and if he could only catch his death in your place—!"

'She suddenly pauses—considers for a while—and springs to her feet, with a cry of triumphant surprise: the wonderful, the unparalleled idea has crossed her mind like a flash of lightning. Make the two men change names and places—and the deed is done! Where are the obstacles? Remove my Lord (by fair means or foul) from his room; and keep him secretly prisoner in the palace, to live or die as future necessity may determine. Place the Courier in the vacant bed, and call in the doctor to see him—ill, in my Lord's character, and (if he dies) dying under my Lord's name!'

The manuscript dropped from Henry's hands. A sickening sense of horror overpowered him. The question which had occurred to his mind at the close of the First Act of the Play assumed a new and terrible interest now. As far as the scene of the Countess's soliloquy, the incidents of the Second Act had reflected the events of his late brother's life as faithfully as the incidents of the First Act. Was the monstrous plot, revealed in the lines which he had just read, the offspring of the Countess's morbid imagination? or had she, in this case also, deluded herself with the idea that she was inventing when she was really writing under the influence of her own guilty remembrances of the past? If the latter interpretation were the true one, he had just read the narrative of the contemplated murder of his brother, planned in cold blood by a woman who was at that moment inhabiting the same house with him. While, to make the fatality complete, Agnes herself had innocently provided the conspirators with the one man who was fitted to be the passive agent of their crime.

Even the bare doubt that it might be so was more than he could endure. He left his room; resolved to force the truth out of the Countess, or to denounce her before the authorities as a murderess at large.

Arrived at her door, he was met by a person just leaving the room. The person was the manager. He was hardly recognisable; he looked and spoke like a man in a state of desperation.

'Oh, go in, if you like!' he said to Henry. 'Mark this, sir! I am not a superstitious man; but I do begin to believe that crimes carry their own curse with them. This hotel is under a curse. What happens in the morning? We discover a crime committed in the old days of the palace. The night comes, and brings another dreadful event with it—a death; a sudden and shocking death, in the house. Go in, and see for yourself! I shall resign my situation, Mr. Westwick: I can't contend with the fatalities that pursue me here!'

Henry entered the room.

The Countess was stretched on her bed. The doctor on one side, and the chambermaid on the other, were standing looking at her. From time to time, she drew a heavy stertorous breath, like a person oppressed in sleeping. 'Is she likely to die?' Henry asked.

'She is dead,' the doctor answered. 'Dead of the rupture of a blood-vessel on the brain. Those sounds that you hear are purely mechanical—they may go on for hours.'

Henry looked at the chambermaid. She had little to tell. The Countess had refused to go to bed, and had placed herself at her desk to proceed with her writing. Finding it useless to remonstrate with her, the maid had left the room to speak to the manager. In the shortest possible time, the doctor was summoned to the hotel, and found the Countess dead on the floor. There was this to tell—and no more.

Looking at the writing-table as he went out, Henry saw the sheet of paper on which the Countess had traced her last lines of writing. The characters were almost illegible. Henry could just distinguish the words, 'First Act,' and 'Persons of the Drama.' The lost wretch had been thinking of her Play to the last, and had begun it all over again!

XXVII

Henry returned to his room.

His first impulse was to throw aside the manuscript, and never to look at it again. The one chance of relieving his mind from the dreadful uncertainty that oppressed it, by obtaining positive evidence of the truth, was a chance annihilated by the Countess's death. What good purpose could be served, what relief could he anticipate, if he read more?

He walked up and down the room. After an interval, his thoughts took a new direction; the question of the manuscript presented itself under another point of view. Thus far, his reading had only informed him that the conspiracy had been planned. How did he know that the plan had been put in execution?

The manuscript lay just before him on the floor. He hesitated; then picked it up; and, returning to the table, read on as follows, from the point at which he had left off.

'While the Countess is still absorbed in the bold yet simple combination of circumstances which she has discovered, the Baron returns. He takes a serious view of the case of the Courier; it may be necessary, he thinks, to send for medical advice. No servant is left in the palace, now the English maid has taken her departure. The Baron himself must fetch the doctor, if the doctor is really needed.

'"Let us have medical help, by all means," his sister replies. "But wait and hear something that I have to say to you first." She then electrifies the Baron by communicating her idea to him. What danger of discovery have they to dread? My Lord's life in Venice has been a life of absolute seclusion: nobody but his banker knows him, even by personal appearance. He has presented his letter of credit as a perfect stranger; and he and his banker have never seen each other since that first visit. He has given no parties, and gone to no parties. On the few occasions when he has hired a gondola or taken a walk, he has always been alone. Thanks to the atrocious suspicion which makes him ashamed of being seen with his wife, he has led the very life which makes the proposed enterprise easy of accomplishment.

'The cautious Baron listens—but gives no positive opinion, as yet. "See what you can do with the Courier," he says; "and I will decide when I hear the result. One valuable hint I may give you before you go. Your man is easily tempted by money—if you only offer him enough. The other day, I asked him, in jest, what he would do for a thousand pounds. He answered, 'Anything.' Bear that in mind; and offer your highest bid without bargaining."

'The scene changes to the Courier's room, and shows the poor wretch with a photographic portrait of his wife in his hand, crying. The Countess enters.

'She wisely begins by sympathising with her contemplated accomplice. He is duly grateful; he confides his sorrows to his gracious mistress. Now that he believes himself to be on his death-bed, he feels remorse for his neglectful treatment of his wife. He could resign himself to die; but despair overpowers him when he remembers that he has saved no money, and that he will leave his widow, without resources, to the mercy of the world.

'On this hint, the Countess speaks. "Suppose you were asked to do a perfectly easy thing," she says; "and suppose you were rewarded for doing it by a present of a thousand pounds, as a legacy for your widow?"

'The Courier raises himself on his pillow, and looks at the Countess with an expression of incredulous surprise. She can hardly be cruel enough (he thinks) to joke with a man in his miserable plight. Will she say plainly what this perfectly easy thing is, the doing of which will meet with such a magnificent reward?

'The Countess answers that question by confiding her project to the Courier, without the slightest reserve.

'Some minutes of silence follow when she has done. The Courier is not weak enough yet to speak without stopping to think first. Still keeping his eyes on the Countess, he makes a quaintly insolent remark on what he has just heard. "I have not hitherto been a religious man; but I feel myself on the way to it. Since your ladyship has spoken to me, I believe in the Devil." It is the Countess's interest to see the humorous side of this confession of faith. She takes no offence. She only says, "I will give you half an hour by yourself, to think over my proposal.

You are in danger of death. Decide, in your wife's interests, whether you will die worth nothing, or die worth a thousand pounds."

'Left alone, the Courier seriously considers his position—and decides. He rises with difficulty; writes a few lines on a leaf taken from his pocket-book; and, with slow and faltering steps, leaves the room.

'The Countess, returning at the expiration of the half-hour's interval, finds the room empty. While she is wondering, the Courier opens the door. What has he been doing out of his bed? He answers, "I have been protecting my own life, my lady, on the bare chance that I may recover from the bronchitis for the third time. If you or the Baron attempts to hurry me out of this world, or to deprive me of my thousand pounds reward, I shall tell the doctor where he will find a few lines of writing, which describe your ladyship's plot. I may not have strength enough, in the case supposed, to betray you by making a complete confession with my own lips; but I can employ my last breath to speak the half-dozen words which will tell the doctor where he is to look. Those words, it is needless to add, will be addressed to your Ladyship, if I find your engagements towards me faithfully kept."

'With this audacious preface, he proceeds to state the conditions on which he will play his part in the conspiracy, and die (if he does die) worth a thousand pounds.

'Either the Countess or the Baron are to taste the food and drink brought to his bedside, in his presence, and even the medicines which the doctor may prescribe for him. As for the promised sum of money, it is to be produced in one bank-note, folded in a sheet of paper, on which a line is to be written, dictated by the Courier. The two enclosures are then to be sealed up in an envelope, addressed to his wife, and stamped ready for the post. This done, the letter is to be placed under his pillow; the Baron or the Countess being at liberty to satisfy themselves, day by day, at their own time, that the letter remains in its place, with the seal unbroken, as long as the doctor has any hope of his patient's recovery. The last stipulation follows. The Courier has a conscience; and with a view to keeping it easy, insists that he shall be left in ignorance of that part of the plot which relates to the sequestration of my Lord. Not that he cares particularly what becomes of his miserly master—but he does dislike taking other people's responsibilities on his own shoulders.

'These conditions being agreed to, the Countess calls in the Baron, who has been waiting events in the next room.

'He is informed that the Courier has yielded to temptation; but he is still too cautious to make any compromising remarks. Keeping his back turned on the bed, he shows a bottle to the Countess. It is labelled "Chloroform." She understands that my Lord is to be removed from his room in a convenient state of insensibility. In what part of the palace is he to be hidden? As they open the door to go out, the Countess whispers that question to the Baron. The Baron whispers back, "In the vaults!" The curtain falls.'

XXVIII

So the Second Act ended.

Turning to the Third Act, Henry looked wearily at the pages as he let them slip through his fingers. Both in mind and body, he began to feel the need of repose.

In one important respect, the later portion of the manuscript differed from the pages which he had just been reading. Signs of an overwrought brain showed themselves, here and there, as the outline of the play approached its end. The handwriting grew worse and worse. Some of the longer sentences were left unfinished. In the exchange of dialogue, questions and answers were not always attributed respectively to the right speaker. At certain intervals the writer's failing intelligence seemed to recover itself for a while; only to relapse again, and to lose the thread of the narrative more hopelessly than ever.

After reading one or two of the more coherent passages Henry recoiled from the ever-darkening horror of the story. He closed the manuscript, heartsick and exhausted, and threw himself on his bed to rest. The door opened almost at the same moment. Lord Montbarry entered the room.

'We have just returned from the Opera,' he said; 'and we have heard the news of that miserable woman's death. They say you spoke to her in her last moments; and I want to hear how it happened.'

'You shall hear how it happened,' Henry answered; 'and more than that. You are now the head of the family, Stephen; and I feel bound, in the position which oppresses me, to leave you to decide what ought to be done.'

With those introductory words, he told his brother how the Countess's play had come into his hands. 'Read the first few pages,' he said. 'I am anxious to know whether the same impression is produced on both of us.'

Before Lord Montbarry had got half-way through the First Act, he stopped, and looked at his brother. 'What does she mean by boasting of this as her own invention?' he asked. 'Was she too crazy to remember that these things really happened?'

This was enough for Henry: the same impression had been produced on both of them. 'You will do as you please,' he said. 'But if you will be guided by me, spare yourself the reading of those pages to come, which describe our brother's terrible expiation of his heartless marriage.'

'Have you read it all, Henry?'

'Not all. I shrank from reading some of the latter part of it. Neither you nor I saw much of our elder brother after we left school; and, for my part, I felt, and never scrupled to express my feeling, that he behaved infamously to Agnes. But when I read that unconscious confession of the murderous conspiracy to which he fell a victim, I remembered, with something like remorse, that the same mother bore us. I have felt for him to-night, what I am ashamed to think I never felt for him before.'

Lord Montbarry took his brother's hand.

'You are a good fellow, Henry,' he said; 'but are you quite sure that you have not been needlessly distressing yourself? Because some of this crazy creature's writing accidentally tells what we know to be the truth, does it follow that all the rest is to be relied on to the end?'

'There is no possible doubt of it,' Henry replied.

'No possible doubt?' his brother repeated. 'I shall go on with my reading, Henry—and see what justification there may be for that confident conclusion of yours.'

He read on steadily, until he had reached the end of the Second Act. Then he looked up.

'Do you really believe that the mutilated remains which you discovered this morning are the remains of our brother?' he asked. 'And do you believe it on such evidence as this?'

Henry answered silently by a sign in the affirmative.

Lord Montbarry checked himself—evidently on the point of entering an indignant protest.

'You acknowledge that you have not read the later scenes of the piece,' he said. 'Don't be childish, Henry! If you persist in pinning your faith on such stuff as this, the least you can do is to make yourself thoroughly acquainted with it. Will you read the Third Act? No? Then I shall read it to you.'

He turned to the Third Act, and ran over those fragmentary passages which were clearly enough written and expressed to be intelligible to the mind of a stranger.

'Here is a scene in the vaults of the palace,' he began. 'The victim of the conspiracy is sleeping on his miserable bed; and the Baron and the Countess are considering the position in which they stand. The Countess (as well as I can make it out) has raised the money that is wanted by borrowing on the security of her jewels at Frankfort; and the Courier upstairs is still declared by the Doctor to have a chance of recovery. What are the conspirators to do, if the man does recover? The cautious Baron suggests setting the prisoner free. If he ventures to appeal to the law, it is easy to declare that he is subject to insane delusion, and to call his own wife as witness. On the other hand, if the Courier dies, how is the sequestrated and unknown nobleman to be put out of the way? Passively, by letting him starve in his prison? No: the Baron is a man of refined tastes; he dislikes needless cruelty. The active policy remains—say, assassination by the knife of a hired bravo? The Baron objects to trusting an accomplice; also to spending money on anyone but himself. Shall they drop their prisoner into the canal? The Baron declines to trust water; water will show him on the surface. Shall they set his bed on fire? An excellent idea; but the smoke might be seen. No: the circumstances being now entirely altered, poisoning him presents the easiest way out of it. He has simply become a superfluous person. The cheapest poison will do.—Is it possible, Henry, that you believe this consultation really took place?'

Henry made no reply. The succession of the questions that had just been read to him, exactly followed the succession of the dreams that had terrified Mrs. Norbury, on the two nights which she had passed in the hotel. It was useless to point out this coincidence to his brother. He only said, 'Go on.'

Lord Montbarry turned the pages until he came to the next intelligible passage.

'Here,' he proceeded, 'is a double scene on the stage—so far as I can understand the sketch of it. The Doctor is upstairs, innocently writing his certificate of my Lord's decease, by the dead Courier's bedside. Down in the vaults, the Baron stands by the corpse of the poisoned lord, preparing the strong chemical acids which are to reduce it to a heap of ashes—Surely, it is not worth while to trouble ourselves with deciphering such melodramatic horrors as these? Let us get on! let us get on!'

He turned the leaves again; attempting vainly to discover the meaning of the confused scenes that followed. On the last page but one, he found the last intelligible sentences.

'The Third Act seems to be divided,' he said, 'into two Parts or Tableaux. I think I can read the writing at the beginning of the Second Part. The Baron and the Countess open the scene. The Baron's hands are mysteriously concealed by gloves. He has reduced the body to ashes by his own system of cremation, with the exception of the head—'

Henry interrupted his brother there. 'Don't read any more!' he exclaimed.

'Let us do the Countess justice,' Lord Montbarry persisted. 'There are not half a dozen lines more that I can make out! The accidental breaking of his jar of acid has burnt the Baron's hands severely. He is still unable to proceed to the destruction of the head—and the Countess is woman enough (with all her wickedness) to shrink from attempting to take his place—when the first news is received of the coming arrival of the commission of inquiry despatched by the insurance offices. The Baron feels no alarm. Inquire as the commission may, it is the natural death of the Courier (in my Lord's character) that they are blindly investigating. The head not being destroyed, the obvious alternative is to hide it—and the Baron is equal to the occasion. His studies in the old library have informed him of a safe place of concealment in the palace. The Countess may recoil from handling the acids and watching the process of cremation; but she can surely sprinkle a little disinfecting powder—'

'No more!' Henry reiterated. 'No more!'

'There is no more that can be read, my dear fellow. The last page looks like sheer delirium. She may well have told you that her invention had failed her!'

'Face the truth honestly, Stephen, and say her memory.'

Lord Montbarry rose from the table at which he had been sitting, and looked at his brother with pitying eyes.

'Your nerves are out of order, Henry,' he said. 'And no wonder, after that frightful discovery under the hearth-stone. We won't dispute about it; we will wait a day or two until you are quite yourself again. In the meantime, let us understand each other on one point at least. You leave the question of what is to be done with these pages of writing to me, as the head of the family?'

'I do.'

Lord Montbarry quietly took up the manuscript, and threw it into the fire. 'Let this rubbish be of some use,' he said, holding the pages down with the poker. 'The room is getting chilly—the Countess's play will set some of these charred logs flaming again.' He waited a little at the fire-place, and returned to his brother. 'Now, Henry, I have a last word to say, and then I have done. I am ready to admit that you have stumbled, by an unlucky chance, on the proof of a crime committed in the old days of the palace, nobody knows how long ago. With that one concession, I dispute everything else. Rather than agree in the opinion you have formed, I won't believe anything that has happened. The supernatural influences that some of us felt when we first slept in this hotel—your loss of appetite, our sister's dreadful dreams, the smell that overpowered Francis, and the head that appeared to Agnes—I declare them all to be sheer delusions! I believe in nothing, nothing, nothing!' He opened the door to go out, and looked back into the room. 'Yes,' he resumed, 'there is one thing I believe in. My wife has committed a breach of confidence—I believe Agnes will marry you. Good night, Henry. We leave Venice the first thing to-morrow morning.

So Lord Montbarry disposed of the mystery of The Haunted Hotel.

POSTSCRIPT

A last chance of deciding the difference of opinion between the two brothers remained in Henry's possession. He had his own idea of the use to which he might put the false teeth as a means of inquiry when he and his fellow-travellers returned to England.

The only surviving depositary of the domestic history of the family in past years, was Agnes Lockwood's old nurse. Henry took his first opportunity of trying to revive her personal recollections of the deceased Lord Montbarry. But the nurse had never forgiven the great man of the family for his desertion of Agnes; she flatly refused to consult her memory. 'Even the bare sight of my lord, when I last saw him in London,' said the old woman, 'made my finger-nails itch to set their mark on his face. I was sent on an errand by Miss Agnes; and I met him coming out of his dentist's door—and, thank God, that's the last I ever saw of him!'

Thanks to the nurse's quick temper and quaint way of expressing herself, the object of Henry's inquiries was gained already! He ventured on asking if she had noticed the situation of the house. She had noticed, and still remembered the situation—did Master Henry suppose she had lost the use of her senses, because she happened to be nigh on eighty years old? The same day, he took the false teeth to the dentist, and set all further doubt (if doubt had still been possible) at rest for ever. The teeth had been made for the first Lord Montbarry.

Henry never revealed the existence of this last link in the chain of discovery to any living creature, his brother Stephen included. He carried his terrible secret with him to the grave.

There was one other event in the memorable past on which he preserved the same compassionate silence. Little Mrs. Ferrari never knew that her husband had been—not, as she supposed, the Countess's victim—but the Countess's accomplice. She still believed that the late Lord Montbarry had sent her the thousand-pound note, and still recoiled from making use of a present which she persisted in declaring had 'the stain of her husband's blood on it.' Agnes, with the widow's entire approval, took the money to the Children's Hospital; and spent it in adding to the number of the beds.

In the spring of the new year, the marriage took place. At the special request of Agnes, the members of the family were the only persons present at the ceremony. There was no wedding breakfast—and the honeymoon was spent in the retirement of a cottage on the banks of the Thames.

During the last few days of the residence of the newly married couple by the riverside, Lady Montbarry's children were invited to enjoy a day's play in the garden. The eldest girl overheard (and reported to her mother) a little conjugal dialogue which touched on the topic of The Haunted Hotel.

'Henry, I want you to give me a kiss.'

'There it is, my dear.'

'Now I am your wife, may I speak to you about something?'

'What is it?'

'Something that happened the day before we left Venice. You saw the Countess, during the last hours of her life. Won't you tell me whether she made any confession to you?'

'No conscious confession, Agnes—and therefore no confession that I need distress you by repeating.'

'Did she say nothing about what she saw or heard, on that dreadful night in my room?'

'Nothing. We only know that her mind never recovered the terror of it.'

Agnes was not quite satisfied. The subject troubled her. Even her own brief intercourse with her miserable rival of other days suggested questions that perplexed her. She remembered the Countess's prediction. 'You have to bring me to the day of discovery, and to the punishment that is my doom.' Had the prediction simply faded, like other mortal prophecies?—or had it been fulfilled on the terrible night when she had seen the apparition, and when she had innocently tempted the Countess to watch her in her room?

Let it, however, be recorded, among the other virtues of Mrs. Henry Westwick, that she never again attempted to persuade her husband into betraying his secrets. Other men's wives, hearing of this extraordinary conduct (and being trained in the modern school of morals and manners), naturally regarded her with compassionate contempt. They spoke of Agnes, from that time forth, as 'rather an old-fashioned person.'

Is that all?

That is all.

Is there no explanation of the mystery of The Haunted Hotel?

Ask yourself if there is any explanation of the mystery of your own life and death.—Farewell.

THE END

THE RED HOUSE MYSTERY

BY

A. A. MILNE

TO JOHN VINE MILNE MY DEAR FATHER,

Like all really nice people, you have a weakness for detective stories, and feel that there are not enough of them. So, after all that you have done for me, the least that I can do for you is to write you one. Here it is: with more gratitude and affection than I can well put down here.

~ A. A. M.

CHAPTER I

MRS. STEVENS IS FRIGHTENED

In the drowsy heat of the summer afternoon the Red House was taking its siesta. There was a lazy murmur of bees in the flower-borders, a gentle cooing of pigeons in the tops of the elms. From distant lawns came the whir of a mowing-machine, that most restful of all country sounds; making ease the sweeter in that it is taken while others are working.

It was the hour when even those whose business it is to attend to the wants of others have a moment or two for themselves. In the housekeeper's room Audrey Stevens, the pretty parlour-maid, re-trimmed her best hat, and talked idly to her aunt, the cook-housekeeper of Mr. Mark Ablett's bachelor home.

"For Joe?" said Mrs. Stevens placidly, her eye on the hat. Audrey nodded. She took a pin from her mouth, found a place in the hat for it, and said, "He likes a bit of pink."

"I don't say I mind a bit of pink myself," said her aunt. "Joe Turner isn't the only one."

"It isn't everybody's colour," said Audrey, holding the hat out at arm's length, and regarding it thoughtfully. "Stylish, isn't it?"

"Oh, it'll suit you all right, and it would have suited me at your age. A bit too dressy for me now, though wearing better than some other people, I daresay. I was never the one to pretend to be what I wasn't. If I'm fifty-five, I'm fifty-five—that's what I say."

"Fifty-eight, isn't it, auntie?"

"I was just giving that as an example," said Mrs. Stevens with great dignity.

Audrey threaded a needle, held her hand out and looked at her nails critically for a moment, and then began to sew.

"Funny thing that about Mr. Mark's brother. Fancy not seeing your brother for fifteen years." She gave a self-conscious laugh and went on, "Wonder what I should do if I didn't see Joe for fifteen years."

"As I told you all this morning," said her aunt, "I've been

here five years, and never heard of a brother. I could say that before everybody if I was going to die to-morrow. There's been no brother here while I've been here."

"You could have knocked me down with a feather when he spoke about him at breakfast this morning. I didn't hear what went before, naturally, but they was all talking about the brother when I went in—now what was it I went in for—hot milk, was it, or toast?—well, they was all talking, and Mr. Mark turns to me, and says—you know his way—'Stevens,' he says, 'my brother is coming to see me this afternoon; I'm expecting him about three,' he says. 'Show him into the office,' he says, just like that. 'Yes, sir,' I says quite quietly, but I was never so surprised in my life, not knowing he had a brother. 'My brother from Australia,' he says—there, I'd forgotten that. From Australia."

"Well, he may have been in Australia," said Mrs. Stevens, judicially; "I can't say for that, not knowing the country; but what I do say is he's never been here. Not while I've been here, and that's five years."

"Well, but, auntie, he hasn't been here for fifteen years. I heard Mr. Mark telling Mr. Cayley. 'Fifteen years,' he says. Mr. Cayley having arst him when his brother was last in England. Mr. Cayley knew of him, I heard him telling Mr. Beverley, but didn't know when he was last in England see? So that's why he arst Mr. Mark."

"I'm not saying anything about fifteen years, Audrey. I can only speak for what I know, and that's five years Whitsuntide. I can take my oath he's not set foot in the house since five years Whitsuntide. And if he's been in Australia, as you say, well, I daresay he's had his reasons."

"What reasons?" said Audrey lightly.

"Never mind what reasons. Being in the place of a mother to you, since your poor mother died, I say this, Audrey—when a gentleman goes to Australia, he has his reasons. And when he stays in Australia fifteen years, as Mr. Mark says, and as I know for myself for five years, he has his reasons. And a respectably brought-up girl doesn't ask what reasons."

"Got into trouble, I suppose," said Audrey carelessly. "They were saying at breakfast he'd been a wild one. Debts. I'm glad

Joe isn't like that. He's got fifteen pounds in the post-office savings' bank. Did I tell you?"

But there was not to be any more talk of Joe Turner that afternoon. The ringing of a bell brought Audrey to her feet—no longer Audrey, but now Stevens. She arranged her cap in front of the glass.

"There, that's the front door," she said. "That's him. 'Show him into the office,' said Mr. Mark. I suppose he doesn't want the other ladies and gentlemen to see him. Well, they're all out at their golf, anyhow—Wonder if he's going to stay—P'raps he's brought back a lot of gold from Australia—I might hear something about Australia, because if anybody can get gold there, then I don't say but what Joe and I—"

"Now, now, get on, Audrey."

"Just going, darling." She went out.

To anyone who had just walked down the drive in the August sun, the open door of the Red House revealed a delightfully inviting hall, of which even the mere sight was cooling. It was a big low-roofed, oak-beamed place, with cream-washed walls and diamond-paned windows, blue-curtained. On the right and left were doors leading into other living-rooms, but on the side which faced you as you came in were windows again, looking on to a small grass court, and from open windows to open windows such air as there was played gently. The staircase went up in broad, low steps along the right-hand wall, and, turning to the left, led you along a gallery, which ran across the width of the hall, to your bedroom. That is, if you were going to stay the night. Mr. Robert Ablett's intentions in this matter were as yet unknown.

As Audrey came across the hall she gave a little start as she saw Mr. Cayley suddenly, sitting unobtrusively in a seat beneath one of the front windows, reading. No reason why he shouldn't be there; certainly a much cooler place than the golf-links on such a day; but somehow there was a deserted air about the house that afternoon, as if all the guests were outside, or—perhaps the wisest place of all—up in their bedrooms, sleeping. Mr. Cayley, the master's cousin, was a surprise; and, having given a little exclamation as she came suddenly upon him, she blushed, and said, "Oh, I beg your pardon, sir, I didn't see you at first," and he looked up from his book and smiled at her. An attractive smile it was on that big ugly face. "Such a gentleman, Mr. Cayley," she thought to herself as she went on, and wondered what the master would do without him. If this brother, for instance, had to be bundled back to Australia, it was Mr. Cayley who would do most of the bundling.

"So this is Mr. Robert," said Audrey to herself, as she came in sight of the visitor.

She told her aunt afterwards that she would have known him anywhere for Mr. Mark's brother, but she would have said that in any event. Actually she was surprised. Dapper little Mark, with his neat pointed beard and his carefully curled moustache; with his quick-darting eyes, always moving from one to the other of any company he was in, to register one more smile to his credit when he had said a good thing, one more expectant look when he was only waiting his turn to say it; he was a very different man from this rough-looking, ill-dressed colonial, staring at her soloweringly.

"I want to see Mr. Mark Ablett," he growled.

It sounded almost like a threat. Audrey recovered herself and smiled reassuringly at him. She had a smile for everybody.

"Yes, sir. He is expecting you, if you will come this way."

"Oh! So you know who I am, eh?"

"Mr. Robert Ablett?"

"Ay, that's right. So he's expecting me, eh? He'll be glad to see me, eh?"

"If you will come this way, sir," said Audrey primly.

She went to the second door on the left, and opened it.

"Mr. Robert Ab—" she began, and then broke off. The room was empty. She turned to the man behind her. "If you will sit down, sir, I will find the master. I know he's in, because he told me that you were coming this afternoon."

"Oh!" He looked round the room. "What d'you call this place, eh?"

"The office, sir."

"The office?"

"The room where the master works, sir."

"Works, eh? That's new. Didn't know he'd ever done a stroke of work in his life."

"Where he writes, sir," said Audrey, with dignity. The fact that Mr. Mark "wrote," though nobody knew what, was a matter of pride in the housekeeper's room.

"Not well-dressed enough for the drawing-room, eh?"

"I will tell the master you are here, sir," said Audrey decisively.

She closed the door and left him there.

Well! Here was something to tell auntie! Her mind was busy at once, going over all the things which he had said to her and she had said to him—quiet-like. "Directly I saw him I said to myself—" Why, you could have knocked her over with a feather. Feathers, indeed, were a perpetual menace to Audrey.

However, the immediate business was to find the master. She walked across the hall to the library, glanced in, came back a little uncertainly, and stood in front of Cayley.

"If you please, sir," she said in a low, respectful voice, "can you tell me where the master is? It's Mr. Robert called."

"What?" said Cayley, looking up from his book. "Who?"

Audrey repeated her question.

"I don't know. Isn't he in the office? He went up to the Temple after lunch. I don't think I've seen him since."

"Thank you, sir. I will go up to the Temple."

Cayley returned to his book.

The "Temple" was a brick summer-house, in the gardens at the back of the house, about three hundred yards away. Here Mark meditated sometimes before retiring to the "office" to put his thoughts upon paper. The thoughts were not of any great value; moreover, they were given off at the dinner-table more often than they got on to paper, and got on to paper more often than they got into print. But that did not prevent the master of The Red House from being a little pained when a visitor treated the Temple carelessly, as if it had been erected for the ordinary purposes of flirtation and cigarette-smoking. There had been an occasion when two of his guests had been found playing fives in it. Mark had said nothing at the time, save to ask with a little less than his usual point—whether they couldn't find anywhere else for their game, but the offenders were never asked to The Red House again.

Audrey walked slowly up to the Temple, looked in and walked slowly back. All that walk for nothing. Perhaps the master was upstairs in his room. "Not well-dressed enough for the drawing-room." Well, now, Auntie, would you like anyone in your drawing-room with a red handkerchief round his neck and great big dusty boots, and—listen! One of the men shooting rabbits. Auntie was partial to a nice rabbit, and onion sauce. How hot it was; she wouldn't say no to a cup of tea. Well, one thing, Mr. Robert wasn't staying the night; he hadn't any luggage. Of course Mr. Mark could lend him things; he had clothes enough for six. She would have known him anywhere for Mr. Mark's brother.

She came into the house. As she passed the housekeeper's room on her way to the hall, the door opened suddenly, and a rather frightened face looked out.

"Hallo, Aud," said Elsie. "It's Audrey," she said, turning into the room.

"Come in, Audrey," called Mrs. Stevens.

"What's up?" said Audrey, looking in at the door.

"Oh, my dear, you gave me such a turn. Where have you been?"

"Up to the Temple."

"Did you hear anything?"

"Hear what?"

"Bangs and explosions and terrible things."

"Oh!" said Audrey, rather relieved. "One of the men shooting rabbits. Why, I said to myself as I came along, 'Auntie's partial to a nice rabbit,' I said, and I shouldn't be surprised if—"

"Rabbits!" said her aunt scornfully. "It was inside the house, my girl."

"Straight it was," said Elsie. She was one of the housemaids. "I said to

Mrs. Stevens—didn't I, Mrs. Stevens?—'That was in the house,' I said."

Audrey looked at her aunt and then at Elsie.

"Do you think he had a revolver with him?" she said in a hushed voice.

"Who?" said Elsie excitedly.

"That brother of his. From Australia. I said as soon as I set eyes on him, 'You're a bad lot, my man!' That's what I said, Elsie. Even before he spoke to me. Rude!" She turned to her aunt. "Well, I give you my word."

"If you remember, Audrey, I always said there was no saying with anyone from Australia." Mrs. Stevens lay back in her chair, breathing rather rapidly. "I wouldn't go out of this room now, not if you paid me a hundred thousand pounds."

"Oh, Mrs. Stevens!" said Elsie, who badly wanted five shillings for a new pair of shoes, "I wouldn't go as far as that, not myself, but—"

"There!" cried Mrs. Stevens, sitting up with a start. They listened anxiously, the two girls instinctively coming closer to the older woman's chair.

A door was being shaken, kicked, rattled.

"Listen!"

Audrey and Elsie looked at each other with frightened eyes.

They heard a man's voice, loud, angry.

"Open the door!" it was shouting. "Open the door! I say, open the door!"

"Don't open the door!" cried Mrs. Stevens in a panic, as if it was her door which was threatened. "Audrey! Elsie! Don't let him in!"

"Damn it, open the door!" came the voice again.

"We're all going to be murdered in our beds," she quavered. Terrified, the two girls huddled closer, and with an arm round each, Mrs. Stevens sat there, waiting.

CHAPTER II

MR. GILLINGHAM GETS OUT AT THE WRONG STATION

Whether Mark Ablett was a bore or not depended on the point of view, but it may be said at once that he never bored his company on the subject of his early life. However, stories get about. There is always somebody who knows. It was understood—and this, anyhow, on Mark's own authority—that his father had been a country clergyman. It was said that, as a boy, Mark had attracted the notice, and patronage, of some rich old spinster of the neighbourhood, who had paid for his education, both at school and university. At about the time when he was coming down from Cambridge, his father had died;

leaving behind him a few debts, as a warning to his family, and a reputation for short sermons, as an example to his successor. Neither warning nor example seems to have been effective. Mark went to London, with an allowance from his patron, and (it is generally agreed) made acquaintance with the money-lenders. He was supposed, by his patron and any others who inquired, to be "writing"; but what he wrote, other than letters asking for more time to pay, has never been discovered. However, he attended the theatres and music halls very regularly—no doubt with a view to some serious articles in the "Spectator" on the decadence of the English stage.

Fortunately (from Mark's point of view) his patron died during his third year in London, and left him all the money he wanted. From that moment his life loses its legendary character, and becomes more a matter of history. He settled accounts with the money-lenders, abandoned his crop of wild oats to the harvesting of others, and became in his turn a patron. He patronized the Arts. It was not only usurers who discovered that Mark Ablett no longer wrote for money; editors were now offered free contributions as well as free lunches; publishers were given agreements for an occasional slender volume, in which the author paid all expenses and waived all royalties; promising young painters and poets dined with him; and he even took a theatrical company on tour, playing host and "lead" with equal lavishness.

He was not what most people call a snob. A snob has been defined carelessly as a man who loves a lord; and, more carefully, as a mean lover of mean things—which would be a little unkind to the peerage if the first definition were true. Mark had his vanities undoubtedly, but he would sooner have met an actor-manager than an earl; he would have spoken of his friendship with Dante—had that been possible—more glibly than of his friendship with the Duke. Call him a snob if you like, but not the worst kind of snob; a hanger-on, but to the skirts of Art, not Society; a climber, but in the neighbourhood of Parnassus, not Hay Hill.

His patronage did not stop at the Arts. It also included Matthew Cayley, a small cousin of thirteen, whose circumstances were as limited as had been Mark's own before his patron had rescued him. He sent the Cayley cousin to school and

Cambridge. His motives, no doubt, were unworldly enough at first; a mere repaying to his account in the Recording Angel's book of the generosity which had been lavished on himself; a laying-up of treasure in heaven. But it is probable that, as the boy grew up, Mark's designs for his future were based on his own interests as much as those of his cousin, and that a suitably educated Matthew Cayley of twenty-three was felt by him to be a useful property for a man in his position; a man, that is to say, whose vanities left him so little time for his affairs.

Cayley, then, at twenty-three, looked after his cousin's affairs. By this time Mark had bought the Red House and the considerable amount of land which went with it. Cayley superintended the necessary staff. His duties, indeed, were many. He was not quite secretary, not quite land-agent, not quite business-adviser, not quite companion, but something of all four. Mark leant upon him and called him "Cay," objecting quite rightly in the circumstances to the name of Matthew. Cay, he felt was, above all, dependable; a big, heavy-jawed, solid fellow, who didn't bother you with unnecessary talk—a boon to a man who liked to do most of the talking himself.

Cayley was now twenty-eight, but had all the appearance of forty, which was his patron's age. Spasmodically they entertained a good deal at the Red House, and Mark's preference—call it kindliness or vanity, as you please—was for guests who were not in a position to repay his hospitality. Let us have a look at them as they came down to that breakfast, of which Stevens, the parlour-maid, has already given us a glimpse.

The first to appear was Major Rumbold, a tall, grey-haired, grey-moustached, silent man, wearing a Norfolk coat and grey flannel trousers, who lived on his retired pay and wrote natural history articles for the papers. He inspected the dishes on the side-table, decided carefully on kedgeree, and got to work on it. He had passed on to a sausage by the time of the next arrival. This was Bill Beverly, a cheerful young man in white flannel trousers and a blazer.

"Hallo, Major," he said as he came in, "how's the gout?"

"It isn't gout," said the Major gruffly.

"Well, whatever it is."

The Major grunted.

"I make a point of being polite at breakfast," said Bill, helping himself largely to porridge. "Most people are so rude. That's why I asked you. But don't tell me if it's a secret. Coffee?" he added, as he poured himself out a cup.

"No, thanks. I never drink till I've finished eating."

"Quite right, Major; it's only manners." He sat down opposite to the other. "Well, we've got a good day for our game. It's going to be dashed hot, but that's where Betty and I score. On the fifth green, your old wound, the one you got in that frontier skirmish in '43, will begin to trouble you; on the eighth, your liver, undermined by years of curry, will drop to pieces; on the twelfth—"

"Oh, shut up, you ass!"

"Well, I'm only warning you. Hallo; good morning, Miss Norris. I was just telling the Major what was going to happen to you and him this morning. Do you want any assistance, or do you prefer choosing your own breakfast?"

"Please don't get up," said Miss Norris. "I'll help myself. Good morning, Major." She smiled pleasantly at him. The Major nodded.

"Good morning. Going to be hot."

"As I was telling him," began Bill, "that's where—Hallo, here's Betty. Morning, Cayley."

Betty Calladine and Cayley had come in together. Betty was the eighteen-year-old daughter of Mrs. John Calladine, widow of the painter, who was acting hostess on this occasion for Mark. Ruth Norris took herself seriously as an actress and, on her holidays, seriously as a golfer. She was quite competent as either. Neither the Stage Society nor Sandwich had any terrors for her.

"By the way, the car will be round at 10.30," said Cayley, looking up from his letters. "You're lunching there, and driving back directly afterwards. Isn't that right?"

"I don't see why we shouldn't have—two rounds," said Bill hopefully.

"Much too hot in the afternoon," said the Major. "Get back comfortably for tea."

Mark came in. He was generally the last. He greeted them and sat down to toast and tea. Breakfast was not his meal. The others chattered gently while he read his letters.

"Good God!" said Mark suddenly.

There was an instinctive turning of heads towards him. "I beg your pardon, Miss Norris. Sorry, Betty."

Miss Norris smiled her forgiveness. She often wanted to say it herself, particularly at rehearsals.

"I say, Cay!" He was frowning to himself—annoyed, puzzled. He held up a letter and shook it. "Who do you think this is from?"

Cayley, at the other end of the table, shrugged his shoulders. How could he possibly guess?

"Robert," said Mark.

"Robert?" It was difficult to surprise Cayley. "Well?"

"It's all very well to say 'well?' like that," said Mark peevishly. "He's coming here this afternoon."

"I thought he was in Australia, or somewhere."

"Of course. So did I." He looked across at Rumbold. "Got any brothers, Major?"

"No."

"Well, take my advice, and don't have any."

"Not likely to now," said the Major.

Bill laughed. Miss Norris said politely: "But you haven't any brothers, Mr. Ablett?"

"One," said Mark grimly. "If you're back in time you'll see him this afternoon. He'll probably ask you to lend him five pounds. Don't."

Everybody felt a little uncomfortable.

"I've got a brother," said Bill helpfully, "but I always borrow from him."

"Like Robert," said Mark.

"When was he in England last?" asked Cayley.

"About fifteen years ago, wasn't it? You'd have been a boy, of course."

"Yes, I remember seeing him once about then, but I didn't know if he had been back since."

"No. Not to my knowledge." Mark, still obviously upset, returned to his letter.

"Personally," said Bill, "I think relations are a great mistake."

"All the same," said Betty a little daringly, "it must be rather fun having a skeleton in the cupboard."

Mark looked up, frowning.

"If you think it's fun, I'll hand him over to you, Betty. If he's anything like he used to be, and like his few letters have been—

well, Cay knows."

Cayley grunted.

"All I knew was that one didn't ask questions about him."

It may have been meant as a hint to any too curious guest not to ask more questions, or a reminder to his host not to talk too freely in front of strangers, although he gave it the sound of a mere statement of fact. But the subject dropped, to be succeeded by the more fascinating one of the coming foursome. Mrs. Calladine was driving over with the players in order to lunch with an old friend who lived near the links, and Mark and Cayley were remaining at home—on affairs. Apparently "affairs" were now to include a prodigal brother. But that need not make the foursome less enjoyable.

At about the time when the Major (for whatever reasons) was fluffing his tee-shot at the sixteenth, and Mark and his cousin were at their business at the Red House, an attractive gentleman of the name of Antony Gillingham was handing up his ticket at Woodham station and asking the way to the village. Having received directions, he left his bag with the station-master and walked off leisurely. He is an important person to this story, so that it is as well we should know something about him before letting him loose in it. Let us stop him at the top of the hill on some excuse, and have a good look at him.

The first thing we realize is that he is doing more of the looking than we are. Above a clean-cut, clean-shaven face, of the type usually associated with the Navy, he carries a pair of grey eyes which seem to be absorbing every detail of our person. To strangers this look is almost alarming at first, until they discover that his mind is very often elsewhere; that he has, so to speak, left his eyes on guard, while he himself follows a train of thought in another direction. Many people do this, of course; when, for instance, they are talking to one person and trying to listen to another; but their eyes betray them. Antony's never did.

He had seen a good deal of the world with those eyes, though never as a sailor. When at the age of twenty-one he came into his mother's money, 400 pounds a year, old Gillingham looked up from the "Stockbreeders' Gazette" to ask what he was going to do.

"See the world," said Antony.

"Well, send me a line from America, or wherever you get to."

"Right," said Antony.

Old Gillingham returned to his paper. Antony was a younger son, and, on the whole, not so interesting to his father as the cadets of certain other families; Champion Birket's, for instance. But, then, Champion Birket was the best Hereford bull he had ever bred.

Antony, however, had no intention of going further away than London. His idea of seeing the world was to see, not countries, but people; and to see them from as many angles as possible. There are all sorts in London if you know how to look at them. So Antony looked at them—from various strange corners; from the view-point of the valet, the newspaper-reporter, the waiter, the shop-assistant. With the independence of 400 pounds a year behind him, he enjoyed it immensely. He never stayed long in one job, and generally closed his connection with it by telling his employer (contrary to all etiquette as understood between master and servant) exactly what he thought of him. He had no difficulty in finding a new profession. Instead of experience and testimonials he offered his personality and a sporting bet. He would take no wages the first month, and—if he satisfied his employer—double wages the second. He always got his double wages.

He was now thirty. He had come to Waldheim for a holiday, because he liked the look of the station. His ticket entitled him to travel further, but he had always intended to please himself in the matter. Waldheim attracted him, and he had a suit-case in the carriage with him and money in his pocket. Why not get out?

The landlady of 'The George' was only too glad to put him up, and promised that her husband would drive over that afternoon for his luggage.

"And you would like some lunch, I expect, sir."

"Yes, but don't give yourself any trouble about it. Cold anything-you've-got."

"What about beef, sir?" she asked, as if she had a hundred varieties of meat to select from, and was offering him her best.

"That will do splendidly. And a pint of beer."

While he was finishing his lunch, the landlord came in to ask about the luggage. Antony ordered another pint, and soon had him talking.

"It must be rather fun to keep a country inn," he said,

thinking that it was about time he started another profession.

"I don't know about fun, sir. It gives us a living, and a bit over."

"You ought to take a holiday," said Antony, looking at him thoughtfully.

"Funny thing your saying that," said the landlord, with a smile. "Another gentleman, over from the Red House, was saying that only yesterday. Offered to take my place 'n all." He laughed rumblingly.

"The Red House? Not the Red House, Stanton?"

"That's right, sir. Stanton's the next station to Waldheim. The Red House is about a mile from here—Mr. Ablett's."

Antony took a letter from his pocket. It was addressed from "The Red House, Stanton," and signed "Bill."

"Good old Bill," he murmured to himself. "He's getting on."

Antony had met Bill Beverley two years before in a tobacconist's shop. Gillingham was on one side of the counter and Mr. Beverley on the other. Something about Bill, his youth and freshness, perhaps, attracted Antony; and when cigarettes had been ordered, and an address given to which they were to be sent, he remembered that he had come across an aunt of Beverley's once at a country-house. Beverley and he met again a little later at a restaurant. Both of them were in evening-dress, but they did different things with their napkins, and Antony was the more polite of the two. However, he still liked Bill. So on one of his holidays, when he was unemployed, he arranged an introduction through a mutual friend. Beverley was a little inclined to be shocked when he was reminded of their previous meetings, but his uncomfortable feeling soon wore off, and he and Antony quickly became intimate. But Bill generally addressed him as "Dear Madman" when he happened to write.

Antony decided to stroll over to the Red House after lunch and call upon his friend. Having inspected his bedroom which was not quite the lavender-smelling country-inn bedroom of fiction, but sufficiently clean and comfortable, he set out over the fields.

As he came down the drive and approached the old red-brick front of the house, there was a lazy murmur of bees in the flower-borders, a gentle cooing of pigeons in the tops of the elms, and from distant lawns the whir of a mowing-machine, that most restful of all country sounds....

And in the hall a man was banging at a locked door, and shouting, "Open the door, I say; open the door!"

"Hallo!" said Antony in amazement.

CHAPTER III

TWO MEN AND A BODY

Cayley looked round suddenly at the voice.

"Can I help?" said Antony politely.

"Something's happened," said Cayley. He was breathing quickly. "I heard a shot—it sounded like a shot—I was in the library. A loud bang—I didn't know what it was. And the door's locked." He rattled the handle again, and shook it. "Open the door!" he cried. "I say, Mark, what is it? Open the door!"

"But he must have locked the door on purpose," said Antony. "So why should he open it just because you ask him to?"

Cayley looked at him in a bewildered way. Then he turned to the door again. "We must break it in," he said, putting his shoulder to it. "Help me."

"Isn't there a window?"

Cayley turned to him stupidly.

"Window? Window?"

"So much easier to break in a window," said Antony with a smile. He looked very cool and collected, as he stood just inside the hall, leaning on his stick, and thinking, no doubt, that a great deal of fuss was being made about nothing. But then, he had not heard the shot.

"Window—of course! What an idiot I am."

He pushed past Antony, and began running out into the drive. Antony followed him. They ran along the front of the house, down a path to the left, and then to the left again over the grass, Cayley in front, the other close behind him. Suddenly Cayley looked over his shoulder and pulled up short.

"Here," he said.

They had come to the windows of the locked room, French windows which opened on to the lawns at the back of the house. But now they were closed. Antony couldn't help feeling a thrill of excitement as he followed Cayley's example, and put his face close up to the glass. For the first time he wondered if there really had been a revolver shot in this mysterious room. It had all seemed so absurd and melodramatic from the other side of the door. But if there had been one shot, why should there not be two more?—at the careless fools who were pressing their noses against the panes, and asking for it.

"My God, can you see it?" said Cayley in a shaking voice. "Down there.

Look!"

The next moment Antony saw it. A man was lying on the floor at the far end of the room, his back towards them. A man? Or the body of a man?

"Who is it?" said Antony.

"I don't know," the other whispered.

"Well, we'd better go and see." He considered the windows for a moment. "I should think, if you put your weight into it, just where they join, they'll give all right. Otherwise, we can kick the glass in."

Without saying anything, Cayley put his weight into it. The window gave, and they went into the room. Cayley walked quickly to the body, and dropped on his knees by it. For the moment he seemed to hesitate; then with an effort he put a hand on to its shoulder and pulled it over.

"Thank God!" he murmured, and let the body go again.

"Who is it?" said Antony.

"Robert Ablett."

"Oh!" said Antony. "I thought his name was Mark," he added, more to himself than to the other.

"Yes, Mark Ablett lives here. Robert is his brother." He shuddered, and said, "I was afraid it was Mark."

"Was Mark in the room too?"

"Yes," said Cayley absently. Then, as if resenting suddenly these questions from a stranger, "Who are you?"

But Antony had gone to the locked door, and was turning the handle. "I suppose he put the key in his pocket," he said, as he came back to the body again.

"Who?"

Antony shrugged his shoulders.

"Whoever did this," he said, pointing to the man on the floor. "Is he dead?"

"Help me," said Cayley simply.

They turned the body on to its back, nerving themselves to look at it. Robert Ablett had been shot between the eyes. It was not a pleasant sight, and with his horror Antony felt a sudden pity for the man beside him, and a sudden remorse for the careless, easy way in which he had treated the affair. But then one always went about imagining that these things didn't happen—except to other people. It was difficult to believe in them just at first, when they happened to yourself.

"Did you know him well?" said Antony quietly. He meant, "Were you fond of him?"

"Hardly at all. Mark is my cousin. I mean, Mark is the brother I know best."

"Your cousin?"

"Yes." He hesitated, and then said, "Is he dead? I suppose he is. Will you—do you know anything about—about that sort of thing? Perhaps I'd better get some water."

There was another door opposite to the locked one, which led, as Antony was to discover for himself directly, into a passage from which opened two more rooms. Cayley stepped into the passage, and opened the door on the right. The door from the office, through which he had gone, remained open. The door, at the end of the short passage was shut. Antony, kneeling by the body, followed Cayley with his eyes, and, after he had disappeared, kept his eyes on the blank wall of the passage, but he was not conscious of that at which he was looking, for his mind was with the other man, sympathizing with him.

"Not that water is any use to a dead body," he said to himself, "but the feeling that you're doing something, when there's obviously nothing to be done, is a great comfort."

Cayley came into the room again. He had a sponge in one hand, a handkerchief in the other. He looked at Antony. Antony nodded. Cayley murmured something, and knelt down to bathe the dead man's face. Then he placed the handkerchief over it. A little sigh escaped Antony, a sigh of relief.

They stood up and looked at each other.

"If I can be of any help to you," said Antony, "please let me."

"That's very kind of you. There will be things to do. Police, doctors—I don't know. But you mustn't let me trespass on your kindness. Indeed, I should apologise for having trespassed so much already."

"I came to see Beverley. He is an old friend of mine."

"He's out playing golf. He will be back directly." Then, as if he had only just realized it, "They will all be back directly."

"I will stay if I can be of any help."

"Please do. You see, there are women. It will be rather painful. If you would—" He hesitated, and gave Antony a timid little smile, pathetic in so big and self-reliant a man. "Just your moral support, you know. It would be something."

"Of course." Antony smiled back at him, and said cheerfully, "Well, then, I'll begin by suggesting that you should ring up the police."

"The police? Y-yes." He looked doubtfully at the other. "I suppose—"

Antony spoke frankly.

"Now, look here, Mr.—er—"

"Cayley. I'm Mark Ablett's cousin. I live with him."

"My name's Gillingham. I'm sorry, I ought to have told you before. Well now, Mr. Cayley, we shan't do any good by pretending. Here's a man been shot—well, somebody shot him."

"He might have shot himself," mumbled Cayley.

"Yes, he might have, but he didn't. Or if he did, somebody was in the room at the time, and that somebody isn't here now. And that somebody took a revolver away with him. Well, the police will want to say a word about that, won't they?"

Cayley was silent, looking on the ground.

"Oh, I know what you're thinking, and believe me I do sympathize with you, but we can't be children about it. If your cousin Mark Ablett was in the room with this"—he indicated the body—"this man, then—"

"Who said he was?" said Cayley, jerking his head up suddenly at Antony.

"You did."

"I was in the library. Mark went in—he may have come out again—I know nothing. Somebody else may have gone in—"

"Yes, yes," said Antony patiently, as if to a little child. "You know your cousin; I don't. Let's agree that he had nothing to do with it. But somebody was in the room when this man was shot, and—well, the police will have to know. Don't you think—" He looked at the telephone. "Or would you rather I did it?"

Cayley shrugged his shoulders and went to the telephone.

"May I—er—look round a bit?" Antony nodded towards the open door.

"Oh, do. Yes." He sat down and drew the telephone towards him. "You must make allowances for me, Mr. Gillingham. You see, I've known Mark for a very long time. But, of course, you're quite right, and I'm merely being stupid." He took off the receiver.

Let us suppose that, for the purpose of making a first acquaintance with this "office," we are coming into it from the hall, through the door which is now locked, but which, for our special convenience, has been magically unlocked for us. As we stand just inside the door, the length of the room runs right and left; or, more accurately, to the right only, for the left-hand wall is almost within our reach. Immediately opposite to us, across the breadth of the room (some fifteen feet), is that other door, by which Cayley went out and returned a few minutes ago. In the right-hand wall, thirty feet away from us, are the French windows. Crossing the room and going out by the opposite door, we come into a passage, from which two rooms lead. The one on the right, into which Cayley went, is less than half the length of the office, a small, square room, which has evidently been used some time or other as a bedroom. The bed is no longer there, but there is a basin, with hot and cold taps, in a corner; chairs; a cupboard or two, and a chest of drawers. The window faces the same way as the French windows in the next room; but anybody looking out of the bedroom window has his view on the immediate right shut off by the outer wall of the office, which projects, by reason of its greater length, fifteen feet further into the lawn.

The room on the other side of the bedroom is a bathroom. The three rooms together, in fact, form a sort of private suite; used, perhaps, during the occupation of the previous owner, by some invalid, who could not manage the stairs, but allowed by Mark to fall into disuse, save for the living-room. At any rate, he never slept downstairs.

Antony glanced at the bathroom, and then wandered into the bedroom, the room into which Cayley had been. The window was open, and he looked out at the well-kept grass beneath him, and the peaceful stretch of park beyond; and he felt very sorry for the owner of it all, who was now mixed up in so grim a business.

"Cayley thinks he did it," said Antony to himself. "That's obvious. It explains why he wasted so much time banging on the door. Why should he try to break a lock when it's so much easier to break a window? Of course he might just have lost his head; on the other hand, he might—well, he might have wanted to give his cousin a chance of getting away. The same about the police, and—oh, lots of things. Why, for instance, did we run all the way round the house in order to get to the windows? Surely there's a back way out through the hall. I must have a look later on."

Antony, it will be observed, had by no means lost his head.

There was a step in the passage outside, and he turned round, to see Cayley in the doorway. He remained looking at him for a moment, asking himself a question. It was rather a curious question. He was asking himself why the door was open.

Well, not exactly why the door was open; that could be explained easily enough. But why had he expected the door to be shut? He did not remember shutting it, but somehow he was surprised to see it open now, to see Cayley through the doorway, just coming into the room. Something working sub-consciously in his brain had told him that it was surprising. Why?

He tucked the matter away in a corner of his mind for the moment; the answer would come to him later on. He had a wonderfully retentive mind. Everything which he saw or heard seemed to make its corresponding impression somewhere in his brain; often without his being conscious of it; and these photographic impressions were always there ready for him when he wished to develop them.

Cayley joined him at the window.

"I've telephoned," he said. "They're sending an inspector or some one from Middleston, and the local police and doctor from Stanton." He shrugged his shoulders. "We're in for it now."

"How far away is Middleston?" It was the town for which

Antony had taken a ticket that morning—only six hours ago. How absurd it seemed.

"About twenty miles. These people will be coming back soon."

"Beverley, and the others?"

"Yes. I expect they'll want to go away at once."

"Much better that they should."

"Yes." Cayley was silent for a little. Then he said, "You're staying near here?"

"I'm at 'The George,' at Waldheim."

"If you're by yourself, I wish you'd put up here. You see," he went on awkwardly, "you'll have to be here—for the—the inquest and—and so on. If I may offer you my cousin's hospitality in his—I mean if he doesn't—if he really has—"

Antony broke in hastily with his thanks and acceptance.

"That's good. Perhaps Beverley will stay on, if he's a friend of yours. He's a good fellow."

Antony felt quite sure, from what Cayley had said and had hesitated to say, that Mark had been the last to see his brother alive. It didn't follow that Mark Ablett was a murderer. Revolvers go off accidentally; and when they have gone off, people lose their heads and run away, fearing that their story will not be believed. Nevertheless, when people run away, whether innocently or guiltily, one can't help wondering which way they went.

"I suppose this way," said Antony aloud, looking out of the window.

"Who?" said Cayley stubbornly.

"Well, whoever it was," said Antony, smiling to himself. "The murderer. Or, let us say, the man who locked the door after Robert Ablett was killed."

"I wonder."

"Well, how else could he have got away? He didn't go by the windows in the next room, because they were shut."

"Isn't that rather odd?"

"Well, I thought so at first, but—" He pointed to the wall jutting out on the right. "You see, you're protected from the rest of the house if you get out here, and you're quite close to the shrubbery. If you go out at the French windows, I imagine you're much more visible. All that part of the house—" he waved his right hand—"the west, well, north-west almost, where the kitchen parts are—you see, you're hidden from them here. Oh, yes! he knew the house, whoever it was, and he was quite right to come out of this window. He'd be into the shrubbery at once."

Cayley looked at him thoughtfully.

"It seems to me, Mr. Gillingham, that you know the house pretty well, considering that this is the first time you've been to it."

Antony laughed.

"Oh, well, I notice things, you know. I was born noticing. But I'm right, aren't I, about why he went out this way?"

"Yes, I think you are." Cayley looked away—towards the shrubbery. "Do you want to go noticing in there now?" He nodded at it.

"I think we might leave that to the police," said Antony gently.

"It's—well, there's no hurry."

Cayley gave a little sigh, as if he had been holding his breath for the answer, and could now breathe again.

"Thank you, Mr. Gillingham," he said.

CHAPTER IV

THE BROTHER FROM AUSTRALIA

Guests at the Red House were allowed to do what they liked within reason—the reasonableness or otherwise of it being decided by Mark. But when once they (or Mark) had made up their minds as to what they wanted to do, the plan had to be kept. Mrs. Calladine, who knew this little weakness of their host's, resisted, therefore, the suggestion of Bill that they should have a second round in the afternoon, and drive home comfortably after tea. The other golfers were willing enough, but Mrs. Calladine, without actually saying that Mr. Ablett wouldn't like it, was firm on the point that, having arranged to be back by four, they should be back by four.

"I really don't think Mark wants us, you know," said the

Major. Having played badly in the morning, he wanted to prove to himself in the afternoon that he was really better than that. "With this brother of his coming, he'll be only too glad to have us out of the way."

"Of course he will, Major." This from Bill. "You'd like to play, wouldn't you, Miss Norris?"

Miss Norris looked doubtfully at the hostess.

"Of course, if you want to get back, dear, we mustn't keep you here. Besides, it's so dull for you, not playing."

"Just nine holes, mother," pleaded Betty.

"The car could take you back, and you could tell them that we were having another round, and then it could come back for us," said Bill brilliantly.

"It's certainly much cooler here than I expected," put in the Major.

Mrs. Calladine fell. It was very pleasantly cool outside the golf-house, and of course Mark would be rather glad to have them out of the way. So she consented to nine holes; and the match having ended all-square, and everybody having played much better than in the morning, they drove back to the Red House, very well pleased with themselves.

"Halo," said Bill to himself, as they approached the house, "isn't that old Tony?"

Antony was standing in front of the house, waiting for them. Bill waved, and he waved back. Then as the car drew up, Bill, who was in front with the chauffeur, jumped down and greeted him eagerly.

"Hallo, you madman, have you come to stay, or what?" He had a sudden idea. "Don't say you're Mark Ablett's long-lost brother from Australia, though I could quite believe it of you." He laughed boyishly.

"Hallo, Bill," said Antony quietly. "Will you introduce me? I'm afraid I've got some bad news."

Bill, rather sobered by this, introduced him. The Major and Mrs. Calladine were on the near side of the car, and Antony spoke to them in a low voice.

"I'm afraid I'm going to give you rather a shock," he said. "Robert Ablett, Mr. Mark Ablett's brother, has been killed." He jerked a thumb over his shoulder. "In the house."

"Good God!" said the Major.

"Do you mean that he has killed himself?" asked Mrs. Calladine. "Just now?"

"It was about two hours ago. I happened to come here,"—he half-turned to Beverley and explained—"I was coming to see you, Bill, and I arrived just after the—the death. Mr. Cayley and I found the body. Mr. Cayley being busy just now—there are police and doctors and so on in the house—he asked me to tell you. He says that no doubt you would prefer, the house-party having been broken up in this tragic way, to leave as soon as possible." He gave a pleasant apologetic little smile and went on, "I am putting it badly, but what he means, of course, is that you must consult your own feelings in the matter entirely, and please make your own arrangements about ordering the car for whatever train you wish to catch. There is one this evening, I understand, which you could go by if you wished it."

Bill gazed with open mouth at Antony. He had no words in his vocabulary to express what he wanted to say, other than those the Major had already used. Betty was leaning across to Miss Norris and saying, "Who's killed?" in an awe-struck voice, and Miss Norris, who was instinctively looking as tragic as she looked on the stage when a messenger announced the death of one of the cast, stopped for a moment in order to explain. Mrs. Calladine was quietly mistress of herself.

"We shall be in the way, yes, I quite understand," she said; "but we can't just shake the dust of the place off our shoes because something terrible has happened there. I must see Mark, and we can arrange later what to do. He must know how very deeply we feel for him. Perhaps we—" she hesitated.

"The Major and I might be useful anyway," said Bill. "Isn't that what you mean, Mrs. Calladine?"

"Where is Mark?" said the Major suddenly, looking hard at Antony.

Antony looked back unwaveringly—and said nothing.

"I think," said the Major gently, leaning over to Mrs. Calladine, "that it would be better if you took Betty back to London to-night."

"Very well," she agreed quietly. "You will come with us, Ruth?"

"I'll see you safely there," said Bill in a meek voice. He didn't quite know what was happening, and, having expected to stay at the Red House for another week, he had nowhere to go to in London, but London seemed to be the place that everyone was going to, and when he could get Tony alone for a moment, Tony no doubt would explain.

"Cayley wants you to stay, Bill. You have to go anyhow, to-morrow, Major Rumbold?"

"Yes. I'll come with you, Mrs. Calladine."

"Mr. Cayley would wish me to say again that you will please not hesitate to give your own orders, both as regard the car and as regard any telephoning or telegraphing that you want done." He smiled again and added, "Please forgive me if I seem to have taken a good deal upon myself, but I just happened to be handy as a mouthpiece for Cayley." He bowed to them and went into the house.

"Well!" said Miss Norris dramatically.

As Antony re-entered the hall, the Inspector from Middleston was just crossing into the library with Cayley. The latter stopped and nodded to Antony.

"Wait a moment, Inspector. Here's Mr. Gillingham. He'd better come with us." And then to Antony, "This is Inspector Birch."

Birch looked inquiringly from one to the other.

"Mr. Gillingham and I found the body together," explained Cayley.

"Oh! Well, come along, and let's get the facts sorted out a bit. I like to know where I am, Mr. Gillingham."

"We all do."

"Oh!" He looked at Antony with interest. "D'you know where you are in this case?"

"I know where I'm going to be."

"Where's that?"

"Put through it by Inspector Birch," said Antony with a smile.

The inspector laughed genially.

"Well, I'll spare you as much as I can. Come along."

They went into the library. The inspector seated himself at a writing-table, and Cayley sat in a chair by the side of it. Antony made himself comfortable in an armchair and prepared to be interested.

"We'll start with the dead man," said the Inspector. "Robert

Ablett, didn't you say?" He took out his notebook.

"Yes. Brother of Mark Ablett, who lives here."

"Ah!" He began to sharpen a pencil. "Staying in the house?"

"Oh, no!"

Antony listened attentively while Cayley explained all that he knew about Robert. This was news to him. "I see. Sent out of the country in disgrace. What had he done?"

"I hardly know. I was only about twelve at the time. The sort of age when you're told not to ask questions."

"Inconvenient questions?"

"Exactly."

"So you don't really know whether he had been merely wild or—or wicked?"

"No. Old Mr. Ablett was a clergyman," added Cayley. "Perhaps what might seem wicked to a clergyman might seem only wild to a man of the world."

"I daresay, Mr. Cayley," smiled the Inspector. "Anyhow, it was more convenient to have him in Australia?"

"Yes."

"Mark Ablett never talked about him?"

"Hardly ever. He was very much ashamed of him, and—well, very glad he was in Australia."

"Did he write Mark sometimes?"

"Occasionally. Perhaps three or four times in the last five years."

"Asking for money?"

"Something of the sort. I don't think Mark always answered them. As far as I know, he never sent any money."

"Now your own private opinion, Mr. Cayley. Do you think that Mark was unfair to his brother? Unduly hard on him?"

"They'd never liked each other as boys. There was never any affection between them. I don't know whose fault it was in the first place—if anybody's."

"Still, Mark might have given him a hand?"

"I understand," said Cayley, "that Robert spent his whole life asking for hands."

The inspector nodded.

"I know that sort. Well, now, we'll go on to this morning. This letter that Mark got—did you see it?"

"Not at the time. He showed it to me afterwards."

"Any address?"

"No. A half-sheet of rather dirty paper."

"Where is it now?"

"I don't know. In Mark's pocket, I expect."

"Ah!" He pulled at his beard. "Well, we'll come to that. Can you remember what it said?"

"As far as I remember, something like this: 'Mark, your loving brother is coming to see you to-morrow, all the way from Australia. I give you warning so that you will be able to conceal your surprise, but not I hope, your pleasure. Expect him at three, or thereabouts.'"

"Ah!" The inspector copied it down carefully. "Did you notice the postmark?"

"London."

"And what was Mark's attitude?"

"Annoyance, disgust—" Cayley hesitated.

"Apprehension?"

"N-no, not exactly. Or, rather, apprehension of an unpleasant interview, not of any unpleasant outcome for himself."

"You mean that he wasn't afraid of violence, or blackmail, or anything of that sort?"

"He didn't appear to be."

"Right.... Now then, he arrived, you say, about three o'clock?"

"Yes, about that."

"Who was in the house then?"

"Mark and myself, and some of the servants. I don't know which. Of course, you will ask them directly, no doubt."

"With your permission. No guests?"

"They were out all day playing golf," explained Cayley. "Oh, by the way," he put in, "if I may interrupt a moment, will you want to see them at all? It isn't very pleasant for them now, naturally, and I suggested—" he turned to Antony, who nodded back to him. "I understand that they want to go back to London this evening. There's no objection to that, I suppose?"

"You will let me have their names and addresses in case I want to communicate with them?"

"Of course. One of them is staying on, if you would like to see him later, but they only came back from their golf as we crossed the hall."

"That's all right, Mr. Cayley. Well, now then, let's go back to three o'clock. Where were you when Robert arrived?"

Cayley explained how he had been sitting in the hall, how Audrey had asked him where the master was, and how he had said that he had last seen him going up to the Temple.

"She went away, and I went on with my book. There was a step on the stairs, and I looked up to see Mark coming down. He went into the office, and I went on with my book again. I went into the library for a moment, to refer to another book, and when I was in there I heard a shot. At least, it was a loud bang, I wasn't sure if it was a shot. I stood and listened. Then I came slowly to the door and looked out. Then I went back again, hesitated a bit, you know, and finally decided to go across to the office, and make sure that it was all right. I turned the handle of the door and found it was locked. Then I got frightened, and I banged at the door, and shouted, and—well, that was when Mr. Gillingham arrived." He went on to explain how they had found the body.

The inspector looked at him with a smile.

"Yes, well, we shall have to go over some of that again, Mr. Cayley. Mr. Mark, now. You thought he was in the Temple. Could he have come in, and gone up to his room, without your seeing him?"

"There are back stairs. He wouldn't have used them in the ordinary way, of course. But I wasn't in the hall all the afternoon. He might easily have gone upstairs without my knowing anything about it."

"So that you weren't surprised when you saw him coming down?"

"Oh, not a bit."

"Well, did he say anything?"

"He said, 'Robert's here?' or something of the sort. I suppose he'd heard the bell, or the voices in the hall."

"Which way does his bedroom face? Could he have seen him coming down the drive?"

"He might have, yes."

"Well?"

"Well, then, I said 'Yes,' and he gave a sort of shrug, and said, 'Don't go too far away, I might want you'; and then went in."

"What did you think he meant by that?"

"Well, he consults me a good deal, you know. I'm his sort of unofficial solicitor in a kind of way."

"This was a business meeting rather than a brotherly one?"

"Oh, yes. That's how he regarded it, I'm sure."

"Yes. How long was it before you heard the shot?"

"Very soon. Two minutes, perhaps."

The inspector finished his writing, and then regarded Cayley thoughtfully. Suddenly he said:

"What is your theory of Robert's death?"

Cayley shrugged his shoulders.

"You've probably seen more than I've seen," he answered. "It's your job. I can only speak as a layman—and Mark's friend."

"Well?"

"Then I should say that Robert came here meaning trouble, and bringing a revolver with him. He produced it almost at once, Mark tried to get it from him, there was a little struggle perhaps, and it went off. Mark lost his head, finding himself there with a revolver in his hand and a dead man at his feet. His one idea was to escape. He locked the door almost instinctively, and then, when he heard me hammering at it, went out of the window."

"Y-yes. Well, that sounds reasonable enough. What do you say, Mr. Gillingham?"

"I should hardly call it 'reasonable' to lose your head," said Antony, getting up from his chair and coming towards them.

"Well, you know what I mean. It explains things."

"Oh, yes. Any other explanation would make them much more complicated."

"Have you any other explanation?"

"Not I."

"Are there any points on which you would like to correct Mr. Cayley?—anything that he left out after you arrived here?"

"No, thanks. He described it all very accurately."

"Ah! Well now, about yourself. You're not staying in the house, I gather?"

Antony explained his previous movements.

"Yes. Did you hear the shot?"

Antony put his head on one side, as if listening. "Yes. Just as I came in sight of the house. It didn't make any impression at the time, but I remember it now."

"Where were you then?"

"Coming up the drive. I was just in sight of the house."

"Nobody left the house by the front door after the shot?"

Antony closed his eyes and considered.

"Nobody," he said. "No."

"You're certain of that?"

"Absolutely," said Antony, as though rather surprised that he could be suspected of a mistake.

"Thank you. You're at 'The George,' if I want you?"

"Mr. Gillingham is staying here until after the inquest," explained Cayley.

"Good. Well now, about these servants?"

CHAPTER V

MR. GILLINGHAM CHOOSES A NEW PROFESSION

As Cayley went over to the bell, Antony got up and moved to the door.

"Well, you won't want me, I suppose, inspector," he said.

"No, thank you, Mr. Gillingham. You'll be about, of course?"

"Oh, yes."

The inspector hesitated.

"I think, Mr. Cayley, it would be better if I saw the servants alone. You know what they are; the more people about, the more they get alarmed. I expect I can get at the truth better by myself."

"Oh, quite so. In fact, I was going to ask you to excuse me. I feel rather responsible towards these guests of ours. Although Mr. Gillingham very kindly—" He smiled at Antony, who was waiting at the door, and left his sentence unfinished.

"Ah, that reminds me," said the Inspector. "Didn't you say that one of your guests—Mr. Beverley was it?—a friend of Mr. Gillingham's, was staying on?"

"Yes; would you like to see him?"

"Afterwards, if I may."

"I'll warn him. I shall be up in my room, if you want me. I have a room upstairs where I work—any of the servants will show you. Ah, Stevens, Inspector Birch would like to ask you a few questions."

"Yes, sir," said Audrey primly, but inwardly fluttering. The housekeeper's room had heard something of the news by this time, and Audrey had had a busy time explaining to other members of the staff exactly what he had said, and what she had said. The details were not quite established yet, but this much at least was certain: that Mr. Mark's brother had shot himself and spirited Mr. Mark away, and that Audrey had seen at once that he was that sort of man when she opened the door to him. She had passed the remark to Mrs. Stevens. And Mrs. Stevens—if you remember, Audrey—had always said that people didn't go away to Australia except for very good reasons. Elsie agreed with both of them, but she had a contribution of her own to make. She had actually heard Mr. Mark in the office, threatening his brother.

"You mean Mr. Robert," said the second parlour-maid. She had been having a little nap in her room, but she had heard the bang. In fact, it had woken her up—just like something going off, it was.

"It was Mr. Mark's voice," said Elsie firmly.

"Pleading for mercy," said an eager-eyed kitchen-maid hopefully from the door, and was hurried out again by the others, wishing that she had not given her presence away. But it was hard to listen in silence when she knew so well from her novelettes just what happened on these occasions.

"I shall have to give that girl a piece of my mind," said Mrs. Stevens.

"Well, Elsie?"

"He said, I heard him say it with my own ears, 'It's my turn now,' he said, triumphant-like."

"Well, if you think that's a threat, dear, you're very particular, I must say."

But Audrey remembered Elsie's words when she was in front of Inspector Birch. She gave her own evidence with the readiness of one who had already repeated it several times, and was examined and cross-examined by the Inspector with considerable skill. The temptation to say, "Never mind about what you said to him," was strong, but he resisted it, knowing that in this way he would discover best what he said to her. By this time both his words and the looks he gave her were getting their full value from Audrey, but the general meaning of them seemed to be well-established.

"Then you didn't see Mr. Mark at all."

"No, sir; he must have come in before and gone up to his room. Or come in by the front door, likely enough, while I was going out by the back."

"Yes. Well, I think that's all that I want to know, thank you very much. Now what about the other servants?"

"Elsie heard the master and Mr. Robert talking together," said Audrey eagerly. "He was saying—Mr. Mark, I mean—"

"Ah! Well, I think Elsie had better tell me that herself. Who is Elsie, by the way?"

"One of the housemaids. Shall I send her to you, sir?"

"Please."

Elsie was not sorry to get the message. It interrupted a few remarks from Mrs. Stevens about Elsie's conduct that afternoon which were (Elsie thought) much better interrupted. In Mrs. Stevens' opinion any crime committed that afternoon in the office was as nothing to the double crime committed by the unhappy Elsie.

For Elsie realized too late that she would have done better to have said nothing about her presence in the hall that afternoon. She was bad at concealing the truth and Mrs. Stevens was good at discovering it. Elsie knew perfectly well that she had no business to come down the front stairs, and it was no excuse to say that she happened to come out of Miss Norris' room just at the head of the stairs, and didn't think it would matter, as there was nobody in the hall, and what was she doing anyhow in Miss Norris' room at that time? Returning a magazine? Lent by Miss Norris, might she ask? Well, not exactly lent. Really, Elsie!—and this in a respectable house! In vain for poor Elsie to plead that a story by her favourite author was advertised on the cover, with a picture of the villain falling over the cliff. "That's where you'll go to, my girl, if you aren't careful," said Mrs. Stevens firmly.

But, of course, there was no need to confess all these crimes to Inspector Birch. All that interested him was that she was passing through the hall, and heard voices in the office.

"And stopped to listen?"

"Certainly not," said Elsie with dignity, feeling that nobody really understood her. "I was just passing through the hall, just as you might have been yourself, and not supposing they was talking secrets, didn't think to stop my ears, as no doubt I ought to have done." And she sniffed slightly.

"Come, come," said the Inspector soothingly, "I didn't mean to suggest—"

"Everyone is very unkind to me," said Elsie between sniffs, "and there's that poor man lying dead there, and sorry they'd have been, if it had been me, to have spoken to me as they have done this day."

"Nonsense, we're going to be very proud of you. I shouldn't be surprised if your evidence were of very great importance. Now then, what was it you heard? Try to remember the exact words."

Something about working in a passage, thought Elsie.

"Yes, but who said it?"

"Mr. Robert."

"How do you know it was Mr. Robert? Had you heard his voice before?"

"I don't take it upon myself to say that I had had any acquaintance with Mr. Robert, but seeing that it wasn't Mr. Mark, nor yet Mr. Cayley, nor any other of the gentlemen, and Miss Stevens had shown Mr. Robert into the office not five minutes before—"

"Quite so," said the Inspector hurriedly. "Mr. Robert, undoubtedly. Working in a passage?"

"That was what it sounded like, sir."

"H'm. Working a passage over—could that have been it?"

"That's right, sir," said Elsie eagerly. "He'd worked his passage over."

"Well?"

"And then Mr. Mark said loudly—sort of triumphant-like—'It's my turn now. You wait.'"

"Triumphantly?"

"As much as to say his chance had come."

"And that's all you heard?"

"That's all, sir—not standing there listening, but just passing through the hall, as it might be any time."

"Yes. Well, that's really very important, Elsie. Thank you."

Elsie gave him a smile, and returned eagerly to the kitchen.

She was ready for Mrs. Stevens or anybody now.

Meanwhile Antony had been exploring a little on his own. There was a point which was puzzling him. He went through the hall to the front of the house and stood at the open door, looking out on to the drive. He and Cayley had run round the house to the left. Surely it would have been quicker to have run round to the right? The front door was not in the middle of the house, it was to the end. Undoubtedly they went the longest way round. But perhaps there was something in the way, if one went to the right—a wall, say. He strolled off in that direction, followed a path round the house and came in sight of the office windows. Quite simple, and about half the distance of the other way. He went on a little farther, and came to a door, just beyond the broken-in windows. It opened easily, and he found himself in a passage. At the end of the passage was another door. He opened it and found himself in the hall again.

"And, of course, that's the quickest way of the three," he said to himself. "Through the hall, and out at the back; turn to the left and there you are. Instead of which, we ran the longest way round the house. Why? Was it to give Mark more time in which to escape? Only, in that case—why run? Also, how did Cayley know then that it was Mark who was trying to escape? If he had guessed—well, not guessed, but been afraid—that one had shot the other, it was much more likely that Robert had shot Mark. Indeed, he had admitted that this was what he thought. The first thing he had said when he turned the body over was, 'Thank God! I was afraid it was Mark.' But why should he want to give Robert time in which to get away? And again—why run, if he did want to give him time?"

Antony went out of the house again to the lawns at the back, and sat down on a bench in view of the office windows.

"Now then," he said, "let's go through Cayley's mind carefully, and see what we get."

Cayley had been in the hall when Robert was shown into the office. The servant goes off to look for Mark, and Cayley goes on with his book. Mark comes down the stairs, warns Cayley to stand by in case he is wanted, and goes to meet his brother. What does Cayley expect? Possibly that he won't be wanted at all; possibly that his advice may be wanted in the matter, say, of paying Robert's debts, or getting him a passage back to Australia;

possibly that his physical assistance may be wanted to get an obstreperous Robert out of the house. Well, he sits there for a moment, and then goes into the library. Why not? He is still within reach, if wanted. Suddenly he hears a pistol-shot. A pistol-shot is the last noise you expect to hear in a country-house; very natural, then, that for the moment he would hardly realize what it was. He listens—and hears nothing more. Perhaps it wasn't a pistol-shot after all. After a moment or two he goes to the library door again. The profound silence makes him uneasy now. Was it a pistol-shot? Absurd! Still—no harm in going into the office on some excuse, just to reassure himself. So he tries the door—and finds it locked!

What are his emotions now? Alarm, uncertainty. Something is happening. Incredible though it seems, it must have been a pistol-shot. He is banging at the door and calling out to Mark, and there is no answer. Alarm—yes. But alarm for whose safety? Mark's, obviously. Robert is a stranger; Mark is an intimate friend. Robert has written a letter that morning, the letter of a man in a dangerous temper. Robert is the tough customer; Mark the highly civilized gentleman. If there has been a quarrel, it is Robert who has shot Mark. He bangs at the door again.

Of course, to Antony, coming suddenly upon this scene, Cayley's conduct had seemed rather absurd, but then, just for the moment, Cayley had lost his head. Anybody else might have done the same. But, as soon as Antony suggested trying the windows, Cayley saw that that was the obvious thing to do. So he leads the way to the windows—the longest way.

Why? To give the murderer time to escape? If he had thought then that Mark was the murderer, perhaps, yes. But he thinks that Robert is the murderer. If he is not hiding anything, he must think so. Indeed he says so, when he sees the body; "I was afraid it was Mark," he says, when he finds that it is Robert who is killed. No reason, then, for wishing to gain time. On the contrary, every instinct would urge him to get into the room as quickly as possible, and seize the wicked Robert. Yet he goes the longest way round. Why? And then, why run?

"That's the question," said Antony to himself, as he filled his pipe, "and bless me if I know the answer. It may be, of course, that Cayley is just a coward. He was in no hurry to get close to Robert's revolver, and yet wanted me to think that he was bursting with eagerness. That would explain it, but then that makes Cayley out a coward. Is he? At any rate he pushed his face up against the window bravely enough. No, I want a better answer than that."

He sat there with his unlit pipe in his hand, thinking. There were one or two other things in the back of his brain, waiting to be taken out and looked at. For the moment he left them undisturbed. They would come back to him later when he wanted them.

He laughed suddenly, and lit his pipe.

"I was wanting a new profession," he thought, "and now I've found it.

Antony Gillingham, our own private sleuthhound. I shall begin to-day."

Whatever Antony Gillingham's other qualifications for his new profession, he had at any rate a brain which worked clearly and quickly. And this clear brain of his had already told him that he was the only person in the house at that moment who was unhandicapped in the search for truth. The inspector had arrived in it to find a man dead and a man missing. It was extremely probable, no doubt, that the missing man had shot the dead man. But it was more than extremely probable, it was almost certain that the Inspector would start with the idea that this extremely probable solution was the one true solution, and that, in consequence, he would be less disposed to consider without prejudice any other solution. As regards all the rest of them—Cayley, the guests, the servants—they also were prejudiced; in favour of Mark (or possibly, for all he knew, against Mark); in favour of, or against, each other; they had formed some previous opinion, from what had been said that morning, of the sort of man Robert was. No one of them could consider the matter with an unbiased mind.

But Antony could. He knew nothing about Mark; he knew nothing about Robert. He had seen the dead man before he was told who the dead man was. He knew that a tragedy had happened before he knew that anybody was missing. Those first impressions, which are so vitally important, had been received solely on the merits of the case; they were founded on the evidence of his senses, not on the evidence of his emotions or of other people's senses. He was in a much better position for getting at the truth than was the Inspector.

It is possible that, in thinking this, Antony was doing Inspector Birch a slight injustice. Birch was certainly prepared to believe that Mark had shot his brother. Robert had been shown into the office (witness Audrey); Mark had gone in to Robert (witness Cayley); Mark and Robert had been heard talking (witness Elsie); there was a shot (witness everybody); the room had been entered and Robert's body had been found (witness Cayley and Gillingham). And Mark was missing. Obviously, then, Mark had killed his brother: accidentally, as Cayley believed, or deliberately, as Elsie's evidence seemed to suggest. There was no point in looking for a difficult solution to a problem, when the easy solution had no flaw in it. But at the same time Birch would have preferred the difficult solution, simply because there was more credit attached to it. A "sensational" arrest of somebody in the house would have given him more pleasure than a commonplace pursuit of Mark Ablett across country. Mark must be found, guilty or not guilty. But there were other possibilities. It would have interested Antony to know that, just at the time when he was feeling rather superior to the prejudiced inspector, the Inspector himself was letting his mind dwell lovingly upon the possibilities in connection with Mr. Gillingham. Was it only a coincidence that Mr. Gillingham had turned up just when he did? And Mr. Beverley's curious answers when asked for some account of his friend. An assistant in a tobacconist's, a waiter! An odd man, Mr. Gillingham, evidently. It might be as well to keep an eye on him.

CHAPTER VI

OUTSIDE OR INSIDE?

The guests had said good-bye to Cayley, according to their different manner. The Major, gruff and simple: "If you want me, command me. Anything I can do—Good-bye"; Betty, silently sympathetic, with everything in her large eyes which she was too much overawed to tell; Mrs. Calladine, protesting that she did not know what to say, but apparently finding plenty; and Miss Norris, crowding so much into one despairing gesture that Cayley's unvarying "Thank you very much" might have been taken this time as gratitude for an artistic entertainment.

Bill had seen them into the car, had taken his own farewells (with a special squeeze of the hand for Betty), and had wandered out to join Antony on his garden seat.

"Well, this is a rum show," said Bill as he sat down.

"Very rum, William."

"And you actually walked right into it?"

"Right into it," said Antony.

"Then you're the man I want. There are all sorts of rumours and mysteries about, and that inspector fellow simply wouldn't keep to the point when I wanted to ask him about the murder, or whatever it is, but kept asking me questions about where I'd met you first, and all sorts of dull things like that. Now, what really happened?"

Antony told him as concisely as he could all that he had already told the Inspector, Bill interrupting him here and there with appropriate "Good Lords" and whistles.

"I say, it's a bit of a business, isn't it? Where do I come in, exactly?"

"How do you mean?"

"Well, everybody else is bundled off except me, and I get put through it by that inspector as if I knew all about it—what's the idea?"

Antony smiled at him.

"Well, there's nothing to worry about, you know. Naturally Birch wanted to see one of you so as to know what you'd all been doing all day. And Cayley was nice enough to think that you'd be company for me, as I knew you already. And well, that's all."

"You're staying here, in the house?" said Bill eagerly. "Good man. That's splendid."

"It reconciles you to the departure of some of the others?"

Bill blushed.

"Oh, well, I shall see her again next week, anyway," he murmured.

"I congratulate you. I liked her looks. And that grey dress. A nice comfortable sort of woman."

"You fool, that's her mother."

"Oh, I beg your pardon. But anyhow, Bill, I want you more than she does just now. So try and put up with me."

"I say, do you really?" said Bill, rather flattered. He had a great admiration for Antony, and was very proud to be liked by him.

"Yes. You see, things are going to happen here soon."

"Inquests and that sort of thing?"

"Well, perhaps something before that. Hallo, here comes Cayley."

Cayley was walking across the lawn towards them, a big, heavy-shouldered man, with one of those strong, clean-shaven, ugly faces which can never quite be called plain. "Bad luck on Cayley," said Bill. "I say, ought I to tell him how sorry I am and all that sort of thing? It seems so dashed inadequate."

"I shouldn't bother," said Antony.

Cayley nodded as he came to them, and stood there for a moment.

"We can make room for you," said Bill, getting up.

"Oh, don't bother, thanks. I just came to say," he went on to Antony, "that naturally they've rather lost their heads in the kitchen, and dinner won't be till half-past eight. Do just as you like about dressing, of course. And what about your luggage?"

"I thought Bill and I would walk over to the inn directly, and see about it."

"The car can go and fetch it as soon as it comes back from the station."

"It's very good of you, but I shall have to go over myself, anyhow, to pack up and pay my bill. Besides, it's a good evening for a walk. If you wouldn't mind it, Bill?"

"I should love it."

"Well, then, if you leave the bag there, I'll send the car round for it later."

"Thanks very much."

Having said what he wanted to say, Cayley remained there a little awkwardly, as if not sure whether to go or to stay. Antony wondered whether he wanted to talk about the afternoon's happenings, or whether it was the one subject he wished to avoid. To break the silence he asked carelessly if the Inspector had gone.

Cayley nodded. Then he said abruptly, "He's getting a warrant for Mark's arrest."

Bill made a suitably sympathetic noise, and Antony said with a shrug of the shoulders, "Well, he was bound to do that, wasn't he? It doesn't follow that—well, it doesn't mean anything. They naturally want to get hold of your cousin, innocent or guilty."

"Which do you think he is, Mr. Gillingham?" said Cayley, looking at him steadily.

"Mark? It's absurd," said Bill impetuously.

"Bill's loyal, you see, Mr. Cayley."

"And you owe no loyalty to anyone concerned?"

"Exactly. So perhaps I might be too frank."

Bill had dropped down on the grass, and Cayley took his place on the seat, and sat there heavily, his elbows on his knees, his chin on his hands, gazing at the ground.

"I want you to be quite frank," he said at last. "Naturally I am prejudiced where Mark is concerned. So I want to know how my suggestion strikes you who have no prejudices either way."

"Your suggestion?"

"My theory that, if Mark killed his brother, it was purely accidental as I told the Inspector."

Bill looked up with interest.

"You mean that Robert did the hold-up business," he said, "and there was a bit of a struggle, and the revolver went off, and then Mark lost his head and bolted? That sort of idea?"

"Exactly."

"Well, that seems all right." He turned to Antony. "There's nothing wrong with that, is there? It's the most natural explanation to anyone who knows Mark."

Antony pulled at his pipe.

"I suppose it is," he said slowly. "But there's one thing that worries me rather."

"What's that?" Bill and Cayley asked the question simultaneously.

"The key."

"The key?" said Bill.

Cayley lifted his head and looked at Antony. "What about the key?" he asked.

"Well, there may be nothing in it; I just wondered. Suppose Robert was killed as you say, and suppose Mark lost his head and thought of nothing but getting away before anyone could see him. Well, very likely he'd lock the door and put the key in his pocket. He'd do it without thinking, just to gain a moment's time."

"Yes, that's what I suggest."

"It seems sound enough," said Bill. "Sort of thing you'd do without thinking. Besides, if you are going to run away, it gives you more of a chance."

"Yes, that's all right if the key is there. But suppose it isn't there?"

The suggestion, made as if it were already an established fact, startled them both. They looked at him wonderingly.

"What do you mean?" said Cayley.

"Well, it's just a question of where people happen to keep their keys. You go up to your bedroom, and perhaps you like to lock your door in case anybody comes wandering in when you've only got one sock and a pair of braces on. Well, that's natural enough. And if you look round the bedrooms of almost any house, you'll find the keys all ready, so that you can lock yourself in at a moment's notice. But downstairs people don't lock themselves in. It's really never done at all. Bill, for instance, has never locked himself into the dining-room in order to be alone with the sherry. On the other hand, all women, and particularly servants, have a horror of burglars. And if a burglar gets in by the window, they like to limit his activities to that particular room. So they keep the keys on the outside of the doors, and lock the doors when they go to bed." He knocked the ashes out of his pipe, and added, "At least, my mother always used to."

"You mean," said Bill excitedly, "that the key was on the outside of the door when Mark went into the room?"

"Well, I was just wondering."

"Have you noticed the other rooms—the billiard-room, and library, and so on?" said Cayley.

"I've only just thought about it while I've been sitting out here. You live here—haven't you ever noticed them?"

Cayley sat considering, with his head on one side.

"It seems rather absurd, you know, but I can't say that I have." He turned to Bill. "Have you?"

"Good Lord, no. I should never worry about a thing like that."

"I'm sure you wouldn't," laughed Antony. "Well, we can have a look when we go in. If the other keys are outside, then this one was probably outside too, and in that case well, it makes it more interesting."

Cayley said nothing. Bill chewed a piece of grass, and then said, "Does it make much difference?"

"It makes it more hard to understand what happened in there. Take your accidental theory and see where you get to. No instinctive turning of the key now, is there? He's got to open the door to get it, and opening the door means showing his head to anybody in the hall—his cousin, for instance, whom he left there two minutes ago. Is a man in Mark's state of mind, frightened to death lest he should be found with the body, going to do anything so foolhardy as that?"

"He needn't have been afraid of me," said Cayley.

"Then why didn't he call for you? He knew you were about. You could have advised him; Heaven knows he wanted advice. But the whole theory of Mark's escape is that he was afraid of you and of everybody else, and that he had no other idea but to get out of the room himself, and prevent you or the servants from coming into it. If the key had been on the inside, he would probably have locked the door. If it were on the outside, he almost certainly wouldn't."

"Yes, I expect you're right," said Bill thoughtfully. "Unless he took the key in with him, and locked the door at once."

"Exactly. But in that case you have to build up a new theory entirely."

"You mean that it makes it seem more deliberate?"

"Yes; that, certainly. But it also seems to make Mark out an absolute idiot. Just suppose for a moment that, for urgent reasons which neither of you know anything about, he had wished to get rid of his brother. Would he have done it like that? Just killed him and then run away? Why, that's practically suicide—suicide whilst of unsound mind. No. If you really wanted to remove an undesirable brother, you would do it a little bit more cleverly than that. You'd begin by treating him as a friend, so as to avoid suspicion, and when you did kill him at last, you would try to make it look like an accident, or suicide, or the work of some other man. Wouldn't you?"

"You mean you'd give yourself a bit of a run for your money?"

"Yes, that's what I mean. If you were going to do it deliberately, that is to say and lock yourself in before you began."

Cayley had been silent, apparently thinking over this new idea. With his eyes still on the ground, he said now: "I hold to my opinion that it was purely accidental, and that Mark lost his head and ran away."

"But what about the key?" asked Bill.

"We don't know yet that the keys were outside. I don't at all agree with Mr. Gillingham that the keys of the down-stairs rooms are always outside the doors. Sometimes they are, no doubt; but I think we shall probably find that these are inside."

"Oh, well, of course, if they are inside, then your original theory is probably the correct one. Having often seen them outside, I just wondered that's all. You asked me to be quite frank, you know, and tell you what I thought. But no doubt you're right, and we shall find them inside, as you say.

"Even if the key was outside," went on Cayley stubbornly, "I still think it might have been accidental. He might have taken it in with him, knowing that the interview would be an unpleasant one, and not wishing to be interrupted."

"But he had just told you to stand by in case he wanted you; so why should he lock you out? Besides, I should think that if a man were going to have an unpleasant interview with a threatening relation, the last thing he would do would be to barricade himself in with him. He would want to open all the doors and say, 'Get out of it'"

Cayley was silent, but his mouth looked obstinate. Antony gave a little apologetic laugh and stood up.

"Well, come on, Bill," he said; "we ought to be stepping." He held out a hand and pulled his friend up. Then, turning to Cayley, he went on, "You must forgive me if I have let my thoughts run on rather. Of course, I was considering the matter purely as an outsider; just as a problem, I mean, which didn't concern the happiness of any of my friends."

"That's all right, Mr. Gillingham," said Cayley, standing up too. "It is for you to make allowances for me. I'm sure you will. You say that you're going up to the inn now about your bag?"

"Yes." He looked up at the sun and then round the parkland stretching about the house. "Let me see; it's over in that direction, isn't it?" He pointed southwards. "Can we get to the village that way, or must we go by the road?"

"I'll show you, my boy," said Bill.

"Bill will show you. The park reaches almost as far as the village. Then I'll send the car round in about half an hour."

"Thanks very much."

Cayley nodded and turned to go into the house. Antony took hold of Bill's arm and walked off with him in the opposite direction.

CHAPTER VII

PORTRAIT OF A GENTLEMAN

They walked in silence for a little, until they had left the house and gardens well behind them. In front of them and to the right the park dipped and then rose slowly, shutting out the rest of the world. A thick belt of trees on the left divided them from the main road.

"Ever been here before?" said Antony suddenly.

"Oh, rather. Dozens of times."

"I meant just here where we are now. Or do you stay indoors and play billiards all the time?"

"Oh Lord, no!"

"Well, tennis and things. So many people with beautiful parks never by any chance use them, and all the poor devils passing by on the dusty road think how lucky the owners are to have them, and imagine them doing all sorts of jolly things inside." He pointed to the right. "Ever been over there?"

Bill laughed, as if a little ashamed.

"Well, not very much. I've often been along here, of course, because it's the short way to the village."

"Yes.... All right; now tell me something about Mark."

"What sort of things?"

"Well, never mind about his being your host, or about your being a perfect gentleman, or anything like that. Cut out the Manners for Men, and tell me what you think of Mark, and how you like staying with him, and how many rows your little house-party has had this week, and how you get on with Cayley, and all the rest of it."

Bill looked at him eagerly.

"I say, are you being the complete detective?"

"Well, I wanted a new profession," smiled the other.

"What fun! I mean," he corrected himself apologetically, "one oughtn't to say that, when there's a man dead in the house, and one's host—" He broke off a little uncertainly, and then rounded off his period by saying again, "By Jove, what a rum show it is. Good Lord!"

"Well?" said Antony. "Carry on, Mark."

"What do I think of him?"

"Yes."

Bill was silent, wondering how to put into words thoughts which had never formed themselves very definitely in his own mind. What did he think of Mark? Seeing his hesitation, Antony said:

"I ought to have warned you that nothing that you say will be taken down by the reporters, so you needn't bother about a split infinitive or two. Talk about anything you like, how you like. Well, I'll give you a start. Which do you enjoy more a week-end here or at the Barrington's, say?"

"Well; of course, that would depend—"

"Take it that she was there in both cases."

"Ass," said Bill, putting an elbow into Antony's ribs. "It's a little difficult to say," he went on. "Of course they do you awfully well here."

"Yes."

"I don't think I know any house where things are so

comfortable. One's room—the food—drinks—cigars—the way everything's arranged: All that sort of thing. They look after you awfully well."

"Yes?"

"Yes." He repeated it slowly to himself, as if it had given him a new idea: "They look after you awfully well. Well, that's just what it is about Mark. That's one of his little ways. Weaknesses. Looking after you."

"Arranging things for you?"

"Yes. Of course, it's a delightful house, and there's plenty to do, and opportunities for every game or sport that's ever been invented, and, as I say, one gets awfully well done; but with it all, Tony, there's a faint sort of feeling that well, that one is on parade, as it were. You've got to do as you're told."

"How do you mean?"

"Well, Mark fancies himself rather at arranging things. He arranges things, and it's understood that the guests fall in with the arrangement. For instance, Betty—Miss Calladine—and I were going to play a single just before tea, the other day. Tennis. She's frightfully hot stuff at tennis, and backed herself to take me on level. I'm rather erratic, you know. Mark saw us going out with our rackets and asked us what we were going to do. Well, he'd got up a little tournament for us after tea—handicaps all arranged by him, and everything ruled out neatly in red and black ink—prizes and all—quite decent ones, you know. He'd had the lawn specially cut and marked for it. Well, of course Betty and I wouldn't have spoilt the court, and we'd have been quite ready to play again after tea—I had to give her half-fifteen according to his handicap—but somehow—" Bill stopped and shrugged his shoulders.

"It didn't quite fit in?"

"No. It spoilt the effect of his tournament. Took the edge off it just a little, I suppose he felt. So we didn't play." He laughed, and added, "It would have been as much as our place was worth to have played."

"Do you mean you wouldn't have been asked here again?"

"Probably. Well, I don't know. Not for some time, anyway."

"Really, Bill?"

"Oh, rather! He's a devil for taking offence. That Miss Norris, did you see her? She's done for herself. I don't mind betting what you like that she never comes here again."

"Why?"

Bill laughed to himself.

"We were all in it, really—at least, Betty and I were. There's supposed to be a ghost attached to the house. Lady Anne Patten. Ever heard of her?"

"Never."

"Mark told us about her at dinner one night. He rather liked the idea of there being a ghost in his house, you know; except that he doesn't believe in ghosts. I think he wanted all of us to believe in her, and yet he was annoyed with Betty and Mrs. Calladine for believing in ghosts at all. Rum chap. Well, anyhow, Miss Norris—she's an actress, some actress too—dressed up as the ghost and played the fool a bit. And poor Mark was frightened out of his life. Just for a moment, you know."

"What about the others?"

"Well, Betty and I knew; in fact, I'd told her—Miss Norris I mean—not to be a silly ass. Knowing Mark. Mrs. Calladine wasn't there—Betty wouldn't let her be. As for the Major, I don't believe anything would frighten him."

"Where did the ghost appear?"

"Down by the bowling-green. That's supposed to be its haunt, you know. We were all down there in the moonlight, pretending to wait for it. Do you know the bowling-green?"

"No."

"I'll show it to you after dinner."

"I wish you would.... Was Mark very angry afterwards?"

"Oh, Lord, yes. Sulked for a whole day. Well, he's just like that."

"Was he angry with all of you?"

"Oh, yes sulky, you know."

"This morning?"

"Oh, no. He got over it he generally does. He's just like a child. That's really it, Tony; he's like a child in some ways. As a matter of fact, he was unusually bucked with himself this morning. And yesterday."

"Yesterday?"

"Rather. We all said we'd never seen him in such form."

"Is he generally in form?"

"He's quite good company, you know, if you take him the

right way. He's rather vain and childish well, like I've been telling you and self-important; but quite amusing in his way, and—" Bill broke off suddenly. "I say, you know, it really is the limit, talking about your host like this."

"Don't think of him as your host. Think of him as a suspected murderer with a warrant out against him."

"Oh! but that's all rot, you know."

"It's the fact, Bill."

"Yes, but I mean, he didn't do it. He wouldn't murder anybody. It's a funny thing to say, but well, he's not big enough for it. He's got his faults, like all of us, but they aren't on that scale."

"One can kill anybody in a childish fit of temper."

Bill grunted assent, but without prejudice to Mark. "All the same," he said, "I can't believe it. That he would do it deliberately, I mean."

"Suppose it was an accident, as Cayley says, would he lose his head and run away?"

Bill considered for a moment.

"Yes, I really think he might, you know. He nearly ran away when he saw the ghost. Of course, that's different, rather."

"Oh, I don't know. In each case it's a question of obeying your instinct instead of your reason."

They had left the open land and were following a path through the bordering trees. Two abreast was uncomfortable, so Antony dropped behind, and further conversation was postponed until they were outside the boundary fence and in the high road. The road sloped gently down to the village of Waldheim a few red-roofed cottages, and the grey tower of a church showing above the green.

"Well, now," said Antony, as they stepped out more quickly, "what about Cayley?"

"How do you mean, what about him?"

"I want to see him. I can see Mark perfectly, thanks to you, Bill. You were wonderful. Now let's have Cayley's character. Cayley from within."

Bill laughed in pleased embarrassment, and protested that he was not a blooming novelist.

"Besides," he added, "Mark's easy. Cayley's one of these heavy, quiet people, who might be thinking about anything.

Mark gives himself away.... Ugly, black-jawed devil, isn't he?"

"Some women like that type of ugliness."

"Yes, that's true. Between ourselves, I think there's one here who does. Rather a pretty girl at Jallands" he waved his left hand "down that way."

"What's Jallands?"

"Well, I suppose it used to be a farm, belonging to a bloke called Jalland, but now it's a country cottage belonging to a widow called Norbury. Mark and Cayley used to go there a good deal together. Miss Norbury—the girl—has been here once or twice for tennis; seemed to prefer Cayley to the rest of us. But of course he hadn't much time for that sort of thing."

"What sort of thing?"

"Walking about with a pretty girl and asking her if she's been to any theatres lately. He nearly always had something to do."

"Mark kept him busy?"

"Yes. Mark never seemed quite happy unless he had Cayley doing something for him. He was quite lost and helpless without him. And, funnily enough, Cayley seemed lost without Mark."

"He was fond of him?"

"Yes, I should say so. In a protective kind of way. He'd sized Mark up, of course his vanity, his self-importance, his amateurishness and all the rest of it but he liked looking after him. And he knew how to manage him."

"Yes.... What sort of terms was he on with the guests—you and Miss Norris and all of them?"

"Just polite and rather silent, you know. Keeping himself to himself. We didn't see so very much of him, except at meals. We were here to enjoy ourselves, and well, he wasn't."

"He wasn't there when the ghost walked?"

"No. I heard Mark calling for him when he went back to the house. I expect Cayley stroked down his feathers a bit, and told him that girls will be girls....—Hallo, here we are."

They went into the inn, and while Bill made himself pleasant to the landlady, Antony went upstairs to his room. It appeared that he had not very much packing to do, after all. He returned his brushes to his bag, glanced round to see that nothing else had been taken out, and went down again to settle his bill. He had decided to keep on his room for a few days; partly to save the landlord and his wife the disappointment of losing a guest so suddenly, partly in case he found it undesirable later on to remain at the Red House. For he was taking himself seriously as a detective; indeed, he took himself seriously (while getting all the fun out of it which was possible) at every new profession he adopted; and he felt that there might come a time after the inquest, say when he could not decently remain at the Red House as a guest, a friend of Bill's, enjoying the hospitality of Mark or Cayley, whichever was to be regarded as his host, without forfeiting his independent attitude towards the events of that afternoon. At present he was staying in the house merely as a necessary witness, and, since he was there, Cayley could not object to him using his eyes; but if, after the inquest, it appeared that there was still work for a pair of independent and very keen eyes to do, then he must investigate, either with his host's approval or from beneath the roof of some other host; the landlord of 'The George,' for instance, who had no feelings in the matter.

For of one thing Antony was certain. Cayley knew more than he professed to know. That is to say, he knew more than he wanted other people to know he knew. Antony was one of the "other people"; if, therefore, he was for trying to find out what it was that Cayley knew, he could hardly expect Cayley's approval of his labours. It would be 'The George,' then, for Antony after the inquest.

What was the truth? Not necessarily discreditable to Cayley, even though he were hiding something. All that could be said against him at the moment was that he had gone the longest way round to get into the locked office and that this did not fit in with what he had told the Inspector. But it did fit in with the theory that he had been an accessory after the event, and that he wanted (while appearing to be in a hurry) to give his cousin as much time as possible in which to escape. That might not be the true solution, but it was at least a workable one. The theory which he had suggested to the Inspector was not.

However, there would be a day or two before the inquest, in which Antony could consider all these matters from within The Red House. The car was at the door. He got in with Bill, the landlord put his bag on the front seat next to the chauffeur, and they drove back.

CHAPTER VIII

"DO YOU FOLLOW ME, WATSON?"

Anthony's bedroom looked over the park at the back of the house. The blinds were not yet drawn while he was changing his clothes for dinner, and at various stages of undress he would pause and gaze out of the window, sometimes smiling to himself, sometimes frowning, as he turned over in his mind all the strange things that he had seen that day. He was sitting on his bed, in shirt and trousers, absently smoothing down his thick black hair with his brushes, when Bill shouted an "Hallo!" through the door, and came in.

"I say, buck up, old boy, I'm hungry," he said.

Antony stopped smoothing himself and looked up at him thoughtfully.

"Where's Mark?" he said.

"Mark? You mean Cayley."

Antony corrected himself with a little laugh. "Yes, I mean Cayley. Is he down? I say, I shan't be a moment, Bill." He got up from the bed and went on briskly with his dressing. "Oh, by the way," said Bill, taking his place on the bed, "your idea about the keys is a wash-out."

"Why, how do you mean?"

"I went down just now and had a look at them. We were asses not to have thought of it when we came in. The library key is outside, but all the others are inside."

"Yes, I know."

"You devil, I suppose you did think of it, then?"

"I did, Bill," said Antony apologetically.

"Bother! I hoped you'd forgotten. Well, that knocks your theory on the head, doesn't it?"

"I never had a theory. I only said that if they were outside, it would probably mean that the office key was outside, and that in that case Cayley's theory was knocked on the head."

"Well, now, it isn't, and we don't know anything. Some were outside and some inside, and there you are. It makes it much less exciting. When you were talking about it on the lawn, I really got quite keen on the idea of the key being outside and Mark taking it in with him."

"It's going to be exciting enough," said Antony mildly, as he transferred his pipe and tobacco into the pocket of his black coat. "Well, let's come down; I'm ready now."

Cayley was waiting for them in the hall. He made some polite inquiry as to the guest's comfort, and the three of them fell into a casual conversation about houses in general and The Red House in particular.

"You were quite right about the keys," said Bill, during a pause. He was less able than the other two, perhaps because he was younger than they, to keep away from the subject which was uppermost in the minds of them all.

"Keys?" said Cayley blankly.

"We were wondering whether they were outside or inside."

"Oh! oh, yes!" He looked slowly round the hall, at the different doors, and then smiled in a friendly way at Antony. "We both seem to have been right, Mr. Gillingham. So we don't get much farther."

"No." He gave a shrug. "I just wondered, you know. I thought it was worth mentioning."

"Oh, quite. Not that you would have convinced me, you know. Just as Elsie's evidence doesn't convince me."

"Elsie?" said Bill excitedly. Antony looked inquiringly at him, wondering who Elsie was.

"One of the housemaids," explained Cayley. "You didn't hear what she told the Inspector? Of course, as I told Birch, girls of that class make things up, but he seemed to think she was genuine."

"What was it?" said Bill.

Cayley told them of what Elsie had heard through the office door that afternoon.

"You were in the library then, of course," said Antony, rather to himself than to the other. "She might have gone through the hall without your hearing."

"Oh, I've no doubt she was there, and heard voices. Perhaps heard those very words. But—" He broke off, and then added impatiently, "It was accidental. I know it was accidental. What's the good of talking as if Mark was a murderer?" Dinner was announced at that moment, and as they went in, he added, "What's the good of talking about it at all, if it comes to that?"

"What, indeed?" said Antony, and to Bill's great disappointment they talked of books and politics during the meal.

Cayley made an excuse for leaving them as soon as their cigars were alight. He had business to attend to, as was natural. Bill would look after his friend. Bill was only too willing. He offered to beat Antony at billiards, to play him at piquet, to show him the garden by moonlight, or indeed to do anything else with him that he required.

"Thank the Lord you're here," he said piously. "I couldn't have stood it alone."

"Let's go outside," suggested Antony. "It's quite warm. Somewhere where we can sit down, right away from the house. I want to talk to you."

"Good man. What about the bowling-green?"

"Oh, you were going to show me that, anyhow, weren't you? Is it somewhere where we can talk without being overheard?"

"Rather. The ideal place. You'll see."

They came out of the front door and followed the drive to the left. Coming from Waldheim, Antony had approached the house that afternoon from the other side. The way they were going now would take them out at the opposite end of the park, on the high road to Stanton, a country town some three miles away. They passed by a gate and a gardener's lodge, which marked the limit of what auctioneers like to call "the ornamental grounds of the estate," and then the open park was before them.

"Sure we haven't missed it?" said Antony. The park lay quietly in the moonlight on either side of the drive, wearing a little way ahead of them a deceptive air of smoothness which retreated always as they advanced.

"Rum, isn't it?" said Bill. "An absurd place for a bowling green, but I suppose it was always here."

"Yes, but always where? It's short enough for golf, perhaps, but—Hallo!"

They had come to the place. The road bent round to the right, but they kept straight on over a broad grass path for twenty yards, and there in front of them was the green. A dry ditch, ten feet wide and six feet deep, surrounded it, except in the one place where the path went forward. Two or three grass steps led down to the green, on which there was a long wooden beach for the benefit of spectators.

"Yes, it hides itself very nicely," said Antony. "Where do you keep the bowls?"

"In a sort of summer house place. Round here."

They walked along the edge of the green until they came to it a low wooden bunk which had been built into one wall of the ditch.

"H'm. Jolly view."

Bill laughed.

"Nobody sits there. It's just for keeping things out of the rain."

They finished their circuit of the green "Just in case anybody's in the ditch," said Antony and then sat down on the bench.

"Now then," said Bill, "We are alone. Fire ahead."

Antony smoked thoughtfully for a little. Then he took his pipe out of his mouth and turned to his friend.

"Are you prepared to be the complete Watson?" he asked.

"Watson?"

"Do-you-follow-me-Watson; that one. Are you prepared to have quite obvious things explained to you, to ask futile questions, to give me chances of scoring off you, to make brilliant discoveries of your own two or three days after I have made them myself all that kind of thing? Because it all helps."

"My dear Tony," said Bill delightedly, "need you ask?" Antony said nothing, and Bill went on happily to himself, "I perceive from the strawberry-mark on your shirt-front that you had strawberries for dessert. Holmes, you astonish me. Tut, tut, you know my methods. Where is the tobacco? The tobacco is in the Persian slipper. Can I leave my practice for a week? I can."

Antony smiled and went on smoking. After waiting hopefully for a minute or two, Bill said in a firm voice:

"Well then, Holmes, I feel bound to ask you if you have deduced anything. Also whom do you suspcct?"

Antony began to talk.

"Do you remember," he said, "one of Holmes's little scores over Watson about the number of steps up to the Baker Street lodging? Poor old Watson had been up and down them a thousand times, but he had never thought of counting them, whereas Holmes had counted them as a matter of course, and knew that there were seventeen. And that was supposed to be the difference between observation and non-observation. Watson was crushed again, and Holmes appeared to him more amazing than ever. Now, it always seemed to me that in that matter Holmes was the ass, and Watson the sensible person. What on earth is the point of keeping in your head an unnecessary fact like that? If you really want to know at any time the number of steps to your lodging, you can ring up your landlady and ask her. I've been up and down the steps of the club a thousand times, but if you asked me to tell you at this moment how many steps there are I couldn't do it. Could you?"

"I certainly couldn't," said Bill.

"But if you really wanted to know," said Antony casually, with a sudden change of voice, "I could find out for you without even bothering to ring up the hall-porter."

Bill was puzzled as to why they were talking about the club steps, but he felt it his duty to say that he did want to know how many they were.

"Right," said Antony. "I'll find out."

He closed his eyes.

"I'm walking up St James' Street," he said slowly. "Now I've come to the club and I'm going past the smoking-room—windows-one-two three four. Now I'm at the steps. I turn in and begin going up them. One-two-three-four-five-six, then a broad step; six-seven-eight-nine, another broad step; nine-ten-eleven. Eleven I'm inside. Good morning, Rogers. Fine day again." With a little start he opened his eyes and came back again to his present surroundings. He turned to Bill with a smile. "Eleven," he said. "Count them the next time you're there. Eleven and now I hope I shall forget it again."

Bill was distinctly interested.

"That's rather hot," he said. "Expound."

"Well, I can't explain it, whether it's something in the actual eye, or something in the brain, or what, but I have got rather an uncanny habit of recording things unconsciously. You know that game where you look at a tray full of small objects for three minutes, and then turn away and try to make a list of them. It means a devil of a lot of concentration for the ordinary person, if he wants to get his list complete, but in some odd way I manage to do it without concentration at all. I mean that my eyes seem to do it without the brain consciously taking any part. I could look at the tray, for instance, and talk to you about golf at the same time, and still get my list right."

"I should think that's rather a useful gift for an amateur detective. You ought to have gone into the profession before."

"Well, it is rather useful. It's rather surprising, you know, to a stranger. Let's surprise Cayley with it, shall we?"

"How?"

"Well, let's ask him—" Antony stopped and looked at Bill comically, "let's ask him what he's going to do with the key of the office."

For a moment Bill did not understand.

"Key of the office?" he said vaguely. "You don't mean—Tony! What do you mean? Good God! do you mean that Cayley—But what about Mark?"

"I don't know where Mark is—that's another thing I want to know—but I'm quite certain that he hasn't got the key of the office with him. Because Cayley's got it."

"Are you sure?"

"Quite."

Bill looked at him wonderingly.

"I say," he said, almost pleadingly, "don't tell me that you can see into people's pockets and all that sort of thing as well."

Antony laughed and denied it cheerfully.

"Then how do you know?"

"You're the perfect Watson, Bill. You take to it quite naturally. Properly speaking, I oughtn't to explain till the last chapter, but I always think that that's so unfair. So here goes. Of course, I don't really know that he's got it, but I do know that he had it. I know that when I came on him this afternoon, he had just locked the door and put the key in his pocket."

"You mean you saw him at the time, but that you've only just remembered it—reconstructed it in the way you were explaining just now?"

"No. I didn't see him. But I did see something. I saw the key of the billiard-room."

"Where?

"Outside the billiard-room door."

"Outside? But it was inside when we looked just now."

"Exactly."

"Who put it there?"

"Obviously Cayley."

"But—"

"Let's go back to this afternoon. I don't remember noticing the billiard-room key at the time; I must have done so without knowing. Probably when I saw Cayley banging at the door I may have wondered subconsciously whether the key of the room next to it would fit. Something like that, I daresay. Well, when I was sitting out by myself on that seat just before you came along, I went over the whole scene in my mind, and I suddenly saw the billiard-room key there outside. And I began to wonder if the office-key had been outside too. When Cayley came up, I told you my idea and you were both interested. But Cayley was just a shade too interested. I daresay you didn't notice it, but he was."

"By Jove!"

"Well, of course that proved nothing; and the key business didn't really prove anything, because whatever side of the door the other keys were, Mark might have locked his own private room from the inside sometimes. But I piled it on, and pretended that it was enormously important, and quite altered the case altogether, and having got Cayley thoroughly anxious about it, I told him that we should be well out of the way for the next hour or so, and that he would be alone in the house to do what he liked about it. And, as I expected, he couldn't resist it. He altered the keys and gave himself away entirely."

"But the library key was still outside. Why didn't he alter that?"

"Because he's a clever devil. For one thing, the Inspector had been in the library, and might possibly have noticed it already. And for another—" Antony hesitated.

"What?" said Bill, after waiting for him to go on.

"It's only guesswork. But I fancy that Cayley was thoroughly upset about the key business. He suddenly realized that he had been careless, and he hadn't got time to think it all over. So he didn't want to commit himself definitely to the statement that the key was either outside or inside. He wanted to leave it vague. It was safest that way."

"I see," said Bill slowly.

But his mind was elsewhere. He was wondering suddenly about Cayley. Cayley was just an ordinary man—like himself. Bill had had little jokes with him sometimes; not that Cayley was much of a hand at joking. Bill had helped him to sausages, played tennis with him, borrowed his tobacco, lent him a putter.... and here was Antony saying that he was what? Well, not an ordinary man, anyway. A man with a secret. Perhaps a murderer. No, not a murderer; not Cayley. That was rot, anyway. Why, they had played tennis together.

"Now then, Watson," said Antony suddenly. "It's time you said something."

"I say, Tony, do you really mean it?"

"Mean what?"

"About Cayley."

"I mean what I said, Bill. No more."

"Well, what does it amount to?"

"Simply that Robert Ablett died in the office this afternoon, and that Cayley knows exactly how he died. That's all. It doesn't follow that Cayley killed him."

"No. No, of course it doesn't." Bill gave a sigh of relief. "He's just shielding Mark, what?"

"I wonder."

"Well, isn't that the simplest explanation?"

"It's the simplest if you're a friend of Cayley and want to let him down lightly. But then I'm not, you see."

"Why isn't it simple, anyhow?"

"Well, let's have the explanation then, and I'll undertake to give you a simpler one afterwards. Go on. Only remember the key is on the outside of the door to start with."

"Yes; well, I don't mind that. Mark goes in to see his brother, and they quarrel and all the rest of it, just as Cayley was saying. Cayley hears the shot, and in order to give Mark time to get away, locks the door, puts the key in his pocket and pretends that Mark has locked the door, and that he can't get in. How's that?"

"Hopeless, Watson, hopeless."

"Why?"

"How does Cayley know that it is Mark who has shot Robert, and not the other way round?"

"Oh!" said Bill, rather upset. "Yes." He thought for a moment, "All right. Say that Cayley has gone into the room first, and seen Robert on the ground."

"Well?"

"Well, there you are."

"And what does he say to Mark? That it's a fine afternoon; and could he lend him a pocket-handkerchief? Or does he ask him what's happened?"

"Well, of course, I suppose he asks what happened," said Bill reluctantly.

"And what does Mark say?"

"Explains that the revolver went off accidentally during a struggle."

"Whereupon Cayley shields him by doing what, Bill? Encouraging him to do the damn silliest thing that any man could possibly do—confess his guilt by running away!"

"No, that's rather hopeless, isn't it?" Bill thought again. "Well," he said reluctantly, "suppose Mark confessed that he'd murdered his brother?"

"That's better, Bill. Don't be afraid of getting away from the accident idea. Well then, your new theory is this. Mark confesses to Cayley that he shot Robert on purpose, and Cayley decides, even at the risk of committing perjury, and getting into trouble himself, to help Mark to escape. Is that right?"

Bill nodded.

"Well then, I want to ask you two questions. First, is it possible, as I said before dinner, that any man would commit such an idiotic murder—a murder that puts the rope so very tightly round his neck? Secondly, if Cayley is prepared to perjure himself for Mark (as he has to, anyway, now), wouldn't it be simpler for him to say that he was in the office all the time, and that Robert's death was accidental?"

Bill considered this carefully, and then nodded slowly again.

"Yes, my simple explanation is a wash-out," he said. "Now let's have yours."

Antony did not answer him. He had begun to think about something quite different.

CHAPTER IX

POSSIBILITIES OF A CROQUET SET

"What's the matter?" said Bill sharply.

Antony looked round at him with raised eyebrows.

"You've thought of something suddenly," said Bill. "What is it?"

Antony laughed.

"My dear Watson," he said, "you aren't supposed to be as clever as this."

"Oh, you can't take me in!"

"No.... Well, I was wondering about this ghost of yours, Bill. It seems to me—"

"Oh, that!" Bill was profoundly disappointed. "What on earth has the ghost got to do with it?"

"I don't know," said Antony apologetically. "I don't know what anything has got to do with it. I was just wondering. You shouldn't have brought me here if you hadn't wanted me to think about the ghost. This is where she appeared, isn't it?"

"Yes." Bill was distinctly short about it.

"How?"

"What?"

"I said, 'How?'"

"How? How do ghosts appear? I don't know. They just appear."

"Over four or five hundred yards of open park?"

"Well, but she had to appear here, because this is where the original one—Lady Anne, you know—was supposed to walk."

"Oh, never mind Lady Anne! A real ghost can do anything. But how did Miss Norris appear suddenly over five hundred yards of bare park?"

Bill looked at Antony with open mouth.

"I—I don't know," he stammered. "We never thought of that."

"You would have seen her long before, wouldn't you, if she had come the way we came?"

"Of course we should."

"And that would have spoilt it rather. You would have had

time to recognize her walk."

Bill was interested now.

"That's rather funny, you know, Tony. We none of us thought of that."

"You're sure she didn't come across the park when none of you were looking?"

"Quite. Because, you see, Betty and I were expecting her, and we kept looking round in case we saw her, so that we should all be playing with our backs to her."

"You and Miss Calladine were playing together?"

"I say, however do you know that?"

"Brilliant deductive reasoning. Well, then you suddenly saw her?"

"Yes, she walked across that side of the lawn." He indicated the opposite side, nearer to the house.

"She couldn't have been hiding in the ditch? Do you call it the moat, by the way?"

"Mark does. We don't among ourselves. No, she couldn't. Betty and I were here before the others, and walked round a bit. We should have seen her."

"Then she must have been hiding in the shed. Or do you call it the summer-house?"

"We had to go there for the bowls, of course. She couldn't have been there."

"Oh!"

"It's dashed funny," said Bill, after an interval for thought. "But it doesn't matter, does it? It has nothing to do with Robert."

"Hasn't it?"

"I say, has it?" said Bill, getting excited again.

"I don't know. We don't know what has, or what hasn't. But it has got something to do with Miss Norris. And Miss Norris—" He broke off suddenly.

"What about her?"

"Well, you're all in it in a kind of way. And if something unaccountable happens to one of you a day or two before something unaccountable happens to the whole house, one is well, interested." It was a good enough reason, but it wasn't the reason he had been on the point of giving.

"I see. Well?"

Antony knocked out his pipe and got up slowly.

"Well then, let's find the way from the house by which Miss Norris came."

Bill jumped up eagerly.

"By Jove! Do you mean there's a secret passage?"

"A secluded passage, anyway. There must be."

"I say, what fun! I love secret passages. Good Lord, and this afternoon I was playing golf just like an ordinary merchant! What a life! Secret passages!"

They made their way down into the ditch. If an opening was to be found which led to the house, it would probably be on the house side of the green, and on the outside of the ditch. The most obvious place at which to begin the search was the shed where the bowls were kept. It was a tidy place as anything in Mark's establishment would be. There were two boxes of croquet things, one of them with the lid open, as if the balls and mallets and, hoops (neatly enough put away, though) had been recently used; a box of bowls, a small lawn-mower, a roller and so forth. A seat ran along the back of it, whereon the bowls-players could sit when it rained.

Antony tapped the wall at the back.

"This is where the passage ought to begin. It doesn't sound very hollow, does it?"

"It needn't begin here at all, need it?" said Bill, walking round with bent head, and tapping the other walls. He was just too tall to stand upright in the shed.

"There's only one reason why it should, and that is that it would save us the trouble of looking anywhere else for it. Surely Mark didn't let you play croquet on his bowling-green?" He pointed to the croquet things.

"He didn't encourage it at one time, but this year he got rather keen about it. There's really nowhere else to play. Personally I hate the game. He wasn't very keen on bowls, you know, but he liked calling it the bowling-green, and surprising his visitors with it."

Antony laughed.

"I love you on Mark," he said. "You're priceless."

He began to feel in his pockets for his pipe and tobacco, and then suddenly stopped and stiffened to attention. For a moment he stood listening, with his head on one side, holding up a finger to bid Bill listen too.

"What is it?" whispered Bill.

Antony waved him to silence, and remained listening. Very quietly he went down on his knees, and listened again. Then he put his ear to the floor. He got up and dusted himself quickly, walked across to Bill and whispered in his ear:

"Footsteps. Somebody coming. When I begin to talk, back me up."

Bill nodded. Antony gave him an encouraging pat on the back, and stepped firmly across to the box of bowls, whistling loudly to himself. He took the bowls out, dropped one with a loud bang on the floor, said, "Oh, Lord!" and went on:

"I say, Bill, I don't think I want to play bowls, after all."

"Well, why did you say you did?" grumbled Bill.

Antony flashed a smile of appreciation at him.

"Well, I wanted to when I said I did, and now I don't want to."

"Then what do you want to do?"

"Talk."

"Oh, right-o!" said Bill eagerly.

"There's a seat on the lawn—I saw it. Let's bring these things along in case we want to play, after all."

"Right-o!" said Bill again. He felt safe with that, not wishing to commit himself until he knew what he was wanted to say.

As they went across the lawn, Antony dropped the bowls and took out his pipe.

"Got a match?" he said loudly.

As he bent his head over the match, he whispered, "There'll be somebody listening to us. You take the Cayley view," and then went on in his ordinary voice, "I don't think much of your matches, Bill," and struck another. They walked over to the seat and sat down.

"What a heavenly night!" said Antony.

"Ripping."

"I wonder where that poor devil Mark is now."

"It's a rum business."

"You agree with Cayley that it was an accident?"

"Yes. You see, I know Mark."

"H'm." Antony produced a pencil and a piece of paper and began to write on his knee, but while he wrote, he talked. He said that he thought Mark had shot his brother in a fit of anger, and that Cayley knew, or anyhow guessed, this and had tried to give his cousin a chance of getting away.

"Mind you, I think he's right. I think it's what any of us would do. I shan't give it away, of course, but somehow there are one or two little things which make me think that Mark really did shoot his brother I mean other than accidentally."

"Murdered him?"

"Well, manslaughtered him, anyway. I may be wrong. Anyway, it's not my business."

"But why do you think so? Because of the keys?"

"Oh, the keys are a wash-out. Still, it was a brilliant idea of mine, Wasn't it? And it would have been rather a score for me if they had all been outside."

He had finished his writing, and now passed the paper over to Bill. In the clear moonlight the carefully printed letters could easily be read:

"GO ON TALKING AS IF I WERE HERE. AFTER A MINUTE OR TWO, TURN ROUND AS IF I WERE SITTING ON THE GRASS BEHIND YOU, BUT GO ON TALKING."

"I know you don't agree with me," Antony went on as Bill read, "but you'll see that I'm right."

Bill looked up and nodded eagerly. He had forgotten golf and Betty and all the other things which had made up his world lately. This was the real thing. This was life. "Well," he began deliberately, "the whole point is that I know Mark. Now, Mark—"

But Antony was off the seat and letting himself gently down into the ditch. His intention was to crawl round it until the shed came in sight. The footsteps which he had heard seemed to be underneath the shed; probably there was a trap-door of some kind in the floor. Whoever it was would have heard their voices, and would probably think it worth while to listen to what they were saying. He might do this merely by opening the door a little without showing himself, in which case Antony would have found the entrance to the passage without any trouble to himself. But when Bill turned his head and talked over the back of the seat, it was probable that the listener would find it necessary to put his head outside in order to hear, and then Antony would be able to discover who it was. Moreover, if he should venture out of his hiding-place altogether and peep at them over the top of the bank, the fact that Bill was talking over the back of the seat would mislead the watcher into thinking that Antony was still there, sitting on the grass, no doubt, behind the seat, swinging his legs over the side of the ditch.

He walked quickly but very silently along the half-length of the bowling-green to the first corner, passed cautiously round, and then went even more carefully along the width of it to the second corner. He could hear Bill hard at it, arguing from his knowledge of Mark's character that this, that and the other must have happened, and he smiled appreciatively to himself. Bill was a great conspirator worth a hundred Watsons. As he approached the second corner he slowed down, and did the last few yards on hands and knees. Then, lying at full length, inch by inch his head went round the corner.

The shed was two or three yards to his left, on the opposite side of the ditch. From where he lay he could see almost entirely inside it. Everything seemed to be as they left it. The bowls-box, the lawn-mower, the roller, the open croquet-box, the—

"By Jove!" said Antony to himself, "that's neat."

The lid of the other croquet-box was open, too. Bill was turning round now; his voice became more difficult to hear. "You see what I mean," he was saying. "If Cayley—"

And out of the second croquet-box came Cayley's black head.

Antony wanted to shout his applause. It was neat, devilish neat. For a moment he gazed, fascinated, at that wonderful new kind of croquet-ball which had appeared so dramatically out of the box, and then reluctantly wriggled himself back. There was nothing to be gained by staying there, and a good deal to be lost, for Bill showed signs of running down. As quickly as he could Antony hurried round the ditch and took up his place at the back of the seat. Then he stood up with a yawn, stretched himself and said carelessly, "Well, don't worry yourself about it, Bill, old man. I daresay you're right. You know Mark, and I don't; and that's the difference. Shall we have a game or shall we go to bed?"

Bill looked at him for inspiration, and, receiving it, said, "Oh, just let's have one game, shall we?"

"Right you are," said Antony.

But Bill was much too excited to take the game which followed very seriously. Antony, on the other hand, seemed to be thinking of nothing but bowls. He played with great deliberation for ten minutes, and then announced that he was going to bed. Bill looked at him anxiously.

"It's all right," laughed Antony. "You can talk if you want to. Just let's put 'em away first, though."

They made their way down to the shed, and while Bill was putting the bowls away, Antony tried the lid of the closed croquet-box. As he expected, it was locked.

"Now then," said Bill, as they were walking back to the house again,

"I'm simply bursting to know. Who was it?"

"Cayley."

"Good Lord! Where?"

"Inside one of the croquet-boxes."

"Don't be an ass."

"It's quite true, Bill." He told the other what he had seen.

"But aren't we going to have a look at it?" asked Bill, in great disappointment. "I'm longing to explore. Aren't you?"

"To-morrow and to-morrow and to-morrow. We shall see Cayley coming along this way directly. Besides, I want to get in from the other end, if I can. I doubt very much if we can do it this end without giving ourselves away. Look, there's Cayley."

They could see him coming along the drive towards them. When they were a little closer, they waved to him and he waved back.

"I wondered where you were," he said, as he got up to them. "I rather thought you might be along this way. What about bed?"

"Bed it is," said Antony.

"We've been playing bowls," added Bill, "and talking, and—and playing bowls. Ripping night, isn't it?"

But he left the rest of the conversation, as they wandered back to the house, to Antony. He wanted to think. There seemed to be no doubt now that Cayley was a villain. Bill had never been familiar with a villain before. It didn't seem quite fair of Cayley, somehow; he was taking rather a mean advantage of his friends. Lot of funny people there were in the world funny people with secrets. Look at Tony, that first time he had met him in a tobacconist's shop. Anybody would have thought he was a tobacconist's assistant. And Cayley. Anybody would have thought that Cayley was an ordinary decent sort of person. And Mark. Dash it! one could never be sure of anybody. Now, Robert was different. Everybody had always said that Robert was a shady fellow.

But what on earth had Miss Norris got to do with it? What had Miss Norris got to do with it? This was a question which Antony had already asked himself that afternoon, and it seemed to him now that he had found the answer. As he lay in bed that night he reassembled his ideas, and looked at them in the new light which the events of the evening threw upon the dark corners in his brain.

Of course it was natural that Cayley should want to get rid of his guests as soon as the tragedy was discovered. He would want this for their own sake as well as for his. But he had been a little too quick about suggesting it, and about seeing the suggestion carried out. They had been bustled off as soon as they could be packed. The suggestion that they were in his hands, to go or stay as he wished, could have been left safely to them. As it was, they had been given no alternative, and Miss Norris, who had proposed to catch an after-dinner train at the junction, in the obvious hope that she might have in this way a dramatic cross-examination at the hands of some keen-eyed detective, was encouraged tactfully, but quite firmly, to travel by the earlier train with the others. Antony had felt that Cayley, in the tragedy which had suddenly befallen the house, ought to have been equally indifferent to her presence or absence. But he was not; and Antony assumed from this that Cayley was very much alive to the necessity for her absence.

Why?

Well, that question was not to be answered off-hand. But the fact that it was so had made Antony interested in her; and it was for this reason that he had followed up so alertly Bill's casual mention of her in connection with the dressing-up business. He felt that he wanted to know a little more about Miss Norris and the part she had played in the Red House circle. By sheer luck, as it seemed to him, he had stumbled on the answer to his question.

Miss Norris was hurried away because she knew about the secret passage.

The passage, then, had something to do with the mystery of

Robert's death. Miss Norris had used it in order to bring off her dramatic appearance as the ghost. Possibly she had discovered it for herself; possibly Mark had revealed it to her secretly one day, never guessing that she would make so unkind a use of it later on; possibly Cayley, having been let into the joke of the dressing-up, had shown her how she could make her appearance on the bowling-green even more mysterious and supernatural. One way or another, she knew about the secret passage. So she must be hurried away.

Why? Because if she stayed and talked, she might make some innocent mention of it. And Cayley did not want any mention of it.

Why, again? Obviously because the passage, or even the mere knowledge of its existence, might provide a clue.

"I wonder if Mark's hiding there," thought Antony; and he went to sleep.

CHAPTER X

MR. GILLINGHAM TALKS NONSENSE

Antony came down in a very good humour to breakfast next morning, and found that his host was before him. Cayley looked up from his letters and nodded.

"Any word of Mr. Ablett—of Mark?" said Antony, as he poured out his coffee.

"No. The inspector wants to drag the lake this afternoon."

"Oh! Is there a lake?"

There was just the flicker of a smile on Cayley's face, but it disappeared as quickly as it came.

"Well, it's really a pond," he said, "but it was called 'the lake.'"

"By Mark," thought Antony. Aloud he said, "What do they expect to find?"

"They think that Mark—" He broke off and shrugged his shoulders.

"May have drowned himself, knowing that he couldn't get

away? And knowing that he had compromised himself by trying to get away at all?"

"Yes; I suppose so," said Cayley slowly.

"I should have thought he would have given himself more of a run for his money. After all, he had a revolver. If he was determined not to be taken alive, he could always have prevented that. Couldn't he have caught a train to London before the police knew anything about it?"

"He might just have managed it. There was a train. They would have noticed him at Waldheim, of course, but he might have managed it at Stanton. He's not so well-known there, naturally. The inspector has been inquiring. Nobody seems to have seen him."

"There are sure to be people who will say they did, later on. There was never a missing man yet but a dozen people come forward who swear to have seen him at a dozen different places at the same time."

Cayley smiled.

"Yes. That's true. Anyhow, he wants to drag the pond first." He added dryly, "From what I've read of detective stories, inspectors always do want to drag the pond first."

"Is it deep?"

"Quite deep enough," said Cayley as he got up. On his way to the door he stopped, and looked at Antony. "I'm so sorry that we're keeping you here like this, but it will only be until to-morrow. The inquest is to-morrow afternoon. Do amuse yourself how you like till then. Beverley will look after you."

"Thanks very much. I shall really be quite all right."

Antony went on with his breakfast. Perhaps it was true that inspectors liked dragging ponds, but the question was, did Cayleys like having them dragged? Was Cayley anxious about it, or quite indifferent? He certainly did not seem to be anxious, but he could hide his feelings very easily beneath that heavy, solid face, and it was not often that the real Cayley peeped out. Just a little too eager once or twice, perhaps, but there was nothing to be learnt from it this morning. Perhaps he knew that the pond had no secrets to give up. After all, inspectors were always dragging ponds.

Bill came in noisily.

Bill's face was an open book. Excitement was written all over it.

"Well," he said eagerly, as he sat down to the business of the meal, "what are we going to do this morning?"

"Not talk so loudly, for one thing," said Antony. Bill looked about him apprehensively. Was Cayley under the table, for example? After last night one never knew.

"Is er—" He raised his eyebrows.

"No. But one doesn't want to shout. One should modulate the voice, my dear William, while breathing gently from the hips. Thus one avoids those chest-notes which have betrayed many a secret. In other words, pass the toast."

"You seem bright this morning."

"I am. Very bright. Cayley noticed it. Cayley said, 'Were it not that I have other business, I would come gathering nuts and may with thee. Fain would I gyrate round the mulberry-bush and hop upon the little hills. But the waters of Jordan encompass me and Inspector Birch tarries outside with his shrimping-net. My friend William Beverley will attend thee anon. Farewell, a long farewell to all—thy grape-nuts.' He then left up-centre. Enter W. Beverley, R."

"Are you often like this at breakfast?"

"Almost invariably. Said he with his mouth full. 'Exit W. Beverley, L."

"It's a touch of the sun, I suppose," said Bill, shaking his head sadly.

"It's the sun and the moon and the stars, all acting together on an empty stomach. Do you know anything about the stars, Mr. Beverley? Do you know anything about Orion's Belt, for instance? And why isn't there a star called Beverley's Belt? Or a novel? Said he masticating. Re-enter W. Beverley through trap-door."

"Talking about trap-doors—"

"Don't," said Antony, getting up. "Some talk of Alexander and some of Hercules, but nobody talks about—what's the Latin for trap-door?—Mensa a table; you might get it from that. Well, Mr. Beverley,"—and he slapped him heartily on the back as he went past him—"I shall see you later. Cayley says that you will amuse me, but so far you have not made me laugh once. You must try and be more amusing when you have finished your breakfast. But don't hurry. Let the upper mandibles have time to do the work." With those words Mr. Gillingham then left the spacious apartment.

Bill continued his breakfast with a slightly bewildered air. He did not know that Cayley was smoking a cigarette outside the windows behind him; not listening, perhaps; possibly not even overhearing; but within sight of Antony, who was not going to take any risks. So he went on with his breakfast, reflecting that Antony was a rum fellow, and wondering if he had dreamed only of the amazing things which had happened the day before.

Antony went up to his bedroom to fetch his pipe. It was occupied by a housemaid, and he made a polite apology for disturbing her. Then he remembered.

"Is it Elsie?" he asked, giving her a friendly smile.

"Yes, sir," she said, shy but proud. She had no doubts as to why it was that she had achieved such notoriety.

"It was you who heard Mr. Mark yesterday, wasn't it? I hope the inspector was nice to you?"

"Yes, thank you, sir."

"'It's my turn now. You wait,'" murmured Antony to himself.

"Yes, sir. Nasty-like. Meaning to say his chance had come."

"I wonder."

"Well, that's what I heard, sir. Truly."

Antony looked at her thoughtfully and nodded.

"Yes. I wonder. I wonder why."

"Why what, sir?"

"Oh, lots of things, Elsie.... It was quite an accident your being outside just then?"

Elsie blushed. She had not forgotten what Mrs. Stevens had said about it.

"Quite, sir. In the general way I use the other stairs."

"Of course."

He had found his pipe and was about to go downstairs again when she stopped him.

"I beg your pardon, sir, but will there be an inquest?"

"Oh, yes. To-morrow, I think."

"Shall I have to give my evidence, sir?"

"Of course. There's nothing to be frightened of."

"I did hear it, sir. Truly."

"Why, of course you did. Who says you didn't?"

"Some of the others, sir, Mrs. Stevens and all."

"Oh, that's just because they're jealous," said Antony with a smile.

He was glad to have spoken to her, because he had recognized at once the immense importance of her evidence. To the Inspector no doubt it had seemed only of importance in that it had shown Mark to have adopted something of a threatening attitude towards his brother. To Antony it had much more significance. It was the only trustworthy evidence that Mark had been in the office at all that afternoon.

For who saw Mark go into the office? Only Cayley. And if Cayley had been hiding the truth about the keys, why should he not be hiding the truth about Mark's entry into the office? Obviously all Cayley's evidence went for nothing. Some of it no doubt was true; but he was giving it, both truth and falsehood, with a purpose. What the purpose was Antony did not know as yet; to shield Mark, to shield himself, even to betray Mark it might be any of these. But since his evidence was given for his own ends, it was impossible that it could be treated as the evidence of an impartial and trustworthy onlooker. Such, for instance, as Elsie appeared to be.

Elsie's evidence, however, seemed to settle the point. Mark had gone into the office to see his brother; Elsie had heard them both talking; and then Antony and Cayley had found the body of Robert.... and the Inspector was going to drag the pond.

But certainly Elsie's evidence did not prove anything more than the mere presence of Mark in the room. "It's my turn now; you wait." That was not an immediate threat;—it was a threat for the future. If Mark had shot his brother immediately afterwards it must have been an accident, the result of a struggle, say, provoked by that "nasty-like" tone of voice. Nobody would say "You wait" to a man who was just going to be shot. "You wait" meant "You wait, and see what's going to happen to you later on." The owner of the Red House had had enough of his brother's sponging, his brother's blackmail; now it was Mark's turn to get a bit of his own back. Let Robert just wait a bit, and he would see. The conversation which Elsie had overheard might have meant something like this. It couldn't have meant murder. Anyway not murder of Robert by Mark.

"It's a funny business," thought Antony. "The one obvious solution is so easy and yet so wrong. And I've got a hundred things in my head, and I can't fit them together. And this afternoon will make a hundred and one. I mustn't forget this afternoon."

He found Bill in the hall and proposed a stroll. Bill was only too ready. "Where do you want to go?" he asked.

"I don't mind much. Show me the park."

"Righto."

They walked out together.

"Watson, old man," said Antony, as soon as they were away from the house, "you really mustn't talk so loudly indoors. There was a gentleman outside, just behind you, all the time."

"Oh, I say," said Bill, going pink. "I'm awfully sorry. So that's why you were talking such rot."

"Partly, yes. And partly because I do feel rather bright this morning. We're going to have a busy day."

"Are we really? What are we going to do?"

"They're going to drag the pond—beg its pardon, the lake. Where is the lake?"

"We're on the way to it now, if you'd like to see it."

"We may as well look at it. Do you haunt the lake much in the ordinary way?"

"Oh, no, rather not. There's nothing to do there."

"You can't bathe?"

"Well, I shouldn't care to. Too dirty."

"I see.... This is the way we came yesterday, isn't it? The way to the village?"

"Yes. We go off a bit to the right directly. What are they dragging it for?"

"Mark."

"Oh, rot," said Bill uneasily. He was silent for a little, and then, forgetting his uncomfortable thoughts in his sudden remembrance of the exciting times they were having, said eagerly, "I say, when are we going to look for that passage?"

"We can't do very much while Cayley's in the house."

"What about this afternoon when they're dragging the pond? He's sure to be there."

Antony shook his head.

"There's something I must do this afternoon," he said. "Of course we might have time for both."

"Has Cayley got to be out of the house for the other thing

too?"

"Well, I think he ought to be."

"I say, is it anything rather exciting?"

"I don't know. It might be rather interesting. I daresay I could do it at some other time, but I rather fancy it at three o'clock, somehow. I've been specially keeping it back for then."

"I say, what fun! You do want me, don't you?"

"Of course I do. Only, Bill don't talk about things inside the house, unless I begin. There's a good Watson."

"I won't. I swear I won't."

They had come to the pond—Mark's lake—and they walked silently round it. When they had made the circle, Antony sat down on the grass, and relit his pipe. Bill followed his example.

"Well, Mark isn't there," said Antony.

"No," said Bill. "At least, I don't quite see why you know he isn't."

"It isn't 'knowing,' it's 'guessing,'" said Antony rapidly. "It's much easier to shoot yourself than to drown yourself, and if Mark had wanted to shoot himself in the water, with some idea of not letting the body be found, he'd have put big stones in his pockets, and the only big stones are near the water's edge, and they would have left marks, and they haven't, and therefore he didn't, and oh, bother the pond; that can wait till this afternoon. Bill, where does the secret passage begin?"

"Well, that's what we've got to find out, isn't it?"

"Yes. You see, my idea is this."

He explained his reasons for thinking that the secret of the passage was concerned in some way with the secret of Robert's death, and went on:

"My theory is that Mark discovered the passage about a year ago—the time when he began to get keen on croquet. The passage came out into the floor of the shed, and probably it was Cayley's idea to put a croquet-box over the trap-door, so as to hide it more completely. You know, when once you've discovered a secret yourself, it always seems as if it must be so obvious to everybody else. I can imagine that Mark loved having this little secret all to himself and to Cayley, of course, but Cayley wouldn't count and they must have had great fun fixing it up, and making it more difficult for other people to find out. Well then, when Miss Norris was going to dress-up, Cayley gave it away. Probably he told her that she could never get down to the bowling-green without being discovered, and then perhaps showed that he knew there was one way in which she could do it, and she wormed the secret out of him somehow."

"But this was two or three days before Robert turned up."

"Exactly. I am not suggesting that there was anything sinister about the passage in the first place. It was just a little private bit of romance and adventure for Mark, three days ago. He didn't even know that Robert was coming. But somehow the passage has been used since, in connection with Robert. Perhaps Mark escaped that way; perhaps he's hiding there now. And if so, then the only person who could give him away was Miss Norris. And she of course would only do it innocently not knowing that the passage had anything to do with it."

"So it was safer to have her out of the way?"

"Yes."

"But, look here, Tony, why do you want to bother about this end of it? We can always get in at the bowling-green end."

"I know, but if we do that we shall have to do it openly. It will mean breaking open the box, and letting Cayley know that we've done it. You see, Bill, if we don't find anything out for ourselves in the next day or two, we've got to tell the police what we have found out, and then they can explore the passage for themselves. But I don't want to do that yet."

"Rather not.

"So we've got to carry on secretly for a bit. It's the only way." He smiled and added, "And it's much more fun."

"Rather!" Bill chuckled to himself.

"Very well. Where does the secret passage begin?"

CHAPTER XI

THE REVEREND THEODORE USSHER

"There's one thing, which we have got to realize at once," said Antony, "and that is that if we don't find it easily, we shan't find it at all."

"You mean that we shan't have time?"

"Neither time nor opportunity. Which is rather a consoling thought to a lazy person like me."

"But it makes it much harder, if we can't really look properly."

"Harder to find, yes, but so much easier to look. For instance, the passage might begin in Cayley's bedroom. Well, now we know that it doesn't."

"We don't know anything of the sort," protested Bill.

"We—know for the purposes of our search. Obviously we can't go tailing into Cayley's bedroom and tapping his wardrobes; and obviously, therefore, if we are going to look for it at all, we must assume that it doesn't begin there."

"Oh, I see." Bill chewed a piece of grass thoughtfully. "Anyhow, it wouldn't begin on an upstairs floor, would it?"

"Probably not. Well, we're getting on."

"You can wash out the kitchen and all that part of the house," said Bill, after more thought. "We can't go there."

"Right. And the cellars, if there are any."

"Well, that doesn't leave us much."

"No. Of course it's only a hundred-to-one chance that we find it, but what we want to consider is which is the most likely place of the few places in which we can look safely."

"All it amounts to," said Bill, "is the living-rooms downstairs—dining-room, library, hall, billiard-room and the office rooms."

"Yes, that's all."

"Well, the office is the most likely, isn't it?"

"Yes. Except for one thing."

"What's that?"

"Well, it's on the wrong side of the house. One would expect the passage to start from the nearest place to which it is going. Why make it longer by going under the house first?"

"Yes, that's true. Well, then, you think the dining-room or the library?"

"Yes. And the library for choice. I mean for our choice. There are always servants going into dining-rooms. We shouldn't have much of a chance of exploring properly in there. Besides, there's another thing to remember. Mark has kept this a secret for a year. Could he have kept it a secret in the dining-room? Could Miss Norris have got into the dining-room and used the secret door just after dinner without being seen? It would have been much too risky."

Bill got up eagerly.

"Come along," he said, "let's try the library. If Cayley comes in, we can always pretend we're choosing a book."

Antony got up slowly, took his arm and walked back to the house with him.

The library was worth going into, passages or no passages. Antony could never resist another person's bookshelves. As soon as he went into the room, he found himself wandering round it to see what books the owner read, or (more likely) did not read, but kept for the air which they lent to the house. Mark had prided himself on his library. It was a mixed collection of books. Books which he had inherited both from his father and from his patron; books which he had bought because he was interested in them or, if not in them, in the authors to whom he wished to lend his patronage; books which he had ordered in beautifully bound editions, partly because they looked well on his shelves, lending a noble colour to his rooms, partly because no man of culture should ever be without them; old editions, new editions, expensive books, cheap books, a library in which everybody, whatever his taste, could be sure of finding something to suit him.

"And which is your particular fancy, Bill?" said Antony, looking from one shelf to another. "Or are you always playing billiards?"

"I have a look at 'Badminton' sometimes," said Bill.

"It's over in that corner there." He waved a hand.

"Over here?" said Antony, going to it.

"Yes." He corrected himself suddenly.—"Oh, no, it's not. It's over there on the right now. Mark had a grand re-arrangement of his library about a year ago. It took him more than a week, he told us. He's got such a frightful lot, hasn't he?"

"Now that's very interesting," said Antony, and he sat down and filled his pipe again.

There was indeed a "frightful lot" of books. The four walls of the library were plastered with them from floor to ceiling, save only where the door and the two windows insisted on living their own life, even though an illiterate one. To Bill it seemed the most hopeless room of any in which to look for a secret opening.

"We shall have to take every blessed book down," he said, "before we can be certain that we haven't missed it."

"Anyway," said Antony, "if we take them down one at a time, nobody can suspect us of sinister designs. After all, what does one go into a library for, except to take books down?"

"But there's such a frightful lot."

Antony's pipe was now going satisfactorily, and he got up and walked leisurely to the end of the wall opposite the door.

"Well, let's have a look," he said, "and see if they are so very frightful. Hallo, here's your 'Badminton.' You often read that, you say?"

"If I read anything."

"Yes." He looked down and up the shelf. "Sport and Travel chiefly. I like books of travel, don't you?"

"They're pretty dull as a rule."

"Well, anyhow, some people like them very much," said Antony, reproachfully. He moved on to the next row of shelves. "The Drama. The Restoration dramatists. You can have most of them. Still, as you well remark, many people seem to love them. Shaw, Wilde, Robertson—I like reading plays, Bill. There are not many people who do, but those who do are usually very keen. Let us pass on."

"I say, we haven't too much time," said Bill restlessly.

"We haven't. That's why we aren't wasting any. Poetry. Who reads poetry nowadays? Bill, when did you last read 'Paradise Lost'?"

"Never."

"I thought not. And when did Miss Calladine last read 'The Excursion' aloud to you?"

"As a matter of fact, Betty—Miss Calladine—happens to be jolly keen on what's the beggar's name?"

"Never mind his name. You have said quite enough. We pass on."

He moved on to the next shelf.

"Biography. Oh, lots of it. I love biographies. Are you a member of the Johnson Club? I bet Mark is. 'Memories of Many Courts' I'm sure Mrs. Calladine reads that. Anyway, biographies are just as interesting as most novels, so why linger? We pass on." He went to the next shelf, and then gave a sudden whistle.

"Hallo, hallo!"

"What's the matter?" said Bill rather peevishly.

"Stand back there. Keep the crowd back, Bill. We are getting amongst it. Sermons, as I live. Sermons. Was Mark's father a clergyman, or does Mark take to them naturally?"

"His father was a parson, I believe. Oh, yes, I know he was."

"Ah, then these are Father's books. 'Half-Hours with the Infinite' I must order that from the library when I get back. 'The Lost Sheep,' 'Jones on the Trinity,' 'The Epistles of St. Paul Explained.' Oh, Bill, we're amongst it. 'The Narrow Way, being Sermons by the Rev. Theodore Ussher' hal-LO!"

"What is the matter?"

"William, I am inspired. Stand by." He took down the Reverend Theodore Ussher's classic work, looked at it with a happy smile for a moment, and then gave it to Bill.

"Here, hold Ussher for a bit."

Bill took the book obediently.

"No, give it me back. Just go out into the hall, and see if you can hear Cayley anywhere. Say 'Hallo' loudly, if you do."

Bill went out quickly, listened, and came back.

"It's all right."

"Good." He took the book out of its shelf again. "Now then, you can hold Ussher. Hold him in the left hand so. With the right or dexter hand, grasp this shelf firmly so. Now, when I say 'Pull,' pull gradually. Got that?"

Bill nodded, his face alight with excitement.

"Good." Antony put his hand into the space left by the stout Ussher, and fingered the back of the shelf. "Pull," he said.

Bill pulled.

"Now just go on pulling like that. I shall get it directly. Not hard, you know, but just keeping up the strain."

His fingers went at it again busily.

And then suddenly the whole row of shelves, from top to bottom, swung gently open towards them.

"Good Lord!" said Bill, letting go of the shelf in his amazement.

Antony pushed the shelves back, extracted Ussher from Bill's fingers, replaced him, and then, taking Bill by the arm, led him to the sofa and deposited him in it. Standing in front of him, he bowed gravely.

"Child's play, Watson," he said; "child's play."

"How on earth—"

Antony laughed happily and sat down on the sofa beside him.

"You don't really want it explained," he said, smacking him on the knee; "you're just being Watsonish. It's very nice of you, of course, and I appreciate it."

"No, but really, Tony."

"Oh, my dear Bill!" He smoked silently for a little, and then went on, "It's what I was saying just now—a secret is a secret until you have discovered it, and as soon as you have discovered it, you wonder why everybody else isn't discovering it, and how it could ever have been a secret at all. This passage has been here for years, with an opening at one end into the library, and at the other end into the shed. Then Mark discovered it, and immediately he felt that everybody else must discover it. So he made the shed end more difficult by putting the croquet-box there, and this end more difficult by—" he stopped and looked at the other "by what, Bill?"

But Bill was being Watsonish.

"What?"

"Obviously by re-arranging his books. He happened to take out 'The Life of Nelson' or 'Three Men in a Boat,' or whatever it was, and by the merest chance discovered the secret. Naturally he felt that everybody else would be taking down 'The Life of Nelson' or 'Three Men in a Boat.' Naturally he felt that the secret would be safer if nobody ever interfered with that shelf at all. When you said that the books had been re-arranged a year ago just about the time the croquet-box came into existence; of course, I guessed why. So I looked about for the dullest books I could find, the books nobody ever read. Obviously the collection of sermon-books of a mid-Victorian clergyman was the shelf we wanted."

"Yes, I see. But why were you so certain of the particular place?"

"Well, he had to mark the particular place by some book. I thought that the joke of putting 'The Narrow Way' just over the entrance to the passage might appeal to him. Apparently it did."

Bill nodded to himself thoughtfully several times. "Yes, that's very neat," he said. "You're a clever devil, Tony."

Tony laughed.

"You encourage me to think so, which is bad for me, but very delightful."

"Well, come on, then," said Bill, and he got up, and held out a hand.

"Come on where?"

"To explore the passage, of course."

Antony shook his head.

"Why ever not?"

"Well, what do you expect to find there?"

"I don't know. But you seemed to think that we might find something that would help."

"Suppose we find Mark?" said Antony quietly.

"I say, do you really think he's there?"

"Suppose he is?"

"Well, then, there we are."

Antony walked over to the fireplace, knocked out the ashes of his pipe, and turned back to Bill. He looked at him gravely without speaking.

"What are you going to say to him?" he said at last.

"How do you mean?"

"Are you going to arrest him, or help him to escape?"

"I—I—well, of course, I—" began Bill, stammering, and then ended lamely, "Well, I don't know."

"Exactly. We've got to make up our minds, haven't we?"

Bill didn't answer. Very much disturbed in his mind, he walked restlessly about the room, frowning to himself, stopping now and then at the newly discovered door and looking at it as if he were trying to learn what lay behind it. Which side was he on, if it came to choosing sides—Mark's or the Law's?

"You know, you can't just say, 'Oh er hallo!' to him," said Antony, breaking rather appropriately into his thoughts.

Bill looked up at him with a start.

"Nor," went on Antony, "can you say, 'This is my friend Mr. Gillingham, who is staying with you. We were just going to have a game of bowls.'"

"Yes, it's dashed difficult. I don't know what to say. I've been rather forgetting about Mark." He wandered over to the window and looked out on to the lawns. There was a gardener clipping the grass edges. No reason why the lawn should be untidy just because the master of the house had disappeared. It was going to be a hot day again. Dash it, of course he had forgotten Mark. How could he think of him as an escaped murderer, a fugitive from justice, when everything was going on just as it did yesterday, and the sun was shining just as it did when they all drove off to their golf, only twenty-four hours ago? How could he help feeling that this was not real tragedy, but merely a jolly kind of detective game that he and Antony were playing?

He turned back to his friend.

"All the same," he said, "you wanted to find the passage, and now you've found it. Aren't you going into it at all?"

Antony took his arm.

"Let's go outside again," he said. "We can't go into it now, anyhow. It's too risky, with Cayley about. Bill, I feel like you—just a little bit frightened. But what I'm frightened of I don't quite know. Anyway, you want to go on with it, don't you?"

"Yes," said Bill firmly. "We must."

"Then we'll explore the passage this afternoon, if we get the chance. And if we don't get the chance, then we'll try it to-night."

They walked across the hall and out into the sunlight again.

"Do you really think we might find Mark hiding there?" asked Bill.

"It's possible," said Antony. "Either Mark or—" He pulled himself up quickly. "No," he murmured to himself, "I won't let myself think that—not yet, anyway. It's too horrible."

CHAPTER XII

A SHADOW ON THE WALL

In the twenty hours or so at his disposal Inspector Birch had been busy. He had telegraphed to London a complete description of Mark in the brown flannel suit which he had last been seen wearing; he had made inquiries at Stanton as to whether anybody answering to this description had been seen leaving by the 4.20; and though the evidence which had been volunteered to him had been inconclusive, it made it possible that Mark had indeed caught that train, and had arrived in London before the police at the other end had been ready to receive him. But the fact that it was market-day at Stanton, and that the little town would be more full than usual of visitors, made it less likely that either the departure of Mark by the 4.20, or the arrival of Robert by the 2.10 earlier in the afternoon, would have been particularly noticed. As Antony had said to Cayley, there would always be somebody ready to hand the police a circumstantial story of the movements of any man in whom the police were interested.

That Robert had come by the 2.10 seemed fairly certain. To find out more about him in time for the inquest would be difficult. All that was known about him in the village where he and Mark had lived as boys bore out the evidence of Cayley. He was an unsatisfactory son, and he had been hurried off to Australia; nor had he been seen since in the village. Whether there were any more substantial grounds of quarrel between the two brothers than that the younger one was at home and well-to-do, while the elder was poor and an exile, was not known, nor, as far as the inspector could see, was it likely to be known until Mark was captured.

The discovery of Mark was all that mattered immediately. Dragging the pond might not help towards this, but it would certainly give the impression in court to-morrow that Inspector Birch was handling the case with zeal. And if only the revolver with which the deed was done was brought to the surface, his trouble would be well repaid. "Inspector Birch produces the weapon" would make an excellent headline in the local paper.

He was feeling well-satisfied with himself, therefore, as he walked to the pond, where his men were waiting for him, and quite in the mood for a little pleasant talk with Mr. Gillingham and his friend, Mr. Beverley. He gave them a cheerful "Good afternoon," and added with a smile, "Coming to help us?"

"You don't really want us," said Antony, smiling back at him.

"You can come if you like."

Antony gave a little shudder.

"You can tell me afterwards what you find," he said. "By the way," he added, "I hope the landlord at 'The George' gave me a good character?"

The Inspector looked at him quickly.

"Now how on earth do you know anything about that?"

Antony bowed to him gravely.

"Because I guessed that you were a very efficient member of the Force."

The inspector laughed.

"Well, you came out all right, Mr. Gillingham. You got a clean bill. But I had to make certain about you.

"Of course you did. Well, I wish you luck. But I don't think you'll find much at the pond. It's rather out of the way, isn't it, for anybody running away?"

"That's just what I told Mr. Cayley, when he called my attention to the pond. However, we shan't do any harm by looking. It's the unexpected that's the most likely in this sort of case."

"You're quite right, Inspector. Well, we mustn't keep you. Good afternoon," and Antony smiled pleasantly at him.

"Good afternoon, sir."

"Good afternoon," said Bill.

Antony stood looking after the Inspector as he strode off, silent for so long that Bill shook him by the arm at last, and asked him rather crossly what was the matter.

Antony shook his head slowly from side to side.

"I don't know; really I don't know. It's too devilish what I keep thinking. He can't be as cold-blooded as that."

"Who?"

Without answering, Antony led the way back to the garden-seat on which they had been sitting. He sat there with his head in his hands.

"Oh, I hope they find something," he murmured. "Oh, I hope they do."

"In the pond?"

"Yes."

"But what?"

"Anything, Bill; anything."

Bill was annoyed. "I say, Tony, this won't do. You really mustn't be so damn mysterious. What's happened to you suddenly?"

Antony looked up at him in surprise.

"Didn't you hear what he said?"

"What, particularly?"

"That it was Cayley's idea to drag the pond."

"Oh! Oh, I say!" Bill was rather excited again. "You mean that he's hidden something there? Some false clue which he wants the police to find?"

"I hope so," said Antony earnestly, "but I'm afraid—" He stopped short.

"Afraid of what?"

"Afraid that he hasn't hidden anything there. Afraid that—"

"Well?"

"What's the safest place in which to hide anything very important?"

"Somewhere where nobody will look."

"There's a better place than that."

"What?"

"Somewhere where everybody has already looked."

"By Jove! You mean that as soon as the pond has been dragged, Cayley will hide something there?"

"Yes, I'm afraid so."

"But why afraid?"

"Because I think that it must be something very important, something which couldn't easily be hidden anywhere else."

"What?" asked Bill eagerly.

Antony shook his head.

"No, I'm not going to talk about it yet. We can wait and see what the Inspector finds. He may find something—I don't know what—something that Cayley has put there for him to find. But if he doesn't, then it will be because Cayley is going to hide something there to-night."

"What?" asked Bill again.

"You will see what, Bill," said Antony; "because we shall be there."

"Are we going to watch him?"

"Yes, if the Inspector finds nothing."

"That's good," said Bill.

If it were a question of Cayley or the Law, he was quite decided as to which side he was taking. Previous to the tragedy of yesterday he had got on well enough with both of the cousins, without being in the least intimate with either. Indeed, of the two he preferred, perhaps, the silent, solid Cayley to the more volatile Mark. Cayley's qualities, as they appeared to Bill, may have been chiefly negative; but even if this merit lay in the fact that he never exposed whatever weaknesses he may have had, this is an excellent quality in a fellow-guest (or, if you like, fellow-host) in a house where one is continually visiting. Mark's weaknesses, on the other hand, were very plain to the eye, and Bill had seen a good deal of them.

Yet, though he had hesitated to define his position that morning in regard to Mark, he did not hesitate to place himself on the side of the Law against Cayley. Mark, after all, had done him no harm, but Cayley had committed an unforgivable offence. Cayley had listened secretly to a private conversation between himself and Tony. Let Cayley hang, if the Law demanded it.

Antony looked at his watch and stood up.

"Come along," he said. "It's time for that job I spoke about."

"The passage?" said Bill eagerly.

"No; the thing which I said that I had to do this afternoon."

"Oh, of course. What is it?"

Without saying anything, Antony led the way indoors to the office.

It was three o'clock, and at three o'clock yesterday Antony and Cayley had found the body. At a few minutes after three, he had been looking out of the window of the adjoining room, and had been surprised suddenly to find the door open and Cayley behind him. He had vaguely wondered at the time why he had expected the door to be shut, but he had had no time then to worry the thing out, and he had promised himself to look into it at his leisure afterwards. Possibly it meant nothing; possibly, if it meant anything, he could have found out its meaning by a visit to the office that morning. But he had felt that he would be more likely to recapture the impressions of yesterday if he chose as far as possible the same conditions for his experiment. So he had decided that three o'clock that afternoon should find him once more in the office.

As he went into the room, followed by Bill, he felt it almost as a shock that there was now no body of Robert lying there between the two doors. But there was a dark stain which showed where the dead man's head had been, and Antony knelt down over it, as he had knelt twenty-four hours before.

"I want to go through it again," he said. "You must be Cayley.

Cayley said he would get some water. I remember thinking that water wasn't much good to a dead man, and that probably he was only too glad to do anything rather than nothing. He came back with a wet sponge and a handkerchief. I suppose he got the handkerchief from the chest of drawers. Wait a bit."

He got up and went into the adjoining room; looked round it, pulled open a drawer or two, and, after shutting all the doors, came back to the office.

"The sponge is there, and there are handkerchiefs in the top right-hand drawer. Now then, Bill, just pretend you're Cayley. You've just said something about water, and you get up."

Feeling that it was all a little uncanny, Bill, who had been kneeling beside his friend, got up and walked out. Antony, as he had done on the previous day, looked up after him as he went. Bill turned into the room on the right, opened the drawer and got the handkerchief, damped the sponge and came back.

"Well?" he said wonderingly.

Antony shook his head.

"It's all different," he said. "For one thing, you made a devil of a noise and Cayley didn't."

"Perhaps you weren't listening when Cayley went in?"

"I wasn't. But I should have heard him if I could have heard him, and I should have remembered afterwards."

"Perhaps Cayley shut the door after him."

"Wait!"

He pressed his hand over his eyes and thought. It wasn't anything which he had heard, but something which he had seen. He tried desperately hard to see it again.... He saw Cayley getting up, opening the door from the office, leaving it open and walking into the passage, turning to the door on the right, opening it, going in, and then—What did his eyes see after that? If they would only tell him again!

Suddenly he jumped up, his face alight. "Bill, I've got it!" he cried.

"What?"

"The shadow on the wall! I was looking at the shadow on the wall. Oh, ass, and ten times ass!"

Bill looked uncomprehendingly at him. Antony took his arm and pointed to the wall of the passage.

"Look at the sunlight on it," he said. "That's because you've left the door of that room open. The sun comes straight in through the windows. Now, I'm going to shut the door. Look! D'you see how the shadow moves across? That's what I saw the shadow moving across as the door shut behind him. Bill, go in and shut the door behind you quite naturally. Quick!"

Bill went out and Antony knelt, watching eagerly.

"I thought so!" he cried. "I knew it couldn't have been that."

"What happened?" said Bill, coming back.

"Just what you would expect. The sunlight came, and the shadow moved back again all in one movement."

"And what happened yesterday?"

"The sunlight stayed there; and then the shadow came very slowly back, and there was no noise of the door being shut."

Bill looked at him with startled eyes.

"By Jove! You mean that Cayley closed the door afterwards—as an afterthought—and very quietly, so that you couldn't hear?"

Antony nodded.

"Yes. That explains why I was surprised afterwards when I went into the room to find the door open behind me. You know how those doors with springs on them close?"

"The sort which old gentlemen have to keep out draughts?"

"Yes. Just at first they hardly move at all, and then very, very slowly they swing to— well, that was the way the shadow moved, and subconsciously I must have associated it with the movement of that sort of door. By Jove!" He got up, and dusted his knees. "Now, Bill, just to make sure, go in and close the door like that. As an afterthought, you know; and very quietly, so that I don't hear the click of it."

Bill did as he was told, and then put his head out eagerly to hear what had happened.

"That was it," said Antony, with absolute conviction. "That was just what I saw yesterday." He came out of the office, and joined Bill in the little room.

"And now," he said, "let's try and find out what it was that Mr. Cayley was doing in here, and why he had to be so very careful that his friend Mr. Gillingham didn't overhear him."

CHAPTER XIII

THE OPEN WINDOW

Anthony's first thought was that Cayley had hidden something; something, perhaps, which he had found by the body, and but that was absurd. In the time at his disposal, he could have done no more than put it away in a drawer, where it would be much more open to discovery by Antony than if he had kept it in his pocket. In any case he would have removed it by this time, and hidden it in some more secret place. Besides, why in this case bother about shutting the door?

Bill pulled open a drawer in the chest, and looked inside.

"Is it any good going through these, do you think?" he asked.

Antony looked over his shoulder.

"Why did he keep clothes here at all?" he asked. "Did he ever change down here?"

"My dear Tony, he had more clothes than anybody in the world. He just kept them here in case they might be useful, I expect. When you and I go from London to the country we carry our clothes about with us. Mark never did. In his flat in London he had everything all over again which he has here. It was a hobby with him, collecting clothes. If he'd had half a dozen houses, they would all have been full of a complete gentleman's town and country outfit."

"I see."

"Of course, it might be useful sometimes, when he was busy in the next room, not to have to go upstairs for a handkerchief or a more comfortable coat."

"I see. Yes." He was walking round the room as he answered, and he lifted the top of the linen basket which stood near the wash basin and glanced in. "He seems to have come in here for a collar lately."

Bill peered in. There was one collar at the bottom of the basket.

"Yes. I daresay he would," he agreed. "If he suddenly found that the one he was wearing was uncomfortable or a little bit dirty, or something. He was very finicking."

Antony leant over and picked it out.

"It must have been uncomfortable this time," he said, after examining it carefully. "It couldn't very well be cleaner." He dropped it back again. "Anyway, he did come in here sometimes?"

"Oh, yes, rather."

"Yes, but what did Cayley come in for so secretly?"

"What did he want to shut the door for?" said Bill. "That's what I don't understand. You couldn't have seen him, anyhow."

"No. So it follows that I might have heard him. He was going to do something which he didn't want me to hear."

"By Jove, that's it!" said Bill eagerly.

"Yes; but what?"

Bill frowned hopefully to himself, but no inspiration came.

"Well, let's have some air, anyway," he said at last, exhausted by the effort, and he went to the window, opened it, and looked out. Then, struck by an idea, he turned back to Antony and said, "Do you think I had better go up to the pond to make sure that they're still at it? Because—"

He broke off suddenly at the sight of Antony's face.

"Oh, idiot, idiot!" Antony cried. "Oh, most super-excellent of Watsons!

Oh, you lamb, you blessing! Oh, Gillingham, you incomparable ass!"

"What on earth—"

"The window, the window!" cried Antony, pointing to it.

Bill turned back to the window, expecting it to say something. As it said nothing, he looked at Antony again.

"He was opening the window!" cried Antony.

"Who?"

"Cayley, of course." Very gravely and slowly he expounded. "He came in here in order to open the window. He shut the door so that I shouldn't hear him open the window. He opened the window. I came in here and found the window open. I said, 'This window is open. My amazing powers of analysis tell me that the murderer must have escaped by this window.' 'Oh,' said Cayley, raising his eyebrows. 'Well,' said he, 'I suppose you must be right.' Said I proudly, 'I am. For the window is open,' I said. Oh, you incomparable ass!"

He understood now. It explained so much that had been puzzling him.

He tried to put himself in Cayley's place—Cayley, when Antony had first discovered him, hammering at the door and crying, "Let me in!" Whatever had happened inside the office, whoever had killed Robert, Cayley knew all about it, and knew that Mark was not inside, and had not escaped by the window. But it was necessary to Cayley's plans—to Mark's plans if they were acting in concert—that he should be thought so to have escaped. At some time, then, while he was hammering (the key in his pocket) at the locked door, he must suddenly have remembered—with what a shock!—that a mistake had been made. A window had not been left open!

Probably it would just have been a horrible doubt at first. Was the office window open? Surely it was open! Was it?.... Would he have time now to unlock the door, slip in, open the French windows and slip out again? No. At any moment the servants might come. It was too risky. Fatal, if he were discovered. But servants were stupid. He could get the windows safely open while they were crowding round the body. They wouldn't notice. He could do it somehow.

And then Antony's sudden appearance! Here was a complication. And Antony suggesting that they should try the window! Why, the window was just what he wanted to avoid. No wonder he had seemed dazed at first.

Ah, and here at last was the explanation why they had gone the longest way round and yet run. It was Cayley's only chance of getting a start on Antony, of getting to the windows first, of working them open somehow before Antony caught him up. Even if that were impossible, he must get there first, just to make sure. Perhaps they were open. He must get away from Antony and see. And if they were shut, hopelessly shut, then he must have a moment to himself, a moment in which to think of some other plan, and avoid the ruin which seemed so suddenly to be threatening.

So he had run. But Antony had kept up with him. They had broken in the window together, and gone into the office. But Cayley was not done yet. There was the dressing-room window! But quietly, quietly. Antony mustn't hear.

And Antony didn't hear. Indeed, he had played up to Cayley splendidly. Not only had he called attention to the open window, but he had carefully explained to Cayley why Mark had chosen this particular window in preference to the office window. And Cayley had agreed that probably that was the reason. How he must have chuckled to himself! But he was still a little afraid. Afraid that Antony would examine the shrubbery. Why? Obviously because there was no trace of anyone having broken through the shrubbery. No doubt Cayley had provided the necessary traces since, and had helped the Inspector to find them. Had he even gone as far as footmarks in Mark's shoes? But the ground was very hard. Perhaps footmarks were not necessary. Antony smiled as he thought of the big Cayley trying to squeeze into the dapper little Mark's shoes. Cayley must have been glad that footmarks were not necessary.

No, the open window was enough; the open window and a broken twig or two. But quietly, quietly. Antony mustn't hear. And Antony had not heard.... But he had seen a shadow on the wall.

They were outside on the lawn again now, Bill and Antony, and Bill was

listening open-mouthed to his friend's theory of yesterday's happenings.

It fitted in, it explained things, but it did not get them any further. It only gave them another mystery to solve.

"What's that?" said Antony.

"Mark. Where's Mark? If he never went into the office at all, then where is he now?"

"I don't say that he never went into the office. In fact, he must have gone. Elsie heard him." He stopped and repeated slowly, "She heard him, at least she says she did. But if he was there, he came out again by the door."

"Well, but where does that lead you?"

"Where it led Mark. The passage."

"Do you mean that he's been hiding there all the time?" Antony was silent until Bill had repeated his question, and then with an effort he came out of his thoughts and answered him.

"I don't know. But look here. Here is a possible explanation. I don't know if it is the right one—I don't know, Bill; I'm rather frightened. Frightened of what may have happened, of what may be going to happen. However, here is an explanation. See if you can find any fault with it."

With his legs stretched out and his hands deep in his pockets, he lay back on the garden-seat, looking up to the blue summer sky above him, and just as if he saw up there the events of yesterday being enacted over again, he described them slowly to Bill as they happened.

"We'll begin at the moment when Mark shoots Robert. Call it an accident; probably it was. Mark would say it was, anyhow. He is in a panic, naturally. But he doesn't lock the door and run away. For one thing, the key is on the outside of the door; for another, he is not quite such a fool as that. But he is in a horrible position. He is known to be on bad terms with his brother; he has just uttered some foolish threat to him, which may possibly have been overheard. What is he to do? He does the natural thing, the thing which Mark would always do in such circumstances. He consults Cayley, the invaluable, inevitable Cayley.

"Cayley is just outside, Cayley must have heard the shot, Cayley will tell him what to do. He opens the door just as Cayley is coming to see what is the matter. He explains rapidly. 'What's to be done, Cay? What's to be done? It was an accident. I swear it was an accident. He threatened me. He would have shot me if I hadn't. Think of something, quick!'

"Cayley has thought of something. 'Leave it to me,' he says. 'You clear out altogether. I shot him, if you like. I'll do all the explaining. Get away. Hide. Nobody saw you go in. Into the passage, quick. I'll come to you there as soon as I can.'

"Good Cayley. Faithful Cayley! Mark's courage comes back. Cayley will explain all right. Cayley will tell the servants that it was an accident. He will ring up the police. Nobody will suspect Cayley—Cayley has no quarrel with Robert. And then Cayley will come into the passage and tell him that it is all right, and Mark will go out by the other end, and saunter slowly back to the house. He will be told the news by one of the servants. Robert accidentally shot? Good Heavens!

"So, greatly reassured, Mark goes into the library. And Cayley goes to the door of the office…. and locks it. And then he bangs on the door and shouts, 'Let me in!'"

Antony was silent. Bill looked at him and shook his head.

"Yes, Tony, but that doesn't make sense. What's the point of Cayley behaving like that?"

Antony shrugged his shoulders without answering.

"And what has happened to Mark since?"

Antony shrugged his shoulders again.

"Well, the sooner we go into that passage, the better," said Bill.

"You're ready to go?"

"Quite," said Bill, surprised.

"You're quite ready for what we may find?"

"You're being dashed mysterious, old boy."

"I know I am." He gave a little laugh, and went on, "Perhaps I'm being an ass, just a melodramatic ass. Well, I hope I am." He looked at his watch.

"It's safe, is it? They're still busy at the pond?"

"We'd better make certain. Could you be a sleuthhound, Bill—one of those that travel on their stomachs very noiselessly? I mean, could you get near enough to the pond to make sure that Cayley is still there, without letting him see you?"

"Rather!" He got up eagerly. "You wait."

Antony's head shot up suddenly. "Why, that was what Mark said," he cried.

"Mark?"

"Yes. What Elsie heard him say."

"Oh, that."

"Yes I suppose she couldn't have made a mistake, Bill? She did hear him?"

"She couldn't have mistaken his voice, if that's what you mean."

"Oh?"

"Mark had an extraordinary characteristic voice."

"Oh!"

"Rather high-pitched, you know, and well, one can't explain, but—"

"Yes?"

"Well, rather like this, you know, or even more so if anything." He rattled these words off in Mark's rather monotonous, high-pitched voice, and then laughed, and added in his natural voice, "I say, that was really rather good."

Antony nodded quickly. "That was like it?" he said.

"Exactly."

"Yes." He got up and squeezed Bill's arm. "Well just go and see about Cayley, and then we'll get moving. I shall be in the library."

"Right."

Bill nodded and walked off in the direction of the pond. This was glorious fun; this was life. The immediate programme could hardly be bettered. First of all he was going to stalk Cayley. There was a little copse above the level of the pond, and about a hundred yards away from it. He would come into this from the back, creep cautiously through it, taking care that no twigs cracked, and then, drawing himself on his stomach to the edge, peer down upon the scene below him. People were always doing that sort of thing in books, and he had been filled with a hopeless envy of them; well, now he was actually going to do it himself. What fun!

And then, when he had got back unobserved to the house and reported to Antony, they were going to explore the secret passage! Again, what fun! Unfortunately there seemed to be no chance of buried treasure, but there might be buried clues. Even if you found nothing, you couldn't get away from the fact that a secret passage was a secret passage, and anything might happen in it. But even that wasn't the end of this exciting day. They were going to watch the pond that night; they were going to watch Cayley under the moonlight, watch him as he threw into the silence of the pond what? The revolver? Well, anyhow, they were going to watch him. What fun!

To Antony, who was older and who realized into what deep waters they were getting, it did not seem fun. But it was amazingly interesting. He saw so much, and yet somehow it was all out of focus. It was like looking at an opal, and discovering with every movement of it some new colour, some new gleam of light reflected, and yet never really seeing the opal as a whole. He was too near it, or too far away; he strained his eyes and he relaxed his eyes; it was no good. His brain could not get hold of it.

But there were moments when he almost had it.... and then turned away from it. He had seen more of life than Bill, but he had never seen murder before, and this which was in his mind now, and to which he was afraid to listen, was not just the hot-blooded killing which any man may come to if he lose control. It was something much more horrible. Too horrible to be true. Then let him look again for the truth. He looked again but it was all out of focus.

"I will not look again," he said aloud, as he began to walk towards the house. "Not yet, anyway." He would go on collecting facts and impressions. Perhaps the one fact would come along, by itself which would make everything clear.

CHAPTER XIV

MR. BEVERLEY QUALIFIES FOR THE STAGE

Bill had come back, and had reported, rather breathless, that Cayley was still at the pond.

"But I don't think they're getting up much except mud," he said. "I ran most of the way back so as to give us as much time as possible."

Antony nodded.

"Well, come along, then," he said. "The sooner, the quicker."

They stood in front of the row of sermons. Antony took down the Reverend

Theodore Ussher's famous volume, and felt for the spring. Bill pulled.

The shelves swung open towards them.

"By Jove!" said Bill, "it is a narrow way."

There was an opening about a yard square in front of them, which had something the look of a brick fireplace, a fireplace raised about two feet from the ground. But, save for one row of bricks in front, the floor of it was emptiness. Antony took a torch from his pocket and flashed it down into the blackness.

"Look," he whispered to the eager Bill. "The steps begin down there. Six feet down."

He flashed his torch up again. There was a handhold of iron, a sort of large iron staple, in the bricks in front of them.

"You swing off from there," said Bill. "At least, I suppose you do. I wonder how Ruth Norris liked doing it."

"Cayley helped her, I should think.... It's funny."

"Shall I go first?" asked Bill, obviously longing to do so.

Antony shook his head with a smile.

"I think I will, if you don't mind very much, Bill. Just in case."

"In case of what?"

"Well in case."

Bill, had to be content with that, but he was too much excited to wonder what Antony meant.

"Righto," he said. "Go on."

"Well, we'll just make sure we can get back again, first. It really wouldn't be fair on the Inspector if we got stuck down here for the rest of our lives. He's got enough to do trying to find Mark, but if he has to find you and me as well—"

"We can always get out at the other end."

"Well, we're not certain yet. I think I'd better just go down and back. I promise faithfully not to explore."

"Right you are."

Antony sat down on the ledge of bricks, swung his feet over, and sat there for a moment, his legs dangling. He flashed his torch into the darkness again, so as to make sure where the steps began; then returned it to his pocket, seized the staple in front of him and swung himself down. His feet touched the steps beneath him, and he let go.

"Is it all right?" said Bill anxiously.

"All right. I'll just go down to the bottom of the steps and back. Stay there."

The light shone down by his feet. His head began to disappear. For a little while Bill, craning down the opening, could still see faint splashes of light, and could hear slow uncertain footsteps; for a little longer he could fancy that he saw and heard them; then he was alone….

Well, not quite alone. There was a sudden voice in the hall outside.

"Good Lord!" said Bill, turning round with a start, "Cayley!"

If he was not so quick in thought as Antony, he was quick enough in action. Thought was not demanded now. To close the secret door safely but noiselessly, to make sure that the books were in the right places, to move away to another row of shelves so as to be discovered deep in "Badminton" or "Baedeker" or whomever the kind gods should send to his aid the difficulty was not to decide what to do, but to do all this in five seconds rather than in six.

"Ah, there you are," said Cayley from the doorway.

"Hallo!" said Bill, in surprise, looking up from the fourth volume of

"The Life and Works of Samuel Taylor Coleridge." "Have they finished?"

"Finished what?"

"The pond," said Bill, wondering why he was reading Coleridge on such a fine afternoon. Desperately he tried to think of a good reason.... verifying a quotation—an argument with Antony—that would do. But what quotation?

"Oh, no. They're still at it. Where's Gillingham?"

'The Ancient Mariner'—water, water, everywhere—or was that something else? And where was Gillingham? Water, water everywhere...

"Tony? Oh, he's about somewhere. We're just going down to the village. They aren't finding anything at the pond, are they?"

"No. But they like doing it. Something off their minds when they can say they've done it."

Bill, deep in his book, looked up and said "Yes," and went back to it again. He was just getting to the place.

"What's the book?" said Cayley, coming up to him. Out of the corner of his eye he glanced at the shelf of sermons as he came. Bill saw that glance and wondered. Was there anything there to give away the secret?

"I was just looking up a quotation," he drawled. "Tony and I had a bet about it. You know that thing about—er water, water everywhere, and—er—not a drop to drink." (But what on earth, he wondered to himself, were they betting about?)

"'Nor any drop to drink,' to be accurate."

Bill looked at him in surprise. Then a happy smile came on his face.

"Quite sure?" he said.

"Of course."

"Then you've saved me a lot of trouble. That's, what the bet was about." He closed the book with a slam, put it back in its shelf, and began to feel for his pipe and tobacco. "I was a fool to bet with Tony," he added. "He always knows that sort of thing."

So far, so good. But here was Cayley still in the library, and there was Antony, all unsuspecting, in the passage. When Antony came back he would not be surprised to find the door closed, because the whole object of his going had been to see if he could open it easily from the inside. At any moment, then, the bookshelf might swing back and show Antony's head in the gap. A nice surprise for Cayley!

"Come with us?" he said casually, as he struck a match. He pulled vigorously at the flame as he waited for the answer, hoping to hide his anxiety, for if Cayley assented, he was done.

"I've got to go into Stanton."

Bill blew out a great cloud of smoke with an expiration which covered also a heartfelt sigh of relief.

"Oh, a pity. You're driving, I suppose?"

"Yes. The car will be here directly. There's a letter I must write first." He sat down at a writing table, and took out a sheet of notepaper.

He was facing the secret door; if it opened he would see it. At any moment now it might open.

Bill dropped into a chair and thought. Antony must be warned. Obviously. But how? How did one signal to anybody? By code. Morse code. Did Antony know it? Did Bill know it himself, if it came to that? He had picked up a bit in the Army not enough to send a message, of course. But a message was impossible, anyhow; Cayley would hear him tapping it out. It wouldn't do to send more than a single letter. What letters did he know? And what letter would convey anything to Antony?.... He pulled at his pipe, his eyes wandering from Cayley at his desk to the Reverend Theodore Ussher in his shelf. What letter?

C for Cayley. Would Antony understand? Probably not, but it was just worth trying. What was C? Long, short, long, short. Umpty-iddy-umpty-iddy. Was that right? C yes, that was C. He was sure of that. C. Umpty-iddy-umpty-iddy.

Hands in pockets, he got up and wandered across the room, humming vaguely to himself, the picture of a man waiting for another man (as it might be his friend Gillingham) to come in and take him away for a walk or something. He wandered across to the books at the back of Cayley, and began to tap absent-mindedly on the shelves, as he looked at the titles. Umpty-iddy-umpty-iddy. Not that it was much like that at first; he couldn't get the rhythm of it.... Umpt-y-iddy-umpt-y-iddy. That was better. He was back at Samuel Taylor Coleridge now. Antony would begin to hear him soon. Umpt-y-iddy-umpt-y-iddy; just the aimless tapping of a man who is wondering what book he will take out with him to read on the lawn. Would Antony hear? One always heard the man in the next flat knocking out his pipe. Would Antony understand? Umpt-y-iddy-umpt-y-iddy. C. for Cayley, Antony. Cayley's here. For God's sake, wait.

"Good Lord! Sermons!" said Bill, with a loud laugh.

(Umpt-y-iddy-umpt-y-iddy) "Ever read 'em, Cayley?"

"What?" Cayley looked up suddenly. Bill's back moved slowly along, his fingers beating a tattoo on the shelves as he walked.

"Er no," said Cayley, with a little laugh. An awkward, uncomfortable little laugh, it seemed to Bill.

"Nor do I." He was past the sermons now past the secret door but still tapping in the same aimless way.

"Oh, for God's sake sit down," burst out Cayley. "Or go outside if you want to walk about."

Bill turned round in astonishment.

"Hallo, what's the matter?"

Cayley was slightly ashamed of his outburst.

"Sorry, Bill," he apologized. "My nerves are on edge. Your constant tapping and fidgeting about—"

"Tapping?" said Bill with an air of complete surprise.

"Tapping on the shelves, and humming. Sorry. It got on my nerves."

"My dear old chap, I'm awfully sorry. I'll go out in the hall."

"It's all right," said Cayley, and went on with his letter. Bill sat down in his chair again. Had Antony understood? Well, anyhow, there was nothing to do now but wait for Cayley to go. "And if you ask me," said Bill to himself, much pleased, "I ought to be on the stage. That's where I ought to be. The complete actor."

A minute, two minutes, three minutes.... five minutes. It was safe now.

Antony had guessed.

"Is the car there?" asked Cayley, as he sealed up his letter.

Bill strolled into the hall, called back "Yes," and went out to talk to the chauffeur. Cayley joined him, and they stood there for a moment.

"Hallo," said a pleasant voice behind them. They turned round and saw Antony.

"Sorry to keep you waiting, Bill."

With a tremendous effort Bill restrained his feelings, and said casually enough that it was all right.

"Well, I must be off," said Cayley. "You're going down to the village?"

"That's the idea."

"I wonder if you'd take this letter to Jallands for me?"

"Of course."

"Thanks very much. Well, I shall see you later."

He nodded and got into the car.

As soon as they were alone Bill turned eagerly to his friend.

"Well?" he said excitedly.

"Come into the library."

They went in, and Tony sank down into a chair.

"You must give me a moment," he panted. "I've been running."

"Running?"

"Well, of course. How do you think I got back here?"

"You don't mean you went out at the other end?"

Antony nodded.

"I say, did you hear me tapping?"

"I did, indeed. Bill, you're a genius."

Bill blushed.

"I knew you'd understand," he said. "You guessed that I meant Cayley?"

"I did. It was the least I could do after you had been so brilliant. You must have had rather an exciting time."

"Exciting? Good Lord, I should think it was."

"Tell me about it."

As modestly as possible, Mr. Beverley explained his qualifications for a life on the stage.

"Good man," said Antony at the end of it. "You are the most perfect Watson that ever lived. Bill, my lad," he went on dramatically, rising and taking Bill's hand in both of his, "There is nothing that you and I could not accomplish together, if we gave our minds to it."

"Silly old ass."

"That's what you always say when I'm being serious. Well, anyway, thanks awfully. You really saved us this time."

"Were you coming back?"

"Yes. At least I think I was. I was just wondering when I heard you tapping. The fact of the door being shut was rather surprising. Of course the whole idea was to see if it could be opened easily from the other side, but I felt somehow that you wouldn't shut it until the last possible moment—until you saw me coming back. Well, then I heard the taps, and I knew it must mean something, so I sat tight. Then when C began to come along I said, 'Cayley, b'Jove'—bright, aren't I?—and I simply hared to the other end of the passage for all I was worth. And hared back again. Because I thought you might be getting rather involved in explanations—about where I was, and so on."

"You didn't see Mark, then?"

"No. Nor his—No, I didn't see anything."

"Nor what?"

Antony was silent for a moment.

"I didn't see anything, Bill. Or rather, I did see something; I saw a door in the wall, a cupboard. And it's locked. So if there's anything we want to find, that's where it is."

"Could Mark be hiding there?"

"I called through the keyhole in a whisper 'Mark, are you there?' he would have thought it was Cayley. There was no answer.

"Well, let's go down and try again. We might be able to get the door open."

Antony shook his head.

"Aren't I going at all?" said Bill in great disappointment.

When Antony spoke, it was to ask another question:

"Can Cayley drive a car?"

"Yes, of course. Why?"

"Then he might easily drop the chauffeur at his lodge and go off to Stanton, or wherever he wanted to, on his own?"

"I suppose so if he wanted to."

"Yes." Antony got up. "Well, look here, as we said we were going into the village, and as we promised to leave that letter, I almost think we'd better do it."

"Oh!.... Oh, very well."

"Jallands. What were you telling me about that? Oh, yes; the Widow Norbury."

"That's right. Cayley used to be rather keen on the daughter. The letter's for her."

"Yes; well, let's take it. Just to be on the safe side."

"Am I going to be done out of that secret passage

altogether?" asked Bill fretfully.

"There's nothing to see, really, I promise you."

"You're very mysterious. What's upset you? You did see something down there, I'm certain of it."

"I did and I've told you about it."

"No, you haven't. You only told me about the door in the wall."

"That's it, Bill. And it's locked. And I'm frightened of what's behind it."

"But then we shall never know what's there if we aren't going to look."

"We shall know to-night," said Antony, taking Bill's arm and leading him to the hall, "when we watch our dear friend Cayley dropping it into the pond."

CHAPTER XV

MRS. NORBURY CONFIDES IN DEAR MR. GILLINGHAM

They left the road, and took the path across the fields which sloped gently downwards towards Jallands. Antony was silent, and since it is difficult to keep up a conversation with a silent man for any length of time, Bill had dropped into silence too. Or rather, he hummed to himself, hit at thistles in the grass with his stick and made uncomfortable noises with his pipe. But he noticed that his companion kept looking back over his shoulder, almost as if he wanted to remember for a future occasion the way by which they were coming. Yet there was no difficulty about it, for they remained all the time in view of the road, and the belt of trees above the long park wall which bordered its further side stood out clearly against the sky.

Antony, who had just looked round again, turned back with a smile.

"What's the joke?" said Bill, glad of the more social atmosphere.

"Cayley. Didn't you see?"

"See what?"

"The car. Going past on the road there."

"So that's what you were looking for. You've got jolly good eyes, my boy, if you recognize the car at this distance after only seeing it twice."

"Well, I have got jolly good eyes."

"I thought he was going to Stanton."

"He hoped you'd think so obviously."

"Then where is he going?"

"The library, probably. To consult our friend Ussher. After making quite sure that his friends Beverley and Gillingham really were going to Jallands, as they said."

Bill stopped suddenly in the middle of the path.

"I say, do you think so?"

Antony shrugged his shoulders.

"I shouldn't be surprised. We must be devilishly inconvenient for him, hanging about the house. Any moment he can get, when we're definitely somewhere else, must be very useful to him."

"Useful for what?"

"Well, useful for his nerves, if for nothing else. We know he's mixed up in this business; we know he's hiding a secret or two. Even if he doesn't suspect that we're on his tracks, he must feel that at any moment we might stumble on something."

Bill gave a grunt of assent, and they went slowly on again.

"What about to-night?" he said, after a lengthy blow at his pipe.

"Try a piece of grass," said Antony, offering it to him. Bill pushed it through the mouthpiece, blew again, said, "That's better," and returned the pipe to his pocket.

"How are we going to get out without Cayley knowing?"

"Well, that wants thinking over. It's going to be difficult. I wish we were sleeping at the inn.... Is this Miss Norbury, by any chance?"

Bill looked up quickly. They were close to Jallands now, an old thatched farmhouse which, after centuries of sleep, had woken up to a new world, and had forthwith sprouted wings; wings, however, of so discreet a growth that they had not brought with them any obvious change of character, and Jallands even with a bathroom was still Jallands. To the outward view, at any rate. Inside, it was more clearly Mrs. Norbury's.

"Yes Angela Norbury," murmured Bill. "Not bad-looking, is she?"

The girl who stood by the little white gate of Jallands was something more than "not bad-looking," but in this matter Bill was keeping his superlatives for another. In Bill's eyes she must be judged, and condemned, by all that distinguished her from Betty Calladine. To Antony, unhampered by these standards of comparison, she seemed, quite simply, beautiful.

"Cayley asked us to bring a letter along," explained Bill, when the necessary handshakings and introductions were over. "Here you are."

"You will tell him, won't you, how dreadfully sorry I am about what has happened? It seems so hopeless to say anything; so hopeless even to believe it. If it is true what we've heard."

Bill repeated the outline of events of yesterday.

"Yes…. And Mr. Ablett hasn't been found yet?" She shook her head in distress. "It still seems to have happened to somebody else; somebody we didn't know at all." Then, with a sudden grave smile which included both of them, "But you must come and have some tea."

"It's awfully decent of you," said Bill awkwardly, "but we—er—"

"You will, won't you?" she said to Antony.

"Thank you very much."

Mrs. Norbury was delighted to see them, as she always was to see any man in her house who came up to the necessary standard of eligibility. When her life-work was completed, and summed up in those beautiful words: "A marriage has been arranged, and will shortly take place, between Angela, daughter of the late John Norbury…." then she would utter a grateful Nunc dimittis and depart in peace to a better world, if Heaven insisted, but preferably to her new son-in-law's more dignified establishment. For there was no doubt that eligibility meant not only eligibility as a husband.

But it was not as "eligibles" that the visitors from the Red House were received with such eagerness to-day, and even if her special smile for "possibles" was there, it was instinctive rather than reasoned. All that she wanted at this moment was news—news of Mark. For she was bringing it off at last; and, if the engagement columns of the "Morning Post" were preceded, as in the case of its obituary columns, by a premonitory bulletin, the announcement of yesterday would have cried triumphantly to the world, or to such part of the world as mattered: "A marriage has very nearly been arranged (by Mrs. Norbury), and will certainly take place, between Angela, only daughter of the late John Norbury, and—Mark Ablett of the Red House." And, coming across it on his way to the sporting page, Bill would have been surprised. For he had thought that, if anybody, it was Cayley.

To the girl it was neither. She was often amused by her mother's ways; sometimes ashamed of them; sometimes distressed by them. The Mark Ablett affair had seemed to her particularly distressing, for Mark was so obviously in league with her mother against her. Other suitors, upon whom her mother had smiled, had been embarrassed by that championship; Mark appeared to depend on it as much as on his own attractions; great though he thought these to be. They went a-wooing together. It was a pleasure to turn to Cayley, that hopeless ineligible.

But alas! Cayley had misunderstood her. She could not imagine Cayley in love until she saw it, and tried, too late, to stop it. That was four days ago. She had not seen him since, and now here was this letter. She dreaded opening it. It was a relief to feel that at least she had an excuse for not doing so while her guests were in the house.

Mrs. Norbury recognized at once that Antony was likely to be the more sympathetic listener, and when tea was over, and Bill and Angela had been dispatched to the garden with the promptness and efficiency of the expert, dear Mr. Gillingham found himself on the sofa beside her, listening to many things which were of even greater interest to him than she could possibly have hoped.

"It is terrible, terrible," she said. "And to suggest that dear Mr.

Ablett—"

Antony made suitable noises.

"You've seen Mr. Ablett for yourself. A kinder, more warmhearted man—"

Antony explained that he had not seen Mr. Ablett.

"Of course, yes, I was forgetting. But, believe me, Mr.

Gillingham, you can trust a woman's intuition in these matters."

Antony said that he was sure of this.

"Think of my feelings as a mother."

Antony was thinking of Miss Norbury's feelings as a daughter, and wondering if she guessed that her affairs were now being discussed with a stranger. Yet what could he do? What, indeed, did he want to do except listen, in the hope of learning? Mark engaged, or about to be engaged! Had that any bearing on the events of yesterday? What, for instance, would Mrs. Norbury have thought of brother Robert, that family skeleton? Was this another reason for wanting brother Robert out of the way?

"I never liked him, never!"

"Never liked?" said Antony, bewildered.

"That cousin of his Mr. Cayley."

"Oh!"

"I ask you, Mr. Gillingham, am I the sort of woman to trust my little girl to a man who would go about shooting his only brother?"

"I'm sure you wouldn't, Mrs. Norbury."

"If there has been any shooting done, it has been done by somebody else."

Antony looked at her inquiringly.

"I never liked him," said Mrs. Norbury firmly. "Never." However, thought

Antony to himself, that didn't quite prove that Cayley was a murderer.

"How did Miss Norbury get on with him?" he asked cautiously.

"There was nothing in that at all," said Miss Norbury's mother emphatically. "Nothing. I would say so to anybody."

"Oh, I beg your pardon. I never meant—"

"Nothing. I can say that for dear Angela with perfect confidence. Whether he made advances—" She broke off with a shrug of her plump shoulders.

Antony waited eagerly.

"Naturally they met. Possibly he might have—I don't know. But my duty as a mother was clear, Mr. Gillingham."

Mr. Gillingham made an encouraging noise.

"I told him quite frankly that—how shall I put it?—that he

was trespassing. Tactfully, of course. But frankly."

"You mean," said Antony, trying to speak calmly, "that you told him that—er—Mr. Ablett and your daughter—?"

Mrs. Norbury nodded several times.

"Exactly, Mr. Gillingham. I had my duty as a mother."

"I am sure, Mrs. Norbury, that nothing would keep you from doing your duty. But it must have been disagreeable. Particularly if you weren't quite sure—"

"He was attracted, Mr. Gillingham. Obviously attracted."

"Who would not be?" said Antony, with a charming smile. "It must have been something of a shock to him to—"

"It was just that which made me so glad that I had spoken. I saw at once that I had not spoken a moment too soon."

"There must have been a certain awkwardness about the next meeting," suggested Antony.

"Naturally, he has not been here since. No doubt they would have been bound to meet up at the Red House sooner or later."

"Oh,—this was only quite lately?"

"Last week, Mr. Gillingham. I spoke just in time."

"Ah!" said Antony, under his breath. He had been waiting for it.

He would have liked now to have gone away, so that he might have thought over the new situation by himself; or, perhaps preferably, to have changed partners for a little while with Bill. Miss Norbury would hardly be ready to confide in a stranger with the readiness of a mother, but he might have learnt something by listening to her. For which of them had she the greater feeling, Cayley or Mark? Was she really prepared to marry Mark? Did she love him or the other—or neither? Mrs. Norbury was only a trustworthy witness in regard to her own actions and thoughts; he had learnt all that was necessary of those, and only the daughter now had anything left to tell him. But Mrs. Norbury was still talking.

"Girls are so foolish, Mr. Gillingham," she was saying. "It is fortunate that they have mothers to guide them. It was so obvious to me from the beginning that dear Mr. Ablett was just the husband for my little girl. You never knew him?"

Antony said again that he had not seen Mr. Ablett.

"Such a gentleman. So nice-looking, in his artistic way. A regular Velasquez—I should say Van Dyck. Angela would have it that she could never marry a man with a beard. As if that mattered, when—" She broke off, and Antony finished her sentence for her.

"The Red House is certainly charming," he said.

"Charming. Quite charming. And it is not as if Mr. Ablett's appearance were in any way undistinguished. Quite the contrary. I'm sure you agree with me?"

Antony said that he had never had the pleasure of seeing Mr. Ablett.

"Yes. And quite the centre of the literary and artistic world. So desirable in every way."

She gave a deep sigh, and communed with herself for a little. Antony was, about to snatch the opportunity of leaving, when Mrs. Norbury began again.

"And then there's this scapegrace brother of his. He was perfectly frank with me, Mr. Gillingham. He would be. He told me of this brother, and I told him that I was quite certain it would make no difference to my daughter's feelings for him.... After all, the brother was in Australia."

"When was this? Yesterday?" Antony felt that, if Mark had only mentioned it after his brother's announcement of a personal call at the Red House, this perfect frankness had a good deal of wisdom behind it.

"It couldn't have been yesterday, Mr. Gillingham. Yesterday—" she shuddered, and shook her head.

"I thought perhaps he had been down here in the morning."

"Oh, no! There is such a thing, Mr. Gillingham, as being too devoted a lover. Not in the morning, no. We both agreed that dear Angela—Oh, no. No; the day before yesterday, when he happened to drop in about tea-time."

It occurred to Antony that Mrs. Norbury had come a long way from her opening statement that Mark and Miss Norbury were practically engaged. She was now admitting that dear Angela was not to be rushed, that dear Angela had, indeed, no heart for the match at all.

"The day before yesterday. As it happened, dear Angela was out. Not that it mattered. He was driving to Middleston. He hardly had time for a cup of tea, so that even if she had been in—"

Antony nodded absently. This was something new. Why did

Mark go to

Middleston the day before yesterday? But, after all, why shouldn't he? A hundred reasons unconnected with the death of Robert might have taken him there.

He got up to go. He wanted to be alone—alone, at least, with Bill. Mrs. Norbury had given him many things to think over, but the great outstanding fact which had emerged was this: that Cayley had reason to hate Mark,—Mrs. Norbury had given him that reason. To hate? Well, to be jealous, anyhow. But that was enough.

"You see," he said to Bill, as they walked back, "we know that Cayley is perjuring himself and risking himself over this business, and that must be for one of two reasons. Either to save Mark or to endanger him. That is to say, he is either whole-heartedly for him or whole-heartedly against him. Well, now we know that he is against him, definitely against him."

"But, I say, you know," protested Bill, "one doesn't necessarily try to ruin one's rival in love."

"Doesn't one?" said Antony, turning to him with a smile.

Bill blushed.

"Well, of course, one never knows, but I mean—"

"You mightn't try to ruin him, Bill, but you wouldn't perjure yourself in order to get him out of a trouble of his own making."

"Lord! no."

"So that of the two alternatives the other is the more likely."

They had come to the gate into the last field which divided them from the road, and having gone through it, they turned round and leant against it, resting for a moment, and looking down at the house which they had left.

"Jolly little place, isn't it?" said Bill.

"Very. But rather mysterious."

"In what way?"

"Well, where's the front door?"

"The front door? Why, you've just come out of it."

"But isn't there a drive, or a road or anything?"

Bill laughed.

"No; that's the beauty of it to some people. And that's why it's so cheap, and why the Norburys can afford it, I expect. They're not too well off."

"But what about luggage and tradesmen and that kind of

thing?"

"Oh, there's a cart-track, but motor-cars can't come any nearer than the road" he turned round and pointed "up there. So the week-end millionaire people don't take it. At least, they'd have to build a road and a garage and all the rest of it, if they did."

"I see," said Antony carelessly, and they turned round and continued their walk up to the road. But later on he remembered this casual conversation at the gate, and saw the importance of it.

CHAPTER XVI

GETTING READY FOR THE NIGHT

What was it which Cayley was going to hide in that pond that night?

Antony thought that he knew now. It was Mark's body.

From the beginning he had seen this answer coming and had drawn back from it. For, if Mark had been killed, it seemed such a cold-blooded killing. Was Cayley equal to it? Bill would have said "No," but that was because he had had breakfast with Cayley, and lunch with him, and dinner with him; had ragged him and played games with him. Bill would have said "No," because Bill wouldn't have killed anybody in cold blood himself, and because he took it for granted that other people behaved pretty much as he did. But Antony had no such illusions. Murders were done; murder had actually been done here, for there was Robert's dead body. Why not another murder?

Had Mark been in the office at all that afternoon? The only evidence (other than Cayley's, which obviously did not count) was Elsie's. Elsie was quite certain that she had heard his voice. But then Bill had said that it was a very characteristic voice—an easy voice, therefore, to imitate. If Bill could imitate it so successfully, why not Cayley?

But perhaps it had not been such a cold-blooded killing, after all. Suppose Cayley had had a quarrel with his cousin that afternoon over the girl whom they were both wooing. Suppose

Cayley had killed Mark, either purposely, in sudden passion, or accidentally, meaning only to knock him down. Suppose that this had happened in the passage, say about two o'clock, either because Cayley had deliberately led him there, or because Mark had casually suggested a visit to it. (One could imagine Mark continually gloating over that secret passage.) Suppose Cayley there, with the body at his feet, feeling already the rope round his neck; his mind darting this way and that in frantic search for a way of escape; and suppose that suddenly and irrelevantly he remembers that Robert is coming to the house at three o'clock that afternoon—automatically he looks at his watch—in half an hour's time.... In half an hour's time. He must think of something quickly, quickly. Shall he bury the body in the passage and let it be thought that Mark ran away, frightened at the mere thought of his brother's arrival? But there was the evidence of the breakfast table. Mark had seemed annoyed at this resurrection of the black sheep, but certainly not frightened. No; that was much too thin a story. But suppose Mark had actually seen his brother and had a quarrel with him; suppose it could be made to look as if Robert had killed Mark—

Antony pictured to himself Cayley in the passage, standing over the dead body of his cousin, and working it out. How could Robert be made to seem the murderer, if Robert were alive to deny it? But suppose Robert were dead, too?

He looks at his watch again. (Only twenty-five minutes now.) Suppose Robert were dead, too? Robert dead in the office, and Mark dead in the passage how does that help? Madness! But if the bodies were brought together somehow and Robert's death looked like suicide?.... Was it possible?

Madness again. Too difficult. (Only twenty minutes now.) Too difficult to arrange in twenty minutes. Can't arrange a suicide. Too difficult.... Only nineteen minutes....

And then the sudden inspiration! Robert dead in the office, Mark's body hidden in the passage—impossible to make Robert seem the murderer, but how easy to make Mark! Robert dead and Mark missing; why, it jumped to the eye at once. Mark had killed Robert—accidentally; yes, that would be more likely—and then had run away. Sudden panic.... (He looks at his watch again. Fifteen minutes, but plenty of time now. The thing arranges itself.)

Was that the solution, Antony wondered. It seemed to fit in with the facts as they knew them; but then, so did that other theory which he had suggested to Bill in the morning.

"Which one?" said Bill.

They had come back from Jallands through the park and were sitting in the copse above the pond, from which the Inspector and his fishermen had now withdrawn. Bill had listened with open mouth to Antony's theory, and save for an occasional "By Jove!" had listened in silence. "Smart man, Cayley," had been his only comment at the end.

"Which other theory?"

"That Mark had killed Robert accidentally and had gone to Cayley for help, and that Cayley, having hidden him in the passage, locked the office door from the outside and hammered on it."

"Yes, but you were so dashed mysterious about that. I asked you what the point of it was, and you wouldn't say anything." He thought for a little, and then went on, "I suppose you meant that Cayley deliberately betrayed Mark, and tried to make him look like a murderer?"

"I wanted to warn you that we should probably find Mark in the passage, alive or dead."

"And now you don't think so?"

"Now I think that his dead body is there."

"Meaning that Cayley went down and killed him afterwards after you had come, after the police had come?"

"Well, that's what I shrink from, Bill. It's so horribly cold-blooded.

Cayley may be capable of it, but I hate to think of it."

"But, dash it all, your other way is cold-blooded enough. According to you, he goes up to the office and deliberately shoots a man with whom he has no quarrel, whom he hasn't seen for fifteen years!"

"Yes, but to save his own neck. That makes a difference. My theory is that he quarrelled violently with Mark over the girl, and killed him in sudden passion. Anything that happened after that would be self-defense. I don't mean that I excuse it, but that I understand it. And I think that Mark's dead body is in the passage now, and has been there since, say, half-past two yesterday afternoon. And to-night Cayley is going to hide it in the pond."

Bill pulled at the moss on the ground beside him, threw away a handful or two, and said slowly, "You may be right, but it's all guess-work, you know."

Antony laughed.

"Good Lord, of course it is," he said. "And to-night we shall know if it's a good guess or a bad one."

Bill brightened up suddenly.

"To-night," he said. "I say, to-night's going to be rather fun. How do we work it?"

Antony was silent for a little.

"Of course," he said at last, "we ought to inform the police, so that they can come here and watch the pond to-night."

"Of course," grinned Bill.

"But I think that perhaps it is a little early to put our theories before them."

"I think perhaps it is," said Bill solemnly.

Antony looked up at him with a sudden smile.

"Bill, you old bounder."

"Well, dash it, it's our show. I don't see why we shouldn't get our little bit of fun out of it."

"Neither do I. All right, then, we'll do without the police to-night."

"We shall miss them," said Bill sadly, "but 'tis better so."

There were two problems in front of them: first, the problem of getting out of the house without being discovered by Cayley, and secondly, the problem of recovering whatever it was which Cayley dropped into the pond that night.

"Let's look at it from Cayley's point of view," said Antony. "He may not know that we're on his track, but he can't help being suspicious of us. He's bound to be suspicious of everybody in the house, and more particularly of us, because we're presumably more intelligent than the others."

He stopped for a moment to light his pipe, and Bill took the opportunity of looking more intelligent than Mrs. Stevens.

"Now, he has got something to hide to-night, and he's going to take good care that we aren't watching him. Well, what will he do?"

"See that we are asleep first, before he starts out."

"Yes. Come and tuck us up, and see that we're nice and

comfortable."

"Yes, that's awkward," said Bill. "But we could lock our doors, and then he wouldn't know that we weren't there."

"Have you ever locked your door?"

"Never."

"No. And you can bet that Cayley knows that. Anyway, he'd bang on it, and you wouldn't answer, and then what would he think?"

Bill was silent; crushed.

"Then I don't see how we're going to do it," he said, after deep thought. "He'll obviously come to us just before he starts out, and that doesn't give us time to get to the pond in front of him."

"Let's put ourselves in his place," said Antony, puffing slowly at his pipe. "He's got the body, or whatever it is, in the passage. He won't come up the stairs, carrying it in his arms, and look in at our doors to see if we're awake. He'll have to make sure about us first, and then go down for the body afterwards. So that gives us a little time."

"Y-yes," said Bill doubtfully. "We might just do it, but it'll be a bit of a rush."

"But wait. When he's gone down to the passage and got the body, what will he do next?"

"Come out again," said Bill helpfully.

"Yes; but which end?"

Bill sat up with a start.

"By Jove, you mean that he will go out at the far end by the bowling-green?"

"Don't you think so? Just imagine him walking across the lawn in full view of the house, at midnight, with a body in his arms. Think of the awful feeling he would have in the back of the neck, wondering if anybody, any restless sleeper, had chosen just that moment to wander to the window and look out into the night. There's still plenty of moonlight, Bill. Is he going to walk across the park in the moonlight, with all those windows staring at him? Not if he can help it. But he can get out by the bowling green, and then come to the pond without ever being in sight of the house, at all."

"You're right. And that will just about give us time. Good. Now, what's the next thing?"

"The next thing is to mark the exact place in the pond where he drops whatever he drops."

"So that we can fish it out again."

"If we can see what it is, we shan't want to. The police can have a go at it to-morrow. But if it's something we can't identify from a distance, then we must try and get it out. To see whether it's worth telling the police about."

"Y-yes," said Bill, wrinkling his forehead. "Of course, the trouble with water is that one bit of it looks pretty much like the next bit. I don't know if that had occurred to you.

"It had," smiled Antony. "Let's come and have a look at it."

They walked to the edge of the copse, and lay down there in silence, looking at the pond beneath them.

"See anything?" said Antony at last.

"What?"

"The fence on the other side."

"What about it?"

"Well, it's rather useful, that's all."

"Said Sherlock Holmes enigmatically," added Bill. "A moment later, his friend Watson had hurled him into the pond."

Antony laughed.

"I love being Sherlocky," he said. "It's very unfair of you not to play up to me."

"Why is that fence useful, my dear Holmes?" said Bill obediently.

"Because you can take a bearing on it. You see— "

"Yes, you needn't stop to explain to me what a bearing is."

"I wasn't going to. But you're lying here," he looked up "underneath this pine-tree. Cayley comes out in the old boat and drops his parcel in. You take a line from here on to the boat, and mark it off on the fence there. Say it's the fifth post from the end. Well, then I take a line from my tree we'll find one for me directly and it comes on to the twentieth post, say. And where the two lines meet, there shall the eagles be gathered together. Q.E.D. And there, I almost forgot to remark, will the taller eagle, Beverley by name, do his famous diving act. As performed nightly at the Hippodrome."

Bill looked at him uneasily.

"I say, really? It's beastly dirty water, you know."

"I'm afraid so, Bill. So it is written in the book of Jasher."

"Of course I knew that one of us would have to, but I hoped, well, it's a warm night."

"Just the night for a bathe," agreed Antony, getting up. "Well now, let's have a look for my tree."

They walked down to the margin of the pond and then looked back. Bill's tree stood up and took the evening, tall and unmistakable, fifty feet nearer to heaven than its neighbours. But it had its fellow at the other end of the copse, not quite so tall, perhaps, but equally conspicuous.

"That's where I shall be," said Antony, pointing to it. "Now, for the

Lord's sake, count your posts accurately."

"Thanks very much, but I shall do it for my own sake," said Bill with feeling. "I don't want to spend the whole night diving."

"Fix on the post in a straight line with you and the splash, and then count backwards to the beginning of the fence."

"Right, old boy. Leave it to me. I can do this on my head."

"Well, that's how you will have to do the last part of it," said Antony with a smile.

He looked at his watch. It was nearly time to change for dinner. They started to walk back to the house together.

"There's one thing which worries me rather," said Antony. "Where does Cayley sleep?"

"Next door to me. Why?"

"Well, it's just possible that he might have another look at you after he's come back from the pond. I don't think he'd bother about it in the ordinary way, but if he is actually passing your door, I think he might glance in."

"I shan't be there. I shall be at the bottom of the pond, sucking up mud."

"Yes.... Do you think you could leave something in your bed that looked vaguely like you in the dark? A bolster with a pyjama-coat round it, and one arm outside the blanket, and a pair of socks or something for the head. You know the kind of thing. I think it would please him to feel that you were still sleeping peacefully."

Bill chuckled to himself.

"Rather. I'm awfully good at that. I'll make him up something really good. But what about you?"

"I'm at the other end of the house; he's hardly likely to bother about me a second time. And I shall be so very fast asleep at his first visit. Still, I may as well to be on the safe side."

They went into the house. Cayley was in the hall as they came in. He nodded, and took out his watch.

"Time to change?" he said.

"Just about," said Bill.

"You didn't forget my letter?"

"I did not. In fact, we had tea there."

"Ah!" He looked away and said carelessly, "How were they all?"

"They sent all sorts of sympathetic messages to you, and—and all that sort of thing."

"Oh, yes."

Bill waited for him to say something more, and then, as nothing was coming, he turned round, said, "Come on, Tony," and led the way upstairs.

"Got all you want?" he said at the top of the stairs.

"I think so. Come and see me before you go down."

"Righto."

Antony shut his bedroom door behind him and walked over to the window. He pushed open a casement and looked out. His bedroom was just over the door at the back of the house. The side wall of the office, which projected out into the lawn beyond the rest of the house, was on his left. He could step out on to the top of the door, and from there drop easily to the ground. Getting back would be little more difficult. There was a convenient water-pipe which would help.

He had just finished his dressing when Bill came in. "Final instructions?" he asked, sitting down on the bed. "By the way, how are we amusing ourselves after dinner? I mean immediately after dinner."

"Billiards?"

"Righto. Anything you like."

"Don't talk too loud," said Antony in a lower voice. "We're more or less over the hall, and Cayley may be there." He led the way to the window. "We'll go out this way to-night. Going downstairs is too risky. It's easy enough; better put on tennis-shoes."

"Right. I say, in case I don't get another chance alone with you what do I do when Cayley comes to tuck me up?"

"It's difficult to say. Be as natural as you can. I mean, if he just knocks lightly and looks in, be asleep. Don't overdo the snoring. But if he makes a hell of a noise, you'll have to wake up and rub your eyes, and wonder what on earth he's doing in your room at all. You know the sort of thing."

"Right. And about the dummy figure. I'll make it up directly we come upstairs, and hide it under the bed."

"Yes.... I think we'd better go completely to bed ourselves. We shan't take a moment dressing again, and it will give him time to get safely into the passage. Then come into my room."

"Right.... Are you ready?"

"Yes."

They went downstairs together.

CHAPTER XVII

MR. BEVERLEY TAKES THE WATER

Cayley seemed very fond of them that night. After dinner was over, he suggested a stroll outside. They walked up and down the gravel in front of the house, saying very little to each other, until Bill could stand it no longer. For the last twenty turns he had been slowing down hopefully each time they came to the door, but the hint had always been lost on his companions, and each time another turn had been taken. But in the end he had been firm.

"What about a little billiards?" he said, shaking himself free from the others.

"Will you play?" said Antony to Cayley.

"I'll watch you," he said, and he had watched them resolutely until the game, and then another game after that, had been played.

They went into the hall and attacked the drinks.

"Well, thank heaven for bed," said Bill; putting down his glass. "Are you coming?"

"Yes," said Antony, and finished his drink. He looked at Cayley.

"I've just got one or two little things to do," said Cayley. "I shan't be long following you."

"Well, good night, then."

"Good night."

"Good night," called Bill from half-way up the stairs. "Good night, Tony."

"Good night."

Bill looked at his watch. Half-past eleven. Not much chance of anything happening for another hour. He pulled open a drawer and wondered what to wear on their expedition. Grey flannel trousers, flannel shirt, and a dark coat; perhaps a sweater, as they might be lying out in the copse for some time. And good idea a towel. He would want it later on, and meanwhile he could wear it round his waist.

Tennis-shoes.... There. Everything was ready. Now then for the dummy figure.

He looked at his watch again before getting into bed. Twelve-fifteen. How long to wait before Cayley came up? He turned out the light, and then, standing by the door in his pyjamas, waited for his eyes to become accustomed to the new darkness.... He could only just make out the bed in the corner of the room. Cayley would want more light than that if he were to satisfy himself from the door that the bed was occupied. He pulled the curtains a little way back. That was about right. He could have another look later on, when he had the dummy figure in the bed.

How long would it be before Cayley came up? It wasn't that he wanted his friends, Beverley and Gillingham, to be asleep before he started on his business at the pond; all that he wanted was to be sure that they were safely in their bedrooms. Cayley's business would make no noise, give no sign, to attract the most wakeful member of the household, so long as the household was really inside the house. But if he wished to reassure himself about his guests, he would have to wait until they were far enough on their way to sleep not to be disturbed by him as he came up to reassure himself. So it amounted to the same thing, really. He would wait until they were asleep.... until they were asleep.... asleep....

With a great effort Bill regained the mastery over his wandering thoughts and came awake again. This would never do. It would be fatal if he went to sleep.... if he went to sleep.... to sleep .... And then, in an instant, he was intensely awake. Suppose Cayley never came at all!

Suppose Cayley was so unsuspicious that, as soon as they had gone upstairs, he had dived down into the passage and set about his business. Suppose, even now, he was at the pond, dropping into it that secret of his. Good heavens, what fools they had been! How could Antony have taken such a risk? Put yourself in Cayley's place, he had said. But how was it possible? They weren't Cayley. Cayley was at the pond now. They would never know what he had dropped into it.

Listen!.... Somebody at the door. He was asleep. Quite naturally now. Breathe a little more loudly, perhaps. He was asleep.... The door was opening. He could feel it opening behind him.... Good Lord, suppose Cayley really was a murderer! Why, even now he might be—no, he mustn't think of that. If he thought of that, he would have to turn round. He mustn't turn round. He was asleep; just peacefully asleep. But why didn't the door shut? Where was Cayley now? Just behind him? And in his hand no, he mustn't think of that. He was asleep. But why didn't the door shut?

The door was shutting. There was a sigh from the sleeper in the bed, a sigh of relief which escaped him involuntarily. But it had a very natural sound—a deep breath from a heavy sleeper. He added another one to it to make it seem more natural. The door was shut.

Bill counted a hundred slowly and then got up. As quickly and as noiselessly as possible he dressed himself in the dark. He put the dummy figure in the bed, arranged the clothes so that just enough but not too much of it was showing, and stood by the door looking at it. For a casual glance the room was just about light enough. Then very quietly, very slowly he opened the door. All was still. There was no light from beneath the door of Cayley's room. Very quietly, very carefully he crept along the passage to Antony's room. He opened the door and went in.

Antony was still in bed. Bill walked across to wake him up, and then stopped rigid, and his heart thumped against his ribs. There was somebody else in the room.

"All right, Bill," said a whispering voice, and Antony stepped out from the curtains.

Bill gazed at him without saying anything.

"Rather good, isn't it?" said Antony, coming closer and pointing to the bed. "Come on; the sooner we get out now, the better."

He led the way out of the window, the silent Bill following him. They reached the ground safely and noiselessly, went quickly across the lawn and so, over the fence, into the park. It was not until they were out of sight of the house that Bill felt it safe to speak.

"I quite thought it was you in bed," he said.

"I hoped you would. I shall be rather disappointed now if Cayley doesn't call again. It's a pity to waste it."

"He came all right just now?"

"Oh, rather. What about you?"

Bill explained his feelings picturesquely.

"There wouldn't have been much point in his killing you," said Antony prosaically. "Besides being too risky."

"Oh!" said Bill. And then, "I had rather hoped that it was his love for me which restrained him."

Antony laughed.

"I doubt it.... You didn't turn up your light when you dressed?"

"Good Lord, no. Did you want me to?"

Antony laughed again and took him by the arm.

"You're a splendid conspirator, Bill. You and I could take on anything together."

The pond was waiting for them, more solemn in the moonlight. The trees which crowned the sloping bank on the far side of it were mysteriously silent. It seemed that they had the world very much to themselves.

Almost unconsciously Antony spoke in a whisper.

"There's your tree, there's mine. As long as you don't move, there's no chance of his seeing you. After he's gone, don't come out till I do. He won't be here for a quarter of an hour or so, so don't be impatient."

"Righto," whispered Bill.

Antony gave him a nod and a smile, and they walked off to their posts.

The minutes went by slowly. To Antony, lying hidden in the undergrowth at the foot of his tree, a new problem was presenting itself. Suppose Cayley had to make more than one journey that night? He might come back to find them in the boat; one of them, indeed, in the water. And if they decided to wait in hiding, on the chance of Cayley coming back again, what was the least time they could safely allow? Perhaps it would be better to go round to the front of the house and watch for his return there, the light in his bedroom, before conducting their experiments at the pond. But then they might miss his second visit in this way, if he made a second visit. It was difficult.

His eyes were fixed on the boat as he considered these things, and suddenly, as if materialized from nowhere, Cayley was standing by the boat. In his hand was a small brown bag.

Cayley put the bag in the bottom of the boat, stepped in, and using an oar as a punt-pole, pushed slowly off. Then, very silently, he rowed towards the middle of the pond.

He had stopped. The oars rested on the water. He picked up the bag from between his feet, leant over the nose of the boat, and rested it lightly on the water for a moment. Then he let go. It sank slowly. He waited there, watching; afraid, perhaps, that it might rise again. Antony began to count....

And now Cayley was back at his starting-place. He tied up the boat, looked carefully round to see that he had left no traces behind him, and then turned to the water again. For a long time, as it seemed to the watchers, he stood there, very big, very silent, in the moonlight. At last he seemed satisfied. Whatever his secret was, he had hidden it; and so with a gentle sigh, as unmistakable to Antony as if he had heard it, Cayley turned away and vanished again as quietly as he had come.

Antony gave him three minutes, and stepped out from the trees. He waited there for Bill to join him.

"Six," whispered Bill.

Antony nodded.

"I'm going round to the front of the house. You get back to your tree and watch, in case Cayley comes again. Your bedroom is the left-hand end one, and Cayley's the end but one? Is that right?"

Bill nodded.

"Right. Wait in hiding till I come back. I don't know how long I shall be, but don't be impatient. It will seem longer than it is." He patted Bill on the shoulder, and with a smile and a nod of the head he left him there.

What was in the bag? What could Cayley want to hide other than a key or a revolver? Keys and revolvers sink of themselves; no need to put them in a bag first. What was in the bag? Something which wouldn't sink of itself; something which needed to be helped with stones before it would hide itself safely in the mud.

Well, they would find that out. There was no object in worrying about it now. Bill had a dirty night's work in front of him. But where was the body which Antony had expected so confidently or, if there were no body, where was Mark?

More immediately, however, where was Cayley? As quickly as he could Antony had got to the front of the house and was now lying in the shrubbery which bordered the lawn, waiting for the light to go up in Cayley's window. If it went up in Bill's window, then they were discovered. It would mean that Cayley had glanced into Bill's room, had been suspicious of the dummy figure in the bed, and had turned up the light to make sure. After that, it was war between them. But if it went up in Cayley's room—

There was a light. Antony felt a sudden thrill of excitement. It was in Bill's room. War!

The light stayed there, shining vividly, for a wind had come up, blowing the moon behind a cloud, and casting a shadow over the rest of the house. Bill had left his curtains undrawn. It was careless of him; the first stupid thing he had done, but—

The moon slipped out again.... and Antony laughed to himself in the bushes. There was another window beyond Cayley's, and there was no light in it. The declaration of war was postponed.

Antony lay there, watching Cayley into bed. After all it was only polite to return Cayley's own solicitude earlier in the night. Politeness demanded that one should not disport oneself on the pond until one's friends were comfortably tucked up.

Meanwhile Bill was getting tired of waiting. His chief fear was that he might spoil everything by forgetting the number "six." It was the sixth post. Six. He broke off a twig and divided it into six pieces. These he arranged on the ground in front of him. Six. He looked at the pond, counted up to the sixth post, and murmured "six" to himself again. Then he looked down at his twigs. One-two-three-four-five-six-seven. Seven! Was it seven?

Or was that seventh bit of a twig an accidental bit which had been on the ground anyhow? Surely it was six! Had he said "six" to Antony? If so, Antony would remember, and it was all right. Six. He threw away the seventh twig and collected the other six together. Perhaps they would be safer in his pocket. Six. The height of a tall man—well, his own height. Six feet. Yes, that was the way to remember it. Feeling a little safer on the point, he began to wonder about the bag, and what Antony would say to it, and the possible depth of the water and of the mud at the bottom; and was still so wondering, and saying, "Good Lord, what a life!" to himself, when Antony reappeared.

Bill got up and came down the slope to meet him.

"Six," he said firmly. "Sixth post from the end."

"Good," smiled Antony. "Mine was the eighteenth—a little way past it."

"What did you go off for?"

"To see Cayley into bed."

"Is it all right?"

"Yes. Better hang your coat over the sixth post, and then we shall see it more easily. I'll put mine on the eighteenth. Are you going to undress here or in the boat?"

"Some here, and some in the boat. You're quite sure that you wouldn't like to do the diving yourself?"

"Quite, thanks."

They had walked round to the other side of the pond. Coming to the sixth post of the fence, Bill took off his coat and put it in position, and then finished his undressing, while Antony went off to mark the eighteenth post. When they were ready, they got into the boat, Antony taking the oars.

"Now, Bill, tell me as soon as I'm in a line with your two marks."

He rowed slowly towards the middle of the pond.

"You're about there now," said Bill at last.

Antony stopped rowing and looked about him.

"Yes, that's pretty well right." He turned the boat's nose round until it was pointing to the pine-tree under which Bill had lain. "You see my tree and the other coat?"

"Yes," said Bill.

"Right. Now then, I'm going to row gently along this line until we're dead in between the two. Get it as exact as you can—

for your own sake."

"Steady!" said Bill warningly. "Back a little.... a little more .... a little more forward again.... Right." Antony left the oars on the water and looked around. As far as he could tell, they were in an exact line with each pair of landmarks.

"Now then, Bill, in you go."

Bill pulled off his shirt and trousers, and stood up.

"You mustn't dive from the boat, old boy," said Antony hastily. "You'll shift its position. Slide in gently."

Bill slid in from the stern and swam slowly round to Antony.

"What's it like?" said Antony.

"Cold. Well, here's luck to it."

He gave a sudden kick, flashed for a moment in the water, and was gone.

Antony steadied the boat, and took another look at his landmarks.

Bill came up behind him with a loud explosion. "It's pretty muddy," he protested.

"Weeds?"

"No, thank the Lord."

"Well, try again."

Bill gave another kick and disappeared. Again Antony coaxed the boat back into position, and again Bill popped up, this time in front of him.

"I feel that if I threw you a sardine," said Antony, with a smile, "you'd catch it in your mouth quite prettily."

"It's awfully easy to be funny from where you are. How much longer have I got to go on doing this?"

Antony looked at his watch.

"About three hours. We must get back before daylight. But be quicker if you can, because it's rather cold for me sitting here."

Bill flicked a handful of water at him and disappeared again. He was under for almost a minute this time, and there was a grin on his face when it was visible again.

"I've got it, but it's devilish hard to get up. I'm not sure that it isn't too heavy for me."

"That's all right," said Antony. He brought out a ball of thick string from his pocket. "Get this through the handle if you can, and then we can both pull."

"Good man." He paddled to the side, took one end of the string and paddled back again. "Now then."

Two minutes later the bag was safely in the boat. Bill clambered in after it, and Antony rowed back. "Well done, Watson," he said quietly, as they landed. He fetched their two coats, and then waited, the bag in his hand, while Bill dried and dressed himself. As soon as the latter was ready, he took his arm and led him into the copse. He put the bag down and felt in his pockets.

"I shall light a pipe before I open it," he said. "What about you?"

"Yes."

With great care they filled and lit their pipes. Bill's hand was a little unsteady. Antony noticed it and gave him a reassuring smile.

"Ready?"

"Yes."

They sat down, and taking the bag between his knees, Antony pressed the catch and opened it.

"Clothes!" said Bill.

Antony pulled out the top garment and shook it out. It was a wet brown flannel coat.

"Do you recognize it?" he asked.

"Mark's brown flannel suit."

"The one he is advertised as having run away in?"

"Yes. It looks like it. Of course he had a dashed lot of clothes."

Antony put his hand in the breast-pocket and took out some letters. He considered them doubtfully for a moment.

"I suppose I'd better read them," he said. "I mean, just to see—" He looked inquiringly at Bill, who nodded. Antony turned on his torch and glanced at them. Bill waited anxiously.

"Yes. Mark…. Hallo!"

"What is it?"

"The letter that Cayley was telling the Inspector about. From Robert.

'Mark, your loving brother is coming to see you—' Yes, I suppose I had better keep this. Well, that's his coat. Let's have out the rest of it."

He took the remaining clothes from the bag and spread them

out.

"They're all here," said Bill. "Shirt, tie, socks, underclothes, shoes—yes, all of them."

"All that he was wearing yesterday?"

"Yes."

"What do you make of it?"

Bill shook his head, and asked another question.

"Is it what you expected?"

Antony laughed suddenly.

"It's too absurd," he said. "I expected—well, you know what I expected. A body. A body in a suit of clothes. Well, perhaps it would be safer to hide them separately. The body here, and the clothes in the passage, where they would never betray themselves. And now he takes a great deal of trouble to hide the clothes here, and doesn't bother about the body at all." He shook his head. "I'm a bit lost for the moment, Bill, and that's the fact."

"Anything else there?"

Antony felt in the bag.

"Stones and—yes, there's something else." He took it out and held it up. "There we are, Bill."

It was the office key.

"By Jove, you were right."

Antony felt in the bag again, and then turned it gently upside down on the grass. A dozen large stones fell out—and something else. He flashed down his torch.

"Another key," he said.

He put the two keys in his pocket, and sat there for a long time in silence, thinking. Bill was silent, too, not liking to interrupt his thoughts, but at last he said:

"Shall I put these things back?"

Antony looked up with a start.

"What? Oh, yes. No, I'll put them back. You give me a light, will you?"

Very slowly and carefully he put the clothes back in the bag, pausing as he took up each garment, in the certainty, as it seemed to Bill, that it had something to tell him if only he could read it. When the last of them was inside, he still waited there on his knees, thinking.

"That's the lot," said Bill.

Antony nodded at him.

"Yes, that's the lot," he said; "and that's the funny thing about it.

You're sure it is the lot?"

"What do you mean?"

"Give me the torch a moment." He took it and flashed it over the ground between them. "Yes, that's the lot. It's funny." He stood up, the bag in his hands. "Now let's find a hiding-place for these, and then—" He said no more, but stepped off through the trees, Bill following him meekly.

As soon as they had got the bag off their hands and were clear of the copse, Antony became more communicative. He took the two keys out of his pocket.

"One of them is the office key, I suppose, and the other is the key of the passage cupboard. So I thought that perhaps we might have a look at the cupboard."

"I say, do you really think it is?"

"Well, I don't see what else it can be."

"But why should he want to throw it away?"

"Because it has now done its work, whatever it was, and he wants to wash his hands of the passage. He'd throw the passage away if he could. I don't think it matters much one way or another, and I don't suppose there's anything to find in the cupboard, but I feel that we must look."

"Do you still think Mark's body might be there?"

"No. And yet where else can it be? Unless I'm hopelessly wrong, and Cayley never killed him at all."

Bill hesitated, wondering if he dare advance his theory.

"I know you'll think me an ass—"

"My dear Bill, I'm such an obvious ass myself that I should be delighted to think you are too."

"Well, then, suppose Mark did kill Robert, and Cayley helped him to escape, just as we thought at first. I know you proved afterwards that it was impossible, but suppose it happened in a way we don't know about and for reasons we don't know about. I mean, there are such a lot of funny things about the whole show that—well, almost anything might have happened."

"You're quite right. Well?"

"Well, then, this clothes business. Doesn't that seem rather to bear out the escaping theory? Mark's brown suit was known to the police. Couldn't Cayley have brought him another one in the passage, to escape in, and then have had the brown one on his hands? And thought it safest to hide it in the pond?"

"Yes," said Anthony thoughtfully. Then: "Go on."

Bill went on eagerly:

"It all seems to fit in, you know. I mean even with your first theory—that Mark killed him accidentally and then came to Cayley for help. Of course, if Cayley had played fair, he'd have told Mark that he had nothing to be afraid of. But he isn't playing fair; he wants to get Mark out of the way because of the girl. Well, this is his chance. He makes Mark as frightened as possible, and tells him that his only hope is to run away. Well, naturally, he does all he can to get him well away, because if Mark is caught, the whole story of Cayley's treachery comes out."

"Yes. But isn't it overdoing it rather to make him change his underclothes and everything? It wastes a good deal of time, you know."

Bill was pulled up short, and said, "Oh!" in great disappointment.

"No, it's not as bad as that, Bill," said Antony with a smile. "I

daresay the underclothes could be explained. But here's the difficulty.

Why did Mark need to change from brown to blue, or whatever it was, when Cayley was the only person who saw him in brown?"

"The police description of him says that he is in a brown suit."

"Yes, because Cayley told the police. You see, even if Mark had had lunch in his brown suit, and the servants had noticed it, Cayley could always have pretended that he had changed into blue after lunch, because only Cayley saw him afterwards. So if Cayley had told the Inspector that he was wearing blue, Mark could have escaped quite comfortably in his brown, without needing to change at all."

"But that's just what he did do," cried Bill triumphantly. "What fools we are!"

Antony looked at him in surprise, and then shook his head.

"Yes, yes!" insisted Bill. "Of course! Don't you see? Mark did change after lunch, and, to give him more of a chance of getting away, Cayley lied and said that he was wearing the brown suit in which the servants had seen him. Well, then he was afraid that the police might examine Mark's clothes and find the brown suit still there, so he hid it, and then dropped it in the pond afterwards."

He turned eagerly to his friend, but Antony said nothing. Bill began to speak again, and was promptly waved into silence.

"Don't say anything more, old boy; you've given me quite enough to think about. Don't let's bother about it to-night. We'll just have a look at this cupboard and then get to bed."

But the cupboard had not much to tell them that night. It was empty save for a few old bottles.

"Well, that's that," said Bill.

But Antony, on his knees with the torch in his hand, continued to search for something.

"What are you looking for?" asked Bill at last.

"Something that isn't there," said Antony, getting up and dusting his trousers. And he locked the door again.

CHAPTER XVIII
GUESS-WORK

The inquest was at three o'clock; thereafter Antony could have no claim on the hospitality of the Red House. By ten o'clock his bag was packed, and waiting to be taken to 'The George.' To Bill, coming upstairs after a more prolonged breakfast, this early morning bustle was a little surprising.

"What's the hurry?" he asked.

"None. But we don't want to come back here after the inquest. Get your packing over now and then we can have the morning to ourselves."

"Righto." He turned to go to his room, and then came back again. "I say, are we going to tell Cayley that we're staying at 'The George'?"

"You're not staying at 'The George,' Bill. Not officially. You're going back to London."

"Oh!"

"Yes. Ask Cayley to have your luggage sent in to Stanton, ready for you when you catch a train there after the inquest. You can tell him that you've got to see the Bishop of London at once. The fact that you are hurrying back to London to be confirmed will make it seem more natural that I should resume my interrupted solitude at 'The George' as soon as you have gone."

"Then where do I sleep to-night?"

"Officially, I suppose, in Fulham Place; unofficially, I suspect, in my bed, unless they've got another spare room at 'The George.' I've put your confirmation robe—I mean your pyjamas and brushes and things—in my bag, ready for you. Is there anything else you want to know? No? Then go and pack. And meet me at ten-thirty beneath the blasted oak or in the hall or somewhere. I want to talk and talk and talk, and I must have my Watson."

"Good," said Bill, and went off to his room.

An hour later, having communicated their official plans to Cayley, they wandered out together into the park.

"Well?" said Bill, as they sat down underneath a convenient tree. "Talk away."

"I had many bright thoughts in my bath this morning," began Antony. "The brightest one of all was that we were being damn fools, and working at this thing from the wrong end altogether."

"Well, that's helpful."

"Of course it's very hampering being a detective, when you don't know anything about detecting, and when nobody knows that you're doing detection, and you can't have people up to cross-examine them, and you have neither the energy nor the means to make proper inquiries; and, in short, when you're doing the whole thing in a thoroughly amateur, haphazard way."

"For amateurs I don't think we're doing at all badly," protested Bill.

"No; not for amateurs. But if we had been professionals, I believe we should have gone at it from the other end. The Robert end. We've been wondering about Mark and Cayley all the time. Now let's wonder about Robert for a bit."

"We know so little about him."

"Well, let's see what we do know. First of all, then, we know vaguely that he was a bad lot—the sort of brother who is hushed up in front of other people."

"Yes."

"We know that he announced his approaching arrival to Mark

in a rather unpleasant letter, which I have in my pocket."

"Yes."

"And then we know rather a curious thing. We know that Mark told you all that this black sheep was coming. Now, why did he tell you?"

Bill was thoughtful for a moment.

"I suppose," he said slowly, "that he knew we were bound to see him, and thought that the best way was to be quite frank about him."

"But were you bound to see him? You were all away playing golf."

"We were bound to see him if he stayed in the house that night."

"Very well, then. That's one thing we've discovered. Mark knew that Robert was staying in the house that night. Or shall we put it this way—he knew that there was no chance of getting Robert out of the house at once."

Bill looked at his friend eagerly.

"Go on," he said. "This is getting interesting."

"He also knew something else," went on Antony. "He knew that Robert was bound to betray his real character to you as soon as you met him. He couldn't pass him off on you as just a travelled brother from the Dominions, with perhaps a bit of an accent; he had to tell you at once, because you were bound to find out, that Robert was a wastrel."

"Yes. That's sound enough."

"Well, now, doesn't it strike you that Mark made up his mind about all that rather quickly?"

"How do you mean?"

"He got this letter at breakfast. He read it; and directly he had read it he began to confide in you all. That is to say, in about one second he thought out the whole business and came to a decision—to two decisions. He considered the possibility of getting Robert out of the way before you came back, and decided that it was impossible. He considered the possibility of Robert's behaving like an ordinary decent person in public, and decided that it was very unlikely. He came to those two decisions instantaneously, as he was reading the letter. Isn't that rather quick work?"

"Well, what's the explanation?"

Antony waited until he had refilled and lighted his pipe before answering.

"What's the explanation? Well, let's leave it for a moment and take another look at the two brothers. In conjunction, this time, with Mrs. Norbury."

"Mrs. Norbury?" said Bill, surprised.

"Yes. Mark hoped to marry Miss Norbury. Now, if Robert really was a blot upon the family honour, Mark would want to do one of two things. Either keep it from the Norburys altogether, or else, if it had to come out, tell them himself before the news came to them indirectly. Well, he told them. But the funny thing is that he told them the day before Robert's letter came. Robert came, and was killed, the day before yesterday—Tuesday. Mark told Mrs. Norbury about him on Monday. What do you make of that?"

"Coincidence," said Bill, after careful thought. "He'd always meant to tell her; his suit was prospering, and just before it was finally settled, he told her. That happened to be Monday. On Tuesday he got Robert's letter, and felt jolly glad that he'd told her in time."

"Well, it might be that, but it's rather a curious coincidence. And here is something which makes it very curious indeed. It only occurred to me in the bath this morning. Inspiring place, a bathroom. Well, it's this—he told her on Monday morning, on his way to Middleston in the car."

"Well?"

"Well."

"Sorry, Tony; I'm dense this morning."

"In the car, Bill. And how near can the car get to Jallands?"

"About six hundred yards."

"Yes. And on his way to Middleston, on some business or other, Mark stops the car, walks six hundred yards down the hill to Jallands, says, 'Oh, by the way, Mrs. Norbury, I don't think I ever told you that I have a shady brother called Robert,' walks six hundred yards up the hill again, gets into the car, and goes off to Middleston. Is that likely?"

Bill frowned heavily.

"Yes, but I don't see what you're getting at. Likely or not likely, we know he did do it."

"Of course he did. All I mean is that he must have had some

strong reason for telling Mrs. Norbury at once. And the reason I suggest is that he knew on that morning—Monday morning, not Tuesday—that Robert was coming to see him, and had to be in first with the news.

"But—but—"

"And that would explain the other point—his instantaneous decision at breakfast to tell you all about his brother. It wasn't instantaneous. He knew on Monday that Robert was coming, and decided then that you would all have to know."

"Then how do you explain the letter?"

"Well, let's have a look at it."

Antony took the letter from his pocket and spread it out on the grass between them.

"Mark, your loving brother is coming to see you to-morrow, all the way from Australia. I give you warning, so that you will be able to conceal your surprise but not I hope your pleasure. Expect him at three or thereabouts."

"No date mentioned, you see," said Antony. "Just to-morrow."

"But he got this on Tuesday."

"Did he?"

"Well, he read it out to us on Tuesday."

"Oh, yes! he read it out to you."

Bill read the letter again, and then turned it over and looked at the back of it. The back of it had nothing to say to him.

"What about the postmark?" he asked.

"We haven't got the envelope, unfortunately."

"And you think that he got this letter on Monday."

"I'm inclined to think so, Bill. Anyhow, I think—I feel almost certain—that he knew on Monday that his brother was coming."

"Is that going to help us much?"

"No. It makes it more difficult. There's something rather uncanny about it all. I don't understand it." He was silent for a little, and then added, "I wonder if the inquest is going to help us.

"What about last night? I'm longing to hear what you make of that. Have you been thinking it out at all?"

"Last night," said Antony thoughtfully to himself. "Yes, last night wants some explaining."

Bill waited hopefully for him to explain. What, for instance, had Antony been looking for in the cupboard?

"I think," began Antony slowly, "that after last night we must give up the idea that Mark has been killed; killed, I mean, by Cayley. I don't believe anybody would go to so much trouble to hide a suit of clothes when he had a body on his hands. The body would seem so much more important. I think we may take it now that the clothes are all that Cayley had to hide."

"But why not have kept them in the passage?"

"He was frightened of the passage. Miss Norris knew about it."

"Well, then, in his own bedroom, or even, in Mark's. For all you or I or anybody knew, Mark might have had two brown suits. He probably had, I should think."

"Probably. But I doubt if that would reassure Cayley. The brown suit hid a secret, and therefore the brown suit had to be hidden. We all know that in theory the safest hiding-place is the most obvious, but in practice very few people have the nerve to risk it."

Bill looked rather disappointed.

"Then we just come back to where we were," he complained. "Mark killed his brother, and Cayley helped him to escape through the passage; either in order to compromise him, or because there was no other way out of it. And he helped him by telling a lie about his brown suit."

Antony smiled at him in genuine amusement.

"Bad luck, Bill," he said sympathetically. "There's only one murder, after all. I'm awfully sorry about it. It was my fault for—"

"Shut up, you ass. You know I didn't mean that."

"Well, you seemed awfully disappointed."

Bill said nothing for a little, and then with a sudden laugh confessed.

"It was so exciting yesterday," he said apologetically, "and we seemed to be just getting there, and discovering the most wonderful things, and now—"

"And now?"

"Well, it's so much more ordinary."

Antony gave a shout of laughter.

"Ordinary!" he cried. "Ordinary! Well, I'm dashed! Ordinary! If only one thing would happen in an ordinary way, we might do something, but everything is ridiculous." Bill brightened up again.

"Ridiculous? How?"

"Every way. Take those ridiculous clothes we found last night. You can explain the brown suit, but why the under clothes. You can explain the underclothes in some absurd way, if you like—you can say that Mark always changed his underclothes whenever he interviewed anybody from Australia—but why, in that case, my dear Watson, why didn't he change his collar?"

"His collar?" said Bill in amazement.

"His collar, Watson."

"I don't understand."

"And it's all so ordinary," scoffed Antony.

"Sorry, Tony, I didn't mean that. Tell me about the collar."

"Well, that's all. There was no collar in the bag last night. Shirt, socks, tie—everything except a collar. Why?"

"Was that what you were looking for in the cupboard?" said Bill eagerly.

"Of course. 'Why no collar?' I said. For some reason Cayley considered it necessary to hide all Mark's clothes; not just the suit, but everything which he was wearing, or supposed to be wearing, at the time of the murder. But he hadn't hidden the collar. Why? Had he left it out by mistake? So I looked in the cupboard. It wasn't there. Had he left it out on purpose? If so, why?—and where was it? Naturally I began to say to myself, 'Where have I seen a collar lately? A collar all by itself?' And I remembered—what, Bill?"

Bill frowned heavily to himself, and shook his head.

"Don't ask me, Tony. I can't—By Jove!" He threw up his head, "In the basket in the office bedroom!"

"Exactly."

"But is that the one?"

"The one that goes with the rest of the clothes? I don't know. Where else can it be? But if so, why send the collar quite casually to the wash in the ordinary way, and take immense trouble to hide everything else? Why, why, why?"

Bill bit hard at his pipe, but could think of nothing to say.

"Anyhow," said Antony, getting up restlessly, "I'm certain of one thing.

Mark knew on the Monday that Robert was coming here."

CHAPTER XIX

THE INQUEST

The Coroner, having made a few commonplace remarks as to the terrible nature of the tragedy which they had come to investigate that afternoon, proceeded to outline the case to the jury. Witnesses would be called to identify the deceased as Robert Ablett, the brother of the owner of the Red House, Mark Ablett. It would be shown that he was something of a ne'er-do-well, who had spent most of his life in Australia, and that he had announced, in what might almost be called a threatening letter, his intention of visiting his brother that afternoon. There would be evidence of his arrival, of his being shown into the scene of the tragedy—a room in the Red House, commonly called "the office"—and of his brother's entrance into that room. The jury would have to form their own opinion as to what happened there. But whatever happened, happened almost instantaneously. Within two minutes of Mark Ablett's entrance, as would be shown in the evidence, a shot was heard, and when—perhaps five minutes later—the room was forced open, the dead body of Robert Ablett was found stretched upon the floor. As regards Mark Ablett, nobody had seen him from the moment of his going into the room, but evidence would be called to show that he had enough money on him at the time to take him to any other part of the country, and that a man answering to his description had been observed on the platform of Stanton station, apparently waiting to catch the 3.55 up train to London. As the jury would realize, such evidence of identity was not always reliable. Missing men had a way of being seen in a dozen different places at once. In any case, there was no doubt that for the moment Mark Ablett had disappeared.

"Seems a sound man," whispered Antony to Bill. "Doesn't talk too much."

Antony did not expect to learn much from the evidence—he

knew the facts of the case so well by now—but he wondered if Inspector Birch had developed any new theories. If so, they would appear in the Coroner's examination, for the Coroner would certainly have been coached by the police as to the important facts to be extracted from each witness. Bill was the first to be put through it.

"Now, about this letter, Mr. Beverley?" he was asked when his chief evidence was over. "Did you see it at all?"

"I didn't see the actual writing. I saw the back of it. Mark was holding it up when he told us about his brother."

"You don't know what was in it, then?"

Bill had a sudden shock. He had read the letter only that morning. He knew quite well what was in it. But it wouldn't do to admit this. And then, just as he was about to perjure himself, he remembered: Antony had heard Cayley telling the Inspector.

"I knew afterwards. I was told. But Mark didn't read it out at breakfast."

"You gathered, however, that it was an unwelcome letter?"

"Oh, yes!"

"Would you say that Mark was frightened by it?"

"Not frightened. Sort of bitter—and resigned. Sort of 'Oh, Lord, here we are again!'"

There was a titter here and there. The Coroner smiled, and tried to pretend that he hadn't.

"Thank you, Mr. Beverley."

The next witness was summoned by the name of Andrew Amos, and Antony looked up with interest, wondering who he was.

"He lives at the inner lodge," whispered Bill to him.

All that Amos had to say was that a stranger had passed by his lodge at a little before three that afternoon, and had spoken to him. He had seen the body and recognized it as the man.

"What did he say?"

"'Is this right for the Red House?' or something like that, sir."

"What did you say?"

"I said, 'This is the Red House. Who do you want to see?' He was a bit rough-looking, you know, sir, and I didn't know what he was doing there."

"Well?"

"Well, sir, he said, 'Is Mister Mark Ablett at home?' It doesn't sound much put like that, sir, but I didn't care about the way he said it. So I got in front of him like, and said, 'What do you want, eh?' and he gave a sort of chuckle and said, 'I want to see my dear brother Mark.' Well, then I took a closer look at him, and I see that p'raps he might be his brother, so I said, 'If you'll follow the drive, sir, you'll come to the house. Of course I can't say if Mr. Ablett's at home.' And he gave a sort of nasty laugh again, and said, 'Fine place Mister Mark Ablett's got here. Plenty of money to spend, eh?' Well, then I had another look at him, sir, because gentlemen don't talk like that, and if he was Mr. Ablett's brother—but before I could make up my mind, he laughed and went on. That's all I can tell you, sir."

Andrew Amos stepped down and moved away to the back of the room, nor did Antony take his eyes off him until he was assured that Amos intended to remain there until the inquest was over.

"Who's Amos talking to now?" he whispered to Bill.

"Parsons. One of the gardeners. He's at the outside lodge on the Stanton road. They're all here to-day. Sort of holiday for 'em.

"I wonder if he's giving evidence too," thought Antony. He was. He followed Amos. He had been at work on the lawn in front of the house, and had seen Robert Ablett arrive. He didn't hear the shot—not to notice. He was a little hard of hearing. He had seen a gentleman arrive about five minutes after Mr. Robert.

"Can you see him in court now?" asked the Coroner. Parsons looked round slowly. Antony caught his eye and smiled.

"That's him," said Parsons, pointing.

Everybody looked at Antony.

"That was about five minutes afterwards?"

"About that, sir."

"Did anybody come out of the house before this gentleman's arrival?"

"No, sir. That is to say I didn't see 'em."

Stevens followed. She gave her evidence much as she had given it to the Inspector. Nothing new was brought out by her examination. Then came Elsie. As the reporters scribbled down what she had overheard, they added in brackets "Sensation" for the first time that afternoon.

"How soon after you had heard this did the shot come?" asked the Coroner.

"Almost at once, sir."

"A minute?"

"I couldn't really say, sir. It was so quick."

"Were you still in the hall?"

"Oh, no, sir. I was just outside Mrs. Stevens' room. The housekeeper, sir."

"You didn't think of going back to the hall to see what had happened?"

"Oh, no, sir. I just went in to Mrs. Stevens, and she said, 'Oh, what was that?' frightened-like. And I said, 'That was in the house, Mrs. Stevens, that was.' Just like something going off, it was."

"Thank you," said the Coroner.

There was another emotional disturbance in the room as Cayley went into the witness-box; not "Sensation" this time, but an eager and, as it seemed to Antony, sympathetic interest. Now they were getting to grips with the drama.

He gave his evidence carefully, unemotionally—the lies with the same slow deliberation as the truth. Antony watched him intently, wondering what it was about him which had this odd sort of attractiveness. For Antony, who knew that he was lying, and lying (as he believed) not for Mark's sake but his own, yet could not help sharing some of that general sympathy with him.

"Was Mark ever in possession of a revolver?" asked the Coroner.

"Not to my knowledge. I think I should have known if he had been."

"You were alone with him all that morning. Did he talk about this visit of Robert's at all?"

"I didn't see very much of him in the morning. I was at work in my room, and outside, and so on. We lunched together and he talked of it then a little."

"In what terms?"

"Well—" he hesitated, and then went on. "I can't think of a better word than 'peevishly.' Occasionally he said, 'What do you think he wants?' or 'Why couldn't he have stayed where he was?' or 'I don't like the tone of his letter. Do you think he means trouble?' He talked rather in that kind of way."

"Did he express his surprise that his brother should be in England?"

"I think he was always afraid that he would turn up one day."

"Yes.... You didn't hear any conversation between the brothers when they were in the office together?"

"No. I happened to go into the library just after Mark had gone in, and

I was there all the time."

"Was the library door open?"

"Oh, yes."

"Did you see or hear the last witness at all?"

"No."

"If anybody had come out of the office while you were in the library, would you have heard it?"

"I think so. Unless they had come out very quietly on purpose."

"Would you call Mark a hasty-tempered man?"

Cayley considered this carefully before answering.

"Hasty-tempered, yes," he said. "But not violent-tempered."

"Was he fairly athletic? Active and quick?"

"Active and quick, yes. Not particularly strong."

"Yes.... One question more. Was Mark in the habit of carrying any considerable sum of money about with him?"

"Yes. He always had one 100 pound note on him, and perhaps ten or twenty pounds as well."

"Thank you, Mr. Cayley."

Cayley went back heavily to his seat. "Damn it," said Antony to himself, "why do I like the fellow?"

"Antony Gillingham!"

Again the eager interest of the room could be felt. Who was this stranger who had got mixed up in the business so mysteriously?

Antony smiled at Bill and stepped up to give his evidence.

He explained how he came to be staying at 'The George' at Waldheim, how he had heard that the Red House was in the neighbourhood, how he had walked over to see his friend Beverley, and had arrived just after the tragedy. Thinking it over afterwards he was fairly certain that he had heard the shot, but it had not made any impression on him at the time. He had come to the house from the Waldheim end and consequently had seen nothing of Robert Ablett, who had been a few minutes in front of him. From this point his evidence coincided with Cayley's.

"You and the last witness reached the French windows together and found them shut?"

"Yes."

"You pushed them in and came to the body. Of course you had no idea whose body it was?"

"No."

"Did Mr. Cayley say anything?"

"He turned the body over, just so as to see the face, and when he saw it, he said, 'Thank God.'"

Again the reporters wrote "Sensation."

"Did you understand what he meant by that?"

"I asked him who it was, and he said that it was Robert Ablett. Then he explained that he was afraid at first it was the cousin with whom he lived—Mark."

"Yes. Did he seem upset?"

"Very much so at first. Less when he found that it wasn't Mark."

There was a sudden snigger from a nervous gentleman in the crowd at the back of the room, and the Coroner put on his glasses and stared sternly in the direction from which it came. The nervous gentleman hastily decided that the time had come to do up his bootlace. The Coroner put down his glasses and continued.

"Did anybody come out of the house while you were coming up the drive?"

"No."

"Thank you, Mr. Gillingham."

He was followed by Inspector Birch. The Inspector, realizing that this was his afternoon, and that the eyes of the world were upon him, produced a plan of the house and explained the situation of the different rooms. The plan was then handed to the jury.

Inspector Birch, so he told the world, had arrived at the Red House at 4.42 p.m. on the afternoon in question. He had been received by Mr. Matthew Cayley, who had made a short statement to him, and he had then proceeded to examine the scene of the crime. The French windows had been forced from outside. The door leading into the hall was locked; he had searched the room thoroughly and had found no trace of a key.

In the bedroom leading out of the office he had found an open window. There were no marks on the window, but it was a low one, and, as he found from experiment, quite easy to step out of without touching it with the boots. A few yards outside the window a shrubbery began. There were no recent footmarks outside the window, but the ground was in a very hard condition owing to the absence of rain. In the shrubbery, however, he found several twigs on the ground, recently broken off, together with other evidence that some body had been forcing its way through. He had questioned everybody connected with the estate, and none of them had been into the shrubbery recently. By forcing a way through the shrubbery it was possible for a person to make a detour of the house and get to the Stanton end of the park without ever being in sight of the house itself.

He had made inquiries about the deceased. Deceased had left for Australia some fifteen years ago, owing to some financial trouble at home. Deceased was not well spoken of in the village from which he and his brother had come. Deceased and his brother had never been on good terms, and the fact that Mark Ablett had come into money had been a cause of great bitterness between them. It was shortly after this that Robert had left for Australia.

He had made inquiries at Stanton station. It had been market-day at Stanton and the station had been more full of arrivals than usual. Nobody had particularly noticed the arrival of Robert Ablett; there had been a good many passengers by the 2.10 train that afternoon, the train by which Robert had undoubtedly come from London. A witness, however, would state that he noticed a man resembling Mark Ablett at the station at 3.53 p.m. that afternoon, and this man caught the 3.55 up train to town.

There was a pond in the grounds of the Red House. He had dragged this, but without result….

Antony listened to him carelessly, thinking his own thoughts all the time. Medical evidence followed, but there was nothing to be got from that. He felt so close to the truth; at any moment something might give his brain the one little hint which it wanted. Inspector Birch was just pursuing the ordinary. Whatever else this case was, it was not ordinary. There was something uncanny about it.

John Borden was giving evidence. He was on the up platform

seeing a friend off by the 3.55 on Tuesday afternoon. He had noticed a man on the platform with coat collar turned up and a scarf round his chin. He had wondered why the man should do this on such a hot day. The man seemed to be trying to escape observation. Directly the train came in, he hurried into a carriage. And so on.

"There's always a John Borden at every murder case," said Antony to himself.

"Have you ever seen Mark Ablett?"

"Once or twice, sir."

"Was it he?"

"I never really got a good look at him, sir, what with his collar turned up and the scarf and all. But directly I heard of the sad affair, and that Mr. Ablett was missing, I said to Mrs. Borden, 'Now I wonder if that was Mr. Ablett I saw at the station?' So then we talked it over and decided that I ought to come and tell Inspector Birch. It was just Mr. Ablett's height, sir."

Antony went on with his thoughts....

The Coroner was summing up. The jury, he said, had now heard all the evidence and would have to decide what had happened in that room between the two brothers. How had the deceased met his death? The medical evidence would probably satisfy them that Robert Ablett had died from the effects of a bullet-wound in the head. Who had fired that bullet? If Robert Ablett had fired it himself, no doubt they would bring in a verdict of suicide, but if this had been so, where was the revolver which had fired it, and what had become of Mark Ablett? If they disbelieved in this possibility of suicide, what remained? Accidental death, justifiable homicide, and murder. Could the deceased have been killed accidentally? It was possible, but then would Mark Ablett have run away? The evidence that he had run away from the scene of the crime was strong. His cousin had seen him go into the room, the servant Elsie Wood had heard him quarrelling with his brother in the room, the door had been locked from the inside, and there were signs that outside the open window some one had pushed his way very recently through the shrubbery. Who, if not Mark? They would have then to consider whether he would have run away if he had been guiltless of his brother's death. No doubt innocent people lost their heads sometimes. It was possible that if it were proved afterwards that Mark Ablett had shot his brother, it might also be proved that he was justified in so doing, and that when he ran away from his brother's corpse he had really nothing to fear at the hands of the Law. In this connection he need hardly remind the jury that they were not the final tribunal, and that if they found Mark Ablett guilty of murder it would not prejudice his trial in any way if and when he was apprehended.... The jury could consider their verdict.

They considered it. They announced that the deceased had died as the result of a bullet-wound, and that the bullet had been fired by his brother Mark Ablett.

Bill turned round to Antony at his side. But Antony was gone. Across the room he saw Andrew Amos and Parsons going out of the door together, and Antony was between them.

CHAPTER XX

MR. BEVERLEY IS TACTFUL

The inquest had been held at the "Lamb" at Stanton; at Stanton Robert Ablett was to be buried next day. Bill waited about outside for his friend, wondering where he had gone. Then, realizing that Cayley would be coming out to his car directly, and that a farewell talk with Cayley would be a little embarrassing, he wandered round to the yard at the back of the inn, lit a cigarette, and stood surveying a torn and weather-beaten poster on the stable wall. "GRAND THEATRICAL ENTER" it announced, to take place on "Wednesday, Decem." Bill smiled to himself as he looked at it, for the part of Joe, a loquacious postman, had been played by "William B. Beverl," as the remnants of the poster still maintained, and he had been much less loquacious than the author had intended, having forgotten his words completely, but it had all been great fun. And then he stopped smiling, for there would be no more fun now at the Red House.

"Sorry to keep you waiting," said the voice of Antony behind him. "My old friends Amos and Parsons insisted on giving me a drink."

He slipped his hand into the crook of Bill's arm, and smiled happily at him.

"Why were you so keen about them?" asked Bill a little resentfully. "I couldn't think where on earth you had got to."

Antony didn't say anything. He was staring at the poster.

"When did this happen?" he asked.

"What?"

Antony waved to the poster.

"Oh, that? Last Christmas. It was rather fun."

Antony began to laugh to himself.

"Were you good?"

"Rotten. I don't profess to be an actor."

"Mark good?"

"Oh, rather. He loves it."

"Rev. Henry Stutters—Mr. Matthew Cay," read Antony.

"Was that our friend Cayley?"

"Yes."

"Any good?"

"Well, much better than I expected. He wasn't keen, but Mark made him."

"Miss Norris wasn't playing, I see."

"My dear Tony, she's a professional. Of course she wasn't."

Antony laughed again.

"A great success, was it?"

"Oh, rather!"

"I'm a fool, and a damned fool," Antony announced solemnly. "And a damned fool," he said again under his breath, as he led Bill away from the poster, and out of the yard into the road. "And a damned fool. Even now—" He broke off and then asked suddenly, "Did Mark ever have much trouble with his teeth?"

"He went to his dentist a good deal. But what on earth—"

Antony laughed a third time.

"What luck!" he chuckled. "But how do you know?"

"We go to the same man; Mark recommended him to me. Cartwright, in Wimpole Street."

"Cartwright in Wimpole Street," repeated Antony thoughtfully. "Yes, I can remember that. Cartwright in Wimpole Street. Did Cayley go to him too, by any chance?"

"I expect so. Oh, yes, I know he did. But what on earth—"

"What was Mark's general health like? Did he see a doctor much?"

"Hardly at all, I should think. He did a lot of early morning exercises which were supposed to make him bright and cheerful at breakfast. They didn't do that, but they seemed to keep him pretty fit. Tony, I wish you'd—"

Antony held up a hand and hushed him into silence.

"One last question," he said. "Was Mark fond of swimming?"

"No, he hated it. I don't believe he could swim. Tony, are you mad, or am I? Or is this a new game?"

Antony squeezed his arm.

"Dear old Bill," he said. "It's a game. What a game! And the answer is Cartwright in Wimpole Street."

They walked in silence for half a mile or so along the road to Waldheim.

Bill tried two or three times to get his friend to talk, but Antony had only grunted in reply. He was just going to make another attempt, when

Antony came to a sudden stop and turned to him anxiously.

"I wonder if you'd do something for me," he said, looking at him with some doubt.

"What sort of thing?"

"Well, it's really dashed important. It's just the one thing I want now."

Bill was suddenly enthusiastic again.

"I say, have you really found it all out?"

Antony nodded.

"At least, I'm very nearly there, Bill. There's just this one thing I want now. It means your going back to Stanton. Well, we haven't come far; it won't take you long. Do you mind?"

"My dear Holmes, I am at your service."

Antony gave him a smile and was silent for a little, thinking.

"Is there another inn at Stanton—fairly close to the station?"

"The 'Plough and Horses'—just at the corner where the road goes up to the station—is that the one you mean?"

"That would be the one. I suppose you could do with a drink, couldn't you?"

"Rather!" said Bill, with a grin.

"Good. Then have one at the 'Plough and Horses.' Have two,

if you like, and talk to the landlord, or landlady, or whoever serves you. I want you to find out if anybody stayed there on Monday night."

"Robert?" said Bill eagerly.

"I didn't say Robert," said Antony, smiling. "I just want you to find out if they had a visitor who slept there on Monday night. A stranger. If so, then any particulars you can get of him, without letting the landlord know that you are interested—"

"Leave it to me," broke in Bill. "I know just what you want."

"Don't assume that it was Robert—or anybody else. Let them describe the man to you. Don't influence them unconsciously by suggesting that he was short or tall, or anything of that sort. Just get them talking. If it's the landlord, you'd better stand him a drink or two."

"Right you are," said Bill confidently. "Where do I meet you again?"

"Probably at 'The George.' If you get there before me, you can order dinner for eight o'clock. Anyhow we'll meet at eight, if not before."

"Good." He nodded to Antony and strode off back to Stanton again.

Antony stood watching him with a little smile at his enthusiasm. Then he looked round slowly, as if in search of something. Suddenly he saw what he wanted. Twenty yards farther on a lane wandered off to the left, and there was a gate a little way up on the right-hand side of it. Antony walked to the gate, filling his pipe as he went. Then he lit his pipe, sat on the gate, and took his head in his hands.

"Now then," he said to himself, "let's begin at the beginning."

It was nearly eight o'clock when William Beverley, the famous sleuth-hound, arrived, tired and dusty, at 'The George,' to find Antony, cool and clean, standing bare-headed at the door, waiting for him.

"Is dinner ready?" were Bill's first words.

"Yes."

"Then I'll just have a wash. Lord, I'm tired."

"I never ought to have asked you," said Antony penitently.

"That's all right. I shan't be a moment." Half-way up the stairs he turned round and asked, "Am I in your room?"

"Yes. Do you know the way?"

"Yes. Start carving, will you? And order lots of beer." He disappeared round the top of the staircase. Antony went slowly in.

When the first edge of his appetite had worn off, and he was able to spare a little time between the mouthfuls, Bill gave an account of his adventures. The landlord of the "Plough and Horses" had been sticky, decidedly sticky—Bill had been unable at first to get anything out of him. But Bill had been tactful; lorblessyou, how tactful he had been.

"He kept on about the inquest, and what a queer affair it had been, and so on, and how there'd been an inquest in his wife's family once, which he seemed rather proud about, and I kept saying, 'Pretty busy, I suppose, just now, what?' and then he'd say, 'Middlin',' and go on again about Susan—that was the one that had the inquest—he talked about it as if it were a disease—and then I'd try again, and say, 'Slack times, I expect, just now, eh?' and he'd say 'Middlin' again, and then it was time to offer him another drink, and I didn't seem to be getting much nearer. But I got him at last. I asked him if he knew John Borden—he was the man who said he'd seen Mark at the station. Well, he knew all about Borden, and after he'd told me all about Borden's wife's family, and how one of them had been burnt to death—after you with the beer; thanks—well, then I said carelessly that it must be very hard to remember anybody whom you had just seen once, so as to identify him afterwards, and he agreed that it would be 'middlin' hard,' and then—"

"Give me three guesses," interrupted Antony. "You asked him if he remembered everybody who came to his inn?"

"That's it. Bright, wasn't it?"

"Brilliant. And what was the result?"

"The result was a woman."

"A woman?" said Antony eagerly.

"A woman," said Bill impressively. "Of course I thought it was going to be Robert—so did you, didn't you?—but it wasn't. It was a woman. Came quite late on Monday night in a car—driving herself—went off early next morning."

"Did he describe her?"

"Yes. She was middlin'. Middlin' tall, middlin' age, middlin' colour, and so on. Doesn't help much, does it? But still—a woman. Does that upset your theory?"

Antony shook his head.

"No, Bill, not at all," he said.

"You knew all the time? At least, you guessed?"

"Wait till to-morrow. I'll tell you everything to-morrow."

"To-morrow!" said Bill in great disappointment.

"Well, I'll tell you one thing to-night, if you'll promise not to ask any more questions. But you probably know it already."

"What is it?"

"Only that Mark Ablett did not kill his brother."

"And Cayley did?"

"That's another question, Bill. However, the answer is that Cayley didn't, either."

"Then who on earth—"

"Have some more beer," said Antony with a smile. And Bill had to be content with that.

They were early to bed that evening, for both of them were tired. Bill slept loudly and defiantly, but Antony lay awake, wondering. What was happening at the Red House now? Perhaps he would hear in the morning; perhaps he would get a letter. He went over the whole story again from the beginning—was there any possibility of a mistake? What would the police do? Would they ever find out? Ought he to have told them? Well, let them find out; it was their job. Surely he couldn't have made a mistake this time. No good wondering now; he would know definitely in the morning.

In the morning there was a letter for him.

CHAPTER XXI

CAYLEY'S APOLOGY

"My Dear Mr. Gillingham,

"I gather from your letter that you have made certain discoveries which you may feel it your duty to communicate to the police, and that in this case my arrest on a charge of murder would inevitably follow. Why, in these circumstances, you should give me such ample warning of your intentions I do not understand, unless it is that you are not wholly out of sympathy with me. But whether or not you sympathize, at any rate you will want to know—and I want you to know—the exact manner in which Ablett met his death and the reasons which made that death necessary. If the police have to be told anything, I would rather that they too knew the whole story. They, and even you, may call it murder, but by that time I shall be out of the way. Let them call it what they like.

"I must begin by taking you back to a summer day fifteen years ago, when I was a boy of thirteen and Mark a young man of twenty-five. His whole life was make-believe, and just now he was pretending to be a philanthropist. He sat in our little drawing-room, flicking his gloves against the back of his left hand, and my mother, good soul, thought what a noble young gentleman he was, and Philip and I, hastily washed and crammed into collars, stood in front of him, nudging each other and kicking the backs of our heels and cursing him in our hearts for having interrupted our game. He had decided to adopt one of us, kind Cousin Mark. Heaven knows why he chose me. Philip was eleven; two years longer to wait. Perhaps that was why.

"Well, Mark educated me. I went to a public school and to Cambridge, and I became his secretary. Well, much more than his secretary as your friend Beverley perhaps has told you: his land agent, his financial adviser, his courier, his—but this most of all—his audience. Mark could never live alone. There must always be somebody to listen to him. I think in his heart he hoped I should be his Boswell. He told me one day that he had made me his literary executor—poor devil. And he used to write me the absurdest long letters when I was away from him, letters which I read once and then tore up. The futility of the man!

"It was three years ago that Philip got into trouble. He had been hurried through a cheap grammar school and into a London office, and discovered there that there was not much fun to be got in this world on two pounds a week. I had a frantic letter from him one day, saying that he must have a hundred at once, or he would be ruined, and I went to Mark for the money. Only to borrow it, you understand; he gave me a good salary and I could have paid it back in three months. But no. He saw nothing for himself in it, I suppose; no applause, no admiration. Philip's gratitude would be to me, not to him. I begged, I threatened, we argued; and while we were arguing, Philip was arrested. It killed my mother—he was always her favourite—but Mark, as usual, got his satisfaction out of it. He preened himself on his judgment of character in having chosen me and not Philip twelve years before!

"Later on I apologized to Mark for the reckless things I had said to him, and he played the part of a magnanimous gentleman with his accustomed skill, but, though outwardly we were as before to each other, from that day forward, though his vanity would never let him see it, I was his bitterest enemy. If that had been all, I wonder if I should have killed him? To live on terms of intimate friendship with a man whom you hate is dangerous work for your friend. Because of his belief in me as his admiring and grateful protege and his belief in himself as my benefactor, he was now utterly in my power. I could take my time and choose my opportunity. Perhaps I should not have killed him, but I had sworn to have my revenge—and there he was, poor vain fool, at my mercy. I was in no hurry.

"Two years later I had to reconsider my position, for my revenge was being taken out of my hands. Mark began to drink. Could I have stopped him? I don't think so, but to my immense surprise I found myself trying to. Instinct, perhaps, getting the better of reason; or did I reason it out and tell myself that, if he drank himself to death, I should lose my revenge? Upon my word, I cannot tell you; but, for whatever motive, I did genuinely want to stop it. Drinking is such a beastly thing, anyhow.

"I could not stop him, but I kept him within certain bounds, so that nobody but myself knew his secret. Yes, I kept him outwardly decent; and perhaps now I was becoming like the cannibal who keeps his victim in good condition for his own ends. I used to gloat over Mark, thinking how utterly he was mine to ruin as I pleased, financially, morally, whatever way would give me most satisfaction. I had but to take my hand away from him and he sank. But again I was in no hurry.

"Then he killed himself. That futile little drunkard, eaten up with his own selfishness and vanity, offered his beastliness to the truest and purest woman on this earth. You have seen her, Mr. Gillingham, but you never knew Mark Ablett. Even if he had not been a drunkard, there was no chance for her of happiness with him. I had known him for many years, but never once had I seen him moved by any generous emotion. To have lived with that shrivelled little soul would have been hell for her; and a thousand times worse hell when he began to drink.

"So he had to be killed. I was the only one left to protect her, for her mother was in league with Mark to bring about her ruin. I would have shot him openly for her sake, and with what gladness, but I had no mind to sacrifice myself needlessly. He was in my power; I could persuade him to almost anything by flattery; surely it would not be difficult to give his death the appearance of an accident.

"I need not take up your time by telling you of the many plans I made and rejected. For some days I inclined towards an unfortunate boating accident in the pond—Mark, a very indifferent swimmer, myself almost exhausted in a gallant attempt to hold him up. And then he himself gave me the idea, he and Miss Norris between them, and so put himself in my hands; without risk of discovery, I should have said, had you not discovered me.

"We were talking about ghosts. Mark had been even more vain, pompous and absurd than usual, and I could see that Miss Norris was irritated by it. After dinner she suggested dressing up as a ghost and frightening him. I thought it my duty to warn her that Mark took any joke against himself badly, but she was determined to do it. I gave way reluctantly. Reluctantly, also, I told her the secret of the passage. (There is an underground passage from the library to the bowling-green. You should exercise your ingenuity, Mr. Gillingham, in trying to discover it. Mark came upon it by accident a year ago. It was a godsend to him; he could drink there in greater secrecy. But he had to tell me about it. He wanted an audience, even for his vices.)

"I told Miss Norris, then, because it was necessary for my plan that Mark should be thoroughly frightened. Without the passage she could never have got close enough to the bowling-green to alarm him properly, but as I arranged it with her she made the most effective appearance, and Mark was in just the state of rage and vindictiveness which I required. Miss Norris, you understand, is a professional actress. I need not say that to her I appeared to be animated by no other feeling than a boyish desire to bring off a good joke—a joke directed as much against the others as against Mark.

"He came to me that night, as I expected, still quivering with indignation. Miss Norris must never be asked to the house again; I was to make a special note of it; never again. It was outrageous. Had he not a reputation as a host to keep up, he would pack her off next morning. As it was, she could stay; hospitality demanded it; but never again would she come to the Red House—he was absolutely determined about that. I was to make a special note of it.

"I comforted him, I smoothed down his ruffled feathers. She had behaved very badly, but he was quite right; he must try not to show how much he disapproved of her. And of course she would never come again—that was obvious. And then suddenly I began to laugh. He looked up at me indignantly.

"'Is there a joke?" he said coldly.

"I laughed gently again.

"'I was just thinking,' I said, 'that it would be rather amusing if you—well, had your revenge."

"'My revenge? How do you mean?'

"'Well, paid her back in her own coin.'

"'Do you mean try and frighten her?'

"'No, no; but dressed up and pulled her leg a bit. Made her look a fool in front of the others.' I laughed to myself again. 'Serve her jolly well right.'

"He jumped up excitedly.

"'By Jove, Cay!' he cried. 'If I could! How? You must think of a way.

"I don't know if Beverley has told you about Mark's acting. He was an amateur of all the arts, and vain of his little talents, but as an actor he seemed to himself most wonderful. Certainly he had some ability for the stage, so long as he had the stage to himself and was playing to an admiring audience. As a professional actor in a small part he would have been hopeless; as an amateur playing the leading part, he deserved all that the local papers had ever said about him. And so the idea of giving us a private performance, directed against a professional actress who had made fun of him, appealed equally to his vanity and his desire for retaliation. If he, Mark Ablett, by his wonderful acting could make Ruth Norris look a fool in front of the others, could take her in, and then join in the laugh at her afterwards, he would indeed have had a worthy revenge!

"It strikes you as childish, Mr. Gillingham? Ah, you never knew Mark Ablett.

"'How, Cay, how?' he said eagerly.

"'Well, I haven't really thought it out,' I protested. 'It was just an idea.'

"He began to think it out for himself.

"'I might pretend to be a manager, come down to see her—but I suppose she knows them all. What about an interviewer?'

"'It's going to be difficult,' I said thoughtfully. 'You've got rather a characteristic face, you know. And your beard—'

"'I'd shave it off,' he snapped.

"'My dear Mark!'

"He looked away, and mumbled, 'I've been thinking of taking it off, anyhow. And besides, if I'm going to do the thing, I'm going to do it properly.'

"'Yes, you always were an artist,' I said, looking at him admiringly.

"He purred. To be called an artist was what he longed for most. Now I knew that I had him.

"'All the same,' I went on, 'even without your beard and moustache you might be recognizable. Unless, of course—' I broke off.

"'Unless what?'

"'You pretend to be Robert.' I began to laugh to myself again. 'By Jove!' I said, 'that's not a bad idea. Pretend to be Robert, the wastrel brother, and make yourself objectionable to Miss Norris Borrow money from her, and that sort of thing.'

"He looked at me, with his bright little eyes, nodding eagerly.

"'Robert,' he said. 'Yes. How shall we work it?'

"There was really a Robert, Mr. Gillingham, as I have no doubt you and the Inspector both discovered. And he was a wastrel and he went to Australia. But he never came to the Red House on Tuesday afternoon. He couldn't have, because he died (unlamented) three years ago. But there was nobody who knew this, save Mark and myself, for Mark was the only one of the family left, his sister having died last year. Though I doubt, anyhow, if she knew whether Robert was alive or dead. He was not talked about.

"For the next two days Mark and I worked out our plans. You understand by now that our aims were not identical. Mark's endeavour was that his deception should last for, say, a couple of hours; mine that it should go to the grave with him. He had only to deceive Miss Norris and the other guests; I had to deceive the world. When he was dressed up as Robert, I was going to kill him. Robert would then be dead, Mark (of course) missing. What could anybody think but that Mark had killed Robert? But you see how important it was for Mark to enter fully into his latest (and last) impersonation. Half-measures would be fatal.

"You will say that it was impossible to do the thing thoroughly enough. I answer again that you never knew Mark. He was being what he wished most to be—an artist. No Othello ever blacked himself all over with such enthusiasm as did Mark. His beard was going anyhow—possible a chance remark of Miss Norbury's helped here. She did not like beards. But it was important for me that the dead man's hands should not be the hands of a manicured gentleman. Five minutes playing upon the vanity of the artist settled his hands. He let the nails grow and then cut them raggedly. 'Miss Norris would notice your hands at once,' I had said. 'Besides, as an artist—'

"So with his underclothes. It was hardly necessary to warn him that his pants might show above the edge of his socks; as an artist he had already decided upon Robertian pants. I bought them, and other things, in London for him. Even if I had not cut out all trace of the maker's name, he would instinctively have done it. As an Australian and an artist, he could not have an East London address on his underclothes. Yes, we were doing the thing thoroughly, both of us; he as an artist, I as a—well, you may say murderer, if you like. I shall not mind now.

"Our plans were settled. I went to London on the Monday and wrote him a letter from Robert. (The artistic touch again.) I also bought a revolver. On the Tuesday morning he announced the arrival of Robert at the breakfast-table. Robert was now alive—we had six witnesses to prove it; six witnesses who knew that he was coming that afternoon. Our private plan was that Robert should present himself at three o'clock, in readiness for the return of the golfing-party shortly afterwards. The maid would go to look for Mark, and having failed to find him, come back to the office to find me entertaining Robert in Mark's absence. I would explain that Mark must have gone out somewhere, and would myself introduce the wastrel brother to the tea-table. Mark's absence would not excite any comment, for it would be generally felt—indeed Robert would suggest it—that he had been afraid of meeting his brother. Then Robert would make himself amusingly offensive to the guests, particularly, of course, Miss Norris, until he thought that the joke had gone far enough.

"That was our private plan. Perhaps I should say that it was Mark's private plan. My own was different.

"The announcement at breakfast went well. After the golfing-party had gone off, we had the morning in which to complete our arrangements. What I was chiefly concerned about was to establish as completely as possible the identity of Robert. For this reason I suggested to Mark that, when dressed, he should go out by the secret passage to the bowling-green, and come back by the drive, taking care to enter into conversation with the lodge-keeper. In this way I would have two more witnesses of Robert's arrival—first the lodge-keeper, and secondly one of the gardeners whom I would have working on the front lawn. Mark, of course, was willing enough. He could practise his Australian accent on the lodge-keeper. It was really amusing to see how readily he fell into every suggestion which I made. Never was a killing more carefully planned by its victim.

"He changed into Robert's clothes in the office bedroom. This was the safest way—for both of us. When he was ready, he called me in, and I inspected him. It was extraordinary how well he looked the part. I suppose that the signs of his dissipation had already marked themselves on his face, but had been concealed hitherto by his moustache and beard; for now that he was clean-shaven they lay open to the world from which we had so carefully hidden them, and he was indeed the wastrel which he was pretending to be.

"'By Jove, you're wonderful,' I said.

"He smirked, and called my attention to the various artistic touches which I might have missed.

"'Wonderful,' I said to myself again. 'Nobody could possibly guess.'

"I peered into the hall. It was empty. We hurried across to the library; he got into the passage and made off. I went back to the bedroom, collected all his discarded clothes, did them up in a bundle and returned with them to the passage. Then I sat down in the hall and waited.

"You heard the evidence of Stevens, the maid. As soon as she was on her way to the Temple in search of Mark, I stepped into the office. My hand was in my side-pocket, and in my hand was the revolver.

"He began at once in his character of Robert—some rigmarole about working his passage over from Australia; a little private performance for my edification. Then in his natural voice, gloating over his well-planned retaliation on Miss Norris, he burst out, 'It's my turn now. You wait.' It was this which Elsie heard. She had no business to be there and she might have ruined everything, but as it turned out it was the luckiest thing which could have happened. For it was the one piece of evidence which I wanted; evidence, other than my own, that Mark and Robert were in the room together.

"I said nothing. I was not going to take the risk of being heard to speak in that room. I just smiled at the poor little fool, and took out my revolver, and shot him. Then I went back into the library and waited—just as I said in my evidence.

"Can you imagine, Mr. Gillingham, the shock which your sudden appearance gave me? Can you imagine the feelings of a 'murderer' who has (as he thinks) planned for every possibility, and is then confronted suddenly with an utterly new problem? What difference would your coming make? I didn't know. Perhaps none; perhaps all. And I had forgotten to open the window!

"I don't know whether you will think my plan for killing Mark a clever one. Perhaps not. But if I do deserve any praise in the matter, I think I deserve it for the way I pulled myself together in the face of the unexpected catastrophe of your arrival. Yes, I got a window open, Mr. Gillingham, under your very nose; the right window too, you were kind enough to say. And the keys—yes, that was clever of you, but I think I was cleverer. I deceived you over the keys, Mr. Gillingham, as I learnt when I took the liberty of listening to a conversation on the bowling-green between you and your friend Beverley. Where was I? Ah, you must have a look for that secret passage, Mr. Gillingham.

"But what am I saying? Did I deceive you at all? You have found out the secret—that Robert was Mark—and that is all that matters. How have you found out? I shall never know now. Where did I go wrong? Perhaps you have been deceiving me all the time. Perhaps you knew about the keys, about the window, even about the secret passage. You are a clever man, Mr. Gillingham.

"I had Mark's clothes on my hands. I might have left them in the passage, but the secret of the passage was now out. Miss Norris knew it. That was the weak point of my plan, perhaps, that Miss Norris had to know it. So I hid them in the pond, the Inspector having obligingly dragged it for me first. A couple of keys joined them, but I kept the revolver. Fortunate, wasn't it, Mr. Gillingham?

"I don't think that there is any more to tell you. This is a long letter, but then it is the last which I shall write. There was a time when I hoped that there might be a happy future for me, not at the Red House, not alone. Perhaps it was never more than an idle day-dream, for I am no more worthy of her than Mark was. But I could have made her happy, Mr. Gillingham. God, how I would have worked to make her happy! But now that is impossible. To offer her the hand of a murderer would be as bad as to offer her the hand of a drunkard. And Mark died for that. I saw her this morning. She was very sweet. It is a difficult world to understand.

"Well, well, we are all gone now—the Abletts and the Cayleys. I wonder what old Grandfather Cayley thinks of it all. Perhaps it is as well that we have died out. Not that there was anything wrong with Sarah—except her temper. And she had the Ablett nose—you can't do much with that. I'm glad she left no children.

"Good-bye, Mr. Gillingham. I'm sorry that your stay with us was not of a pleasanter nature, but you understand the difficulties in which I was placed. Don't let Bill think too badly of me. He is a good fellow; look after him. He will be surprised. The young are always surprised. And thank you for letting me end my own way. I expect you did sympathize a little, you know. We might have been friends in another world—you and I, and I and she. Tell her what you like. Everything or nothing. You will know what is best. Good-bye, Mr. Gillingham.

"MATTHEW CAYLEY.

"I am lonely to-night without Mark. That's funny, isn't it?"

CHAPTER XXII

MR. BEVERLEY MOVES ON

"Good Lord!" said Bill, as he put down the letter.

"I thought you'd say that," murmured Antony.

"Tony, do you mean to say that you knew all this?"

"I guessed some of it. I didn't quite know all of it, of course."

"Good Lord!" said Bill again, and returned to the letter. In a moment he was looking up again. "What did you write to him? Was that last night? After I'd gone into Stanton?"

"Yes."

"What did you say? That you'd discovered that Mark was Robert?"

"Yes. At least I said that this morning I should probably telegraph to Mr. Cartwright of Wimpole Street, and ask him to—"

Bill burst in eagerly on the top of the sentence. "Yes, now what was all that about? You were so damn Sherlocky yesterday all of a sudden. We'd been doing the thing together all the time, and you'd been telling me everything, and then suddenly you become very mysterious and private and talk enigmatically—is that the word?—about dentists and swimming and the 'Plough and Horses,' and—well, what was it all about? You simply vanished out of sight; I didn't know what on earth we were talking about."

Antony laughed and apologized.

"Sorry, Bill. I felt like that suddenly. Just for the last half-hour; just to end up with. I'll tell you everything now. Not that there's anything to tell, really. It seems so easy when you know it—so obvious. About Mr. Cartwright of Wimpole Street. Of course he was just to identify the body."

"But whatever made you think of a dentist for that?"

"Who could do it better? Could you have done it? How could you? You'd never gone bathing with Mark; you'd never seen him stripped. He didn't swim. Could his doctor do it? Not unless he'd had some particular operation, and perhaps not then. But his dentists could—at any time, always—if he had been to his dentist fairly often. Hence Mr. Cartwright of Wimpole Street."

Bill nodded thoughtfully and went back again to the letter.

"I see. And you told Cayley that you were telegraphing to Cartwright to identify the body?"

"Yes. And then of course it was all up for him. Once we knew that Robert was Mark we knew everything."

"How did you know?"

Antony got up from the breakfast table and began to fill his pipe.

"I'm not sure that I can say, Bill. You know those problems in Algebra where you say, 'Let x be the answer,' and then you work it out and find what x is. Well, that's one way; and another way, which they never give you any marks for at school, is to guess the answer. Pretend the answer is 4—well, will that satisfy the conditions of the problem? No. Then try 6; and if 6 doesn't either, then what about 5?—and so on. Well, the Inspector and the Coroner and all that lot had guessed their answer, and it seemed to fit, but you and I knew it didn't really fit; there were several conditions in the problem which it didn't fit at all. So we knew that their answer was wrong, and we had to think of another—an answer which explained all the things which were puzzling us. Well, I happened to guess the right one. Got a match?"

Bill handed him a box, and he lit his pipe.

"Yes, but that doesn't quite do, old boy. Something must have put you on to it suddenly. By the way, I'll have my matches back, if you don't mind."

Antony laughed and took them out of his pocket.

"Sorry.... Well then, let's see if I can go through my own mind again, and tell you how I guessed it. First of all, the clothes."

"Yes?"

"To Cayley the clothes seemed an enormously important clue. I didn't quite see why, but I did realize that to a man in

Cayley's position the smallest clue would have an entirely disproportionate value. For some reason, then, Cayley attached this exaggerated importance to the clothes which Mark was wearing on that Tuesday morning; all the clothes, the inside ones as well as the outside ones. I didn't know why, but I did feel certain that, in that case, the absence of the collar was unintentional. In collecting the clothes he had overlooked the collar. Why?"

"It was the one in the linen-basket?"

"Yes. It seemed probable. Why had Cayley put it there? The obvious answer was that he hadn't. Mark had put it there. I remembered what you told me about Mark being finicky, and having lots of clothes and so on, and I felt that he was just the sort of man who would never wear the same collar twice." He paused, and then asked, "Is that right, do you think?"

"Absolutely," said Bill with conviction.

"Well, I guessed it was. So then I began to see an x which would fit just this part of the problem—the clothes part. I saw Mark changing his clothes; I saw him instinctively dropping the collar in the linen-basket, just as he had always dropped every collar he had ever taken off, but leaving the rest of the clothes on a chair in the ordinary way; and I saw Cayley collecting all the clothes afterwards—all the visible clothes—and not realizing that the collar wasn't there."

"Go on," said Bill eagerly.

"Well, I felt pretty sure about that, and I wanted an explanation of it. Why had Mark changed down there instead of in his bedroom? The only answer was that the fact of his changing had to be kept secret. When did he change? The only possible time was between lunch (when he would be seen by the servants) and the moment of Robert's arrival. And when did Cayley collect the clothes in a bundle? Again, the only answer was 'Before Robert's arrival.' So another x was wanted—to fit those three conditions."

"And the answer was that a murder was intended, even before Robert arrived?"

"Yes. Well now, it couldn't be intended on the strength of that letter, unless there was very much more behind the letter than we knew. Nor was it possible a murder could be intended without any more preparation than the changing into a different suit in which to escape. The thing was too childish. Also, if Robert was to be murdered, why go out of the way to announce his existence to you all—even, at the cost of some trouble, to Mrs. Norbury? What did it all mean? I didn't know. But I began to feel now that Robert was an incident only; that the plot was a plot of Cayley's against Mark—either to get him to kill his brother, or to get his brother to kill him—and that for some inexplicable reason Mark seemed to be lending himself to the plot." He was silent for a little, and then said, almost to himself, "I had seen the empty brandy bottles in that cupboard."

"You never said anything about them" complained Bill.

"I only saw them afterwards. I was looking for the collar, you remember. They came back to me afterwards; I knew how Cayley would feel about it.... Poor devil!"

"Go on," said Bill.

"Well, then, we had the inquest, and of course I noticed, and I suppose you did too, the curious fact that Robert had asked his way at the second lodge and not at the first. So I talked to Amos and Parsons. That made it more curious. Amos told me that Robert had gone out of his way to speak to him; had called to him, in fact. Parsons told me that his wife was out in their little garden at the first lodge all the afternoon, and was certain that Robert had never come past it. He also told me that Cayley had put him on to a job on the front lawn that afternoon. So I had another guess. Robert had used the secret passage—the passage which comes out into the park between the first and second lodges. Robert, then, had been in the house; it was a put-up job between Robert and Cayley. But how could Robert be there without Mark knowing? Obviously, Mark knew too. What did it all mean?"

"When was this?" interrupted Bill. "Just after the inquest—after you'd seen Amos and Parsons, of course?"

"Yes. I got up and left them, and came to look for you. I'd got back to the clothes then. Why did Mark change his clothes so secretly? Disguise? But then what about his face? That was much more important than clothes. His face, his beard—he'd have to shave off his beard—and then—oh, idiot! I saw you looking at that poster. Mark acting, Mark made-up, Mark disguised. Oh, priceless idiot! Mark was Robert.... Matches, please."

Bill passed over the matches again, waited till Antony had relit his pipe, and then held out his hand for them, just as they were going into the other's pocket.

"Yes," said Bill thoughtfully. "Yes.... But wait a moment. What about the 'Plough and Horses'?" Antony looked comically at him.

"You'll never forgive me, Bill," he said. "You'll never come clue-hunting with me again."

"What do you mean?"

Antony sighed.

"It was a fake, Watson. I wanted you out of the way. I wanted to be alone. I'd guessed at my x, and I wanted to test it—to test it every way, by everything we'd discovered. I simply had to be alone just then. So—" he smiled and added, "Well, I knew you wanted a drink."

"You are a devil," said Bill, staring at him. "And your interest when I told you that a woman had been staying there—"

"Well, it was only polite to be interested when you'd taken so much trouble."

"You brute! You—you Sherlock! And then you keep trying to steal my matches. Well, go on."

"That's all. My x fitted."

"Did you guess Miss Norris and all that?"

"Well, not quite. I didn't realize that Cayley had worked for it from the beginning—had put Miss Norris up to frightening Mark. I thought he'd just seized the opportunity."

Bill was silent for a long time. Then, puffing at his pipe, he said slowly, "Has Cayley shot himself?"

Antony shrugged his shoulders.

"Poor devil," said Bill. "It was decent of you to give him a chance. I'm glad you did."

"I couldn't help liking Cayley in a kind of way, you know."

"He's a clever devil. If you hadn't turned up just when you did, he would never have been found out."

"I wonder. It was ingenious, but it's often the ingenious thing which gets found out. The awkward thing from Cayley's point of view was that, though Mark was missing, neither he nor his body could ever be found. Well, that doesn't often happen with a missing man. He generally gets discovered in the end; a professional criminal; perhaps not—but an amateur like Mark!

He might have kept the secret of how he killed Mark, but I think it would have become obvious sooner or later that he had killed him."

"Yes, there's something in that.... Oh, just tell me one thing. Why did Mark tell Miss Norbury about his imaginary brother?"

"That's puzzled me rather, too, Bill. It may be that he was just doing the Othello business—painting himself black all over. I mean he may have been so full of his appearance as Robert that he had almost got to believe in Robert, and had to tell everybody. More likely, though, he felt that, having told all of you at the house, he had better tell Miss Norbury, in case she met one of you; in which case, if you mentioned the approaching arrival of Robert, she might say, 'Oh, I'm certain he has no brother; he would have told me if he had,' and so spoil his joke. Possibly, too, Cayley put him on to it; Cayley obviously wanted as many people as possible to know about Robert."

"Are you going to tell the police?"

"Yes, I suppose they'll have to know. Cayley may have left another confession. I hope he won't give me away; you see, I've been a sort of accessory since yesterday evening. And I must go and see Miss Norbury."

"I asked," explained Bill, "because I was wondering what I should say to—to Betty. Miss Calladine. You see, she's bound to ask."

"Perhaps you won't see her again for a long, long time," said Antony sadly.

"As a matter of fact, I happen to know that she will be at the Barringtons. And I go up there to-morrow."

"Well, you had better tell her. You're obviously longing to. Only don't let her say anything for a day or two. I'll write to you."

"Righto!"

Antony knocked the ashes out of his pipe and got up.

"The Barringtons," he said. "Large party?"

"Fairly, I think."

Antony smiled at his friend.

"Yes. Well, if any of 'em should happen to be murdered, you might send for me. I'm just getting into the swing of it."

25595581R00285

Made in the USA
San Bernardino, CA
04 November 2015